DARK & BEASTLY FAE

NISSA & KIERDEN'S STORY

To all the fairytales that didn't give me a love story

CHAPTER ONE
KIERDEN

I paced the elven throne room as foreign, violent magic pulsed on the back of my hand. The brand emanating wicked power glowed crimson, forming shapes and glyphs in the language of the lost gods.

"How do we buy ourselves time?" Vayme asked Alida, the elven leader we'd gone to for help.

The other two fae kings had woken up with the same veil-cursed markings I had. Those damn brands were calling cards for the twisted assassins that plagued our world, Evare, which made them death sentences.

"How do we *remove* the magic?" Ravv growled.

"Making it to the eclipse is the only way we know of to break the connection, but no one makes it to the eclipse," Alida said.

"There must be some solution," Vayme countered

"The only chance you have is to conceal your magic. They'll track you through your power's aura, because your connection to them is entirely magical. But there are women with life magic hidden in the human lands—I can sense them through the forests. Bind them to you as your mates, and their magic will hide yours until the eclipse passes, the bonds vanish, and the monsters are released from their vows."

We all went still.

"She's gone mad," I muttered.

"Absolutely insane," Ravv agreed.

"We didn't survive centuries of wars to be killed by our own people because of *mate bonds*," Vayme said.

"It's the only way. Take the humans, or die." She spun on her heels and strode out of the room.

CHAPTER TWO
NISSA

I watched the thick berry vines grow slowly but steadily, right in front of me. Though I wasn't doing anything to make them grow, I could feel the flow of my magic and energy moving into the ground and plants around me.

I willed it to stop moving, but it didn't.

The fuzzy purple berries were already nearly the size of my fists, but they could still get bigger.

My backside was aching after an hour on the rotting, uneven log that functioned as a bench. My ankles and wrists throbbed too, thanks to the rough rope tying them to said bench.

"Take me back to my prison," I told the man behind me. The sharp tip of his massive steel sword was pressed lightly to the center of my back.

His name was Runo, and his weapon was an attempt at overcompensating for his lacking manhood. I knew from past experience that cracking a joke about it would only lead to him actually cutting me with the damn thing, so I didn't bring it up.

"You stay until Fina gives the word," Runo argued. After a long, long pause, he added, "And your home is not a prison. We've been very generous."

Fina.

My dear, dear mother.

The lovely woman who had shut me in a tower on the day of my thirteenth birthday, after I woke up in a room full of flowers, fruits, and vegetables. It had been nine years since then, and I still hadn't managed to free myself.

"A home you're not allowed to leave is a prison, Runo." I continued staring at the berries, willing them with every ounce of effort to *just stop growing*. It failed, of course. "And if you were really generous, I'd be able to leave this damned town. We both know you're not going to kill me, so put the sword away. Everyone would starve without me at this point."

And I was twisted enough that I'd laugh all the way to their graves if they did. A town that would lock me up to save itself the effort of growing its own plants or creating its own goods didn't deserve my pity.

Of course, that was only one of my controversial opinions. None of which had ever done a single good thing for me.

I was still a prisoner.

At least I had outgrown the nightmares about everything I'd lost when I became that.

Runo put the sword away.

A bell chimed at the edge of town, courtesy of my dearest mother, and Runo grabbed my hands by the rope attached to them. When he led me and my weak, shaking legs toward the next rotting log, I didn't fight him. Fighting had never gotten me anything but a little more pain.

"Try to focus on the melons. My wife loves melons," Runo told me, as he tied my ropes to the next rotting, uneven log.

I fought a snort at his words, moving a little on the log in an attempt to regain feeling in my ass.

The melons in front of me began growing rapidly, through no actual effort on my part.

Time passed slowly, as it always did. My energy trickled away bit by bit, draining into the ground, seeds, and existing plants.

A few more hours passed similarly before I was so completely exhausted that I may as well have been a corpse. Runo finally dragged me back to the tower he considered a generous home.

Fina hadn't come outside to see me.

Neither had anyone else, adult, child, or otherwise. They always hid when I was outside, afraid I might infect them with my magic. It was ironic, really, that they feared my power so completely while relying on it wholly to stay alive.

I itched to develop enough control over it to finally make an escape, but that seemed like an impossibility after so many years.

Runo stopped outside the short door that led into my prison, the same way he always did. He untied the bindings on my wrists and ankles, then unceremoniously pushed my exhausted body onto the stone staircase at the base of my tower.

My legs gave out, and my ribs collided hard with the harsh stone. I groaned at the pain of the impact as I saved my face from yet another bruise with my forearms. My waist-length, dark green hair sprawled over the tanned skin on my arms, and it took a minute to pull it all out of the way. Runo closed and locked the door behind me, as always.

After lifting myself to a seated position with my shaking arms, I slowly used the wall to ease myself up to my feet, tugging my dark, oversized dress out from beneath me.

Every muscle I had trembled with the force of my exhaustion as I made my way up the stairs one by one.

There were so many stairs.

And I was so damn tired.

Still, I climbed.

I'd find a way out that night, I promised myself with every step.

When the moons rose, I'd figure out how to leave the town, I vowed, as I put one foot in front of the other.

Left.

Right.

Left.

Right.

Finally, I reached the top of the stairs.

Relief made my shoulders sag as I stumbled to my bed, ignoring the growl in my stomach.

The town's bellies were full.

Their coffers were, too.

And yet there was never enough food left for me. They kept me hungry, drained, and trapped in a tower, all because it made their lives a little easier.

My back collided with the rough, old mattress, and I winced at the smell of mildew that assaulted my nose in retaliation. As despair began to creep into my mind, making my chest feel tight and my breaths shorten, I forced myself to close my eyes.

When I woke up, I'd figure out a way to get free.

It was a lie, but one I had to force myself to believe if I was going to survive another day.

I cracked my eyes open, rubbing the grit in them. The pit in my stomach was deep and yawning, desperate for food that wouldn't come.

My captors would feed me when they pulled me out at sunrise. They'd give me a bowl of some type of grain with a few chunks of the perfectly-ripe fruits and vegetables I'd grown the day before. I may not have been growing things on purpose, but I was damn good at my job. Or my magic was, I supposed.

The food would only give me enough energy for my magic to drain right back into the earth again, but I still yearned for it.

I eased myself out of bed, wincing in pain at the bruises on my ribs, both new and old. I had to believe that I was going to find a way out; there was no other option.

Slowly, I made my way to the window, and then sat down in the seat below it. The seat was simple and made out of stone like the rest of my tower, but compared to the uneven logs I was forced to occupy outside, it might as well have been a throne.

My gaze moved over the portion of town I could see from my window. Both of Evare's moons were up that night, so everything was illuminated enough for me to see the evidence of my magic. One of the moons rose every second night and the other only rose every third, so most of the time they were only up together once a week. I always looked forward to that night.

Thick, vibrant plants bloomed wildly and covered nearly every building, all of them for the sole purpose of growing food and spices. My mother made sure everyone cut down and burned all of the flowers and purposeless plants that grew.

I could see the two dozen guards walking the streets of the town, and silently went over their names, the way I always did. I knew which guards worked which nights every week, and which routes each of them followed.

Coby.

Kelle.

Ren.

Jor...

Who was that?

My gaze caught on a man I'd never seen before.

Even from my window, I could see that he was built much bigger and stronger than any of the others in town.

Though he strode down the middle of the street, he seemed to be dressed in nothing but a simple pair of shorts. Most men wore thick work pants and long-sleeve tunics to protect themselves from all three of our suns, even though those in my town were rarely forced to work in the heat of the day.

Most of them were rarely forced to work *at all*, thanks to me.

My brow furrowed, and I leaned closer until my forehead and nose met the window.

My gaze flicked between the newcomer and the other men and women walking the streets. He didn't seem to be carrying a weapon of any kind, and the way he moved was strange.

Or maybe not strange. Just different.

He didn't walk, or storm; he prowled, like the jungle cat I'd seen on the border where my town met the Broken Woods as a child. The shifters lived in the Woods, so entry was forbidden to any human who wanted to keep their life.

The prowling man in the streets halted abruptly.

My gaze may as well have been bound to him with rope, for all I could pull it away.

His eyes collided with mine, and even from my tower, I could see his gaze glowing dark blue with magic.

My heartbeat picked up.

Every magical being in Evare had eyes that glowed. It was one of the many things that set us apart from the humans and nonmagical creatures, which I was reminded of as I saw my own eyes glowing bright green every time I looked in the mirror.

The magical man didn't look away, and neither did I.

Something in my chest sort of... thrummed.

Was it hope?

Was it something more?

I didn't know, but I still couldn't take my eyes off him.

His gaze jerked to the side, in the same direction one of the guards was moving. After one last lingering look at the tower, at *me*, he began moving again, faster.

"What are you doing?" I whispered, my eyes following his form until he disappeared from my sight. My heart was still beating fast, and that strange feeling was still thrumming inside me.

Was he there to abduct me?

Veil, I hoped so.

A few other towns had tried to take me for my magic, but with the vast amount of food I grew for them, my mother's people had plenty of time to learn how to fight and plenty of money for weapons. They slaughtered everyone who came for me.

But no one with *magic* had ever tried to abduct me before.

I heard a snap as the metal lock on the door beneath me broke, and then a creak as the door opened.

My heartbeat picked up even faster.

Even if he was just going to kill me, I'd be grateful for the freedom of death.

I faced the top of the stairs head-on when the man cleared them.

His shoulders were back and his dark blue eyes glowed with emotion I couldn't read as they slid up and down my figure, slowly.

My face heated at the judgment that was undoubtedly running through his mind.

I was dirty, and shaking a little.

I'd been starving for years, though my oversized dress may have hidden that.

In contrast, he was absolutely gorgeous. Tall and strong, with lightly-tanned skin that practically shimmered with health. His ears were pointed, marking him as a fae, and inky black tattoos snaked up one of his arms before spreading over part of his chest.

His hair was thick and dark, the length of it curling around his ears. Most human men kept theirs cut close to their heads for ease, and the soft curl of the fae's made my lower belly tighten.

"Veil," I whispered. It was a curse, but also the word for the dividing line between our world and the world of our dead.

"You'll come with me," he said. Though his voice was low, it was flooded with the confidence and certainty of an extremely powerful man.

Then again, he was a fae.

I may as well have been a spider to him, ready to be crushed beneath the heel of his bare foot.

Perhaps if I hadn't wanted the same thing he did, I would've protested. Considering he was offering me the very thing I'd wanted for the past nine years, he wasn't going to hear an argument from me.

I crossed the room. My body felt weak, but I tried to control the shaking.

The fae looked a bit taken aback that I hadn't fought him on it, but turned and made his way back down the steps just as silently as I'd expected him to.

I followed him down, leaning heavily against the wall as I went. He was a lot faster than me, but I didn't call out to him. I was too worried about being caught by the guards outside.

He found me halfway down the stairs, his eyes narrowed as if he was about to lecture me for being slow.

"I haven't eaten much tonight," I whispered to him, not wanting to tell him how malnourished I was in case it would change his mind about taking me.

He grabbed my wrist, and an electric current raced through me. I jerked back, and he released me, looking down at his hand and then at my wrist.

My lips parted in shock as I watched a silver handprint appear where he'd touched me... and the shock became horror when it started to *glow*.

When I looked at the man, I found his entire palm glowing the way my wrist was.

Without further ado, he threw me over his shoulder and ran down the stairs, moving faster than I ever had in my life. He was out of the castle and weaving through the town a heartbeat later, dodging the streets with guards on them easily.

There would be a few guards at the gate, but I assumed the fae was going to avoid them somehow.

"Double moon nights are the best to be on duty," one of them remarked, as we neared.

My rescuer didn't slow down even a little.

"Best visibility," another man agreed. He took a bite of something that made a crisp crunching sound, and my stomach rumbled against the fae's shoulder just as he ran past a group of six guards.

They barely had time to gape at us before my rescuer disappeared around the edge of the gate, and ran right into the Broken Woods.

As their name suggested, the Broken Woods were dark and looked dead, despite the life and magic teeming within. The trees and bushes grew without leaves or color, the dirt beneath them was an eerie reddish-brown, and the bugs and animals that called the place home hunted without cover or fear.

My world was spinning madly, and plants sprouted miraculously in our wake. Tree branches grew thicker, and leaves swelled larger.

"Stop using your magic," the fae barked at me.

I had no control over my magic, but I couldn't say that aloud. What if the fae ditched me because of it? I had to wait until we were somewhere I could stay alive—like a city or town.

Not that a fae city would be much safer than the woods. I'd never seen one, but I assumed they were dangerous.

The sounds of my town rallying help and getting ready to pursue us faded rapidly. They had no chance of catching the fae man. There was a reason we humans stayed away from the many magical beings in Evare, and it wasn't because we had superior strength, speed, or senses.

My abductor slowed.

Fear made me nauseous.

Was he going to drop me because of my magic?

My world tilted, and then my ass landed on something warm and hard.

My entire body shuddered.

I looked down and realized what I was sitting on—then I shuddered again, harder.

It was one of the jungle cats. They were bigger than I'd realized, with sleek black fur that had just a hint of a pattern to it.

A massive, warm chest pinned me against the back of the jungle cat's neck as arms wrapped around me and hands gripped the creature's fur lightly.

The cat took off into the trees, hauling me further from my tower-shaped prison and the town that was the only place I'd ever known. Despite the shock and terror of the situation, only one thought rang through my mind:

I was finally free.

CHAPTER THREE
NISSA

s the jungle cat carried us deeper into the forest, flowers bloomed in the dead-looking trees and bushes we passed.

And my energy?

What little I had left drained away steadily.

"By the veil, what is wrong with her?" a masculine voice growled, as my body grew too weak for me to keep holding my head up. It didn't sound like it was in my ear, but where else could it have been?

I had no idea who the voice was talking to, but it sounded like the male fae's.

"She's going to drain herself dry." The gorgeous male voice was getting angrier.

I wondered if I'd started hallucinating, because I honestly thought the voice might've been speaking into my *mind*.

My eyes closed just as the fae behind me jerked my head to the side and said into my ear, "Sillah ovim rett warum."

The words sent tingles down my spine.

I had no idea what they meant, but I could feel them start changing something. Something deep inside me, where my magic was.

Something like... my soul.

That couldn't have been right, though. Could it?

The tingles in my spine turned to pins, and I bit back a scream as the pain grew excruciating. The fae man pressed me against the jungle cat harder, all but *shoving* me against the creature while I bit my cheek.

Something swelled in my middle—something new, hard, dead, and *cold*.

Ice magic, something inside me seemed to whisper. The same icy power I knew all of the fae possessed.

But why could I feel a fae's power inside me?

The fae man swore into my ear, "Veil, what is wrong with your magic?"

I honestly had no idea.

My power was over plants, obviously. But why was it uncontrollable? And why did it drain me so damn fast?

I didn't have answers.

But the ice magic that had appeared in my chest did seem to be slowing the drain of my power, somehow. I was still absolutely exhausted to the point of not functioning, but relief had my body relaxing.

"What did he do?" I wondered, the thought clear and strong.

"Don't speak into my mind, human."

Apparently, I was right about hearing his thoughts.

At least I wasn't going insane.

"I'm not trying to. What did you do to me?" I asked.

"Mated us, temporarily. The next eclipse will remove the bond."

The words made my mind reel and my world spin even more than it was already spinning.

"Mated?" My words sounded faint.

He didn't bother confirming it. We both knew I'd heard him correctly.

I had no idea what it meant to be mated to a fae—I was fairly sure it was their version of marriage—but I also had no energy to figure that out.

So, I just leaned my head against the cat beneath me, closed my eyes, and let myself fall asleep.

The next time I opened my eyes, I found myself staring up at what looked like a chunk of solid ice. If I was surrounded by ice, I logically should've felt cold, but there was no chill in the air.

I sat up slowly, taking stock of my surroundings.

There was... ice.

Just ice.

Everywhere.

I seemed to be in some kind of box made of ice.

My hands lifted to the smooth, hard wall in front of me, and I pressed them against it as I fought my panic.

How was I supposed to get out?

With another look around, I determined that there was no sign of the male fae who captured me.

That wasn't good.

Had he left me for dead in the ice box?

I pushed against the walls, hoping to find the glass thin and easy to shatter. But when I poked, prodded, and smashed it, nothing happened.

I let out a huff as I began running my fingers over the walls and ceiling, trying to find a door of some kind to let me out.

I didn't find anything, though. There was no way out.

My breathing picked up at the thought of being trapped again.

Had I escaped one prison just to be thrown in another?

A moment before my fear turned into panic, the roof of the ice box slid away. The fae from before scowled down at me, then grabbed me by the arms and lifted me out.

He set me down and stepped away, but the weakness in my body had my knees knocking together. My legs gave out, and I stumbled.

Massive hands landed on my waist, catching me before I could fall on my face. My cheeks burned with embarrassment—and then my stomach growled.

Hunger wasn't the most present emotion, though, surprisingly enough.

Something about having his hands on my hips made me feel... calm. Settled, too.

A long moment passed before the fae finally peeled his hands off me and stepped away. Without glancing in my direction, he tossed a huge berry at me.

By some miracle, I caught it without falling again.

My eyes followed him as he walked across a patch of the woods, right over to a pair of jungle cats.

When he sat next to the bigger one and scratched the hair behind its ears, my eyes widened. It started to purr, and they widened even more.

"You're not human at all," the man said, his expression twisted in irritation again.

I looked down at myself.

I mean... I thought I was? Minus the magic and all.

"You have a bonded beast." He gestured toward the second big cat.

I blinked. "That's not mine."

"Don't call her *that*," the man said harshly.

"I'm not a fae. My parents were humans, and I'm pretty sure that makes me human too. I don't know anything about *her*." I gestured toward the creature. "We call them jungle cats."

He went silent for a moment.

I eased myself to the ground, then took a small bite of the berry. I'd never had one that looked like it before, but the black skin was silky and the inside was bursting with flavor.

"They are called esu," he finally said, pronouncing the word *ee-sue*. "Some choose to bond themselves as fae companions."

I gestured to the cat—the esu. "And she thinks I'm a fae, and that we're bonded."

"She does."

I blinked again.

Then I took another bite of my berry, deciding I really didn't have anything to say about that after all.

"No questions?" the man asked me, his expression growing skeptical.

"No." I took another bite.

His skepticism morphed into pure suspicion, but he didn't say anything else.

So I didn't either.

I just needed him to get me to a city. Surely they needed plant-growing magic in icy fae cities. Assuming I got there safely, I could find someone to give me a job and a place to live.

With a job and a place to live, I'd actually be free.

"You're not going to ask why I captured you? Or why I connected us?" His suspicion lowered his voice in a way that made my toes curl and my body warm.

I'd read steamy books before—plenty of them. But none had mentioned someone's voice making me attracted to them.

How unnerving.

I took another bite of my berry, and pointedly did not ask any of those questions.

"You're an assassin," he said, springing to his feet.

The female esu behind him gave a warning growl, and the one next to her joined in.

I eyed them suspiciously, not sure if they were growling at him or me. "If I'm an assassin, I've been very poorly trained."

His glowing blue eyes met my glowing greens.

It was time for a subject change. "Since I'm your captive, you should probably find a place to wash me up. And a new dress for me to wear."

He scoffed. "No."

Very well then.

I took another bite of my fruit.

He stalked back to the esu and sat down.

I found myself staring curiously at the glowing silver mark on his palm and the handprint on my wrist, but didn't ask the fae about it again. He didn't seem like he cared to answer my questions, and I was suspicious about the connection he'd apparently created between us.

A *mate* connection.

I definitely couldn't tell him that he'd saved my life by getting me out of my tower. He might think I owed it to him to be his mate or something.

The fae scowled at me while I finished my fruit. It wasn't anywhere near enough, but I didn't see any other fruit hiding in the trees or bushes nearby.

He rose to his feet while I was looking around, and when I turned my head, I found him climbing on his esu. "We're leaving," he said.

My bonded esu—whatever that meant—prowled over to me.

I eyed her uneasily as she bowed her head toward me.

"You want me to climb on?" I asked.

She bobbed her head.

Guess I was climbing on.

She crouched down, and I slipped onto her back. The moment I touched her fur, my eyes closed and I felt another tingle up my spine.

A soft, warm consciousness met mine before it spoke into my mind. *"Hello, Nissa."*

"Hello." My voice was a lot more tentative than hers. *"Do you have a name?"*

"I do. I am Brightfangs. The king's companion is Deathjaws. Most fae know us only by the first portion of our names."

So Bright, and Death.

Because that wasn't terrifying at all.

She began walking slowly. My eyes slid over to the fae man and his esu as I adjusted my grip on her fur. I didn't want to hurt her, but also didn't want to fall off her back.

"That fae is the king? Do you know his name?" I paused. *"And do esu have magic the way fae do?"*

"Esu have no magic of our own, though we are impervious to all other magics. And yes, Deathjaws' companion is Kierden Jirev, king of the tree fae."

She pronounced his name keer-din jer-ev.

"Tree fae?" I asked.

"There are three branches of fae. Though they all have the same magic, they organize themselves into three kingdoms. Esu know them based on where they live—they have a kingdom in the trees, one inside the mountains, and a third on an island of ice a ways off the sea's shore."

Damn.

We humans had always been told that the fae just lived in the jungle called the Endless Wilds. I guess we weren't completely wrong, if they did have a city in the trees.

"Is that where we're going?" I asked her. *"To the tree fae city?"*

"Yes. Deathjaws asked me to follow him to Jirev."

"Is he the esu king, since Kierden is the fae king?"

She made a chuffing sound that reminded me a little of a laugh. *"Esu have no rulers. I respect his request because he carries your mate."*

"What does it mean to be a fae's mate?

"There haven't been mated fae for many centuries, but their mate bonds connect their minds and magic."

I grimaced. *"Why did Kierden start a mate bond with me then, even if it's temporary?"*

"I'm uncertain. I'll ask Deathjaws what he knows, but he may not share something if his companion doesn't wish him to. They've been bonded for many, many years."

"That's alright. It's probably better not to make him suspicious. I don't want to cause you any problems with him."

I felt her amusement roll across our connection. *"He'll expect me to inquire for you. Their companion is the top priority for an esu until he or she has taken a mate, and even then, the connection is treasured greatly."*

"Is that why you were in the forest waiting for me? How long were you there?" I asked.

"I felt drawn to you when you were a child, and have kept as close an eye on you as I could since then. The shifters didn't like having me in their woods, so I had to move around continuously and wasn't able to see you often."

"Well, thank you for waiting for me, Bright."

"It was a privilege, Nissa. I rather enjoy watching the plants bloom around you."

"I do too," I admitted. *"I just wish I had some control over it."*

"You will learn." Her simple belief in me was foreign after so many years in that damn tower. It made my throat swell with emotion.

She started to move faster—to jog, then to run, and we both grew quiet. My mind calmed as I felt the plants around me explode with life when we passed them.

I was fairly certain that our mate connection had given me access to Kierden's magic, because the pull of my power was still much slower, as if the ice was chilling it somehow.

That made me appreciate our bond, at least a little bit.

We ran until the moment my stomach rumbled. When it did, Bright stopped abruptly next to a fruit tree and murmured, *"You need to build your strength. You are very light."*

She was right, so I grabbed a piece of fruit.

Kierden and Death caught up to us a moment later. The king was glaring at me, and Death looked absolutely unsurprised to find me eating. I wondered if he'd spoken mentally to Bright when he realized she wasn't behind him anymore.

"Did you tell them my name?" I asked Bright.

I was coming to like our bond tremendously, already.

"I did not. Neither of them asked me."

Veil, what giant asses.

"Don't tell them, please. If the king decides he cares about my name, he needs to ask for it himself."

She chuffed again, and I took a large, irritated bite of the fruit in my hands.

Kierden scowled at me. "You ate less than an hour ago."

I took another bite.

It felt incredibly good to eat, even if I was still annoyed with the king.

"Deathjaws wants to know why your stomach growled so quickly after eating," Bright said.

"They starved me in the tower," I admitted.

Her rage rolled through me and made my own anger about the years of mistreatment feel justified.

At least I knew I had *someone* on my side.

"I'm sorry, Nissa. If I had known, I would've intervened sooner."

"It's not your fault," I assured her. *"I don't want Kierden to know, since he doesn't care enough to ask my name."*

She didn't seem convinced, but didn't argue. *"I won't tell Deathjaws or the king."*

"Thank you."

I finished the fruit, and then Bright carried me to a river to wash my hands. I ended up splashing my face and arms too, attempting to wash myself, and made her chuff a little more.

Both of us ignored the glaring males beside us.

When I was satisfied that I was as clean as I was going to get without a true bath, I slipped onto Bright's back again, and we took off.

The rest of the day was littered with stops for food. Kierden got angrier with every one of them—and I started to enjoy the power that Bright gave me just by existing even more.

I suppose *freedom* would be a better description than *power*, but freedom felt a lot like power after the life I'd lived.

When Bright stopped and let Death know that I needed to sleep, Kierden slipped off the back of his esu, muttering curses under his breath.

I pretended not to hear him cursing, settling on a fallen log with yet another piece of fruit in my hands.

With a moment of focus, he created another box-shaped shelter that had an opening on one side. If not for his magic tangled with mine, I'd have frozen to death in the structure. Thanks to his power, I didn't seem to feel the cold at all.

"Do you have any questions now?" the man growled at me as I ate.

"Not any you seem willing to answer." Maybe I had a bit of a stubborn streak. Or a lot of one.

He crouched in front of me and grabbed the mass of my hair, which hung to my hips in wild tangles. Before I could push him away, he'd lifted the strands away from my face and was studying my ears.

His expression twisted with some emotion I couldn't read. Probably distaste.

"I told you, I'm human." I pulled my hair out of his grip—or at least tried to. His hands tightened so I let go, shooting him a glare. "Don't touch me."

His eyes flashed with something I couldn't read, and he dug his fingers into my hair so he had complete control over my head's position. With a surprisingly gentle motion, he tilted my face back and exposed my neck.

I was too surprised and confused to bother fighting his hold.

Veil, maybe I was even a little turned on by it.

Bright gave a low, warning growl.

Death started growling with her, too, but neither of the esu made a move to attack either me or Kierden.

"Your magic is draining me dry," he said. "Cut it off, now."

"Give me a reason to."

He glared at me.

I waited.

Finally, he said through gritted teeth, "I started the mate bond because there was no way around it. I was told that I had to ignite the connection between us, or let myself be hunted by the Beast of the Endless Wilds."

It took a moment for the title to set in.

The Beast of the Endless Wilds...

"One of the elves' assassins is looking for you?" I asked, growing alarmed.

Everyone had heard stories about the three monsters the elves had created for protection. According to the legends I'd heard, the creatures had grown too strong and then slaughtered a lot of the elves. Supposedly, they now prowled all of Evare, glutting themselves on the blood and power of any living creatures they could find.

"*Hunting* me." He tilted his head toward a mark I hadn't noticed on the back of his hand—the glowing one that wasn't buried in my hair. "The assassins can only kill those they've been paid to hunt."

My face paled. "And he's coming for you?"

"He was, until I bonded us as mates. Now your magic will conceal mine from him until he manages to track me another way."

Veil.

"Why would being mates change that? What does being mates even mean?" I asked, wanting his definition on top of the vague one Bright had already given me.

"A mate bond is a death sentence among the fae. You'll keep it a secret until the suns' eclipse erases it. Our connection means nothing."

"If you want me to keep it a secret, tell me what it actually *is*. I want concrete answers, Kierden."

He growled, "A sealed bond is a soul-deep connection that lasts through this life and every other that follows after you cross the veil. What I created between us is the start of a connection. It will vanish entirely with the next eclipse unless you seal it by repeating what I said back—which you will not be doing."

Those foreign words ran through my mind as if I'd just heard them. *"Sillah ovim rett warumm."*

"Obviously I have no desire to do that. Why is a mate bond a death sentence? And how does it protect you against a *magical assassin?*"

He scowled, still holding his grip on my hair. "Because your magic is life and mine is death, yours is supposed to hide mine. A mate bond alters the magic of both parties. I'm sure you can feel my ice strengthening you even as your damned plants strangle me slowly. Centuries ago, a cult formed that killed anyone who created a mate bond. Most of the cult was eradicated afterward in revenge, but some of its members slipped through the cracks. All around Evare, they still hunt down mated pairs and slay them mercilessly."

My eyebrows shot upward. "So you're risking *my* life in an attempt to save yourself."

"Yes." He didn't seem apologetic, not even a little.

"Well, at least you can admit that you're a bastard."

He wasn't fazed by the insult. "I gave you the information you wanted. Now cut off the magic."

Guess it was time for honesty. "I can't."

His grip on my hair tightened, and I inhaled sharply at the suddenness of it. Maybe it should've scared me, but for whatever reason, I wasn't afraid of the king in the slightest. *"Now, human."*

A furry, muscular body slammed into the king's side. He released me as the force of the esu rolled both of them. My eyes widened as I watched the king and Bright wrestle, her teeth snapping insanely close to his throat while he only defended himself.

"Enough." A low growl rolled through my mind, and my attention jerked to Death, who was prowling toward the wrestling fae and esu.

Kierden released his hold on Bright. She remained on top of him as she snarled into his face, snapping her teeth at him but not biting him. Fury edged her voice as she said, *"A male esu would sooner skin himself alive than physically hurt his mate. A king should know better, even if your bond is temporary."*

Kierden growled back, "Your companion is *draining me*, and I didn't grip her hair tightly enough to hurt her."

"She's draining you unintentionally, and humans are hurt more easily than fae," Bright snapped. *"You're the one who created the bond, so you have no one to blame but yourself. Apologize."*

"I am a *king*. I apologize to no one."

"No one except your bonded esu—and your bonded mate." She bared her teeth at him, sharp white fangs practically glistening.

"Brightfangs is correct. You bound yourself to the human; she's now your responsibility until the eclipse erases the bond," Death said, still speaking loud enough for me to hear him.

Kierden snarled, but when Bright climbed off him, he covered the distance between me and him in the blink of an eye. His eyes burned with some emotion I couldn't read—probably anger—and he gritted out, "I was not trying to harm you. It won't happen again."

Well, that was a terrible apology.

But something told me it was the best I was going to get, and I really didn't want Bright to kill the fae before he led me to his city.

So, I simply nodded once, and then went back to eating.

CHAPTER FOUR

NISSA

Kierden's temper calmed as he ate too. We didn't speak to each other, but Bright came over and sat next to me. I found myself stroking her fur and leaning against her.

It had been so long since I felt loved. Or even like I really mattered to someone. And in such a short time she had already made sure I had time to eat and sleep, and defended me too.

Kierden finished his food, then strode to the shelter he'd created. He folded himself inside easily, though he barely fit in the thing.

Not at all interested in snuggling with the big old bastard, I curled up on the ground.

"The shifters could hunt you down if you're not in the shelter," Bright said into my mind. *"You'll need to sleep next to the king."*

"That shelter is tiny," I protested.

"It takes a great amount of magic to keep a small shelter up while a fae sleeps. The king is sacrificing to protect you, even if it doesn't seem like it."

Oh.

"Can't the shifters still smell us, though? Or just follow the trail of my plants?"

"Yes. But when they see me and Deathjaws beside the king's shelter, they will leave. Getting past two esu and through thick ice walls would be no small feat, even for a pack of wolves."

So it was about intimidation on top of physical protection.

Which meant I was going to have to climb into that tiny shelter with Kierden.

I heaved a sigh, then stood up slowly and made my way over on reluctant legs.

The king was taking up the entire space, which meant I was going to have to literally lay on him.

Thanks to all my years in the tower, I had never shared a bed with anyone. Or kissed anyone. Or done anything else resembling sex. I'd read a bunch of books about it though, and overheard a long discussion about it between two adults when I was fifteen, so I had a basic understanding of how everything worked.

I'd tested some things on myself to make sure my body functioned, too. Everyone got lusty when an eclipse happened, so after I'd matured, I had the option of dealing with it or just waiting for the desire to fade. There had been a clear winner.

But that didn't make it any less intimidating to face the fact that I was going to have to literally climb on top of a king.

I walked up to the shelter and peered inside.

Yeah.

Wow.

Not much room.

A sigh escaped me.

The king gave me an annoyed growl but said nothing.

Part of me itched to warn him that I would figure out a way to literally rip him apart with my vines if he trapped me inside it alone again. For obvious reasons, I didn't do well with the thought of being imprisoned again.

But Kierden didn't seem to have realized the purpose of my tower, so I wasn't going to bring it up.

I bit my lip to hide my cringe as I climbed right in on top of the king. My dress tangled around my calves, and I knew I probably smelled terrible, but I ignored those things.

His chest felt insanely good beneath my hands.

I blamed that on the bond.

He gave me a dark look while I tried to get comfortable on top of him, and my cringe grew apologetic. "Sorry."

He muttered something I didn't understand, and I decided not to ask him about it as I finally collapsed on his chest. He was significantly bigger than me, so my forehead nestled against his neck.

"If you're an assassin, I'll make your end incredibly painful," he grumbled to me.

"If I'm an assassin, someone forgot to train me," I mumbled back against his throat. The brush of my lips on his skin made me shiver a little, and one of his hands landed on my lower back.

My toes curled, and I fought hard to ignore the warmth blossoming in my chest.

Something hardened against my belly, and my eyes opened wide.

He was turned on.

I'd turned him on.

"The damn bond is affecting my body," he growled at me.

"Same," I whispered back. I was pretty sure fae senses were good enough that he could probably smell my own growing desire. At least I wasn't the only one who had to deal with that awkwardness.

"You smell terrible," he added.

It sounded like he was trying to convince himself, though.

"So do you," I lied.

The smell on his skin was something deep and wild, and enticed me far, far too much.

I couldn't say that, though.

So we both just went to sleep.

The second day went a lot like the first one.

Kierden only spoke to me to grumble about how many stops I made him take. He didn't ask my name, or about my tower. I didn't ask about his kingdom, or his friends.

We just traveled.

And made an incredible number of stops for food, all of which frustrated the king. They made me happy, though.

We spent the second night the same way we had the first, with both of us denying our growing lust, and then began another day that went exactly the way the first two had gone.

We made it out of the Broken Woods as the last sun set on the third night, and camped near the beginning of a massive strip of desert called the Timeless Sands. It was a no-man's-land of sorts, where humans and magical beings would go to trade or simply coexist. I knew it was full of crime, and had never wanted to see it for myself.

It wasn't safe for the esu to sleep outside alone there, so we all packed together in Kierden's shelter. I ended up trapped between Bright and the king. Her sharp claws and teeth led me to burrow against Kierden, and despite a few grumbles, he didn't tell me to move.

We all woke up a little more tired the next day, and resumed our journey in grim silence.

Halfway through the morning, we approached a small town. Kierden made me wait a short distance away with the esu while he went in, and a few minutes later, he came back with a big bag of assorted food items for me.

I thanked him profusely, and it seemed to soften him a little. He was much less bitter as we made our way through the desert over the next two and a half days with significantly fewer stops for food. There wasn't much growing anyway, outside of the cacti. My magic made fruits and flowers blossom on the spiky green plants, but we didn't eat them.

Kierden and I didn't become friends, but I had stopped disliking him so much, at least.

He relaxed much more when we finally made it through the desert and into the fiercely-beautiful jungle that was the Endless Wilds. Thick, massive trees packed the space, climbing so far into the sky that they concealed the suns entirely. Their branches and trunks were wrapped in winding vines that brought color everywhere the vibrant human-sized leaves did not.

The esu moved much faster through the jungle, rejuvenated by the thick trees and branches they ran through. The jungle was their home, and it showed.

Kierden and I still didn't talk more than was necessary, or share stories. Despite the hardness I felt against my belly every night when we went to sleep, and the warmth that flooded my body, neither of us acknowledged our physical responses to each other again, or made an effort to become friends.

Both of us knew what our connection was—his selfish attempt to save his own life.

And even though I hadn't admitted it to him, he was saving my life too.

. . .

Eight days had gone by when Bright finally warned me that we were approaching the city. Just a little light from one of our moons filtered through the leaves and branches above us, but my eyesight seemed to have gotten better after the connection with Kierden was established, because I could see just fine.

Traveling with a grumpy fae king was a world's improvement from the awful life I'd lived in that tower. My belly was full and there were no ropes on my wrists or ankles. The temporary mate bond was a chain of its own, but for some reason it didn't feel like one.

Hope made my eyes bright and my stomach curl with excitement. Getting closer to a city where I could start fresh with a chance to actually live my life... veil, it was a rush.

Bright and Death moved quickly, climbing higher into the branches, and my eyes widened when I caught my first glimpse of the city.

It was literally built into the trees, with branches and bridges working as pathways, and buildings *carved* into the living giants around us.

The vines thickened as we neared them, slowly crawling further over the branches and trunks. Kierden muttered curses in his mind loudly enough that I could hear him damning my magic, and my lips curved upward.

"Don't destroy my city," he growled into my mind.

"Did you figure out how to control my magic while I wasn't looking?" I shot back.

He didn't answer.

The bastard knew I had no control over it, hadn't attempted to teach me any control, and had failed in every effort to gain control of it himself. He'd decided that he didn't think we would be able to use each other's magic unless we sealed the bond, which we agreed was *not* going to happen.

So yeah, whatever happened to his city was his own fault.

He added, *"Hide the handprint. If anyone asks why I brought you here, tell them the kings have planned an event in their competition that requires humans."*

My forehead knitted. *"An event? I'm not doing an event. What does that even mean?"*

As much as I liked to argue with him, I wasn't taking the risk of getting murdered by some cultist. I wrapped my non-glowing arm over my glowing wrist, so it covered the silver handprint entirely.

"The three fae kingdoms have been at war for centuries. The other kings and I finally settled on a peace treaty a few weeks ago, and had our people put together a bunch of violent events to turn the tension into entertainment. That's why there are so many fae here right now—I was the only one willing to host it."

My eyes scanned the trees around us with some amount of interest as we passed group after group of fae, as well as a ton of trees carved into buildings. There was ice scattered in the trees too, used as bridges or decorations, though most of it seemed to be in some stage of melting.

"So there are three cities-worth of fae here?" I asked him.

I had no idea how many fae there usually were to a city, so that didn't really mean much to me.

"Three kingdoms'-worth. Each kingdom has only one massive city, which is always given the surname of its current king. There used to be more before the war according to the legends, but very few of us remember those times."

"And you left the other kings to run this whole thing so you could come find me?" My skepticism was heavy.

"No. All three of us were targeted by the assassins so we all left to hunt humans with life magic. There were enough people I trusted here to run the city while I was gone and the events were already planned, so it should've gone smoothly."

I felt like *should've* was the most important word there.

"No one's fighting, so it seems to have worked," Kierden added, looking past me as we continued.

"I guess that's a good sign..."

"It is. My people are fine."

I nodded, like I believed him. Maybe I did. I supposed that would be determined when I met whoever he trusted.

Assuming he didn't lock me up in his castle.

My body went stiff at the realization that was a possibility. *"Do you think he'll trap me again?"* I asked Bright.

"I don't know," she admitted. *"I can eat him, if he does."*

I tried to smile but failed.

Veil, I hoped he didn't try to lock me up.

If he did, the reluctant peace we had established was going to change drastically. I'd make that bastard regret picking me as his temporary mate, somehow.

The esu carried us through the city for nearly an hour before we reached the largest tree I'd ever seen. It had to be nearly as big as my town, with a house-sized entrance carved into the front. The tree's trunk was dotted with what appeared to be windows, and there were thick vines wrapped around many of its branches, growing toward the tree as if trying to reach out and touch it.

"This is the castle," Bright told me.

Flowers blossomed on the tree and vines as we passed through the open doorway, and Kierden growled a few more curses as we left them behind.

The king had to take at least some of the blame for that. It wasn't my fault he'd combined our magics, making mine work so much better than it usually did, without exhausting me so quickly.

Bright and Death carried us through a maze of hallways before we finally blazed through a door and into a massive room. We'd passed many fae, but none of them bowed at Kierden. They just looked at us both curiously.

The doors to the room closed behind us as I slipped off Bright's back. Kierden dismounted too, and we both gave the esu an affectionate scratch behind the ears while I looked around. The room was made entirely of wood, as was to be expected considering we were in a gigantic tree. The wood was smooth, and sealed with something that made it just a little shiny.

Without saying a word to me about where we were or exactly what we were doing there, Kierden strode toward a large pool of water off to the side of the room. It had to be at least as big as *two* of my tower.

"You're bathing," he told me as he went.

I blinked at him before my gaze moved back to the room. It had to be Kierden's room, based on the way he was making himself at home in it.

It was as big as three homes in my town, with a bed nearly the size of my tower up against one wall, a closet and bathroom up against the second, and the dark stone bathing pool in the corner where the other two met.

There were no windows, but that seemed intentional. It was large, and I could tell everything was made with the utmost luxury. But it seemed... bland.

Even my tower had a few simple decorations.

A pretty blue bowl someone had once sent with my food in it, on the table in the tiny kitchen I'd never had enough food to use.

A small ribbon I'd tied my wild, wavy dark green hair back with as a child.

The many books the town gave me to keep me from going insane.

Kierden's room had none of those things.

My gaze moved back to the pool. If that was his bathtub, perhaps small decorations weren't good enough for him.

My eyes widened when the king pushed his shorts down his thighs, and my cheeks began to burn. Part of me felt like I should jerk my head and look away, but the part of me that warmed every time we shared a bed kept me watching.

I wasn't sure what most men's asses looked like but damn, his was nice. I suddenly understood the appeal of a strong backside.

Self-consciousness had me patting my own.

Nope, it certainly wasn't strong. Or soft.

Guess I'd be leaving my dress on.

"I'll bathe after you," I told the king, finally forcing myself to look away as I turned and began to rub the fur on Bright's head. She leaned toward me as I did.

A chuff escaped her when Death crossed the room rapidly and then dove into the pool in a sleek motion. My gaze followed the esu.

Kierden ignored my words, disappearing beneath the water. Soap bubbled up to the surface as he scrubbed his skin and hair, and I wondered if it took him any effort to stop his ice magic from just leaking out and freezing the water. I couldn't imagine having an ice power that worked the way my own magic did. What a nightmare.

The king broke the surface after a moment and then climbed out of the pool while facing away from me. My eyes followed the water down his back, to his ass, to his thighs, and I found myself wiping at my mouth just to make sure I wasn't drooling.

I wasn't, thankfully.

He grabbed a towel I hadn't noticed hanging nearby and dragged it over his head. I watched as he dried his arms off, and then wrapped the towel around his waist. Before he was done, I made sure to turn myself toward Bright and focused on scratching her ears so he wouldn't realize I'd been staring at him.

But damn, I had really wanted him to turn toward me. I'd never actually seen a cock before, and I was curious.

That was probably a bad thing to admit, but I didn't particularly care if it made me terrible.

As he strode toward the closet, the entry doors burst open and a gorgeous fae woman walked through with a massive esu at her side. All she had on was a black binding around her chest and tiny black shorts. Relief gleamed in the woman's eyes, until they landed on me.

Then, that relief morphed into suspicion.

I knew she couldn't have been his mate, because Bright told me fae didn't take mates. And because of the bond between us, obviously.

But what if she was his lover? No one had told me whether or not fae took companions of the other sex without starting mate bonds.

She and Kierden looked nothing alike. Where he was tan with dark, wavy hair, she was pale with straight white-blonde hair that had streaks of vibrant blue throughout it, matching the electric blue that glowed in her eyes.

"You are a *fool*, Kier," the woman finally said, looking away from me and back at the king. "An utter fool. How could you think this was a good idea? Do you know how many brawls I had to fight to keep the damned Vuuths from tearing our city to shreds?"

"This was the *only* idea. You know it wasn't mine." He disappeared into the closet. "And I'm sure you enjoyed the brawls."

She followed him. Between the nickname and following him in while he got dressed?

Yeah, definitely his lover.

They didn't close the door behind them, so I could see the large gap between them as Kierden faced away from her. He pulled on a pair of tight, small shorts that must've been his undergarments, followed by longer shorts like the ones he'd been wearing since we met.

"My enjoyment doesn't matter because those brawls were unnecessary, and a risk to the peace. I—*veil*, what is on your hand?" She grabbed his wrist as he started to step past her, and there was a long moment's pause before she released it. "Damn. You really are mated."

"Temporarily."

She dragged a hand through the top of her smooth, straight hair. Since she was facing me then, I saw her expression grow considerate. At least until she wrinkled her nose while glancing at me. "You'll need to wash his scent off your skin, along with all that filth. You reek."

I blinked.

Was she talking to me?

She had to be talking to me, right? She hadn't even acknowledged me earlier though, so I was having a hard time believing it.

"She speaks, right?" the fae woman glanced at Kierden.

"Yes, Eisley." He pronounced her name *eyes-lee*. "I already told her to bathe. She didn't listen." The king wound some fabric around his hand, then tied it into place with his teeth. It covered his palm entirely, blocking the glow of our bond and the brand on the back of his hand.

"What's her name?"

My face heated at the way they were talking about me.

"I haven't asked." With that he strode out of the room, abandoning me to the mercy of his lover. Death followed him out, walking confidently at the king's side.

What a damn asshole.

CHAPTER FIVE
NISSA

The door shut behind them, and Eisley looked at me again. "He didn't even ask for your name? You were traveling for six or seven days, right?"

"Eight," I admitted. "And no, he didn't."

She scoffed. "Bastard."

At least we'd found something to agree on. That would ease the awkwardness of the mate-vs-lover thing. Considering the size of her muscles and the fact that she was a fae, I did *not* want to start a fight with her.

An ache bloomed in my wrist where the glowing handprint was, and I rubbed it absently.

"So, what's your name? You really do have to take a bath, by the way. I don't know how humans are about cleanliness, but you stink badly. And right now, wearing a male's scent on your skin when it's not the eclipse will get you gutted around here."

"I'm Nissa," I said. "I'd rather the king not know my name until he's asked me himself."

"Ohhh, good revenge. I won't tell him." She gave me a wicked grin.

I gave her a small smile in return. "Thank you. Are you guys together, or..." I trailed off, not wanting to come right out and ask if they were lovers.

"Nope." She made a disgusted face. "I'm the bastard's sister."

Ah.

Siblings.

I'd always hoped for one. After I'd lost my family altogether and been locked up, I would've taken just about anything. Sibling, aunt, grandmother, second-cousin-twice-removed...

"Are fae really lax about nudity?" I asked.

Her eyes glittered with amusement. "Yup. Everyone's seen everyone's naked bits a thousand times over. They all look pretty much the same, so no one's worried about it around here."

That made the closet situation more understandable, I supposed.

Since I really did want to take a bath, I headed to the pool. The fae I'd seen so far were extremely muscular, so their naked bits would *not* look like mine. Even as a child, I'd never been particularly skinny or strong. I was decidedly average among humans.

And something told me that I'd never look like the fae, even if I worked hard at it.

"I'll go find you something to wear. Oh, and there's another human woman in the castle with one of the other kings; you can meet her when you don't stink like my brother."

Eisley left the room without waiting for my thanks, and I noticed the gleam of metal on the inside of her thigh, and the back of her arm.

Were those *knives*?

Her bonded esu remained for a moment as he studied me with narrowed eyes. He was just as tall as Death but built even thicker, which made him even more terrifying somehow.

I shivered as he turned around and left the room. The door swung shut behind him, apparently built to allow the esu to come and go as they wished.

"*I don't know whether to be nervous or excited about meeting another magical human,*" I said to Bright as I stripped and then sat down on the ledge of the pool. It had been a long, long time since I last swam. Even as a child, I hadn't been great at it. Something about deep water had always scared me a little.

"*I'm sure it'll be nice not to feel so alone,*" Bright said, and then dove in the same way Death had. She swam around for a minute before climbing out and shaking off. My lips stretched in a grin as water splattered all over Kierden's perfectly-clean floors.

The ache in the marking on my wrist had graduated to a dull throb, which I wasn't a fan of, but I continued to ignore it. I didn't know what was causing it, so there wasn't anything I could do about it.

My thoughts churned a bit. "*I don't know what I'm supposed to do while I'm here. I'd like to find a place to belong, where I can be useful and comfortable. Kierden only brought me so he doesn't get killed before the eclipse, so what does that mean for me after the bond is gone?*" I slipped into the water and found a simple seat below the surface. The temperature was a perfect neutral, and the seat was just deep enough that the top of the water rose a little above my chin.

"*The fae still have to grow their food. Make a deal to take over as the farmer and you could live a very comfortable life here or in any of the other fae lands. Kierden's kingdom is known to be the most welcoming as far as the fae go, so this one may be the best choice.*"

"*What if I want to go back to the humans?*" I asked. As the words left my lips, I knew that wasn't a possibility. I'd never forget what my own family had done to me, or how my town had starved me to feed and clothe themselves. I hoped they'd all rot without me, even though I knew it was a terrible hope to have.

But some awful feelings were reasonable ones.

"*Then we'll find a better town, or a large kingdom.*"

"He only needs my magic, right?" I asked her. *"Maybe I can leave before the eclipse as long as I stay bonded to him. I don't really want to deal with his grumpiness for the next two and a half months."*

"If he was okay with that, he'd have left you in your town after starting the bond with you."

I wished she wasn't right.

When I found a bar of soap on a ledge near my face, I took it and used it to scrub myself clean. The throbbing in my wrist morphed into a sharp, stabbing pain.

There was nothing to be done about it though, so I did my best to ignore it as I surfaced and started to clean my hair.

After a few minutes, it grew so painful that I had to sit still and squeeze my eyes shut while I waited for it to pass.

"Are you alright?" Bright asked me. She was sitting beside the pool, drying off.

"I don't know. The handprint on my wrist feels like someone's stabbing a knife into it."

She gave a low growl. *"I'll find the king."*

"You don't need to—" I cut myself off as the door shut behind her, leaving me entirely alone.

I leaned the back of my head against the hard stone of the bathing pool and stared up at the wood ceiling.

The pain was bad enough to cloud my mind, and I focused on breathing as I waited for it to abate.

In.

Out.

In.

Out.

I didn't know how much time passed. Five minutes, maybe ten?

The doors to Kierden's room finally opened again, and Eisley came walking back through. She had a bundle of fabric tossed over her arm, and her angry-looking bonded esu at her side.

She frowned when she saw me. "Are you okay?"

I let out a slow breath, not sure I could speak through the pain.

After another minute passed I managed to say, "The handprint is causing me pain."

Her forehead furrowed and she glanced at her esu. He gave me a long glower before slinking away, and she patted his back as he left.

"We'll get Kier back in here."

I closed my eyes. "Sounds like a good way to make him angry."

She laughed. "He's usually angry. It's a requirement when you're a violent fae warrior who's been leading others into battles for hundreds of years. The anger keeps all the other shitty emotions at bay."

I supposed that was decent logic.

Choose anger, and you wouldn't have to acknowledge whatever else you were feeling.

"Sounds like a good way to make yourself miserable," I murmured.

She grinned. "Yup. Come on; let's get you dressed and moving, in case Kier ignores Sharp and we have to hunt him down."

"Sharp?"

"My bonded esu. Sharpclaws. I asked him to try to drag my brother back."

Ohhh.

"Bright went too," I admitted as I eased myself carefully out of the pool. Though I tried not to put pressure on my hand, I mostly failed. "She's my bonded esu, I guess. I'm still trying to wrap my mind around everything."

Eisley looked at my bare body with a deep frown. My face warmed as I quickly wrapped myself in the towel and attempted to wring my hair out with one of the flaps of it.

"Everyone knows Bright," she said.

"Really? Why?"

"She's something of a legend among the fae. She fought fiercely along-side us for centuries but always refused to bond with any of us. None of the fae have even heard her speak before, as far as I know. When there are no battles to fight, she disappears, and no one can find her. Two decades ago, she vanished entirely. No one had seen her since then until today."

Well, that took me aback.

"Why?"

Eisley shrugged. "People would always say that she was waiting for her companion to be born. The assumption was that she must have a soul-deep connection with her companion, one that lasted beyond the veil separating us from the life before and the life after. But fae aren't *born* anymore. We stopped procreating when the last of the mated pairs were murdered, shortly after my birth. Between the horror of that and everyone's focus on the war, there haven't been any new babies, so we didn't know if she'd ever meet her companion."

"People in my town would see an esu in the woods behind our village every now and then while I was growing up," I admitted. "I felt an itch to go out looking for her my entire life, but my father kept me in the village as a kid, and then..." I bit my lip. "Well, it didn't happen."

I didn't want to tell her about my tower.

I didn't even want to *think* about that prison.

"Does Kier know you've been starving?" Eisley asked, abruptly.

My throat swelled.

So much for avoiding that conversation. "I don't think so."

Eisley bobbed her head. "Don't tell him. Mated fae are driven to care for their mates, so he'd make you insane by shoving food in your face constantly until your ribs aren't showing." She handed me the fabric bundle in her hands. "This will probably be too big, but it'll cover more of your skin than anything else I have. We can find you some clothes of your own after tonight's event is over. It already went long, and with Kier there, it's going to go even longer."

I dropped my towel and dressed quickly. The fae undergarments were smaller than human ones, just triangles of fabric that barely covered the important bits, but I wasn't entirely surprised given what Eisley was wearing. She said they called their undergarments "scanties," and according to her, most of Evare did too.

The pain in my wrist was still pretty fierce, but it had faded enough that I could function a little.

"What's the event?"

Eisley grinned. "A wrestling tournament. We started with weapons two weeks ago, and finally graduated to physical fighting without anything but your hands."

Ah.

"It probably doesn't sound interesting to a human since you aren't as violent as us, but picture this—dozens of naked fae males rolling around together as they try to establish dominance."

My cheeks went pink at her description as I tugged the dress into place. It was made up of rich black fabric with a top that arched over my breasts, a voluminous skirt that fell to the middle of my thighs, and two puffy sleeves that wrapped around my biceps and only connected to the dress with tiny strips of fabric.

"You look absolutely killer in black," Eisley said with a grin. Despite what she'd expected, the dress wasn't too big at all. In my starving state, I was about as wide around as a healthy fae woman. I'd definitely be more curvaceous than them when I gained a little of the weight back.

My stomach rumbled as if on cue, and I spread a hand over my abdomen.

Eisley's grin vanished. "Let's find you something fattening to eat, and you can meet the other human."

She handed me a thick metal cuff bracelet to go around my wrist and cover up the handprint as we headed out of the room.

We found the other human woman sitting in a chair in the castle's dining hall when we got there. She was alone at a massive table, with enough plates in front of her to feed the largest family in my town.

She waved when she saw me and Eisley, barely taking her attention off the food in front of her to do so. She wore a dress similar to mine, but hers was tight and the off-shoulder sleeves were long. Her skin was paler than anyone's I'd ever seen, and her hair was somehow both red and orange at the same time.

Eisley gestured for me to sit next to the other human, so I slipped into a chair while she introduced us. "Laeli, this is Nissa. Nissa, this is Laeli."

"You're stuck with a fae bastard too?" Laeli asked me, cutting into something that smelled absolutely incredible.

My stomach rumbled again, louder. "Unfortunately."

She nodded. "It sucks, but at least there's food. I've been locked in a damn cellar since my magic came in, and my town rarely bothered to feed me."

"I was trapped in a tower," I admitted.

She shivered. "I do *not* do well with heights, so I don't envy you. Here." She pushed one of her plates over to me.

Eisley pushed the plate back to Laeli. "I'll have the kitchen make her something." She strode away, leaving me alone with the other human.

"So what's your power?" Laeli asked, pushing the plate back to me.

I didn't hesitate to grab one of the strange-looking pastries off it. "Plants. They grow around me, draining my magic in a few hours. I have no control over it."

Her eyes brightened with interest. "Damn, that's lucky. My magic is uncontrollable too, but it's fire magic. You can feel the heat in the air around me constantly, and if I feel anything too strongly, I burn."

"Really? Have you ever burned yourself?"

She grinned. "I've tried, but the fire dodges me. I'll show you if you're ever around when I light up."

I suddenly found myself hoping she would lose her temper.

The pain in my wrist suddenly flared, and I swore, clutching the pastry so tightly that it balled in my fist. "Veil."

"Do you have a handprint too? These things are miserable." She tugged the top of her sleeve down, showing a silver handprint on her bicep and then quickly covering it again. "I told Ravv that if he keeps walking away from me, I'm going to melt his ice castle. He's stayed close enough not to ignite the pain since then. He's a grumpy asshole, but he doesn't seem to want to start another war."

"Is walking away what triggers it?" I asked, taking a bite of the crumpled pastry and then setting it on the plate so I could massage the aching handprint.

"Mmhm. Physical distance seems to do it."

I nodded, considering what she'd said. It had started after Kierden left me, so I supposed that made sense.

"Does it cause the men pain too?"

"Yep. They like to pretend they don't feel it, though. Makes them feel better about themselves and those tiny fae cocks."

I snorted, and she flashed me a grin.

I'd never seen a man's cock before, but considering the size of the fae men, it seemed safe to assume theirs wouldn't be small.

"Alright, here you go." Eisley stepped back up to me with a full plate in her hands that matched one of Laeli's. I didn't hesitate to dig into the unfamiliar food. If the plates they'd given us were any indication, the fae ate a lot more bread, pasta, and other grains than they did fruits and vegetables. I'd never complain if there was pasta and bread on the table.

Eisley dropped into the chair next to me. "How's the wrist?"

I didn't want to complain about it, so I took a massive bite of a strange-looking bread instead of answering.

"Bad," Laeli said for me, popping another bite of something in her mouth. "Someone needs to find her king."

"He's helping judge the wrestling tournament, and maybe participating in it," Eisley explained. "We'll have to go to him."

Laeli shrugged. "Ravv must've skipped it."

"She said the men wrestling are all naked," I told her.

Her eyes took on a wicked gleam, and she stood suddenly. "Let's get you out of pain, then."

I laughed.

Eisley rolled her eyes. "Sit down."

"Why? We haven't established whether fae men are as possessive as their bonded animals are with their mates," Laeli pointed out. "This seems like the perfect opportunity to test the theory on someone who can't burn the jungle down." She pointed to me.

"I'm sure they're not possessive of females they're temporarily bonded to," Eisley countered.

"Kierden is disgusted by my ears, let alone the rest of me. Pretty sure possessiveness is off the table," I said.

Even as I said it, I remembered the feel of his hardness against my lower belly as I draped myself over his body.

"Everyone's just called him Kier since he was a kid. He doesn't even introduce himself as Kierden. Did he ask you to call him by his full name?" Eisley asked, her expression a bit curious.

My face warmed. "No. Bright introduced him to me that way, and I guess it stuck. He never actually told me his name himself."

"Hmm." She studied me.

I'd called him that out loud at least once or twice. Why hadn't he corrected me?

"I'm still stuck on the possessiveness, ladies. We need to know, and this is the perfect way to find out," Laeli said with a grin.

I shelved the nickname thing for later, deciding not to worry about it yet. Then I ate as much food as I could possibly handle... until the pain in my wrist grew so bad that I gave in, and off we went.

CHAPTER SIX
NISSA

My pain faded as we approached the stadium that had been carved into a massive tree just for the sake of the violent events the fae had come up with to promote peace.

It was pretty late at night by then, but none of the fae seemed ready to go home. Between the moonlight, my improved eyesight, and some magical lights I didn't have a name for that floated around the forest at random, it was illuminated enough to see without a problem.

And thanks to my pain and the excitement I had about being in a new city, I wasn't anywhere near ready to sleep.

Eisley and I had both asked our bonded esu to come back and carry us to the stadium since they weren't making any progress with Kierden. Because Laeli wasn't bonded to an animal, she rode with Eisley on our way there.

"The wrestling has gotten brutal," Bright murmured to me as she wove through the city. *"Someone convinced Kierden to join, and it grew much bloodier. They do seem to be having a good time though."*

I grimaced at the thought of someone bleeding and *enjoying it.*

Then again, it didn't surprise me at all that the king could find it entertaining. He was technically a warrior, even if his kingdom wasn't at war at the moment.

"Tell me if it makes you nauseous. We don't need you throwing up all that food," she added.

I thanked her, though I was still trying to wrap my head around it. I'd known fae existed my entire life and yet still felt like I'd been dragged into an entirely new world.

Then again, a new world was far preferable to my old one. So, the fresh start was a good thing. Eisley had been kind, and that meant there was a good chance I could convince her to find me a job after the mate connection was gone.

My eyes caught on a clump of vibrantly-colored flowers as we passed them. They were... different. I hadn't seen anything like them in the Endless Wilds or in the Broken Woods before. Flowers seemed hard to come by in the parts of our land full of magical beings.

But around me, they were everywhere. In bright pinks, reds, yellows, and oranges. In deep purples, and vibrant blues.

The vines were thicker and longer, brighter green, too. The leaves on the trees looked even more massive than usual as well.

My magic was still leaking out of me. And maybe out of Kierden too, I realized when we reached the stadium. The outside of the tree that housed it had way more flowers than any of the others we'd passed, and more vines too.

Inside the stadium the fae were roaring wildly, standing on benches that had been carved along the outer edges as they watched someone fighting in the middle. Looking at the enthusiastic group from afar, I never would've guessed there was bad blood between any of them.

Then again, one could never get the full picture from afar. If they could, Kierden would've realized I was a starving prisoner when he found me in my tower. Though there was always a chance he *did* realize I had been a prisoner and simply didn't care.

Bright followed at Eisley's bonded esu's tail. His name was Sharp, if I remembered right.

Sharp maneuvered smoothly to an empty bench right outside the huge metal cage the men were fighting in. We were as close as you could possibly get to the fight, and I—

My thoughts cut off as I slid off off Bright's back and surged toward the thick bars separating us from the fighters.

That was *Kierden's* bare backside. *Kierden's* hair. *His* arm of tattoos, too.

He was wrestling a man who looked just as large as him, and the king seemed to have the upper hand. Or the other man was beneath him, at least.

"By the veil," I breathed as I watched the man buck fiercely against the king's hold. Kierden moved with him a bit, letting the other man fight, but had no problem holding his grip on the guy.

There was blood dripping off both of them in a few different locations, though I couldn't see the wounds that were the source of it. It smeared on the ground as they moved a bit, and finally, the man beneath Kierden slapped his hand on the smooth wooden floor four times.

The king released the other man and rose to his feet smoothly. His lips were stretched in a wicked grin, and the other guy wore a grimace that somehow looked satisfied.

The roaring of the crowd grew deafening as the king wiped blood off his lip, which was definitely swollen. That was the source of some of the blood, but only a little.

My eyes moved slowly over the king's figure and my body heated as I took him in. *All* of him. His cock wasn't hard, but damn, he was still impressive.

He had a few small bleeding cuts on his arms and legs but didn't pay them any mind. The fabric he'd wrapped around his hand still remained, looking a lot bloodier than it had the last time I saw it.

Kierden offered the losing fae a hand, which he accepted. When the king had helped tug him to his feet, he and Kierden clapped each other on the back in a strange hug before he strode off the field.

Kierden turned back to the crowd, opening his arms as he faced them in all his gorgeous, naked glory and roared, "Who will challenge me?"

The words nearly started a frenzy.

"Do it," Laeli whispered to me, nudging me with her shoulder. I had been so lost in looking at Kierden's body that I'd forgotten we were there to test the fae males' possessiveness somehow. "Challenge him. You know you want to roll around with all of that."

My body flushed hotter. "No thanks."

"He would *ravage* her," Eisley tossed out.

Laeli snorted.

I couldn't help but laugh.

Eisley just grinned at me before turning back to watch the fight.

Someone else came out to wrestle Kierden. I didn't see them, because in that moment, his eyes collided with mine.

My breath halted in my lungs, and my body went still.

Kierden's gaze went from bloodthirsty to just plain furious in a heart-beat. His gaze jerked to his sister as his lips twisted in a snarl.

His chest heaved as he turned to face the new challenger.

I couldn't bring myself to look away when he and the man lunged for each other.

They moved so fast it made me dizzy.

Strong arms flexed, thick thighs moved and rolled and swung. Blood spurted, and the fae's back hit the ground so hard I could almost hear the thud over the sound of the fae roaring all around us.

Kierden was back on his feet a moment later, wiping at his nose. He ignored the crowd, his gaze meeting mine once again with even more fury. His mind touched mine—the feeling was foreign and strangely intimate. It had been more than a week since we'd spoken mentally, and that had been an accident.

This was on purpose, and the connection felt thicker and stronger.

"Get out of here now," Kierden snarled into my mind. He was turning toward another challenger as he spoke to me, but he sounded *livid*. I'd never seen or heard him that angry before, and wasn't sure what to think about it.

A thick, furry head bumped lightly against my hip. When I looked beside me I found Bright there, with Death just a short distance away from her. *"Kierden asked Death to remove you from the arena,"* she murmured.

I opened my lips to protest, but noticed that my new friend was gone and looked at Eisley instead. "What happened to Laeli?"

"You didn't hear Ravv show up? He was pissed." She grabbed my arm. "We need to go. Kier looks like he wants to kill me, and I'm usually the one person he *doesn't* want dead."

"I'd rather stay."

"Please? We can find you something new to eat. And some clothes that actually fit." Despite asking politely, she was already tugging me away.

With a sigh, I slipped onto Bright's back. She streaked out of the stadium and then into the trees, once again following Sharp closely.

The marking on my wrist started to ache as we ran. It was still only in the throbbing stage when we stopped in what I assumed was their version of a marketplace. I hadn't been to a market since I was a kid, but I'd always liked walking around to see everything.

The marketplace was a cluster of small shops built into trees and connected by dozens of bridges, ropes, and vines. There were a few icy walkways too. Those were all dripping water, so I wouldn't be going near them. With a little bit of moonlight streaming down on everything through the trees and those small floating lights moving around lazily, it was absolutely beautiful.

My eyes moved over one shop after another. Some had food and others held clothing or jewelry.

Eisley climbed off Sharp's back and led me inside the marketplace. It was flooded with fae and their companions, and I noticed there were three different types of animals. The esu, along with creatures that looked like huge white bears, and some that seemed to be monster-sized wolves with gray fur.

"What kind of animals are those?" I asked Eisley, tilting my head toward one of the busiest shops.

"Oh, the giant wolves are called xuno. Xuno bond with the fae who live in Vayme Vuuth's city beneath the mountains." She pronounced xuno like zoo-no. "The bears are called idorr, and they bond with the fae in the ice city on the ocean that Ravv Loire is the king of." She pronounced idorr, eye-door.

Ravv was the one bonded to Laeli, if I remembered right.

My lips curved upward at the irony of a male fae who lived in an ice castle needing a human woman with fire magic to keep him alive.

I didn't have anything to say though, so I just nodded in response to her explanation.

"We'll find clothes first. Hopefully, that'll give some of these fae time to marvel over the sight of a human so they don't obsess over you when we sit down," Eisley added.

I agreed, and then followed her into a building full of dresses and shorts. All of the clothing hung from large wooden racks around the space, which intrigued me. My fingers brushed the rich fabrics, all of them smoother and more luxurious than the clothes humans created.

My town had held me captive for so long to feed them and make money for them, yet they could still never have had the funds to buy the kind of clothing the fae wore. It was a pity for them but gave me a sense of satisfaction.

Perhaps that satisfaction wasn't healthy, but I didn't particularly care.

"What do you like?" Eisley asked, gesturing around the shop. Much of the clothing was brown, black, or dark green. I supposed the fae *were* warriors, and the dark colors would help them hide better.

But my eyes were drawn to the bright colors on a rack in the corner.

"I'm not particular," I told her, pulling my gaze back to the racks nearest to me.

"Nonsense. Everyone is particular, whether they like to admit it or not. Pick what you like, Nissa."

I reluctantly walked to the back of the room.

Having opinions was dangerous when you were a prisoner. And even if I technically wasn't one any longer, it still felt like I was. Not because of Kierden or Eisley, but because of the darkness in my mind.

"Just grab two or three dresses. We're going to get some meat on those bones fast, and then you'll need new clothes again," Eisley said.

I nodded and started looking through the dress options. They were short and fairly scandalous by human standards, but that didn't really matter. I'd get over showing more of my body sooner than I'd get over the years in the tower.

"Which ones are your favorite?" Eisley checked, when I'd gone through all of them.

"I'm not sure," I admitted, rubbing the silky fabric of an extremely pink dress between my fingers. It reminded me of the flowers I'd seen in the jungle—and the ones I'd watched my mother burn so many times from my tower.

She always said they were useless, but they *weren't*. They made me smile, and that meant something. It meant a lot.

Eisley sent me an exasperated look.

My lips curved upward a bit.

She wanted me to have opinions.

Fine; I'd have opinions.

I wanted the dresses that reminded me most of the flowers my village had cut down, the ones that had grown back again, again, and again. The ones that made me happy and brought me hope. I wasn't going to dress like a fae; I was going to dress like a damn *flower*.

"This one," I said, pulling the pink dress off the rack. Two more steps, and I grabbed a vibrant orange one, and a purple one too.

"Perfect. Reo?" Eisley looked toward the corner of the store.

A tall, elegant fae man stood up. He had a mass of curly hair that looked like actual art, brown skin, and eyes that glowed lavender. Unlike the other fae males, he was wearing full-length pants and a fancy shirt. "Ready?"

"Yup. Our little human is trying to gain some weight, so it'd be great if you could leave her some room to grow."

He nodded. "Of course."

They led me into a room, and I tried not to feel weird when the man measured my waist, breasts, and hips with a thin rope, making notes on the wall afterward. My eyes moved over the wood and widened when I saw hundreds of sets of measurements, all written in different places on the wall. Mine was off to the left side, near the middle vertically.

"You keep track of people's sizes?" I asked.

"Of course. I don't want to remeasure when they need new clothing. Take your current dress off; I'll need to alter the clothes while you wear them to make sure everything fits right."

I looked at Eisley for help, and she just nodded.

Guess I was stripping for the stranger.

He stepped back, and I pulled the dress on. He tsked his tongue as it fell into place. "You have a lot of weight to gain, my dear."

"Yeah." I bit my lip, cheeks flushing.

"You'll likely need new dresses in a week or two with more fabric than these have. They'll need to be custom. Do all humans starve?" There was some kind of morbid curiosity in his eyes.

"Reo," Eisley protested.

My cheeks flushed hotter. "It's fine. No, most humans don't starve. The others trapped me because of my magic, so they could use me."

His curiosity was replaced with pity. "Welcome to Jirev then, human. What's your name?"

"Nissa."

He wrote it next to my measurements while I tugged the first dress on.

I watched in fascination as he focused his magic to create needles of ice, threading them in the process. He began tucking some pieces of fabric and untucking others, altering the dress's waistline a bit and adjusting the sleeves so it fit my shorter human body. He left the skirt portion's length where it was when I asked him to, without batting an eye at the request.

A few minutes later, I changed into the next dress and we restarted the process.

After Reo had finished with the final two dresses, Eisley paid the man, and we headed out. Two of my new dresses and the one she'd loaned me were tucked inside a cloth bag that hung over my shoulder. My bright orange dress swayed around my legs with every step I took, and I found myself enjoying the soft motion.

Maybe I liked wearing bright colors and short dresses.

I was feeling much more hopeful about everything after my trip into the dress shop. Something about the way Reo acknowledged me without insulting me made me feel a little more confident in my place with the fae.

My connection with Kierden was... a mess. One I had no idea how to deal with. We were civil most of the time, but friendliness wasn't a thing. All we had was lusty attraction and forced nearness, both of which were useless considering that developing feelings for each other could lead to us getting *murdered*.

But my issues with him didn't mean I couldn't fit in with the fae. My magic was the opposite of theirs, but it was still magic. And I had a bonded esu who already saw me as one of them, so I belonged.

I did.

I just needed to stop letting my fear control me and start acting like it.

So, as we walked to a cute little shop serving food that looked like some type of soup, I lifted my chin and put my shoulders back.

I hadn't escaped the way I hoped, but I *had* escaped. I wasn't a prisoner anymore, and I wasn't hiding either.

We sat down at a table, and I felt eyes on me.

One glance around the room proved it was a *lot* of eyes.

A female fae brought fancy bread and bowls of soup over and set them down in front of us. We thanked her, and she gave me a curious look. "You're the human who's been growing flowers all over the Wilds?"

"Yep." I gave her a small smile, though part of me worried about her reaction.

She smiled. "I love seeing the flowers everywhere. You should stick around after your event with the other humans."

My smile grew at her invitation to stay, even though I wasn't thrilled to hear her mention the competition I was theoretically going to be participating in. "I'll think about it."

"Did you try the berries she already grew over by the falls?" someone asked at the table next to ours. "They were incredible."

Well, that made me feel good.

Hope swelled in my chest.

I was going to find a place. I was going to build a life. A real one, not one trapped in a tower, hoping for everything to change.

And I was going to find it with the fae.

CHAPTER SEVEN
NISSA

As we finished eating, a male fae came and sat down beside me. My face warmed at the short distance between us—and the size of him.

Damn, fae men were huge.

I'd adjusted to Kierden enough that his size didn't affect me other than turning me on sometimes, but the same wasn't true for the rest of the fae. This guy in particular had long, curly dark blue hair gathered in a bun on top of his head, and light brown skin. His cheekbones were insanely chiseled, and he was grinning at me.

Honestly, the grin alone made me like him. I'd never had a man look at me like that.

"Hello," he said.

"Hi." I bit my lip to hide a smile.

He reached over and tugged my lip free from my teeth, his grin widening. Having his hands on my skin made me feel weird, to say the least. But also kind of good. "What's your name, Beautiful?"

Ohh.

He was pulling out the big guns already, calling me *Beautiful*.

"Nissa. What's yours?" I leaned back away from him, just so he didn't get any big ideas.

"Uron. How do you like our city?" He gestured to the forest around us.

"It's kind of magical," I admitted, glancing out the window nearby and looking at the vibrant jungle around us. Everything was even greener than it had been when I arrived, and I could see some of my colorful flowers out there too, bringing it to life even more.

"*Kind of* magical? You haven't seen enough of it, then."

My lips curved upward.

"Stop flirting with her, Uron." Eisley threw a chunk of her bread at him. He caught it easily, his grin stretching wider as he threw it back.

"Why? I'd like to be at the top of her list when she decides who to spend the eclipse with." He winked at me, and my smile grew.

He found me attractive, despite the way I'd been starving and imprisoned and everything else.

"It's two and a half months away. I don't think you need to start now," Eisley drawled back.

"Sure I do. Half the fae in Jirev already want to see what kind of plants Nissa grows when she climaxes."

Heat bloomed on my cheeks, and Eisley scoffed.

"Can I see your ears?" Uron asked, leaning closer to me.

I wasn't sure that I should be encouraging him after his last comment, but it wasn't like my ears were sacred. They were just ears. So, I pulled part of my hair up to let him see one of them.

The look in his eyes morphed to fascination as he reached toward it. My toes curled in anticipation...

But a massive hand grabbed his wrist out of the air, halting the fingers a breath from my ear. I recognized the fabric wrapped around that giant hand just as a low, masculine voice growled, "I didn't bring this little human here for you to bed her, Uron."

"We're a long way from any bed," Uron replied without missing a beat. His grin was back. "And I wasn't doing anything she didn't want."

A long, tense moment passed before Kierden finally forced himself to release Uron's hand. He didn't even look at me before saying flatly, "We're leaving."

I knew he was talking to me based on the complete and utter lack of respect in his voice.

Something inside me wanted to fight back against that lack of respect. To show him that I wasn't a damn object—that he couldn't order me around like I didn't matter.

"*Careful, Nissa,*" Bright murmured into my mind. My intentions must've shown on my face.

"Why don't you guys have sex outside of the eclipse?" I asked Uron, remaining in my chair.

"To make procreating an impossibility," Eisley answered for him as she stood smoothly.

I leaned over the table a little, my fingers splayed wide. "There are herbs to prevent that, though. Humans have them, so I'm sure you do too."

Uron set his hand on mine and opened his mouth to answer.

Kierden ripped the man's hand away from mine, cutting him off with a sharp answer to my question. "We've been at war as long as any of us can remember. Sex was a risk because of the emotions it could inspire. It might create attachments with someone that could be snatched away at any moment."

"But you're not at war now."

The king jerked his head in a nod. "When our peace has been solidified, we'll reconsider our stance against protected sex outside of the eclipse."

"When?" a woman across the room asked.

His gaze lifted to her, and mine did too. We both wanted to hear the answer.

"What day, exactly? A lot of us would like to know," the woman clarified.

Damn, I was impressed with her for standing up to him.

And impressed with him for not seeming surprised or annoyed by her question. If anything, he became slightly less angry after she asked it.

Some of the fae in the shop weren't even from Kierden's city, but they looked curious about his answer too.

"As soon as the other cities have cleared out. I understand the importance of that freedom, and I appreciate the sacrifice all of us have made to prevent distractions and focus on the war. We lost far less fae than we could have."

The mood in the shop grew solemn with his words, and I saw a few of the fae nodding.

"Thank you," the woman said, bowing her head toward him slightly.

Others followed her, until most of the fae in the shop had bowed their heads toward him.

I didn't bow, of course.

The man didn't need any kind of confirmation that he was bigger, better, or more powerful than me. He already acted like I was nothing more than an annoyance.

"Let's go," the king said.

I didn't have to look at him to know he was talking to me.

And something told me it would be a bad idea to protest after everyone had bowed and so clearly offered him their support.

I grabbed my bag of clothes off the floor near my feet and stood. Bright and I followed Kierden, Death, Eisley, and Sharp out of the shop and then we all headed back to the castle.

• • •

Kierden and Eisley exchanged a few quiet, angry words before he growled at me to follow him and then strode in the direction I knew his room was.

"Do you think I can convince him to give me my own room?" I asked Bright. *"I'd like some space from the big, angry bastard."*

"I don't see why not." She brushed her side against my leg and I scratched her behind her ears. It was probably early in the morning, but I was still full of arrival-adrenaline, so I didn't feel tired.

Death held the door to Kierden's room open for me with his big, furry body, and I murmured a thank you as I passed him. He surprised me by brushing the side of his head against my thigh. It was the first bit of affection he had ever given me, and I had no idea what I was supposed to think about it.

I stopped abruptly inside the room when I slammed into Kierden's chest. As I stumbled backward, he caught me by the waist. After I was steady I tried to step away, but his grip tightened to stop me.

Bright and Death slipped past us to get into the room. She only brushed up against me, but he made a point of rubbing against both of us.

"What was that?" Kierden glared down at me.

I had to tilt my head back to look him in the eyes, and it made me feel small. That feeling was frustrating, reminding me of the way it had been between me and the men who held me captive in my mother's town. "What was *what*?"

"You and Uron, in the shop."

"He was just being nice." I took a step back, and the king held onto my hips as he stepped with me, ending up even closer to me.

I quickly took another step back, then another, and another, until I was pinned between Kierden and the wall. His body was hard against mine —every inch of him. It made me warmer than I cared to admit.

"You let him touch you," the king said, his voice low and his eyes nearly feral.

"He was being *nice* to me," I repeated, emphasizing the words. "I'm not against being touched by nice men."

The king's lips twisted in a snarl.

His chest was rising and falling faster, his thoughts spilling into my mind.

"She's mine."

"I want her."

"My female."

"My mate."

The thoughts moved rapidly, and so powerfully that it made my mind spin. It made me want him—and I couldn't let myself want him.

"What's my name?" I asked aloud, my attempt at halting his thoughts and my own lust.

The words leaking through our connection stopped abruptly, but he didn't answer.

"You don't get to care who I talk to or touch when you don't know anything about me," I said. "We're not friends or family, Kierden. I don't owe you anything. This mate bond isn't real, and—"

My words cut off when one of his hands lifted to my face. His fingers dug into my hair, his grip firm and unyielding. "A temporary bond is still *real*. Tell me your name."

The command only angered me further. "No."

He stepped closer, pressing his body harder to mine.

I inhaled sharply as his erection pressed against my belly, his muscles pressed close to me.

Maybe I wasn't as impervious to the difference in our sizes as I thought.

"Back up," I breathed.

He didn't back up.

Kierden tilted my head back further instead. "Tell me your name." His fingers started moving slowly on my hip, stroking my skin lightly.

Veil, it felt incredible.

My body grew warmer at the foreign pleasure of his touch. "No."

"I can smell your desire for me in the air, little human. You'll tell me, or I'll make you." His hand dragged down my hip until he found the bare skin on my thigh.

"Go ahead and try." He could do whatever he wanted to me; I wouldn't bend on that. But I was enjoying the way he was touching me far too much to even think about telling him to stop.

Considering what he'd said to his fae in the market, I knew he wouldn't actually have sex with me. And the closest he'd ever gotten to hurting me was gripping my hair, so he could go ahead and do his worst.

His eyes dilated with the challenge, and his erection throbbed against my belly.

Kierden took a small step to the side and then began sliding his hand further up my thigh. My body clenched and my toes curled as I silently urged him higher and higher.

His fingers dragged over the sensitive crease at the top of my thigh, and I took in a sharp breath.

The esu slipped past us again, and the doors swung shut behind them as they left us. I barely even noticed.

"Tell me your name," he said.

"No."

Finally, his fingers brushed the thin fabric covering my core.

My body trembled. My dress hid the view of his hand touching me, but the sight of it disappearing beneath my skirt was still overwhelming in the absolute best way.

"So wet for me already, little human," Kierden growled into my ear, stroking me again through the fabric. "You want my fingers on your bare skin, don't you?"

My chest rose and fell rapidly, his body still holding me in place.

I didn't answer him.

I couldn't admit it.

But we both knew he was right; I wanted more.

He continued touching me, his fingers slow but confident. The pleasure swelled inside me as I neared the edge of my climax.

But then his touch stilled.

"Tell me your name, and I'll let you shatter." His lips brushed my ear as they formed the words.

I clamped my mouth shut, still refusing to give him what he wanted despite my intense need and pleasure.

He wasn't going to break me, or manipulate me through sex.

I was stronger than my desire.

He gave me another slow, long stroke.

A soft cry escaped me and his fingers paused again, halting my pleasure.

I was so close.

So close.

"Tell me, or you'll have no release." His teeth caught my earlobe and dragged slowly, making me shudder.

"No." I clenched my jaw.

Kierden might have been the king, but he wasn't *my* king. He couldn't just give me orders and expect me to follow them.

If he wanted to know something, the bastard would have to earn it, or at the very least ask politely with a sincere apology for not giving a shit about me when we first met.

He released my earlobe, pressing lightly against my core again, making me bite back a groan.

But then he pulled his hand away.

My body cried out for more immediately, but I gritted my teeth against the desire.

Kierden stepped away from me. His eyes were hot as he lifted his fingers to his mouth and licked the wetness of my desire off of them.

"I need my own room," I managed to say without sounding too off balance.

"So you can lock a door behind you and give yourself that release? No. You'll stay with me."

"I'm *not* sleeping with you again."

"Then you'll sleep on the floor."

It was wooden, and obviously very hard. For the sake of my pride, I'd make it work. "Fine."

He strode to his bathroom, but I stepped between him and the escape. His erection was raging and throbbing enough that I knew he was going to take care of it as soon as that door shut between us. "If I don't get to touch myself, neither do you."

His eyes flashed with warning. "How do you intend to enforce that?"

Shit.

He had me.

Veil, this was a terrible idea.

"No closed doors between us."

His gaze turned wicked. "Lovely." With one smooth motion, he turned on his heels and strode to the bathing pool instead.

My throat swelled and my body flushed hotter as he stripped his shorts down his thighs, exposing his perfect ass to me. There was still dried blood on him, I realized, and my eyes narrowed in on one particularly bad cut on his back before he turned.

My mind may as well have frozen altogether when I saw his erection jutting out proudly and straining with the force of his desire.

His desire for *me*.

Veil, he was gorgeous.

There was another cut on his thigh, I noticed. It was worse than the one on his back.

"You need to see a healer," I managed to get out.

"No." He slipped into the water. I let out a breath when it covered him entirely so I wasn't staring at his cock anymore.

As much as I enjoyed staring at it, there was always the chance staring might lead to me doing something I shouldn't.

Like licking it.

Or somehow managing to fall on top of it.

"How much faster do fae heal than humans?" I asked. I found myself taking a few steps toward the pool, ignoring the ache of unmet need in my body.

"I don't know." He spread his arms out over the dark brown stone that made up the inside and outer ledge of the pool, leaning back against the wall of the bath and closing his eyes.

"How long will it take your wounds to heal?" I asked him, growing irritated.

"A day or two."

Knowing him, he probably refused to admit any weakness. So, he'd probably underestimated the healing time.

Even if he thought he'd heal twice as fast as he really would, three or four days was incredible for wounds like those. I'd seen a man die from a shallow cut as a kid, and he'd had the wound that killed him for nearly two weeks before the infection took him. My stomach still turned at the memory of how quickly he'd passed after the infection set in.

"At least let me look at them to make sure your life's not at risk," I said.

Kierden didn't argue, which I thought was probably the closest I'd get to an agreement out of him.

I sat down on the edge of the pool. When he didn't move to show me his back immediately, I debated for a few seconds, and then finally put a hand between his shoulder blades and pushed him forward.

The king reluctantly leaned for me and exposed a large wound. There was already a skin-colored patch of some sort covering it, but he'd bled through the fabric. It was stained dark red with blood, not thick enough to stop more from trickling down his back.

"Can I take this off?" I whispered to him, my stomach turning at the sight of the blood.

He grunted, which I decided meant yes.

Carefully, I peeled the bandage away from his skin. The edges were incredibly sticky, but I eventually managed to get it off.

"How did you get this from *wrestling*?" I asked.

He didn't answer right away.

I scooped up some water and used it to rinse the blood off his back, assuming he wasn't going to tell me at all.

After a few minutes, he finally said, "Vayme returned with his human female. He was struggling to control his rage so he challenged me to a match with weapons. First one to draw blood won."

I assumed Vayme was the king who still hadn't gotten back yet when I met Laeli. "You have *two* wounds."

Kierden couldn't have lost twice, could he? He was so damn massive.

"We fought seven rounds. He got the upper hand twice."

Huh.

He hadn't boasted about his strength or about defeating the other man, which seemed out of character.

Then again, all I really knew about him was that he was a king, a warrior, and angry about the fact that we'd bonded. And angry about being hunted by the Beast of the Endless Wilds, though I figured anyone would have the right to be angry about that.

"So you won."

"He was blinded by rage. It made him weak."

Oh, the irony.

When was Kierden not blind with rage when it came to me? And yet, it hadn't made him weak. Not that I could tell.

"Do you have more bandages somewhere?"

"In the bathroom."

I walked over to it. My eyebrows lifted when I found a simple basket full of fresh bandages sitting near the door. I supposed that a centuries-long war meant a lot of wounds, and a lot of wounds meant a lot of bandages.

After returning to Kierden, I kneeled down and splashed his cut again to clean the blood off.

"If the skin's wet, the bandage will stick to it," he said.

It surprised me that he told me before I asked. But I wasn't about to acknowledge any positive feelings for the man, so I changed the subject. "Why did you fight seven rounds if he kept losing?"

"His rage hadn't faded. He lost the first four, then had calmed enough to win the fifth. I took the sixth, and after he won the seventh, his female fainted. He thanked me for my help, then brought her back to the castle to rest."

My eyebrows shot upward as I finished wetting his back and then dried my fingers carefully on my dress. "Why did she faint?"

He grunted again when I pressed the bandage to his wound and held it in place. Part of me expected it to fall off when I let go, but it stayed where I put it as I withdrew my fingers. A quick brush against the edges of the fabric proved that it was stuck tight.

Kierden said, "She's tiny and weak. Not assertive, like you are. Apparently the blood scared her."

My heart went out to the poor girl. If she'd been trapped the way Laeli and I had, I didn't blame her at all for being *tiny*, *weak*, or *not assertive*. Then again, even if she hadn't been trapped, I wouldn't blame her for those things.

Not everyone needed to be strong or stubborn. I didn't even consider myself either of those things, yet apparently Kierden found me attractive. Or at least attractive enough to touch intimately without demanding anything in return except my name.

"I'm not assertive. I just don't let you mistreat me." I tried to change the subject. "Give me your leg. I saw a cut there too."

He grumbled a bit but pulled himself out of the water. I forced myself not to make eye contact with his erection as I studied the cut on his thigh. It was bigger than the last one, so I looked for a bandage to fit it.

"Of course you're assertive. You're wearing an orange dress. Do you know how many fae I've ever seen wear orange?"

My face warmed as I pulled out a bandage. "Only a few?"

He chuckled. "None."

And he was practically ancient, so there must not have been any fae who wore bright colors—at least not in his kingdom.

Whoops.

I leaned over his cut again. It was leaking blood, so I scooped water out of the pool in an attempt to clean it. "Eisley forced me to choose what I liked the most, so it's her fault."

"The fact that you wanted the color in the first place speaks volumes about your personality. You hold back your fire, but it still burns."

"I don't want to *burn* anyone," I countered.

"Does a fire hurt by merely existing?"

The words surprised me.

I didn't have an answer for him.

Kierden added, "Anyone who touches the fire or steps into it burns, but does that put the fire at fault?"

My forehead wrinkled and I forgot about his wound for a moment. "I think you're telling me not to hide my feelings and emotions, in a roundabout way."

He made a noise of amusement. "I'm telling you that you can't hurt anyone by existing, little human. If someone is hurt by opinions that don't belong to them, they are responsible for their own perceived pain."

"That sounds like a perspective only a fae can live by. Humans try not to hurt each other... or at least the good ones do." I finally looked back at his wound and washed it off again.

"Perhaps. Fae do not live our lives with an intent to please anyone; we simply exist. No one is responsible for someone else's peace of mind."

That sounded kind of nice, honestly.

I'd like to be able to see the world that way, even though I didn't know how I'd ever get to that point.

"You said you're always at war, though, and you guys are pretty violent. That's the opposite of peace of mind."

He chuckled. "No one remembers the purpose of our war. We didn't fight over offenses or glory; we fought because it was a tradition, and it's hard to break tradition after that many centuries. Now that we've broken it, we fight for fun."

I supposed I wasn't going to win that argument. Surprisingly enough, I didn't mind.

"So do you hate my orange dress?" I tried to lighten the mood. "I feel like you insulted it."

As soon as the words slipped out, I wondered why I cared what his opinions about my dress were. Maybe I was just trying to stir the pot or stoke the flames.

He grunted as I pressed the bandage over the cut on his leg and held it in place for a moment. "The color doesn't bother me, though I'd prefer you wear nothing at all."

My eyes widened, and then caught on the thick length of his erection.

I couldn't ignore it any longer.

My hand lingered on his thigh, though the bandage had to have been secured for ages already.

"There's curiosity in your eyes," Kierden said.

"I've never seen a cock before," I admitted, immediately biting my lip and regretting the admission.

"Then this is quite the treat for you," he drawled.

The sarcasm relaxed my shoulders, and I bit back a laugh as my face heated "Oh, yes."

He chuckled. The sound surprised me so much that I looked up at him, and found his lips curved upward slightly.

My gaze dipped back to his erection, and I wondered if the romance books had lied to me about the way cocks felt. Steel and silk, they always claimed.

The king said, "Your forehead is creased. You're welcome to throw a towel over me if I'm bothering you."

I warred with my conscience for a moment before deciding not to hide what I wanted. "Can I touch you?"

His gaze was scorching. "You don't ever need to ask to give me pleasure. The answer is always yes."

My face flushed. "I'm not going to get you off. You left me all frustrated."

"Tell me your name and I can fix that."

I blushed hotter. "No."

He chuckled. "You don't have to make me climax to touch me, little human. Any touch would be a pleasure."

I wanted to turn him down and walk away...

But I was too curious.

So I lifted my hand off his thigh and carefully wrapped it around his erection. He throbbed in my grip, just as hard and soft as the books had promised me. "Damn, Kierden," I whispered, trying to ignore the wetness between my thighs.

"You approve?" Kierden was trying to make a joke, I thought, but his voice was too low and intense for it to hit right.

"You feel incredible." I slowly slid my hand down the length of him, and then back up again.

He growled at me, catching one of my knees and using it to open my thighs for him. His fingers dragged over my core again through the fabric that covered them, and I bit back a moan.

I wanted more.

But I couldn't let him manipulate me.

Still... I could brush the edge a little. I could tease him, and let him tease me.

I stroked his cock again.

Kierden found my clit despite the fabric covering me, and teased me there.

I continued touching him lightly, careful not to take him too close to his release.

His fingers worked me harder and faster until they froze on my clit, leaving me right on the edge of my climax. I could've moved my hips and used him to get myself off...

But I wasn't ready to let him win, or to push him into taking our little standoff to further heights by claiming the pleasure I wanted so desperately.

So, I let go of him and stood up quickly. "I'm going to go to bed. On the floor, as promised."

His voice was strained when he growled back, "Don't take any of my pillows."

He would go back to being an asshole, I supposed. Not that he'd ever really stopped. I'd just... adjusted.

Yet as I walked to the empty corner of the room across from the bed, I found myself realizing that I didn't hate Kierden. Not even a little.

...Of course, that didn't mean I *liked* him. That would've been simply ridiculous.

CHAPTER EIGHT

KIERDEN

My female was tossing and turning on the ground, making soft, adorable huffing noises. I was drying off slowly in my closet, fighting the urge to hang my little human's clothing up with my own.

Of course, I needed to stop thinking of her as mine.

And I needed to convince her to share the bed with me without giving away how fiercely I wanted her.

I wasn't sure how to make either of those things happen, though. I couldn't let myself truly pursue her the way my instincts were driving me to.

For a male like me, there was no uncertainty. She was either mine in every damn way, or she was nothing.

I wanted everything—yet claiming her the way I wanted to would be the end for both of us.

So I couldn't acknowledge my desire.

I had to keep pushing her away as much as I could manage.

Our bond would disappear when the eclipse came around, along with the itch of the wicked magic pulsing beneath my skin.

The urge to study the silver glow of our connection struck me hard. I gritted my teeth and grabbed a pair of shorts, tugging them up my thighs and then tucking my erection below the tight waistband. The fabric would hide nothing, but I didn't want to hide from my human.

Even more than I itched to be free of the Beast's wicked magic, I wanted to know her. I wanted to ask her questions and hear her perspective. I wanted to see her smile and make her laugh.

And I wanted to know her damn *name*.

But knowing any of that would only take me closer to the one thing I truly desired, yet could never have:

A mate.

It irritated me that she had refused to give me her name, though pride swelled in my chest for the same reason.

She wouldn't let me control her.

It was perhaps the most infuriating thing about her, as well as one of the sexiest.

Even in the Broken Woods, she had refused my control. She had dodged my every attempt to assert dominance over her, sometimes simply by meeting my eyes and saying nothing at all.

I crossed the room and slipped beneath the luxurious blankets on my bed. Though I had no real need for the luxury, it eased the nightmares that plagued me at times.

My human continued tossing and turning.

Even if I'd closed my eyes, I wouldn't have been able to sleep. Not while she was on the floor. I hadn't managed to fall asleep before her while we slept together yet, my mind constantly struggling with the driving need to touch her.

Her scent and skin had been difficult to resist in the forest, even with the dirt and sweat clouding it.

Now, resistance was growing impossible.

I ached badly for her. I'd never had urges intense enough to feel like *needs* before. The need to taste her. To touch her. To watch her unravel on my fingers, tongue, and cock, repeatedly.

My cock throbbed as I remembered the soft noises she'd made, and the way she'd reacted to my touch.

Veil, I'd wanted her.

I still did.

There was nothing to be done about it, so I tried to settle myself.

I was failing.

"Did the bond cause you pain when I was fighting?" I asked her, unable to stay silent while she continued tossing and turning. I could nearly *smell* the woman's frustration.

"Yes. Bright and Sharp tried to bring you back to me." She didn't bother acting like she was asleep—or hiding the frustration in her voice.

She had every right to be exactly that, too. I hadn't even thanked her for tending my wounds, something only a sibling or healer would normally do.

I had treated her terribly in my attempt to prevent myself from falling in love with her. As much as I despised hurting her, my intention had been to keep her alive.

But she would hate me if I didn't find another way to maintain that distance, and some part of me couldn't stand the idea of her hatred.

"Death didn't tell me until after the fights had ended. I'll stay closer from now on."

There was a long pause, as if she was debating what to say. She finally settled on, "Thank you." After another pause, she asked, "Did it hurt you too?"

The pain had melded with the twisted magic of the Beast's tracking rune on my skin. It was brutal, but I couldn't tell her that. Not while I still felt like a monster for leaving her hurting for so long.

"Some," I said.

"The fighting probably distracted you."

She was right, though she didn't sound happy about it.

The doors swung open, and both of our bonded esu came walking back into the room.

"That ended quickly," Death drawled into my mind.

My lips curved wickedly at his sarcasm. *"Asshole."*

"Likewise. I assume your female fought back when you pinned her?"

"She enjoyed it, actually."

He leapt onto the bed smoothly and silently, settling in the spot he always claimed as his. *"Not enough to sleep beside you again."*

"She wanted her own room. I said no. This was her revenge."

He chuffed, showing his amusement. *"I like her."*

"I noticed."

"You know how I feel about fae not taking mates. Perhaps you should reconsider your stance." He settled his head on top of his paws.

"You find it unnatural," I agreed. *"And yet you lack a mate of your own."*

"I've pursued Brightfangs multiple times, as you know. I only lack a mate because I have yet to persuade her to see things as they really are."

"And how are things really?"

"She belongs at my side, as I belong at hers. Our souls were meant to be one. The fact that our bonded companions are in the same position is merely a push from someone on the other side of the veil."

Death rarely waxed romantic, but when he did, he did it fiercely.

"So you want me to believe that my human and I are merely side characters in your love story?" I asked.

"Of course. And the fact that you just called her yours only emphasizes my point."

"I know. It's a problem I haven't gotten under control yet."

"Technically, the marking on both of you does declare her yours. So you're not wrong."

I let out a long breath. *"You are terrible backup, my friend."*

"As are you." He adjusted the position of his head. *"Figure out a way to tell Brightfangs that she's meant to be mine without angering her. She still refuses to believe me when I say it."*

"You'd be better off convincing her human."

"I intend to."

Off in my human's corner, I heard a cute, frustrated huffing noise.

She cleared her throat and said, "I'm not sure if you're aware, Kierden, but Death is trying to convince Bright that you want me in your bed."

I jerked my gaze back to the esu.

He batted his eyes, completely unrepentant.

"Death wants Bright in the bed and has resorted to underhanded methods to make it happen, then," I said.

Death stared at me for a moment before letting out a huff.

There was a long pause before my human finally said, "Oh."

She stood slowly, still wearing the same orange dress she'd had on earlier. Most female fae slept in their scanties, but I wasn't about to ask her to strip. The last thing I needed was more temptation where she was concerned.

She crossed the room, sat down on the edge of the bed, and gave Death a quick smile. "Can I talk to Kierden for a second?"

He pretended to consider it. Finally, he licked her on the nose and slipped past her, heading straight for Bright. The female esu made a noise of amusement as he plopped down beside her.

My human leaned closer and whispered, "We could share the bed for their sake. Bright insists she's not interested in him as a mate, but it sounds like she's been alone for a long time, so it could be a good thing."

I murmured back, "They can both hear you from here."

Her head whipped around, and her cheeks blushed a gorgeous crimson color that made me itch to run my fingers over them. I ignored the itch.

She turned back to me, glared, and announced loudly, "I'm sleeping over here."

Her feet slipped under the blankets, and both esu joined us on the bed.

Just as I turned toward my female, Bright stepped between us and plopped down on her belly in Death's usual spot. Her eyes narrowed suspiciously at me, but she said nothing. Esu could only broadcast their thoughts directly to their bonded fae or to everyone nearby, which meant she and I couldn't have a private conversation then and there.

Something told me that if we could, she would've threatened me.

"Get her name if you can," I told Death quietly.

"Mmhm." His eyes remained open and fixed on Bright as he settled on the other side of me and dropped his head on my abdomen so he could watch Bright.

My human's eyes shut. She snuggled up against her bonded esu, and her breathing leveled out almost immediately.

As I watched her chest rise and fall evenly, I was forced to admit the truth.

I *did* want my human to be my mate... even if I couldn't act on it without getting us both killed.

CHAPTER NINE
NISSA

I expected Kierden to be gone when I woke up, but he wasn't.

When I silently studied him from between my cracked eyelids, I was surprised to find him awake *and* still there.

He was sitting up in bed with his back to the wall and a book open in his hands. The quick way his eyes moved over the paper told me he must've been enjoying whatever he was reading.

I assumed that meant he was reading fiction, and some part of me softened.

Something about the possibility that he liked fictional stories too made him seem more like a real person to me and less like a mystical fae warrior-king.

His dark hair was messy, and his eyes were a bit sleepy. Something about the complete and utter relaxation in his posture made me feel strangely comfortable waking up in bed with him. I could still hear both of the esu snoring softly, so we may as well have been completely alone.

Minus the large, warm, furry bodies in bed with us, of course.

Kierden's eyes flicked to me and lingered. He lifted a hand off his book and pressed a finger to his lips in the universal sign to be quiet.

"Did their snoring keep you up?" he asked me.

Feeling his words in my mind was soft, comfortable, and intimate.

I wasn't entirely sure I liked that.

Then again, some other part of me was absolutely certain I loved it.

"No."

"Yesterday was a long day, so I'm not surprised. At least we're not traveling today."

I felt like I'd woken up in an alternate universe, with an alternate man. Had a good night's sleep in his own bed really been all he needed to remember how to be kind? If so, we should've moved faster on our way back to his kingdom.

My stomach rumbled softly, and the esu didn't budge. They were the ones who had been running while we traveled, so I wasn't surprised that they were exhausted. I'd need weeks to recover if I did what they had.

I stretched quietly, then eased myself out of the bed and padded to the bathroom, using the facilities and then changing.

When I emerged, I stared for a long moment at the bed. It held a gorgeous, mostly-naked fae king who was reading quietly while snuggling with both of our bonded esu.

Nope, I could *not* get back in there without developing some kind of positive feelings about our situation.

Not wanting to stop and chat, I slipped out of the room as silently as possible. I was pretty sure I knew where to find the dining hall, and didn't think it was far enough away to cause either of us any pain.

My stomach rumbled again as I maneuvered through the halls.

"Where are you going?" the king asked, falling into step beside me.

Damn, I'd hoped for a little space from him. Guess that wasn't happening.

"The dining hall."

"Always so hungry," he said, his voice almost... playful.

That joke did *not* hit right.

If he'd been starving for as many years as me, he'd be hungry all the time too.

But I didn't want to explain anything about my past to him, so I didn't say anything.

We stepped into the dining hall and only found one other couple inside. I didn't recognize either of them, though that wasn't a surprise.

The woman's skin was as pale as Laeli's, and she was wearing a long human-style dress that looked supremely uncomfortable, though not dirty. Her vibrant blue hair was gathered up in a bun on top of her head. A few of the strands had escaped, and seemed to be blowing in a breeze that had absolutely no place in the castle.

I looked around the room, trying to find the source of the breeze, but found nothing.

Guess I knew what her magic was.

"That's Vayme and his human," Kierden murmured into my mind.

I nodded, and the king motioned to someone in the kitchen as he walked beside me to the table.

Like Kierden, Vayme had his hand wrapped in fabric. Unlike my king, Vayme wore a pair of thick-looking pants instead of loose shorts, and his brown hair was long and thick, falling to his shoulders. He had a beard too, but it was trimmed fairly short.

"Hi," I said, as we approached the table.

Vayme shot me a dark look, and Kierden's hand lifted to my lower back as he stepped closer to me. When I glanced sideways at him, I found his eyes narrowed and his body tensed.

Vayme finally lifted two fingers in a tiny wave and grunted before returning to his food.

"Hello," his human whispered, and my attention went to her. Veil, she looked even skinnier than me and Laeli. I itched to ask for her story, but didn't want to share mine while Kierden was right there. "I'm Kaelle," she said, pronouncing it kay-elle. "I think Laeli told me about you. You have plant magic, right?"

"Yep." I gave her a quick smile, and she returned it, though hers was faint.

My heart ached for her.

"He hasn't hurt you, right?" I sat down beside her, gesturing toward Vayme.

The king's glare snapped up to me.

Kierden murmured into my mind, *"Careful."*

"No, he's fine. Thanks for asking, though." She carefully took my hand and squeezed it lightly. I felt the breeze blowing off her skin, and it caught me off-guard a little, but I nodded.

Someone brought out plates of food for me and Kierden, and the tension dissipated as he pulled a chair up to sit next to me. Kaelle released my hand so I could eat, and silence reigned as all of us focused on our meal.

"Were you glad to leave your city?" Kaelle asked me softly, as she set her fork down next to her plate.

"I was," I said simply.

She nodded, and the empathy in her eyes as she looked between me and Kierden told me she understood the space I was trying to put between us. "Has he hurt you?" Her voice was barely above a whisper.

Kierden growled in response .

I put a hand to his chest, stopping him before he could rise to his feet. "No. He hasn't."

She nodded, eyeing the food that remained on Vayme's plate. He wordlessly moved some of it to hers.

I removed my hand from Kierden's chest and went back to my own food. "Do *you* miss your city?" I asked her. Though I'd been from a small town, it wasn't surprising that she'd come from a larger one. There were a lot in the human lands, and some of the biggest considered themselves their own kingdom. If any of those places had learned about my magic, they would likely have slaughtered my town to take me.

I'd wished for that to happen more times than I wanted to admit.

"Oh, I'm from a teeny, tiny town." She bit her lip, as if to stop herself from saying something, and then added a moment later, "Laeli was from a big city though, so I assumed you were too."

"My town was small, too. They would kill anyone who got close enough to try to take me."

Her eyes widened. "So they protected you?"

I wasn't sure how to explain without giving away things I didn't want Kierden to know. "In a way, yes."

"What does that mean?" His voice was low in my mind, making me shiver.

Kaelle nodded, her expression growing empathetic. She started eating the food Vayme had put on her plate, and all of us grew silent again. It hadn't passed my notice that the kings didn't really acknowledge each other, but the last thing I wanted to do was start another fight between them. Since they'd been at war for a long time, it wasn't surprising they didn't like each other much.

"Have you seen any sign of the Monster?" Kierden asked Vayme, finally addressing the other king as we all finished our food.

"Not yet." The man's forehead wrinkled, his gaze disturbed. "The ache in the rune has gotten worse, though."

"Mine as well," Kierden admitted. "I assume they'll search the human lands after losing the trail of our magic there, and then return here."

Vayme nodded slowly. "Should you need a place to hide, my castle is open to you and the female. They won't expect us to rely on each other."

"Thank you." Kierden's expression was grim, but his words did seem genuine.

"The Monster is hunting you?" I asked Vayme as my curiosity grew. He was another of the elves' assassins, who had all been created from other beings in Evare.

The twisted wolf shifter hunting Kierden was called the Beast of the Endless Wilds.

The dragon shifter assassin was called the Demon of the Weeping Skies. Everyone despised dragons for their harshness and cruelty, so he was the one I'd be most afraid of.

The Monster of the Aching Chasm had been a gargoyle before he was transformed.

At least, that was what the stories I'd heard as a kid said.

"Yes." Vayme dipped his head in a nod, though his face twisted in a scowl.

"Does he really drink *blood*?" Kaelle shivered a little as she asked.

"I don't know. Pray we don't find out."

Kierden grabbed his empty plate as well as mine. "The events will start in a few hours." He left me where I was as he went to return the plates to the kitchen.

Kaelle sighed.

I figured that was my cue to leave, so I gave the other woman a quick smile and fell into step beside Kierden as he strode out of the dining hall.

When we'd turned down another hallway, Kierden opened a door I didn't recognize and gestured for me to go inside. I stepped in, and he shut the door behind himself.

A quick glance around showed that we'd found an empty bedroom.

Hope beat in my chest.

Was he going to give it to me?

"About what happened in the forest," Kierden said, slipping his hands in the pockets of his shorts.

Oh.

This wasn't about the room at all.

"When you grabbed my hair?" I frowned.

"Yes. I don't apologize often, but..." He let out a long breath.

Was he actually going to apologize?

He hadn't even hurt me.

"It wasn't my intention to cause pain. I *am* sorry." His words seemed genuine, though unnecessary. And I believed him when he said he didn't apologize often, so I wasn't going to tell him not to.

"You didn't really hurt me, but thanks for apologizing."

Relief crossed his face, and he changed the subject abruptly. I figured he was glad to be done talking about it. "I plan to spend all day at the event. You're coming, to avoid the pain of our separation."

Guess he was back to giving me orders. I didn't mind it as much as I had the day before, for some reason. "Alright. Does everyone always fight naked?"

He scowled. "At the events, yes."

I flashed him a smile. "Then it's my lucky day."

His scowl deepened.

I hoped he was remembering the way I'd touched him the night before, because I was.

He opened the door for me, still looking unhappy about my question.

My lips curved upward at his discomfort, though. At least I could bother him as much as he bothered me.

. . .

We headed out shortly after that, taking a walking path through the city so our bonded esu could continue catching up on sleep. There were fae with their companion animals everywhere, and a lot of their eyes lit up when they saw me and Kierden. Many of them were picking fruit, and some even had flowers tucked behind their ears. I wasn't sure which of us they were smiling at, but considering the silent, respectful nods they gave him, I assumed it was me.

Walking through the trees and over bridge after bridge connecting them was fascinating. I looked at everything, unable to decide what to focus on. It really was an entirely different world than the one I'd grown up in.

"My farmers have already asked that you be assigned to their fields in the hours since you've been here," Kierden told me, after we'd walked for a while in silence. It wasn't a short distance, but I appreciated the chance to get out and move.

"Really? That would be perfect." I smiled, waving back at a fae woman who waved at me.

Kierden said into my mind. *"It would not be perfect. If you focus your magic on our fields, you'll drain us both faster."*

"I have no control over my magic. Focusing it doesn't do anything, remember? It drains consistently into whatever is around me, so if I lived on a field, I could grow food. Then your people wouldn't want me to leave."

His scowl deepened. *"You could learn control."*

"How? I had nothing but time to learn it in my town. My magic flooded out of me in just a few hours, leaving me exhausted constantly. If I couldn't figure it out then, how would I figure it out now?"

There was a long pause.

The king finally heaved a great big sigh and said, *"I'll try to teach you."*

"We'd just end up arguing. And besides, I don't think your magic works the same way mine does. It feels really different."

"Perhaps if you learn how to stop draining my magic, we'll get along better."

"Maybe if you stop being an asshole to me, we'll get along better," I shot back.

The look he shot me was a weary one.

I changed the subject. *"How many more days until the fighting is over? I'm thinking this place will be a sex fest as soon as you give the word."*

The king's expression turned disgruntled. *"You think correctly."*

"You'll have to give me my own room, then. I'm not sharing the bed you sleep with other women in."

He scowled. *"So you can invite the likes of Uron into your room? No."*

My anger rose quickly, along with something that felt like... jealousy.

I wasn't calling it that though. And I'd never admit it. *"It wouldn't be wrong for me to have sex with an attractive man who's been kind to me,"* I argued. *"I bet you've hooked up with dozens of these fae secretly, even while your ridiculous anti-sex law was in place."*

"I have kept every one of my laws, and that one wasn't my idea to begin with."

"Because you'd rather have a new woman in your bed every night. Maybe even two," I spat.

My anger had been rising steadily, and I didn't know why. Not jealousy; definitely not jealousy.

Probably because he was trying to tell me what to do, and I wanted freedom.

"Because I have no taste for casual sex," he snarled back. *"I grew up with mated parents. I saw how they loved each other. Sex with no emotion behind it is deadening for me."*

His words shocked me right into silence.

My mind went back to the way he'd touched me, in his room. And the way he'd let me touch him.

If he had no taste for it, he had only agreed to it to get what he wanted... and because he knew it was what *I* wanted.

New anger hit me hard, but I kept it silent.

I was done with him. Absolutely done. When our bond broke, I'd be thrilled if I never saw the bastard again.

He didn't say anything else to me as our walk continued, and I didn't say anything else to him.

The event started an hour or two after we arrived. I remained on the bench in the area that seemed to be reserved for Kierden, the one Eisley had brought me to the night before. He left me there to go figure out the logistics of something when someone asked him for help, and I stayed where I was, entirely alone.

My anger cooled as I sat there, and I settled into a calm state of trying to determine how I was going to act with Kierden. It sounded like he was going to force me to continue sleeping in his room, to prevent me from having casual sex while we were bonded. I could survive another two months or so of that; it wasn't the end of the world. I hadn't had sex before, anyway, so I wasn't entirely sure what I was missing out on.

Then again, I could always spend a bunch of time out at the shops meeting new people. If more of them were as friendly as Uron, I might eventually develop feelings for one of them enough to trust them to take my virginity.

Or perhaps I'd just get tired of holding out and ask someone to show me how it worked.

There were many options, regardless of where I slept.

As I considered my options, I decided to show Kierden the same quiet indifference I gave him in the forest after he rescued me, rather than allowing myself to fight with him again. The fighting only made us both feel things more strongly, which wasn't good for us.

Eisley joined me after a while, her gaze a bit bleary. She didn't say much to me at first, but sniffed the air and gave me a weird look.

"What?" I frowned at her.

She leaned closer and sniffed me, then made a face. "You smell like Kier again."

Oh.

I hadn't bathed after he... well, touched me. Against the wall and by the pool. *Intimately.*

"There's only one bed in the room, and he's too paranoid to let me sleep anywhere else."

Understanding dawned in her gaze. "Veil."

"Yeah."

She rubbed her eyes. "It's fine. You don't smell that strong right now. Just don't get too close to anyone so they don't pick up on it. And start bathing every morning."

I nodded, and she leaned against me a bit as we both stared out at the empty cage.

Shortly after that, Kierden joined us on the bench, and the fighting began. They were doing some kind of specialized hand-to-hand combat, with smooth, graceful motions. It was fascinating to watch, honestly.

And the nudity made it even more fascinating.

Hours and hours passed, and it was dark again by the time we left. Despite the lunch we'd been fed in the middle of the day, and the part of hers that Eisley gave me, I was starving.

Our esu had joined us partway through the day, so they carried us back to the castle, and we poured into the dining hall with a group of other fae.

As I ate, I learned that no one except the king and his sister technically lived in the castle, but that it was always open for anyone who needed a break or wanted an escape for a few days. There was a massive pool inside it somewhere, as well as a bunch of space for training, and a huge library.

Since everyone was welcome, there were constantly people coming in and out. There were usually only a few fae staying there, but everyone had done so at one point or another.

It fascinated me that they could rely on each other like that and surprised me to hear that Kierden was so welcoming.

But then again, I supposed I didn't really know him. It had been less than two weeks since he saved me from my tower, after all.

After we finished eating, Kierden and I went to his room and collapsed in bed. We didn't talk—he still seemed frustrated about our conversation earlier, and I was still absolutely not interested in being his friend.

Both of us fell asleep snuggled with our bonded esu, and despite the tension between us, I still slept so much better than I ever had in my tower.

CHAPTER TEN
NISSA

The following two weeks passed quickly.

I was quiet, but observed the fae and tried to learn as much as I could about their land.

Kierden was still grumpy, but surprisingly enough, not angry or cruel.

I still didn't give him my name, and he only asked once a day or so. He didn't try to persuade me to give it to him with his hands or body again, either.

By some miracle, we also didn't fight. It still felt like a few steps back after the way we'd talked and touched each other while I cleaned his wounds, but that was my goal. What he'd said in the forest about not being interested in casual sex made it pretty damn clear that he had been trying to manipulate me even more than I'd realized, and I wasn't involving myself with someone like that.

Even when I patched his wounds again after he fought a few more times, we only exchanged surface-level pleasantries about the many flowers and fruits I was accidentally growing, our favorite foods, and other similar topics.

We spent our days at the friendly fighting events, and then started training for the *human fight* the kings had used as a cover when they brought us to Kierden's city. Me and the other girls were absolutely terrible with weapons of every kind, so they decided they were just going to have to give us all swords and see what happened.

On the fifteenth day since we'd arrived, my stomach clenched as Bright approached the arena.

Kierden didn't seem worried for me, but Bright was still trying to give me strategies to help me win the fight.

I really didn't care about winning. I was just concerned with the surviving part, considering that Laeli had fire magic and Kaelle had wind. They could wreck me, and the worst I could possibly do was wrap them in vines. It was more likely that I'd just end up growing them a damn snack.

Kierden had also tried to teach me to control my magic, but we hadn't gotten anywhere. He wouldn't admit it, but I was pretty sure he had adjusted to my magic draining him slowly. He didn't seem worse for wear, despite his moodiness.

The drain on my power would get worse again after the eclipse. I'd need to convince someone else to bond with me when that came around just so I could live a normal life. I still had two more months to worry about that, luckily.

"I have a bad feeling about this fight," I said quietly to Bright as she wove through the benches, toward a room behind the fighting cage. We would get ready inside the room.

There were already a few fae in the stands, and they wished me luck when they saw us. I waved a little but couldn't manage a smile.

"You've never fought before," she reminded me. *"All of us have bad feelings about new things."*

I sighed softly. *"Laeli and Kaelle's magic is unpredictable."*

"So is yours."

"Not in the same way theirs is, though."

"Believe in yourself," she said simply. *"And know that if anything goes wrong, we will get you out quickly."*

"You and who else? Kierden obviously doesn't care that my life's going to be at risk."

"Have you seen the other women with their swords? They're just as bad as you. No one accidentally dies in a fight."

I didn't think that was true. Maybe none of the fae, who were all badass fighters with centuries of experience, died *accidentally* in a fight. But a couple of human women with uncontrollable magic and no experience? We were a very different story.

What guarantee was there that Kaelle wouldn't accidentally throw a gust of wind that impaled me with her sword? What guarantee was there that Laeli wouldn't get stressed and catch on fire, then light *me* on fire?

"I hope you're right," I said to Bright, as she slipped into the room behind Death.

Kierden and I were the first ones there, so he went over and picked the first sword off a rack near the wall for me.

Bright licked my knee and prowled over to the corner of the room, where she plopped down on her belly and set her head on her paws so she could watch me.

Eisley arrived just after us, carrying three sets of clothing hidden by thick bags and wearing a massive grin. I heard metal clanging inside the clothing bags and fought a groan.

"I don't like that face," I warned her, waving my finger toward her expression. "You look downright wicked."

She laughed. Honestly, it was almost a cackle. "You're going to hate it."

I groaned.

Vayme and Kaelle arrived then, distracting me from Eisley, her evil smile, and whatever she had in those clothing bags. Ravv and Laeli were just behind them, and I could hear the crowd outside getting louder.

My nerves churned my stomach, but I tried hard to ignore them. After a few weeks of regular meals, I had filled out a lot more. My stomach was starting to get a little softer and my thighs were filling out a bit, although I could still see my ribs when I looked at myself in the mirror. If I ate more, I could have filled out faster, but Kierden's playfulness about how often I ate meant I was careful not to act as hungry as I was.

Unlike me, Laeli and Kaelle were gaining weight and growing curves rapidly. I'd noticed Vayme silently loading Kaelle's plate with his own food on multiple occasions and Laeli stealing food from Ravv's, who usually looked grumpy about it. I didn't think Kierden had noticed it; I knew him well enough to be nearly confident that he would have fed me more than I could ever eat if he knew why I was so hungry.

"You can't look partial to any of the women. As far as anyone knows, you only captured them for this and have no real connection to them," Eisley told the kings, waving them out of the room. The kings glowered and glared at her but all made their way out. Their companions stayed in the room: Death, Gleam (Ravv's bonded idorr), and Strong (Vayme's bonded xuno).

Kaelle and Laeli hadn't bonded with any animals yet, but the other kings' companions were a lot more protective of them than Death was of me. He was mostly focused on trying to convince Bright to be his mate, which I thought was kind of adorable.

And though Death wasn't protective of me, he was always affectionate, brushing up against my side and licking me whenever he passed me. He'd even started taking Bright's place between me and Kierden at night.

When the kings were gone, Eisley said cheerfully, "I brought your outfits for the fight. I'm sure it won't be super exciting, considering how terrible you all are, so the outfits are meant to distract everyone with your soft, bouncy bodies."

Compared to Laeli's and Kaelle's, my body wasn't soft or bouncy, but I understood the concept. If I'd been eating five huge meals a day like they were, I would've grown just as fast.

I didn't think that had occurred to Eisley any more than it had occurred to Kierden, though. She would've done something about it if it had. She just didn't understand humans well.

And yeah... Kierden was going to be *furious* if he found out that my town had starved me. I didn't plan on him finding out, though.

At least, I didn't plan on it until Eisley unzipped the bag.

I groaned at the sight of the outfit. I couldn't even call it a dress. It was just a pair of fancy scanties. The top portion was made with thin strips of metal that curved and would barely cover my nipples. The bottom portion had three strips—one over each hip, and one that would cover my lower bits, for the most part.

"Oh, that's terrible," Laeli said with a grin. "The kings are going to lose it."

Kaelle shivered. "I can already imagine the look of utter shame and disappointment on Vayme's face."

Laeli snorted. "Veil, not a chance. Barely-contained lust, sure."

"He isn't attracted to me," Kaelle said.

"Of course he is. You'll see."

They both looked at me to see my reaction.

I was still grimacing, trying hard to think my way out of the situation I'd just landed myself in.

There was no way, other than refusing to wear the outfit. And Eisley would literally wrestle me into it if I refused when she was that excited.

"Hello?" Eisley waved a hand at me.

I wordlessly lifted my short orange dress to my breasts and pointed to my ribs.

All of the girls went silent.

"You haven't gained much weight yet?" Eisley frowned, deeply.

"Kierden doesn't know the truth about the tower. I'm pretty sure he thinks it was to protect me because of my magic. If I suggest an extra meal, he'll make jokes about it or ask questions. And he's never seen me naked, so..." I shrugged helplessly, letting my dress fall back into place.

Death prowled over to me, his chest rumbling with a warning growl. He brushed the hem of my dress with his nose, and I sighed, lifting it.

He bumped my ribs, asking for an explanation without using words.

"I was starving," I told him. "For a really long time."

His eyes widened with what was clearly horror.

"Don't tell him. I didn't want him to know." I dropped my dress again.

With a low, angry rumble, he stepped up closer and leaned against me. It was the closest thing he could offer to a hug, and I reluctantly wrapped my arms around him. His chest was still rumbling with unhappiness as I did.

"We can just fight in our normal dresses," Kaelle said. "Kier doesn't need to know."

"Actually, I think this would be the perfect opportunity to show him how much of an asshole he is," Laeli said, a wicked glint in her eyes. "All of his people will be able to see how humans look when we're being fed properly—even if we aren't quite there yet. Everyone will know that Kier hasn't been feeding you enough."

Well, when she put it like that, it sounded downright vicious.

And... I kind of loved it.

Eisley's forehead wrinkled with alarm.

Kaelle moved between her and the door, blocking her path out. Eisley probably could've killed the small blue-haired human with her little finger alone, but she wouldn't. We all knew that.

"Fighting in your dresses is a *great* idea," Eisley said quickly.

Laeli looked at me, and I nodded.

She plucked the metal outfits out of the fae woman's hands, and Eisley sighed. "He's going to kill me."

Laeli snorted. "In your dreams, maybe." She handed me and Kaelle our outfits.

I released Death, but he just snuggled up closer to me. The poor guy probably felt bad. I didn't blame him for not knowing; if he had, he would've made Kierden do something about it a long time ago.

When I started changing, Death gave me space. He went back to Bright and sat down next to her. The way her eyes narrowed told me he was talking to her, possibly saying something she didn't like.

"Thank you for letting me have my secrets," I murmured to her. *"I know keeping them wasn't the smartest decision, but it was important to me."*

"You couldn't make your own choices for too much of your life, Nissa," Bright replied, her voice smooth and sure. *"I couldn't make that one for you. It was for the sake of your pride, and I understood that, even if I didn't always agree."*

"This is going to be terrible," Eisley muttered, as she took all our original dresses from us and then tied strips of glittering fabric over our glowing handprints to hide them from the rest of the fae.

"This was *your* idea," Laeli said, flashing Eisley a grin while she adjusted the metal outfit to cover her nipples better.

"Oh, I'm not going down for this. I will pin it on you, because I *know* your king will protect you." She pointed at Laeli, who was honestly the most plausible one of us to pin it on, if we weren't blaming Eisley.

And Ravv would definitely defend her. He was the only king who had shown any sign of the possessiveness that was apparently supposed to be expected.

"Did you hear that?" Kaelle's face jerked toward the caged area we would be fighting in.

"Did we hear what?" I asked her.

"I don't know. It sounded... strange." She frowned.

"I'm sure it's just the crowd. They get really rowdy."

A female fae rapped on the door and called out, "Ready?"

We all looked at each other.

"I guess," Laeli called back.

Eisley grimaced deeply as we grabbed our swords. The fact that I was going to get some sort of revenge on Kierden during the fight made me forget the bad feeling I'd had about it.

The male fae at the door stepped in and took one look at us before his face went red. His eyes were glued to Laeli. The fae were all used to being nearly naked, but with their constant warring, they were all muscular and thin. And that was a direct contrast to the natural soft-ness of humans.

Eisley cleared her throat, and he jerked his gaze to her.

Coughing a bit, he nodded respectfully at us all, and then stepped through the door that led out into the cage. A deafening roar went through the crowd, making my stomach roll.

He gave a quick introduction about the humans the kings had abducted for them, and then Eisley pushed us all out together.

We didn't stumble, by some miracle.

We also didn't jog or move with any other kind of enthusiasm. But the crowd didn't care—their yelling and roaring and stomping had me fighting back a small smile.

When we reached the middle of the cage I turned, and my eyes met Kierden's. He was up against the bars of the cage, his eyes burning as he gripped the metal.

Good.

He'd noticed.

Kaelle said something, but I didn't hear it. Her wind was blowing harder than I'd ever felt it though, which didn't seem like a great omen.

The fae man set us up across from each other, so we formed a triangle, and then he announced the start of the fight with a booming yell.

None of us moved as he crossed the cage, and then closed the door.

Only one of Kaelle's hands was on her sword. The other one was pressed to her temple, and she grimaced like she was in pain.

The crowd's roaring started to die down.

I looked at Laeli.

She shrugged, lifting her sword.

Guess we were still doing it.

I lifted mine too, and then Kaelle's eyes flew open, her wind whipping through the area. "He's here," she whispered.

The crowd had gone quiet enough for us to hear.

"Who?" Laeli asked, frowning.

"One of the assassins. I can feel him."

My eyes widened. "How can you feel him? How do you know?"

"I see and feel auras," she said quietly. "My wind comes from them. And his is *terrible*."

"What are you waiting for?" Ravv shouted from beside Kierden.

They couldn't hear us.

They didn't know what she was saying.

"What do we do?" I asked.

Kaelle's eyes darted around the cage. "I don't know."

"We need to get everyone out," Laeli said. Steam was coming off her arms and hands, a good sign that she was close to catching on fire.

"Oh, it's far too late for that," a low, masculine voice purred. The voice's owner appeared beside us, and we all stumbled backward. "Which one of you is connected to Kier Jirev?"

The man was absolutely gorgeous, with tan skin, wavy black hair, and even bigger muscles than the fae kings. He looked more like a god than a monster. His eyes glowed red, and his lips lifted in a feral grin that spoke of sex and sin.

"The Beast of the Endless Wilds," Laeli whispered.

The crowd in the stands was deadly silent.

His grin widened, and I saw his fangs. Was he a vampire somehow, too? "Hello, sweetheart. Is Kier using your magic to hide his?"

She said nothing, her eyes wide with panic. Flames danced just off her skin, not burning her but getting close.

As if on cue, yells and shouts erupted above us, and the fae started to *move*. The door we'd come through to get into the cage rattled as if someone was trying to get through it, but the Beast must've locked it from the inside. I heard snarling and roaring from fae around us—maybe the kings—but assumed that if they hadn't left yet, they would soon.

Kierden certainly needed to.

They were all warriors, but a smart warrior knew when to run. And clearly, that moment had come.

The wind blew against us as if we were in a ferocious storm. Laeli had caught fire, and was burning brightly.

Kaelle started to open her mouth, and I had the feeling she was going to lie for me. I couldn't let that happen.

"I'm mated to Kier," I blurted. "It's me."

His lips curved upward wickedly. "See how easy that was?" I blinked, and he was gone.

A massive hand closed over my shoulder, and another covered my mouth to muffle my scream. "You smell absolutely delicious, don't you?"

My head was wrenched to the side a moment later, and I felt a sharp pain in my shoulder before a feeling of bliss overwhelmed me.

The pain vanished for a moment, but the bliss remained. Something rumbled against me as a male voice mused, "Surely a fae king of any worth would at least attempt to defend the female he's claimed as his. Come out and fight, Kier."

Another sharp pain stung my shoulder, and then my eyes closed as even more bliss followed.

Some part of me wondered if I was really going to die before Kierden even learned my name.

CHAPTER ELEVEN
KIERDEN

The blood pounding in my ears and the fear burning my lungs were unlike anything I'd ever felt before. There was a record of every battle I'd ever fought on my arm, in ink, and yet I had never been afraid of a loss the way I was in the moment the Beast appeared beside my mate.

My concern had nothing to do with my life, and *everything* to do with hers.

Death was snarling in my mind, him and the rest of our bonded animals already ramming the gate to the cage, trying to get through.

But it was made of gargoyle steel. When locked from the inside it was impenetrable, created to protect its occupants during the vulnerable moments of their fight.

The other kings and I charged the door. For once, we were preparing to fight together instead of against one another.

"He's here for you," Vayme snarled, as we ran. "You need to go."

"I won't leave her," I snarled back.

"Then we fight."

"We can't break it," Death growled to everyone as we reached the door, finding the animals' sides bloody and their chests heaving. Eisley and a few of the other kings' allies were there too, each of them holding weapons. *"Tell your females to get it open."*

I gave the command to my human as I lunged for the walls of the room, gripping the bars while I tried to see into the cage.

She didn't respond, and I couldn't see through the other humans' magic.

Ravv's female was burning brightly enough to take up half the space. Vayme's female had her wind blowing so fiercely that it worked with the fire to conceal everything.

Veil, I hoped she wasn't on fire or in the arms of the Beast. He would play with his food before consuming my magic, and there was no better way to break the mind of a male than to torture his female.

"Come on, little human," I demanded. *"Open the door."*

Still, I received no response.

A small form ran through the wind and fire. A moment later, the little human with blue hair burst through it. Vayme caught her in his arms, and hugged her fiercely.

"Nissa told him she was bonded to you, and he bit her. He's drinking her blood," the girl said, lifting her watering eyes to mine. "We didn't know he was a vampire. I didn't know. I should've warned everyone."

Her wind blew more fiercely, and the cage started to rattle around us.

Nissa.

My human.

She was talking about my mate.

"Laeli's on fire," Vayme's human added, her voice starting to shake as the wind grew even fiercer. "She can't stop it. I—"

We couldn't fight in that wind. Not against the Beast.

"Get her out of here. Go to the elves," I said to Vayme, my voice cold as the calm of battle began to seep into my mind, body, and blood. "Tell them if their assassins kill any of our people, *including* our mates, we will consider it an act of war and will come for them as one."

Our magic wasn't as strong as theirs, but they were soft. They didn't know how to fight.

And we were weapons, down to our very souls.

Together, no group of creatures could stand against us.

He jerked his head in a nod, then threw his female onto the back of his bonded xuno.

"We destroy the Beast, and then tame my female's flames," Ravv said, as we sprinted into the cage. Both of us threw ice out to protect ourselves against his human's flames.

I tapped into my magic to create both long, icy blades I preferred to fight with. Though Ravv and I had never fought *together*, we had fought each other enough times to know one another's strengths and weaknesses. He was ferocious; he would take the offense, without a shred of defense.

So he would distract the Beast, and I would free my female.

My sister was behind me, with all of our bonded animals. They were the only ones I would trust with my human.

My *Nissa*.

Ravv roared as he lunged for the Beast, massive claws of ice over his fingers, knuckles, knees, and forehead. More were blossoming; the man used his entire body as a weapon.

I saw the Beast through the crowd, and my vision went red when I saw the bastard's teeth buried in my unconscious female's shoulder. The elves' assassins had been made with some variation of the curse that could turn humans into vampires, so they all relied on blood for sustenance.

Him feeding on Nissa only heightened my rage.

The Beast saw Ravv coming and dropped my female, moving in the blink of an eye. Fae were much faster than humans, but the assassins were even faster than fae.

Eisley caught my female as the Beast appeared behind Ravv, grabbing the king by his throat. The Beast snarled, and the smell of his tainted blood flooded the air as Ravv's ice tore into his hands and arms.

The Beast threw himself backward, ice still lodged in his limbs as he moved. Death and Gleam launched at him, and he vanished just in time to dodge them.

I sensed him behind me just before his hands landed on my shoulders. The ice of one sword sliced through his abdomen as I spun, slashing at his throat with the other.

The bastard barely had time to duck away.

He charged toward Eisley, who had a knife out and wore a face that said she'd make the Beast regret his vow to hunt me down.

A screaming, flaming human woman threw herself between Eisley and the Beast before he could reach her.

Ravv roared and tried to grab his female, but wasn't fast enough. She collided with the Beast, and an unearthly scream escaped him.

A moment later, he was gone.

Ravv caught his human, gripping her to his chest as he dragged her further from the rest of us. Her magic wouldn't hurt him, because their bond had knitted it with his like mine with Nissa's.

I covered the distance between me and my female in a heartbeat, dropping to my knees beside her and taking her from Eisley's arms. With her fragile body pressed to mine, I slowly inhaled her scent. The way it had mixed with the Beast's was nearly enough to drive me mad, but I couldn't allow myself to lose control.

Not when the Beast could still be in my city.

I had no idea how quickly he could heal, or how soon he would return.

Nissa was breathing steadily. Her skin was ashen, but her heartbeat was normal.

My body trembled slightly as I slowly lowered my forehead to hers, simply closing my eyes and holding her close for a long, long moment.

I had nearly lost her.

The assassins technically couldn't kill anyone they hadn't vowed to end, but they worked around it by *nearly* killing anyone they wanted to and then letting nature do the rest of the work.

"Please take Nissa to my room," I asked Bright in a low voice.

She dipped her head, and I looked at Eisley. "I need you to get Dirue while I secure the perimeter." Dirue was the healer, and the oldest fae in our city. Though she had no healing magic, she knew more about herbs and wounds than anyone else.

"I can secure it so you can get her and stay with Nissa," Eisley said, unshaken despite the insanity that had just gone down. She was a damn good warrior, and that was the reason she was my second-hand, not because of our shared blood.

"I need you with my mate. The Beast could very well still be here, and I won't risk letting him near her for a second time," I said.

"Alright. I'll do it." Eisley jerked her head in a nod.

It killed me not to be at Nissa's side while she was in pain, but there was no alternative. I couldn't risk her life again for my own desires.

"I'll follow the Beast's scent trail to make sure he's gone," Ravv said, his jaw tight as he gripped a shaking Laeli even tighter.

I agreed.

He asked one of his most trusted fae, Elwynne, to stay with Laeli. After she agreed, he whispered something to his mate, and her flames slowly receded. When they were gone completely, her eyes looked haunted and she was still shaking badly, clearly traumatized.

I lifted my female carefully up to Bright's back, and Bright slipped out with Eisley and Sharp.

Ravv handed his mate to Elwynne, and both women left on the back of her bonded idorr.

A long, slow breath escaped me.

The other king looked at me and nodded.

I nodded back.

It was all the acknowledgement either of us were ready to give at the moment. Merely fighting together was a difficult task, considering all of the pain we'd caused each other over the centuries. But in this situation, we were all united in being completely at the mercy of our bonds.

Both the bonds we despised that connected us to the assassins... and the ones we were still trying to figure out with the humans.

Death and I ran two circles around our city's perimeter, then snaked our way through the bridges and paths. We were both quiet, though there was no anger between us, only solemn contemplation.

Ultimately, I had allowed my little human to be in that cage. I had gone with the lie that we brought the humans back for that event alone, and there was no one to blame but me.

The weight of responsibility for that choice was heavy on my shoulders. As was the weight of her health, which I'd never questioned until the truth of it was before my eyes.

"You saw her ribs?" Death asked me as we began another loop.

"I did."

I'd never seen her bare before, or in anything that showed her abdomen. And she was the same size as Eisley, so I'd assumed she was healthy.

I'd been trying to keep my distance to avoid getting her murdered... and I'd hurt her in doing so.

Veil, I'd *starved* her.

"You didn't starve her. She's eaten every meal with you," Death said as if reading my mind. *"She chose not to tell you because she wanted you to ask. The female wants to be chased, but you've kept her at an arm's length for her safety."* We'd known each other long enough that he didn't need to hear my thoughts to know what I was thinking most of the time.

"She needed more food. I should've realized there was a reason for her hunger," I said bitterly.

My father would've noticed immediately if my mother wasn't eating enough or if she had seemed hungrier than normal. He had noticed everything about her.

Then again, they had been mated for a long time before they had me.

Regardless, I was at fault.

Completely and utterly at fault.

"You were trying not to let yourself feel anything for her. A useless feat, as I said from the beginning. All creatures are meant to take mates," Death said.

"She'll never forgive me for this."

"Perhaps not. But if you had known, you would've fed her. A fact she is doubtlessly aware of. She was waiting for you to pay attention to her."

I grimaced. *"After this, she's going to beg me to ignore her again."*

Death chuffed. *"Perhaps. But she's a stubborn enough female to appreciate your strong will, even if it takes her time to admit it."*

Ravv found us soon after that, and we exchanged reports. The Beast was still bleeding badly when he disappeared into the Wilds, and Ravv had followed his scent trail for an hour before heading back when there was no sign of it turning around. I hadn't found evidence of the Monster or the Demon, either.

Both of us itched to check on our mates, so we headed back to the castle to set up an assload of patrols.

When we approached, we found Eisley standing outside the castle, arguing vocally with a massive group of my fae. Ravv headed in another direction, but Death went down there without a second thought.

"What's going on?" I asked, raising my voice as I slid off Death's back and stepped up beside Eisley.

"We want to know what the Beast was doing here," a woman at the front of the group said. Her name was Tal, and she had been a pain in my ass since I turned down her invitation to spend the eclipse with her two centuries earlier.

They deserved the truth, even if it made them angry. And I doubted they would take the risk of selecting a new king so soon after the war ended, regardless of any anger they felt.

"Someone made a bargain with the Beast to kill me," I said bluntly, as I unwound the fabric from my hand and then lifted it up to show them both the brand and my glowing palm.

Their gasps were audible at the sight of it.

I added, "Someone made bargains with *all* of the elves' assassins, one to kill each of the kings. Apparently a few fae in the other kingdoms were willing to sacrifice their lives for the sake of our deaths."

The responding silence was so thick and heavy, it may as well have been alive.

None of my fae had gone missing or been found drained of life, so I knew none of them had made the deadly bargain.

"After we woke up with the brands, we went to the elf Alida and asked her for a way to buy time. She directed us to the humans with life magic. Their power neutralizes the death of the ice in our veins to hide us from the assassins when combined with ours as mates."

A long pause followed the explanation, and I added, "I have bonded with the human female Nissa, under the advice of Alida, and it is protecting me from the Beast. When the eclipse comes, it will erase both the Beast's brand, and our temporary bond."

Some eyes were narrowed in anger.

Some were wide with shock.

No one was afraid; we'd faced far too many battles for that.

"Have you had sex with her?" someone demanded.

"I have not and will not, unless we all agree to remove the law against it," I said firmly. "You know I am a male of honor. I gave you my word, and I have kept it."

A few murmured agreements sounded.

"Let's remove the law," a male voice called out. "If the Beast is hunting you, he's hunting all of us. And if I'm going to die at the hands of an assassin, I'd like to do so after spending the night in someone's bed."

A few chuckles followed his request.

"Get me proof of everyone's agreement, and we'll remove it," I said.

"I've got it," someone else called out. The crowd parted and Weva slipped through, then handed me a thick roll of paper. "Everyone signed it, except you."

"Even Eisley?" I lifted an eyebrow.

"She was the first one." She gave me an impish grin, and I chuckled.

"Alright." I didn't bother opening it. There weren't any of my people who would be unwilling to sign it; I knew that without a doubt. "The law is removed. Have at it."

A few people whooped, though it was half-hearted after the drama of all that had just happened.

Eisley leaned closer to me, her expression anxious as she whispered, "Nissa isn't doing well. I was coming to find you."

My heart dropped into my abdomen.

"I can run a rotation of patrols through the jungle to keep an eye out for the assassins," Jor said from behind a few of the other males. "See if you can help her. We heard the Beast drank from her."

Murmurs of agreement sounded.

I dipped my head toward him. "Thank you. And yes, she decided to tell the Beast that she was bonded to me. Probably saved the other humans' lives."

"Then she could've very well prevented another war, too," a female I couldn't see murmured.

"Plus, she grows the most delicious fruit. You've got to convince her to stay here, even after your bond breaks," someone added.

A few people chuckled. I didn't let myself react, afraid I'd make an admission that would let them know just how large my aversion was to the thought of letting her go.

"I'll see what I can do." With that, I headed into the castle to find my female.

I moved quickly through the hallways with Eisley, Sharp, and Death as we headed to my room.

"Dirue can't get her to respond to anything," Eisley said as we went. "When I told her you two had bonded, she said your blood can heal Nissa. Something about the magic of mate bonds."

Dirue knew mate bonds better than the rest of us, since she was one of the only fae old enough to remember the details about them.

"What about Ravv's human?" I asked.

"She's not hurt in any way, just shaken up."

"Good."

I pushed the door to my room open.

My eyes landed on my female, and fear struck me hard.

She looked like death itself had come for her.

Her tan skin was grayish, and she was so damn still in my bed that it terrified me.

"Veil," I snarled. "Someone should've come for me *hours* ago."

Dirue had no bonded esu anymore; she had lost hers in a battle centuries earlier, so there was no beast to growl at me for getting angry with her.

"Her heart is still beating, but you'll need to give her your blood; it will heal her much faster than anyone or anything else can. In the past, mates would share blood every month or two to strengthen each other," Dirue said much more calmly than I felt.

"How do I feed it to her?" I growled at the healer as I sat beside Nissa on the bed. Bright was already next to her, with her head resting on my human's shoulder.

"If she were conscious, it would be better for her to drink from here." She tapped the place where her neck met her shoulder.

The place where Nissa had been bitten by the Beast.

"She's obviously not conscious," I gritted out.

"You'll need to cut yourself and hold the wound to her mouth. It will be rather intimate, but she does need a lot of blood. When she wakes, lift her up and have her drink from here." She tapped her neck again.

"Fine. Get out," I barked.

Conjuring a blade of ice took less than a heartbeat, and slicing through my wrist with it was just as fast.

My fingers were gentle on Nissa's soft, fragile lips as I parted them and then pressed my weeping wound to her mouth. My blood dripped down her chin, but onto her tongue, too.

She stirred a little as soon as she tasted me. After a few moments, she started to drink.

There was a thick, satisfying pleasure in the way the color slowly returned to her face as she swallowed my blood.

A few minutes passed, and then her eyes flew open. She gripped my wrist, holding it tighter to her mouth.

My cock hardened as she sucked, her eyes dazed but hot.

When I was sure she was conscious enough, I pulled my wrist from her grip and lifted her onto my lap. "Bite me, female." My chest rumbled with the thickness of my desire as I spoke.

I felt the tug of magic in our connection as she sank her teeth into my skin. The magic must've lengthened them because her small, human teeth weren't made for biting the way most magical beings' were.

My eyes caught on something near the door. It took a moment to recognize that Dirue was standing near the entrance to my room, watching us.

Death and Bright had already slipped out, and I could hear one or both of them growling from outside the room.

Possessive rage crashed into me when I realized the healer was witnessing my female and I in a vulnerable, intimate moment.

"Get out," I roared at her, nearly shaking the bed with my fury.

My human didn't so much as flinch at my anger. Dirue dipped her head in a small bow and then slipped away. It made me proud that Nissa didn't fear me—that she knew I wasn't going to hurt her.

I clutched her tightly to my chest as she continued drinking, my cock throbbing against her core where she straddled me. I wouldn't acknowledge my desire while she was hurting, but there would be no hiding it.

She pulled away, sucking in a deep breath of air. Her eyes were mostly clear when she looked at me.

"Take more," I growled at her.

She started to hesitate, but when I tugged her head back to my shoulder, she bit me again.

There was fierce pleasure in providing something for my mate that no one else could. Fiercer than the thrill of any battle won or enemy defeated. Perhaps the fiercest joy I had ever felt.

I held her tight and didn't plan to let go until she forced me to.

CHAPTER TWELVE
NISSA

When I lifted my face from Kierden's shoulder the second time, I felt alive again. My body was still shaking from trauma and blood loss, but I could move. I could breathe unobstructed. I could *feel*.

At least, I could feel enough that drinking his blood was turning me on. That was annoying to say the least, since I was still trying to hate the bastard.

"More," he ordered me as I sucked in air. I could feel blood dripping down my chin, and was still trembling.

"I need a few minutes," I said, reaching a shaking hand toward my mouth.

Kierden's fingers beat mine, my body going still as he slowly wiped the blood from my face then slid his finger into my mouth.

I fought a groan.

Why did his blood taste so damn good?

Even his skin tasted good.

I found myself sucking on his finger, and decided I'd deny it if he ever brought it up again.

When I'd finally developed the strength to release him, I leaned back a bit. My head started to tilt, but Kierden caught it with his gigantic hand and held it up for me.

"I guess I probably have to tell you my name, since you just saved my life," I murmured.

"You do."

"It's Nissa. Not long or complicated. Just Nissa."

"It suits you," he said.

I wasn't sure if that was an insult or a compliment.

His voice lowered. "And I must admit that Kaelle gave it to me when the Beast had you."

"That was pretty bad, huh?" I whispered. "I didn't know he would drink my blood. Telling him I'm bonded to you was a risk."

"Not a measured one," he growled.

"Of course it was measured. He would've grabbed one of the other women if I hadn't, and I couldn't risk their lives." My voice was growing softer as my exhaustion set in.

When Kierden pulled my face gently to his neck, on the side I hadn't bitten, I rested it against him without a fight.

There was no reason to fight when his skin felt so good on mine.

It probably wasn't the answer he wanted to hear, but I was too exhausted to be thinking clearly.

"I would prefer you risk *everyone's* lives before yours," he said. I felt something on my cheek that reminded me of the way my father used to kiss my forehead as a child, strangely enough. Perhaps I imagined it.

"Well, you're the only one who feels that way," I whispered back.

"And the only one whose opinion matters when it comes to your life, Nissa."

The words would've stunned me if I'd been more conscious. I wasn't, so I didn't fully understand them.

I felt him move, and supposed he had climbed out of bed. The world spun a bit. My body wasn't recovered enough for the motion to feel natural. "Where are you going?"

"I'm bathing you. If you want me to leave your scanties on, I will." His voice grew grumpier when he said the last bit.

My lips turned downward. "You say that like you're actually interested in me being naked."

He moved my thigh just slightly, so his erection pressed against my leg as he walked. "I can assure you that I am."

"You don't do casual sex. You only pinned me to that wall to control me," I mumbled.

He scoffed. "We're halfway *mated*, Nissa. There would be nothing casual about us having sex. It would electrify our bond, and probably strengthen it too."

Oh.

I hadn't thought of it like that.

And damn, I liked the way he said my name. Like it wasn't just a word but was something important. Something that *mattered*.

He stripped his shorts off with one hand, then sat down on the ledge of the bathing pool with me on his lap.

Trying to ignore the feel of his bare thighs against my legs, I asked, "So you actually liked touching me?"

"I've hardly thought of anything else since," he growled. "Having you beside me constantly is the only thing that's kept me from stroking myself to the memory of it day in and day out."

Damn, I loved that.

And as much as I didn't want it to, it erased the bitterness I'd felt toward him when I thought he'd feigned interest in touching me. The same bitterness I'd been using to keep myself from growing too fond of him or starting to like him in any way.

"Maybe you can stroke yourself to the memory of it sometime while I watch," I mumbled.

My exhaustion was making things come out of my mouth that I wouldn't have said otherwise.

"Any day and any time, little human." I felt that feeling again—the feeling of his lips on my cheek. "Am I removing your scanties, or not?"

He dragged my mind back to the bathing pool. We were still sitting on the ledge.

"I can take them off. They're too uncomfortable to leave on." I started to pull my head away, but he tugged it back and tucked it against his neck again.

"No." His hands were gentle as they slid down my back to the metal over my lower bits.

I shivered slightly, and his cock responded to my movement. The throb of it made me warmer. I was too exhausted for anything steamy to happen, but I still liked feeling his body's reaction to me.

"Stay still. I'm going to break it with ice." He smoothed a hand over my lower back again and made me shiver once more.

"Ice can break metal?"

"Ice can break just about anything if you try hard enough. A few flimsy strips of metal aren't a problem." His knuckles brushed my skin with a little pressure, and then I felt a gentle snap near my hip. He moved to the other side and repeated the motion.

Then his hand slid between our bodies.

I clenched at his nearness to my core.

"Stay still, Nissa."

He snapped the metal there, and then carefully eased it down and under me. The backs of his fingers brushed my clit, making me feel all hot and fluttery.

"You smell divine," he said as he tossed the metal away. My backside landed on his thighs, and I inhaled unevenly at the pressure of his bare cock against my core.

Veil, that was blissful.

"I'm sure I smell like blood and the Beast."

"You did." Kierden found the latch at the back of the piece that wrapped around my breasts. He snapped the thin bands that went over my shoulders, and then eased me away from his chest so he could pull the metal away. "Now, all I can smell is your desire."

He pulled me back against his chest, then slipped into the water. My throat closed at the intense feeling of my breasts pressed against his warm, hard, bare chest.

I tried to clear my throat, and failed, so I distracted myself from my desire by asking, "Can the Beast hurt you or find you through me?"

"No. He can only hunt his target, just as he can only purposefully kill that person or creature. The elves thought that little rule would protect them from their assassins. As you saw, there are ways around it."

Veil.

"He was terrifying," I admitted. "But strangely attractive. I always assumed monsters were ugly."

"What good is an ugly monster? The more attractive it is, the more efficiently it can lure its pray or lull it into comfort."

"Well, that's a scary thought," I murmured.

"Aren't fae beautiful? And elves, demons, and dragons? The beauty of a creature distracts others from seeing the truth."

"I don't know if *that's* the case. I thought you were beautiful when we first met, but I still knew you were a bastard when you opened your mouth," I murmured.

He chuckled. "Perhaps you're a monster too, then." His finger trailed up my tailbone. I shivered against him, making his cock throb again.

"I don't think I'm beautiful enough to be a monster," I admitted. "I'll never look like you guys. And I have the ugly round ears, which I obviously can't change."

"If you knew how many times I've imagined tracing those round ears with my tongue, I doubt you'd find them ugly."

"You're the one who told me they were ugly!" I exclaimed.

He scoffed. "I did *not*."

"Yes, you did. You pulled my hair away from them on the first day and gave me this look of complete and utter disgust. I thought you might vomit."

He snorted. "Because of your *ears*? How weak did you think I was?"

"I didn't think you were weak. I thought you were an asshole, disgusted by my ears, and a fae elitist," I said matter-of-factly. "I still believe two of those things."

"I don't even want to know which ones," he grumbled. "If I made a disgusted face, it's because I was disgusted by how badly I wanted to taste them."

"You did not want to *taste* my *ears*."

He leaned his head down and slowly dragged the tip of his tongue over the curve of my ear. I shivered, hard. With my bare body literally in his hands, the moment was very, very intimate.

And I wasn't entirely certain I didn't like it.

I fought to keep my voice even. "I bet it tastes like an ear."

"Want to try it?" He pulled my face away from his neck.

When I opened my mouth to ask how he thought I would taste my own ear, he slid his tongue between my lips... and licked the length of mine.

Then he withdrew and pulled my head back to rest against his throat.

My mind spun again at the sudden increase in intimacy. "You just *licked* my *tongue*."

"After I licked your ear."

"You're supposed to hate me," I whispered against his neck.

"Tomorrow, perhaps."

Panic swelled in my chest. "No. You can't be nice to me today and then go back to being an asshole tomorrow. I won't know what to think or how to feel."

"I don't value kindness the way humans do, Nissa. If someone deserves my respect, I give it to them, but I'm not going to walk around smiling and asking people how their day is. I'll probably always be an asshole."

He misunderstood me. "I know *that*. I just meant you can't go back to being an asshole *to me*. I don't like the push and pull of it; it doesn't make me feel safe."

"I apologize for making you feel unsafe. That was never my intention, and it won't happen again." His voice was quiet, but I didn't question him. Kierden had never been a liar. "What else did your people do to you?"

Well, that was a dangerous question.

"What do you mean, what else?" I asked. If he wanted vulnerable answers from me at that point, he was going to have to ask directly and share vulnerable answers of his own.

"I know they starved you, little human. I saw the evidence on your body. It infuriates me that I didn't put the pieces together sooner—and frustrates me that you didn't attack me for the first comment I made about your hunger."

Hurt curled in my abdomen at the reminder, but I didn't move away from him. His body still felt too damn good against mine to move away. "Why *did* you make those comments?"

He let out a long breath. "I am immensely attracted to you. I was trying to make you hate me, because your hate made it easier to stay away."

"It didn't make me *hate* you, it frustrated me. I knew that if I told you the truth, you'd start loading my plate with your food. I just didn't want you to find out unless you cared about me enough to ask."

"If you knew I would've fed you, doesn't that imply that I would've cared?" he countered.

"Maybe? I don't know. I was just hurt, and I didn't understand the way you were treating me."

A moment passed before he admitted, "I've told you before that those who seal mate bonds in my kingdom are murdered. Despite the danger, some couples choose to create a bond secretly. No matter what they do to hide it, we always find them dead in their bed within a few days, with glowing golden handprints confirming their connection."

Sadness flooded me for their sake.

Though I couldn't imagine a love strong enough to make me risk my life for it, I still ached for them.

Kierden admitted, "Sometimes they tell me after they create the bond, in hopes that I can help protect them. Even when I guard them myself, they still die. We've never found the cultist who must be hiding among our people. It's the greatest shame of my life."

"Do you think they use poison?"

"They must, though I haven't figured out what kind, or how they use it. Even when I watch them cook for themselves and no one else knows about their bond, they always end up dead."

If he'd seen that many couples die because of a mate bond, I had to think he was probably afraid for our lives because of ours. And that kind of fear would change a person; I knew, because I'd looked it in the face when I was alone, starving, and locked in that damn tower.

"So you were an ass to me to protect me," I said.

"Yes."

"That's a shitty way to protect someone, Kierden." I closed my eyes, but my lips curved upward just slightly with his low chuckle. The rumble of it against my bare breasts felt incredible.

"I know. It won't happen again."

I bit my lip. "It might have to, though. If anyone finds out we're together..."

"I had to tell my people about the bond. There was no way around it. As far as they know, we have no feelings for each other and plan to separate when the eclipse comes. No one is killed over silver bonds, only golden ones."

Damn.

"*Do* we have feelings for each other?" I asked, after a long moment.

He didn't answer immediately, so I waited.

Kierden finally said, "I suppose we're still figuring that out." He added, "Don't think I didn't notice you avoid telling me about your town."

Damn.

"Can we talk about it tomorrow? Or after I sleep? I don't know what time it is, but I'm too exhausted for that conversation."

"I suppose. Let me clean you and get you to bed, little human."

"I need something to sleep in," I mumbled to him, as he started slowly washing my back with soap and water. "I'm tired of sleeping in my dresses."

"Most fae sleep in their scanties."

My eyes closed at the blissful peace of him touching me like that. "Too uncomfortable."

He considered it as he continued washing the wound where my shoulder met my neck very carefully. It didn't hurt as much as I had expected it to. "I have a few old shirts. I haven't worn them in a long, long time, but they might work."

"That sounds nice."

He chuckled. "You are absolutely stunning."

My lips curved upward. "Ears and all?"

"Mmhm." He licked the curve of my ear again, making me laugh softly.

When he was done washing me, he dried me off and then carried me to the closet.

He pulled a shirt out of the back of his closet, then set me down on my feet just long enough to dry my hair with a towel and tug the shirt into place. The fabric was loose and soft, exactly what I'd wanted. It barely fell to the middle of my thighs, but I didn't mind showing skin thanks to the dresses I'd been wearing.

"You're going to need to drink more of my blood before you go to sleep," he told me as he set me down again in the bathroom. I was only on my feet long enough for him to get out a bandage, wet my skin, and then cover the puncture wounds on my neck with it.

"Am I? I feel fine."

"It's supposed to help you heal faster. Unless you'd rather eat?"

I made a face. "I don't think I can choke anything down."

His eyes gleamed wickedly, and I got the feeling he was holding back a sex joke as he said, "Blood it is, then."

Kierden carried me back to the bed, setting me on his lap and tilting his head to the side. I frowned at the wounds I'd left on him. They were already partway healed, but still looked terrible.

"I don't want to hurt you again," I said.

His hands skimmed my bare thighs, sliding toward my ass and making me warmer. "Think of it as revenge for the times I treated you poorly."

"Going out in the metal outfit was revenge, and look where that got me."

He stroked my ass, his hands just below the hem of my shirt. "That was *brilliant* revenge. The Beast's interference wasn't your fault."

I made a noise of agreement. "Did it bother you?"

"Learning about my own errors alongside the rest of my kingdom? Immensely." He squeezed my ass lightly in his hands.

"I expected you to yell at me."

"Why would I yell when I can think of far better punishments?" He squeezed my ass again, harder.

The tight grip made me hotter. "In the Woods when we first met, you didn't correct me when I called you by your full name. Why?"

"The way it sounded on your lips was too perfect for me to ask you to shorten it."

"I can call you Kier. Or at least, I can try."

"Don't. It makes me hard when you say my name." He used his grip on my ass to drag me against his erection just a little harder.

"You must be hard a lot around me, then," I said.

"Constantly. Now, stop changing the subject and bite me, Nissa."

My face flushed bright red, but I finally followed the command.

The taste of his blood was even better than I remembered. It calmed me and made me hot for him at the same time, and I found myself rocking against his erection as I drank from him.

He never pulled away from me or pushed me to stop, letting me take as much as I wanted.

My mind spun when I finally released his neck, my body flushed but full and relaxed.

He pulled me to his chest, lowering us to the bed on our sides. His front was pressed tightly to my back and his erection nestled between my thighs as he pulled the blankets over us.

"Veil, you want me," he rumbled.

My face flushed. "I don't."

We both knew it was a lie.

"My shorts are drenched with your desire, little human." His lips brushed my ear, and I shivered against him. He was right; I wanted him fiercely. "I owe you a climax. Let me give it to you."

My heart skipped a beat. "I don't know if I'm ready to reciprocate."

"I didn't ask you to."

There was no way I could deny that I wanted what he was offering. His touch and a release, nothing more. I whispered, "Okay."

His chest rumbled again. He pulled one of my legs over his hip, opening me up. The blankets still covered me, and his hand slid down the front of my thigh before stopping a breath away from my core.

"Tell me I can touch you, Nissa." He dragged his tongue over the curve of my ear again. "Tell me your body is mine to relax and relieve. Tell me you want to feel my fingers inside you when I bring you to climax."

My body flushed hotter. "I already gave you permission."

His fingers brushed my clit lightly—so lightly. "I want to hear you say it again."

I inhaled sharply as he brushed my clit once more with that same soft, teasing touch. My body was tense, every damn part of me clenched and waiting and *desperate*.

So I gave him what he'd asked for. "I want you to touch me, Kierden. I want you to make me climax. I want you to bury your fingers inside me and prove that you like the way I feel."

He gave me a satisfied growl and *finally* lowered his fingers to my center.

I sucked in a breath when he stroked my clit lightly. The feel of his huge, warm fingers on my folds was unreal, and my pleasure swelled almost instantly.

His cock throbbed between my thighs as he stroked me again and again, murmuring, "You're so damn wet for me, little human."

I couldn't form a single word to reply. The pleasure built so fast I couldn't believe it.

He rumbled, "So hot and slick. Veil, I can't wait to have you wrapped around my cock." He teased my slit with a thick digit while he continued stroking me, and it was just too much.

I cried out, my hips jerking against his hand as I climaxed harder than I'd ever dreamed was possible.

My chest heaved as I came down from the high, my world spinning again. I had never felt so damn relaxed before, though there was enough desire still curling in my abdomen that I wanted to urge Kierden to keep going.

He slid his fingers out from between my thighs and returned my leg to its original positon. "Sleep now, Nissa."

I sighed but nodded and then started drifting off to sleep.

The bed dipped a few minutes later, when Death and Bright slipped into the room. Both of them snuggled up against me instead of taking their own sides, and my lips curved upward slowly.

I'd nearly been killed by the Beast of the Endless Wilds... and yet I would risk myself again if I knew it would bring me back to everything that had happened afterward.

CHAPTER THIRTEEN
NISSA

I woke up in the same position I'd fallen asleep in, with my back pressed to Kierden's front. His erection was still tucked between my legs, and his hands had started moving slowly over my thighs again at some point.

I couldn't remember ever feeling so content when I woke before.

Foreign words crossed my mind, and I felt a soft urge to speak them.

Sillah ovim rett warum.

I didn't voice them, but there was a light pressure of some sort pushing me to.

It took a moment, but I realized where I'd heard them before—when Kierden started the bond between us. If I spoke them, it would seal our connection.

And theoretically also send murderers after us, on top of the Beast that was already hunting us.

So obviously, I couldn't say the words.

Kierden murmured into my ear, "Eisley brought food."

Apparently he'd realized I was awake.

"Okay." I made no move to get up. For once, I wasn't very hungry. I felt good, honestly. Really good. Better than I had in a long time.

He rolled away from me and lifted me to a sitting position.

Guess I was eating after all.

Kierden left me on the bed while he crossed the room and opened the door, angling his body so no one could see past him when he did.

"How is she?" Eisley asked quietly.

"Fine, now." He didn't budge.

"Please let me see her. I know I should've sent someone for you sooner, but Dirue said not to. It was a moment of poor judgment for both of us. We didn't realize how fragile humans are."

"A moment of poor judgment that could've cost Nissa her *life*," the king growled.

Maybe I'd been closer to death than I realized.

But Eisley had helped keep me sane since I'd been in Kierden's kingdom, so I couldn't leave her to deal with him on her own. I slipped out of bed and padded toward the door.

"You knew she had been starved too," Kierden said flatly.

His sister didn't answer immediately.

I pulled the door away from the king and stepped out in front of him, flashing Eisley a small smile. There was a rolling cart next to her, and the food on it looked absolutely incredible. My stomach rumbled, unsurprisingly. "I'm fine, Eisley. And I'm sure you had a good reason for everything you did or didn't do. No one here knows how to deal with humans."

Her gaze moved to me, grateful.

Kierden's hand landed on my hip, his grip tight as he pulled me back two steps until I collided with his chest.

"Thank you for the food." I caught Eisley's hand long enough to squeeze it, then grabbed the handle of the cart. "I really am fine. I'm sure he'll get tired of me and let me out of here soon." With that, I stepped backward.

Kierden didn't move, though, so all I managed to do was press my ass to the erection waiting for me.

"We'll talk later," Kierden warned her.

I looked up at him long enough to flash him a glare, and he met my eyes for the briefest moment before looking back to Eisley. "And..." He paused for a moment. "Thank you."

Her expression softened, and she dipped her head in a nod.

He set a hand on the cart's handle too and then took a few steps back, pulling me and the food inside with him before closing the door unceremoniously.

"You're not shaking anymore," he said, picking me up easily and carrying me toward the bed.

"Which means I can walk on my own feet."

He set me down on the mattress—next to the snoring esu, who had ended up snuggling together at some point. When he sat down on the other side, he pulled the food cart closer. His gaze moved over it like he was cataloguing everything.

I started to reach for a bowl of fruit on the side closest to me, but before I could grab it, he plucked a plate off the cart and set it in my hands.

I blinked down at the food.

It was some kind of breakfast cake, with thick chocolate sauce drizzled over it and nuts sprinkled over that.

"Why?" I asked him, not bothering to explain what I was questioning. We both knew I was asking why he'd picked that.

"Your diet will mainly consist of things to help you gain weight until you've recovered from the trauma you don't want to tell me about." He grabbed a bowl of some strange gel-like substance and set it next to me, then plucked another three plates off the cart and added it to the others he'd given me.

"I already feel better than I have in ages," I told him. "I think your blood might have healed the effects of that *trauma I don't want to tell you about.* Or at least made a dent in it."

When I looked down at my thigh, I honestly thought it looked a little thicker.

He leaned closer to me, grabbed the hem of my shirt, and lifted it up.

Some part of me wanted to shrink at the sudden intensity of his stare. But he had bathed with me the night before, and given me a climax too, so there wasn't really anything to hide from.

"You do look healthier," he said, with approval in his voice. "Your ribs are nearly hidden. But the other humans had more curve, so you still need to eat a lot."

With that, he dropped my dress.

My face burned. "So you looked at the other women and then decided I wasn't good enough?"

His eyes narrowed at me. "No. I saw your ribs, and then looked at the other women to see if theirs were visible. My attention was purely scientific. I felt no desire for them."

My responding gaze was skeptical.

"I was standing right next to the other kings. Either of them would've attacked me if they thought I was looking at their mate with interest. Take the fact that they didn't as your evidence."

"Kaelle doesn't think Vayme is even attracted to her," I countered.

"She's wrong," he said bluntly.

The look I gave him said I didn't believe him.

"Even if he isn't, fae are territorial. Having a mate makes that worse." Kierden added another plate to the crowd of them he'd already put in front of me.

"Are you saying you feel territorial of me?"

"Of course." He looked at me like the question was ludicrous.

I looked at him the same way.

Neither of us gave in for a long, long moment.

I was waiting for him to clarify vocally. The fact that I was still sleeping in his room at his insistence seemed like evidence enough of him being territorial, but I wanted him to say that.

He was waiting for... me to call him out, maybe?

For me to say I didn't believe he was territorial?

When another minute passed without either of us giving in, he finally looked away from me just long enough to cut into my chocolate-covered cake and lift the bite to my mouth.

I narrowed my eyes at him.

He narrowed his back.

Reluctantly, I took the bite.

"You're mine," he finally said. "The feelings and emotions behind that knowledge are complex, but the certainty remains. You belong to me. All else seems inconsequential, unless it puts your life at risk."

"And that's why you've been an asshole to me?"

"Moreso than I typically am," he agreed. "My kindness could be your end, and that made the distance between us a necessity."

Damn.

Death started to stir beside me, but I stroked his head, and he fell back asleep with a rumble of contentment.

"If we were to be together, we'd either have to let our bond break with the eclipse or seal it and keep it a secret," I said.

"We would." Kierden didn't deny it.

"Well, I don't want to be anyone's secret mate."

He lifted another bite of food toward me, and I snagged the utensil from his hand so I could feed myself.

I added, "In the extremely unlikely situation of us deciding we want to be together, I wouldn't be willing to do so in hiding. I was trapped for far too long to let the fear of someone's reaction hold me captive."

His expression darkened. "*Trapped?*"

I supposed I'd have to tell him about my past after all. I found myself actually *wanting* to tell him some of it, though.

"The tower you found me in was my prison. My mother ran the town, and she made sure I was kept starving and locked away so I could keep growing food for everyone."

His expression grew murderous. "I would've killed all of them if I'd realized. I thought the tower and guards were for your safety."

"They were for the *town's* safety. To keep everyone else from trying to steal their food source, and to make sure I wouldn't get more than a few feet away if I tried to escape on my own."

I scooped another bite of the cake. It was probably the best thing I'd ever tasted, and I'd had some incredible things in the time I'd been in Jirev.

"As soon as I'm free of the beast, I'll return to your town with a few of my warriors and end them all," he said. Though his voice was calm, I believed him completely.

"I don't want you to kill them all. The worst punishment would be to force them to relearn how to grow their own plants. But my plants shouldn't be too hard to tend to—and the town has so much money from selling my food that I don't think they'll even need to start any new farms. You should see the size of the gemstones the women have started wearing. A lot of them would've been big enough to feed the whole town with for months, before my magic came in."

"Then we'll burn your plants down, steal their money, and take their finery for ourselves," Kierden said bluntly.

My lips curved upward. "I appreciate that, but I don't want the kids in town to suffer. They don't know anything about the kind of hard work we put in before I was locked in the tower."

"Then they'll have to learn. Even if you leave them your plants and the gemstones you bought them, eventually, the money will run out. With the way humans age, it'll be the children in a few generations who suffer if you leave the plants, not the ones who wronged you. How long did they hold you?"

I grimaced. "Nine years."

His scowl deepened, his anger rising. "They *will* suffer for it. I'll ask a few warriors to remain in the Broken Woods to make sure the children don't go hungry, but the ones old enough to make a conscious decision to use you will pay."

"I just want to be done with my past, Kierden. I don't want to go back there for any reason, including revenge."

"Then you'll remain here, while I deal with it." He wasn't fazed even slightly by my reluctance.

"Alright." I leaned back against the wall.

He reached over, maneuvered my hand back to the cake, and scooped more food with my utensil.

We ate quietly for a bit, and my mind returned to what I'd said earlier about how I wasn't willing to be his secret mate. Kierden hadn't acknowledged that refusal—and I suspected it was because he had no solution for it.

Ultimately, nothing he'd ever said or done led me to believe he was willing to risk my life.

That put us in an impossible situation. The only way not to risk our lives was to keep any actual feelings for each other a secret.

According to Kierden, his people seemed to have accepted it when he told them that the bond was only to protect him from the Beast. That certainly didn't mean they would accept him taking me as a permanent mate.

"You didn't mention your father," Kierden remarked as I finished up with my food. I hadn't made it through everything he gave me, but I'd made a dent in it.

"I haven't," I agreed.

He waited.

I took another bite.

And another.

"You'll tell me eventually," he finally said.

Maybe he was right.

I guess that depended on what we decided to do when we were finally forced to make a decision about our mate bond.

We spent the next two days doing nothing of real worth. Kierden made me stay in his room to rest, since he was unconvinced that I'd already recovered. We chatted a little—him, mostly. I dodged pretty much all of the questions he asked me, since most of them were about my past, and I didn't want to keep talking about it. Particularly when he hadn't shared any pieces of his own history.

So, we settled on reading books and discussing them afterward, with our bonded esu snuggling up with us and offering the occasional thought.

It surprised me to find out how many emotions the king had when it came to fictional worlds. Especially because I had many emotions of my own. Many times, books had been what kept me sane in my tower, and they were the only real thing of value that my town had given me.

Then again, those books usually arrived after days where I'd gotten particularly agitated... and perhaps seemed slightly insane. So, my mother had probably been hoping the books would keep me docile.

On top of the reading, Kierden fed me a *lot*. We had five meals a day, and after I was certain I couldn't eat anything else, he fed me dessert.

It probably should've driven me mad to be stuck in his room, but I didn't feel trapped. I felt cared for, strangely enough. It was a foreign feeling, but one I loved.

And the fact that he slipped his hand between my thighs and gave me a climax every night before we fell asleep, without asking for anything in return, definitely didn't hurt.

CHAPTER FOURTEEN
NISSA

When a knock came on the third day and Eisley said she needed us immediately, I was honestly a little sad.

We assumed the elves had arrived. As disappointing as it was, I'd known that life would eventually have to return to our version of normal, where Kierden ignored me, and I acted like I wasn't attracted to him.

I stepped into the bathroom to change, and took off the massive shirt I'd borrowed from the king. When I slipped into my orange dress, it caught on my hips. I had to tug hard to get it over them, which made me frown.

A glance at myself in the mirror made my eyes widen.

The dress *fit*.

Veil, it didn't even *fit*. It was *too tight*.

I beamed at my reflection as I turned sideways to see my profile, and the curves in it.

Damn, I looked good.

I definitely wasn't the same size or shape as any fae woman I had met, but I loved the flare of my hips, the softness of my belly, and the fullness of my breasts. They were healthy, human, and *alive*.

Kierden was waiting for me on the edge of the bed when I stepped out, and slowly, his eyes moved down my figure.

And then back up.

And then down again.

When they finally collided with mine, he couldn't have missed my grin.

His own lips curved upward slowly, until they formed a smirk. "Your dress is too tight; I suppose you'll have to wear the metal lingerie again."

I laughed. "Too bad you broke it."

We slipped out—him first and me second, with both esu behind me—but halted when we found a grave-looking Eisley waiting in the hallway.

"What happened?" Kierden's growl was immediate, every ounce of humor gone.

"We found another couple," Eisley said.

The sickness in her expression told me they'd probably found the couple mated and murdered.

Veil.

We'd thought she was there because of the *elves*.

"Who?"

Eisley gave two names I didn't recognize, but Kierden swore viciously.

Ice crept over his fists as he stormed down the hallway. Eisley kept his pace without a problem.

Death and Bright remained beside me as I stared behind them for a moment, then Bright bumped the side of my leg with her nose.

Right.

I needed to stick with them, because of the pain that would come from the bond if we were separated too much.

So I slipped onto Bright's back, leaning toward her and burying my fingers in her fur as she and Death caught up to the fae.

"You'll need to act indifferent," Bright murmured to me. *"Don't let anyone see that you and the king have gotten closer."*

I agreed.

Eisley and Kierden climbed onto the backs of their bonded esu, and then we were all moving quickly through the trees. I couldn't help but stare at the vibrant flowers that had spread through the jungle all around us. The further we ran, the more flowers I noticed.

None of them had been there before me. *I* had grown them and made the beauty of the jungle even more vibrant and alive.

I was proud of that, even if the tiniest bit of fear was curling in my belly at the fact that we were headed toward the bodies of two mated fae who had been killed.

We reached a small house built inside a tree. There were a few fae already standing on the platform just outside it. A few of them were crying, a few looked hollow... and a few looked absolutely furious.

Everyone parted for Kierden and Eisley, and their bonded esu stepped through the crowd and into the house.

Bright and I remained outside with the other fae. We hoped it would show respect for their dead and put distance between me and the king. A few of the fae glowered at me, and I tried not to shrink under the weight of their hatred. Most of them ignored me, so that made it slightly better.

"They're just mourning," Bright said quietly.

"She told me she wasn't going to seal the bond," one of the women near us said, wiping tears away with shaky hands. "She knew this could happen. Why did she seal it?"

"Why do any of them seal it?" another woman asked bitterly.

When no one answered, I realized it was a genuine question.

I remembered the itch in my mind to speak the words Kierden had said to me. The desire to seal the bond, even when I knew I didn't want that.

If I was in love with him, or actually wanted a sealed bond... veil, it would've been impossible to fight.

"They seal it because the magic pushes them to," I said quietly.

Everyone on the platform looked at me.

I explained, "There's an urge in your mind. It's unconscious, almost. You find yourself thinking the words you'd have to say to seal it, while the magic pushes you to speak them aloud. Even if you don't want it, you find yourself itching to do it. I'm so sorry for your loss, but it's not their fault; the magic most-likely made the decision for them."

Slowly, all of their gazes lowered to the glowing handprint around my wrist. Someone had taken my bracelet off me at some point while I was healing, and I hadn't thought about putting it back on.

My face warmed, slightly.

Kierden and Eisley emerged from the house, still on the backs of their bonded esu. Everyone was silent as they looked at the king.

There was something in his eyes—some combination of fury, horror, and guilt.

"Just like the last times," he said. His stance remained strong, and his gaze grew harder.

"The laws against sex helped prevent this," one of the male fae said.

"Refusing to start a bond in the first place is the only way to really stop it," another woman said solemnly.

"We should be free to create bonds if we want to." Eisley's face was pale, but her jaw was set firmly. "We should be allowed to take mates if it's something we desire."

"Not if it gets us killed," one of the men spat. "We need to catch the bastard who's doing this. We need to hunt again."

"We never *stopped* hunting, we just didn't find any damn leads," Kierden growled, his body tense.

"No one in the city could kill you," one of the women said. "If you sealed your bond with the human, we would have a chance of finally finding and ending the killer."

Everyone looked at me again.

Everyone except Kierden.

They wanted me to volunteer, to offer myself up as bait.

"No." Kierden's voice cut through the silence like a weapon. "Nissa is a human who's only lived a fraction of the time the rest of us have. After our bond dies with the eclipse, I'll mate with someone willing to risk their life for an answer."

His words stunned me.

And *veil*, they hurt me.

We'd been in bed together for days, talking for days, *touching* for days, and he just... volunteered to mate with someone else?

From what he'd told me, no one was killed until their bond was complete. And a complete bond was permanent.

I understood that what was happening was a tragedy, and that they needed a solution, but that didn't mean he needed to volunteer to mate with someone.

And he hadn't even *considered* choosing me permanently. After he'd spent days telling me he was attracted to me, he wanted me, he found me beautiful... the bastard may as well have slapped me in the face.

Nods went around the group of fae.

His people *approved* of his plan, and I couldn't question him without becoming either a target or a laughingstock.

I needed to get out of there. To get away from the king and clear my mind.

"The elves are approaching!" a voice called from somewhere deeper in the jungle.

"We'll comb the bodies and homes for any sign of magic or interference after I speak with the elves," Kierden said. He called three names and told them they would guard the home, and that they'd be working with him afterward. They agreed, and then Kierden, Eisley, and I headed off to meet the elves with our bonded esu.

Part of me wondered whether he'd even notice if Bright and I slipped away.

But then he glanced over his shoulder, looking me up and down. His voice touched my mind and he asked, *"Are you okay?"*

I stared at him.

What was I supposed to say?

Another mated couple had been murdered, solidifying the fact that Kierden and I could *not* seal our bond. Which I didn't want anyway, right?

And he had basically just told me we didn't have a future. We couldn't admit the truth of our developing feelings to his people, but if he really wanted me, he could've just gone along with volunteering me as the damn bait.

If we didn't have a future, what was I doing there at all? I couldn't watch him mate with another woman and just be friends with him after everything we'd done and been through.

Though I was nowhere near ready to seal our bond, some part of me had still been holding on to the possibility that I could be with Kierden in some capacity. Even if we were just lovers. I hated the idea of being mates in secret, but if we did break our bond, we could share a bed, share a home, share a life... it would have perks.

Perks that I could no longer allow myself to consider.

"I'm feeling sick," I lied. *"I'm going to go back to the castle and rest while you meet with the elves."*

His forehead wrinkled in concern. *"I'll ask Eisley to go with you."*

"No. I'd prefer to be alone."

He studied me for a moment, and then finally nodded and turned back.

"Let's go to the marketplace," I told Bright quietly. *"I need to get away from Kierden for a while."*

"We can ask Reo to make you dresses that fit," she suggested.

It sounded like the perfect way to distract myself for a bit, so I agreed, and she ran.

We reached the marketplace a few minutes later. The handprint on my wrist was throbbing thanks to my distance from Kierden, but I ignored it as well as I could. A lot less people were at the marketplace than the last time—and the ones who were there seemed much more subdued.

Kieren had told me he was certain the elves would agree to protect the fae kingdoms from their assassins when threatened with war. The elves weren't warriors. He also assumed they would send the other kings back to their own lands to make that protection easier, so the assassins couldn't work together. Because of that, I figured most people would be gathered together to hear how the meeting went.

Personally, I wasn't interested in fae politics, or elven politics, or... well, *anyone's* politics. I just wanted to live a peaceful life and spend the rest of my days with plenty of food to eat. How I was going to make that happen, I wasn't entirely sure.

Although if Kierden was going to mate with someone else, I supposed he was going to make my decision easy. I'd find a farm, convince someone to let me run it, and spend the rest of my life feasting on berries and vegetables.

I would miss the castle chef's incredible food and desserts, but I could sacrifice chocolate for safety and security.

There was no one in a few of the shops I passed, so I assumed those ones were closed. Reo's shop was open, so I slipped off Bright's back and walked toward a huge wooden bridge we'd need to cross to get there. Vines and flowers wrapped around nearly every inch of the bridge, but even that didn't really help my mood.

"*What's wrong?*" Bright asked me as we went.

"*He said he was going to choose another mate,*" I admitted quietly.

"*I heard. He may have just been trying to calm the other fae.*"

"*I don't think so. He told me that the couples being murdered are one of his greatest shames. It doesn't seem like a stretch that he would risk his life trying to fix it, especially now that the war is over and the fae are trying to figure out how they want to live. A lot of them probably want to take mates.*"

"*Perhaps. You'll need to talk to him, to find out,*" she mused.

"*It seems like he'll say anything he can to get what he wants, though. I don't know if I can trust him.*"

"*What does he want?*"

"*I don't know. Sex?*"

"*If all he wanted was sex, he would've asked or tried to make a move on you at night,*" she pointed out. Though she and Death always left when things got steamy, I'd kept her updated on the developments between us because she was the only woman I could really talk to.

Or female, at least.

I would've liked to find Kaelle or Laeli and talk to them, but Kaelle was gone with Vayme, and Kierden hadn't let me out of our room since things started progressing. Eisley was obviously out too, since she was his sister. She wasn't hanging out in the room reading books with us or anything, so even if I wanted to talk to her, I couldn't.

I heaved a sigh. "*Stop being reasonable, Bright.*"

She chuffed as we walked into the clothing shop. "*Esu are not like fae. We don't appreciate drama. If a male esu wants you, he tells you. Kierden has told you that he wants you, so trust him. He's never lied to you before.*"

"But if there's really a chance he's going to mate with someone else after the eclipse, I can't risk letting myself develop any more feelings for him. I'd rather not have him than have him and lose him."

She rubbed her side against mine. *"I understand."*

We walked up to Reo, who was sitting in a chair with a book in his hands. The back of his chair was leaned up against a wall, and one of his ankles was draped over his knee. He lifted his eyes as we approached, and his lips curved upward just a tiny bit. "Hello."

"Hi. I need a few more dresses," I said apologetically. "Mine don't fit. I don't have any money, but—"

"You're keeping our king alive, from what I hear. I'll send him the bill." He winked at me, and I relaxed. "Come with me."

Bright and I followed him into the room where he'd taken my measurements the last time. At his command, I stripped. My face heated as I looked down at myself.

Yeah, *everything* was too tight. Scanties included.

"This will only take a moment," Reo said absentmindedly, as he started measuring my different parts. I fixed my gaze on one of the lights moving lazily through the room, and for the first time since I'd been in Jirev, I wondered what they were made of.

"Where do the lights come from?" I asked him, as he finished up his measurements.

He held up a finger, going back to the wall and scribbling some things down. When he returned, he said simply, "We call them glow bugs. In the language of the lost gods, they're named *huvin*." He held a hand out toward the creature.

After a moment, the bug descended slowly. Finally, it landed on his palm.

I stepped closer, eyes widening in fascination as I looked at it. We didn't have a human equivalent for it, but it was big and round, with a bit of fuzz on its body and two teeny antennae. Its entire body glowed, and seemed to brighten as he held it.

"What makes them glow?"

"They feed on our magic," he explained.

I blinked, resisting the urge to jerk away from the creature.

Reo's lips curved upward again, and he lifted my dress off the floor before he handed it back to me. "It doesn't hurt. The amount of magic they can take is so minute you won't even feel it. Quite handy to have around though, hmm?"

"Definitely." I tugged my dress back over my head. "Thank you for doing this. I should be able to get by with three more dresses, since I'm not sure if I'm finished growing or not."

He nodded, and we started walking toward the exit. "What colors?"

"Whatever you have that matches the flowers outside."

He assured me that wouldn't be a problem, and I headed out.

As I slipped onto Bright's back, I asked her, *"Do you know where we could go to talk to someone with a farm? I'd like to be able to use my magic to grow food for the kingdom, if they're interested in my help."*

"Of course." She headed down a bridge I hadn't crossed before, one just as covered in flowers and vines as the last one we'd walked. *"It'll be good for you to find your own place here, in case Kierden ends up being a worse man than I think he is."*

"You have a lot of faith in him," I grumbled at her.

She chuffed. *"I have a lot of faith in the power of mate bonds."*

I supposed that was good enough reasoning.

CHAPTER FIFTEEN
NISSA

The pain in the handprint on my wrist grew fiercer as Bright carried me to the farm. It was on the ground, at the base of the town-sized tree the castle was built into. There was another farm in the treetops too, according to Reo, but it was on the far end of the city. That was too far from Kierden, so I knew it wasn't a possibility for me.

I ignored the stabbing pain as my gaze moved over the many rows of crops in awe. I'd helped my dad in the fields as a kid, so standing in front of them again felt a lot like coming home.

My town had been a mess of fruit and vegetable plants, all of which had been allowed to grow wildly and without reason so long as they produced something edible or sellable. In Jirev, even with my magic making everything grow better, they were still being kept neat and orderly.

I'd planned to walk out to the middle of the fields and sit down for a while, taking the time to try to figure out how to control my magic again. Staring out at the plants, I was no longer sure I could make my way out there without messing up any of the crops. And I really didn't want to piss off the farmer, so...

Guess we were staying near the castle.

Bright plopped down and closed her eyes, readying herself for a nap.

I noticed a wide door built into the tree's trunk and figured it must be the house of whoever the farmer was, so I walked up and knocked.

After a long moment, the door opened.

A beautiful male fae opened the door, his expression dark and grumpy. He had tousled, curly navy-blue hair, light brown skin, and wore nothing but a pair of shorts.

"Hi," I said, fighting the urge to take a quick step back and shrink in on myself a little.

"Ignore his attitude," a gorgeous female fae said, slipping out from behind him and giving me a massive smile. Her hair was tied in a thick, messy bun made up of small braids, her skin was dark brown, and her eyes glowed a soft purple color. All she had on was a pair of fancy scanties that looked as if they'd been pulled on in a hurry.

She looked happy, I thought.

Really, really happy.

His hand landed on her hip, and he stepped closer to her, eyeing me with less anger and more curiosity. "You're the human who's bonded to King Kier."

"Yes. I didn't mean to bother you—I was just wondering if I could sit in your fields while I practice with my magic. I figured I might as well grow something useful while I try." The pain in my wrist flared as I finished speaking, and I bit down on the inside of my cheek to stop from wincing.

Kierden must've started moving. He hadn't mentally demanded to know where I was though, so he hadn't figured me out yet.

Probably.

The woman's smile widened. "Of course; sit anywhere. Your magic has already made our job a lot easier. Don't be afraid to mess things up, either. We'll come out and fix anything we need to later."

"Thanks." I gave them both a quick smile, then turned and strode out into the fields as if my wrist didn't hurt like a fiend. The soil was soft and damp beneath my toes, and something about it made my lips curve upward.

Being there felt... right.

Something about the fields made my heart settle, and the ache in my chest calm.

I was exactly where I was supposed to be.

The pain in my wrist eased to just an ache as Bright followed me out. I figured Kierden was headed back toward the castle, and assumed he'd reach out into my mind all grumpy and growly when he realized I wasn't there.

But I needed the space from him, so I could think without the heaviness of his presence looming over me. While I liked that heavy presence, I had to be careful not to let it overshadow me and what I wanted.

"I love it out here," I admitted to Bright, as I sat down on the soil before lowering my back to the ground. With the plants around me and the trees above me, it was calm and beautiful. I almost wondered if I'd somehow managed to cross the veil and find a more perfect world than Evare without realizing it.

"It suits you." She licked my arm.

"I wish there was a way to stay here. The fields still feel like home to me."

"The last time I was here, the fae were arguing about who would be stuck tending the gardens when the rest of them went to fight. Perhaps they'd still like someone else to take over." With that, she put her head back down on her paws and fell asleep quickly. Esu needed more sleep than humans or fae, I'd realized—or maybe they just enjoyed it more than us.

I considered her idea as I stared up at the trees.

With the fields just below the castle, it wasn't an ideal living space. I'd be closer than I wanted to be to Kierden, considering we weren't going to be mated. But my mind gave me an image—a blissful one—of me spending my days in the fields and my nights in the castle with Kierden. We'd read and talk. We'd kiss, and bathe. We'd...

I closed my eyes and let out a long breath.

We weren't going to be together after the eclipse came around.

That was a hard thing to accept, but a necessary one.

And if I didn't create the life I wanted to live, I wasn't going to enjoy the one I ended up in.

So I formed a plan in my mind as I stared up at the trees above me and decided that I was going to make the farm my home, regardless of the cost.

I let a good chunk of time go by—without hearing from Kierden, though the pain had vanished—before I got up, dusted as much soil off my back and ass as possible, then walked back to the building.

I'd tried to make my magic respond to me again, but it was like there was no connection between me and it. I tried to stop it, and it ignored me. I tried to increase the flow of it, but that was useless, too.

I had a plan to persuade the farmers to let me take over their job. The chance of said plan succeeding was slim, but why not take the chance?

Rejection was the worst thing that could happen, and rejection was nothing compared to the misery I had already survived.

My fist rapped on the wood of the door again. This time, the tree's inhabitants opened it faster, and both of them looked slightly more put-together than the last time. The woman still wasn't wearing clothes, but I was used to seeing fae women in their scanties, so I really didn't care.

"Hi again," I said, giving them the biggest smile I could muster. "My bonded esu told me that you don't love working the fields, so I was wondering, would you be interested in handing the job over to me?"

They blinked at me.

"I'm sure you have a system, but I can learn it," I said quickly. "I'd—"

"It's all yours," the woman said, grinning broadly as she stepped back and gestured for me to come inside. "The fields, the house... veil, anything you want. Take it, *please*."

It was my turn to blink at her. "Just like that?"

She laughed.

The man grinned.

"The rest of the kingdom forced us down here because we refused to follow their laws against having sex during wartimes," she explained. "We're not mated, but we would be if we could do it without getting killed."

The look she gave my glowing handprint was a lingering one, and it made my heart ache a little for her.

"So this was a *punishment* for you?" I asked, a bit incredulous as I looked around the house. It was small but spacious, and looked cozy and comfortable.

There were two long windows built into the front walls and partially covered by thick, white curtains. The bed off to the side of the room was nearly as big as Kierden's. The kitchen was large and nice, the floors and walls were polished wood of course, and frames holding beautiful, dried flowers were displayed throughout the space.

"Yup." The man pointed to the kitchen, and I noticed one of the walls looked like it was covered in writing, like the one in Reo's dress shop. "There's the schedule for when people come to pick their produce. You don't have to harvest anything you don't want to eat yourself; your job is just to grow the plants. It used to be a lot more difficult than it is right now."

The woman winked at me.

My lips stretched widely. "I think I can manage that."

She laughed, crossed the room, and then pulled me in for a fierce hug. "Thank you so much. We'll just grab our things and get out of your hair."

The next few minutes were a whirlwind. They packed up much faster than I expected—even taking the sheets and blankets off the bed—and then left me alone.

Alone with the plants, the trees, and the esu who had become my most trusted friend.

"Well, that was easier than I expected," I mused to Bright.

She chuffed. *"I told you no one wanted the job."*

"I'm really glad you're right."

I opened the curtains and windows to air out the smells of strangers, and then went outside and picked a few of my flowers. They'd probably grow inside the house if I left them there, and I liked the idea of that.

I set them around the room, hoping they'd help freshen up the scent while I headed up to the castle to grab some bedding and my clothes.

There were a lot of fae moving around throughout the castle when Bright carried me inside again. A few of them waved at me, and though I waved back, none of them stopped me to talk.

I sat down and ate a meal in the dining room, surrounded by strangers, all of whom had a bonded esu with them. I took that to mean they were all from Kierden's kingdom.

A bunch of them were in the middle of a discussion, and I listened in long enough to learn that the king had been right. A few elves had agreed to go to each of the kingdoms to defend the land from the assassins, and so the fae from those kingdoms had all filed out with their kings, Laeli, and Kaelle.

The subject changed to the murders, and everyone's voices grew hopeful as they talked about Kierden agreeing to mate with someone after my bond with him broke. They all seemed certain that he would be able to end the murderer when that person came for him, easily.

I wasn't sure it would be that simple, but I tried not to let their emotions sway my own too much. It was a little difficult to hear them talk about Kierden mating with someone other than me, but I'd be fine.

I had to believe that.

When I'd finished my meal, I slipped out of the dining hall and headed to the nearest room. I knocked on the door and found the space empty of fae and personal belongings, confirming that it was open.

Quickly, I stripped the blankets off the bed, followed by the pillows. Tying everything in a bundle was a bit of a struggle, and it ended up nearly as big as me, but I managed.

After I grabbed some toiletries too, I made a quick stop in Kierden's room for the rest of my things, including the three big shirts of his I'd claimed. I packed all of it into a bag, then climbed up onto Bright's back, struggling to hold everything while maintaining my balance.

Her amusement swelled alongside mine as she carried me out of the castle. We got a few curious looks, but no one followed us down to the fields, thankfully.

My heart was beating fast and my lips were stretched in a massive grin when I slammed the door behind us.

I was already imagining Kierden's fury when he realized I'd moved out of his room without his permission... and veil, it made my grin even wider.

My excitement faded into peaceful happiness as I set up my new home. The blankets went on the bed, the toiletries in the bathroom, and the clothing in the closet.

When I was done, my happiness had faded too, and I found myself frowning at the home I'd claimed.

It was beautiful, and comfortable. Far more of a home than my tower had ever been. And the door worked properly—I'd made sure it couldn't be locked from the outside.

But something about it felt sort of... lonely.

I supposed that was to be expected, after sharing a bed with Kierden for nearly a month. I just wasn't used to being on my own anymore.

Deciding that I wasn't going to let that affect me, I threw myself into reading the couple's notes about the fields. When I finished reading, I walked the length of them on my own two feet, forcing myself to chat with Bright about anything and everything I could think of as we went. There were miles and miles of fields, and even though my wrist hurt, I kept moving.

If Kierden had changed his mind about wanting me, that was his problem. He had bigger things to deal with than a mate bond he hadn't wanted, and I did too.

Or at least, I tried to convince myself of that.

When the sun faded from the sky and the jungle grew quiet around me, I sat down on the edge of the bed and finally forced myself to admit the truth:

I loved the plants, but I was *lonely*.

I kept remembering the way I'd felt sitting in that bed with Kierden, talking about fictional worlds and characters as if they were real ones, and I missed that.

I missed it a lot.

Not just the conversation, though. The feeling that I wasn't alone. That someone liked me and cared about me, on top of it.

After spending nine years almost entirely alone, I'd finally spent a month living with someone else. Even when I hadn't liked Kierden, I had liked that he was next to me.

And... I wasn't willing to be alone any longer.

I wasn't willing to be his secret mate, and I wasn't willing to wait for him to reject me, either. When our bond disappeared, my magic would take control of me again without anyone's ice to slow it. If that happened, I'd only have a few solid hours of consciousness a day.

Which meant I was going to have to find someone else to bond with.

My stomach clenched at the thought, but there really wasn't an alternative. Even if there was, I didn't think I would settle for it.

I wanted a male to lay in bed with me and talk about books. To bathe with me when I felt sick and tell me I looked beautiful when I felt terrible. I wanted a husband; I wanted a *mate*. And when Kierden and his pretty fae woman stopped the murderers, I decided I was going to have exactly that.

Surely, I could talk *someone* into not despising farming. Some grumpy, battle-hardened warrior who needed a soft human to snuggle and take care of. Or some brilliant fae male who wanted a woman who'd discuss vague topics she didn't really understand with a great deal of passion and stubbornness...

I refused to admit to myself that Kierden functioned as both of those men in my mind.

So, I put on my pink dress and slipped back out of my house.

Bright carried me up to the nearest tavern. She seemed amused by my determination to meet a nice man. *"If you're really that desperate for a male, you can have one of my suitors,"* she drawled, as I climbed off her back just outside. It was near the marketplace, so my hand was aching something fierce, but I ignored the pain yet again.

Laughing, I said, *"Sure, I'll take Death off your hands right now."*

She gave me a feline grin. *"Not that one."*

"Think you might keep him?"

"Perhaps."

She was completely in love with him but still playing hard to get, which I got a kick out of.

We slipped inside the tavern, and I was surprised by the noise. It was large, and built into a tree like all the other homes in the city, which somehow made the whole kingdom feel like home to me. Some of my vines and flowers seemed to have invaded the place already, climbing down the walls and wrapping around the furniture.

One side of the space was taken up by a long countertop with a row of stools in front of it. Beside each stool was a cushion for an esu to sit on. Most of them were occupied, with only a few empty seats remaining.

The other side of the room was filled with tables of varying sizes, all of which were surrounded by multiple chairs.

Every table and most of the chairs were full of fae. Some were talking loudly and laughing. Others were quiet, seeming lost in their minds.

Off in the corner by the tables, a female fae was playing a smooth, soulful song on a stringed instrument I'd never seen before. The music filled the air and made the whole place feel more welcoming.

I didn't see anyone I knew in the tavern, so I just headed over to one of the empty chairs and sat down.

The man to my right looked over and grinned. "You're the king's human?"

Well, that was a *great* way to be identified. "For now."

He laughed.

A female fae brought me a drink, but stopped before she handed it over, and eyed me with some suspicion. "I'm not sure how our ale will affect a human."

"I'm not completely human," I said. "Other than the ears, of course."

The magic was a fairly distinctive difference.

The man next to me grinned, and the woman holding the ale looked curious.

Assuming that curiosity was for said ears, I dutifully pulled my hair away from one of them, turning to the side.

"Damn," the woman admired.

The man next to me ran a finger over the curve of my ear without asking permission first. I shuddered a little, but not because it felt good. Something about his touch just felt *wrong*. Especially after Keirden had dragged his tongue over that same curve.

"Don't touch her while she's the king's," the man on the other side of me growled, reaching past me to smack the other fae's hand away. "Do you *want* him to kill you?"

"He's just using me for my magic. I really don't think he'd care," I said, though the words felt bitter on my tongue.

I honestly wasn't sure how he'd feel.

"He'll be territorial with the bond between you, even though he doesn't want you," the man who hadn't touched me said.

I tried not to shrink at his words.

Even though he doesn't want you.

I reached over and took the drink from the woman's hand, and she leaned over the countertop for a moment. "If the king shows up furious and asks who served you, point to him." She pointed to a mean-looking guy handing out drinks on the other end of the counter.

I nodded.

But I was pretty sure that if the king showed up and got furious, his anger wouldn't be for the person who served me. It would just be for *me*.

"So what are you doing here?" the man who'd touched my ear asked. "Kier doesn't have you chained to his side while he looks into the murders?"

"Nope." I dodged his first question about what I was doing there, electing to lift the drink to my nose and sniff it.

It smelled so strong it made my eyes water, so I set it right back down. If I experimented with fae ale, I wasn't going to do it surrounded by strangers. For all I knew, they could lock me up and make me grow their crops too.

Then again, it wasn't as if I'd be difficult for them to trap if they wanted to. They were immortal fae warriors, after all.

The man who'd touched my ear took my drink, since his own was gone, and swallowed it in three loud gulps.

Maybe he wasn't the best choice to sit next to.

"You didn't say why you're here," he pointed out.

"I was lonely," I admitted.

He grinned at me, leaning closer. "I can keep you company."

The guy who'd smacked his hand leaned past me again and shoved at the other man's chest, hard. "Go home, or I'll kick your ass for the king."

The drunk man laughed, but he climbed out of his chair and swaggered off.

"Guess he's afraid of you," I told the man sitting next to me.

"Guess so." He grunted.

"I'm going to have to start a new bond after the eclipse," I told him, the words blurting out of my mouth. "If I don't, I'll lose control of my magic again, and I'll be unconscious most of the time."

"Damn."

"Yeah. I..." I bit my lip. "I'm Nissa." I offered him a hand.

He eyed it but didn't shake it. "Noin," he said. "And I'm sure the king will be here soon. I wouldn't mention looking for a new bond until after your current one is broken if you don't want to get locked in the castle."

He paused for a moment, then added, "And you should put ale on your ear; if Kier smells another man on your skin, he'll go hunting."

Veil.

"Thanks," I said weakly.

The woman who'd given me the first drink showed up with a new glass and set it down in front of me. "I found some weak ale in the back. It should be safer for you."

"Thank you." I gave her a small smile, and she left me with the ale.

I sipped a tiny bit, making a face at the strange, bitter taste.

Maybe going to a tavern wasn't such a good idea after all, because somehow, doing so had only managed to make me feel even lonelier. And the constant pain in my wrist only made that worse.

I wished Kierden was there... even though I knew I needed to move on.

CHAPTER SIXTEEN
KIERDEN

I rubbed the exhaustion out of my eyes, staring at the sheet-covered bodies as if merely looking at them would produce the answers I needed.

After the elves had ridden in with their glittering magic and unreasonably delicate dresses, they'd formed an invisible shield over my city. The warriors and kings who'd been in my kingdom for the events had gone home soon after, thankfully.

When that was done, I'd gone back to the castle and spent the rest of my day trying to figure out the damned murders that had been plaguing us for so long.

I itched to go find my female, who must've been in and out of the castle all day if the ache in my palm was any sign. I knew she'd be safe with Bright, and I had a responsibility to my people to look for any evidence.

As always, there had been none.

The kings before me hadn't taken the killings seriously enough, and that gave the damn murderer time to perfect their method long before I was ever in a situation to find the killer.

The rest of the fae had already gone home or out to taverns, looking to drink away the stress of the day. We'd continue searching when morning came around, but the fact that we hadn't found anything was far from a good omen.

The door opened, and Eisley stepped in. Her expression was clouded as she sat down in the chair beside me.

A long, heavy moment passed between us before she finally said, "You didn't hear this from me, but I heard people talking about seeing Bright and Nissa in a tavern."

I blinked.

A *tavern*?

Why would Nissa go to a tavern?

I had no idea if our ale would affect her. Or if the other males would try to charm her in an attempt to share a bed with her. I'd lied to them about taking a mate, and they thought I wasn't interested in her. If any of them tried anything...

Veil, I'd kill them.

"Thanks," I told her, already striding across the room toward Death, who was sitting in the hallway.

He was up and waiting for me when I made it through the doors. I threw a leg over his back, and he took off through the castle. We were in the trees a moment later, running toward our females.

It didn't take long to get there. As soon as my feet hit the ground, I was striding into the tavern. My eyes landed on my female immediately, finding her small, soft form and her long, dark green hair without a problem.

She looked calm, with her hands wrapped around a glass of ale that was the wrong color.

Had someone drugged it?

I fought the urge to snarl at everyone and whisk her out of there, to make sure she was alright. She'd told me she wasn't feeling well—and when I stopped by the room to check on her after talking to the elves, she wasn't there. I had assumed she started feeling better and went out to do something, not that she'd gone to a *tavern*.

Apparently, I should've reached out to her mind or asked Death to find her instead.

There was an empty chair on one side of her, and Noin sat on the other. Rather than throwing her over my shoulder and stealing her away like I wanted to, I forced myself to calmly cross the tavern and take the seat next to her.

She glanced over at me, and then looked over again with surprise lighting those gorgeous green eyes. Her cheeks were flushed beautifully, but she said nothing.

If she wasn't bothering with a greeting, neither was I.

I plucked her glass from her hands, ignoring her weak protest as I lifted it to my nose and sniffed. It smelled like... watery ale. I only allowed myself to drink once or twice a year—usually at the eclipse—but I still knew the scent well.

"What is this?" I asked.

"Weak ale. It's gross, huh?" She tried to take it back anyway.

I hadn't smelled anything suspicious on the liquid, and I believed that.

I moved it away from her. "Why are you in a *tavern*, Nissa? You told me you were ill."

She opened her mouth to speak, then glanced around the room.

"Little human," I warned.

"I'm a farmer now," she finally said. "Farmers drink ale." She tried to steal the drink from me again, but the attempt was almost humorously ridiculous.

"What does that mean?" I was still itching to grab her and get out of there.

She huffed at me. "You don't care."

Before I could tell her she was wrong, the woman sitting beside me set her hand on mine. I jerked toward the woman with a growl as I ripped my hand away.

"Did you find any evidence, Kier?" Tal asked me, batting her eyelashes.

"Not yet." My annoyance flared.

"I would be willing to mate with you. If someone has to make the sacrifice, I'll do it."

"I have a mate," I growled back at her, the response so immediate and harsh that she leaned away from me, her eyes flooded with surprise.

"She's nothing more than a shield," Tal said. "You're a warrior, and you deserve to be mated to one too."

I didn't want a veil-damned warrior—I wanted my human.

I couldn't say that, though.

"I'll mate with whomever I choose should the necessity arrive. That is none of your concern, as you damn well know," I told her bluntly, turning away from her.

When I looked back at Nissa, I found her chair empty.

Bright was gone too.

"They left," Death told me.

"Clearly," I growled back. *"Where did they go?"*

"I don't know. Your female looked upset, and Bright told me she'd flay me if I followed her."

"You'd be thrilled if she flayed you." I abandoned the glass of human ale and strode toward the door as I reached out for my human's mind.

I'd find her—and I'd get the answers I wanted from her.

My lips curved upward wickedly as I considered the many ways I could do exactly that.

CHAPTER SEVENTEEN
NISSA

I slammed the door behind me and collapsed against the wood, breathing fast. The ale was not sitting well in my stomach—not well at all. I'd only had a few sips, and all it had managed to do was make me feel dizzy and flushed, which was miserable.

And then Kierden had shown up and made me feel all strange, and that *woman* had touched his hand...

I shuddered.

I'd never wanted to physically hurt anyone before. That really wasn't my personality. Sure, I had hoped my town would be burned down on many occasions, but I'd never actually wanted to do the burning myself.

And yet, I wanted to wrap my hands around that woman's neck and squeeze until the life had drained out of her.

Veil, what had possessed me?

Despite my horror at my own reactions, something inside me was still repeating:

He's mine.

He's mine.

He's mine.

"Veil," I groaned, squeezing my eyes shut and hoping Kierden couldn't hear those damn thoughts.

I never should've accepted that ale.

I never should've let myself start to care about the damn fae king.

What was I supposed to do now?

"Are you alright?" Bright asked me, sounding somewhere between amused and concerned.

At least one of us was enjoying the night.

"Fantastic," I lied.

She chuffed.

"Where are you, Nissa?" Kierden's voice echoed in my mind, low, growly, and making me shiver all over again.

I ignored him.

He wasn't getting a single damn answer from me.

Eventually, he'd follow my scent trail and find me.

Still, the longer it took him, the longer I'd have to try to gather my loose, ale-drowned wits.

I forced myself to remember why I'd moved out of his room.

He'd promised to mate with some random fae woman.

He hadn't considered even asking me if I'd be willing to just seal our bond instead.

He'd lied to me about wanting me—he only wanted sex.

Even if Bright didn't think that last part was true, I still felt like it was. Why else would he be so damn certain that he had to choose a fae female? Why else would he have told his people that he'd be in some other woman's bed as soon as the eclipse removed our connection?

My mind was moving too fast, spinning too quickly.

The room was moving a little, too.

Why did I think the ale was a good idea?

"Tell me where you are, or I'll have no choice but to start hunting you, little human," Kierden purred into my mind.

I shuddered yet again.

The mental bond was only getting more intimate, not less.

And what in the veil was I going to do about that?

"He's looking for you," Bright said, her voice almost... pleased.

"How do I stop him?" I asked her.

She chuffed. *"I don't think you do."*

I was in trouble.

Deep, deep trouble.

"Last chance," Kierden said into my mind.

He sounded just as pleased as Bright did.

"Just go home," I finally told him, a little desperation in my voice. *"I'm done."*

The door behind me flew open, shoving me forward with it. A thick arm caught me by the waist before I could land on my face, and then a hard chest was pressed to my back as my feet were lifted off the ground.

"You are *terrible* at hiding," the king growled into my ear. He stepped inside the house, and I heard him inhale deeply. "Why does it smell like you in here?"

I tried to keep my voice even as I said, "I moved out."

"You *what?*" His humor and playfulness were gone.

"I moved out of your room. The people living here offered me their house when I said I'd take over growing the food, and I accepted. I belong here, now. Among the plants."

"You're not a veil-damned *plant*, Nissa. You're not living among them," he growled into my ear, gripping my waist even tighter. "You're coming back to my room."

"I'm *not*," I shot back. "I'm *not* living with you for the next two months just so you don't have to deal with your own territorial feelings before you jump in bed with another woman as soon as the eclipse is over. I'm *not* going to let you touch me again before you abandon me. I'm *not* going to be the woman you only care about in secret, or the one you ignore as soon as you leave your bedroom, or the one you lie to just to enjoy a few months of sex with a bonded mate."

My eyes started stinging, and I reached up and wiped at them angrily. He was still holding me up off the floor, his lips near my ear, but he said nothing.

A moment of silence passed.

A long, long moment of silence.

I finally added in a shaky voice, "You don't get to use me, Kierden. No one gets to use me anymore. You're no better than my mother, using my magic to protect yourself without giving a damn about me. My feelings matter—I matter. Even if I'm not as important as you."

Another silent moment followed.

Despite the anger and bitterness I was feeling, getting the words out in the open made me feel... free.

Really free.

I felt like I could breathe again.

Kierden finally set me down on my feet.

I expected him to argue.

To tell me that I was wrong—that he thought I mattered, too. To say that he hadn't just used me or my magic, that he'd also protected me and taken care of me and more recently, fed me.

But he didn't.

Instead, he walked away.

I turned around in time to see Death disappear into the darkness of the trees.

My eyes stung more, they stung *worse*. A few tears dripped down my cheeks as I shut the door. Silently, I walked over to the edge of my bed and then sat down on the mattress.

I was fine.

I was going to be fine.

Kierden was only one man, and there were so many others out there. Others who would treat me better. Others I would like more.

But my mind kept going back to the way he had washed me in the bathing pool. To how gentle his hands had been, and how he hadn't been angry with me for risking my life when the Beast asked who was bonded to him.

My thoughts returned to the way he'd offered to wreck my mother's town, so the people could get what they deserved for the way they'd used and mistreated me.

A few more tears dripped out.

Despite the pain I was feeling, Kierden *had* been good to me. He hadn't—

The door opened again.

I blinked, wiping the water from beneath my eyes once more.

Kierden stood in the doorway with a bag thrown over his shoulder and steel in his eyes.

I blinked again.

He stepped inside.

Bright slipped out, knocking the door shut behind her and murmuring, *"Good luck."*

My throat swelled with emotion.

Why had he come back?

Neither of us said a word as he dropped his bag and then crossed the room in three massive steps.

He sank to his knees in front of me. The man was so insanely large that even kneeling while I sat on the bed, his eyes were only a few inches below mine.

He took my face in his hands, his grip firm and strong, but gentle too. "I'm sorry," he said, his voice low and honest. "I'm *sorry*, Nissa. When I first took you from your town, I *did* use you for your magic, and I am sorry for that. But I'm not your mother. I revel in the fire burning in your chest and the way you argue with me, as I always have. I care about your comfort, your health, and your happiness—and I have never tried to use you for sex, as you know well."

My eyes started watering again.

Dammit, he was right.

He hadn't tried to use me for sex.

It was an easy excuse to make, but not an honest one.

"It hurt you when I told my people I would mate with someone else," he said.

I squeezed my eyes shut for a moment, trying not to let my face contort with emotion. "It did."

His forehead met mine, the pressure comfortable. "I have never lied to you, and I never will. It didn't occur to me that my words might hurt you, but if I had told my people that I would mate with you to hunt down my killers, they would've realized what you mean to me already. I wasn't willing to take the chance that they could use it against both of us."

He admitted, "I don't know who the killer is; it could be anyone in my whole damn kingdom. If I give away my emotions, I put you at risk, and that's not something I'm willing to do at this point. Perhaps we'll decide to mate to hunt down the killer, and perhaps we won't. Either way, it will be *our* decision. Not theirs. I assumed you would see the deception for what it was, knowing that I care for you, and I'm sorry that I didn't make sure you understood. That was my fault, and it won't happen again."

My eyes stung. "That was a lot of apologies."

He gave me a rough, rueful chuckle. "I suppose I have a lot to apologize for."

"So you're not really going to mate with a fae woman after the eclipse is over?"

"No. I've been with my people for centuries, Nissa. If I were interested in pairing off with one of them, I would certainly have her in my bed by now."

My lips curved upward, just a tiny bit.

He had *me* in his bed. Which meant he was interested in pairing off with me, if his previous statements were to be trusted. I didn't know whether they were or not, but I still liked the sound of it.

"I have no experience with romantic relationships," Kierden squeezed my face between his palms lightly. "If I do something wrong, I need you to tell me so I can fix it. I won't get everything right the first time—veil, at this rate, I'll probably get everything wrong the first time. But I am trying, Nissa. I swear that to you."

"Is that what we have?" I asked him, still feeling vulnerable. "A romantic relationship?"

"Yes." He didn't have any doubt, and that made me feel a little more secure. "Though I seem to be failing at it, if you aren't sure. Perhaps I should spend more time in the nude so you can see exactly how you affect me."

My lips curved upward, slightly. "I'm sure that would help."

He tilted my head back slightly with his grip on my face, then captured my lips in his.

There was no hesitation. No pause. No fear. No question. Just his mouth on mine.

It was soft at first. He was giving me time to push him away, I supposed.

But I didn't want to push him away. I wanted him, the same way he wanted me.

It was my first kiss, but I wasn't nervous. Not with his grip on my face and his mouth on mine. I trusted him to take care of me.

He parted my lips, and we groaned together as his tongue stroked mine. The contact was strange, but perfect. Nothing like I'd expected, and yet so much more than I'd hoped for at the same time.

Kierden pulled away after a few minutes, and it made me fiercely proud when I saw his chest rising and falling almost as quickly as my own. He took a step back, burying his hand in his hair and gripping tightly, as if trying to resist grabbing me again.

His gaze was hot as it moved up and down my skin slowly. "How much ale did you drink?"

I lifted a shoulder. "Not much." Though I still felt flushed and a little dizzy, I found myself not minding it anymore.

"That was your first glass?"

I nodded.

"And it was watered down?"

"Yes. Why are you asking me this?" I eyed him, wishing he'd go back to kissing me already. While I looked at him, I debated the merits of throwing myself at him, so he had no choice but to start kissing me again.

"I'm trying to decide how much of an asshole I'd be if I stripped you bare and licked you until you unraveled on my tongue," he growled back.

Oh.

Ohhhh.

"Not an asshole," I said quickly. "Not at all."

Veil, I was *dying* to know how that would feel.

"A drunk female would feel the same way." He slid his hands into his pockets.

I was losing him.

If I didn't convince him immediately, my night was going to end in more talking.

And... I didn't want to talk anymore. I wanted to be distracted. Preferably by his fingers and mouth.

"You could touch me again," I said.

He narrowed his eyes at me. "A drunk female would say that, too. The last thing I want is for you to wake up feeling violated."

Damn him for caring.

Even though I really did appreciate that. I just... well, I wanted to be violated by him.

"I let you touch me before," I told him. "So technically, I already gave you permission to do that."

His gaze was skeptical.

I rose to my feet and stepped toward him until our chests collided. His hands landed on my hips, and his skepticism grew softer.

"That woman touched you," I said. "I saw it. She touched you and she offered to be your mate, so I left. What did you say to her after I was gone?"

His expression morphed into a scowl. "I told her that I already had a mate, and that I wasn't interested in her. I moved my hand away as soon as she touched me; it's not as if I encouraged her."

"I saw that part, too. You didn't hold her hand, which makes me feel better. But something inside me sort of... lost it when she touched you. I wanted to *kill* her, which obviously wouldn't work out, since she's a warrior and I'm a farmer."

His eyes gleamed wickedly. "If you wanted to end her, I would hold her down for you."

I laughed. "How romantic."

"She's been a thorn in my side for a long, long time. I suppose I should admit, she propositioned me once to spend the eclipse with her."

My eyebrows shot upward, and every ounce of humor and desire I'd felt vanished. "You had *sex* with *her*?"

"No. She propositioned me, and I turned her down. I haven't had sex in..." He thought about it for a moment and then finally admitted, "A long time."

"How long, exactly?" My curiosity was rising.

"Nearly four centuries, at my best guess."

I nearly choked on my own spit. "You're ancient."

"Time means little to me. So much of my life has been spent in war that I feel like I still haven't truly lived."

"Why did the war start in the first place?"

"No one remembers, yet we were all too old and too stubborn to stop, until recently. Vayme lost his twin brother a few years ago, and he came to me, pleading with me to consider putting an end to the fighting before we made ourselves extinct. It took a lot of time to convince our people, and ourselves, but it seems to have worked." He paused, and then added, "As long as you ignore that someone sent assassins after us as punishment for creating peace."

I gave him a sad smile. "I wouldn't live very long here if war broke out again."

He dragged me closer. "Actually, with your ability to grow food for us, you would be our highest priority to protect even if you weren't my mate. The other kingdoms wouldn't try to kill you—they would try to take you, for the advantage of your magic."

I grimaced. "Well, that might be even worse than dying."

Kierden chuckled, lowering his lips to mine and capturing my mouth again.

CHAPTER EIGHTEEN
NISSA

My thoughts vanished entirely as I wrapped my arms around the man's neck and deepened the kiss.

He began slowly walking us backward while our mouths moved together, stopping only when my ass met a wall. I hooked a leg around his hip, and he lifted me up without breaking the kiss. His erection met my core, and I wrapped my other leg around his ass as I ground against him. I was already wet with desire, and there was no way he hadn't realized it.

The kiss grew rougher, and Kierden lifted one of my hands to his hair. I dug my fingers into the thick, soft strands as he released my mouth to move down the column of my throat, sucking, licking, and biting me.

He eased my core away from his cock, unwrapping my legs enough to take a step to the side and open me up to him.

"Your skin is so damn delicious, little human." His lips worked their way back up my throat, then tugged my hair out of the way so he could trace the curve of my ear with his tongue.

I shuddered against him.

He withdrew for a moment—long enough to growl, "Why does your ear taste like ale?"

Veil.

"Must've spilled," I mumbled.

"Nissa," he growled.

"Just kiss me."

He chuckled, low and deep. His hand slid down the front of my dress, stopping to squeeze my breast lightly before following the curve of my hip and wrapping around my ass. I rocked my hips a bit. "Tell me, if you want me to keep touching you."

"Asshole," I breathed.

"Oh, I'll play with that too."

I arched as his hand slid between my legs from behind, his knuckles slowly teasing my slit without giving me the contact I wanted.

Considering we'd shared difficult truths already, I supposed I had to give him the answer he wanted. "Someone at the tavern touched my ear. I used the ale to clean it."

He snarled. "Who? I'll end them for touching you."

"It doesn't matter," I said quickly.

"It does. You are *mine* to touch."

"You don't even know if you want to be with me. I was looking for a mate, Kierden. If I don't take a mate when the eclipse comes, I'll be completely at the mercy of my magic, and I can't risk that again.

"You're wrong." His gaze was steady, his voice low and growly. "You belong to me, and I know what I want; I want someone I can ravage any time I feel the urge. Someone who will drench my fingers, tongue, and cock with their release day or night, whether in our bed, in an empty bedroom, or in the castle's pool."

My body only grew hotter with every word he said. "You want a mate."

His hand slipped out from behind me, and he moved me further to the side as he finally dragged a finger over my clit. Fabric still separated us, but damn, it felt incredible. "No. I want *you* to be my mate. Permanently."

I cried out as he slowly teased me, dragging slow circles around my clit while I gripped his hair tightly and panted. He made me want more, and more, until he finally pinched my clit, and I shattered.

Kierden gripped my core in his hand while my back arched, loud cries escaping me as I lost control. The pleasure seemed to go on forever.

When I finally slumped back against the wall, I was sucking in deep breaths of air, trying hard to recover.

He brushed a few strands of hair from my face with his free hand. The other was still gripping my core like it belonged to him. "Veil, you are *stunning* when you climax."

"Thanks, I guess," I murmured.

My eyes flew open when he carried me to the bed. The base of his palm moved as he walked, grinding against my clit. My body responded much faster than I expected it to, and desire swelled within me again as he lowered me to the edge of the mattress.

Kierden slid his shorts down his thighs. "Take your dress off."

I didn't respond to his command, my gaze fixed on his cock as it sprung free.

Veil, he was so damn thick.

"Dress off, Nissa." He slowly dragged his fist down the length of his erection.

My mouth dried at the sight, and I nearly shivered again.

He stepped closer, his cock bobbing for me as he finally grabbed the bottom hem of my dress and peeled it over my head for me.

The fabric hit the ground, and I glanced down at myself. My breasts were nearly bursting from the triangles of fabric that covered them. Even without looking, I knew my ass was the same.

Kierden growled, "Veil, look at those curves. Touch yourself for me, little human."

"I'd rather watch you," I breathed.

He grabbed my legs, tossing them up onto the bed before climbing up himself. He kneeled in front of me, his cock jutting out proudly as he opened my legs wide.

I nearly froze as he leaned forward and dragged his tongue over the fabric covering me. It was so thin that I could feel the heat of his lick—and I was so wet I knew he'd taste me.

His chest rumbled in appreciation as his eyes locked with mine, and he waited.

Need flooded me, hot and fast.

"Keep going," I breathed.

"No. If you want a climax or you want to see my release, you show me how you touch yourself."

I groaned, and his lips curved wickedly. We held each other's stare for a long, long moment as we both waited for the other to give in.

Finally, I slid a hand beneath the damp fabric covering me. My breath hitched as I slowly teased myself.

Kierden's gaze dropped to my hand, his eyes hot and needy. "How does that feel, Nissa?"

"So good," I whispered, my hips jerking slightly.

Something about having his eyes on me made it so much hotter.

"Show me how you touch yourself," I told him, my chest rising and falling rapidly. Unlike me, he didn't protest—he just kept watching me as he wrapped his hand around his cock.

My breathing grew frantic as I watched his powerful body react to every stroke of his hand. I was wetter than I'd ever been before, and dying to lose control, but the fabric of my scanties was in my way.

I pushed at them with shaky hands, and Kierden growled, grabbing the fabric and yanking it down my legs. He used my knees to open me up wider for him so he could see every wet inch of me.

My hand found my clit again a moment later, and then I was arching and crying out as I lost control.

Kierden stroked himself harder and faster until he found his release, roaring with me as he coated my core, ass, and the blanket beneath me with his pleasure.

His release felt blissfully warm on my sensitive skin.

I rubbed it around my clit, and my hips rocked.

Something about having his pleasure on me felt so damn right.

Desire curled in my lower belly.

I needed him.

"Touch me," I breathed to him.

"No. You drank the ale, you deal with the consequences. I don't know how it's affected your reasoning," he growled back.

I narrowed my eyes at him—then started touching myself again, too turned on to stop even if Kierden wasn't willing to participate.

His erection bobbed.

Human men needed to rest after climaxing, but I knew from the books I'd read that magical beings didn't have the same problem.

He took his cock in his fist and started stroking again.

The pleasure built up so insanely fast, it made my mind spin.

"Slide a finger inside yourself," the king commanded me.

I did as he said, and he snarled, "Another."

When I'd followed that one too, panting and rocking a little, he grabbed my wrist and tugged my fingers free so he could suck my pleasure off my skin while he touched himself.

He rumbled at the taste of me—of both of us—and a heartbeat later my ass was hanging off the edge of the bed. His mouth found my core, his face between my thighs as he devoured me. His tongue was so damn hot on my clit, his massive hands squeezing my thighs and ass as he worked me.

The feeling was absolutely surreal, and the sight was nearly as good. I lost control with another cry, and Kierden didn't pause for even a moment. He feasted on me, dragging my pleasure out and then reigniting my flame as his tongue carried me higher and higher.

I shattered again with more hoarse cries, and he finally let go of me— just long enough to stand over me and stroke his cock. He climaxed again quickly, covering me in his release once more as he roared his pleasure.

My body was blissfully warm and relaxed as Kierden collapsed in bed with me. He held my back to his chest, wrapping his arms around me.

"That was..." I trailed off.

I wasn't sure I had words for it.

"The best moment of your life?" he murmured to me.

"Yes," I admitted.

"Mine as well." His arms tightened around me. "You'll never be free of me now. I intend to make you mine in every way there is."

"I still don't even feel like I know you," I whispered back. "I mean, I know your personality sometimes. But not well enough for me to promise you the rest of our lives."

"A mate bond is eternal. To seal ours would be to make a promise that would last far beyond our lives in Evare, Nissa. You would belong to me on this side of the veil and the next, regardless of what the future holds in this world or the one that follows."

"And you would belong to me too?" I asked, feeling slightly vulnerable.

"In every way there is." His grip on my abdomen loosened, and his fingers started moving slowly over my ribcage. The brush of them was light, gentle, and absolutely blissful.

"What would that really mean for us in real life, though?" I couldn't picture it. Or... any future for us, honestly.

"It would mean you could demand my cock, fingers, or tongue anywhere, at any time." He nipped lightly at my ear. A long moment passed, and then he added, "It would mean that I'd take care of you before myself. You would be fed the most delicious foods. Your closet would be full of colorful dresses, more than you could wear in a life-time. I would brush your hair, feed you as often as you let me, and rub your shoulders when they're tight."

My throat felt thick.

All of that sounded incredible, honestly.

"What if I wanted to be a farmer?"

He made a noise of amusement. "Then all we would need to do is move the rest of my things down here. At this point, I'm not sure we'll ever be able to stop your magic from draining us."

My lips curved upward.

"If we were truly mated, I would do as much as I can to ensure that there's never a repeat of today," he added, a bit more quietly. "I should've told you what I was thinking about my people. I only stopped by to check on you once, and I didn't reach out when I didn't find you in our room. I regret that. I have a tendency to get slightly... obsessed, when I'm working on something or trying to solve a problem."

"You? Obsessed?" I teased him, my voice soft.

He chuckled, pulling an arm away enough to squeeze my hip lightly.

"If we were really mated, I would need to practice speaking my mind instead of getting angry or defensive," I admitted. "I should've stayed with you to talk to the elves, and offered my help with the murders, even though I'd probably be useless in that situation. And I definitely should've told you what I was thinking."

"I'd rather not have you near the bodies." He squeezed my hip again. "It's far too much risk, since we have no idea what killed them. And you are still human."

My lips curved downward. "Would it even be possible for us to be mated, considering my humanity?"

"Our magic has already connected. If we were to seal the bond, it would become one, and the magic fueling my immortality would fuel yours as well."

Well, I didn't hate the sound of that.

"Can you undo the back of my scanties?"

"Mmhm." He rumbled against me, and my lips curved upward.

Kierden undid it quickly, then slid it off my skin and pulled me closer. His arms wrapped around my middle again, his hands cupping my bare breasts, and I relaxed against his body. His cock was still hard, pressed lightly against my backside, and I loved the feel of it.

"Do you guys have the same birth control herbs that we have?" I asked him softly.

"We do. Dirue, our healer, hands them out without blinking an eye, as she always has, even when the law was in place."

"I think I'll visit her soon, then."

His chest rumbled in satisfaction, and his erection throbbed against my ass. "I look forward to it, little human."

My heart about melted at the soft, sultry nickname. It had seemed like an insult at first, but knowing that he wanted me—not just for sex, but permanently, as his mate—erased any bad feelings I'd had toward it.

"Will you tell me about your life?" I asked him. "I'd like to know you as more than the battle-hardened king who loves books."

He was silent for a moment, and then finally said, "When I was a child, my parents were very vocal about wanting peace. They led a small resistance, protesting our endless war. The incidents they staged to demonstrate war's brutality cost many fae their lives on every side. They were not good people, though perhaps they had good intentions. The kings and queens at that time hunted them for many decades without success."

"That was when people were still mated, and still having children?" I asked.

"Yes. Mated couples began being hunted shortly before I was born. The kings and queens who despised my parents were eventually murdered by those hunters, which bought my family a little more time. I was ten and Eisley was four when members of the cult caught up to us. We were in the forest—the four of us, and two cultists—but my father and mother had sworn away their magic in their effort to create peace. My mother didn't touch her power at all while she was pregnant with Eisley, so my sister had no ice of her own. I had no idea how to use my magic, but I could feel it in my veins, and I knew that if I couldn't protect us, we were going to get slaughtered."

My eyes were wide, my throat so swollen I doubted I could've spoken even if I tried.

He admitted, "I threw everything I had at them, but I was an untrained ten-year-old, and it wasn't enough. Their ice cut through mine with ease, and it was all I could do to throw a protective shelter over myself and Eisley before they could kill us too. I left her inside when I knew the killers were gone, and then buried our parents myself in earth and ice, the way our people always do. With no other options left, I carried Eisley to the nearest kingdom—this one. It was called Prive at the time. A group of warriors led us to the castle, where we were housed with the other orphans and taught to fight."

My eyes stung with tears. "*Veil*, Kierden."

"It was a long time ago. Don't weep for me, Nissa." He gently wiped the tears from my cheeks. "You may be able to imagine the rest. My magic was very strong, ironically. I became the fiercest warrior in the kingdom, though I made certain that my sister was a close second, since she had no magic to protect herself with."

He continued, his voice still soft, "After one of our kings died, our people elected me to take his place. We vowed to put an end to all distractions, and our numbers stopped falling. We haven't lost a fae during battle in nearly a century."

"And I thought nine years in a tower was difficult," I said, wiping at my own tears.

He growled at me, captured my hand, and lifted it to his lips to kiss my palm. "Do not discount your own struggles because they sound less vicious than someone else's. If I were thrown in a tower for nearly a decade, I can tell you without question that I would come out a rabid, savage beast with little sense of myself. Losing all control like that would scar the fiercest warrior, and yet here you are, still sane, functioning, and *kind*."

"I don't sound so bad when you put it like that," I told him, still wiping away my tears.

"You are *not* bad, Nissa. Not at all." His grip on my hip and abdomen tightened. "I may have been terrible at proving it thus far, but I feel extremely lucky to have found you. After so many centuries without a shred of interest in the females I've known and fought with, I started to wonder if perhaps I'd never be capable of feeling for someone the way I do you."

"Maybe you should've started considering the males," I mumbled.

His chest rumbled with amusement. "I am not attracted to men, love. I've been alive long enough to be certain of that." He squeezed my hip again. "Tell me about your father, please?"

I grimaced. "It's not a happy story."

"Then it'll fit right in with mine."

I sighed. "My magic came in on my thirteenth birthday, and I woke up surrounded by vines, fruit, and flowers. It wasn't exciting; it was terrifying. I couldn't even get out of my room. My mother left as soon as she saw the plants, and my father spent an hour freeing me from them. By the time he finally got me out of the room, my mother had gotten the rest of the people in the town together. They held tools as weapons while she told me that my magic was a curse sent from the other side of the veil to punish me for the crimes of a past life, but that the town could use my curse to ease their struggles."

I continued, "My father tried to protest, but there were so many of them. When they started leading me around the town by my hand, he couldn't do anything but walk by my side until I collapsed after the magic had drained me dry. My feet were blistered when I woke up, and I could hardly move. We weren't in our home, but someone else's. When the people came to get me again, my father argued with them, but they shoved past him and took me anyway. We saw the base of the tower, then—and saw everyone working on it."

My eyes closed, and I let out a long breath.

Kierden's fingers massaged my hip gently, and the touch calmed me a little.

My voice was quiet when I admitted, "It only took them two weeks to build it. My mother told me and my father that it would be my new home the evening before it was ready. I told her I didn't want to live there, and she told me she didn't care, reminding me that I was cursed. That night, my dad woke me up before dawn and told me that we were leaving for my safety. He said that my mother had gone mad—that I was blessed, not cursed. He already had our things packed, so we left."

"She anticipated it, though. There were guards waiting for us at the edge of town. Everything happened so quickly. They swung at my father, and he fought back. There were three of them, and he was a farmer, not a fighter. I don't remember who stabbed him or what weapon they used. It felt like only a heartbeat later I was kneeling beside him, sobbing as he breathed his last breaths. He held me as tightly as he could, telling me he loved me while repeating over and over that I was a blessing, not a curse." Tears leaked from my eyes.

I had never told anyone any of that before, and getting it out made me feel... fresh. Stronger, too. Cleansed, maybe.

I felt like I could *breathe*, again.

So I continued. "They threw me into the tower, still covered in his blood. My mother and I had never been close before I got my magic, but she became the monster who stole everything from me. The town made her their leader, and she stayed away from me. I rarely saw her, even when they tied me up and led me around to make sure my magic would grow everything. I could be actively bleeding from the blisters on my feet, and no one would bat an eye. I meant *nothing* to them. They only cared about my power."

I squeezed my eyes shut. "I tried to escape every time I could, and I never forgot what my father said to me. I am *not* a curse. My magic is a part of me, but it's only one part. I knew you thought you were abducting me when you showed up in my tower, but you saved me. You saved my life."

"You would've figured out a way to save yourself eventually," he told me, his voice low and edged with fury.

That fury wasn't geared toward me, but to the people who had used me for so long.

"Maybe."

Even as I said the word, I knew it was a lie.

The only way out for me on my own would've been death.

"Tell me about your attempts at escape," he said.

He cared about what had happened to me.

He cared about *me*.

So I opened my mouth, and I told him.

With every story I told and every one he told me, I felt closer to him. By the time I fell asleep, I wondered if it was possible for a single conversation to change a person's life... because it felt like that one had changed mine entirely.

CHAPTER NINETEEN

NISSA

I woke with a gentle hand on my arm and a warm kiss to my cheek. Soft orange light streamed in from the windows I'd left open the night before, bathing my skin and the blankets around us.

"I have to go back to the castle to continue my search for the murderer," Kierden murmured.

Goosebumps broke out on my skin at the sultry tone to his voice. "Okay."

The words to seal the mating bond slipped into my mind again.

"Sillah ovim rett warum."

I ignored them.

He stroked my arm lightly. "Come to the castle for breakfast, and let me know when you're there. We'll meet for your other four meals as well."

"I think three meals is enough now. I haven't been as hungry."

"Four, then."

"Fine." I gave him a dramatic sigh.

The words repeated themselves in my mind again—

"Sillah ovim rett warum."

The urge to say them was getting stronger, but I could still fight it.

Kierden leaned over and captured my lips before reluctantly getting out of bed, oblivious to the way the bond pushed at my mind.

I watched him closely, my body warming as he moved. Noticing me watching him, he dragged a hand over his erection for me.

I bit my lip to fight a grin, and bit it harder when he gave me a gorgeous smirk.

Kierden pulled a clean pair of shorts from his bag and tugged them on before heading out. He stopped in the doorway to look back at me for a long moment before saying, "Stay safe, and let me know what you're up to so I don't worry."

I lifted an eyebrow. "I'm not going to update you every time I use the toilet, Kierden."

"Pity." He slipped out, and I snorted.

Bright stepped back inside as he left, and he gave her a friendly pat on the head in passing.

She jumped onto the bed and snuggled up next to me. I scratched her behind the ears absentmindedly, not in any hurry to get up.

"It seems like you worked things out," she said to me, eyes gleaming with interest.

"Seems like it."

I wouldn't really know how much the night had meant to Kierden until we had interacted in front of his people again—and even then, I didn't know how sure I could be, because he had to put on an act of some kind for them.

"Are we supposed to pretend we don't like each other in front of everyone else again?" I asked him mentally. The connection seemed to come much easier than it had the last time I used it, which was nice.

"No. I've been aiming for neutrality," he said.

"Damn. If that's your definition of neutrality, you must've been a miserable bastard to be around for the past century or three."

He laughed into my mind—loudly. *"I never claimed to be cheerful or polite, Nissa. My people are not the kind who obey calm, measured words. If you want them to get their asses in line, you bark, yell, or snarl at them. They're used to it; it doesn't offend them."*

"So you're going to bark at me?" I checked.

"No. I'm done pretending not to have feelings for you. There are a few couples in the kingdom who have been lovers very openly for hundreds of years. The murderer hasn't touched them because they haven't created a bond. He or she only cares about a permanent connection—it seems to be the only thing that inspires them to kill."

"Are there people in the other kingdoms with mate bonds?" I asked curiously.

"I don't know. If there are, they won't dare come here. To do so would be a death sentence."

"Have the mated couples tried leaving the city?"

"Yes. We find their bodies buried with our other fallen, identified by their ice gravestones."

"Well, that's terrifying."

"When you and I decide to seal our bond, there will be nothing that can peel me from your side until the killer is dead," Kierden vowed.

Surprisingly enough, I didn't hate the sound of that.

Even though I wasn't quite sure whether to be excited or alarmed by his use of the word *"when"* where I would've put an *"if"*.

"Alright. Good luck," I told him.

I sort of *felt* it when his mind disconnected from mine, and the feeling was an unpleasant one that made me shiver a bit. There was no pain in my wrist, at least. Just a slight ache.

I stayed in bed for a little while, lounging around while I convinced Bright to give me the details about her night with Death. As it turned out, he had propositioned her, she had refused again, and then they'd spent hours running through the trees together, fighting and playing. He had tried to convince her to be his mate once more at the end of the night, and she'd turned him down yet again.

"What are you waiting for?" I asked her curiously.

She flashed me a wickedly sharp grin. *"Eventually, he'll grow certain enough to tell me that I belong to him and will no longer accept my refusal. That will be my guarantee that he won't change his mind."*

A laugh escaped me.

She *did* have a point.

We spent an hour or two walking around in the fields, when we finally got out of bed. They were among the most peaceful hours I'd ever lived.

Though my stomach rumbled a few times, I was enjoying it so much that I only headed back when Kierden's mind touched mine. *"You'd better not be trying to skip a meal, little human."*

My lips curved upward, my fingers sliding over the bumpy rind of a huge citrus as I passed it. It shuddered at my touch, swelling much larger. *"I'm not skipping a meal. Just enjoying my new life as a fae farmer."*

He chuckled. *"I'm glad."*

"I'm heading up now. Did you find anything?"

"Nothing." His voice grew frustrated. *"My sister is bothering me about socializing with the elves. Would you be willing to eat in the dining room?"*

"Sure. I guess she's the diplomatic one between the two of you."

"Undoubtedly. There has never been much need for diplomacy before, which makes it that much worse now."

"I can imagine. Will the elves be offended by my curved ears?"

"Only if they want my swords in their chests," he grumbled. *"They're aware of my bond to you, and most elves pride themselves in being graceful and polite."*

"So the opposite of fae?" I teased.

"Exactly. One of the elven leaders is here too—Alida. She's half shifter, so less uptight. She's the one who told me and the other kings that we needed to mate with humans. Unlike the rest of the elves, she's trustworthy, and visits the fae kingdoms often."

"Have you asked the elves for help with your murders?"

"Yes. The killer doesn't seem to use magic, so the elves haven't found anything. He or she also doesn't use weapons, so we believe it's some sort of poison, though we have yet to find any proof of it."

"I could take a look," I suggested. *"If it's plant-related, maybe I could find something?"*

"If we don't find anything in the next few days, I suppose it's worth a try." His response was grudging, but I already knew he didn't like the idea of having me around the bodies. It wasn't that he didn't want my help, he just thought it was risky for me because of my humanity.

Bright reached the castle, and I looked around the entrance in surprise. My vines were spreading much farther down the hallways than they had been the day before—and the flowers on them were bigger, brighter, and more vibrant.

Kierden and Death waited for us near the entrance, and the king greeted me with a fierce hug that made me smile.

"When did the flowers get like this?" I asked, gesturing to the vines as he lifted me off Bright's back like I didn't have legs of my own.

"Last night." The look he gave me was wicked, and my face heated at the memory of what we'd done together. "The fruit looked much bigger, too."

I supposed it had.

I flashed him a grin. "You must have a really great farmer."

"The best."

When he took my hand in his and started down the hallway, I noticed a few of his warriors, both men and women, were gaping at us.

The heat in my cheeks flared a bit, but I did my best to ignore it. If Kierden was willing to hold my hand in public, he must've accepted the consequences of it.

"They're staring at us," I told him as we walked.

"They should. You're too damn gorgeous in that dress not to." He glanced over at me, making a show of looking me up and down.

"Reo is making me a few that fit better," I admitted.

"I know. He sent a fae over earlier to ask me if I had any color preferences." Kierden adjusted his grip on my hand, pushing his fingers between mine. The hold was comfortable—really comfortable.

"What did you say?"

"Black."

"Asshole." When I flashed him a glare, I found him smirking and realized it was a joke. My lips curved upward.

"I told him to give you whatever colors you asked for, with a little less fabric," he said.

I rolled my eyes at him. *"You didn't."*

He chuckled. *"Alright, I told him that your clothing is your choice. I'm sure he'll make you something you love; he's famous among the fae for that, and travels back and forth between the kingdoms. I think it's just his way of avoiding fighting a battle, but I can't say I blame him."*

"Neither do I."

We walked into the dining hall, and more eyes turned to us.

Kierden squeezed my hand lightly, not stumbling for even one beat as we walked toward the large table Eisley was seated at.

I knew male elves didn't exist, only females, and my gaze slid over all five of the women as I tried to determine which of them was Alida. They had a variety of skin and hair colors, all of them soft-looking and curvy in the same places a healthy human was. Like mine, their builds were a direct opposite to the slim, muscular ones of the female fae.

"Look at that pretty, glittering bond between you two," one of the elves purred, leaning over the table toward us. Her long, straight hair was a deep shade of black, her skin was light brown, and her eyes glowed a stunning hazel. Her gaze landed on me, and lingered. "Veil, the magic just *pours* off of you, doesn't it?"

"Unfortunately. I haven't figured out a way to control it," I admitted, taking the only remaining empty seat at the table. Kierden left for a moment to grab another chair.

"No, and I don't think you will," she mused.

"Well that's encouraging," Eisley drawled. "Thanks for bringing the sunshine, Alida."

"Some magic isn't meant to be controlled," the elf said simply. "It's not a bad thing. It just *is*. The wilds around you thrum with the energy of your power now. It's quite beautiful."

"We could certainly use some of these flowers in our corner," another elf murmured.

"Nah, we're going to keep them." Eisley slung an arm over my shoulder, tugging me close. "I don't know if my brother's going to let her go."

Kierden put his chair beside mine, sat down, and set his hand on my thigh possessively. "I'm not."

Eisley grimaced. "Just don't do anything insane, like sealing that damn bond."

Alida's eyes glittered. "Oh, but bonds are *meant* to be sealed. The magic will grow stronger, and the urge to say the words will become irresistible."

"You knew this was going to happen, didn't you?" Eisley asked Alida.

The elf grinned wickedly. "You'll never know."

"Alida sees the future," Eisley explained, looking at me. "She's a pain in everyone's ass."

Alida cackled.

"She only sees the tiniest flashes of the future," one of the other elves corrected. "But she can see mate bonds—both fated and nonfated ones. And relationships between people too, both positive and negative."

"Fated?" I asked, curious.

When I glanced over at Kierden, he shook his head. "Fated mates are just a legend." His mind touched mine. *"Don't tell them anything about how our bond started."*

"To some people. Not to me." Alida's eyes flashed green. "A mate bond between a fated couple will ignite before they've said the words to create a connection. Did yours?"

I thought about it, but wasn't sure what the sign was of a bond igniting.

Kierden drawled, "No, Alida."

Her eyes gleamed. "Is that so?"

"Yes." His gaze met hers, steely.

"What's special about fated mate bonds?" I asked her. Since Kierden was worried about them knowing the truth about the beginning of our relationship, I had to guess that meant we were fated, and he didn't want anyone to know.

"It's said that the souls of fated mates choose each other in the life before this one," one of the elves explained.

I found that concept absolutely beautiful.

"What does it look like when fated mates meet, then?" I asked them. "How does the bond ignite?"

"It always starts with a handprint." One of the women gestured to my glowing wrist. "If a couple is fated, the print appears the first time they touch. It's the place their souls meet again for the first time in this world, and that makes it sacred. If you're not fated, the print forms after you say the words, marking the place your souls meet for the first time as mates."

My mind whirled.

I could distinctly remember Kierden grabbing me in my tower, before he said the words that officially started the bond between us. And when he grabbed me, the handprint appeared.

"It has to stay a secret," he said to me.

I held the elves' gaze. "The handprint definitely appeared *after* he started our bond."

One of them looked slightly suspicious. Alida didn't look even a little bit convinced.

"Fated mate bonds are known to be more powerful than normal ones," Alida said, studying us. "If the couple seals their bond, their power not only combines, but grows stronger as well. It makes them great rulers —and incredible villains."

"Then the cult probably went after them first, right?" I asked.

Expressions around the table grew grim.

"Indeed," Alida said quietly.

"Do fated bonds still disappear when the eclipse comes?"

"They do. A bond can only be sealed by choice, even if that choice is made under the influence of the bond's magic." Alida gave me a small smile. "An unwanted bond will never become permanent."

I nodded.

My first instinct was to be angry with Kierden for keeping that secret from me, but ultimately, he had been determined that he wasn't going to seal the bond with me. And if we didn't seal the bond, knowing we were fated would only hurt me more.

That made the secret feel like more of a kindness than anything else.

One of the elves remarked, "The strongest males and females of all magical beings usually have fated mates out there somewhere. Alida sees the connection stretching away from them."

"It's true," Alida agreed. "I saw the king's bond; he has a fated mate."

Interesting.

If she could see bonds, and she was known for visiting the fae fairly often, maybe she could be the killer...

Then again, he said he trusted her, and he didn't trust easily.

"Well, I suppose Kierden had better get out and start looking for him or her, then," I said, flashing him a teasing smile that I hoped everyone thought was real.

He chuckled. "Not going to happen, little human." Squeezing my thigh, he said into my mind, *"How angry are you?"*

"Not angry. I understand why you didn't tell me." I paused before adding, *"And I don't think it really changes anything, unless you're only with me for the hope of an eventual boost to your magic."*

"Without a war to fight, I have no need for more ice, Nissa."

"Then I don't have any reason to be angry."

Eisley changed the subject, thankfully. "Have you seen any sign of the Beast outside your forcefield?" she asked.

"Not yet, though I'm sure he's here," Alida said easily.

I grimaced. "How long can you hold him off?"

"Two months, we hope."

"How did they get so powerful?" I asked.

"We made an error when we created them," Alida began.

Someone interrupted us as they brought our food out, and we all paused for a moment to thank them before we started eating.

Alida resumed, "It's a long story, but we made them dependent on their contracts to stay alive. They gain energy through killing, and it keeps them functioning. We didn't factor in the possibility that the energy wasn't their own by nature, so it won't ever fade from them."

My eyes widened. "So they're constantly getting stronger?"

"Yes. What an error to make, right? Eventually, those bastards are going to be strong enough to destroy our world—and we have no way of knowing exactly when that will be."

Damn.

"I need to get back to our work as soon as we're done eating," Kierden told the elves, changing the subject again. They offered to help look at the bodies again, and he agreed readily.

We ended up talking about the differences between clothing styles in all the different lands while we ate. And honestly, it was a lot more fun than I expected.

CHAPTER TWENTY
NISSA

The next two weeks passed by quickly. Kierden spent most of his time with the elves, looking into anything and everything that could possibly be a lead. They found nothing, though none of them gave up.

Eisley left soon after the elves started helping Kierden and the other fae search. Neither she nor her brother would tell me where she was going, but she took a group of fae with her. Though I didn't voice my suspicion, I was guessing that Kierden had sent her to my town for the revenge he had mentioned.

Part of me hoped my suspicion was right, because that part of me wanted them to suffer for what they'd done to me.

Another part of me hoped I was wrong, and we could all just let go of what happened. I wanted to be done with it more than I wanted revenge.

Kierden most definitely didn't feel that way, though.

I spent my days in the fields, growing plants and helping harvest them. We had an excess of crops, and they were all getting too big, so we sent two groups of fae out to the other kingdoms with massive carts full of produce. I worried the esu would be grumpy about pulling the heavy carts, but they were excited to have something to do, and really excited to see the kingdoms without being at war.

When we finished harvesting, it would be time to replant my fields. It would take me *weeks* to get everything planted, and I was absolutely thrilled that I'd get to spend all that time with my hands in the dirt. I never felt more at ease than I did surrounded by my plants.

Kierden and I spent every night together, splitting our time between his room in the castle and my home just off the farm. I'd started considering them both *our* homes, but it felt like a stretch since we hadn't officially bound ourselves together in any way.

The itch to seal our bond grew stronger, and I had to fight harder not to say the words with every damn day that passed.

The desire to have sex grew stronger too—we made love every night with our fingers and mouths but hadn't taken it any further. I was putting off a visit to the healer, Dirue, because it just seemed awkward.

I kept hoping a fertility-suppressing plant would just appear outside my house overnight, but that had yet to happen. Kierden had offered to go, but he was busy with the elves, so I turned him down.

After one night when we had a particularly hard time restraining from graduating to full-on sex, I finally decided it was time to swallow my discomfort and visit Dirue.

Bright and I made our way to the healer's house. She was amused by my reluctance... so at least one of us was entertained by my misfortune.

I knocked tentatively on the door. It was on the far end of the kingdom, so my wrist was hurting something fierce. Kierden had assured me mentally that she wouldn't want to chat for long, so I was ignoring the pain. He and Bright both insisted that she wouldn't mind the intrusion, but I was still a bit nervous.

I scratched Bright lightly behind the ears as I waited.

The thick wooden door opened a moment later, and my gaze collided with that of a beautiful fae woman with light skin and vibrant pink hair. She was nearly as tall as Kierden, though obviously not as large.

"Nissa," the healer said, her voice warm as her mouth curved upward. "I wondered when I'd get to see you healthy."

I blinked.

"I was the one who sent for Kierden, so you could drink his blood and recover from your meeting with the Beast," the woman explained.

"Thank you, then."

"Of course. Come in." She opened the door, and I walked inside a bit cautiously.

My eyes slid over the interior of the large tree she had made her home. It looked a lot like all the others, with the smooth wood floors and walls. There were no dividers between the bed and living area.

My gaze was drawn to three large shelves of plants at the far end of the space, near a slim window that let in just a tiny bit of light. The bright green plants sat in matching white pots. Their leaves were small and delicate, growing off long, thin branches that stretched over the sides and grew down toward the ground.

"I'm Dirue," she said. "What can I help you with?"

My cheeks warmed. "I'm hoping you might be willing to share some of the fertility-suppressing herb, actually."

Her smile widened. "Of course." She picked up a fabric bag from a pile to the left of the plants, and slowly looked over all of them. "You don't intend to seal your mate bond, do you?"

"Oh, definitely not," I said quickly.

She nodded.

A moment of silence followed. It was an awkward one, honestly.

"Have King Kier and the elves found anything about the murders yet?" Dirue asked, making conversation as she slowly and carefully began pulling a leaf from one of the plants.

"Not yet, but I'm sure they will." Another awkward silence followed, and I felt inclined to fill it. "It's surprising that someone here is willing to kill people just because they fall in love. Among humans, love is treasured."

Or at least in an ideal world it was.

"Love isn't what's getting them killed," Dirue said absentmindedly. "The cult never feared or hated love—they just believed a mated pair could destroy our world."

Kierden had told me that, but he hadn't given many other details. "How was the cult destroyed?"

"Oh, the elves' numbers were being decimated by the cult. The elves used to form mate bonds with the gargoyles; it was a vital part of their culture, so they were a large target. They grew desperate after their queen was killed, and created their assassins to hunt the cult members down. The cultists were picked off one by one until the elves lost control of the assassins, and that gave the rest of them time to go into hiding."

"Damn, that's terrible," I murmured. My eyes swept over the plants again, lingering on one in the middle. Though it looked identical to the others, something about it just sort of *felt* the tiniest bit different to me. When I focused on the flow of my magic and followed it to the plant, I realized its energy was different than the others.

I assumed it was the original plant, perhaps one that had been taken from the human lands since the fertility-suppressing herbs grew wildly there. "Would you mind if I took a clipping so I could grow my own?"

"Unfortunately, these plants are too delicate to clip, even for someone as gifted as yourself." She winked at me and finally tied the top of the pouch. "You're welcome to come back any time you need more. Tuck a leaf beneath your tongue for about ten minutes once a week, and you won't find yourself with child. Swallow it if you want, or discard it. It'll work the same either way. And you can take them twice a week for extra protection, if desired."

"Thank you." I gave her a quick smile as I tucked the pouch of leaves into the top of my dress. Reo had come through with some gorgeous ones that actually fit me, in colors that made me ridiculously happy. "I've got to get back, but it was nice to meet you."

"And you as well." She led me to the door, waving at me as I slipped onto Bright's back. I waved too, and then held on as Bright began to move.

"That was odd. I'm sure her plants aren't that delicate. The herbs taste good —we plucked wild ones all the time as children without damaging anything, and we were never careful."

"She's probably just protective of them because they enable her to hold her role as healer," Bright mused. *"If you started growing them for everyone, no one would need to visit her, and she might feel purposeless. Magical beings are known to start losing their minds when they get too old. Given how long the wars have been going, there may be some insanity beginning to brew for a lot of the warriors. They call that insanity immis."*

She pronounced the word ihm-iss.

Well, that sounded terrifying.

"Immis doesn't happen for esu?"

"Oh, no. We're smart enough to take mates before immis begins to set in," she said with a chuff. *"And we have our bonds with the fae to ground us, too."*

"Taking a mate prevents insanity?"

"It does. Your mate becomes your purpose. Even on your worst day, you feel a drive to make sure they've had enough to eat and drink. You feel a desire to spend time with them and experience things together. Having a mate enriches your life enough to protect against immis entirely."

"Maybe a lot of the fae will start taking mates now that they don't have any more wars to fight, then," I murmured.

"Maybe the wars were started in an effort to avoid immis without taking a mate in the first place," Bright countered.

I wondered if she had a point.

"Would it be terrible if I grew my own plants from the leaves Dirue gave me? I don't want to take her place or make her lose her mind, but I don't want to be reliant on her plants either."

Bright chuffed. *"No. I wouldn't want to return to her in a few weeks when those run out either. She only put four in there."*

My lips curved upward.

We neared the castle, and I reached out to Kierden. *"Are you ready for me to look at the bodies?"*

He and the elves had exhausted their ideas, so he was finally ready to take the "risk" of having me see if I could sense anything. It was unlikely, but my magic was unique so there was always some small chance it would work.

He sighed. *"Unfortunately. They're frozen, and I've covered them with sheets; if there are any plants, you should be able to sense them without seeing them, right?"*

"I think so."

"We'll find out, then."

I didn't want to see the bodies unless I had to, so I was grateful that he covered them.

When we reached the castle, I slipped off Bright's back, and she led me through a maze of hallways.

Bright didn't want to go in with the bodies, so when we reached the room and found Death already sitting outside the doors, the two of them decided to slip into the jungle together for a few hours. She still hadn't admitted that she was in love with him, but everyone knew, including Death. He wasn't sure why she still wouldn't mate with him, but he was getting closer to refusing her "no" every day, just like she wanted him to.

The room was much emptier than I'd expected. There were no elves in sight; it was just Kierden and a few other fae I didn't know. On one side of the space, there were a few long desks. On the other side, there were two tables set up parallel to each other, holding two bodies hidden beneath sheets.

I could see the bright golden glow of their bond showing through the fabric covering them.

"Their bond is still glowing?" I asked Kierden mentally, not wanting to disturb the grim silence in the room.

"A sealed mate bond doesn't break with death, little human. The magic of it holds through every world and every life that follows."

My throat swelled with emotion.

He'd told me that before, but it never occurred to me that a bond could be so eternal that the glow of it didn't vanish.

What had happened to them was horrible, but at least they were still together, permanently.

Kierden stepped up to me, his hand landing on my lower back as he waited for me to decide whether I was going to approach them or not.

I let out a slow breath, and finally walked over to the tables. Despite the nausea in my stomach, I was there for a purpose.

"Do you feel anything?" Kierden asked me quietly, as we stood between the fae. I assumed he'd spoken aloud for everyone else's sake.

"Give me a minute," I murmured.

Closing my eyes, I focused on my magic. I was usually surrounded by so many plants that I had never bothered with trying to find them individually.

As I followed the energy of my magic, I could feel the life in the walls and floors of the room, along with every other inch of the tree that made up the castle. Whoever created it had done so with extreme care, making sure not to hurt the tree in the slightest, and had put magic into place to prevent its growth from contorting the castle's shape. My magic had rejuvenated the tree, strengthening it without affecting the shape or size of it.

It took a few minutes for me to guide my mind through the massive flow of my power. Navigating through it as I tried to pinpoint smaller bits of growth felt like running uphill.

I felt the vines and flowers, growing over the walls inside the castle.

I felt the large variety of herbs growing in the kitchen, bursting with life even as someone plucked a few of the leaves.

Finally, I felt the room I was in. It was nearly empty as far as plants went. Besides the living, breathing being that was the tree we occupied, and the herb pouch tucked in my dress, I felt only two tiny twinges.

Both seemed to have been set on the table furthest from me. The twinges felt familiar; I recognized the plants, though I couldn't say what they were from where I was in the moment.

"There's nothing in the bodies that I can feel," I said quietly. "Just two things over there." Letting out another long breath, I pulled my mind away from my magic and opened my eyes. "What are they?"

"The fertility-suppressant plants. Most males take them too, when they're with a partner."

I nodded. "Can I see?"

He captured my hand and pulled me over to a small tray with two leaves on them.

I slipped my pouch out of my dress and pulled one of my own leaves from it, leaning closer and comparing them. Visually, they looked identical.

"And you studied them to make sure no one has poisoned them?" I asked.

"Dirue does every time," he confirmed. "We check for magical tampering, too, but haven't found anything."

My throat swelled. "What if she's the killer?"

"Dirue? No. She's been alive longer than any of the rest of us, and has been taking care of our people with medicinal herbs and plants throughout the years. The woman has an entire garden dedicated to it."

I held my leaf between two of my fingers, and picked up one of the other ones with my free hand.

"Veil, Nissa," Kierden growled, trying to rip the leaf from my hand. I took a few quick steps back and closed my eyes, focusing on the tiny blip of energy coursing through both leaves.

"These are *not* the same, Kierden. They grow the same and look the same, but their energy is different. I noticed a strange plant between the others in Dirue's house—and this feels like it came from *that* plant."

He ripped both leaves from my hand and dropped them on the table as he covered my fingers with ice, like he was trying to cleanse them. The ice cracked and fell away quickly, vanishing before it could clatter to the ground.

"She's not the killer—And don't risk your damn *life*." He snarled that last part at me, grabbing my pouch of the herbs off the counter and shoving it in his pocket.

I could feel the eyes of every other fae in the room on us, but I didn't let myself acknowledge that. "I didn't say she's the killer," I told him, my voice calm and even. "I said that those leaves came from two different plants. Which they did. Maybe mated couples need stronger fertility suppressants; I don't know. But the plants she gave me are not the ones she gave the couple who died."

He stared at me, eyes narrowed and chest heaving.

I met his stare without flinching.

"I'll get mine so we can determine which ones are different," one of the female fae in the room with us said quietly. I turned my head, looking away from Kierden and meeting her eyes. They glowed a brilliant teal, a gorgeous contrast to her vibrant purple hair and dark brown skin.

"I need to go back for more," one of the men said. He had tan skin, purple eyes, and gleaming white hair. "I'll mention that I wish I could make Eiva my mate, and ask her what she knows of the bond outside of the murders, so we can find out if fertility increases."

"My house is close enough to hers that I can sit on my porch and read while keeping an eye on her without raising suspicion," another female offered. Her amber gaze met Kierden's glowing blues as she stood and slipped her hands into the pockets of her simple, black dress. "None of us want to believe Dirue could be behind this, but this is the only real clue we've *ever* had. And when you think about it, haven't all of the bodies had the same leaves? If they're really different than the ones the rest of us take..." she shook her head, her eyes pooling with tears. "We've lost too many people. No one will make sense as the murderer after this long."

She turned and left the room, her words hanging heavy in the air around all of us.

"It *could* be a coincidence," the male fae with the white hair said. "But we'd be fools not to look deeper into it. Nissa doesn't know any of us; she's perhaps the only person in our kingdom who could see the deaths from a neutral perspective. I'll report back after I've talked to Dirue— we all need to spread the word that we've given up on our search without finding any clues."

Nods went around the room, but I looked at Kierden.

He jerked his head too, and finally admitted, "It's a good idea. Thank you. Come and find me if you have news."

Murmurs of agreement followed, and the rest of the fae filed out of the room until it was just me and the king.

I braced myself for his anger as I turned toward him.

Instead, I saw him rake his fingers through his hair as he swore under his breath.

"I'm sorry," I said quietly.

"It's not your fault. None of this shit is your fault." He grabbed me by the hips and dragged me to his chest. I realized he was hugging me a moment later than I should've, and wrapped my arms around him too.

I wasn't sure we'd ever just *hugged*. Maybe when I was recovering from the Beast's bite? I wasn't sure. But honestly, it felt incredible. I could definitely get used to hugs.

"It's going to be a long few hours." His voice was weary.

"No one would expect you to go to a tavern to drink away your worries?"

"No. I only drink on eclipses, and only to dull the desire," he rested his chin on the top of my head, holding me securely. "I usually just sit in here and pace, trying to work out a damn solution in my mind until I'm exhausted enough to collapse. Then I return the bodies to their loved ones, and I mourn with them."

"You're a good king," I murmured.

"They'd flay me if I wasn't." His voice was tired. So damn tired.

He let go of me long enough to lead me out of the room with a hand on my back, and then dragged me into his arms again as he leaned up against the wall in the hallway. The space was empty, but I didn't think he would've done anything different if it wasn't.

"You'd probably enjoy the challenge if they tried to flay you," I teased him lightly.

His lips curved upward slightly. "I suppose."

"What do you do when you want to relax?"

"I read, remember?" He dragged a hand slowly over my back.

"What else?"

"I train a lot, though that feels nearly pointless without a battle in our future."

I got the feeling those were *really* the only things he did for relaxation.

"Alright. Well... you have a pool here, don't you? You mentioned that before, but I've never seen it." He'd mentioned a library too, but I didn't think books would be a good enough distraction at the moment.

"Yes." His chest rumbled. "It's a large hot spring the original king paid the elves to create a millennium ago, and the only source of warm water in the city. Most fae don't enjoy the heat, so it's rarely used."

"Well, *I* would enjoy the heat. And maybe it would take your mind off everything while we wait?"

As the words slipped out, I found my cheeks warming a bit.

I'd asked him to do something with me, for what was probably the first time in the entire month and a half we'd known each other.

"I suppose it's worth a try." He let out a long sigh. "Alright. Let's go to the pool."

"You sound positively thrilled," I teased him.

He chuckled and took my hand, sliding his fingers between mine without hesitation as he led me out of the room.

CHAPTER TWENTY-ONE
NISSA

S team rose off the swirling water in the hot pool, and I stared at it in utter fascination. Something in the water foamed enough to cloud the surface completely, and it smelled strangely good. We hadn't had anything like that in my town—just a small river off to one side.

The pool was in a massive room that also contained the training area, so when we'd walked in, I got an eyeful of gorgeous fae warriors fighting with weapons of ice.

"Why don't you guys use your magic for anything other than weapons?" I asked Kierden, as I tugged my dress over my head. He took the fabric from me and folded it smoothly before setting it down on the side of the pool.

I couldn't help but watch him as he took off his shorts and put them by my dress. He still had on the tight undershorts he always wore, but the view certainly didn't disappoint.

"Because we have no need of it." He captured my hand as I started to step down toward the water. *"Be careful. I don't want you bleeding again."*

"Why don't you need your magic?"

"Ice magic is death personified," Kierden said, stepping into the water after me and wincing at the heat. As I sank further into the warm bliss of it, he remained standing on one of the steps, adjusting to the temperature the way I would've needed to adjust to cold water before I was bonded with him. *"It's not a magic that can help someone. Ice is hard and cruel. It asks no questions and gives no answers. Even if we were to create our city with it, like our ancestors did in Ravv's, it wouldn't feel alive the way our jungle does."*

"Ice can be beautiful, I'd imagine," I countered.

"Of course. There's something beautifully final about death, isn't there? Even knowing that life continues beyond the veil, the permanence of it is still poetic."

I eyed him with distaste as I settled down on the deepest seat beneath the water. *"Maybe you're the killer."*

He chuckled, finally sitting down beside me. *"I am far from innocent, little human. They didn't choose me to be king for my gentleness."* My hair moved around me in the water, and Kierden snagged a few strands, rubbing them softly between his fingers. *"You, on the other hand..."*

"The picture of innocence?" I drawled back.

He dragged me onto his lap, wrapping a possessive arm around my waist and placing the other on my thigh. *"Oh, yes."*

"You'll ruin me, though." I leaned my head back against his shoulder. *"As long as I don't drink ale."*

His chest rumbled against me as he chuckled again, his hand sliding further up my thigh. *"In every way there is, Nissa."*

Veil, I loved the sound of that.

His erection throbbed against my ass, and his hand slid higher, until his knuckles brushed my clit through the fabric covering me.

I inhaled sharply, my gaze snapping to the warriors on the far side of the room. They were pretty far away, and completely focused on their fighting, but there were at least fifteen of them over there. Maybe even more.

"They could see us," I hissed at him, as his fingers brushed my clit again and desire swelled in my lower belly.

Veil, I wanted him to keep going.

"Only from the waist up. Stay still and quiet, and they won't notice," Kierden said, his tone almost wicked.

I started to protest—but then his fingers brushed my core again, and I had to clamp my mouth down to stop myself from crying out.

"Kierden," I growled into his mind.

"You wanted to distract me, Nissa. This is the only distraction I want."

Damn him.

And damn me for wanting him.

I clenched my jaw tighter as he hooked a finger in the top of my scanties and pulled. The thin triangle of it rolled up and rubbed against my clit as he pulled it higher and higher.

My breathing hitched at the pressure, and my fingers dug into his arms as he lazily dragged a finger down my clit, pressing on the tight fabric.

One of the pairs of warriors strode toward us.

My body tensed, but Kierden's fingers continued slowly stroking my core over the thin roll of fabric, and the tension in my shoulders relaxed even as my lower body clenched tighter.

The warriors nodded at Kierden without stopping to chat, and I felt him nod back.

"You are dead to me," I hissed into his mind.

"You'll change your tune when you're unraveling on my fingers." He kissed my shoulder lightly as he finally eased the fabric away from my core.

"You're supposed to be territorial," I shot back, trying to ignore the short-circuiting in my brain as he slid the cloth down to my knees.

"Oh, I am," he rumbled back. *"Every male who looks this way sees me holding you. He doesn't know that I'm touching you like this, but he knows*

that you're mine—and that if he tried to take you from me, my blade would tear him to shreds."

"I thought possessiveness would mean you want my skin covered more—not that you'd risk touching me in a damn public pool."

His chest rumbled as he chuckled, and *finally*, he dragged his finger over my clit. *"They can look at you and envy me as much as they'd like, so long as they remember that I'm the only one who gets to taste you, fill you, and make you scream."*

My body trembled as I bit back a cry of pleasure. *"You're obsessed."*

"Entirely." His growl and fingers dragged me over the edge, and I shattered with a silent cry. He held me in place with a firm hand, preventing me from bucking or rocking against him the way I so desperately wanted to. Though the fingers on his other hand remained over my clit, he'd stopped stroking me. *"Are you going to take my cock tonight, Nissa?"*

I didn't even have to think about it. *"Veil, yes."*

He made a noise of approval. *"How wet will you be for me?"*

"As wet as you make me."

He chuckled again, his erection throbbing against my ass. *"Good answer."*

My breathing had finally started to level out when he dragged his fingers down my clit again—just as another pair of warriors strode through the room, headed toward the others. They nodded at Kierden like the others had, and he nodded back again.

"What are you doing?" I asked him.

"I'm nowhere near done with you. If you want my cock, you have to take my fingers first, and prove that you can still feel pleasure with them stretching you."

The way my tense stomach fluttered at his words was ridiculous, but I couldn't suppress it.

"What if I can't?"

"Then I get to feel you shatter on them over and over until you can," he growled.

One of his thick fingers brushed up against my slit, making my breath catch.

"Ready?" he asked me.

"Yes."

His finger pushed inside me, so, so slowly.

I clutched his arm, digging my nails into his skin as he slid deeper and deeper, until he was filling me. He stopped when his finger was fully sheathed inside me, his thumb stroking my clit lightly. *"How do you feel?"*

"Incredible," I breathed.

"Good. Show me how well you can climax on my hand, little human."

I bit my cheek to stop myself from groaning. He continued working my clit—and started slowly stroking the inside of my channel, too.

Another pair of warriors walked by, and I barely even noticed them.

Kierden continued touching me, stretching me, and bringing me plea-sure until I shattered. A soft cry escaped me, but by some miracle none of the warriors turned toward us.

"We can't keep doing this here," I told Kierden.

"Would you prefer the dining hall?" he purred to me.

"You're a damned exhibitionist," I spat.

"And I will be, until everyone in my kingdom knows that you belong to me." His voice was casual, but there was more steel in it than I would've expected.

"Stop, Kierden," I hissed at him, as he rubbed my clit harder.

To his credit, he stopped immediately.

My chest rose and fell too rapidly—I was feeling too out of control.

"You don't get to make me climax just to make a statement. If you touch me, it's because you want to make me feel good." I caught his wrist and tugged it away, so his fingers slid out of me. Though I winced at the loss of him, it was the right call.

"Of course I want to make you feel good," he growled back at me. *"A man can have more than one motive."*

"Not if one of them is proving a point." I tried to slide off his lap, but he held me firmly in place.

"I am not human, nor will I ever be. I will always feel a drive to dominate and conquer. As the king, that drive becomes a visceral need. You are either willing to accept that part of me, or you aren't. The time to decide that is now."

When I tried to climb off him again, he released me, though he did so with great reluctance. As I reached for my scanties, he did too—pulling them up my thighs and then smoothing them, making sure they covered me.

The gesture was confusingly sweet after our little argument.

My stomach growled as I stood, and Kierden rose to his feet with me. He took my hand again to steady me as I climbed out.

"I'll train for an hour or two while I wait for my fae to return with news about Dirue. Eat something and think about it." His voice was gentle again.

Something told me he already felt confident that I was going to accept his *drive to dominate and conquer.*

"Tell me as soon as you hear something. I want to be there for all of it," I warned him.

He agreed, and I believed him.

I tugged my dress over my wet skin and walked to the dining hall on shaky legs, wondering what I had been thinking when I decided to develop feelings for a fae king.

. . .

Eisley was sitting at a small table in the corner of the dining hall when I got there, both of us completely alone for once.

She grinned at me when I sat down across from her. "Hey."

"Hi." I gave her a small smile of my own. "Back from your secret mission?"

She winked at me. "I'll never tell."

My smile grew slightly more genuine.

"You look stressed," she remarked.

"Confused, mostly."

She waited.

I sighed.

"Come on, Nissa. I need the distraction." Her words were slightly playful, but the sadness in her eyes told me they were genuine. I had a feeling she was still struggling with the loss of the couple that had died; they had been her friends.

And the fact that her words mirrored Kierden's didn't pass my notice. I felt a little bad for leaving him when he was struggling, but he had upset me. I couldn't just ignore that, or the man would start to think he could make all the calls about everything.

I looked around.

There were only a few other people in the room, and they were far enough away that they wouldn't hear me as long as I didn't raise my voice.

"Kierden told me he feels a drive to dominate and conquer," I said quietly.

She made a face. "Do *not* give me details."

"Sorry," I replied quickly.

She gave me a long look, and then leaned in. "Fine, tell me. Still, no details."

I leaned closer too. "He wanted a distraction. I distracted him. But he pushed me a little too far and I got mad, so he said the thing about needing to dominate and conquer, and told me I had to decide whether I could handle it or not."

She nodded. "Kier has always been very, very intense. I know the reason he hasn't been interested in anyone in so long is because he feels things too strongly. He won't accept casual or half-committed relationships. If he wants something, he's all in, permanently. I'm sure he's shitty at expressing it, but that's the truth. If he wants you, he wants *everything* with you."

"What if I don't like *everything*?" I asked. "What if he tries to do something—" I saw her face and added hastily, "Like cooking me breakfast —and I don't like it? Do you think he'd be angry? Would he push me for more? Would he insist that I keep letting him cook me breakfast because of his desire to dominate and conquer or whatever? I don't want to be trapped, or forced into anything. I really couldn't handle that."

Her eyes softened. "With a sealed mate bond, it would be impossible for him to hurt you. I don't know much about the connections, but I do know that. Even the cruelest, most violent kings couldn't hurt a hair on the heads of their queens. They were teams—as wicked and dark as that sometimes was for everyone."

Maybe that shouldn't have made me feel better, but it did.

"I don't want to make him unhappy, though," I said quietly. "I don't want to agree to this and then change my mind, and have him regret it."

She flashed me a smile—a genuine one. "Kier has never regretted a decision in his life. He's far too *dominant* and *conquering* for that. If he picks you, he's yours, no matter what."

My heart warmed rapidly.

Her gaze lifted to the dining hall's entrance, and her smile grew. "Whatever he did, he must've realized he screwed up."

My head turned just as a thick, warm hand landed on my shoulder.

"I'm sorry," he said into my mind. *"Veil, I am terrible at this."*

"It's alright. I think we just need to talk about it."

"I agree." He sat down next to me.

"You're talking mentally, huh?" Eisley asked knowingly.

"Of course not." Kierden snagged my fork from my fingers, loading it up and lifting it to my mouth. I stole it back from him and ate the food.

"We would never," I agreed as I chewed. "You need to eat something too," I told him.

"Don't worry about me, Nissa." He dropped a hand to my thigh and squeezed.

"I'm supposed to worry about you. We're mates."

He made a noise of disagreement. *"You're my female."*

"And you're my male, right?"

"You guys are *totally* talking mentally. If you weren't so damn adorable, I'd be annoyed," Eisley said, interrupting our conversation.

Err, the conversation we *weren't* having.

"We aren't," I protested as Kierden said into my mind,

"You know I'm yours, little human."

"Mmhm." Eisley didn't sound convinced in the slightest.

Kierden got up for a moment, and she shook her head at me while he was gone. He returned quickly, with a plate of food in his hands.

"So I take it you didn't learn anything about the deaths today?" Eisley looked at her brother.

He inclined his head to the side a little, and I realized he was gesturing toward the room we'd been in earlier. "No, we didn't."

"That's disappointing," she said calmly, though her eyes had widened slightly.

"We'll talk after we tell her what happened," Kierden murmured.

I agreed, and we both focused on our meal.

CHAPTER TWENTY-TWO
NISSA

Eisley made conversation while Kierden and I both ate. When we were done, all three of us went back to the room the bodies were in. One of the fae woman from earlier was already waiting for us inside, and when we entered, she pulled a small pouch nearly identical to mine out of her pocket. She tossed it to me, and I caught it.

"Don't touch the other leaves again," Kierden warned me as he pulled my pouch out of his pocket and handed it to me.

"It'll be easier to match them if I hold them."

"I will drag your ass back to my room if you even think about it," he growled.

Though I gave him a dramatic sigh, I had to admit that he had a point.

I wouldn't touch anything.

"What's going on?" Eisley asked.

"When Nissa was in Dirue's home, she realized one of the fertility-suppressing plants wasn't the same as the others around it. They look the same, but their energy is different," the female fae who'd returned with her leaves explained. Kierden was too busy watching me to make sure I didn't touch any of the leaves to explain it himself.

"Veil," Eisley breathed. "You think *Dirue* is the murderer?"

"We think someone has been murdering couples for a long, long time, and this is the first clue we've ever had," the other woman said.

They continued talking while I set my leaves and the other woman's on tables a few feet away from each other, and then stepped back and closed my eyes.

Letting out a slow breath, I forced myself to follow the flow of my magic again.

It took some time, but eventually, I managed to find the plants in the room again.

I paid close attention to the individual leaves for a few minutes before finally withdrawing from the magic. I'd made sure I was absolutely certain—I wasn't going to be responsible for condemning someone for something they hadn't done.

All three pairs of eyes in the room were focused on me when I opened mine.

"Mine match hers." I gestured to the woman who'd brought hers for comparison. "The couples' leaves feel different than ours."

Eisley's expression grew grave.

"It could still be that the mated couples need stronger plants," the other woman reminded us, though she didn't sound convinced.

"She's the killer," Kierden said, his voice low but sure. "It doesn't make sense, but nothing else does either."

Eisley's grimace deepened. "She supported the unmated couples more than anyone else, and opposed the anti-sex laws more loudly, too. I don't know how she could go from that to murdering all newly-mated couples."

"She told me that the cult didn't have anything against love, they just thought mated couples could destroy Evare," I said quietly.

"Veil." Eisley pushed her hair out of her eyes.

There was a long moment of silence.

Finally, Kierden said, "We don't act until we've heard back from Govind. It'll be a few hours; he's going over there to ask her about the fertility of fully-mated pairs."

The women nodded.

"We'll keep an eye out for him and come find you when he shows," Eisley said, looking at Kierden.

He nodded, grabbing my pouch of leaves and the other woman's too. He tossed hers back, then tucked mine into my dress like I had earlier. My face warmed at the brush of his knuckles on my breast, but he withdrew quickly before taking my hand and slipping his fingers through mine.

"At least this nightmare is almost over," Eisley said quietly, as we slipped out of the room.

"For that, we can thank the veil," the other woman agreed.

Kierden's shoulders were heavy as we walked back to his room. I didn't ask if he was okay; clearly, he wasn't. Some things were far too terrible to ever be okay with.

"Are we moving down to your farm after this ends?" he asked me as he pulled the door to his room open. I got the feeling he was just trying to lighten the mood a little, but he didn't need to do that for me. I was used to dealing with the darkness, and it hadn't overwhelmed me yet, by some miracle.

Or some amount of strength, as silly as that seemed.

"I don't know. Are we?" I glanced at him.

"Perhaps we'll just keep both homes, so you have somewhere other than the tavern to run to when I inevitably screw up."

My lips curved upward a bit. "You didn't screw up in the pool. You just took me by surprise, and I didn't react well. Being defensive seems like my automatic response. I don't think either of us handled it perfectly."

He nodded, and I noticed him eyeing the bathing pool. Though we'd only just been in the water and some of my hair was still damp, I tugged him toward the bath. He'd used it to relax after long days on a few different occasions, so I thought it might calm him. I wasn't hoping for a repeat of earlier—I just wanted to help him feel a little better.

"Haven't you had enough water for the day, little human?" His voice was tired, but slightly playful.

I flashed him a smile as we reached the edge of the bath. "Not yet. Take your clothes off and get in."

He gave me a small grin. "You just want me naked."

"I won't deny that."

After a soft chuckle, he stripped completely, then slipped into the water.

Rather than following his lead, I sat down right behind him with my legs on either side of his arms as he leaned back against the wall of the pool.

He flashed me a curious look as I set my hands on his shoulders. "What are you doing?"

"Attempting to give you a massage. I'm sure I'll be terrible at it. The last massage I even saw was one my father gave my mother when I was eight or nine, and she looked absolutely miserable. He did too."

His expression morphed to surprise. "I'm sure I wouldn't know the difference. I've never had a massage before."

My eyebrows lifted. "Really? But you've had sex before. We always spend a little time in bed together, touching each other a bit, so I assumed it might've happened before for you." I lightly pressed my thumbs into the thick muscles at the base of his neck.

He groaned at the pressure, and I moved my thumbs around a bit. "Veil."

"It's okay?"

"It's incredible."

I grabbed the soap and rubbed it over my hands, so they'd be slicker. He groaned again, even louder, when I set them back on his shoulders and resumed the motions.

"I told you, the sex was only physical. There was no emotion involved. I didn't smell the female's hair, tell her she was beautiful, hold her, or particularly care if she climaxed, just as she didn't care if I did. For the fae, sex is always very selfish. I've never taken pleasure from making a woman unravel the way I do with you—and I've certainly never wanted one's hands on my skin like this before."

I liked that a lot, though I wasn't sure I should admit it. "When have you ever sniffed my hair?"

He groaned again when I slid my hands a bit further apart to massage the tighter parts of his muscles. "Every chance I get."

I didn't bother asking if it felt good, since he was so clearly showing me that it did. "Do I smell good?"

"Better than anything." His words sounded almost reverent.

"And you really think we're fated?" My words were soft, but I wanted to hear him say them aloud.

"I know that we're fated. I can feel it in my chest, my magic, and my very soul."

His words made something within me settle a little.

We both grew quiet, other than Kierden's soft groans and murmurs of how good my hands felt on his skin. I wasn't really thinking about anything, just focused on trying to make him feel good.

After a little time had gone by, he said in a voice so low I could barely make out the words, "I dread what this night will hold, Nissa."

"Do you want to talk about it?"

There was a long pause.

I assumed he was going to say no.

Instead, he admitted quietly, "It's my duty to kill her for what she's done. Though she deserves to die for her actions..."

"She's your friend," I said quietly.

"She's my friend," he repeated, his words slower and heavier than mine.

"Did you have sex with her?" I asked him. If he had, I wouldn't be jealous; it would've been a long time ago, and I only wanted to know so I could be aware of whether it was a factor or not.

"No. We have never been attracted to one another."

"But she's still your friend."

"Indeed." He leaned his head forward for me, and I slid my hands back to the base of his neck, earning a low, rumbly groan.

"I'm sorry," I said softly. "If there was a way for me to make it easier for you, I would do it."

"Thank you." He lifted a hand to rest on my knee. The gesture wasn't sexual; it was one of gratitude, and companionship.

"Is it lonely to be the king? I know you have Eisley, but she's your little sister, and I've never seen you vulnerable with her."

"Eisley is the only person I trust entirely when it comes to the kingdom, but you're right. I don't share my emotions or my burdens with anyone, and it has been lonely. Until now, I suppose."

"Does sharing them feel like ripping your nails off?" I teased him gently.

He chuckled. "Surprisingly, no. It feels like a weight is being lifted off my shoulders. Then again, that could just be those pretty little fingers."

I laughed. "Still flirting with me, huh?"

"As I will be until the bitter end, little human." He squeezed my knee. "We should talk about what happened at the pool earlier."

"Alright. Want me to stop touching you?"

"Never." His answer was quick, and firm. "But if your hands are getting sore, I'd rather you stop."

"I'm alright." They were a little tired, but in a good way. I loved the way he was reacting to my touch, and the way his muscles felt beneath my palms, so I had no desire to let go. "I can accept your need to *dominate* and *conquer*, but if something makes me uncomfortable, I have to be able to draw a line. And I'm not comfortable with you using me to make a statement to your people. If your drive for those things is too strong to accept that, this will never work between us. I'm not an object to be used."

"I know you aren't, and I'm sorry. I like to be in control, but I can only enjoy it if it brings you pleasure too. It wasn't my intention to make you feel like I cared more about the statement I was making than about pleasing you; my focus was on you, not my warriors."

I nodded. "I get it. And the dominating and conquering thing doesn't surprise me, or scare me away. If it gets you off to touch me in random places, I'm not against it, as long as no one actually sees anything and it's about us having fun."

"I can agree with that." There was a gorgeous, growl to his voice that I loved. "Despite my poor reaction, that was among one of the most pleasurable moments of my life."

My body warmed a little. He hadn't even climaxed. "Mine too," I admitted. "I have to admit, I'm curious how we could possibly have sex in the dining room."

He chuckled. "I suppose you'll have to wait and see."

My lips curved upward.

I continued massaging him for a while before I finally stopped and rested my hands on his shoulders. He leaned backward until he found my chest with his shoulder blades, and then tilted his head back so he could look into my eyes.

The gorgeous, dark blue orbs held me enraptured for a long moment before I blinked.

His lips curved upward, just the tiniest bit. "I'd like to spend the next few hours in our bed, holding you in my arms."

"That sounds nice." I brushed some hair off his forehead, and he closed his eyes briefly.

"Despite everything else, I'm not sure I've ever had a moment this peaceful before. I feel... happy." Kierden's voice was soft, his eyes still closed. "Thank you for giving me this."

My throat swelled. "You're welcome."

He opened his eyes, then caught my hand and dragged it to his lips. I gave him a small smile when he brushed a kiss to the backs of my fingers.

After a moment, Kierden released me and turned so he was kneeling on the pool's seat. His hands landed on either side of me, and his lips met mine in a soft kiss. Our tongues tangled, the movements slow and intimate enough to make my toes curl.

He pulled away a few minutes later and scooped me into his arms before he climbed out of the water. I leaned my head against his chest as he crossed the room, and a moment later, I was tucked beneath the blankets. He left me while he dried off, and my gaze lingered on his form as he pulled on a pair of tight shorts and then returned to me.

I moved over to give him room when he slipped under the blankets— and then he pulled me right back to him before putting me completely on top of him, so my chest was pressed against his. His heat warmed me through the thin fabric of my dress, and I lowered my head to rest against his neck.

"If we really decide to complete the bond, our entire lives will change," I whispered to him.

"A warrior without something to fight for is a hopeless wanderer. You give me something to fight for again, so I welcome the change," he murmured back.

"But what if your war starts again?"

"Then I'll finally have a reason not just to fight it, but to end it." His hand stroked my back lightly. "I don't see that happening, though. It's been so long since we've had peace that I think everyone is looking forward to the quiet. We plan on having the friendly fights here every year, to give our people something to train for in case they aren't interested in finding something else to do with themselves."

"Do you think any of them will want to have kids?" I asked, curiously.

"I'm certain that many will. There are couples in the kingdom who have been together for centuries without mating or starting a family, and I would guess that at least a few of those females will be pregnant before the year's end."

"And what about you?"

"What about me?"

"Do you want to have kids?"

He was silent for a moment.

A long, long moment.

"I suppose I've never considered it," he finally admitted. "I've longed for a partner at times. Someone to hold, confide in, and laugh with. A child never even crossed my mind."

"Well, you were so focused on war that you outlawed sex. Kids seem like an impossibility when no one's having sex."

He made a noise of agreement. "Do you want children?"

A soft laugh escaped me. "I have no idea. I feel like I haven't even lived yet. I need to figure out who I am before I so much as *consider* having a kid."

"You know who you are." His voice grew soft, and slightly playful. "You're a farmer."

I smiled; I did love my farm.

"You're as stubborn as any fae warrior," he added, his hand moving gently over my back, as if he were tracing a shape. "Braver, too.

Certainly tougher. A sentence in that tower would've driven any of us mad, and yet here you are."

My smile grew a bit wistful. "I didn't know how much longer I was going to make it. I'm glad you showed up."

"As am I, little human."

"If we seal the bond, I won't really be human anymore."

"Regardless, you will be mine." His lips brushed the top of my head.

"Why are you so certain of that?" I asked him. "What do you even see in me?"

He was silent for a moment.

Part of me cringed, waiting for him to admit that he saw nothing, or just some potential.

Instead, he said, "I see many things when I look at you, Nissa. The one that truly stands out is *hope*. You make my world look brighter, and I need that."

I grew quiet as those words set in.

"What do you see in me?" he asked.

"Physical strength, mental strength, emotional strength... you have everything. When I think about the person I want to spend my life with, I think about someone I can lay in bed and talk about books with, and someone strong enough to protect me, if anyone else ever comes after me for my magic. Someone who will hold me when I need it and push me when I need that too. At this point, it doesn't even work when I try to picture anyone else but you in that place."

"Good. I'd hate to have to behead one of my warriors just because you pictured him as your mate."

I laughed again. "You wouldn't really."

"Perhaps not. I'd want to, though."

"That's fair." I closed my eyes, taking in a deep breath of his scent. My body was completely and entirely relaxed, and I was getting a little sleepy.

"You should rest. I kept you up late last night, and you're still fragile."

"I'm not fragile; I'm thicker than most of your fae," I mumbled back.

"In the best places." He slid his hand down and gave my ass a possessive squeeze. "But it will take more time than this to recover from those years of starvation."

"Unless you convince me to drink more of your blood." My words grew softer as he started stroking my back again.

"I thought I'd have to work up to that."

My lips curved upward. "It was fun. You should try drinking mine too, sometime."

"Definitely thought I'd have to work up to *that*," he said, chest rumbling a bit.

"We'll figure it out later."

He made a noise of agreement and continued to rub my back as I drifted off.

CHAPTER TWENTY-THREE
NISSA

Kierden woke me up an hour or two later. His expression was so solemn that I didn't need to ask whether the male fae had come back from Dirue's house with news.

Both of us were silent as he pulled his shorts on and I adjusted my dress. He took my hand, slipping his fingers between mine while he opened the door.

Eisley and a few of the fae I'd met earlier stood outside with their bonded esu, including the man who had gone to talk to Dirue.

Their expressions were all grave.

"What happened?" Kierden's voice was low, but not angry.

The man who'd visited her explained, "She told me fertility doesn't change after sealing a mate bond, but that taking extra leaves doesn't hurt, so she usually sends them home with more. I went back and searched the couple's home afterward but couldn't find their pouches anywhere."

Kierden grimaced, "She didn't mention giving them different leaves?"

"No."

He nodded slowly. "Is she still home?"

"Yes."

"I'll confront her and give her a chance to explain. Ready?" He looked at the others, and they all nodded.

Then he looked at me.

I was a little surprised he didn't ask me to stay back but nodded too.

"I asked Death to bring Bright back with him while you were sleeping," Kierden told me as we walked.

"Thank you."

"Of course." He squeezed my hand, and I squeezed back.

Our bonded esu reached the castle's entrance as we did, and we slid onto their backs while the other fae with us did the same.

I filled Bright in on what we'd learned while we moved through the city as a pack. She mentioned catching the Beast's scent while she was outside the elves' shield—which terrified me a little, though there was nothing we could do to keep him away from us.

The Beast would keep hunting Kierden until the eclipse, and there was no way around that. According to Kierden and the elves, shifters didn't believe in hurting animals, so the esu were safe outside the magical shield.

When we reached the healer's house, Kierden and Death stopped on Dirue's balcony, and Eisley and Sharp did the same. It made me feel better to know they would watch each other's backs.

Bright stopped on the porch of a tree near Dirue's, close enough that we could see her porch and far enough that she couldn't reach us.

I saw movement in the corner of my eye, and then noticed more fae already gathered in the trees around us. They waited silently, their expressions dark. Someone must've spread the word about Dirue's potential guilt, but since she was still in her home, it obviously hadn't reached her.

Kierden rapped a fist on her door, then gave her a moment to answer.

She opened the door with a smile—but when her gaze met Kierden's and then lifted to the trees, it vanished.

"Please step outside," Kierden told her.

Despite the "please," I knew it wasn't optional. And the look on Dirue's face told me she knew it wasn't either.

She stepped outside.

Kierden's mind touched mine. *"Which plant is it?"*

"The middle one," I said.

He strode into the house, sending me a mental image of them as he grabbed the pot. I confirmed it was right, and then focused my magic just to make sure.

"Be careful," I told him quietly.

Ice covered his hand and arm to keep the plant from touching his skin.

"What's this about?" Dirue asked, her expression a calm neutral the whole time Kierden was gone.

Eisley stared her down. "The murders."

Dirue didn't look surprised, though she didn't say anything incriminating.

Kierden emerged with the pot.

"Please be careful with my plants. Not all of us grow things as easily as the human you brought here," the healer said curtly. The argument was a pointless one, considering my magic had already sprouted massive flowers all around us. There was no way it hadn't affected her plants too.

"Her name is Nissa." Kierden stepped up to Dirue and held out the pot. "Eat one of these leaves."

She studied him.

"The only reason you wouldn't be willing to eat one of your own plant's leaves is if you knew it could kill you, the same way it killed Freive and Woan."

She stayed silent for a long, long moment.

"Do you deny it?" Kierden asked.

She held his gaze. "I do not."

The trees around me seemed to inhale as one as the fae's shock rolled through the air.

"You've killed every mated couple for centuries, when they trusted you. Why?" The king didn't lose his temper, and I respected him for it. My heart was beating rapidly, and I wasn't even really involved in the situation.

"A sealed mate bond gives a couple too much power. Look at you and Nissa. Between her life magic and your death, you could ravage our world. It's a risk no one should be willing to take—one you should be killed for, should you choose to seal your bond." She gestured toward me.

Kierden's eyes flashed with anger. "For murdering our friends and family in cold blood, Dirue, I challenge you. Does anyone protest the challenge?" He raised his voice as he asked the question, but the jungle was thick with silence.

Another look around showed that even more fae had gathered. Nearly the whole damn kingdom had to have been there; I could even see the elves in one of the trees nearest to the ground.

"Can I say a few words, first?" Dirue asked, her voice calm and measured.

Kierden set his jaw, but jerked his head in a nod.

She looked up at the trees. "I have loved all of you and been honest with all of you. I wept for the lives I ended, and mourned their deaths, even though they were necessary ones. I saw the wicked, corrupt power of a mated fae king and queen as a child. They wounded without reason and killed without question. I pray to the veil that one among you will consider taking up my mantle, and—"

A sharp blade of ice sliced through her throat, and her words cut off abruptly. She grabbed at her neck as blood poured from her, and I watched in sick fascination as she fell to her knees.

"Close your eyes," Bright and Kierden both told me.

I closed them.

"May the souls of our lost make your next life a painful one," Kierden growled. "And may the guilt on your conscience turn your future to ash."

There was an awful squelching noise, and then I heard Dirue's body hit the ground.

Silence reigned in the jungle for a long moment.

I opened my eyes.

Kierden dropped the potted plant on the porch, beside Dirue's body. He turned to face the warriors in the trees and said, "We will burn her in her home with her poison, and pray that she's tortured in the next life by the people she murdered so coldly. Should anyone else attempt to hurt a mated couple for no other reason than the bond, we will take great pleasure in tearing them limb from limb, over many weeks. We do not fear strength, we *celebrate* it. And no one's past dictates our future— *we* do."

Murmurs and growls of agreement seemed to echo through the jungle around us.

A male fae brought a burning torch forward as Kierden and Eisley went back into the house for the non-poisonous plants. They emerged quickly, but my gaze remained fixed on Dirue's body while a few other fae joined the man with the torch. Their hands were out as they used their magic to spread their ice over the wood, so they could burn the killer without hurting the tree.

A few more fae brought large bottles of something that looked suspiciously like ale, and slowly drizzled it over Dirue's body and her poisonous plant, before stepping into her home to spread more of it inside.

I watched quietly as they finished and slipped off the porch and into the tree branches—and I stayed silent as the man finally tossed his flaming torch onto the healer's body.

There was a moment's pause before everything went up in flames, and no one said a word as we watched it burn.

A flash of gold off to my right made me turn my head. The couple from the farm was standing together, her back to his chest, and his arms wrapped securely around her middle. A golden handprint rested on her hip, glowing much brighter than the silver one on my wrist—and I could see the glow from the man's hand, too.

My lips curved upward just a tiny bit at the sight. Though my heart was still beating quickly, and there was still a lump in my throat from the violence I'd seen, knowing that mated couples weren't in danger anymore brought me peace.

Eisley and Sharp wove through the branches until they landed next to the couple. She exchanged a few words with them, then all three of them nodded.

I imagined she was inviting them to stay at the castle so she and Kierden could keep an eye out, just to make sure Dirue had been working alone.

"Are you alright?" Kierden asked me quietly.

My eyes met his over the blazing fire below us. He stood on a bridge across from my branch with Death and a bunch of other fae and esu. His arms were full of plants, and if the situation had been different, the sight might have turned me on. *"I am. Are you?"*

"Not really. I've never had to kill one of my people before."

"Do you think anyone's going to try anything because of what she said?"

"I don't." He didn't hesitate. *"If she had been working with anyone, we would've caught them by now. It's much harder for two people to keep a secret than one."*

"I hope you're right."

We all stayed where we were and remained silent until the fire died completely. Though no one spoke for a long moment, everyone was looking at Kierden, waiting for him to give them instructions.

"Nissa will plant the herb throughout the city," Kierden said, looking at me.

I nodded.

"If you want to grow your own, do it. You are in control now. We all are. Our fates are ours to decide, and if we choose mates, we will defend them."

Murmurs of agreement rolled through the trees around us.

Kierden's mind touched mine. *"Follow me."*

I didn't look back at what we'd left behind as we disappeared into the jungle.

When Death headed toward my farm, Bright followed. He stopped at one of the far edges of my recently-harvested land, and Kierden held out one of the potted plants he'd been holding.

"Ready?" he asked me.

"Mmhm." I took a small clipping of the plant—he gave me a small pair of sharp scissors made of ice when I asked him to—and then crouched down.

It only took a moment to make a small divot in the dirt, tuck the plant in, and rebury the roots. I felt my magic wash over it instantly, and saw the plant perk up.

We repeated the motion a few more times around the farmland, far enough from the crops that their roots wouldn't overlap as they continued to grow.

"There are a few high-traffic places we should put them, if you're okay with it," Kierden told me after we'd nearly planted all we could from the first pot. His voice was still low, and though he hadn't said anything about it, I knew he was itching to go back to the castle and to bed. Not to sleep, but to give himself time to process everything that had happened and everything he had done.

I agreed, and our bonded esu took us to the marketplace. I tucked a few of the plants' stems into deep crevices that existed in a few of the tree trunks, where they could grow freely. They wouldn't grow there naturally, but my magic wasn't exactly natural.

When we were done there, Bright and I followed Kierden and Death to a residential portion of the city I'd never seen before. Some of the fae in their homes watched us as we planted, and I waved at them when I saw them. Most waved back, too.

Eisley joined us as we were nearing the end of our stash. She and Kierden exchanged a few quiet words while I continued going through the last of our plants, and then handed him the ones she had picked up too.

She gave me a quick hug before she left again, and Kierden led me to another part of the city that was also full of homes. He watched me for a moment before he began helping me tuck the plants away to get them ready to continue growing.

As we did, I noticed my vines and flowers had somehow managed to grow all the way out where we were. It was much further from the castle than the edges of my town had been from my tower.

That meant my magic was either growing stronger, or it was simply spreading further when the plants near me were strong enough. I hoped for the latter.

We went to a few more locations, planting the herbs everywhere we went until we only had a few small sprouts left. Kierden stopped at the forest's floor to fill two of the pots with dirt, and then we finally went back to the castle.

I didn't bother asking him if he wanted to go to my house by the farm. He needed the comfort of his long-time home, and I needed to be somewhere in the middle of all the new plants. The castle was about as central as it got, and staying central would help make sure my magic reached everything so the herbs would start growing the way they were supposed to.

The door to his room closed behind us, and Kierden let out a long breath. He kneeled near the door, and quickly dumped half of the dirt from the two full pots into the other two, so all four were half-full. After he tucked the sprouts into the soil and buried the roots, he rose to his feet. I leaned over and carefully took one of the few remaining leaves from one of the sprouts, slipping it into my mouth and tucking it under my tongue.

It didn't hurt to be prepared, after all.

The taste was sweet and tangy, reminding me of my happy childhood, before everything had changed. I wasn't sure whether to smile at the memories or embrace the sadness of knowing just how far in the past they were. But, after so many weeks in Jirev, the sadness felt much more distant than it used to.

My gaze moved back to Kierden. He looked absolutely defeated.

I could help him with that, though.

"I think I need a bath. Come with me?" I asked, wrapping my hand around his gigantic bicep. There was a fair amount of dried blood on his skin, and I wasn't climbing in bed with him until we'd washed it off.

Kierden nodded absently, so I led him to the bathing pool.

Bright murmured to me that Death had asked her on a run in the forest, and when I assured her that we'd be fine, the two of them slipped out of the room.

I tugged my dress over my head, dropping it at my feet. Kierden's eyes lowered to my skin and trailed over me slowly as I took off my scanties too—and they heated when I stepped up to him and pushed his shorts down his thighs.

When his erection sprang free, I wanted to touch him, but didn't want to push him after what he'd had to do to Dirue.

"Keep looking at me like you want to eat me, little human, and your tongue and teeth won't be the only things in your mouth," he murmured as he took a seat on the edge of the bathing pool.

My gaze jerked to his, and I found his lips curved slightly, his eyes a little playful. He'd taught me how to please him with my mouth when I demanded it a handful of days earlier, but it wasn't his favorite way to get off. Not because I wasn't good, but because I took control from him, and he was a little obsessive about retaining it. I didn't mind, because he was damn good at being in control... though it did make me feel powerful to be in charge of his pleasure like that.

Though his words had been a joke, I'd been with him long enough to know that a joke about something related to sex meant he wanted it. He was too prideful to ask me to go down on him—and too polite to demand it. I had a feeling the politeness would vanish with the newness of our bond, though.

I kneeled beside him and leaned over, wrapping my lips around his erection. His eyes closed, his head tilted back, and a low groan escaped him. "You suck my cock so damn well."

I made a noise of agreement, bobbing and gripping the base of his cock as I took him deeper. His hands dug into my hair, and he gripped my head firmly. Even when he started moving me the way he wanted me, I still knew I was in control. If I'd resisted at all, he would've stopped and let me take the lead again.

"I fit so perfectly in that little mouth," he growled, as he neared the edge of his climax. I squeezed him, then took him deeper until he hit the back of my throat.

He snarled, his hips jerking and his hands fisting tightly in my hair as he flooded my mouth with his release. I swallowed his pleasure, licking the head of his cock as I slowly pulled away.

Kierden pulled me into his arms, sitting me on his thigh and holding me against him. I listened to the rapid beat of his heart as his chest rose and fell quickly.

"Thank you," he said, his voice low. One of his hands started to slip between my thighs, but I pressed down on it, holding it where it was.

"I did that because I wanted to, Kierden. Not because I wanted you to reciprocate."

He pulled his hand free, and used it to wipe a bit of his pleasure off my lip before slipping it inside my mouth. I sucked, and his lips curved upward slightly. "Veil, you're cute."

I laughed softly. "I hope that's a compliment."

"It is."

He slipped into the water, still holding me tightly to his chest. A few more minutes passed peacefully before he murmured in my ear, "Thank you."

"You already thanked me." I leaned back against him, enjoying the feel of his skin on mine.

"Not for bringing me pleasure; for bringing us the closure we've been seeking since before I was king." His lips brushed the side of my head. "And for letting me hold you like this while pretending you need a bath."

A soft laugh escaped me. "I did no such thing."

"Mmhm." He pressed another kiss to my temple. "Tell me a story from your childhood. Something happy."

It took me a minute to come up with something, but I eventually remembered a day I'd spent helping my dad in his fields, and launched into the story.

CHAPTER TWENTY-FOUR
NISSA

A few hours and a few dozen stories later, we emerged from the bathing pool and got dressed again. I think we could've lasted a bit longer, but my stomach started growling, and my hunger made Kierden grumpy.

So, we headed to the dining hall.

Despite the horror of what had happened a few hours earlier, I felt closer than ever to the king. We'd talked like old friends, and something about hearing stories of the stupid things he'd done when he was younger made him feel more real to me.

"The cooks will have brought out the ale, so prepare yourself," he warned me as we walked. "My fae will be drunk. Very drunk."

"Noted."

Despite my confirmation, I wasn't really prepared for what we walked in on.

The dining hall was absolutely full—I didn't see a single empty seat, anywhere. The walls were lined with even more people, too. They were everywhere.

A group of men and women in one corner were singing loud and drunkenly, at least a dozen of them strumming stringed instruments. They were completely out of rhythm, and the clashing sounds made me cringe a little.

In another corner there were a handful of fae crying together with a pile of tissues on the table in front of them.

The third corner held fae who were playing games with cards and dice, some of them roaring with laughter while others looked angry or grumpy.

The last corner held a buffet of food, and there was another table beside it with dozens of glasses of ale lined up on it.

I whistled.

He pulled me behind him as he began weaving around the tables. Some of the people moved for him, but some were just too drunk. *"The goal is to get food and get out before too many people notice us."*

"What happens if they notice us?"

"They'll convince me to drink with them," he grumbled.

My lips curved upward. *"I kind of want to see you drunk."*

"You will eventually."

When we reached the buffet table, we both loaded our plates quickly. Kierden wasn't satisfied with the amount of food I put on mine, so he piled more on it before he snagged it from me and then started back toward the door.

"King Kier!" one of the male fae exclaimed, his voice extremely slurred.

"I'm busy," Kierden said, as we neared our escape.

"It's okay if you want to spend the evening drinking with them. They knew Dirue the same way you did, and you could all talk about her. It might give you closure," I told him. *"It won't offend me. I understand, and can spend the night with Bright and Death, or—"*

"I don't need closure." He led me out of the dining hall. The noise faded as we walked further from it. *"I got that when I saw her go up in ashes, and I've had all day to accept the truth. Now, I want to be distracted. Preferably by your body."*

I didn't really believe him about having accepted everything, but if he wanted a distraction, I could give him that.

"Alright. If you change your mind, that's okay."

"I'm not going to change my mind, Nissa. I want you bare and writhing with pleasure through the whole damn night." He pushed the door to his room open with his shoulder, and held it for me while I stepped through too.

"Sounds like fun."

"Mmhm." He turned just slightly, only enough for my hip to brush against his erection as I walked past him.

Veil, he was hard.

"Do you think Bright and Death are going to mate soon?" I asked him as we walked to the bed together.

Perhaps it was strange to eat in bed, but it was a habit I hoped we'd never break. Something about having plenty of food to eat, while lounging beneath the blankets, felt like the pinnacle of luxury to me.

Kierden chuckled. "He's going to lose his damn mind if they don't."

I grinned. "She'll give in soon."

We sat down and ate, and though we were quiet, his hand brushed my knee and thigh every now and then, making me feel... well, like I mattered to him.

It was one of the best feelings I'd ever had.

When we finished, he took my plate and set it on the floor before tugging my dress over my head. He dragged my barely-clothed body into his arms before the fabric even hit the floor.

"You're going to take my cock tonight, little human," he murmured to me, moving his hands slowly over my bare thighs and ass as I settled against his erection. I could feel the thickness of his cock against my clit, despite the fabric of his shorts and my undergarments that separated us.

"Sounds like fun." My clit grinded against him as I moved my hips.

"Oh, yes. You'll be drenched and desperate for it long before I fill you." He nipped at my shoulder. "Remember the way my finger feels inside you?"

My body flushed at the memories. "Of course."

"You'll take two when I lick you to climax."

He was right; I was already soaked for him, and achy too.

"Will I?" I managed to ask.

His hands finally found my core, and he dragged a finger lightly up and down the center of me. "Yes. You'll take three after the second climax."

Oh damn.

He hooked a finger in my scanties and tugged them downward. My body rocked at the brush of his skin against my clit, and his chest rumbled in satisfaction.

With one smooth motion, he rolled me to my back. Our eyes were locked as he pulled the fabric down my legs and then tossed it to the floor.

He freed my breasts next, tossing that fabric too before he took thick handfuls of my tits and squeezed. Releasing them, he slid further down my body until he settled between my thighs, opening my legs wider. His burning eyes took in every inch of me like it was the first time he was seeing me, the same way they always did.

He dragged a finger slowly over my clit, and my hips rocked in response. "When you're drenched in your own pleasure, you'll part these gorgeous thighs even wider for me and watch my cock sink inside this pretty little body of yours. Ready, Nissa?"

"Yes," I breathed.

His lips curved upward wickedly. "Good."

He lowered his tongue to my clit and licked me, slowly.

The world stopped.

Everything stopped.

Everything, except my body and Kierden's.

His chest rumbled in approval. "You're absolutely delicious."

He licked me again, and I cried out at the sensation.

"I can see and taste how much you want me, little human. Look how slick you are for me." He dragged a finger down my center, and I cried out again. My hips rocked desperately as he slowly slid a finger inside me while his tongue made love to my clit.

My cries grew more desperate as I shattered, the pleasure hitting hard and fast.

I was panting when I came down from the high, flushed and relaxed but somehow still wound up. Probably because his tongue was still moving lazily over my clit, like he just couldn't stop tasting me.

"That was perfect, Nissa. You're going to take another finger now. Get ready."

Something about the simple way he gave the order was insanely erotic to me, and I found myself nodding.

He slipped his finger out of me—and then slowly slid two inside me.

My body went still at the pressure of it.

His tongue dragged over my clit, and I let out a long, shaky breath. He stretched me further and further, until his fingers were buried deep inside me.

Kierden slowly stroked my inner walls, and I let out a slow moan as my body tensed. The pleasure was fierce, building up rapidly until I lost control with another cry.

He sucked lightly on my clit, making me dizzy as I struggled to catch my breath. "Just one more, little human. Then you'll be ready for me."

I already felt ready for him, but if he was going to keep licking me and touching me, I'd do whatever he wanted.

When he slowly worked his third finger into me, I gasped, reeling at the pleasure of it.

If his fingers felt that good, how would his cock feel?

I moaned at the thought, the sensations, and everything else.

He licked and sucked on my clit, giving it so damn much attention as he filled me with his fingers. The need built again, more slowly but more fiercely, until I unraveled with another desperate cry of pleasure.

I was so unbelievably sated.

So unbelievably drained, too.

But when he slid his fingers out of me, I still whimpered just the tiniest bit at the loss of him.

Kierden gave my clit one last flick with his tongue before he stripped his shorts off, then leaned back over my body and captured my mouth. He kissed me slowly, his hands moving over my skin as he opened my thighs wider. His erection rubbed against my core, and the thick heat of him made me want more, despite everything we'd just done.

He growled against my lips, "Ready, little human?"

"Completely," I breathed.

The head of him pressed against my slit, and everything didn't just stop —it ceased to exist.

The world.

The room.

Even the bed.

Nothing mattered except me and Kierden.

He slowly slid inside me, and all thoughts faded from my mind.

It was just me and him.

Me and my king.

Me and my friend.

Me and my *mate*.

And veil, we fit together perfectly.

My breathing was fast, my body flushed and needy as I wrapped my legs around his hips, pulling him even deeper inside me.

"You're so damn wet and tight. So damn *perfect*." His words were low and gravelly, his lips moving against mine as he spoke them. I struggled for air while he throbbed inside me, staying still while I adjusted to the thickness of him. "How do you feel?"

"So good."

His rumble of approval made me feel even better.

He slowly slid out and back in—and the intensity of it made me gasp.

So he did it again.

And again.

And again.

Until I was bucking my hips, crying out at the ferocity of the climax that took control of me.

It was everything.

He was everything.

Kierden roared with me, slamming into me as he took his pleasure too. The sensation of him flooding me with his release was so damn surreal —and I wanted more before he was even done.

He tried to pull out of me, but I grabbed him by his thick, muscular ass and held him in place. My nails dug into his backside, and his eyes burned into mine as his cock throbbed inside me.

"You need a break," he told me, wiping a bead of sweat from my forehead and then licking it off his thumb.

"No," I whispered, holding him there. His release was leaking out of me, wet and warm on my core and the insides of my thighs. "I want more."

His eyes burned hotter. "Nissa..."

"Give me what I want, Kierden." I squeezed his ass, and he growled at me. In one sharp motion, he'd rolled us over so he was below me.

"*Take* what you want, little human."

Ohhh.

I liked that a lot.

"I don't know what I'm doing," I warned him, as I propped myself up on his chest and rolled my hips a little.

"You're doing it *perfectly*," he growled, grabbing my ass and squeezing, *hard*.

I rolled my hips, and he squeezed my ass again. "Use me for your pleasure, little human. I belong to you."

One of his hands moved to my breast, gripping and massaging as I sat up higher so I could watch our bodies connect as I rode him slowly. The pleasure was building again—he'd made me so damn insatiable.

I rocked my hips, panting as the pleasure grew. Kierden's fingers brushed my back entrance, making me gasp as we neared the edge together.

The touch shattered me. I made sounds I hadn't even realized I was capable of as the climax went on, and on, and on. He lost it with me, flooding me with his release again.

When the bliss had faded, I collapsed on Kierden's chest, catching my breath as he held me tight.

"That was incredible." He squeezed me tightly. "Damn, little human."

I grinned against his chest. "It was. I think you're holding back on me, though."

His whole body rumbled with a deep belly-laugh. "Of course I'm holding back on you. I wasn't even sure you'd like my cock."

My grin widened. "Asshole."

"You're tiny, Nissa. A man my size has to worry, so consider it a compliment."

"How could I consider it a compliment?" I peeled my face off his chest, propping myself up on my forearms as I attempted to give him a dirty look. It failed, because he was still buried inside me, and I was still grinning.

Kierden lifted his hands to cradle my face. "I was worried because I care about you. If I didn't care, I wouldn't worry."

"Okay, you win. It's a compliment."

His lips curved upward, and he pulled me down for a slow, soft kiss before releasing me and tugging my face back down to his chest. "Fate clearly chose right for us. When I'm sure I can stop holding back without hurting you, I'll do exactly that, with great pleasure. Until then, I'm going to hold back."

I sighed dramatically. "Overprotective fae bastard."

He chuckled. "I'll wear the title with pride."

"Kierden Jirev, King of the Fae, Overprotective Bastard of a Mate," I drawled.

"Suits me perfectly."

"It does." I patted him on the chest.

He laughed again for me, and my grin returned. "You are *stunning*, Nissa. I may be holding back, but that was still the most incredible sex I've ever had."

"Liar."

He rolled me over, pinning me to the bed as his body pressed into mine.

Damn, I'd forgotten how *big* he was.

"I've never had sex with a woman who means something to me, and that makes this the most intimate, pleasurable connection I've ever had. Doubt that, and there will be consequences."

"What consequences?" I shot back. "You'll stop holding back?"

He rocked his hips, and a soft groan escaped me as his cock hit the back of my channel. "Consequences like me freezing your wrists above your head, so you can't touch me while I drag you to the edge repeatedly without letting you climax," he growled, thrusting into me again. "Consequences like me sitting you on my face and holding you there while I feast on you until you *beg* for release."

Veil, that sounded hot.

"In all seriousness, I think the bindings might be too much for me," I admitted. "After being tied up so many times..."

"Then there will be no binding until you want to try it." He stroked my hip lightly with one of his hands. "Your pleasure is what matters most to me, little human. Remember that."

"It would bring me pleasure if you stopped holding back."

He studied me. "You're serious about this."

"Of course I'm serious about this. You have tons of experience, and I'm new. I don't want you holding back and then thinking later tonight, *'damn, Nissa is really terrible at sex... I should go back to one of my old fae lovers.'*"

He barked out a laugh. "I never had a *lover*."

"I feel like you just missed the point of the whole conversation," I grumbled.

"I didn't. You want me to treat you like you have experience, to take what I want from you the way I would if you were a fae woman."

"Yes." I nodded emphatically.

He rocked his hips, bottoming out inside me. I swore as I jerked mine in response, and my channel clenched as he pulled out entirely. His arms

were under me a moment later, and then he was striding across the
room.

CHAPTER TWENTY-FIVE

NISSA

My feet hit the ground as we reached the wall, and he spun me around until my breasts kissed the wood. My cheek pressed against it, and Kierden lifted one of my hands up above my head, followed by the other.

"Leave them there," he commanded.

"Okay, I—" The words died in my throat when he grabbed me by the thighs, opening me up before he slammed into me.

I choked on air and pleasure, my breasts smashed against the wood as he slammed into me again and again. His fingers dug into my thighs, and the need inside me built much slower, but it *did* build.

"After a female has given him permission, a male fae takes what he wants, when he wants it," Kierden said into my ear. "If a female needs more, she demands it."

"How?" I gasped.

"Commands. *Slower. Harder. Touch my clit. Don't climax until I have. Fill me with ice. Stop for a moment.*"

"Slower," I breathed.

"Louder, Nissa. You're the queen; act like it."

The title he'd given me didn't process at all.

"Slower, Kierden," I snarled at him.

"Perfect," he growled back, slowing his strokes immediately.

I groaned as he bottomed out inside me.

Even after following my command, he was driving into me harder and faster than he had on the bed. It wasn't better, but it was still incredible —just different.

His breathing was more ragged, his hands rougher on my skin as he grabbed my breasts, hips, and ass whenever he wanted.

"Touch my clit," I ordered him breathlessly.

He ignored me, so I repeated it louder, commanding him again.

He didn't hesitate to give me what I'd wanted, his fingers working me as he slammed home.

The pleasure hit me, and I shattered on his cock even harder than before. A scream tore through my lungs at the fierce intensity of it, and Kierden snarled as he lost control with me.

"Veil," I moaned, collapsing against his chest. "You should never hold back again. I did like it slower too, though. It was more emotional, in a way. So maybe holding back isn't the worst."

"Noted," he rumbled against my back, his hands moving slowly over my breasts. "And I agree."

I huffed a sigh. "I am so damn exhausted."

"I should let you sleep," Kierden agreed. He started lifting me off his cock, but I protested immediately.

"I'm not ready."

"Good; I want you to fall asleep with me buried inside you." He carried me into the bathroom and grabbed a towel, then dampened it as he slid me off his cock. When he set me on my ultra-wobbly legs, kneeling in front of me, I stared down at him. He gently cleaned me off, then leaned in and kissed my clit like he just couldn't help it.

And then he buried a few fingers inside me, like he couldn't help that either.

A laugh escaped me. "Kierden."

"Stop looking and smelling so damn good, and maybe I won't need to touch you so much," he grumbled at me, withdrawing his fingers and licking them clean.

If I wasn't so exhausted, the sight would've turned me on.

Kierden stood back up when I was clean, lifting me off the ground. After a stop in the closet for one of his old shirts—which he tugged over my head himself—he carried me back to the bed.

When he sat down, he tugged the fabric up out of the way so we could both watch as he pulled me down onto his cock again. I sank down much easier than before, and veil, it felt so damn good.

"If you sleep like this, I'm going to wake up partway through the night to get you off. Probably more than once," Kierden warned me as he lowered us both to the bed.

"Feel free," I breathed.

He brushed a kiss to my forehead. "Sleep well, Nissa. Despite the misery of this evening, I'll cherish the memories of tonight as the best of my life."

Emotions swelled in my chest. "Me too."

He kissed my shoulder, and I drifted off with the soft words of our bond echoing in my mind, itching to be spoken.

"Sillah ovim rett warum."

"Sillah ovim rett warum."

"Sillah ovim rett warum."

I pressed my lips to his chest to keep myself silent, and the urge passed as I fell asleep.

. . .

Kierden woke me with his face between my thighs an hour later, and rolled me onto my abdomen before he drove his cock into me from behind, bringing my pleasure to new heights before we fell back asleep.

I woke him an hour after that with my mouth on his erection, tasting us both on his skin before he seated me on his cock backward and slammed into me again, again, and again.

The night passed by in a haze... and quickly rolled into the next day.

The next handful of weeks went by in a whirlwind of farming, delicious food, and sex. We explored the library a bit, but Kierden joined me in the fields most of the days, learning how to harvest and plant with me.

Our breakfasts were spent in the castle's dining hall, conversing with the other fae. Our lunch breaks were full of fresh fruit and conversation, alone in my house just off the farm. Our dinners were always back in the castle, laughing with the elves as they and the fae told story after story of the long lives they'd lived.

They were the most blissful weeks of my life.

We didn't discuss making our bond permanent, but Kierden had told me he planned on reigniting it after the eclipse so my magic didn't overwhelm me.

Bright and Death spent most of their time in the jungle together. Though we missed them, we were thrilled for them. He was pursuing her with every damn ounce of effort he had, and we kept waiting for them to come back mated. They frequently smelled the Beast while out in the Wilds, but as everyone kept reminding me, he wouldn't go near the esu.

A few nights before the eclipse, Bright's panicked cry cut into my mind in the middle of the night, waking me up suddenly. *"Nissa!"*

Jerking upright, I sucked in a deep, staggered breath. *"What happened? What's wrong?"*

"The Beast took Death. We just mated a few hours ago—he's my mate." The fear in her voice was thick. *"He's hurt. I don't know how bad. I can smell Kierden in the Wilds; I think he's on his way. We need to get the elves— they're the only chance we have."*

My head jerked to the side, and I realized the bed was empty.

Terror crashed into me.

The Beast couldn't kill Death, though he could wound him badly.

But he could kill Kierden.

He *needed* to kill Kierden.

It was his last chance to do so, because when the suns eclipsed in the morning, his vow would break if my mate was still alive.

"I'll get Alida," I said, scrambling toward the door in nothing but the massive white shirt I wore as a nightgown. There was a thin layer of ice over the door—Kierden's quick attempt to stop me from going after him, the absolute bastard—but when I rammed it with my shoulder, I broke through easily.

He knew better than to truly trap me anywhere. I would kick his ass to the veil and back, and still be absolutely furious.

My hair and massive shirt swayed and bounced with me as I sprinted down the hallway. I knew the general direction of the elves' rooms, but I'd never been there before, so I yelled as I neared them, "Alida!"

I continued shouting and running until the sleepy, pissed-off elf-shifter burst out of a room as I neared the door.

My chest rose and fell rapidly, my heart beating like a drum in my chest. "The Beast is here. He hurt Death—Kierden's running toward him right now. You have to stop him."

She blinked. "You want me to stop Kierden?"

"No, the Beast. Please, you have to help." Images flickered in my mind, memories of my dad taking his last breaths while I held on to him as if I could anchor him to this side of the veil myself.

That couldn't happen to Kierden.

I couldn't let it happen to Kierden.

Alida's expression darkened. "If there was anything we could do to stop our assassins, we would've done it centuries ago. You'll have to stop the king yourself, or say goodbye."

She took my hand and squeezed lightly. "I'll strengthen the defenses on the city just to be safe."

With that, she disappeared back into her room and left me standing in the hallway alone.

"They can't help us," I whispered to Bright.

She snarled into my mind. *"Then we'll have to save them ourselves."*

"How?"

"The beast wants power, right? You're more powerful than any of the fae in the city. If you offer to mate with him after the eclipse so he can have your power too, it might buy time. We only need a few hours."

"Or it might get me killed," I whispered.

"He can't kill you. Not completely."

He could get really damn close, though, and let my humanity do the rest.

When it came down to it, it was a choice between certain death for Kierden, or a chance that we could both live.

There was no question what I had to do.

Alida burst back through the door, her eyes wide and bright. "Our assassins hunt through magical connections; that's why your bond hides Kierden from the Beast. If you seal it, his magic will meld with yours and change permanently. The beast's contract will dissolve, and he won't be able to kill the king no matter how badly he wants to."

I went still.

If I sealed my bond with Kierden, it would save his life.

But it would change mine permanently, and that was a massive commitment.

If it came down to it, and there was no other choice...

Well, I'd do whatever I had to, to save his life.

"I'm coming," I told Bright.

She picked me up at the castle's entrance a few minutes later and streaked into the Wilds faster than she'd ever run.

"I'll grab Kierden and get him out of there as fast as I can," Bright told me, her voice hard. *"He's on foot, and not far ahead of us. Do whatever you have to. The Beast thought you smelled good, so use that."*

"I probably smell like Kierden now," I whispered back.

She inhaled, and then swore.

"I'll figure something out."

"We're all going to survive this," Bright growled. *"We haven't made it this long to lose our lives to the damn Beast."*

I agreed, though my confidence was fading alongside the distance between us and the Beast.

It was a terrible plan, but if we didn't go, no one would. And we couldn't just sit back and let our mates die; veil, that wasn't even an option.

"Here I am," Kierden's snarl echoed through the jungle ahead of us.

Fear clutched my stomach as the Beast's laughter cut through the Wilds.

Finally, we saw Kierden, the Beast, and an unconscious Death in a small clearing on the floor of the jungle. There was only a short distance between the men—and Death separated them.

Bright launched toward the clearing as the Beast lunged for Kierden, moving so fast I couldn't even see him move. The fae king's ice swords appeared in his hands as he whirled out of the way, slashing his weapons out.

The Beast roared as ice cut through his arm—and his claws caught Kierden's side.

The men spun together, the scent of their blood flooding the air as they fought. I couldn't see who was winning, but Kierden wasn't anywhere near as fast as the Beast, and I knew that meant he would eventually be overtaken.

"Death is breathing. He's unconscious, but I don't smell any blood," Bright said. *"You have to intervene now, if you want me to get Kierden out of here."*

She was right.

Though it went against every one of my instincts, I slipped off Bright's back and called out, "Beast, I have something you'll want more than a fae king's energy."

The asssassin appeared in front of me.

"Get Kierden out of here," I whispered to Bright. *"I don't care what you have to do to him—just get him out."*

She practically flew at the fae king, ramming him. He landed on her back, and she bit down on his leg to hold him there as she sprinted back into the jungle with him.

Kierden was snarling into my mind, but I didn't let myself listen to what he was saying. If I listened, I might get worried, and I couldn't allow myself to be afraid.

I forced myself to focus on the real threat—the man in front of me.

His lips lifted in a feral grin that told me I was going to regret sacrificing myself the way I just had. "You must be very powerful to think you're worth more to me than the man I've vowed to kill. Or just very stupid."

Or a little of both, maybe.

"What do you know about mating?" I asked him, fighting hard to keep my voice even.

"Your mating won't keep me from killing your king, sweetheart."

"Not my mating; *yours*."

His gaze became slightly... curious. "I'm listening."

"Did you know that mating connects two people's magic? If I seal my bond with Kierden, I'll have access to his power, and he'll have access to mine."

The Beast's eyes narrowed.

I added quickly, "The elves' magic changed you. What if you mated with a shifter? Would it balance out that magic so you don't have to take contracts anymore? Would it make your power even stronger?"

His eyes narrowed even further.

The words poured out of me, "I've been where you are. You're trapped by the spells the elves put on you; I was trapped in a literal tower for most of my life. But what if there's a way out? What if taking a mate would free you? Isn't that worth more than this?" I gestured to the jungle around us.

The Beast lifted an eyebrow "You're defending him."

Kierden had grown silent in my head, which worried me, but I couldn't let it distract me. "Of course I am. He's my *mate*."

"Yet he stole you from your home and started a bond between you against your will, to protect himself."

"Most people will do whatever they possibly can to stay alive. I think you're proof of that."

The Beast laughed darkly. "Indeed. I'll even use a fragile little human as bait."

He lunged too fast for me to dodge. One of his arms pinned my hands at my side, and the other gripped my throat as he held my back to his chest. I couldn't breathe with the way he held me, and the pain warred with the panic of being trapped.

"I have your female, Kier," the Beast bellowed into the forest. "For every minute you make me wait, I'll remove a limb. Will you let her bleed for you?"

"I can't stop him," Bright snarled into my mind. *"He's coming for you."*

My eyes collided with Death's.

The esu was conscious, and staring at me.

"When Death moves, duck," Bright commanded me, speaking for her mate.

In the blink of an eye, he launched toward me and the Beast.

My heart lodged in my throat as I threw myself forward. The Beast didn't so much as blink at the weight of my effort—but then Death's body slammed into him, throwing us both backward.

His claws dug into my hip and throat, and a scream burst from me in response to the pain. Death tore into his shoulder, and with a snarl, the Beast threw me aside.

I slammed into a tree, *hard.*

The impact knocked the breath out of me.

I felt something crack—before I felt nothing at all.

When I landed on the jungle's floor on my back, my breathing felt shallow, and feeling slowly started creeping into my limbs again. It wasn't just feeling, it was *pain.* Insane, intense pain.

The scent of my blood flooded the air, and slowly, the pain grew more intense.

Shock clouded my mind as I watched Death fight the Beast. Both creatures bled and snarled, until a moment later, when Kierden and Bright joined the fight.

It was a flurry of blood and pain.

One simple, clear thought crossed my mind as I watched them tear into each other, claws colliding with fangs and swords of ice:

I was dying.

I had no future anymore.

If I sealed our bond I could give Kierden a chance of surviving *hundreds* of years.

And if I did manage to make it through by some miracle...

Well, I would want to spend my life with him. He'd proven that he was willing to try anything if it kept him at my side, including *farming*. And most importantly, he wasn't someone who would change his mind. After he said we belonged to each other, he never wavered. He would fight for us no matter how bad things became.

It would've been terrifying to promise him my life, no matter how long I knew him or how sure I was that everything would work out between us. A bond like that was so much bigger than I could ever understand from our side of the veil.

But there was so damn much hope in it, too.

Even if I was dying, even if I wouldn't see him until he joined me on the other side of the veil in a few centuries, I *wanted* that bond with him.

And I wanted to save his life.

So I parted my lips, and finally whispered the words that the bond had tried so damn hard to get me to say.

"Sillah ovim rett warum."

The handprint on my wrist burned.

The magic in my chest swelled.

I gasped at the pain, at the intensity—and then watched helplessly as everything faded around me, until the world itself was gone.

And perhaps I was gone too.

CHAPTER TWENTY-SIX
KIERDEN

I was covered in blood as I spun and slashed, fighting as one with my bonded esu and his mate.

Death and I had never fought a battle we couldn't win, but perhaps we'd finally found one.

At least when I passed, I would do so fighting for my female.

The Beast was gaining ground on us, wounding us more than we were wounding him, without waning in the slightest despite his own blood loss.

He was a monster, created by magic and fueled by it too. I was simply a warrior, honed through battle but kept alive by the blood and ice in my veins, the warring of life and death.

A whisper sounded behind me—one I shouldn't have heard with my focus trained on the fight. Nissa's voice, softer and weaker than it should've been.

"Sillah ovim rett warum."

Time slowed—and then went still.

Fierce pain burned through my palm—and then Nissa's magic burst to life in my chest, over my skin, and through my blood. It cleansed the dark magic of the brand on my hand as it knitted with mine, her life and my death.

Battle cries echoed through the jungle as my warriors launched into battle. I didn't know who had woken them, or how they'd found us. I didn't have time to be glad they were there, either.

Because as they charged the Beast, I staggered backward. I could feel the fading consciousness of my mate through my mind... and all the way to my damned soul.

She was dying.

My mate was dying.

Nissa was dying.

There was no time to think.

No time to consider my options, or pray to any of the lost gods who might still be listening.

I shoved through the mass of my warriors until I reached her. As I dropped to my knees, I didn't let myself look at her broken body, her bleeding wounds, or the sickly paleness of her tan skin.

There wasn't time for that either.

I sliced through the place my neck met my shoulder with one hand as I hauled her upright with the other, and dragged her face to my bleeding wound.

"Bite me, Nissa," I snarled into her mind and ear with every bit of force and power I had.

She didn't respond.

I refused to accept that.

Diving into our bond, I found the place our minds met. There was a thin wisp of a wall separating us, but I cut through it ruthlessly.

She could hate me for it later.

Later, when she wasn't going to die.

I wouldn't let her leave me.

"Drink my blood," I commanded her, all but taking control of her body with the force of my will.

Her body jolted slightly, and I held her face to my neck.

Finally, she swallowed.

It was the tiniest sip, but it was all the assurance I needed.

It was going to work.

She *was* going to survive.

"Again," I snarled directly into her mind. She couldn't block me out, not while I was inside her so damn intimately.

She took another small swallow.

"More, Nissa."

She drank again, again, and again, until she was sucking my blood down desperately, taking all I had to offer.

My energy faded as she drank, but veil, I couldn't have cared less about myself. As long as she was breathing, as long as she was *living*, I'd walk through that damn veil with pride.

"My fiery little human," I murmured into her mind, stroking her hair lightly as I turned so my back met the tree behind us for support. *"Our months together have been the best of my life. I love you more than I could ever find the words to say."*

Her beautiful eyes were cloudy as they collided with mine, and their appearance stunned me. One was the same gorgeous green it had always been, while the other was my dark blue. My chest burned with pride and relief as I slipped into unconsciousness.

She was alive.

And she was mine in this life, the one that had come before, and every damn one that would follow.

CHAPTER TWENTY-SEVEN

NISSA

"Veil. What happened?" Eisley's voice snapped me out of the daze I was in, staring at Kierden's face. His chest was still rising and falling, though slowly, and he looked paler than he should've. He was unconscious—but just unconscious, I hoped.

"I almost died," I rasped. I could feel Kierden's blood moving through me, *healing* me, but it would take time. "He saved me. Again."

"You saved him first. And then again, too," she pointed out, kneeling next to me and putting two fingers on his throat. She was checking for his pulse, I thought.

Near-death experiences were probably expected for her, at that point. After so many centuries of battle, it must've been inevitable. I supposed that was enough to keep anyone calm when another one arose.

"Slow, but healthy," she told me. "He'll be just fine." She carefully wiped at a bit of blood on my neck, her lips turning down in a grimace.

"Where's the Beast?" My head turned back to where he'd been.

"Even he wasn't fast enough to handle an army of fae warriors. When it became clear that he couldn't win, he took off. With the eclipse coming in a few hours, I doubt he'll attempt to return." Eisley's gaze dipped to Kierden's hand, and her gaze lingered. "The brand's already gone."

I nodded, still a little shaky. "Alida said if we sealed it, the brand would vanish. The connections are through magic, and our magic changed permanently when the bond solidified."

Her eyebrows shot upward. "Damn."

I looked back at Kierden, watching his chest rise and fall again just for the sake of my sanity.

Bright and Death shoved their way past the fae and stepped up on either side of me and Kierden, sniffing both of us as they pressed up against us. I leaned against Death a little, scratching Bright lightly behind the ears as my eyelids started to grow heavy.

"I think I need to rest," I whispered to Eisley.

"Let's get you back to the castle," she agreed, eyeing Bright and Death. Both of them had wounds and were bleeding in multiple places, but they seemed fine otherwise.

Death ducked a head under Kierden's arm, and Bright growled at him.

He stopped and gave her a long look.

She growled at him again, and he lowered his head toward her before he stepped up close to me and inclined his head. My arm went up over his neck, and Eisley lifted me onto his back as he bent down a bit.

My face buried into his fur, and I felt the warm stickiness of his blood against one of my arms as I carefully wrapped them around him.

"I'm sorry," I whispered to him, realizing why Bright had gotten mad at him when he tried to take Kierden. He was more injured than she was.

He licked my arm lightly, and my guilt softened.

"He still wants to help. Stubborn bastard," Bright grumbled as she bent down. Eisley helped shove Kierden's massive body onto Bright's back, and then Bright slipped into the jungle, her movements smooth and careful. A few bands of ice wrapped around her and the other four of us followed.

It took a lot longer to get back to the castle than it normally would've, but I didn't complain.

I was alive and well, and Kierden was too. We needed rest—probably a lot of rest—but we were okay. And that was what mattered.

When Death reached Kierden's room in the castle, I was shivering a little, and could barely keep my eyes open. He carefully placed me on the bed, and Bright did the same with Kierden. My side met his, and I curled toward him as my heavy eyes started to close.

"I'm going to bring you food soon and check on you frequently," Eisley warned me. She brushed a few strands of hair off my face, then placed the back of her hand against my forehead to check my temperature. "I don't know much about how humans heal, but you seem alright," she said. I thought it was more to herself than to me.

"I'm a fae now," I murmured to her, finally giving up on the fight with my eyelids. "Kierden's magic will have changed me in all the ways that matter."

She flipped my hair away from my ear and lightly tapped on the gentle curve of it. "Not here."

My lips curved upward slightly.

Kierden loved my ears.

She smoothed my hair back into place carefully, despite the blood and dirt in it. "Get some rest. I'll be back soon."

I was already lost to sleep.

Eisley woke me up to eat sometime later, and attempted to wake Kierden too. He didn't so much as flinch. When I reached out to his mind to make sure he was alright, I didn't feel anything concerning, so she gave up on it and left us to get more sleep.

· · ·

Kierden's blood must've worked well, because the next time she woke me up, I already felt much, much better. When we looked at my wounds, we were shocked to find them almost entirely healed. Though I still felt sore, I was no longer in terrible pain.

Bright and Death woke up just long enough to scarf down the food Eisley brought them, then fell back to sleep almost instantly when they'd finished.

Once again, we couldn't get Kierden to wake up. Eisley was starting to worry, though she was trying to act like everything was fine for my sake.

"I'm almost healed," I told her quietly, so I wouldn't wake the esu. "If he's not up in a few hours, I'll make him drink my blood the way he made me drink his."

"He'd kill me if I let you do that so soon after you've recovered," she protested. "I'm sure he'll wake up soon."

I didn't argue with her, because she was taking care of me, and I didn't want her to worry that I'd take it into my own hands. But I wasn't concerned with Kierden's potential anger; I could handle it. And if my wounds were healed, I wouldn't die if he drained me the way I'd drained him.

I nodded my agreement, eating the food she'd brought me quickly before handing her my plate. She fussed with my hair, the way she'd taken to doing, and then slipped out of the room.

Though I fell asleep quickly, I did so with one thought in my mind:

Making sure Kierden was alright.

The next time Eisley fed me and the esu, she was even more worried. I didn't mention her concern, because I was going to wake him up as soon as she left.

After the esu went to sleep and she slipped out again, I waited a few minutes to make sure no one else was going to barge in, and then I carefully rolled on top of Kierden. His wounds had only healed a tiny bit, but none were actively bleeding, so I hoped that was a good sign.

He didn't react to me laying on top of him, so I carefully leaned down, pressing the top of my shoulder against his lips as I reached toward his mind.

Instead of his mind, I found... him.

His whole *being*.

I shivered at the intensity of finding him there so completely. His thoughts and emotions were silent because of the deep unconsciousness, but it wasn't just his mind I'd found; it was his *soul*.

We'd have time to explore that part of the bond later, though. After we were both healed, and conscious.

"Kierden," I said quietly, into his mind.

His body stirred below mine, and a huge hand landed on my lower back.

"Bite me, Kierden."

He groaned beneath me.

When I repeated the words louder, making them a full-on command, he finally reacted.

His teeth sank into my neck, and I gasped at the intensity of the feeling. It didn't hurt at all—honestly, it was one of the most pleasant things I'd ever felt. It wasn't like the Beast's bite, where an unfortunate bliss washed over me. Instead, I just felt some mixture of joy, pleasure, and desire.

His hands found my hips as my life flooded into him. He'd given it to me first, though, so the trade only seemed fair.

Some amount of time passed; I wasn't keeping track.

But then he jerked his head away, gasping for breath and rolling me off of him.

The world spun around me as he snarled at me—I was getting a lecture, I thought—but I couldn't keep myself awake. My eyes closed, and I went back to sleep immediately.

"Nissa," Kierden growled into my mind. His hands were on my hips, and I felt my bare chest pressed against his. A thick blanket had been pulled over the top of me, but it didn't feel nearly as nice as the warm body I was laying on. *"You need to wake up and eat."*

"Hmm?" I struggled to rouse myself from sleep.

"Open those pretty eyes, little human." He still sounded angry at me, but I wrestled them open anyway—and then froze when I saw his eyes staring down at me.

One was his gorgeous dark blue... and one was my typical green.

"Veil," I breathed.

Kierden swept hair off my face, then leaned forward and kissed my lips softly. He pulled away before the kiss could grow intense, unfortu-nately, and growled, "I am *furious* with you."

I closed my eyes again. "Tell me later. I'm tired."

"You can sleep after you've eaten."

I sighed heavily.

"Thank you, Eisley. I'll make sure she eats," Kierden told his sister, in a voice much kinder than the one he'd been giving me. Guess I earned his anger by letting him drink from me so soon after my brush against the veil.

I opened my eyes long enough to wave at her, and she winked at me before she closed the door behind herself. She looked much calmer than she had the last time I saw her, so I was glad at least one person appre-ciated what I'd done.

Kierden plucked that thought right out of my mind.

"I *appreciate* you worrying about me enough to feed me your blood." He set my plate on my lap then picked up a sandwich and lifted it to my lips.

I reluctantly bit into it.

He added, "But you should've stopped me before you passed out. You should've snapped me out of it and made sure I didn't hurt you."

"It definitely didn't hurt," I said after I swallowed the food in my mouth.

He let out a long breath, leaning back against the bed's headboard. "You scared me, Nissa. Veil, I've never been so terrified in my damn life."

"You didn't seem scared. Just thirsty." Though I knew he was talking about my near-death experience, I would rather discuss the blood drinking.

He gave me an exasperated look, and I matched it with one of my own as I plucked the sandwich from his hand and took another bite.

He stared at me while I ate it.

I stared back at him.

Finally he shook his head and raked a hand through his hair.

I noticed the dried blood all over him, and the fresh skin where his injuries had been. "We need to bathe."

"I'm worrying about you," he growled at me. "Let me worry."

I put my plate on his lap and tossed the blanket off my body, turning a bit so he could see me. "Look, Kierden. I'm fine. My wounds are healed. My body doesn't hurt anymore."

"You're still pale and covered in dried blood." He tossed a hand toward me. "You were *dying*, Nissa. I felt you *dying*." The grit in his voice was a clear sign of what he was really worried about.

There was nothing I could say to take that memory from him, or to prevent him from worrying. But, I could prove that I was alright.

I slipped out of bed, patting Death's head lightly and scratching Bright behind the ears as I passed them.

Kierden set our food down on the bed and followed me across the room. "What are you doing?"

"Taking a bath. There's nothing like a pool of cold water to revive you after a near-death experience."

He scowled. "It won't feel cold to you. My magic is yours now. I—"

"Ohhhh." I sank into the water, closing my eyes.

Somehow, it felt *warm*.

I leaned back against the inner edge of the bathing pool. "This is even better than the hot pool."

"I know," he grumbled, reluctantly stepping into the bath with me. He had me seated on his lap a moment later, and I leaned against his chest as his arms wrapped around my abdomen.

"I'm sorry I almost died," I told him quietly. "That wasn't my intention. The Beast needed to kill you, and I hoped I could persuade him to leave me alive while Bright saved your life. It clearly didn't work as I hoped."

"Bright told me you were planning to offer yourself up as his mate," Kierden growled at me, his grip tightening.

"It was an option. But Alida told me just before I left that sealing our bond was an option too, so I wasn't rushing into offering myself to him. I didn't know if I was really ready for the bond, and I didn't want to force you into it when I wasn't sure you wanted it, but I was dying. I figured I might as well seal it to save you."

"Veil." He gritted his teeth.

I sighed, leaning my head back against his shoulder. "I'm sorry."

"No. I just—" he cut himself off, growling, "How could you think I wouldn't want the bond? How could you think I'd be *upset* about having your magic in my veins and your thoughts in my mind? I feel blessed, Nissa—so damn *blessed* to be your mate. I hate that I got you hurt, and I despise that I couldn't protect you from the Beast, but I am *thrilled* that you sealed the bond."

Emotion swelled in my chest, lodging itself in my throat.

There was a moment's pause before he admitted, "I probably deserve to die for it, but I'd do it all again if I knew it would bring me back to this moment. Holding you in my arms, smelling my scent on your skin, feeling your heart beating against mine... You're my mate, Nissa. My *mate*." He pressed his lips to my shoulder once, then again, like he just couldn't help himself. "It's surreal."

"It is," I admitted, and he brushed a kiss to my shoulder again. My emotions were thick and fierce, a verified whirlwind. But the strongest of them was relief.

Relief that he wanted me and wasn't angry I'd sealed the bond. That he hadn't changed his mind without the threat of the Beast hanging over our heads.

"Do you feel ready for the connection now?" he asked me.

"I think so? I'm not sure. If we had the option, I would've waited longer. Not because I doubted you, but because I worry I'll decide I want to leave your kingdom and become a nomad, or do something entirely different with my life, while you're tied to the castle."

"I'm tied to nothing but you now, little human. If you want to see all of Evare, we'll see it all. If you want to farm plants and continue growing an absurd amount of flowers all over my kingdom, that's what we'll do. You are my first priority—nothing and no one else. Eisley would be a better queen than I am king, anyway." He kissed my shoulder again.

My lips curved upward. I had no current intention to ask him to sacrifice his throne, but his words made me feel a bit better about my place versus his kingdom's.

"You'll feel more confident after you've recovered," he told me, running a hand lightly down my thigh. "I'm going to wash you, get you fed, and put you back to bed."

My smile grew. "That sounds nice."

"Mmhm." He kissed my throat, and then my cheek, before he started scrubbing me.

As he washed me, I decided that even if shared baths for the rest of my life were the only benefit of a sealed mate bond, I had made a very, very good choice in sealing ours.

CHAPTER TWENTY-EIGHT
NISSA

I slept for most of the the next two days. When I finally woke up long enough for more than a meal and a short conversation with Kierden, I found myself in bed with the gorgeous king, draped over his lap while he read a book.

"When did I become your table?" I murmured to him, looking over my shoulder at the edge of the book he had resting on my back.

He chuckled and his body rumbled against me, making me smile a little. "When you became my mate."

My body felt strangely warm.

A yawn stretched my lips. Kierden lifted his book when I slipped off his side, spreading my arms and legs out to stretch a little. I frowned at the increasing warmness in my body. And... wetness between my thighs? "Why am I horny?"

"Welcome to the eclipse, little human." He slid his hand into my hair and massaged my scalp lightly. I closed my eyes and groaned at the blissfulness of it.

"Has there been any sign of the Beast coming back?" I asked him.

"Luckily for him, no." Kierden's voice was playful, though we both knew it would be no laughing matter if the Beast really did come back. "A few of our warriors followed his trail back toward the Broken Woods."

"Oh, damn. I mentioned mating with a shifter when I was trying to buy time—you don't think he's actually going to do it, do you?"

"I think the shifters can defend themselves just as thoroughly as the fae can. Don't worry about them."

I sighed. "Alright."

"Reo dropped some new clothing off for you yesterday. I put it in our closet, if you'd like to see it," Kierden said, still massaging my scalp.

I sat up quickly. I'd finally stopped gaining weight a few weeks earlier, and my curves had been a little too much for the last batch of dresses. I was *dying* to know what he'd created now that he knew I wouldn't need something new in a few days—pun not intended.

"Let's go."

Kierden grinned, tossing his book to the bed as he slipped out from beneath the blankets with me. I grabbed his hand and towed him to the closet, halting in the doorway. My lips parted when I took in a full row of vibrantly-colored fabrics, in all of the same shades as my flowers. "I love them," I whispered.

Kierden laughed. "You haven't even tried them on." He opened a simple set of drawers and pulled out a pair of scanties, dangling them toward me.

I snagged them from his fingers, then grabbed the first dress I saw— one in the same shade of orange as my old favorite. Stripping out of the simple shirt I had on took all of one moment, and then I tugged the scanties on, followed by the dress.

Kierden followed me to the bathroom as I went to see myself in the mirror. He leaned up against the doorway while I stared at myself for a long, long moment.

I looked... good.

Healthy.

Strong, too.

The dress was cut perfectly to the shape of my body, with sections missing from the sides to show off my figure. The thin, soft sleeves hung off my shoulders and over my arms, and the part over my breasts was heart-shaped, emphasizing the weight of them.

"Veil," I whispered. Slowly, I lifted my eyes to meet Kierden's in the mirror. He wasn't looking at my face when I did, though. "What do you think?"

"It would look a damn lot better on the ground, with you bent over our bed," he said.

My lips stretched in a wide grin, my fresh scanties already damp thanks to the heat of the eclipse. "I'll take that as a compliment."

"You should."

My gaze dipped to his shorts. More accurately, to the fabric tented at the front of them.

My body warmed. "It's been a few days since we've had sex."

"Believe me, I know." The low tone of his voice made me hotter.

I grinned and tugged my dress back over my head. As I did so, my gaze caught on the handprint around my wrist.

My eyes widened as I finally gave it the attention it deserved.

The damn thing glowed, and it glowed brightly.

"Let me see your hand," I told him, tugging it out of his pocket without waiting for him to give it to me, and then staring down at the glow in wonder. "Damn."

"Miraculous, isn't it?"

"It's beautiful," I admitted—and then nearly choked on my own damn spit when he sent me a mental image of his glowing hand between my thighs as he pinned me to our bed and toyed with my clit.

Heat flushed my cheeks when the mental image progressed into a full-on fantasy of us having sex, his hand glowing against my body while we moved.

The eclipse must've been going for a while, if he was already fantasizing about me.

Then again, we'd been having a *lot* of sex before we both nearly died, so he could've just been horny.

He hooked his fingers in the waistband of my scanties and used them to tug me closer. My chest met his, and his lips curved upward. "The suns haven't even overlapped yet, little human—and the eclipse affects fae far more than humans. The wetness between your thighs is just the beginning."

Well damn, I liked the sound of that.

"So should we hold off as long as possible?" I checked.

He dipped his fingers deeper into my scanties, and my body arched as he dragged them lightly over my clit.

Veil, that was more intense than it should've been.

His gaze met mine, and there was a challenge in it. "I'd prefer to get an early start."

"It *is* our first eclipse together. We should make it count."

"Precisely," he rubbed my clit again, his touch still light. I leaned against him, my eyes closing as I grabbed his arms and held on. My body was far more reactive than usual—and it was always reactive for him.

"Veil," I whispered, my breaths coming out rapidly as I already neared the edge of my first climax.

Kierden slid a finger inside me, and I cried out, so damn close to losing it. His finger went still though, and his hand held my hips securely to stop me from using his hand.

I hissed, "Dammit, Kierden."

He chuckled, low and deep. "If you want pleasure today, you take it on my cock."

"Fine." I pushed his shorts down, freeing his cock. "Fill me, then."

His eyes gleamed, and he didn't wait for another invitation. He lifted me up and spun me around until my back met the bathroom wall, hard, as he ripped my scanties off and yanked me down on his cock. The motion was harsh, but with the eclipse already affecting me, it felt incredible.

"You feel so damn good," he growled at me, thrusting into me and taking me over the edge.

I cried out as the pleasure hit me—and then screamed when his teeth sank into my shoulder, dragging the climax out longer and making it insanely intense. His body quaked as he filled me with his release.

I sucked in deep breaths of air when I came down from the high. He released my shoulder, licking the wound clean before capturing my mouth in his. His cock throbbed inside me as he kissed me, our bodies still intertwined as our tongues danced.

His hands lowered to my ass, and one of his fingers brushed my back entrance. I sucked in a harsh breath as another one of his mental images hit me—this one, of me on my hands and knees in front of him. My legs were spread wide, his cock was buried deep inside me, stretching my wet, pink skin... and he held a cylinder of ice inside my ass.

"Veil," I moaned, as his fingers slicked over my asshole. We hadn't tried that yet, but he'd mentioned it in passing. I'd never thought I'd like it...

"You would love it," he growled, answering the thought I hadn't voiced. "There's nothing more intense."

"Prove it," I breathed.

He hauled me back to our bed and set me down on the edge, sliding his cock free before he kneeled in front of me. His pleasure dripped down my thighs, but I knew from experience that he didn't give a damn about the mess unless he thought it might bother me.

He parted my thighs, lowering his face to my core and tilting me back. My forearms collided with the mattress, but I caught myself as he said, "You'll take my finger first."

I opened my mouth to reply, but then his tongue was on my clit, and he was sliding a piece of ice shaped like his cock inside my channel. It wasn't cold; just smooth, and hard.

He worked my clit slowly with his mouth—I could tell he didn't want me to climax again yet, but enjoyed it anyway. His fingers dragged the slickness of our combined pleasure to my back entrance, and then massaged the sensitive skin there lightly.

My pleasure heightened with the touch, and heightened further when the slick tip of his finger stretched me.

I sucked in a sharp breath, and he stopped.

"Don't stop," I demanded.

He licked my clit again, but pulled away before I could climax.

I swore and bucked my hips as his finger sank deeper inside my ass, stretching me wider and wider. The need for release was borderline painful, but in a way I was absolutely feral for. I cried out as ice covered his finger, stretching me further.

"You are so damn beautiful like this," he said, leaning back to look at me. An image from his point of view hit me—my legs spread wide, my body bare, and my channel and back entrance both full of ice. My hips were rocking with need, and his hands were on my thighs, holding me in place.

"Don't torture me," I panted to him.

He chuckled, grabbing the ice in my channel and slowly sliding it free. "I feel your emotions bleeding into mine, little human. You love this."

He was right.

My hips bucked desperately against his grip, my body clenching around nothing as I snarled at him, "Give me your cock, now."

Kierden's eyes burned. "That's right, little human. I'm yours to command—don't forget it."

He flipped me onto my stomach with one motion and tucked my knees up beneath me, before he lifted my ass and slid home slowly enough to make me detonate.

I screamed, my body jerking as he thrust into me harder and faster. The ice in my ass swelled larger, and the pleasure was so intense I could've sworn I touched the veil.

When my climax ended, I collapsed to the mattress with a groan. The eclipse must've been beginning, because my body was somehow even hotter and needier than before.

Kierden slapped my ass lightly, and I shuddered. "How long is the desire going to last?"

"All day and all night. You'll be deliciously sore tomorrow." He thrust in and pulled out.

I shuddered again. "I already want more. This is absolutely insane."

"Soon, your thoughts will fade, and you'll do nothing but *feel*. Prepare to embrace the insanity, Nissa Jirev. You're my mate now; you'll never spend an eclipse out of my arms again."

Heat flooded my body, and I clenched around Kierden's cock, making him growl. "I like the sound of that."

"Good. Now, open your eyes and tilt your head so you can watch me slide in and out of your channel. I want you to see yourself climax."

More heat flared as I did as he said, and sure enough, I watched my body writhe with pleasure only moments later.

There was no thinking that day—only feeling.

And veil, I definitely understood why the fae celebrated eclipses.

CHAPTER TWENTY-NINE
NISSA

It was the middle of the next day before we finally made it into the dining hall, exhausted and sore, but ridiculously content. We talked with the elves—they were heading out later that day—and then chatted with Eisley and a few of the other warriors.

When we were done eating, we headed down to my farm with Bright and Death. They kept brushing up against each other's sides and making these adorable purring noises. Kierden flashed me a grin from where he was planting seeds, and I mirrored his with my own.

Our bonded esu went off together, leaving me and Kierden to the plants near the front end of my farm.

"Have fun," I told Bright.

She chuffed. *"Oh, I will."*

My grin widened.

We finished planting where we were, and then headed out on a short walk. He captured my hand, lacing his fingers between mine and lifting my hand to his lips as we went. *"Thank you for saving me,"* he murmured into my mind.

"You're the one who saved me, remember?" I tilted my head toward him, and a soft breeze caught my hair, dragging the long strands into the air. It made me think of Kaelle. The fae brought me news of her and Laeli when they returned with their empty carts after taking the extra produce to the other kingdoms, but they hadn't told me anything that made me think anyone really knew what was happening to the human women and their kings.

I liked to believe that they were determined enough to forge themselves lives that they loved in those kingdoms, but I'd reach out soon myself to make sure.

Kierden said, *"We saved each other on multiple occasions. It's a good way to begin a life together, though I pray to whatever gods still remain that you never have to risk your life for me again."*

My lips curved upward. *"I'll add my prayers to yours, then."*

He chuckled, and we continued walking. My eyes scanned the jungle above us, following the vines and flowers down every tree trunk. My magic had flooded everything with life, making the colors richer and the plants more energetic. The fruit grew thick and rich, the vegetables monstrous and full of flavor.

Like the jungle, I was still the same as I'd been in my mother's town. I had the same breath in my lungs and heart in my chest, but since I'd come to Jirev, I'd been brought to life.

Thinking of my town... I looked at Kierden. "Did you send your fae to raid my mother?"

His lips curved upward wickedly. "Of course I did."

I heaved a sigh, but it turned into a laugh as I shook my head. "No one died?"

"Not even your mother. My fae distributed the money and produce among the towns nearby that looked worse for the wear. I wanted to do it myself, but Eisley warned me that you may not forgive me for tearing out your mother's throat, so I decided to stay."

"Probably a good choice," I said with a soft smile. "Thank you. And for what it's worth, I love you."

"It's worth a great deal, little human." He leaned over and brushed a kiss to my cheek. "And I love you."

I smiled up at the flowers above me as we continued walking. My magic still emanated from me without my control, but something about it felt settled alongside our mate bond.

I couldn't wait to keep practicing with it, to see if I could learn even a shred of control.

It was a simple thing, really, to look forward to a future. But it was a simple thing I'd never had before—and one I would cherish for the rest of my life.

BONUS SCENE
NISSA—A FEW WEEKS AFTER THE ECLIPSE

"*This is a terrible idea,*" I whispered into Kierden's mind, as he sat me down on his lap in the corner of the dining hall. It was early in the morning, so we were all alone, other than the chefs in the kitchen. I'd finally met them a few days earlier, and they were ridiculously nice.

There was no way of telling how long it would be until someone else walked into the dining hall though—which was what made this idea terrible.

"*This is a fantastic idea.*" He set our plate down in front of us before dropping a hand to my thigh.

Dipping his fingers beneath the hem of my dress, he dragged them lightly over my clit, making me flush. I wasn't wearing any scanties, which had been his idea—and honestly, I supported it.

I grabbed a pastry off our plate and took a big bite of it to keep myself quiet.

Though I was in my longest dress, my longest dress was still extremely short, and that made our current escapade very, very risky.

"My good little human, already drenched for me," Kierden growled, slipping his fingers into my channel, then dragging them over my clit again.

I fought a groan. *"You're already hard for me, too."*

"I'm always hard for you." He rocked my ass against his erection, just a little.

He also wasn't wearing any undergarments. I was still unsure as to whether we'd actually be able to have full-on sex in the dining room, but we'd figured we might as well be prepared.

"Eat, Nissa." He snatched the pastry from me with his free hand and lifted it to my mouth.

I took a bite, choking on the food as I nearly inhaled it when he pinched my clit.

"You're so damn bossy."

He pinched me again. *"You love it."*

I really did love it.

He continued teasing my clit and feeding me. I gripped the edge of the table for dear life, letting him have his way with me as I edged closer to my climax.

Just before I lost control, he lifted my ass for a moment—and then slid me onto his cock.

I choked on a cry at the intense pressure of the tight fit. My legs weren't parted much, thanks to our position and my lack of undergarments. *"Veil."*

"So tight and slick," he growled into my mind as he moved my hips until he was fully sheathed inside me. *"You're too good to me, little human."*

My body trembled.

I wasn't sure I could put words together even if I tried.

His fingers found my clit again. *"Bite the bread and I'll let you climax."*

I bit it, and he worked my clit. His fingers stilled just before I lost control, and I started to growl at him—but then the doors opened.

A pair of male fae came in, their fingers intertwined and their hands glowing gold.

My body went stiff as a board while I tried to reign my need in, and Kierden tugged my skirt down, so it covered us both.

There would be no doubt about what was going on if they came any closer.

They nodded at Kierden, and he nodded back as they grabbed food from the kitchen and then settled in the other corner of the room.

They faced away from us as they ate, and my king's fingers slid to my clit again.

"This is so risky," I hissed at him.

"If you didn't love it, you wouldn't be soaking my cock right now." He sucked lightly on my throat. *"Give me a climax, and I'll let you go."*

I groaned silently. *"Kierden."*

"Nissa." He nipped at my shoulder. *"The longer you wait, the more people will show up."*

"We're going to be sitting here all day then," I said bluntly.

He chuckled. *"Alright. If they don't leave soon, I'll get us to an empty room."*

"Deal."

He stroked my clit slowly, and the pleasure began to build again. Whenever my gaze flicked to the men in the other corner, Kierden would send me a mental image of his cock sliding inside me—or of his tongue between my thighs—or of me, sitting on his face.

The heat built, and built, until I was nearly panting. I started moving my hips a little, clenching around his cock, and he picked up the pace on my clit.

Just before I lost it, the men at the table got up—already done.

I snarled into Kierden's mind as we both froze, and he lifted another piece of bread to my mouth.

I took a violent bite, and we both waved at the men as they left.

As soon as the doors shut behind them, Kierden flung a hand out toward them to freeze them shut. He did the same to the doors to the kitchen as he hauled me up onto the table, pushing the food out of the way. My tits met the wood as he slammed into me, and I cried out into his mind as my climax *finally* hit. He drenched my channel with his release—and then pulled out quickly, yanked my dress back down, and tucked his cock back into his shorts.

"We're leaving," he told me, grabbing our plate and leading me toward the door. My body was positioned in front of his to hide his erection. He pulled the ice down from the doors with a glance at them, opening everything back up.

A big group of people stepped in just as we stepped out, and Kierden grunted a greeting at them as we passed.

He led me into the room nearest to the dining hall. The door shut behind us—and then our plate clattered to the ground as Kierden pinned me to the wall. He kissed me, his mouth brutal on mine.

"That was so damn sexy, little human," he growled into my mind. *"You were perfect."*

He released my mouth, then dragged me to the ground. *"You're going to sit on my face now. I need to hear you scream."*

My face flushed. "I—" I began, but he cut me off with his tongue and teeth on my clit as he held me against his face. A cry escaped me at the first sensation, and then I was lost to the pleasure.

He definitely got what he wanted—but honestly, so did I.

EPILOGUE
KIERDEN—MANY YEARS LATER

"Swords out, swords out, swords out," I bellowed at the hoard of small, yelling warriors who sprinted through the castle's hallway. Our children loved running around like wild animals— and we loved watching them grin like madmen.

The violent events we held to keep the peace every year were going on in the stadium, but Nissa, Kaelle, and Laeli had convinced the other kings and I to spend the day watching our children run around together instead.

It hadn't taken much convincing at all.

"The gourd king has risen!" Ravv barked, as we jogged behind the kids. "Go, go, go!"

We came around the corner, and found Nissa's forehead wrinkled furiously. Her hands were held out toward the massive yellow gourd as she focused her magic on it. Control was still a struggle at times, but she had figured it out for the most part.

All of the kids started hacking at the large, squishy vegetable with their dull icy swords, shouting insults at the *"smelly, rabid beast"*.

I pushed my magic toward Nissa, and she flashed me a quick smile as she took a hold of it. The gourd king swelled even larger, growing just as lopsided as I knew she was hoping it would.

The kids yelled with renewed fury and swung harder and faster, throwing in some punches and kicks too.

"He's falling!" one of my boys hollered. "Harder!"

I tugged Nissa away from the massive vegetable, pulling her back flush against my front just in time for our little warriors to defeat their monster.

Cheers of victory erupted from them, and they started jumping, dancing, and laughing about the king they had slain.

"You're so damn perfect," I murmured to Nissa, brushing a kiss to her cheek.

"I know, I know," she teased me.

I squeezed her tightly, thanking the veil that the Beast had sent me running toward the little human who had brought me more happiness than I could've ever imagined.

THE END
(Keep reading for a peek at Laeli's story, Dark & Dreadful Brutes, and
Kaelle's story, Dark & Deadly Predators!)

DARK & DREADFUL BRUTES
BRUTES
LAELI & RAVV'S STORY

To all the fairytales that ended with just one kiss

CHAPTER ONE
RAVV

I stared at the city in the valley below, watching the streets as humans flooded them. Though the city was smaller than my own, it must've had ten times the population.

And I needed to find one human female among them.

My lips flattened in a line. If there was a way to survive that didn't require taking a mate—such as cutting off a finger or three—I would've done it without batting a damn eye.

But no amount of sacrifice would deter the assassin hunting me. My only chance was a human woman with magic that could hide mine.

So I had to take a mate.

Temporarily, of course.

I gave the city one last look, cursing the elf who sent me after the female, before heading out to find her.

CHAPTER TWO
LAELI

I scrubbed my filthy dress with a rough bar of soap, wondering how I'd been so damn unlucky.

Most people had *some* amount of bad luck, but me?

Mine had yet to be good.

The dented metal bucket I scrubbed my dress in was shallow, and the water in it was filthy, yet I scrubbed anyway.

"You're taking too long," Jern grumbled behind me. Like me, he was a human with magic. Unlike me, he had dark brown skin and a mass of curly blue hair. I was pale, with long hair that was either red or orange, depending on the angle you looked at me from. While his eyes glowed electric blue, mine were the same reddish-orange as my hair.

Both of us were equally skinny thanks to starvation; we were locked in a glorified cellar beneath our kingdom's castle.

It was *below* the dungeon.

And since the floors were dirt, everything was filthy.

Everything.

"Move faster, Laeli." Gora smacked me on the arm, and I flashed her a glare. All I had on was my scratchy undergarment, but it covered all the important bits. It didn't smell great, but we'd get clean clothing in a few days.

I'd rather wait it out than sit around naked while my undergarment dried. Nudity led to discomfort, and discomfort led to losing control of my magic, which was not an option.

Gora was nearly as pale as me, with shaggy brown hair and small eyes that glowed an intense greenish-black.

I said, "I'm really damn tired of the two of you teaming up against me. I would never have supported your relationship if I knew it was going to lead to *this*."

This, meaning, me being the odd woman out. Constantly.

Having to stare at the walls of our jail every time they kissed.

Having to lay in the bed above theirs while they made love.

Veil, if I never had to think about someone having sex again, it would still be too soon.

The veil separated our world from the next, and was commonly used as a curse word.

Some part of me was happy for Gora and Jern, but I would've been much more enthusiastic about their relationship if I wasn't forced to witness every single moment of it.

"Don't boil the water," Gora warned, grabbing the bucket and dragging it away from me.

I scowled at her before looking down at my hands.

Steaming already—just my damn luck.

My magic was absolutely uncontrollable. I radiated heat constantly, up until I felt any kind of strong emotion. When the emotions hit, I turned into a walking campfire.

It was lovely. Very, very lovely.

If one appreciated being on fire, that is.

Which I didn't.

Because of my magic, our beds were stone.

Our walls were stone too.

The books we'd been given to entertain ourselves were hidden beneath a thick, plastic sheet that was meant to protect them if I caught on fire. It didn't happen often, though the steaming hands were damn near constant.

I heaved a sigh.

"I'll get the soap off your dress. Jern, want to read for her?" Gora looked at her lover. Err... betrothed? They planned on getting married the moment we were free, though none of us knew if that would ever happen.

"As long as you'll move faster than she does."

The couple exchanged grins.

"Stop being so nauseatingly adorable," I mumbled.

They laughed together, and Jern grabbed the book we were partway through. I wasn't allowed to hold the books, to make sure I didn't accidentally destroy them, but my friends didn't mind reading aloud for me.

As much as I complained about them, they kept me sane.

Jern started reading. I only heard a few words before I got a strange feeling.

My hand lifted to my chest as my heart started to sort of... hum.

I looked around the room, but saw nothing except our usual stone beds and dirt floors.

"Do you feel that?" I asked the others, interrupting Jern rudely. My hand was still pressed to my chest—and the humming in it seemed to grow louder.

"No..." Gora looked slightly concerned.

All of our heads jerked toward the thick stone door, and we all went silent as we watched something that looked a lot like *ice* crawl over the surface of it.

The ice spread and spread—until it shattered.

All of us ducked, throwing our arms over our heads as chunks of rock and ice flew everywhere. A few of the sharp bits hit my exposed skin, but none of them hurt too badly.

When I lifted my eyes, my body went still.

I was steaming—*definitely* steaming—but there was a man in the empty doorway.

The biggest man I'd ever seen.

He was tall and strong, made completely of muscle that looked chiseled from stone. His eyes glowed an angry violet color, and his light skin was covered almost completely in sharp-looking shards of ice. His blond curls were wild, and the tops of his ears were pointed.

He was a *fae*.

But we were in the human lands, a long way from the Endless Wilds that the fae supposedly called home.

So, what was he doing in our jail cell?

And why did he look so angry?

A massive white bear stepped into the room behind him, and my eyes widened at the sight of it.

Its shoulders were a few inches taller than the fae's head—and its eyes glowed bright pink.

All magical creatures in Evare had glowing eyes, so the bear must've had magic. Or it was magical, in some way.

"I've been looking for you for *hours*," the fae growled.

I had no idea who he was talking to.

Gora and Jern clung to each other. Their magic wasn't the defensive or offensive kind. Not instinctively, at least. Gora could move wickedly-fast, and Jern could lift small objects with his mind sometimes.

"Get up." The man grabbed me by my bare, wimpy bicep—then he wrenched backward as a sharp electric current sliced through my arm where he'd touched me.

I gaped at my bicep as a silver handprint slowly appeared on my skin... and then started to glow too.

The fae snarled the words, *"Sillah ovim rett warum."*

Though I didn't recognize the words, it felt like some buried, ancient part of me did.

They rolled through me, and I took in a long, deep breath as I felt something vital inside me begin to *change*.

Where my magic's fire burned in my middle, something else slowly pooled. Something cold, something like... ice.

All fae had ice magic, if the legends were true, but how was it possible for the man's magic to join mine in my veins?

We should've been opposites. We should've—

Heavy footsteps sounded in the hallway outside our prison.

The fae man wasted no more time.

He plucked me off the ground by my waist, tossed me onto the bear's back, and then jogged out of the cell. I gripped the bear's fur for dear life as it started to run behind the fae.

Veil, they were fast.

I managed to lift my head and see over the bear just in time to watch us collide with a *wave* of humans.

The fae was already cutting through them, spinning and slashing with claws of ice on his hands, elbows, and shoulders. Every inch of him swelled with thicker, sharper shards of it.

The humans were too slow to defend themselves.

They should've run while they had the chance.

A few of them did as the fae reached the end of the hallway, and he let them go.

Then he flashed a scowl over his shoulder.

I knew he wasn't scowling at the bear, but at *me*.

Gora and Jern caught up to us, wheezing and gasping. They'd stepped over the bodies of the humans without batting an eye, and I didn't blame them.

Being held captive for a decade really reduced the amount of empathy you felt for the people who could have freed you.

"You need to run!" I called to them. If the bear wasn't so damn tall, I would've tried to get off its back. But it was massive—and the fae had said he was looking for *me*, which meant he wasn't going to just sit by and watch me run away from him.

Even if he did, the bastard could catch me easily.

The bear I was riding took off down the hall.

I shrieked, gripping its fur even tighter as it skidded around a corner.

It ran hard for a moment, roaring loudly as it burst through a set of doors. The smell of burning fur met my nose, and it occurred to me that I might be burning the creature.

Panic hit me hard, and I let go quickly.

When I let go, I lost my balance, and flew off the creature's back.

My world tilted before I could scream.

I landed hard on my side, and then rolled.

My back slammed into a wall, and I saw stars for a long moment.

Somewhere off to my side, I could hear the bear and fae roaring and snarling. Humans were yelling, too.

When I managed to crack my eyes open, though, the only thing I saw was my thick red-orange hair, my undergarment, my body, and my flames.

Somehow, my bad luck had even managed to wreck the fae's rescue.

Granted, I wasn't sure he considered it a rescue. Perhaps he was abducting me.

There were worse things in the world than being abducted by a gorgeous fae man, though.

Like being locked in a dirt and stone cellar for ten years.

Closing my eyes, I took a deep breath in.

My flames didn't burn away the clothing I was wearing when I caught fire, just as they never burned me. I supposed I needed to consider that a blessing.

But when I got worked up enough to actually catch fire, that fire wouldn't vanish until it managed to drain my energy completely. It knocked me out for most of a day while my body recovered from the intensity of the magic.

Since the fae had touched me, I felt... different, though.

As I leveled my breathing, I opened my eyes again so I could watch my flames begin to shrink.

They'd only been open for a moment when a gorgeous, furious face leaned over me.

I blinked up at the fae man.

He glowered at me. "Stop your fire and end the pull on my magic."

I blinked again.

"She can't stop the fire," Gora said from somewhere behind the fae.

I didn't turn my head to look at her.

Something inside me said that looking away from the man who was legitimately *soaked* with other people's blood would be a bad call.

The fae turned his glower on the couple I'd been forced to live with for far too long.

Jern cleared his throat. "She can't control her magic. It drains her when it wants—and when she catches fire, she burns until it knocks her out."

The fae's attention jerked back to me.

I felt something crawl over my arms—and shuddered when I looked down at myself and realized it was ice.

It spread over my skin, killing the flames as it went.

I breathed rapidly when it closed over my throat. It was just a thin layer, but panic warred inside me anyway.

My fire burned hotter, melting through the ice in a heartbeat.

The fae man swore.

"Her flames react to her emotions. You'll have a better chance of killing the fire if you can calm her down," Gora added.

"We don't have time for this." The fae man scooped me up off the ground and tossed me over his shoulder. My face crashed into his back, and he ran. My flames didn't seem to burn him, which was lucky for him and not particularly great for me.

A moment later, I was squeezing my eyes shut to hide them from the sunlight that washed over us. The warmth from all three of our suns kissed my exposed skin, since I was still wearing nothing but my undergarment.

It felt good.

Veil, no. It felt *incredible*.

And the fae's warm, bare back felt even better.

Until he started running, and my face slammed against it. "Don't leave Gora and Jern!" I cried out, ignoring the stinging in my eyes.

He didn't stop.

Cries and screams echoed through the city as he sprinted through, moving so fast that I doubted anyone could even make out the shape of him well enough to see who and what he was, or why he was on fire.

The man must've run for half an hour, weaving through the city and then up into the barren mountains that rose above the valley.

I was lightheaded—and still burning—when he finally slowed and then stopped beside a small river.

I eyed the water, in too much shock at seeing the real world again to put together why he'd decided to stop there in particular.

He tossed me into the river, and a screech escaped me as I plummeted in.

I hadn't swam since I was a kid.

Would he let me drown?

Why had he gone to the trouble of saving me just to throw me in a river?

The water engulfed me, nowhere near as cold as it could've been. My shoulder brushed soft sand, and I realized how shallow it was.

I'd be fine.

The fae wasn't trying to kill me.

At least, not *yet*.

As if to emphasize that point, he grabbed the back of my undergarment and hauled me onto dry land again.

I gasped for air, my knees knocking as my bare feet hit the ground hard. My fire was out, by some miracle.

The fae growled at me like an animal, grabbing my waist to hold me upright. The motion put our chests fairly close to each other, but I didn't let myself think much of it. He was just trying to keep me from falling over. "Why are you so weak?"

"I was in a cellar for ten years. They barely fed us." My chest still rose and fell rapidly as I sucked in air, but I didn't catch fire again. "You'd be weak too."

His anger faded just the tiniest bit.

"Where's your bear? Did it grab my friends?"

He glared at me. "She's not a *bear*, she's an idorr. And her name is Gleam."

I blinked.

That was... not what I expected to hear.

"What's an idorr, then?" He'd pronounced the word eye-door, so I made an effort to do the same.

"A magical animal much stronger, faster, and smarter than its distant relatives, the bears. They form a mental and soul-deep bond with some fae, becoming our life companions."

I blinked again. "So... you're married to a bear?"

At least he wouldn't want to have sex with me.

Then again, he was gorgeous. Maybe I should've been mourning that fact.

"No," he growled. "To be bonded with a beast is to be connected as friends. Gleam has a mate."

Oh.

"And you don't?"

"Enough questions," he snarled at me.

"You don't get to yell at me for not knowing something and then yell again when I try to learn," I shot back. "*You're* the one who abducted *me*."

"I *rescued* you."

"You and I both know you had some selfish reason for showing up where and when you did. And it probably has something to do with this." I gestured to the silver handprint on my arm, and then to the matching one I'd noticed on his palm.

He glared at me.

I glared back, waiting for an explanation.

Finally, he said through gritted teeth, "It's a mate bond."

Damn.

That was *not* what I expected to hear.

"A *mate bond*?"

"Yes. It appeared when I grabbed you, which means fate has decided for whatever reason that we're meant to be together. I spoke the words necessary to complete my side of the connection—don't repeat them or we'll end up stuck together permanently."

Veil.

"I don't even remember what you said."

Even as the words left my lips, something in my mind whispered,

"Sillah ovim rett warum."

"Good." He jerked his head to the side. "Gleam is here. Prepare to say goodbye to your friends."

"Where am I going? You'd better not kill them."

He flashed me a dark look. "How do you intend to stop me?"

A shiver went up my spine as my magic threatened to surface again.

He released me and strode away.

I wobbled a bit, but managed to stay upright as I followed him down the river's bank. We found his bear—err, idorr—companion setting Jern and Gora on their feet by the river.

The fae scratched his idorr-friend's head, and she rumbled happily as she licked him in the face.

I *must've* imagined the curve of his lips in response to her, because he was a grumpy bastard.

Gora and Jern pulled me in for massive hugs, both saying something about how glad they were that we were all alive and free. I murmured my agreement, though I was still eyeing the fae guy who was apparently my mate.

What *was* a mate, though?

He'd used the word the way I would use husband, and there was no way a handprint could be a marriage.

Right?

The fae guy untied a bag I hadn't noticed hanging from a branch. He must've hidden it in the trees before going into the city, because he didn't bother digging through it before he slung it over his shoulder.

Jern and Gora hid me behind them protectively when the man rumbled, "Time to go."

His eyes narrowed at them when they stepped a bit closer to each other, concealing me completely.

"Laeli stays with us," Gora warned.

I bit my lip.

It was sweet of them to try to protect me, but the fae bastard had hunted *me* down. I didn't know why he had, but I didn't think there was a chance he would leave without me after killing his way through the damn castle to find me.

The man didn't try to cut their throats for disagreeing with him, luckily. Instead, he said, "If you want food and directions to the nearest town, she stays with me."

The couple was silent for a moment.

All three of us were starving. We wouldn't make it far at all without food, even if the fae *wasn't* hunting us down. Which he would be, if we all tried to leave together.

"We can't go to the nearest town," Jern finally said. "Not with our eyes glowing. We'll be dragged right back to the king's cellar."

"I can't take you back with me," the fae said flatly.

"Coarse can take you back to Loire," a feminine voice said into my mind. The way Gora and Jern jumped a bit told me they'd heard it too. *"He's my mate, and he's only a few hours behind us."*

I assumed the voice belonged to Gleam, the idorr.

"We don't need humans in Loire," the fae growled. "They can find a damn human town to take them."

"How long were you imprisoned?" Gleam asked my friends, ignoring the fae.

"Five years for me. Eight for Jern," Gora admitted. "Laeli was there for ten."

The idorr made a noise of sadness. I peeked over Gora's shoulder to watch as Gleam plopped down on the dirt. *"We'll wait for Coarse."*

"Thank you," Jern said. "Laeli needs to stay with us, too."

"Oh, no. You two smell like mates; you can understand that Ravv and Laeli need to stay together." She draped her head over her paws.

I assumed Ravv was the angry fae man's name.

"Mates?" Gora looked over his shoulder at me.

"The handprint thing." I didn't bother looking down at it.

Seeing it glow on my arm kind of freaked me out, honestly.

When I looked over Gora's shoulder again, I saw Ravv with his eyes narrowed at Gleam, who remained where she was without budging an inch. Something told me they were arguing mentally.

Ravv finally dropped his bag beside the idorr and then stormed into the forest, disappearing from our view.

I stared after him.

"Maybe we'll get lucky, and he won't come back," Jern muttered.

Clearly, he was uneducated as far as my bad luck went.

"He's coming back," Gleam said pleasantly. *"There's food in the bag. When Ravv returns, he'll bring more."*

None of us hesitated to open the bag, or to scarf down half the contents like the starving, wild animals we may as well have been.

My upper arm ached for some reason while he was gone—where the handprint was, actually—but I ignored the pain in favor of a full belly.

CHAPTER THREE
LAELI

When Ravv returned a few hours later, there was another idorr at his side. The newcomer was even bigger than Gleam, and his face was twisted in an angry scowl.

Us humans were snacking on fresh berries we'd picked from a bush near the river, our bellies full as we leaned up against a tree. Gora and Jern were holding hands, their shoulders pressed together, and Jern had been fighting a smile for *hours*.

"Stop being so damn adorable," I grumbled at them, the same way I always did.

Except when they were having sex.

Then I just tried to ignore the sounds and the way the bed shook beneath me.

Ignoring it usually failed, and ended up contributing to my sex aversion.

At least *they* had enjoyed our time in the cellar as much as possible.

I stood up and dusted dirt off my ass. My undergarment was still the extent of my clothing, though it was significantly cleaner after my dip in the river.

The angry idorr growled as he stormed over to Gleam. He prodded her with his nose, sniffing, grumbling, and making frustrated noises. She rubbed the side of her face against his fur as he moved, her own noises resembling amusement.

Though I itched to ask what was going on, I didn't want to make either of the grouchy males any angrier, so I stayed quiet.

Gleam said, *"Gora and Jern, you'll go with Coarse. He'll protect you until you get to our city, Loire, and then he'll make sure you're fed and clothed."*

She pronounced the city's name *lore.*

My friends stood behind me, murmuring their thanks and eyeing the angry idorr with a bit of worry.

I was kind of nervous he'd eat them, but it seemed unlikely after how kind Gleam had been. Then again, being eaten by an idorr was probably better than spending another decade in the cellar.

Or at least it was for me. The couple would probably disagree.

"Where are you going?" Gora asked Ravv.

"Jirev," Ravv said flatly, pronouncing the word, *jeer-ev.*

Gora and Jern exchanged looks that I didn't have to read to know they were wondering where Jirev was.

"It's another fae city. Ravv is needed there for the next few weeks," Gleam said smoothly. *"You'll be reunited soon."*

Veil, I hoped she was right.

And I really hoped she didn't intend for me to share a room with Gora and Jern when I got to Loire. Honestly, I'd share with Ravv before them.

It had been way too many years.

"Thank you," Jern said, as he gave Gleam a small smile. He pulled me in for a hug and squeezed me tightly, murmuring, "Do whatever you have to, to protect yourself from him."

"I'll be fine," I whispered back.

Gora wrapped her arms around both of us, squeezing tightly. "We'll see you soon."

My eyes didn't water.

They would later, when everything set in... but for now, I was still in shock that I was outside the cellar and sitting in the forest. The suns were still shining down through the trees, and it felt surreal.

It took them a few minutes to get up on Coarse's back, and Ravv finally had to haul them up by their clothes. Ravv then scratched Coarse behind the ears, and the big, grumpy idorr rubbed up against Gleam one last time before he gave her a warning growl. He looked at me, and his vibrant eyes lingered for a long, long moment before he turned and took off into the forest.

Coarse moved just as fast as Ravv, if not faster.

As soon as he was gone, Ravv shot me a look that said I was about to get threatened.

I raised my hands in surrender. "I'm ready."

His hands landed on my hips when I reached him and Gleam—but instead of lifting me, he gave me an irritated rumble and said through a clenched jaw, "You reek."

"I've been in prison for years," I shot back, my defenses rising. "Dirt and sweat are inevitable."

"I don't mind dirt and sweat." He swept me off my feet, hauling me back to the river.

"Then what's your problem?"

"The smell of your male."

My eyebrows lifted. "Jern is not *mine*."

He muttered something that sounded suspiciously like, *"he'd already be dead if he was,"* before he tossed me back into the river.

I came up sputtering and angry. "What is *wrong* with you?"

A bar of soap came sailing toward me, and I barely managed to dodge the damn thing.

It disappeared into the river with a soft plunk, and I stared after it in disbelief.

There was a splash as Ravv dove in after it.

I groaned, staring up at the sky and asking the veil why my life always went this way.

Would it really be so bad if things worked in my favor just one time?

I'd traded a cellar for an angry fae man, and...

Well, fine.

Ravv was much better than the cellar.

Perhaps I'd had a small stroke of decent luck.

He surfaced with the soap and stalked toward me. Somehow, he managed to look threatening even in the middle of a river, holding a bar of soap.

"Turn around," he said.

I turned around.

His soap met the top of my head, and I winced at the pressure. "Too hard."

He grunted but eased up enough that it felt nice, instead of painful.

"I can wash myself," I told him, as his soap and fingers deftly worked through the thick length of my hair. "You don't even know me."

He ignored my offer and statement.

My eyes closed as his fingers massaged my scalp.

It was truly a bizarre moment. I stood in a river, with a gorgeous fae man cleaning my hair, while Evare's suns filled the sky with light above my head.

Part of me wondered if I was dreaming.

But I clearly remembered the escape. And when his soap and fingers moved down my arm, I clenched my jaw as they ran over the bruises there.

"How long until you heal?" he asked.

"I don't know. Depends how much I eat, probably." I paused. "Did I hurt Gleam? I didn't mean to catch on fire."

"No, she has thick skin. You just burned a little hair."

"It'll grow back," she offered, from where she sat on the dirt.

I grimaced anyway, dunking my head into the water enough to rinse the suds from my hair. "I'm still sorry."

"Take your clothes off," Ravv said, lifting his soap back to my hair and starting all over again there. I had to imagine there was more dirt than one scrub could take care of.

My body stiffened. "We are not having sex. I don't care what the hand-print means. I have a sex aversion."

I didn't know if a sex aversion was really a thing, but I was making it a thing.

"I'm not propositioning you," he growled back. "Your clothes are filthy."

"Oh." I considered it.

The bastard was right—I was utterly disgusting.

I turned my back to him and started undoing the front. The water rose to my waist, so my ass was well-enough hidden that I didn't think he'd see much. "Alright, as long as you're not going to grab me or anything. Do you have spare clothes in your bag? I'd rather not walk around in my undergarment."

"That's an undergarment?"

"Mmhm. What do fae women wear under their clothes?"

"Significantly less fabric."

My face heated.

He'd probably been with hundreds of women.

He was probably *ancient*. He wouldn't even be interested in my body.

"Humans are strange," Ravv grumbled.

"You're the one who showed up in my city without wearing a damn shirt. That makes you the strange one." I tugged my undergarment the rest of the way off. "And I guess that means you don't have spare clothes."

"Only shorts and pants. I'll find you something in the Timeless Sands when we pass through." He plucked my undergarment from my fingers and started scrubbing it with the soap.

My face warmed a bit. "I've never even imagined going that far. How long will it take us to get there? Will we go through the Broken Woods?"

"About three days on Gleam's back to the Sands." He continued scrubbing, making much quicker work of it than I would've. "We're far enough west that we'll dodge the Woods."

I sighed.

I'd always been curious about the Woods.

"Don't be disappointed. The shifters are assholes."

"How?"

"Here." He handed me the soap. "Unless you want me to scrub the rest of you." His eyes gleamed.

I ripped the soap out of his hands, ignoring the obnoxious warming in my nether regions at the wickedness in his gaze. "I'm good."

"What is a *sex aversion*?"

Heat bloomed on my cheeks. "I think I made it up. Maybe it's real; I don't really know. But I was trapped with Gora and Jern, and they were all over each other constantly. I started to dread any mention or thought of sex, and labeled it an aversion to make me feel better about the constant cringing."

He barked a laugh. "Veil."

"Right? It's nothing against them; I'd feel the same way listening to *anyone* having sex so frequently. The bed would literally rock beneath me." I shuddered.

"It was prison and torture in one, then."

"Yeah." I finished scrubbing myself, and handed him the soap. "At least it's over."

He slipped out of the river, taking my underclothes with him and wringing them out. I considered asking him to hang them over a branch or something so he could look away while I dressed... but decided against it. Ravv hadn't made me feel unattractive or self-conscious, and he probably wasn't attracted to me anyway, so there was no reason for modesty.

He had made that comment about cleaning the rest of me, but it was probably just a joke.

I started climbing out of the water, and he was quick to offer me a hand.

When I lifted an eyebrow at him, he rumbled, "So you don't cover yourself in dirt. We'll be riding close enough that your dirt will become mine."

Right.

Ravv squeezed one last bit of water out of my clothing, then gave it to me. He turned away without me asking while I wrestled myself back into my wet undergarment, letting out a relieved huff when I finally fastened it again.

He grabbed his bag off the ground, filled it with some fruit he'd gathered while he was off in the forest, and then threw it over his shoulder again. "Let's go."

I agreed and headed over to Gleam. She batted a big eye at me, and then licked my knee.

My lips curved upward. "Is there any particular way to climb on without hurting you?"

She let out a chuff that reminded me of a laugh. *"You aren't heavy enough to hurt me."*

I didn't bring up my flames.

It was difficult to get my leg up over her back, but I maneuvered myself up with a bit of effort. I was breathing fast when Ravv landed behind me without any effort at all.

Those long legs were a huge advantage.

"You'll need to communicate with Gleam mentally while she's running," he told me, lifting me forward about a foot and then pushing me down until my chest was pressed to her back. He gave her a friendly rub, and she made a happy noise. "Not all beasts can or choose to speak mind-to-mind with someone who isn't their companion, but Gleam does. You and I can communicate mentally too, but I'd rather not. Just tap my knee if you need to stop."

I nodded, and he leaned down with me until his chest rested securely against my back and his arms wrapped around me. I noticed a mark glowing crimson on the back of his hand, but the glyphs embedded in the marking were in a language I couldn't read, so I assumed it was some kind of fae magic.

Gleam walked for a moment, before she started to *run*.

Veil, she was even faster than I'd realized. The wind whipped my hair behind and around me, and my lips stretched into a grin as my exhilaration grew.

A few hours earlier, I'd been trapped in a small stone room with dirt floors... maybe my luck had actually started to turn around.

We ran for hours.

The excitement of it died down as my back started to get sore. The blissful comfort of having Ravv pressed against me didn't fade, though. He braided my hair for me and tucked it in the back of my undergarment at one point, but neither of us commented on that.

When my stomach rumbled, we slowed long enough for me to gorge myself on some fruit and crackers he pulled out of his bag, and then started running again.

By the time we stopped for the night, I was absolutely exhausted.

"Do we just sleep on the dirt?" I mumbled to him, as I plopped down on my ass and stretched my legs out in front of me. My face scrunched as I reached for my toes, pulling on my tight muscles.

"No, you'll sleep in an ice shelter."

I nodded, my eyelids growing heavier.

Hopefully the ice didn't feel cold.

I'd probably melt it whether it did or not.

"Do you catch fire in your sleep?" he asked.

"Nah." I lowered my head to my knee, letting my eyes shut just for a minute.

"Laeli." There was a slight growl to Ravv's voice, and his huge hand landed on my shoulder. I thought the touch was gentler than I would've expected, but I could've imagined that.

When I didn't lift my head, a thick arm slid under my legs.

I felt the ground disappear from beneath me, and leaned up against the fae's warm chest as he carried me.

Something hard met my back. Some part of me registered that it wasn't my stone bed, but it was a small part.

I relaxed against the ice, drifting off quickly.

I woke up in a pool of warm water... with an ice wall above my head.

A huge drop of water plopped onto my eye.

I attempted to wipe it away, but another one landed in the middle of my forehead when I did.

"Guess it's time to get up," I mumbled, lifting myself up onto my forearms in an attempt to find a way out.

I saw... five walls.

Panic swelled in my chest. "Ravv!"

The wall over my head slid away, and an exhausted, scowling man appeared above me.

"I thought I was trapped." I dropped my head back into the puddle. Water flooded my ears, but at least I could see the trees above me.

"You wrecked my shelter."

"I improved it. Every shelter needs a bathtub," I mumbled back.

He scoffed at my joke.

"You're grumpy," I said.

Then again, it seemed like he was always grumpy.

Maybe there was a different word for it, if it was a constant state.

He disappeared from above me.

I forced myself to get up, and winced as I climbed out of the shelter.

Yeah, I was absolutely drenched. My hair dripped water everywhere—including down my face.

I yanked it out of my eyes as I looked around for Ravv—and found him stuffing more fruit into his bag. None of the suns were up yet, but I could see the tiniest sliver of light through the trees, marking the beginning of the first one's rise. "Did you sleep at all?"

He didn't answer me.

"He didn't," Gleam murmured, stretching out her long, heavy legs.

"Why not?"

"He doesn't trust the human lands, and you were out of his sight."

Rav growled at the idorr, and she chuffed, lowering her head back to her paws.

"Should we sleep together in the shelter tonight?" I asked.

"Yes," Gleam said, at the same time Ravv growled, "No."

I blinked again.

"I don't want to wake up in a damn bathtub," he said, closing his bag and throwing it over his shoulder. "Let's get moving."

Gleam and I exchanged knowing looks.

We would get him to sleep in the shelter.

Or at least, she would.

Ravv lifted my sore body onto his bonded idorr's back, and we ate silently while Gleam walked.

Despite my exhaustion and soreness, and the fact that I was soaking wet, I found myself smiling as I watched one of the suns rise while we went.

So much for having terrible luck.

CHAPTER FOUR
LAELI

When we stopped for the second night, Ravv had to literally peel me off Gleam's back.

"Veil," he muttered, easing me into the ice shelter he'd created.

"Just leave me in this cold coffin to die," I mumbled back.

He hid his snort with another scoff. "You're not going to die tonight. Your muscles are just sore."

"Being trapped in a cellar does not prepare you for days of riding an idorr."

He made a noise of agreement, and started to ease away from me.

I dug my fingers into his arms. "You have to sleep too, so you're not grumpy tomorrow."

He grunted. "Ow."

I dug my nails in tighter. "No leaving."

"Fine." He grumbled, but maneuvered himself beneath me.

His body was way more comfortable to lay on than the ice. I relaxed against him, my body warming when I felt his erection against my lower belly.

He *was* attracted to me.

Bet he didn't expect that—a gorgeous fae man, being attracted to a human.

Maybe it was because of our mate bond. He still hadn't told me why he'd created it, but I assumed there was a reasonable answer. Eventually, I'd get it out of him or Gleam.

"Damn, you want me," I whispered.

"Go to sleep," he growled at me.

My lips curved upward, but I went to sleep. We'd probably wake up in a bathtub together, but I didn't mind. His body felt good against mine, and as stupid as it probably was, I trusted him not to do anything I didn't want him to.

The next two days went the same way, and on the fourth night, we camped by a river on the border between the Broken Woods, Timeless Sands, Aching Chasm, and Human Lands. The place we stayed was slanted down toward the Sands and the Woods, making it easier to see the land around us.

When I peered into the Broken Woods, I got to see the massive, dead-looking trees and reddish-brown dirt I'd been curious about since I was a kid.

The Timeless Sands stretching in front of us were made up of massive dunes in every shade of yellow, white, and orange.

The Aching Chasm was only identifiable by the way the ground had slowly started to morph from green to crimson. Eventually, the land would give way to a monstrous drop-off that went further than any being's eyes could see.

Honestly, I was grateful we were headed to the Endless Wilds rather than the Chasm. I shuddered to think about what it'd be like to go inside *that*.

"Eat before you fall asleep," Ravv said, handing me more food than I'd be able to eat in one sitting. Though he was clearly attracted to me, he hadn't done anything that made me think he was interested in pursuing that attraction, so I hadn't brought it up again. "All of that."

"I'm not that hungry," I protested, stunning myself with the admission.

How had I gone from *starving* to *not that hungry* so fast?

Then again, we'd eaten seven or eight times throughout the day. I was fairly certain Ravv was lying about being hungry during most of those meals, but I wasn't going to complain about him feeding me.

"I didn't ask if you were hungry. Eat it."

His eyes narrowed at me.

Mine narrowed back.

But after a long moment, I finally gave up and dropped my gaze.

He could win that one.

I ate while he used his magic to build the shelter.

"You'll sleep alone tonight," Ravv told me.

"No. I'm not sleeping in the watery coffin alone," I said bluntly. "If one of us wakes up in a hot bathtub, we both do."

He scowled at me.

I met his scowl with my unyielding stare.

It was his turn to give in.

He made me wait a long, long while before he finally jerked his head in a nod. "Fine."

"Fine," I repeated.

We washed up quickly before we went to bed together, and I didn't acknowledge his erection at all.

Or the way his arms wrapped around my back.

Or the way I wanted to grind up against him when I woke up.

Maybe my sex aversion wasn't real after all.

When we entered the Timeless Sands, I quickly realized how much I hated sand. It got in my eyes and constantly stung my skin as we ran, making me agitated. That agitation led my power to drain my energy faster as I radiated more heat, making all of us miserable.

"We need to stop at an inn or something. I need a break," I rasped to Ravv during one of our short food breaks. He had filled a large bowl with water for Gleam, and passed me one of his many water skins, making me grateful he had a bag full of supplies.

"We can't stop," he said.

I waited for an explanation, but it didn't come.

"Ravv," I protested.

"Laeli," he mimicked my tone.

I gave him a dark look.

He mirrored that too.

"You said you'd find me something better to wear." I gestured to my undergarment. "That requires going into a city, at least."

"The Timeless Sands aren't safe," he growled back. "You'll stay far outside the city—even while I get your clothes."

I heaved a sigh.

He really wasn't going to change his mind on that.

So finally, I agreed.

We rode for a few more hours before we stopped, and he built an ice shelter for me. After he herded me inside it and threatened not to give me my new clothes if I tried to leave, he headed to the nearest city on foot.

Gleam and I chatted for a few minutes before my exhaustion lulled me to sleep. It was only the middle of the afternoon, but veil, it had been a long few days.

A strange soreness and then *pain* in my arm woke me up shortly after Ravv left. It started as an ache, but graduated into a painful throbbing —and then an excruciating *stabbing*.

The pain was so bad it became a struggle just to breathe.

My heart pounded rapidly, and the heat radiating off me swelled.

The shelter was already dripping all over me. I didn't know how long it would last before holes started appearing in the structure, giving way to the heat of both the suns and *me*.

My mouth dried, and sweat dripped off me alongside the water falling from the ceiling like rain.

Veil, it was *scorching*.

I tried to reach out to Ravv's mind the way I did Gleam's, since we were supposed to share a mental connection, but I failed. We'd never talked mentally before, so I didn't know how to find that bond.

"Laeli." Gleam's low growl distracted me from the pain for a moment. *"There are raiders coming. Stay inside the shelter while I kill them."*

Fear made my stomach clench. *"What are raiders?"*

"Groups of humans and magical beings who roam the Timeless Sands, looking for things and people to steal. Slaves only exist in the Sands, but some of the most ruthless creatures in Evare rule the cities here. Ravv didn't want you to worry."

Veil.

"Do you know how to fight?"

She scoffed, reminding me of Ravv. *"I've fought beside my king and my mate for centuries. The fae are warriors, and so are their companions."*

Her *king?*

I hadn't heard of an idorr king, but growing up, I'd heard a few stories about fae kings and queens, so it wasn't difficult to believe that the idorrs had leaders the same way their fae companions did.

"Okay," I whispered back, my teeth chattering a little. *"But the shelter is melting."*

And the pain in my arm was driving me toward insanity.

She swore. *"Try to stay calm."*

Considering my agony, sweating, and trembling, that wasn't a possibility.

The heat was going to continue.

"Is Ravv coming back?"

"He's just reached the city. I'm not telling him about the raiders until they're gone."

That did *not* seem like a good idea. *"He needs to know."*

"He'll abandon the city to get back to us, and we can't let that happen. If we walk into Jirev without something to cover your arm and his palm, his people will kill you both. There's no way he can reach us in time, anyway. I'll protect us."

Veil, we were in trouble.

Something told me this was going to go very poorly.

I tried to lean into that fear, because the fear was less terrible than the pain in my arm.

A whimper escaped me as the pain grew worse.

My heat flared, and sunlight filtered into my shelter through a hole in the roof.

"Shit," I whispered.

"You'll be alright," Gleam promised.

I didn't believe her, but there was nothing else to do about it. If I caught on fire, it could knock me out—and being unconscious in a melted shelter could definitely lead to me being abducted by someone far worse than Ravv.

A battle cry sounded outside the shelter, and my body tensed as I heard Gleam roar in response.

The awful sounds of swords clashing with claws and claws slashing through skin had me squeezing my eyes shut.

There was a cracking sound, and when my eyes flew open, I found a man with red eyes and horns grinning wickedly.

Demon.

He had to be a demon.

There were a few kinds of demons, and dragons were known as demons even though they technically didn't meet the qualifications, but—

He slammed the butt of his sword into the wall of my ice shelter.

Cracks ran through the ice from the first hit—and when his sword hit it again, it *shattered.*

I screamed as ice shards rained around me. My fire ignited, melting them before they could crash into me.

The demon pulled away from my flames, snarling something to another one of the raiders.

Another man jogged toward me, and I rose on shaky legs.

I needed to run.

The demon stepped in front of me as I threw a foot over the edge of the shelter.

"You come with us," he said, eyes gleaming viciously.

I knew I should've run *toward* him—he was afraid of my fire, because not all demons were fireproof—but I couldn't.

I just couldn't.

I shrunk backward as the other man reached me.

The pain in my arm increased exponentially, and my knees knocked together. I screamed and crashed to the ground, landing back inside the remains of the shelter, still burning.

"She'll be useful in the forges," a gravelly male voice said, as the skin of the man in front of me transformed to thick, gray stone.

Gargoyle.

He was a gargoyle.

Veil, all they needed was a sea dragon and an angel, and they'd have a whole damn party.

The man with the stone skin plucked me off the ground and threw me over his shoulder. It reminded me of the way Ravv had carried me out of the city, but it hurt much more.

Ravv must've been gentler than I realized.

The gargoyle hauled me away from the ice shelter, and I saw a snarling, fighting Gleam.

Though a dozen corpses surrounded her, some kind of magical bindings were around her neck and legs—and there were so many men and women holding those bindings that I didn't think she stood a chance at escaping.

My screams died down as I was carried toward a massive cage on top of a cart.

Veil, were they going to cage me?

Some traumatized, terrified part of me shrunk further at the reminder of how helpless I'd been for so much of my life.

And now, I was right back to where I'd started.

I tried again to find my connection to Ravv—but the pain in my arm grew too intense, and I cried out for a moment before I lost consciousness, unable to fight the fear and pain any longer.

CHAPTER FIVE
RAVV

I gritted my teeth against the stabbing in my palm as I tucked the food, clothing, and other supplies for my female into my bag.

I hadn't been able to resist the urge to buy her things she never would've had in her land—or in her cell.

I wasn't supposed to feel a thing for her, and yet I found myself *liking* her fire. She wasn't afraid to speak her mind to me, and she was blunt about the horror of the mistreatment she had survived.

And the way her eyes lit up when she was happy?

It was becoming my weakness.

At least she couldn't feel the same pain with our separation that I was dealing with. I'd heard that a mate bond's physical urges were more difficult for a male to fight than a female, and that was a mercy for Laeli, because the damn things were going to drive me mad.

Mad with lust.

Mad with the desire to slay everyone who'd mistreated her.

Mad with the itch to hold her in my arms until she'd told me every damn thing there was to know about her.

Veil, even mad with the need to find the male she'd been trapped with —who had clearly been in love with the other woman—and make sure he knew who she belonged to.

"I'm heading back," I said to Gleam. We'd been communicating throughout my journey, so I could keep track of my bonded companion and my mate.

She didn't respond immediately, but I didn't let myself worry yet.

I picked up my pace, and finally, the pain in my palm eased just slightly. *"Gleam?"*

She still didn't respond.

My abdomen clenched.

Ice crawled over my hands, forming the claws I'd need to fight even though I was a few hours from the females.

I wasn't through the city yet, but I started to run anyway. *"Answer me,"* I snarled into Gleam's mind.

"Okay." Her voice was groggy. *"We're okay. I think."*

Veil.

"What happened?"

"Raiders. They took us to a camp of some kind."

I swore viciously and picked up the pace. *"How? Are you hurt? Is Laeli hurt? Why didn't she reach out to me?"*

It didn't surprise me at all that Gleam had stayed quiet about it. I was too far to do anything, and she would've thought she could handle the situation.

I would've thought so too, frankly.

"You told her not to speak to you mentally, and we're both fine. Laeli's on fire, and it looks like her energy is waning, but I don't smell her blood. They drugged me with something, but I'm awake now. I don't think we're far from where you built the shelter."

If we'd stopped near them, it wasn't a shock that they'd come out to see who we were. They would've taken one look at Gleam, realized how much money she'd be worth in their damned trading rings, and done whatever they could to get her.

"I'm coming. Let me know if anything changes."

"Alright." Her voice was still groggy, and I knew she'd need to rest. It would take time for whatever they'd drugged her with to wear off. *"Be careful."*

I found the glimmer of fiery magic in my veins and followed it to Laeli's mind. It took a few minutes, but I had nothing but time as I ran toward the females. Relief had me letting out a long breath when I finally found her mind. *"Laeli,"* I rumbled.

"Ravv?" Her voice was barely a whisper, holding none of the fire I'd come to expect from her.

"Tell me what happened," I growled. *"Has anyone touched you?"*

Images flicked through her mind and into mine rapidly.

The melting shelter.

The demon destroying the walls.

The gargoyle carrying her.

Her fire burning as they caged her.

The bars of the cage melting.

Her being dragged back out—and chained with metal that was melting over her wrists, burning her skin with every damn drop.

My breathing grew ragged. Not because of the running, but because of what had been done to her.

"They will all die," I snarled at her.

She didn't respond—and I felt her pulling away.

"Tell me what your male did in the cellar when your fire grew uncontrollable," I demanded.

"I told you, he's not mine."

"Laeli," I rumbled angrily.

"Jern and Gora would read to me," she whispered. *"Tell me stories. Recite poetry from books."*

I couldn't read to her—and I couldn't have thought up a poem to save my damn life.

But I had stories.

Veil, I had more stories than most people could imagine. It was rare for me to share one, preferring privacy over friendship outside of a few people I trusted, but if it would help her, I'd give her as many stories as she wanted.

"Gleam and I went foraging out on the glacier Loire is built upon," I began.

"Loire is the kingdom we're going to?" Laeli interrupted. Though her voice was still soft, her interruption told me she was going to be alright.

"Yes. All of the city's buildings and many of the decorations are ice," I confirmed. *"The glacier it's built on is massive, with many, many miles of peaks and valleys. There's ocean around the outer edges, where some fae fish for sport. We release the fish to avoid angering the sea dragons below, but there's still sport in trying to catch them. Laeli?"* I hadn't heard her in a moment, and it worried me.

"I'm listening."

"We weren't looking for anything in particular, just a moment away from everyone, to breathe," I explained. *"Gleam was distracted by a flying critter as she ran. You may not have realized it yet, but she can be very distractable—it worries Coarse constantly. She started following the critter, and managed to fall into a crevasse. My heart about broke through my chest as we plummeted."* I paused, waiting for confirmation that she was there.

"I'm listening," she said quickly.

"I managed to morph one of the walls as she fell, so the fall became a slide. I nearly lost my head when we finally reached the bottom of the crevasse and

the slide flung Gleam across the space. Rather than colliding with more ice, we slowed, and then stopped."

"There was a room inside the crevasse?" Laeli asked, her voice much more alert than it had been a few minutes earlier.

Though my fear still blazed brightly, satisfaction melded with it. *"Not just a room, but another city. We'd known one existed beneath the surface of the glacier but had never seen it until then. We found ourselves at a pair of gates made of ice, but the guards in front of them refused us entry seeing that I wasn't mated."*

"They only let mated people in?"

"Yes. It's a haven for the mated. In Loire, mated fae are often killed, so the city was established to protect them."

"Veil. So you're taking me there when you get me out of here?" Laeli was coming back to life in my mind, which gave me immense relief.

"No. We'll have to keep our bond a secret until it breaks with the eclipse."

"Oh."

There was a long pause.

I didn't know why I felt the need to explain myself, so I squashed the urge and remained silent. If I told her who I really was and why the secret had to remain, she would look at me differently.

And for some ridiculous reason, I didn't want her to look at me differently. Not yet, at least. Not until I'd had more time to... veil, I didn't even know what.

To hold her while we slept?

To feed her?

The bond would drive me to continue doing both those things until our connection was broken, so that wasn't it.

I supposed I didn't want to admit the truth, whatever it was.

She interrupted my thoughts. *"How far away are you? And do you know how to kill a gargoyle? They have a gargoyle guarding me."*

"Of course I know how to kill a gargoyle; I'm a fae warrior. All of Evare fears our fighting prowess."

"It was a reasonable question. All you have is ice, and he's made of stone. You broke my cellar's door, but a door isn't a person."

"Ice can break any kind of stone with enough effort. Even a gargoyle."

"Good. That's good." She sighed. *"How far?"*

"Two hours," I admitted.

"I hope my magic doesn't knock me out by then. I'm feeling really weak. The pain in my arm is fading a little bit, at least. Does your silver hand hurt?"

"The distance is causing you pain?" I demanded.

"I think so."

Veil.

"I didn't know it would hurt you, but I'm coming back. Stay conscious; I don't want you unconscious with strange men," I growled at her.

"If I could order myself to stay conscious, I would've done it years ago."

"Alright, I'll come up with another story." It took a moment to think of one that wouldn't lead to more of her questions.

"Tell me about fishing. I'm curious," she said.

Fishing was plenty safe, so I launched into a story about the first time Gleam and I had gone fishing—and I even found myself enjoying the conversation.

But my purpose remained—I would find my mate and my bonded idorr, and I'd free them both. We'd get back on the road to Jirev so I could eventually get my people back home... where we'd have to deal with the civil war.

Two hours later, I told Laeli I needed her to be quiet as I approached the camp. Both of the females I sought would be hidden at the center of the space, protected from intruders. And both would draw attention in their own ways, so it didn't matter which I freed first.

The last sun was almost fully hidden by the horizon, but that wouldn't affect the visibility for any magical beings.

Speed was my main advantage, outside of skill. Most magical beings were faster than humans, but other than the elves' assassins, none were faster than fae. Our speed, paired with our brutal strength and centuries' worth of battle, made us a threat to even the strongest magical beings.

I made it halfway through the camp before the first guard noticed me.

His first mistake was making eye contact.

His second was not crying out a warning to his people, because my claws severed his head from his body without giving him the chance to make a third mistake.

I removed the heads from two more guards before one of them finally had the sense to yell that they had an intruder. His head joined his friends', but by then, there was an unorganized group of raiders sprinting toward me.

"They're coming," Laeli warned me.

"I'll handle it. Don't distract me," I growled back, launching toward the first raider. He reeked of shifter, until the icy spikes on my shoulder caught him by the throat. With one sharp roll, they cut through his heart too, and then he smelled of nothing but blood.

The next raider was in her fox form when she launched toward me.

She fell just as quickly as the first.

I cut through the rest of them, one after another. They weren't warriors; they had no experience with war, or those of us who'd been trained to kill as we learned to walk.

The bodies remained behind as I ran toward Gleam's roaring. Their friends could bury them if they thought the men and women deserved it.

"Get Laeli and get out of here," Gleam snarled into my mind.

I ignored her, just as she knew I would.

My steps slowed when I found two men and a woman holding knives to Gleam's throat.

The men were demons, and the woman smelled like an elf, though her hair was chopped short and her clothing wasn't the long, flowing dresses the magical women usually wore.

"Any closer and we kill your idorr," the woman warned. She was on Gleam's back, her arms around my beast's neck and her blade already cutting slightly into Gleam's throat.

The men stood beside her with their weapons, close enough that if Gleam hadn't been restrained by the magical ropes holding her down, she could've bitten their heads off.

They were fools.

I lifted my hands as I tapped into my magic and formed three spears with my ice.

With one rapid motion, I slammed the ice into the raiders' chests.

The men collapsed to their knees, and a roaring Gleam flung the woman from her back.

I bent down and made quick work of her bindings.

"Are you alive?" Laeli whispered into my mind.

"I'm fine."

"The gargoyle grabbed me and ran."

I snarled, *"What? Why didn't you say something? Has he hurt you?"*

"No, I'm fine. Just being hauled deeper into the dunes. And you told me not to bother you."

"Still on fire?" I barked.

"Yeah."

I threw a leg over Gleam's back, and she shook her fur out before taking off in the direction we could both smell Laeli's scent. *"We're coming."*

"Thank you," she whispered.

"Don't thank me for getting you captured."

"Technically, you captured me first."

I growled into her mind, *"I saved you."*

"By capturing me."

"You're my fated mate. I claimed what already belonged to me."

She scoffed. *"I am not an object to be claimed."*

"No, you're a person to be claimed. By me," I said bluntly.

"Sometimes you're a real bastard, Ravv."

"Most of the time." I leaned closer to Gleam.

"No, you're decent most of the time. Just growly and grumpy."

My grumpiness was an attempt at putting distance between us, but Laeli seemed determined to cross that distance.

If I let myself care too much about her, it could lead to both of our deaths.

My people... veil, I didn't even want to consider what they'd do to us.

"Can you keep talking to me? This gargoyle guy is holding me really tight, and it's going to terrify me if I'm not distracted." Though she tried hard to sound playful, I could hear the fear in her voice.

I snarled again, *"He's going to die."*

She didn't reply.

"Laeli?" I demanded.

"I'm here. I just don't want to talk about murder."

She was going to have a hard time fitting in with my people, then.

"More about fishing?" I growled at her.

"Sure. I liked your fishing story."

I launched into another story about fishing, silently urging Gleam to run faster.

CHAPTER SIX
LAELI

I was starting to think the bruises on my legs might become permanent fixtures on my skin when Ravv finally went silent for a moment.

His silence could only mean they'd caught up to me.

"The moment you're free, run for Gleam," Ravv said. His voice was the kind of calm that would worry anyone with half a brain.

I nodded, my throat swollen with fear.

Helplessness was not pleasant. Not pleasant at all.

Gaining some amount of independence, and then losing it when I was captured, had me questioning everything.

Mostly myself, though.

The gargoyle holding me stumbled, and then went down hard. His body landed on mine, and I cried out.

I could practically feel the bruises developing.

Ravv collided with the gargoyle, and both men rolled off of me. I gaped at them as ice blocked stone and stone blocked ice.

My eyes could barely keep up with them.

Gleam's nose bumped my face. When I glanced at her, she grabbed the back of my undergarment in her teeth and towed me away from the fight. She released me before my fire could burn her, thankfully.

Ravv and the gargoyle moved dizzyingly fast, but the gargoyle was clearly slower. When he turned, I saw a thick shard of ice sticking out of his back—and I watched in fascination as he slowed further, and the ice expanded.

The gargoyle finally went stiff.

He slowly crashed to his knees.

Ravv stepped back and waited there until the man's body was on the sand.

The gray in his skin slowly gave way to the paleness he'd had before he shifted.

Ravv finally created an icy spear in his fist, and then stabbed it into the man's chest.

His body didn't budge; he had been dead before it hit him.

Though my stomach churned, something told me that double-checking was necessary with a gargoyle. Ravv hadn't been violent without reason, yet.

Satisfied that the man was dead, Ravv stormed back to Gleam's side. He lifted me to my feet before he dropped his bag and kneeled in front of me, grabbing my leg.

"What are you doing?" I checked, uncertain but not entirely against the way he was touching me.

"Looking at your wounds," he growled back. "That bastard hurt you."

I glanced down at my leg, and grimaced as I looked at all of my bruises. A few were clearly shaped like handprints—ones that didn't glow, thankfully.

Ravv didn't say another word as he lifted and turned my legs one by one, inspecting them.

He checked my arms out next—and then lifted my hair to look at my back and neck.

The look in his eyes was not a happy one when he finally stepped around to the front of me and started undoing the laces on my undergarment. He didn't pay my fire any mind, since it had never tried to burn him.

"Uh, what are you doing?" I asked him again, though the answer was still obvious.

"Checking your wounds." He didn't even look up from what he was doing.

I plopped a hand down over the laces. "No, you do not have permission to strip me naked. Next time, ask."

He finally looked at me. His eyes held enough silent fury to make me reconsider what I'd said. "You're hurt. It's my fault. I need to see the extent of the damage."

I blinked.

I wasn't...

I mean...

Did I really care if he saw me naked?

No, I decided, I did not. He was ancient, and undoubtedly had plenty of sexual experiences. And he'd proven that he could keep his hands to himself when we slept together at night, so... I trusted him.

Enough to strip, at least.

I finally pulled my hand away.

He made quick work of the fasteners, and then stripped the undergarment off my body. I flushed a little at his attention, despite the ache in my entire body, and by some miracle, the fabric didn't burn.

I tried not to react as his gaze scanned my flame-clad figure clinically, looking at my wounds without paying any attention to the rest of me. My body heated when his gigantic hands landed on my hips and carefully turned me around so he could see my back.

When he released me and stood, his motions were stiff and uncomfortable. He walked back to the backpack he'd dropped next to Gleam, picking it up silently and digging through it.

When he pulled out a long-sleeved dress and some tiny strips of fabric, I frowned. "My flames will probably burn that."

"Not if I'm holding it." Ravv grabbed one of the strips of fabric—it resembled two triangles sewn together, with a few extra bits of glorified string—and maneuvered the glorified string bits over my arms. He adjusted a band of it around my back, and then fastened it between my nearly-nonexistent breasts.

I stayed silent, my body flushing at the contact between his knuckles and my breasts.

He stepped my feet into the other undergarment one at a time, pulling it into place over my ass and lady bits. Then, he slid the dress over my head and slipped my arms through. The fabric was insanely soft and clung in all the right places, form-fitting enough that most human women wouldn't have even considered wearing it.

It fell to my feet, which I thought would make riding with Ravv and Gleam a bit difficult—but Ravv's ice sliced through the skirt, then, cutting its length to the middle of my thighs.

"I don't know how you're preventing that from burning," I told him, as he stepped backward and gave my dress a critical look.

He turned me around with one hand, his gaze lingering on my body. He ignored my remark and said, "You're already gaining a bit of weight."

My face warmed.

I started to say something in my defense, but before I got the words out, he added, "You look good."

The compliment caught me off guard, and I went silent.

He added, "Mates can heal each other by exchanging blood. If you're still bruised by the time we reach Jirev, you'll drink my blood to recover."

I didn't know what to say to that, so I changed the subject. "I can't ride on Gleam's back, obviously." I was still on fire, so that was out of the question.

"No." He hauled me off my feet, with one of his arms beneath my knees and the other around my lower back. It was entirely different from the way the gargoyle had held me, and made me feel closer to him, somehow.

My face pressed to his chest, and I realized the intimacy of it didn't bother me at all.

I trusted him... more than I probably should've.

Enough to relax against him as he started to run.

The sweat and sand coating his skin didn't bother me anymore. If anything, they made me feel safer.

Because they meant that Ravv had come after me when someone tried to take me captive. And someone willing to protect me without stopping to question it was someone I never wanted to walk away from.

Ravv ran through the darkness for a few hours before he finally slowed and then stopped. There were deep circles beneath his eyes, and exhaustion in his shoulders.

He built us a shelter with the last of his energy, then collapsed inside it without so much as a mention of me sleeping alone.

My fire was still burning, so I just sat down on the sand.

After that much running, there was sand everywhere. In my mouth. In my eyes. On my skin. Under my nails.

I may as well have been made of the damn stuff.

"Are you alright?" Gleam asked me, plopping down a few feet away from me. She was just far enough that my fire didn't have a chance of reaching her, which I was immensely glad about.

"I don't know," I admitted, pulling my knees to my chest and wrapping my arms around them.

I had finally started to feel a little less powerless, and then...

My eyes moved over the hand-shaped bruises on my legs.

My sight at night was much better than it had been in the cellar, which I assumed had something to do with my connection to Ravv.

"Get in here so I can close the damn shelter," the male fae growled at me.

I was experienced enough with his grumpiness that my lips curved upward just the tiniest bit.

I rose to my feet slowly, then stepped over the ledge of the shelter and slipped inside. He pulled me down into his arms and held me securely against his chest as he closed us in together.

His ice skimmed my arms and legs, the touch slow and comforting as my chest pressed to his. I felt my flames flicker a few times, before going out entirely.

A long breath escaped me when they were gone. "I don't know how you did that."

"Your magic recognizes mine as its mate." His fingers skimmed my arm, and his erection throbbed lightly against my lower belly.

A few long minutes passed in silence before I said quietly, "Thank you for rescuing me."

"You're my mate. I protect what's mine." His voice was low and gravelly.

For a moment, I let myself believe our connection would be permanent.

Just for one breath, I let myself picture what it would be like if I had the grumpy fae at my side for the rest of my life.

Veil, the idea nearly made my eyes burn.

I wanted that. Someone to protect me. Someone to rescue me when I was taken. Someone to put my fire out when I couldn't do it myself.

"Why did you come for me?" I whispered, a few minutes later.

But by the time the words left my mouth, it was too late. He was already asleep.

I squeezed my eyes shut.

Though it took some time to wind down after everything that had happened, I eventually managed to fall asleep.

We woke up just a few hours later, then started to move again. Gleam seemed more rested than Ravv and I, which was a good thing since she was the one running.

That day and night passed uneventfully. We reached the Endless Wilds in the middle of the day after, and awe struck me as we barreled into the massive jungle.

The trees stretched up so much further than I could see, wrapped in thick vines and sprouting monstrous leaves. The colors were more vibrant than any I'd ever seen, and I found myself watching the scenery go by with much more interest than I had in the Human Lands or the Sands.

Gleam stayed on the jungle's floor, which meant weaving around trunks the size of houses back in my city, along with all the other plants we had to dodge too.

I didn't feel at ease in the jungle, but I vastly preferred it to the desert.

We stopped by a river that night. The water was moving rapidly, and Ravv warned me that there could be predators within, so he carried me in and kept one arm wrapped firmly around my middle. We both scrubbed ourselves clean quickly.

The cleanliness was worth the fear. I felt like an entirely new person without all that sand coating me. My body was still extremely sore and achy, and my bruises were only getting uglier, much to Ravv's irritation, but I hadn't been abducted by anyone new in two whole days. That felt like a victory, as ridiculous as it was.

Ravv and I climbed into his shelter together, still damp but also warm and sticky thanks to the jungle's humidity. I curled up in his arms, and he pulled me into his possessive grip.

"You're going to drink my blood tomorrow," he told me, his voice low but not unsteady in the slightest.

"That didn't sound like a question."

"It wasn't one. Your bruises look even worse today."

I rolled my eyes. "That happens with all human bruises. They look worse before they get better, and healing takes time."

"I'm not walking into Jirev with a bruised mate. Every fae we see will assume *I'm* the one who hurt you."

"You said the mate thing has to be a secret."

"It does."

"Then you can just tell your friends that I tried to run away from you or something. I'm sure your people don't care about humans," I said flatly.

"I would never hurt a weak, fragile, human woman," he growled. "You'll drink my blood. This discussion is over."

I scowled. "I have no desire to drink your blood. I'm not a damn *vampire*, Ravv. Even if I did want to, I'd probably vomit if I tried."

"Exchanging blood is intimate for mates. It's a way to provide each other with life. The moment will be erotic, not nauseating."

I blinked.

And then blinked again.

Sharing blood was *erotic?*

Maybe I did want to try it.

I'd been fighting my body's attraction to Ravv since the first day we met. Maybe acting on it just a little would remove the temptation altogether.

"How erotic?" I asked.

I wasn't really ready to jump in head-first, but why not dip my toes in?

I still didn't trust Ravv completely. There were too many things I didn't know about him for that. He hadn't even told me why he'd come looking for me, or why he'd made me his mate.

But I trusted him to keep me safe, and I trusted him to tell me the truth about things that really mattered.

"I don't know. I've never had a mate before," he said.

And it was probably safe to assume that most couples didn't give details about their love-making sessions following their blood-drinking. Especially if the mated ones were the only ones who shared blood, and they were hidden underground.

Just the thought of drinking Ravv's blood made me shudder.

The idea certainly wasn't an appealing one.

"I'll think about it," I finally said.

"You'll do it," he rumbled back.

I scowled again.

His arms tightened around me. "You're mine, Laeli. Get that through your little human skull. Accept it. Embrace it."

"I'm your *secret*," I countered. "You don't want me embracing anything."

"I know what I said." His voice was frustrated.

Was he annoyed that we needed to keep our connection a secret?

The thought made me curious, but I was too tired to keep pushing him. "Good night. I'll think about it tomorrow."

"You'll *do* it tomorrow." He squeezed me, just once.

And then he muttered something that almost sounded like "Good night."

That would've been far too civil for my grumpy fae abductor-slash-savior, so I had to have imagined it.

We traveled through the next day, and a few hours into the night too, before Gleam finally stopped. She was growing more exhausted by the day, and as we all ate, I scratched her head while I thanked her for carrying us.

She fell asleep quickly, and Ravv gave her one last pat before he created another ice shelter for us—this one bigger, and with thicker walls.

My mind went back to our conversation the night before.

He wanted me to drink his blood.

I halted outside the shelter as he disappeared inside.

"Laeli." His warning rumble flooded the air.

No, I was not ready for that.

I turned and walked right back to Gleam's side, then plopped down next to her. She was snoring loudly enough to scare off all the predators, so I'd just sleep beside her.

He stepped out and leaned up against the side of his shelter, his eyes narrowed at me.

I narrowed mine right back.

There was no way he could force me to drink his blood. Even if there was, I didn't think he'd actually do it. He was grumpy and angry, but never cruel.

"You're covered in bruises. You're tired and achy, too. My blood will fix all of those things."

"I told you, I'm not a vampire."

Vampirism was a curse most humans feared deeply. Using magic we weren't born with would corrupt our bodies and make us vampires, who were hunted and tossed into the Aching Chasm. I wasn't sure what that magic was, or how to find it, but I knew it was deadly.

He was silent for a moment, his eyes still narrowed at me. A long moment passed before he finally said, *"You're scared."*

"No. It's just... new."

Fine, I was scared. In what world would I enjoy drinking his blood? What would be wrong with me if I *did*?

"Would it make you more comfortable if I drank from you first?"

I shuddered. *"No."*

He stared at me.

"We'll just tell everyone what happened with the raiders," I finally said, looking away from him.

An image flickered from his mind to mine—and lingered.

I straddled him while he sat on the ground.

His hands were on my hips, his head was tilted to the side, and my mouth was at the crook where his neck met his shoulder.

Veil, it was intense.

My hand lifted to my throat, and my eyes jerked back to Ravv's.

They looked... hot.

Steam caught my attention, and I swore when I looked down and realized my hands were smoking.

"You actually want to do that?" I asked him, my voice quieter than before. *"Not just because you feel guilty, but because you're attracted to me?"*

"You feel my body's response to you every night, and we're fated mates, Laeli. Of course I'm attracted to you."

I huffed. *"I still don't want to do it."*

"What do you want in exchange?" His voice was more even than I expected.

Then again, he had probably anticipated my rejection.

What did I want?

The most obvious answers flashed through my mind.

Freedom.

Safety.

Security.

Happiness.

Ravv couldn't really give me any of those things, though. I didn't know why he'd come to find me, but it was safe to assume that he would have to answer to someone—his king, at the very least—when we got there.

And that person might want to use me for something terrible. Or they might want to kill me.

Veil, they might even want to send me back to my old kingdom, which sounded even worse than the other options.

So I couldn't ask Ravv for those things.

But there were other things I wanted, weren't there?

I bit my lip to stop myself from blurting out my answer.

Ravv was old, and that meant he was experienced in basically every way.

That meant he wouldn't have any moral issues with giving me what I wanted, hopefully.

I held his gaze. *"I want you to make me climax."*

He blinked.

I could've explained to him that I had never had the privacy to explore my own body. That I had been curious for years, without the freedom to try anything.

But I didn't explain any of that.

"How?" Ravv finally asked me.

"Pretty sure I shouldn't have to give you directions," I drawled back. *"You're an ancient fae, aren't you?"*

His lips curved upward in an expression I'd almost call a smirk. *"I could bring you to climax with my cock, ice, mouth, or fingers. A combination of all four would be even better. I could make you climax once, or five times. I could—"*

"I get it," I interrupted him.

My face was hot, and I was still steaming, but I was more intrigued than bothered.

"One climax," I said. Committing to more, before I'd even had one, seemed like too much. *"And you can use your fingers—that's it."*

Though I was interested in all the other options too, I wasn't ready to jump in completely. I needed to ease in, and I'd feel safest if he was only using his hands.

"Alright. Let's go." He stayed where he was, waiting for me.

There was no way to back out now that he'd agreed to my plan, so I slowly made my way to the shelter.

Ravv followed me inside and sealed us in, then sat down in the middle of the space, and waited. He'd shown me that mental image of me sitting on him, so I knew exactly how he wanted me.

Letting out a slow breath, I finally eased myself onto his lap. I'd never sat on him—or anyone—like that, so it was a little bit dizzying. His bare chest was against my clothed one, his eyes nearly even with mine.

His hands landed on my hips, and he adjusted my position a bit, lining my core up perfectly with his erection. The clothing that separated us didn't hide his desire from me at all.

"What guarantee do I have that you'll uphold your part of the deal?" I asked him, my voice soft and a bit breathy. My body was warming, and I didn't even have a desire to stop it.

"You could make the months until the eclipse very difficult for me if I didn't," he murmured, his eyes lingering on my lips as he spoke. "I need you to keep our bond a secret. You could announce it to everyone. That sounds like a damn good assurance to me."

He wasn't wrong.

"Alright." I put both of my hands on his shoulders, and he tilted his head sideways a little. "What do I do? My teeth aren't sharp like yours." I gestured to his mouth, and his lips curved upward for me, showing off the sharp lines of his fangs.

"The bond will help you. Just bite me."

I heaved a sigh, and he gave me a low chuckle.

"This feels like a bad idea," I whispered, as I lowered my lips to the crook where his neck met his shoulder.

"Every fae warrior knows that feeling far too intimately, and continues anyway."

"I'm not a fae warrior." My lips brushed his skin as I spoke, and I was almost confident I saw him shiver the tiniest bit.

"Bite me." His words were a command, then—and I shouldn't have liked that, but I did.

I squeezed my eyes shut, and bit him.

My teeth lengthened and sharpened as they met his skin, and his blood flooded my mouth. It was surprisingly... good. I liked the taste a lot more than I expected.

"A few swallows will be enough," he growled at me, his mind bumping against mine just long enough for me to hear, *"Veil, she'll be my end."*

Slightly offended, I drank slowly from him.

His blood wiped away the offense I felt, replacing it with thick need and desire. My body flushed quickly, wetness growing at the apex of my thighs.

I had a few swallows, and then I pulled away. My body was warm and trembling, and I could feel blood trickle down from the corner of my lips.

With a shaky finger, I carefully wiped up the dripping blood and stared down at it. I expected my stomach to turn at the sight, but it didn't.

My eyes flicked to Ravv's, and I found him watching me with hot, hooded eyes, waiting to see what I'd do.

I finally lifted my finger back to my lips and wrapped them around the digit, sucking the blood away.

His chest rumbled with satisfaction, and he eased me to the ground before positioning himself on his side. My breathing was already rapid —and then his hand landed on the inside of my thigh.

My breaths grew ragged as he slowly slid his hand up, and up, and up.

His knuckles brushed my core, and my hips jerked.

Ravv's lips curved upward wickedly, and he repeated the motion. *"This will be your first climax?"*

He already had all the power in our relationship.

Admitting the truth to him would give him even more power over me, and I didn't want him to have it.

So I lied. *"No. Jern and I introduced each other to sex years ago, before he was with Gora."*

Ravv's smirk faded, slightly.

His expression morphed back toward his usual anger, and his knuckles brushed me again. I itched to tell him the truth, so he could teach me the things I'd never learned about my body, but I ignored the itch. *"First in years?"*

"Yes."

That seemed to satisfy him a bit. *"You're drenched for me."* His knuckles swept over me again, slower, and I moaned.

He hooked a finger in the bottom portion of my tiny undergarments and tugged them down to my knees. When his knuckles brushed my slick, hot skin, I inhaled sharply.

Veil, I had no idea it would feel that good.

Ravv finally dragged a thick finger down the center of me. A noise escaped me at the touch—one I hadn't realized I could even make.

He lifted the finger to his nose and inhaled deeply. The man couldn't have forced the rumbly groan that escaped him as he smelled me.

My lips parted as he brought his hand to my nose and commanded, "Smell how much you want me."

My nostrils flared of their own accord, and I shuddered.

He lowered his fingers to my lips. "Taste it."

I couldn't argue. My body was too hot, and I was too desperate.

My lips wrapped around his finger, and I sucked.

He gave me another rumble—this one pure, masculine satisfaction. "Good." He slid his finger from between my lips and cupped my chin for a moment as he leaned closer and murmured, "You're going to beg me to taste you soon."

My throat closed as the erotic words hit me.

Ravv finally released my chin. He slid his hand down my front before slipping it between my thighs again. I itched to see him touching me, but with his whole display of dominance, I wasn't willing to risk moving in case it made him stop.

I took another staggered breath in, finding and gripping his arm as he slowly stroked me.

My lower belly tightened—veil, my entire body tightened—as he touched me.

I wanted to ask him what I was feeling.

I wanted to make him tell me what to expect.

But I clamped my jaw shut as the foreign sensations slowly built up inside me, my body growing more and more tense.

Ravv buried his free hand in my hair and turned my head to the side. He pressed his erection against my hip as he lowered his lips to my ear and growled, "You are the most stunning creature I've ever seen."

I shuddered at his words as he continued stroking me. One of his fingers teased my entrance. The tip of it slid inside me—and I lost control.

Cries escaped me as my hips rocked and jerked, the pleasure hitting me so much harder and faster than I'd ever expected. I sucked in air as the pleasure faded, and Ravv lifted his fingers back to my lips.

"If you were in my bed, that would be nothing but the start of our night," he rumbled into my ear. "Clean my fingers."

My body trembled.

I felt good, yet still wanted more.

"Clean them yourself," I whispered back.

He chuckled, low and deep. "The first time I taste you, my face will be between your thighs. Clean my fingers or open your legs for more."

If my body hadn't already been steaming, it was then. "Asshole."

Veil, I wanted more.

I couldn't give him even more power over me, though.

My lips wrapped around his fingers, and his cock throbbed against me. When I released him, he dragged his teeth over my earlobe. "Sleep now, Laeli."

I bit my lip and closed my eyes as he rolled us both, so my back was cradled against his front. His erection was rock hard against my ass, but I'd grown to love feeling that. It was evidence of his desire for me that he couldn't hide, and it made me feel desirable.

It took time but eventually, I fell asleep.

My dreams were full of wicked fingers and a low, husky voice that sounded suspiciously like Ravv's.

CHAPTER SEVEN
LAELI

I woke up wet in every way.

The shelter was dripping on us again, but it was far less annoying than the slickness and ache between my thighs. My undergarments were still around my knees, and somehow his touch had only made me more interested in sex, not less. My bruises were gone, at least.

"Damn, you want me." Ravv's words mimicked my own from that first night I'd felt his erection. His lips were against my ear, and his hardness had made its way between my thighs, straining against the fabric of his shorts.

"I don't," I whispered.

He gave me a low, rumbly chuckle. "Lie to me and I'll be forced to prove it."

My eyes squeezed shut as the memory of his fingers stroking my core warmed me further. "It doesn't mean anything."

"It means you want me." He squeezed my thigh, where I hadn't noticed he was holding me. "And you already know I'm willing to take care of you."

As much as I wanted to agree, I couldn't let him continue making the power dynamic between us any less even. And I wasn't about to offer to take his cock in my hand; my inexperience would be obvious the first time I touched him.

If he realized I was a virgin before we had sex, he would take that power and use it against me even more.

"No thanks." I eased my ass away from him, sliding his erection out from between my thighs as I moved.

"Laeli." His eyes were narrowed at me as I stood. Our shelter had shrunk to its usual size at some point during the night, so there was nowhere for me to go.

"Ravv." I mimicked his tone, giving him a flat look. "Open the roof."

"You enjoyed my touch last night," he said. Though there was no uncertainty in his words, it almost felt like a question.

He probably wasn't used to women turning him down after he gave them the most erotic experience of their life.

Letting him wonder would be a way to steal back some of that power he'd taken from me... so I met his stare with my own and said nothing.

His eyes flashed with some dark emotion I couldn't read.

"Let me out, or I will burn my way out," I finally warned him. He knew I didn't do well when I felt trapped, so if he didn't listen, I would know he was being intentionally cruel.

The roof slid open, the way it always did.

I hid my sigh of relief as I stood up, tugged my undergarments back into place, and then strode toward the river.

No way was I getting on Gleam's back so wet with my own damn desire.

Ravv caught up to me as I reached the water, growling, "Don't even think about getting in alone."

Anger was his normal state, but his voice wasn't as angry as I'd expected. That meant I caught him off guard with my refusal, which was exactly what I'd intended to do.

A feeling of victory washed over me as we waded into the river together.

Ravv could try to control me all he wanted, but I was going to fight back until the bitter end.

...Even if it made me ache again every damn morning.

We rode through the day. It was late afternoon when Gleam started climbing up the thick branches and making her way higher into the trees. Soon enough, I was watching a city come to life around us. The homes were built *inside* the trees, the shapes of them carved perfectly without seeming to harm the wood.

My hair whipped around us as Gleam maneuvered over bridges I never could've imagined, and through the most incredible wood and vine arches. There were some ice bridges and arches too, but most of them seemed to be melting, so we avoided them.

There were fae all over the place too, and I noticed all of the men were dressed like Ravv, and most of the women wore short dresses like mine, or even less clothing. It didn't surprise me, given what he'd already told me about the fae's preferences.

"This is Jirev?" I asked Ravv, just wanting to be certain.

"Yes. Kier's city is impressive—though far too hot and sticky," the man behind me grumbled.

"Who's Kier?"

"Kier Jirev is the king."

Oh.

"King over all the fae?"

"No. Just this kingdom." His voice was flat, but that didn't surprise me.

Anger was his typical state, after all.

"How many fae kingdoms are there?"

"Three. The cities are called Loire, Jirev, and Vuuth, named after their current kings."

Veil, he couldn't have given me that information earlier? I should've been bothering him with questions throughout our entire journey.

"Loire is made of ice, this one is in the trees, and the third..." I trailed off.

"Underground. They live in caves inside the mountains on the border of the Weeping Skies."

I shuddered at the mention of that cursed place. Dragons and winged demons lived in the wicked mountains, and we had all grown up being told stories about the brutality that happened there.

The Demon of the Weeping Skies reigned over the mountains, not as a king, but as a scourge. If the legends were true, he was some kind of twisted dragon that the elves had turned into a magical assassin. He was said to have more power than anyone else in Evare, except the other two assassins who were called the Monster and the Beast.

"I'm glad you're not from that one. I don't think I'd do well underground," I admitted.

"You're stronger than you think."

My head jerked toward him, and I found his eyes scanning the trees. *"What are you looking for?"*

He didn't answer me, of course.

I was beginning to wonder if no one had ever taught the fae how rude it was to ignore someone.

We passed dozens and dozens of other fae. Most of them were with massive creatures—some with idorr, others with gray wolf-looking things, and others with terrifying jungle cats.

Eventually, we approached the biggest tree I'd ever seen. There was a set of massive doors at the front of it, with a huge balcony attached to them. *"What's this place?"*

"Kier's castle."

I found it strange how Ravv didn't call him *King* Kier, but assumed the fae just didn't respect their leaders the way humans were expected to.

I found myself liking the casualness of that. A king who didn't demand respect probably wouldn't have a dungeon, or a cellar beneath it for people with magic they shouldn't have been born with.

"Is it safe for me to be in here?" I asked him, as Gleam landed on the balcony attached to the castle.

"The trees were enchanted by elves when the city was built. Your fire won't be able to hurt them," Ravv said.

That made me feel better about my flames.

Considering that Loire was made of ice, I doubted it would have the same protective enchantments, but I supposed we'd figure that out when we got there.

"Why do we need to be here, anyway? You live in Loire, right?" I asked him, as he slid off Gleam's back and pulled me to my feet with him. He'd wrapped his palm in fabric before we left the riverbed that morning, so the silver on it was hidden, and the long sleeves on my dress hid my handprint.

"We're at peace for the first time in centuries. Kier is holding a month's worth of violent competitions to promote peace." Ravv grabbed me by the arm, nearly in the same place he'd grabbed me in the cellar when he gave me the handprint. *"Walk by my side. Do not argue vocally with me."*

I raised my eyebrows at him as he started walking quickly. I nearly had to jog to keep pace with him, but he didn't slow down.

Asshole.

"Why would violent competitions promote peace?"

"Our people are warriors; we enjoy fighting." He didn't so much as look at me.

We passed a few fae with idorr beside them, and I frowned when I noticed them lower their heads toward Ravv, almost like they were *bowing*.

That couldn't have been right, though.

All of the fae were tall, and ridiculously strong. None of the women were built curvy, or soft at all.

I supposed *centuries* of war meant that the strong were the only fae who had survived.

A fae woman and a large male idorr fell into step with Ravv. Neither of them gave me a second glance, which made me feel sort of... small.

I despised the feeling, though I was certainly well-acquainted with it.

"Who else is back?" Ravv growled at the woman.

"No one. You're the first."

Ravv's chin lifted a bit, his shoulders lowering slightly as he continued striding through the castle, dragging me along. "How many did we lose to fights?"

"None. I worked with Eisley, and we kept the peace well enough to avoid casualty."

Ravv dipped his head. "Well done."

"Thank you."

We reached the end of a hallway, and Ravv and his companions strode into a room, giving me no choice but to enter too. The door was on strange hinges that swung open without a doorknob, revealing a simple room made of sleek, polished wood like the rest of the castle. There was a large bed against one wall, a bathroom and closet against another, and a small pool of sorts in one of the corners.

I was so damn confused that I didn't even know what questions to ask.

"What's your name?" the woman asked, when the doors were closed behind us and Ravv had released his hold on my arm.

It took me longer than I cared to admit to realize she was talking to me.

"Laeli," I finally said, getting a closer look at her now that I wasn't being dragged around. Her eyes glowed an intense shade of blue, and her hair was a vibrant purple at the roots that morphed into a gorgeous hot pink as the strands fell down her back. She had lightly-tanned skin, and looked strong enough to go toe-to-toe with any of the male fae.

Veil, she could probably kill me with the flick of a finger.

"I'm Elwynne." She flashed me a grin. "Your magic is fierce, isn't it? I can see the heat blazing off you."

I glanced down at myself.

"Elwynne sees magic where most fae can only sense it," Ravv said to me, before looking back at the other woman. "And Laeli's power is uncontrollable. We need to figure out a way to prevent her from catching fire randomly."

My flames weren't *random*, and Ravv knew that. They responded to my emotions, and nothing else.

I flashed him an annoyed look.

Elwynne eyed me curiously.

"How do you two know each other?" I asked, looking between them.

If they were together...

Veil.

"I'm the king's right hand. Or his left, if you ask Orvay." Elwynne winked at me.

I was pretty sure she was making a joke, but it didn't hit right. "The king? Is Orvay the king?" I looked at her, and then at Ravv.

When he met my gaze head-on without saying anything, I looked back at her.

Elwynne frowned. "No. Ravv is the king; you know that, right?" She glanced at him, and then back at me. "*Veil.*"

I took a step back.

And then another.

My mouth was dry. Though my thoughts raced with questions, I didn't voice any of them. I couldn't.

"Has there been any sign of the Demon?" Ravv asked her.

"No. There haven't been signs of any of the assassins." Elwynne was still frowning, her gaze lingering on me.

"We need to—" Ravv began, but I cut him off.

"What do you mean, the Demon?" My voice rose. "The Demon of the Weeping Skies?"

"Yes. He's hunting Ravv," Elwynne said. "That's why he went looking for you; your magic is life to his ice's death, so it hides your power from the assassin. You already knew that, right?" she looked to Ravv, but I didn't.

My lips parted.

He really *had* come to abduct me.

He didn't give a damn about me, my safety, or my health. He had protected me and called me his because he was using me to hide himself from a magical assassin.

And he was the damn *king*.

None of which he'd bothered to tell me himself.

Hurt curled in my abdomen, sharp, hot, and fierce.

"Get out," I whispered.

Ravv's hard gaze met mine.

"This is my room, right?" I said, raising my voice again. There were no clothes in the closet, and the bed was made.

Ravv jerked his head in a nod.

"Then get out. Veil, don't even *consider* coming back," I spat, clenching my fists as they started smoking.

Elwynne opened her mouth to say something, but Ravv caught her arm —much more gently than he would've grabbed mine—and led her out without saying another word. Gleam and Elwynne's bonded idorr followed them out silently. When I felt Gleam's mind brush up against mine, I withdrew harshly, making it clear that I had no desire to speak with her.

Tears stung my eyes as the doors swung shut behind them.

I slowly sank to my knees as water rolled down my cheeks. My hands caught fire, but I ignored the flames as they rested on my thighs.

I thought Ravv actually liked me. I let him touch me.

Veil, I should've known.

I squeezed my eyes shut and let the tears fall.

Most people just wanted to trap me so my fire couldn't hurt them. Because he hadn't trapped me, I had been lured into trusting him.

I'd been so *stupid*.

But he'd let me believe it.

He'd never told me the truth, or let me know what he intended.

The tears fell as my sadness morphed into anger.

Ravv was a *king*. He should've made that clear from the beginning, and he should've told me why he was capturing me. He should've known better than to tell me he'd saved me when he knew he'd only abducted me to protect his own ass.

He'd said all that shit and *touched me* when he knew none of it was real for him. The bastard had used me in more ways than one.

And now, he was going to pay for it.

Maybe not that night, or the next night, or the next...

But he would pay.

Because I would do every damn thing I could to piss him off.

The ache returned in my arm—a sure sign that the *king* had gone further from me than our bond wanted him to.

I shoved my way into his mind, and could've sworn I felt him wince at the sudden invasion as I hissed into his mind, *"If you go far enough to cause me pain while this bond is in place, I will spend every moment we're connected and every ounce of my energy melting your ice castle to the ground."*

He didn't reply, but the ache in my arm faded soon after I made the threat.

I wiped angrily at the wetness on my face as a few minutes passed.

That bastard didn't get the pleasure of making me cry.

The next time he saw me, I'd be colder to him than a damn ice fae.

A knock on the door dragged me to my feet, but the door swung open without waiting for an answer. Another fae woman's head peeked in immediately. "Laeli?" she checked.

"Yep." I crossed the room, hoping she couldn't see the evidence of my tears. My hands were still burning, which wasn't ideal, but I'd survive.

She was definitely fae, though she was smaller than some of the others I'd seen and at least a few inches shorter. Her skin was pale, her eyes glowed a bright shade of aqua, and her hair was white-blonde, streaked with strands the same color as her eyes. She flashed me a grin, her gaze lingering on my burning hands. "I'm Eisley. You're human?"

"Unfortunately."

"Elwynne asked me to bring you a dress. She said you need to keep her involvement from Ravv, and I couldn't resist something that might piss off one of the kings." She winked at me, and thankfully set the folded dress on the floor instead of trying to give it to me. Then she slipped out, leaving the doors swinging behind her.

I heaved a sigh, and spent a few minutes trying to figure out how to lock the door before I finally got it in place.

Though I wanted nothing more than to climb into the comfortable-looking bed off to my side, I wasn't willing to risk waking up in a bonfire.

So, I left the dress on the floor and made my way to the pool in the corner of the room. I eyed it as I approached. I hadn't bathed in a tub in more than a decade, but it certainly wasn't a tub. It was more like a tiny pond, though the sides seemed to be made out of stone instead of the wood the rest of the castle boasted.

I couldn't see the bottom of the pool, which made me a bit suspicious. It was still my best chance at getting clean, so I tugged my dress off. I used the bar of soap I found nearby to scrub my undergarments clean, just in case Elwynne hadn't sent any, and then slipped into the water.

It felt lukewarm; not cold, but not hot either. It was nice, I supposed, though I was fairly certain I'd always dream about the hot baths I'd had a few times as a kid.

I refused to let myself think about my childhood for the sake of my sanity, so I forced myself to focus on Ravv.

And what he'd done.

Veil, the bastard was going to regret it. I'd make sure of that.

CHAPTER EIGHT
LAELI

My fire went out at some point during my bath, and thankfully didn't reignite. I collapsed in bed when I was completely clean, satisfied the door was still locked, and didn't get up again until my growling stomach forced me to.

There were no new undergarments, so I started putting mine on—and then decided I'd have a better chance of pissing Ravv off if he found out I didn't have anything on beneath the dress. I tucked them under the blankets on the bed, hiding them just in case someone went into my room while I was gone.

The dress slid over my skin easily, and I sighed at the feel of the soft fabric. It was black and fell to the middle of my thighs, not loose but not tight, and clearly made for a taller and stronger woman than me. It had longish sleeves that hung off my shoulders, though I was confident they were supposed to sit on top. They covered my handprint, so that was all that really mattered.

I smoothed the fabric and slipped out into the hallway. My stomach rumbled painfully, and I patted it, silently promising it I'd fill it soon.

Since I didn't know my way around the castle, I walked up to the first fae I found. They were both male, and both standing with idorr beside them, so I assumed they were Ravv's people.

They weren't supposed to know we were mates, so I kept my mouth shut about that. I wanted revenge, but it would be much sweeter if I drove him mad instead of just going against his wishes.

Both men eyed me curiously. I gave them the biggest, friendliest, most human smile I could manage. "Hi, guys. I'm looking for food, do you know where I can find some?"

"The dining hall is that way." One of them gestured toward a wall.

I supposed I could just wander in that direction, but that sounded like so much work.

And a wicked idea to contribute to my revenge plot was practically boiling in my mind.

"Oh, perfect." I looped my arm through one of the fae's, and his eyebrows lifted. The man was huge, so it was a risk to grab his arm without permission or invitation. I didn't think I could make an ancient fae feel violated by touching his elbow, though. "Lead the way."

The man looked at the other guy.

He shrugged.

We all started walking, and my smile morphed into a grin. "So you guys are from Loire?" I asked them, tapping into what little fae knowledge I possessed.

"We are," the guy whose arm I wasn't holding said. "You're from the Human Lands?"

"Yep. The kingdom I lived in was called Rowain, and it's a fairly unpleasant place," I said cheerfully. "Luckily, your king dragged me back here. You wouldn't know why, by chance, would you?"

Both men looked surprised. The one whose arm I was holding said, "You're going to fight two other humans to end our peace events."

Fight?

That bastard expected me to *fight*?!

Ravv could cross the damn veil for all I cared.

"Great," I forced my grin to remain.

We stopped in front of a pair of doors, and the man I was holding gestured to them. "Here's the dining hall. If no one serves you, go to the kitchen and ask." He eyed me. "Politely, so they don't kill you."

Asshole.

My smile widened. "Perfect. Thank you so much." I started to release his arm, and then paused. Next was the risky part of my plan. Ravv might not be as possessive as he had seemed... but maybe he was. "You know, I've never hugged a fae before. Or kissed one. Would you be willing to kiss me?"

The man looked taken aback.

I fought a snort at his expression.

"I have a life partner," he said.

"Not a mate?" I asked innocently.

"No. She and I can't create a bond without making ourselves a target for the cultists."

Cultists?

Well, everything just got better and better.

Ravv was doing an incredible job at keeping secrets from me.

"Sorry I grabbed you, then." I released the man's arm and patted it lightly in apology.

"I'll kiss you," the other guy offered. "I have no partner or mate. I'd be interested in spending a night with you, too, to see how humans differ from fae."

Oh, dear.

He'd just propositioned me.

I should've seen that coming.

"I'll keep that in mind, but I'm still trying to adjust to all this. Maybe tomorrow?"

The man only looked slightly disappointed, and nodded. "Can I see your ears, then?"

I shrugged, pulling my hair up away from one and turning so he could see it.

His eyes lit with fascination. "Can I touch it?"

"Sure." It was just an ear.

He ran a finger over the curve of it, and I literally felt nothing.

Still just an ear.

"Fascinating," the man said.

His hands landed on my hips, and he turned me. I dropped my hair as my chest met his, and my hands landed awkwardly on his large pectorals.

I'd never actually kissed someone before, so I was glad he was taking initiative.

And it made me feel like I was making a point to Ravv to *choose* the man I was having my first kiss with, even if I didn't actually know him.

The king probably wouldn't even care, but it still mattered to me.

He tilted my chin up with one hand and lowered his lips to mine. The sensation was foreign and strange as his soft mouth brushed against mine, and then his tongue slipped between my lips.

He didn't taste very good, but I supposed that was to be expected, since he was both male and fae.

His hands held me close as we kissed, and my lower belly tensed when I felt him grow hard against me.

The other fae finally cleared his throat, and I pulled away. Both of our chests were rising and falling a bit quickly.

"You have an audience," the man said in a low voice.

My head jerked to the side, and I found a group of fae with a variety of appearances and bonded beasts waiting.

We were blocking the dining hall's entrance.

"Does the human taste different than a fae?" one of the guys in the group asked.

It was a good thing my face was already red, or my embarrassment would've been obvious.

"No. A little softer, though." His expression was thoughtful as he looked at me. "We'll share a bed tomorrow night?"

Had I agreed to that?

I didn't know if I was ready to commit that completely to my revenge plan. I couldn't turn him down with a crowd though, so I flashed him a smile and nodded.

He smiled back. "I'll find you."

With that, he and his friend vanished back into the hallway we'd walked down.

"Uh, sorry, everyone." I waved at our audience before slipping into the dining hall. Since I didn't want to wait and see if anyone would happen to serve me, I headed into the doors that I assumed led to the kitchen and poked my head in.

I was probably still red and flushed, but I didn't really care at that point. My stomach was rumbling fiercely.

My gaze collided with a group of male and female fae who looked like they'd just stopped in the middle of a conversation.

I said quickly, stumbling over my words a bit, "Hi. I was living in a cellar up until a few days ago, so I'm starving. I'll eat anything and everything, and I have no idea what I like. So if you have enough food, I'd love to have some."

There was a moment's pause before a sympathetic-looking woman spoke up. "We'll bring it out. Just sit down at any of the tables."

I nodded. "Thank you so much."

They brought me a dozen plates, loaded with food. My eyes got a little teary every time they brought me something new, and sometimes when I tasted said new food as well.

It was all absolutely incredible.

Fancy savory breads.

Elegant sweet breads.

Soups.

Pastas.

Salads of every kind.

Desserts, desserts, and more desserts.

I must've died and crossed the veil, because damn, it was something out of a dream.

I was already incredibly full when Eisley, the fae who'd brought me the dress, strolled back into the dining room with another woman. She looked just as short as me, and just as skinny too.

My heart went out to her even as I shoved another bite into my mouth, and I gave a quick wave to show that I'd seen her. We were alone in the dining hall at that point, and it would've been rude to ignore her even if we weren't.

Unlike Ravv, I wasn't an asshole.

At least, not most of the time.

Eisley gestured to the chair next to me, and the girl sat down as the fae introduced us. Though we were equally skinny and wimpy-looking, her light skin was a bit tanned and her long, wavy hair was a gorgeous dark green color. "Laeli, this is Nissa. Nissa, this is Laeli."

She looked a bit uncertain, so I figured it was time to be social.

"You're stuck with a fae bastard too?" I asked her, cutting into some sort of casserole.

Nissa's stomach rumbled loudly, and my sympathy grew. "Unfortunately."

I nodded. "It sucks, but at least there's food. I've been locked in a damn cellar since my magic came in, and my town rarely bothered to feed me."

"I was trapped in a tower," she admitted.

I shivered.

A tower?

Veil, I'd rather die.

She did seem to have had some sunlight in her tower though, and I envied that immensely. My prison would've been much more livable with a little sunlight.

Maybe I wouldn't rather die.

"I do *not* do well with heights, so I don't envy you. Here." I pushed one of my plates over to her.

Eisley tried to give me the plate back, so I gave her a dirty look. I had plenty, and Nissa was clearly starving too. "I'll have the kitchen make her something," the fae said, before leaving us.

I pushed the plate back to Nissa as soon as she was gone. "So what's your power?"

She grabbed one of the pastries I wished I could've forced my stomach to take. Those things were incredible. "Plants. They grow around me, draining my magic in a few hours. I have no control over it."

That was epic.

Sunlight, and plants.

Veil, I'd trade my fire and my cellar for her prison any day. I could deal with the heights for that.

"Damn, that's lucky. My magic is uncontrollable too, but it's fire magic. You can feel the heat in the air around me constantly, and if I feel anything too strongly, I burn."

"Really? Have you ever burned yourself?"

I grinned. "I've tried, but the fire dodges me. I'll show you if you're ever around when I light up."

"Veil." Nissa suddenly swore, crunching her pastry in her fist and grabbing her wrist with the other hand. There was a metal bracelet wrapped around it, and I assumed the metal was hiding a mate bond.

I'd reacted much the same when Ravv first walked away from me in the desert, so my heart went out to her for it.

"Do you have a handprint too? These things are miserable." I tugged the top of my sleeve down, showing her my handprint for a second before pulling it back. "I told Ravv that if he keeps walking away from me, I'm going to melt his ice castle. He's stayed close enough not to ignite the pain since then. He's a grumpy asshole, but he doesn't seem to want to start another war."

"Is walking away what triggers it?" Nissa took a bite of her food, then set it down so she could massage her handprint through her bracelet. I wasn't sure how much good the massage would do, because when those things hurt, they *really* hurt.

"Mmhm. Physical distance seems to do it."

"Does it cause the men pain too?"

I nodded and tossed out a joke to lighten the mood. "Yep. They like to pretend they don't feel it, though. Makes them feel better about themselves and those tiny fae cocks."

She snorted, and I grinned at her again.

"Alright, here you go." Eisley gave Nissa a plate and then sat down beside her. "How's the wrist?"

She didn't answer. I assumed it was because she didn't want to admit she was in pain.

I didn't think we needed to water things down for the fae who were using us for protection and treating us like shit. So, I answered for her. "Bad. Someone needs to find her king."

"He's helping judge the wrestling tournament, and maybe participating in it," Eisley said. "We'll have to go to him."

I shrugged. "Ravv must've skipped it."

"She said the men wrestling are all naked," Nissa told me with a guilty grin.

Oooh.

My revenge plan was about to get even sweeter.

I stood. "Let's get you out of pain, then."

Nissa laughed.

Eisley grumbled, "Sit down."

I needed to come up with a logical excuse.

My mind moved quickly.

Considering Ravv's reaction to Jern's scent on me, it was safe to assume he was possessive. But I didn't know if Nissa or Eisley knew that, since it seemed rare for fae to take mates, and Nissa obviously wasn't fae.

So I threw out, "Why? We haven't established whether fae men are as possessive as their bonded animals are with their mates. This seems like the perfect opportunity to test the theory on someone who can't burn the jungle down."

"I'm sure they're not possessive of females they're temporarily bonded to," Eisley countered.

"Kierden is disgusted by my ears, let alone the rest of me. Pretty sure possessiveness is off the table," Nissa said.

Yikes.

The conversation topic changed, but I brought it back to the naked wrestling as soon as I could—and eventually, Nissa's pain got bad enough that we all headed out to enact my revenge plan.

Er, I mean, to see if fae men were possessive.

The stadium where the fae held the events was built into another massive tree. I rode on Eisley's bonded jungle cat with her—which I learned was called an esu, pronounced ee-soo. It wasn't nearly as comfortable as riding with Ravv, not that I would admit it aloud.

Nissa had a bonded esu of her own already, which seemed like a pretty damn good sign to me that she and her king, Kier, were just as fated as me and Ravv, but I couldn't say that out loud either.

I itched to ask if I could meet a few of those magical animals without riders. It would be nice to have a big furry companion of my own to eat anyone who pissed me off. Despite the urge, I decided it was wiser to stay quiet about it until I had established a place for myself with the fae.

After all, I had no intention of going back to my city and being thrown in that cellar again.

It seemed to be the middle of the night, but thanks to my nap, I wasn't all that tired. Between my improved eyesight and some big light bugs I noticed flying all over the place, I could see just fine.

There were flowers blooming around the city, which seemed like a new addition. I assumed Nissa was to blame, since I also saw a few fae marveling over them, and I knew she had plant magic of some sort.

My bicep started to throb as Eisley's bonded esu carried us into a stadium full of roaring fae. She maneuvered down a bunch of rows of benches until we reached a few empty ones. The empty ones were just outside the huge metal cage that held two naked, fighting men.

Though their nudity was appealing, I found myself backing away from the violence. It was close to us—way too close to us.

One of the guys in the ring finally lost the wrestling match, and the crowd cheered even louder. The man who stood up was just as big as Ravv, with tan skin, wavy black hair that fell around his ears, and an arm of tattoos that looked like the ones on Ravv's back.

One of his palms was wrapped up, and when I glanced at Nissa, I noticed her gaze riveted to him, her body pressed as tightly to the bars as possible.

He had to be her king, Kier.

And damn, he was nice to look at.

Kier offered the losing fae a hand, and pulled the guy to his feet before clapping him on the back. The other guy left the cage, and Kier turned back to the crowd, holding his arms out as he roared, "Who will challenge me?"

The crowd's yells and screams grew even more ferocious.

"Do it," I whispered to Nissa, nudging her with one of my shoulders. "Challenge him. You know you want to roll around with all of that."

Honestly, I wanted to see his reaction to her doing it, though I didn't think there was a chance she would.

Her face reddened. "No thanks."

"He would *ravage* her," Eisley threw out.

I snorted.

Nissa fought a laugh of her own.

Eisley grinned at both of us before turning back to watch the fight.

My bicep had stopped aching, so I assumed Ravv was moving closer to avoid the pain, and to avoid me making good on my threat.

Kier noticed Nissa against the cage, and gave me the possessive reaction I'd pretended to be looking for. His gaze jerked to Eisley, and he snarled so viciously I could almost hear it over the sound of the crowd.

My eyes squeezed shut when his next challenger came out. I imagined he was beating the other man to a pulp, with his anger driving him. I'd seen firsthand how a king's anger could make him fight, and it was vicious.

A pair of massive hands landed on my shoulders and wrenched me backward. They held me upright before I could fall, and Ravv's intense, dark purple eyes collided with mine. "What are you doing here?" He inhaled deeply again, and then snarled, "And why do you smell like another male?"

"Neither of those things are any of your business," I shot back, frustration welling inside me.

He snarled again, then threw me over his shoulder and stormed away from the cage.

My ass landed on Gleam's back. The king pressed me tightly to his bonded idorr as she carried us away from the fight. Ravv was breathing hard, his chest rising and falling as he gripped Gleam's fur like it could keep him sane.

I didn't think it could, though.

And for the sake of my revenge, I *hoped* it couldn't.

CHAPTER NINE

LAELI

Gleam ran until we were back in my room in the castle. My dress was still on the floor—and I hoped my undergarments were still tucked beneath the blankets on the bed.

Ravv set me on my feet before stepping up right in front of me. His hands gripped my face, and he tilted my head back so my eyes met his. His grip was tight, but loose enough that I could've broken free if I really tried.

"What in the veil were you thinking?" he snarled.

"I was thinking that I wanted to watch the fae warriors fight, and—"

He cut me off by lowering his nose to my mouth and inhaling.

His responding roar was loud enough it nearly shook the damn ground.

He released me in a heartbeat—and then he was storming toward the door.

Elwynne appeared in the doorway before he made it out, and her massive bonded idorr was behind her. "What happened?" she demanded, looking between us.

Ravv tried to get past her, but her companion stepped in front of him, making him snarl at her.

She narrowed her eyes at him and didn't budge. "What's going on?"

"My mate kissed another male, and had his arms around her," Ravv gritted out.

Her gaze jerked to me. "Are you insane?"

"No, I'm not insane. I'm not the bastard who started a mate bond with a complete stranger and then carried her across the world, lying to her about everything and then expecting her to just go along with it!" I tossed a hand toward Ravv. "Don't blame me for *his* stupid decisions."

"Regardless, you can't kiss someone else while you're mated. You could start another damn war," she shot back, as she and her idorr stepped closer to each other, blocking Ravv more completely.

"He's the one who's losing control," I snapped back.

"Mated fae are protective. If he kissed another woman, you'd lose control too."

Ravv glowered at me. "I wouldn't betray her that way."

I wasn't touching those comments. "Just tell me how to get out of this ridiculous bond and this city, and we'll all be free of each other." I gestured to my arm.

"The eclipse is the only thing that can break it. We're staying out here to make sure neither of you leave." She shot Ravv a warning look. "Talk to her. Fix this."

The door shut behind her and her idorr.

I scoffed, striding back to the bed.

"Don't consider climbing beneath my blankets smelling like another man," Ravv snarled. When I tossed him a glare over my shoulder, I found him striding toward me.

I turned and planted my feet, putting my hands on my hips. "This is *my* bed. You told me it was *my* room."

"That was before you went and kissed Toveo. Now, you're sleeping with me again. In my arms. Where I know you can't touch another damn male."

My hands ignited, and I clenched my fists as they blazed. "You *used* me. You've used me this *entire* time. Someone has to get the stain of your touch off my skin."

He covered the rest of the distance between us and grabbed my face in his hands again. Despite the roughness, his grip didn't hurt in the slightest as he tilted my head back. He was trying to assert his dominance over me, but I wasn't giving in this time.

"I used your *magic* to protect myself from an ancient assassin, after an elf told me it was the only way I could survive."

"You only protected me to protect yourself," I shot back.

His voice went low and dark. "If I didn't care about you, I wouldn't have fed you. I wouldn't have washed you. I wouldn't have given you my blood, or touched you."

"Oh, please. I'm sure you spend every night with a different woman."

"I haven't intimately touched a female or had sex in nearly a century," he growled back.

"Is that supposed to make me think you're a damn saint?" I sneered. "How impressive; you resist your urges with the women you respect. Because I'm just a worthless human, you abduct me, lie to me, use me, and—"

He cut me off by hauling me off my feet and whisking me away from the bed. The bastard tossed me into the bathing pool before I had a chance to shout at him.

I surfaced a moment later, sputtering and shoving hair out of my eyes. "You should've left me to rot in that damned cellar." My voice shook with the fury I had no other way to express. My fire was still burning beneath the water, my flames growing instead of shrinking.

Ravv kneeled at the edge of the pool and leaned toward me. "No, I shouldn't have. Like it or not, fate declared you mine. Now, tell me what happened, or we stay here all night."

"Cross the veil," I spat.

"The only one crossing the veil tonight is Toveo, for touching what's mine."

More rage flooded me, and I grabbed him by the arm, yanking him toward the water. The movement must've surprised him, because I actually managed to pull his heavy ass off balance. He crashed into the water right on top of me, dragging me beneath the surface.

My lungs screamed, but Ravv hauled me back out, spitting, "Dammit, woman."

"Damn *you*." I shoved him away from me, but he only gripped me tighter, treading water to keep both of us afloat. "You are an absolute *bastard*. Not once, in all those times you claimed you saved me, did it occur to you to tell me the truth! To say, 'hey, Lae, I only started this mate bond because I needed your magic to protect mine, so don't get too comfortable'."

He scowled. "Of course it occurred to me."

"But you didn't do it!"

"I had no idea when I was looking for you that you'd be my fated mate —or that I'd find myself *attracted* to you. This situation is difficult for me too, *Lae.* I'm being hunted by one of the very few beings in this world who stand a chance of killing me, and if I die, there's a good chance my kingdom dies with me." His words were low, his chest rumbly and unhappy. "It's not just my life on the line here."

I... hadn't considered that. "Why would your kingdom die? If you would just *talk* to me, we wouldn't be having this issue." I gestured between us, swimming in a tiny but deep bathing pool, fully dressed.

Or at least, as fully dressed as it got when you were a fae.

"It's complicated."

I scowled, pushing out of his arms so I could tread water myself. My back brushed the stone edge of the small bathing pool. "Get out of my room if you're not going to speak to me like I'm your equal."

He growled at me, "You drive me insane, woman."

"The feeling is mutual."

Ravv shoved his curls out of his eyes. "It's not a short story."

"Look at me. I have nothing but time."

"There was a cult that slaughtered mated pairs a few centuries ago. They were afraid of the power mated couples possessed. My mother and father were the queen and king of Loire at that point—and they were fated, so they were one of the first targets. They narrowly dodged multiple attempts on their life before deciding to go underground, literally."

My eyebrows lifted. "The underground city you found?"

"Yes. They ran from battle like cowards—one of the worst shames a fae can take on their shoulders. They left my twin sister and I to determine who would rule, but Ria had already joined the cult."

"Your *sister* tried to kill your parents?"

"Yes. Outside of the cult, our people wouldn't follow her. Most unmated fae didn't despise mates, they just hadn't found anyone they wished to spend their eternity with."

"So you took over."

"Yes. At twenty-years-old."

Damn.

I was twenty-three, and I couldn't imagine ruling over anyone. I could barely keep my own shit together.

Then again, I'd spent much of my life in a cellar, battling my own flames unsuccessfully.

"What did your sister do?"

"Built her own damn army of those who despise mated pairs and set her mind to find the hidden half of our kingdom."

"Did she find them?"

"It took a few decades, but she did. Then, our civil war began."

"Your *civil war*?"

"Yes. My army has been fighting to keep the damned Vuuths and Jirevs from taking over our kingdom, while my sister and her group of bastards have been at war with the mated city beneath our land. Even now while I'm here, they fight. The cult's numbers are dwindling, but they'll war until the bitter end."

"Then who are all the people here?" I gestured toward the hallway. The guy I'd kissed had been single, but his friend had a life partner, so they couldn't have been anti-mate.

"The warriors who care more about survival than a squabble about mating bonds." Ravv's shoulder blades hit the back of the bathing pool, and he pulled himself out. My eyes followed the swell of his biceps as he moved. "If they discover what we are to each other, there's a damn good chance my warriors will be forced to take sides. And if they take sides, the civil war will escalate, instead of continually shrinking."

"And which side would you choose?" I asked him.

"Anyone's but the cult's. I don't condone anyone killing each other for love, of all things. If the cultists feel threatened, they should take mates themselves to make their magic stronger."

"Why are they so strong that the mated couples haven't been able to wipe them out?"

"Many of the mated couples have children. Few of them are willing to leave their fortress of a city to fight—and fewer are willing to kill their old friends and families. There can't be many left, but they are persistent, and they hide well."

"And it won't end until the cultists are gone?"

"Even then, I'm sure they have members hidden among my army." He closed his eyes for a long moment, and I saw the lines in his face. I saw the weight of his stress, and of his throne.

Suddenly, I understood his anger and grumpiness just a little bit.

He'd been holding an entire kingdom together through grit and willpower for *centuries*, fighting a war he didn't want on both fronts.

"Would killing your sister end it? She's the leader, right?" I asked.

"She is, but she's careful to avoid any fights she knows she can't win. Eventually, she'll grow desperate enough to face me, and I'll have the chance to end her."

"Your warriors respect you though, right? If you took a mate, would they side with you?"

He grimaced. "It's unlikely."

"But you don't know."

"I don't. Most would be loyal to me if the truth comes out, but some wouldn't."

That was better than nothing, I supposed.

"So what do we do?" I finally hauled myself out of the bathing pool too. I was a lot less graceful about it than Ravv was, but managed to end up on my ass, with my feet hanging in the water.

"You made that much harder than it needed to be," Ravv drawled, leaning back as he stared at me. Despite his words, there was heat in his eyes, and they were lingering on my thighs. My dress had ridden up, and it barely covered me.

"Not all of us are warrior fae kings," I drawled back.

"Thank the veil for that."

I rolled my eyes at him. "I'm serious. What are we going to do about us?"

"You're going to tell me what you did with Toveo, to start."

"That is still not your business," I said bluntly.

His eyes narrowed at me. "You belong to me. That makes it my business."

"Did you not hear anything you just said? It's not even *possible* for us to be together. And once again, you don't own me."

His eyes were still narrowed at me. "Tell me, *Lae*."

I should never have let my old nickname slip. No one had called me that since...

Well, since all the happy shit in my past that I preferred to pretend had never happened.

I still wasn't going to give in. There was no way I could let him win. "Make me."

His eyes burned into me for a long, long moment.

My gaze jerked down when I felt ice wrapping around my wrists and my thighs, trapping me where I was. I pulled against them, but they were thick and unyielding.

Panic started to rise in my chest as he stood smoothly and strode over to me. Ravv's massive hand landed on my shoulder, and when I looked down again, I found his knees on either side of me.

For some reason, his presence soothed the panic I'd initially felt at being trapped.

His lips brushed my ear. "Tell me, and I free you. Stay silent, and you force me to figure it out myself."

How would he *figure it out* himself?

"What does that mean?" I demanded, though my chest was rising and falling rapidly. The dress clung to nearly every inch of my skin, highlighting the hard buds of my nipples but concealing my core, just barely.

"You think a dip in the water could wipe a male's scent from your skin entirely? I can find out exactly where his body touched yours without releasing you, Lae."

He wasn't giving up on the nickname.

I wasn't sure I wanted him to, as insane as that probably made me.

It was time to lean on my sarcasm again. "So you're going to *smell* me?"

He chuckled, but didn't answer me.

Instead, he lowered his nose to my neck and inhaled deeply. His chest rumbled unhappily, and I breathed in sharply when his tongue dragged slowly over the sensitive flesh there.

My body clenched as heat flooded me.

His tongue left my skin, and I relaxed for a moment—before he inhaled against my ear.

A snarl escaped him, and the silky heat of his tongue dragged over the curve of it.

A moan escaped me, my body clenching again, tighter.

I swore silently, and he chuckled.

He must've heard my curse in his mind.

If he was going to lick every part of me that smelled like the guy I'd been pressed up against...

Veil, he'd lick every inch of me.

My ears.

My belly.

My breasts.

Which meant... I was going to have to give in.

I was going to have to let him win.

Because if he tasted me like that, I wouldn't want it to end. And I'd grow too damn attached to the man who had lied to me and used me without even bothering to let me know what he was doing.

If I told him what I'd done with the fae in the hallway—Toveo, according to Ravv—it would still piss him off.

The whole goal of my revenge plot was to hurt him the way he'd hurt me. Telling him the truth might achieve that, too.

Especially if I embellished a little.

"I asked Toveo to be my first kiss, so I wouldn't have to give it to you," I breathed.

Ravv's body went still.

The man absolutely froze.

His breath still tickled my ear, his chest pressed to my back and his knees at my hips.

"I wrapped my arms around him, pressed my body to his, and took his lips in mine." I let my heartbeat pick up with the stress of the lie, knowing Ravv would interpret it as something entirely different. "His mouth made love to mine while I rubbed myself against him. I wasn't wearing any undergarments, so he felt my bare breasts against his chest. He probably smelled how much I enjoyed it, too. He gripped my ass and squeezed my tits—until I climaxed, without so much as a damn touch of his fingers."

Rav's breathing was ragged as his fury swelled.

He had no way of proving me wrong without leaving the room, and that gave me all the power.

"When I thanked him and pulled away, he invited me to share his bed tomorrow night, and I agreed. As I turned around, I realized we had an audience. Fae from all of the kingdoms had seen me unravel against him, and knew that we'd be bare in his bed the next night. That made it hard to walk away from him, but I forced myself to go."

A slow, low snarl that legitimately sounded like it had come from a wild animal vibrated against my back. Ravv slowly released my shoulder—and then he left the room so quickly, I didn't even see him move.

A relieved breath escaped me when he was gone.

"Wicked little human," Gleam murmured, her mouth parted in what almost resembled a grin.

I hadn't even realized she was still in the room with us, and flashed her a warning look as I tugged again at the ice still holding me captive.

It didn't budge.

"I won't let you control me either," I warned her.

"Good." She lazily rose to her paws. *"Fate knew what it was doing when it paired you. My king has finally met his match."*

With that, she slipped out of the room.

I focused on my anger, trying to force my damn fire to reignite—but all I got was a little steam.

Truthfully, I wasn't all that angry anymore.

Sadness outweighed anger again... and veil, I despised it.

Eventually, my heat melted the ice enough that I managed to slip my wrists and thighs out of the icy restraints. I was exhausted, so I simply locked the door to my room and dropped into bed, curling up in a small ball.

At least the mattress was comfortable.

At least I wasn't in the cellar anymore.

I calmed myself with those reminders, and drifted off to sleep.

CHAPTER TEN
RAVV

Elwynne cursed as she ran behind me, barely managing to keep the pace I set.

I was going to find Toveo, consequences be damned.

He had touched my mate.

He had stolen her first kiss from me.

He had made her *unravel*.

The bastard would pay.

Gleam caught up to me as I reached the castle's exit, and I landed on her back smoothly.

"I don't think this is wise," she murmured to me. *"Laeli may have been lying about the extent of their connection."*

"I smelled him on her skin," I snarled back. *"She has no reason to lie."*

"Of course she does. You lied to her while we traveled. From her perspective, you used her, plainly and simply. That makes you no better than an enemy to her."

"I'm not her damn enemy."

"*Ravv.*" Her voice was amused. "*You may be fated, but you haven't treated her as a mate. You fed her and touched her, but her life is at risk because of you, and her whole world has been turned upside down. If she had done any of those things to you, she'd be your enemy. If she did all of them? She'd be buried in ice and earth already.*"

I shook off her reason, and the guilt that burned in my chest because of it.

My gaze jerked down to my wrist as it started throbbing, and I growled a harsh, "*Turn around. She's in pain.*"

Gleam skidded to a stop in the middle of a large bridge.

Someone yelled at us, but I didn't let myself retaliate.

"*You either want her as your mate, or you don't. If you want her, you'll go back to her room and apologize for losing your head and leaving her trapped in ice restraints. Then you'll apologize for making her feel like you were using her, too. If you want her, your place is to make her feel loved and important, not to lose your mind when she kisses another man in an attempt to get revenge.*"

"*If that was her goal, it clearly worked,*" I growled.

Gleam chuckled. "*Of course it did. She's seen enough of your moods to know how to hurt you.*"

As much as I hated the idea, I had to grudgingly respect her for it.

"*And what if I want her? My people could lose their damn minds and turn on us.*"

"*Many of your people have partners. They wouldn't hate you for having the same,*" Gleam said, starting her walk back in the direction we had come from. "*And if they do, you'll kill them.*"

I barked out a laugh. "*That easy, huh?*"

"*You know I find it sad that fae remain alone for so much of their lives. I'm still trying to convince Coarsefur to consider going into the mated city so he can find a companion. Being without a companion makes him grumpy.*"

"*Everything except you makes him grumpy.*"

"True." She chuffed. *"A mate bond is good for everyone, including fae. We're not at war with Jirev and Vuuth anymore. Even if you do decide to seal your bond with Laeli, you could simply retreat to the mated city until you've had the chance to kill Ria."*

"I suppose."

A furious Elwynne and her playful bonded idorr, Swift, met us on the next bridge. The fae around us ignored us for the most part, thankfully.

"Gleam talked you down?" Elwynne asked, her expression wary.

"She did."

"Veil, what were you thinking? That human is going to hate you, if she doesn't already," she tossed out.

"She probably does," Gleam agreed, broadcasting the thought to all of us.

"She doesn't hate me," I grumbled.

"She'd be a fool not to," Elwynne said, as the idorr began carrying us back toward the castle. "If you want her to go along with your plan now, you're going to have to grovel."

I had never groveled in my life, and I wasn't about to start.

"Bring food when you do. She needs to eat more," Gleam said.

It had been irritating me since I left her side a few hours earlier that I hadn't made sure she ate something. Gleam's words pushed that over the edge.

"I'll apologize with food," I agreed, though not entirely thrilled about it.

I was still angry that she'd kissed another man.

Veil, I was furious about that.

But there was a small chance I had lost control of my jealousy, and over-reacted.

"I'll get the full story on her and Toveo," Elwynne said.

I agreed, and we split up.

After a quick stop in the dining hall for a plate of food, Gleam and I headed back to the bedroom I'd been assigned. When I found the door locked, I opened it with my ice—Laeli hadn't figured out how to secure it properly yet—and slipped inside, scratching Gleam behind the ears before leaving her to sleep in front of the door.

She wanted us to have privacy, and still needed to rest so she could recover from our journey. And no fae would ever hurt a bonded beast outside of a battlefield, so I knew she'd be safe.

Laeli was in the bed, buried beneath the blankets. Her hair was sprawled over half of the mattress, damp and tangled.

I set the plate down on the table beside the bed as I sat on the edge of the mattress, smoothing some of her hair away from her face.

She made a soft noise at the touch, and her eyes cracked open just a little bit.

Her lips curved upward when she saw me, and mine did the same.

Her happiness vanished as soon as it had appeared, and then she groaned and buried her face in the bed. "Go away."

"I brought food."

"Keep your damn food," she mumbled into the blankets.

I slid further onto the mattress, sitting with my back to the wall as my side met hers.

"Unless you're here to apologize for being such an asshole, save us both the trouble and just leave," she added.

I set a hand on her back and slowly started to rub her skin.

She groaned again. "I hate you."

But she didn't ask me to stop, so it was progress.

"I may have lost my temper," I said gruffly.

"Is the guy dead?"

"No."

She paused, and I continued rubbing her back.

After a moment, she asked, "Is he bleeding? Or afraid for his life?"

I scowled. "No. I didn't go to him."

Her shoulders relaxed slightly.

I stopped moving my hand, and she grumbled, "Rub my back or leave."

A low chuckle escaped me as I turned, setting both my hands on her shoulders and pressing my thumbs into her muscles lightly.

Another groan escaped her—a louder one that sent blood rushing straight to my cock. If I wasn't already hard just from the sight of her sprawled across a bed, veil knew the sound alone could give me an erection.

"I still hate you," she mumbled. "And that wasn't a good enough apology."

A few moments passed. Her body was growing boneless beneath my hands, the knots in her muscles fading beneath my touch. "I regret losing my temper," I finally said. "Your actions felt like a betrayal, and I don't do well with betrayal."

"I don't think anyone does well with betrayal." She paused before adding, "I shouldn't have kissed that guy. I only did it to hurt you."

"You did far more than kiss him," I growled back.

She was silent for a moment before she finally admitted, "I may have exaggerated."

My hands stilled.

"There was no groping. Or climaxing. And I didn't promise to spend the night with him," she finally said. "Though he did ask. I guess I didn't really say no, but I wasn't planning on actually going through with it. I just couldn't turn him down with people around."

I forced my body not to quake with renewed fury.

"Ravv?" she peeked over her shoulder at me, and the flash of those gorgeous amber eyes calmed me just slightly.

I gritted my teeth. "Give me a minute."

She turned her head back to the mattress.

When I'd regained control, I slowly began to massage her shoulders again.

Her groans returned, making my cock swell thickly.

"You still kissed him," I finally said. "It wasn't your first?" I assumed if she had been messing around with Jern, they would've done that too, but humans didn't make a whole lot of sense to me.

"It was." Her response was quiet. "You hurt me. Not physically—never physically—but when you lied to me, that hurt. I spent so damn long in that cellar, with no one but Jern and Gora. And then you saved me and protected me. I guess I just wanted you to be a better man than you are, and that's my fault, not yours."

The words were a blow to my chest, and to my damn pride.

I'd never tried to be a good man, but I'd spent my life trying to keep everyone around me alive. I'd given everything for my kingdom, yet I hadn't given the truth to my mate.

"I'm sorry." My voice was lower than it had ever been, and rougher with emotion, too. "I'm sorry, Lae. You were looking at me like I was a damn hero, and I didn't want that look to change. I was selfish—and you deserve more."

"Yeah, I do." Her words were quiet.

I continued rubbing her shoulders, working years and years of knots out of those muscles.

"You should probably go," she whispered.

"No." I dug my thumbs in deeper, and she groaned again.

When she turned to look at me once more, there was confusion in her eyes. "You just said I deserve better. That implies you're going to leave me so I can find better."

"I said you deserve better, implying that I'm going to *be* better. I'm not leaving you to damn *Toveo*; he can't take better care of you than me. No one can."

She groaned again as I worked one of the more resilient knots in her shoulders, and those pretty eyes closed. "I am *not* committing to you."

"You don't need to. My palm and your arm both glow with the statement that we belong to each other."

"You're insane."

"I never claimed not to be."

She heaved a sigh. "Fine. We're setting rules, though. I'm not here for a repeat of the bathing pool incident. If you ever dump me in a pool again, we're done."

"And if you ever come home smelling like another man again, I'll chain you to my damn bed for an entire week, and drag you to the edge of climax on my tongue again, again, and again without letting you find release. Understood?"

"Veil, this is not progress," she muttered, dropping her head to the pillow. "I changed my mind."

"No, you didn't. My rule is that you don't let another man put his hands on you. What's yours?"

"I'm going to regret this." She pushed some hair out of her face, sagging against the pillow as I continued massaging her. "Fine. My rule is that you have to be nice to me. I'm tired of getting snarled at."

I'd done a really terrible job of winning her over, hadn't I?

"*Nice* isn't measurable," I said. "And I'm not practiced in it."

"Then the deal is off." She groaned at my touch.

"No. Come up with a way to measure it." I worked one of the larger knots, and she lost her voice for a moment before finally straining,

"Fine. If I give you a glare or tell you to stop something, you stop. If you don't stop, you've broken the boundary, and you give me as much space as I ask for."

"As much as you ask for? No. One day of as much space as you want, and then I at least get the chance to grovel."

I couldn't believe I was bargaining for the chance to *grovel*.

But... maybe for her, I'd do it.

"Veil, you're stubborn," she grumbled.

"And you're not?"

"Fine, fine. We've officially made rules. I won't touch anyone else, and you'll be nice to me, especially around water."

"And we'll share a bed every night," I added.

"I don't remember agreeing to that one."

"You didn't. That's my rule."

"Alright, if you're making a rule about sharing a room, I need a rule that gives me space from you. I'm still trying to figure out who I am outside the cellar, so I need time apart, too," she said.

I dug my fingers in harder, just to get another groan from her. "It's not safe for you to have time alone here."

"Gleam can stay with me, then," she said. "Or Elwynne. Or anyone you want—I just need some space to make sure this is what I actually want."

"I'll be what you want," I growled.

"It's easy to say that, but harder to prove it. And so far, you haven't proven it." Her words were harsh, but deserved. "It's going to take me time to move past your selfish reasoning for abducting me, even though you rescued me in the process."

When she put it like that, I sounded like an absolute asshole. I supposed I deserved it, too.

"I didn't intend to like you," I admitted. "The goal was just to save myself. One of the elves' leaders felt your magic through the earth, and sent me after you. If it was anyone but the Demon hunting me, I wouldn't have bothered."

"I don't even want to think about the Demon coming after us," Laeli mumbled. "Why is he hunting you?"

"Vayme Vuuth believes someone from his kingdom sent the assassins after us. He'll look into it further when he's back."

"Well, that's reassuring."

"I won't let anything happen to you," I said.

"*You're* afraid of the Demon. How would you protect me from him?" she countered.

"I'd give myself to him before I'd let him touch you."

She groaned at the pressure on her shoulders. "Veil, you're good at this. Don't tell me you learned on your last life partner."

I chuckled. "I've never had a life partner. You'll be the first."

"*Life partner* does not have the same ring to it as *mate*. And I never agreed to be either of those things, as you know." She groaned again. "You've got to stop. I'm not going to be able to sleep without this next time."

My lips curved upward wickedly. "I can think of another way to relax you."

Her foot shot out, kicking me. It didn't hurt in the slightest, but I grumbled at her as if it did. "Another rule: nothing sexual can happen until I've decided I'm willing to consider being with you in a romantic capacity."

"*Something* sexual already happened," I pointed out. "But that's fine; you're going to beg me to taste you soon."

She scowled at me. "I'm not going to beg you for *anything*."

"We'll see, Lae." I dug my thumbs into her muscles again, and she finally pushed my hands away.

"This is all too much."

I dragged her into my arms. She sighed as I tucked her head beneath my chin, holding her close.

"I hate how much I like this," she muttered. "Why do you feel so damn good?"

"Ask fate." My chest rumbled against her back, and I pulled her closer, catching the tiniest bit of Toveo's scent in her hair. "Veil, I need to scrub you clean."

"Tomorrow," she whispered.

"Only if you'll let me touch you to mark you with my scent afterward."

"Fine." She sighed softly. "I should hate your possessiveness."

"You'd be just as angry if you smelled another woman on me."

"I'm not going to think about or acknowledge that statement."

I chuckled. "Go to sleep, Lae."

"My parents used to call me that." Her words were barely audible. "Don't use it if you're going to hurt me again."

My heart clenched.

I ached to hear her story... but I'd have to wait until she was ready to give it to me.

"I won't."

She made a noise of agreement, and then slowly, her breathing evened out. I cradled her to my chest, closing my eyes and focusing on the feel of her in my arms rather than the scent lingering on her skin.

She was mine; she would always be mine.

I'd survive a few hours of another man's scent on her.

CHAPTER ELEVEN
LAELI

"What are you doing?" I groaned, as Ravv lifted me out of bed.

I felt disoriented—I could've fallen asleep a few minutes earlier, a few hours earlier, or a few *days* earlier for all I could tell.

"I can't stand his scent on you for another minute," he growled at me, gripping me tightly to his chest.

"Really, Ravv?"

"It's been nearly twelve hours. I let you sleep, and now I need you clean." He slipped into the water with me, instead of dropping me in. "Go back to sleep if you want. I can wash you whether your eyes are open or not."

I slowly wrestled my head off his shoulder, as his big, soapy hands ran over my back.

A groan escaped me at the feel of his touch—and his erection against my core. "This should *not* turn you on."

He grumbled at me but resumed scrubbing. My dress was still on— which I assumed was because I hadn't given him permission to strip it off me.

At least he had respected that.

"Can I take this off?" He tugged lightly on one of my sleeves.

"Mmhm." I leaned away from him as he slid it over my head and tossed it to the floor.

His eyes collided with my breasts, and he went still.

I glanced down.

Right.

I wasn't wearing anything under my dress.

"Veil, I need to feed you more," he said.

I tried to push him away, but he pulled me tighter.

"Asshole," I snapped.

"I can still see your ribs, Lae."

"You see me naked and your first comment is that I need to eat more? What is your problem?" I tried again to push him away, and he only dragged me closer. My bare chest collided with his, and I sucked in a sharp breath at the delicious heat of it.

"It was an observation, not an insult. You don't want to hear the rest of my thoughts about you," he growled.

My hurt swelled.

His mind opened to me—just opened, like a damn door.

The first thing I saw was a detailed fantasy of him with his fingers buried inside me and his lips wrapped around my nipple. My face was twisted with pleasure, my bare body pinned beneath his.

More images flickered.

His face between my thighs.

His cock filling me.

His mouth on my breasts, my belly, my mouth, and my throat.

Him drinking my blood.

"Breathe, Lae." He squeezed my hips and closed the doors between our minds.

My chest was rising and falling rapidly.

"Don't believe for a second that I'm not interested in your bare body." He lifted me further up his cock so the length of it pressed against my core, though his shorts separated us. "I want you in every damned way there is."

"Okay," I managed.

The words were nearly a squeak.

He eased me away from his erection, set me on the floor so my legs hung off the edge, and then started scrubbing the rest of me down.

I was in too much shock to protest or take over.

His hands were strong but gentle as he slowly cleaned my skin, taking his time to massage my arms, legs, and feet as he went.

When he pulled me back into the bathing pool to work on my hair, my eyes were already closed, and I was relaxing against him. The way he massaged my scalp was blissful.

Ravv finally finished scrubbing me clean, and then held my body to his as I let myself snuggle against him for a few minutes. He was big, hard, and warm—the perfect combination.

And he held me like I mattered to him, which made me feel good, even if I knew I was going to have to retreat physically and emotionally from him as soon as we were up and dressed.

Eventually, I told him we needed to get out. He eased us both from the pool and dried me off before drying himself. I watched him closely, though I didn't want to admit that I was curious to see if he would really treat me differently after our conversation.

I hadn't gotten growled at in a while, which seemed like progress compared to the day before.

"I can get myself dressed," I murmured to him, stepping away to put a little space between us.

He looked like he wanted to protest, but dipped his head in a nod.

Progress.

He dried himself and pulled on a pair of the tight shorts he wore as an undergarment, while I slipped into my own, and then the black dress I'd worn since the Timeless Sands. It was clean and fresh, when it hadn't been the day before, so I assumed he had cleaned it.

That made my chest warm a bit.

"I'd like to have breakfast alone, so we can spend some time apart," I told him, meeting his gaze steadily. "After I eat, you can show me around the city, if you're interested?"

He grimaced but agreed, and I slipped out of the room alone.

Even after our conversation, I was surprised it had been that easy. I scratched Gleam's head as I passed her, and she continued snoring without missing a beat.

As soon as I stepped inside the dining hall, I noticed a tiny blue-haired woman sitting in the corner of the room, looking ill. There were only a few other people inside, and she was so much smaller than them that I had to assume she was human.

She had a gigantic gray wolf sitting next to her with its side pressed against her legs. Though she had three plates of food in front of her, one of her hands was buried in the wolf's fur while the other held her utensil.

After I stopped in the kitchen to ask for a plate of my own, I sat down across from the woman and flashed her a smile. "Hey. You're human, right?"

Veil, she was as pale as I was.

She nodded, and I noticed her hair lift slightly in some kind of breeze. There was no wind in the dining hall, so I didn't know where the breeze was coming from.

Maybe from her?

"I am too. I'm Laeli."

Her shoulders relaxed slightly. "I'm Kaelle." She pronounced it kay-ell. "At least I'm not the only one."

"There's another one of us too—her name's Nissa. She has plant magic, and she's mated to Kier."

Kaelle grimaced. "He's terrifying."

"Is your king not?"

She shuddered. "Vayme is worse."

The poor girl looked absolutely terrified.

"Did he abduct you too? Ravv likes to tell me he rescued me, which is technically true, but I'm pretty sure he would've stolen me away even if I'd been happy in my old life."

"Yeah. My village kept me protected in a cave outside town so I wouldn't kill their crops with my wind. There was never enough food to go around, even before my magic came in," she admitted.

Damn, she hadn't even been a *prisoner*. I knew my luck had been shitty.

"I'm sorry." I reached across the table and squeezed her hand. "The king of my city kept me locked in a cellar beneath their prison, so I can imagine the misery of that."

Her eyes flooded with horror. "Veil."

"Yeah. At least we're free now."

She nodded, though she looked a bit nauseous. "How are you not scared senseless? You don't even look nervous about being here, and I feel like I can barely breathe through the terror."

My lips curved upward, and I leaned toward her. "The best way to stop being afraid is to act like you're not. The more confidently you carry yourself, the more people will believe you're confident, even if you're terrified on the inside."

She sighed. "That sounds... difficult."

"But worth it."

She nodded reluctantly.

Someone brought my food out, and we both grew quiet as we ate. A few minutes into the meal, I let myself look around the room until my gaze caught on a large man.

A familiar large man.

"Dammit, Ravv," I growled into his mind, continuing to eat like nothing was wrong at all.

"You wanted space. I'm giving you space." His words were far calmer than I expected. *"You're free to be alone and do as you wish, and I'm free to know where you are and what you're doing."*

"I told you Gleam or Elwynne could come with me."

"Both of them are sleeping. Just act like I'm not here." He continued eating.

I looked back at Kaelle and found her slouching against her chair, her eyelids barely open. "Are you okay?"

"Yeah. I think I just need to go to bed," she whispered. "It's been a long week."

That felt like the understatement of the century.

"Get out of here, then." I waved her toward the door, and she nodded. She leaned against the giant wolf as she made her way out of the dining hall.

I expected Ravv to come over and sit by me, but he remained where he was.

"What do you call the big, magical wolves?" I asked him.

"Xuno. The one with the blue-haired human is Vayme's bonded beast. His name is Strong."

I took a big bite of my food. *"How well do you and the other kings know each other?"*

"Not well. We've been enemies for centuries, but we've met on the battlefield enough times to know certain facts about each other—and we were forced to get on civil terms as we negotiated for peace. It took a few years to get from peace talks to actually ending the war."

I nodded, then focused on my food.

Eventually, Elwynne showed up at the dining hall and leaned in close to whisper something to Ravv.

I ignored the jealousy that stirred in my lower belly, refusing to envy a woman I didn't know when it came to a man I had never actually decided I wanted. We were mates, but fate wasn't all-powerful. It couldn't always be right.

"A few of my warriors are getting too vicious in today's events," Ravv told me, his voice laced with irritation. Since it wasn't geared toward me, my lips curved upward just a bit. *"I need to go deal with them. Elwynne will show you around the city today—just tell her when the distance starts causing you pain, and she'll take you closer to me. I don't want you at the fights."*

"What if I want to see the fights?" I countered.

"You don't."

He was right.

I didn't want to admit it, but I also didn't want to go to the fights.

"Alright, I'll stay with Elwynne."

"Thank you." I could tell the words were foreign to him. He wasn't someone who thanked people often, but he was trying for me.

And damn, I liked that.

Elwynne sat down across from me, and someone put a plate in front of her a moment later. She thanked them, which warmed me up to her pretty quickly.

Something about the way they'd spoken to each other irked me, though. Her leaning in... it made me curious. And irritated. And... well, I still refused to call it possessive.

"You're not interested in Ravv romantically, right?" I asked her, deciding not to let my resentment build when I might have seen incorrectly.

Her eyebrows shot upward. "Veil, no."

I waited for an explanation.

Her lips slowly stretched in a smile. "You're possessive of him already."

"I'm choosing not to call it that." I took a bite of my food.

She laughed. "I'm not interested in him as anything but a friend. Ravv, Orvay, and I have been friends for so long that Ravv's nearly a brother to me. Orv and I are somewhere between lovers and life partners, anyway. We've spent every eclipse together over the past few centuries."

That made me feel slightly better. "Orvay is Ravv's left-hand man?"

She grinned. "Yes. Say that to his face when you meet him."

Her expression was so contagious that I found myself grinning too.

Maybe Elwynne wasn't so bad.

We headed out as soon as we were done eating, and spent the day wandering the city. Jirev was massive, with a huge marketplace full of shops.

We chatted as we walked around trying a ton of different foods, and Elwynne told me stories about the battles she, Ravv, and Orvay had fought. She bought me three dresses that fit and some more undergarments too, thankfully. I shared stories about my time in the cellar, laughing about Jern and Gora's antics, and didn't touch on anything before that time in my life.

Ravv ended up staying at the events for most of the day to keep the peace, and though the handprint on my shoulder throbbed a bit at our distance, I ignored the pain. He checked in a few times to make sure I was doing alright, and met up with us for lunch, but otherwise gave me the space I requested.

By the time we finally retreated back to the castle, I was exhausted. I fell asleep the moment my head hit the pillow, barely stirring when Ravv slipped into bed with me and pulled my body to his.

The next day went the same, with Elwynne and I chatting and exploring.

But after lunch, Ravv's mind touched mine and asked me to find him. Elwynne led me to the location he named—a building not far from the castle—and when we got there, we found all three of the kings waiting, along with the other humans.

All three men were equally tall and intimidating, though they looked different. Vayme had brown hair and tan skin, was the only one with a beard (though it was trimmed short), and his hair was longer than the other two men's, falling all the way to his shoulders. I had to agree with Kaelle that he did look the scariest, though not by much.

"What are you angry about?" I asked Ravv, noticing the rage in his eyes.

"You're going to start training." Even in our minds, his jaw sounded clenched.

"And that makes you mad because..."

"Because I don't like the idea of other humans swinging swords at you."

Right.

Should've expected that one.

"It's alright, I can probably cook them if they try to hurt me," I said to lighten the mood.

"Your magic doesn't work fast enough. We need to try to control it, too."

"I don't think it's controllable. Nissa mentioned that she can't control hers either, and I noticed Kaelle's hair blowing around, which didn't seem intentional."

Ravv's gaze grew slightly curious, and I realized that at least a little of his anger was just a front to distance himself from the other kings and seem like more of a threat. *"Perhaps humans weren't meant to hold magic as strong as yours."*

"Seems likely," I admitted.

"You still need to prepare for the fight we're using as an excuse for having you here," he told me. *"You'll be training a lot until I'm confident you can go into the cage without dying."*

"Thanks for believing in me," I drawled back.

The kings put swords in our hands, and told us to fight each other to show them what we could do.

We exchanged blank stares.

Those swords were too damn heavy.

They finally decided to start from the basics, and had us run through hour after hour of fighting positions.

My body was screaming by the time we went back to the castle for dinner and sleep, and I collapsed in bed afterward without so much as a word to Ravv.

CHAPTER TWELVE
LAELI

The next two weeks passed in a whirlwind of food and training. We didn't see any sign of the magical assassins hunting the kings, thankfully.

Ravv gave me the space I asked for, and I appreciated it.

I also appreciated the comfortable feel of his skin against mine when we went to bed every night. And the way he massaged my scalp when I let him wash my hair.

My muscles were still sore when we finally entered the cage on the day of the fight the kings had planned, wearing the most ridiculous outfits I'd ever seen. They were literally metal lingerie, made with strips of metal that barely covered the important bits. We had small scarves of glittering fabric tied dramatically over our handprints, too.

Our swords were stupidly heavy, and though I'd gained plenty of weight with our constant eating, I was nowhere near the level of a fae warrior, nor would I ever be.

The crowd roared as we walked deeper into the cage, the sound nearly deafening. A fae man waited for us; he had announced our magic before we even entered.

Kaelle looked nauseous, so I leaned close to her and called out, "Are you alright?"

"I don't know." Her gaze flitted around the massive crowds of fae in the stands. The stadium was so loud, I could barely hear her. The wind that constantly blew around her picked up, whipping all of our hair around our faces. "Something's wrong," she said, her voice barely audible.

"What's going on?" Ravv growled into my mind. *"Why is her wind blowing harder?"*

"I'm not sure."

"I'm getting you out of there."

"I'll be fine." I stopped him quickly, before he did something to make the rest of the fae suspicious about the possibility of a bond.

The announcer dragged us into place until the three of us faced each other, and then he called for the fight to start with a booming yell.

We all stayed where we were while he crossed the cage, then shut the door.

One of Kaelle's hands lifted to her head, pressing to her temple as she leaned her weight against the sword she held in her other hand. Her face was twisted, like she was in pain.

Slowly, the crowd's roaring quieted.

Nissa looked at me.

I had no idea what was wrong with Kaelle, but everyone was staring at us. If we didn't do something fighting-related, they were going to get mad. And then they were going to get suspicious.

I shrugged at Nissa, and lifted my sword.

She did the same.

Before we could take a swing at each other, Kaelle whispered, "He's here."

Her magic whipped around all of us, but I paid no attention to the way it slapped my skin.

The crowd was silent.

"Who?" I asked her.

She breathed, "One of the assassins. I can feel him."

Nissa's eyes went wide. "How can you feel him? How do you know?"

"I see and feel auras," Kaelle admitted. "My wind comes from them. And his aura is *terrible*."

Ravv demanded to know what was going on again, but I didn't answer him.

My confidence was draining away, my body starting to freeze up the way it had when I was captured in the Sands.

The fear hit me hard—so hard I could barely breathe.

"What are you waiting for?" Ravv shouted from the stands. Kaelle's wind was so loud he couldn't hear us. He didn't know there was an assassin there—he didn't know he needed to run.

"What do we do?" Nissa demanded.

"I don't know." Kaelle looked just as terrified as I felt.

I tried to shove my fear away to talk to Ravv, to get him out of there, but couldn't make my mind connect with his.

"We need to get everyone out," I finally told them, my desperation swelling. My arms were already steaming; soon, they'd be flaming.

"Oh, it's far too late for that," a sexy male voice purred. A man appeared next to Kaelle, and I jerked away, stumbling backward. "Which one of you is connected to Kier Jirev?"

The man was gorgeous, with tan skin and wavy dark hair, and he had to be at least a little bigger than the fae kings.

Despite his beauty, his eyes were glowing red, and his lips lifted in a wicked grin.

He was looking for Kier... which meant he wasn't the Demon hunting Ravv.

But veil, he was still right in front of us.

"The Beast of the Endless Wilds," I whispered.

I didn't hear a peep from the stands.

"Get out now," Ravv snarled into my mind, but I didn't move.

I *couldn't* move.

The Beast's grin widened, flashing me a glimpse of his fangs. "Hello, sweetheart. Is Kier using your magic to hide his?"

I didn't say a damn thing.

Shouting erupted above us, and the fae in the stands poured out. They were warriors, but no warrior could compare to the elves' assassins, if the legends were true.

The door to the cage started rattling like someone was trying to get through it. The Beast must've locked it from the inside, trapping us in and keeping everyone else out.

Kaelle's wind had graduated to a ferocious storm, whipping at my fire and making the flames swell larger.

She started to say something, but Nissa blurted,

"I'm mated to Kier. It's me."

The Beast's grin grew wicked. "See how easy that was?"

My magic flared bigger, brighter, and hotter.

I couldn't see a damn thing, and stayed where I was as my flames grew, and grew.

I'd never lost control so completely while wind blew like that, dragging my fire higher and higher.

The Beast called out above the wind and flames, "Surely a fae king of any worth would at least attempt to defend the female he's claimed as his. Come out and fight, Kier."

My fire kept burning.

The wind grew so strong that I had to move to keep myself upright, though my flames concealed everything around me.

"Find the door, Lae. Find the door, and get it open," Ravv commanded me. His anger was gone, and a lethal calm was in its place.

He was locked out.

I saw some part of the cage in front of me, and surged toward it. My hands collided with thick bars, but I still couldn't see through the damn fire.

It didn't feel like a door.

I started moving, trying to feel around in hopes that I'd find it. The Beast still had Nissa—but if I couldn't see the damn door, I couldn't see the assassin, either.

"Stay as far from the Beast as you can," Ravv ordered.

He must've gotten into the room.

The wind started to die down, and I let out a shaky breath as the mass of my flames slowly started to shrink. I turned my back to the cage's bars and remained where I was, hoping it could keep me safe.

Finally, the flames shrank enough that I could see.

Nissa was unconscious, her shoulder bleeding and her skin an unnatural gray.

The Beast moved so fast—and he was close to me. Close enough that I could do something about it.

He had started as a shifter before the elves' magic changed him, which meant he wasn't fireproof, unlike the Demon and the Monster.

Despite the fear in my chest, the panic in my lungs, and the way I could feel my energy fading as my fire literally burned it away, I could do something to help.

With a yell, I launched myself at the Beast as he ran toward someone else.

Time seemed to slow as I crashed into him.

Ravv roared behind me.

The Beast let out an unearthly scream.

Ravv grabbed me, yanking me to his chest and snarling into my ear and mind.

The words didn't register.

Nothing registered except that same damn fear.

It was overwhelming. It made my throat hurt, and my chest ache. It made my mind spin. Veil, it made *everything* spin.

I closed my eyes against the terror, not hearing anything despite the voices sounding around me.

Finally, Ravv's chest rumbled against me as he said to someone else, "I'll follow the Beast's scent trail to make sure he's gone. You'll need to check the city for signs of the Demon and the Monster."

I wanted to say no.

I wanted to ask him to stay with me.

His chest rumbled again as he asked Elwynne to take me back to the castle, and she agreed.

Ravv's lips brushed my ear, and his mind touched mine as he murmured, *"Once, when Gleam and I went fishing, she fell through a hole in the ice and landed in the water. She's a fierce warrior, but she may also very well be the clumsiest idorr you'll ever meet."*

I recognized what he was doing immediately:

Telling me stories about fishing simply because I told him reading aloud would help me.

And veil, maybe it didn't make much sense, but his words distracted me enough that my flames started to retreat just slightly.

"I need you to stop burning so you can get back to our room, where you'll be safe," he said gently, before continuing the story. *"There was a massive sea dragon just below the ice when she fell in. My heart nearly stopped when I saw it—but Gleam just swam down and rubbed against her, greeting the damned shifter like they were old friends."*

My flames faded bit by bit as he continued, until finally, they went out completely.

I was still steaming, and I was fairly confident I'd be hot to the touch, but Ravv didn't waste any time. He handed me to Elwynne as soon as my fire was gone.

She tucked me against her chest as she slid onto the back of her bonded idorr, Swift, and he ran.

Elwynne's skin was red when she finally put me down in my room in the castle.

I crashed to my knees, and my flames erupted again.

"I'm so sorry," I whispered to her, my eyes shining with tears. I was shaking—I was pretty sure I was shaking.

"It's not your fault," she said, her gaze steady and clear despite the burns she wore.

"It is."

I was the one who couldn't control my magic.

I was the one who couldn't control my *fear*.

"You need to find something for your burns," I told her. "And for Swift's, if he has any."

She shook her head.

I glowered at her. "Get something for your damn burns, Elwynne. I won't be able to live with myself if you don't."

She hesitated for a long moment.

Swift finally nudged her arm, and then she dipped her head in a nod, and left.

My body quivered as I struggled to my feet and crossed the room. My hands trembled as I slid the lock into place, shutting it properly, like Elwynne had taught me a few days earlier.

With the door secure and my body still blazing fire, I finally stumbled over to the bathing pool and slipped inside.

Tears trailed down my cheeks, and my body shook with the weight of my terror.

My chest rose and fell rapidly, my heart beating like a drum in my ears.

I was fine.

But the memories the fear brought back...

They were not fine.

My family's home on fire.

The burns on my father's skin as he dropped me in the hay, staring at me with fear in his eyes.

The swords that had cut down the people I loved.

The dirt and stone cellar I'd been thrown into all alone, after losing everyone and everything I loved.

I squeezed my eyes shut and prayed—I prayed to the veil, to any of the lost gods who might still be listening, to *anyone* who could possibly hear me.

I prayed that they'd take my memories, that they'd erase my past, that they'd finally let me forget the horrors I had lived through.

But the memories didn't fade.

The tears continued to fall.

And the agony in my mind, in my heart, in my chest... it lingered.

Eventually, my fire burned through the remainder of my energy and knocked me out.

Through the haze of my exhaustion, I thought I heard someone pounding on the door.

Then I thought I heard Ravv snarling into my mind.

And then there was just warmth, and silence.

Everything was blurry when I opened my eyes.

I found myself cradled in Ravv's arms, tucked beneath blankets that smelled like us.

Memories flooded my mind again, and water pooled in my eyes.

"Lae," Ravv's voice and chest rumbled.

I squeezed my eyes shut and said nothing.

He lifted me to a seated position. I opened my eyes just a crack, and my amber orbs met his worried, intense purples as he growled, "You need to eat."

I wasn't hungry.

It might've been the first time for that, ever.

I didn't say a word as he set a plate on my lap.

Or as he lifted the food to my mouth and commanded me to take a bite.

Or as I noticed the broken doors positioned over the doorway.

I did as he said, slowly eating as much as I could manage before my nausea returned.

My eyes leaked tears every now and then, and Ravv silently wiped them away without questioning them.

He thought I was crying because of the Beast, and I didn't correct him.

I couldn't bring myself to consider saying the words aloud.

So I ate, and then I slept.

He held me through as much of it as he could, updating me about Nissa's recovery when I asked, and telling me that I was stronger than I realized.

I didn't disagree vocally... but my mind was another matter.

A few days passed before Ravv finally murmured to me that it was time to go back to Loire.

He lifted me onto Gleam's back, and followed us out of the castle on foot.

I didn't say goodbye to anyone.

He didn't ask me to.

I buried my face in Gleam's fur when Ravv mounted behind me, and his body pressed to mine as he leaned against me.

Vayme had taken Kaelle to find the elves, and threaten them with war against all three fae kingdoms if they couldn't protect the kings against the assassins they created. The elves had agreed, and sent a handful of their people back to protect us.

The mysterious women traveled with us, all of them outfitted in flowy dresses and riding on the backs of idorr with female fae.

Ravv left me to my thoughts as we rode throughout the Wilds for the rest of that day, finally stopping for the night when both moons were shining their light through the trees.

He set me down on a sturdy rock and then left me for a few minutes. Elwynne and Gleam were both close, though Elwynne was chatting with someone I didn't know, and Gleam was already taking a nap.

I noticed a few of the fae eyeing me. Some looked curious—others looked stricken.

"Is there a reason your people are staring at me?" I asked Ravv, my voice quiet in his mind.

"I had to tell them about the bond after the Beast's attack. They know we intend to let it break with the eclipse, so no one's tried to kill us yet."

Yet.

I didn't love that.

My mind was still dark with the echoes of the memories I was trying to suppress, so I just said, *"Fantastic."*

Ravv didn't reply to that.

He sat down on the dirt beside me a few minutes later, handing me a small bag of various fruits and vegetables. *"Eat, Lae."*

I wasn't hungry, but it wasn't worth the fight, so I ate what I could.

His lips were pressed in a tight line when I handed the bag back, but he didn't ask if I was okay.

He still thought I was just afraid.

A fae woman wove through the crowd, bowing her head slightly when she approached us. The bow was for Ravv, of course. "The Demon was spotted flying overhead," she said.

Ravv's jaw clenched.

The blood drained from my face.

I wasn't ready to face another assassin.

The last one brought back memories that had nearly broken me, and he hadn't even hurt me.

I didn't want to know what the next one could do to me. And if he actually managed to kill Ravv... I'd be entirely alone again.

"The elves' shield is holding?" he asked.

"For now."

"How long will it hold?" I asked quietly.

"If the Demon attacks them, they don't know," the fae woman admitted.

Veil.

"It'll hold." Ravv's voice was steely.

Since he was the king, I supposed he needed to be the voice of hope and whatnot.

The woman dipped her head again and slipped back through the crowd.

I didn't bother disagreeing with Ravv's statement. It wouldn't do anything except make him angry, and I was tired of making him angry.

Veil, I was tired of everything.

Some part of me ached to go home, but I had no home. I didn't have a family to return to, or a safe place to hide.

"In exchange for our bond, I'd like a house in your city after the eclipse," I told Ravv. *"Or a ride back to Jirev, if it's safer there or they have a place for me. I don't care how big it is, or even if there's any furniture—I just a want a place to call home."*

"Of course." He didn't hesitate to agree, and some of my tension dissipated. *"As long as you'll forgive me for dragging you into this mess."*

My lips curved upward, just the tiniest bit. *"I can try."*

"Good enough." He paused for a moment, then added, *"You'll need to stay with me in the castle until the eclipse, though. After our bond is broken, you'll be safe."*

Even if I wasn't safe, I wouldn't be his problem anymore.

I supposed that was all he could offer me. He'd mentioned possibly wanting us to be life partners, but I was pretty sure that was just a possessive, heat of the moment thing. He didn't know me very well, so even if he was truly interested in me, it was just because of the bond.

"That's fair," I agreed.

A few other fae came to talk to Ravv about their planned route for the next day, so he built me an ice shelter before he went off to talk to them.

I eyed Elwynne, who was chatting with someone else, and debated going over to talk. When she noticed me watching her, she waved me over. I gave her a small smile and shook my head, then made my way into the shelter and curled up on the ice.

Ravv closed it without joining me, and my throat swelled. He needed to act like he wasn't interested in me romantically while we were traveling with his warriors, so I'd be sleeping alone.

They might have already started wondering if we had feelings for each other, but I didn't know.

And some part of me was too worried about rejection to ask him if he was coming to share the shelter.

So I just tried to get comfortable on the ice floor, and when that didn't work, I watched the ice drip until I couldn't keep my eyes open anymore.

CHAPTER THIRTEEN
LAELI

The next two days passed incredibly slowly.

The temperature gradually fell as we traveled through the Endless Wilds. We reached the frosty shore where the Wilds met the Glittering Sea that night, and I slept alone.

The next day, we filed onto a slim ice bridge that led toward the huge, frozen castle I could see a long way in the distance. I kept an eye out for the sea dragons that were supposed to live beneath the nearly-frozen water, but didn't see any.

The Demon flew slow, lazy circles over our heads the entire time we were on the bridge, and all of us were tense and quiet as the idorr ran through the day. His glittering red scales caught my eye and terrified me, but thankfully, he hadn't made a move against the elves' shield yet.

"We may need to leave at some point so we can attempt to lose him in the Wilds," Ravv admitted to me, as we finally neared the ice castle. It was even bigger up close, and I couldn't look away from the thick walls that looked like they wrapped around the whole city.

The bridge seemed to lead straight inside the castle. Because we were at the back of the group, Ravv's warriors had been pouring in for nearly an hour by the time we finally made it inside.

"Could the Demon melt the entire city?" I asked him, as Gleam carried us through the gate.

"No. Loire's ice was enchanted by the elves the same way Jirev's trees were."

That was a relief, I supposed.

I took in the castle's first massive room with a bit of surprise. The structure itself was made of smooth ice, of course, but thick, cozy-looking rugs stretched over much of the floors, and colorful landscape paintings hung at random on the walls around what seemed to be... the throne room?

There were a pair of frozen thrones pushed up against one of the walls like an afterthought.

The castle's gates shut behind us, and Ravv slipped off Gleam's back.

I glanced over my shoulder at him while he strode down one of the hallways, his mind brushing mine with the command, *"Rest. I'll find you when I can."*

That was a dismissal if I'd ever heard one.

Gleam carried me down a different hallway, moving faster than I expected. She barged into a room, dropped me on a bed, and then called out, *"I'm going to Coarse. Lock the door behind me,"* before vanishing.

The room suddenly seemed very, very empty.

And I suddenly felt very, very alone.

Theoretically, Jern and Gora were in the city. Part of me wanted to go out and look for them, too.

But with everyone knowing about my connection to Ravv, it likely wasn't safe for me to go out alone.

I tucked my feet beneath the blankets and lowered my head to the pillow.

When I closed my eyes, all I saw was flames.

Veil, I needed to get my mind out of the past. I needed to find a way to shut my memories out again, to *forget.*

But it had been ten years, and I still hadn't forgotten... which made me think I probably never would.

So I opened my eyes and peeked around the room. It was simple but cozy, with a huge, thick rug in a pretty shade of dark blue that reflected on the icy walls, making them look a little bluish too.

Other than the huge bed I occupied, and the rug, there was no other furniture. I could see two doors, which I assumed led to a closet and a bathroom. There were a few calm landscape paintings hanging up, showing images of the glacier the castle had been built on, and the ocean.

There were no books, not that I'd risk reading them if there were, and no other distractions either.

Which meant I needed to leave.

But I didn't want to risk my life, obviously.

So, after a few minutes of debating, I finally reached out to Ravv. I felt his attention the moment I did.

"I need you to find Jern and Gora for me," I told him.

"No." He didn't even consider it.

"I'm not tired enough to fall asleep right now, and I'm not staying in here alone all night. You said you would treat me better; this is your chance." I felt a little bad for tapping into his guilt, but he had left without a real explanation, and he was the reason my life was in danger in the first place.

"It's not safe for you to leave, and I don't want them in our room. Gleam went to Coarse?"

"Yes."

He grumbled but didn't sound surprised in the slightest. *"I'll send Elwynne to you."*

"I'd rather see my friends," I told him, my defenses rising a bit. *"I need to know they're okay."*

"We can find them first thing in the morning, but I'm being briefed about the war right now."

Veil.

I'd forgotten about the war, somehow.

"Elwynne needs to be there, then." I started closing myself off. *"I'll be fine alone."*

He swore. *"I'm sorry, Lae."*

I pulled away from him, then slipped off the bed. After I locked the door, I padded to the bathroom. My dress hit the floor as I walked, my toes digging into the soft carpet, and my undergarments followed.

There was no tub in the bathroom, just a large shower. Our room in Kier's castle had a shower too, so I knew of them, but I'd never used one before.

I watched the strange, large glass shape protruding from the ceiling as I turned the lever to start the water's flow. A moment later, water was raining on me. Though it didn't feel cold thanks to Ravv's magic, it didn't feel warm either.

Closing my eyes, I focused on the sensation. It was strangely soothing.

My body relaxed a bit as the water washed over me, wiping away two and a half days' worth of travel. I had survived—I was fine.

The Demon was probably still flying above our heads, but I would be okay.

He wasn't after me, anyway.

Ravv was in danger, but... well, I still wasn't entirely sure where I stood with him. He seemed to want me, but he didn't really know me, and I wasn't sure if I *wanted* him to know me.

He was grumpy and often angry, but fiercely protective.

He was rough and harsh, but gentle when it mattered.

He was demanding and insistent, but he...

There didn't seem to be a redeeming quality paired with those ones. Maybe confidence? The veil knew he had enough certainty in himself to fuel half a dozen other men.

Despite all of his negative qualities, the good ones seemed to outweigh the bad.

That could be because he saved me, though. As much as I hated to admit it, he *had* rescued me, and that would undoubtedly color my view of him.

Perhaps when I was back with Jern and Gora, they could help me look at the situation objectively.

I scrubbed my skin and hair before drying off and walking back to the bed, where I collapsed in an absolutely unattractive heap of wet hair and hot skin and fell asleep.

My problems could wait until the next day.

CHAPTER FOURTEEN
LAELI

Sunlight woke me in the morning.

It was incredibly disorienting to wake up to that, considering my years in the cellar and then my weeks living in a tree in Jirev.

I liked it, though.

The light made the icy walls and ceiling glitter, and my eyes trailed over the gleam of them before landing on the bed beside me.

Empty, and unwrinkled.

Ravv hadn't come to bed.

Insecurity thrummed unevenly in my chest.

Was he with another woman?

Veil, that was ridiculous to even consider.

But... still.

I had no idea what he was like in his kingdom, or whether or not we would have any kind of relationship at all.

My gut told me to distance myself further from him before he hurt me any more than he already had. I put on a tough façade, but it was just a mask. Beneath it, I was deeply afraid that I would lose everything again. I didn't have much, but I had started to feel like I had Ravv.

Veil, I didn't want to lose him.

But was I willing to fight for him? Was I willing to push him to make time for me? Or to try to get to know him more?

That, I didn't know.

"You're alive, right?" I finally asked him.

"I'm fine." His voice was weary. *"The war grew worse while we were gone, so we've been forming a plan. I'll take you to find Gora and Jern as soon as I get out of here."*

"Do what you need to. I can figure it out on my own," I said, slipping out of bed. My clothes were still on the floor—and still dirty.

"If you leave that room without me, I'll freeze you to the damn bed," he growled into my mind.

"You tried that already, with the floor in Jirev. I'll just melt your chains again."

"Don't, Lae. My people are not trustworthy."

"You do realize that probably says something about you as their leader?" I shot back.

"I'm aware that I'm a problem." His anger was fading. *"Unfortunately, the problem they chose. I'll end the meeting as soon as possible so I can get back to the room; don't do anything you'll regret. Gleam is probably in her room across the hallway—wake her and Coarse if you have to, but don't leave alone. I'm sorry to make you wait."*

"You've been apologizing a lot lately."

"Only to you. As far as everyone else knows, I regret nothing."

My lips curved upward just slightly as he pulled away, probably to focus on his meeting again.

There was nothing to do while I waited, though.

Nothing to occupy my mind.

And my smile disappeared as my thoughts slipped back to the past.

Back to the flames.

To the screams.

To the bodies.

A shudder tore through me.

Distraction—I needed a distraction.

All I had was myself. And I—

I pulled a pillow over my head and forced myself to count the seconds of my breaths.

In...2...3...4...

Out...2...3...4...

In...2...3...4...

Out...2...3...4...

Eventually, the panic subsided.

I continued focusing on my breaths as I waited for Ravv.

Veil, the way I was dealing with my past just seemed to be getting worse. What was I supposed to do about that?

The door rattled a bit when the king finally tugged on it. *"Unlock it, Lae."*

I let out a long breath.

It was fine.

I was going to be fine.

Slipping out of bed, I padded over to the door. My hands shook as I undid the lock.

Ravv pushed the door open and stepped inside, then took one look at me before he wrapped me in a hug.

My body seemed to deflate as he gripped me against his chest. The bedroom door was still open, but he didn't give a damn. My eyes watered at the warm comfort of his hug.

"I'm sorry that took so long," he said into my hair.

"It's okay," I whispered.

It wasn't okay.

I liked him more than I wanted to admit, and he could never put me first. His kingdom would always be his top priority, and veil, I was too much of a mess to be okay with being the second thing someone worried about. I was already that with Jern and Gora, and it was almost as lonely as being completely on my own.

If I could just keep my distance from him until after the eclipse, I could have my own place. I'd have time to move on from Ravv, and time to distance myself from the shitty memories the Beast had dredged up too.

...assuming the Demon didn't kill us first.

I didn't want to consider that option, though.

"What happened with the war?" I asked.

"The cult moved against the mated pairs and managed to break through their city's walls in their latest attack. The mated fae slaughtered the cultists when they came in, razing their numbers. There can't be many of them left at this point. But the cult killed two of the city's fae—one was a child."

"Veil."

"Many of my warriors are trying to persuade me to move against the cult. A war on two sides would be harder for them to fight, and we could strengthen the gates of the mated."

"Assuming none of the cultists managed to fool you into believing they're on your side."

"Exactly." He slid a hand through my hair slowly, and I squeezed my eyes shut at the peaceful bliss of the feeling. "The bonded idorr of cultists almost always abandon them after they've killed a mated fae, but it's not a certainty. A few of the idorr agree with them, which makes it difficult to tell friend from foe."

I could imagine.

"What you need is a way to destroy all of them at once," I murmured. "Like... a really big fire."

Ravv chuckled. "You're not getting involved in my war, Lae. My role is to protect you, not to risk your life."

"My life's already at risk. You saw the Demon flying above us just as much as I did."

His humor faded. "We have a plan for him too, now."

"What is it?" I lifted my face, meeting his gaze.

"We wait for him to attack. When he does, he faces the fury of an army of fae. Even a dragon can't survive our wrath."

"Aren't dragon scales impenetrable?"

"There are solutions one can coat their weapons with to cut through scales. We already have some hidden away in case the sea dragons decide to go to war with us, so we're ready."

I nodded, biting my lip.

There were many ways that plan could go wrong, but what was the alternative?

I didn't know of one, so I had no choice but to go along with it.

"Let's find your friends," he said, though he was already combing his fingers slowly through my hair again.

It was on the tip of my tongue to tell him we needed to stay in so he could rest, but the closer we grew emotionally, the more it would hurt when we separated.

So, I kept my mouth shut as he released my hand and led me out of the room.

"My male, you mean?" I teased him lightly as we walked, bringing back one of our first conversations in the mountains after he'd freed me.

He chuckled. *"Only if you want him to die."*

I rolled my eyes at him, though my lips curved upward a little.

Ravv led me through a few hallways before we finally emerged from the castle. All three of our suns shined down on us, and I found myself squinting against the light. It felt good on my skin, but it would take time for me to readjust to it after so long in Jirev. I'd grown to like the sunlight during our days traveling through the Human Lands and the Timeless sands, so I hoped I'd start to like it again.

Ravv said, *"The idorr want to meet you, as well. Many of them are without companions because most of our fae stopped reproducing. The mated pairs won't allow them in their city without being already bonded to one of those pairs, for their children's safety."*

My stomach curled with excitement. *"Do you think I can bond with one of them?"*

Veil, to have a companion...

It would change everything for me.

The fae could rely on their bonded beasts. They took care of each other, and became each other's closest friends and allies. Having a bonded idorr would mean having protection and security, as well as never being so entirely alone again.

"Kier's human bonded with an esu, so I don't see why not." He continued walking, both of us leaving distance between our bodies so no one would overthink if they saw us together.

My hope had returned though, fiercer than it had been in a long, long time.

My bond with an idorr wouldn't break when the eclipse came around. It would be unbreakable, and soul-deep.

And damn, I wanted it.

"Let's go to the idorr first. Jern and Gora can wait."

His lips curved upward as he glanced at me. *"Alright."*

There weren't many fae in the streets as we made our way through. I assumed most of them were resting or just enjoying being home after so many weeks in Jirev.

The cultists lived somewhere outside the city, according to Ravv. Since the mated pairs lived beneath it, the king's warriors were the only ones who lived inside the walls.

A flash of crimson caught my eye, and my excitement faded as I saw the Demon fly over our heads. His movements were slow and lazy, as if he was making an effort to let us know that he was confident he could kill us at any moment.

"The elves are still holding the shield, right?" I asked Ravv.

"Yes. They've been put in a protected wing of the castle, with guards that we trust implicitly. I doubt even the cultists would try to take the elves down though; no one wants to deal with the Demon."

I didn't blame them, either.

"This section of the city belongs to the idorr," he told me as we approached a large street. *"Most of them are mated at this point, and the mated ones share homes the way fae who are life partners do."*

"Where do Coarse and Gleam live?"

"They have a home here, but they spend most nights snuggled in my bed." Ravv's words were a grumble, but I could tell he wasn't bitter or annoyed. He probably liked having two big fuzzy pillows to cuddle with. *"They have a room across the hall from mine, too. I assume they're in there right now, but Gleam's still asleep so I can't ask."*

We turned onto their street, and I stopped in my tracks for a moment.

Despite the large houses on both sides of us, there were idorr outside. *Everywhere.*

Draped over stairs.

Plopped down on the street.

Walking around lazily.

I even saw two tiny ones wrestling. They must've been babies, and that about melted my heart. Maybe I'd bond to an adorable, tiny idorr.

"How do you choose one?" I asked Ravv.

"You don't choose. When it's right, your souls catch on each other and the bond forms. There's no fighting it or swaying it. Fate decides."

Well, I guessed that was good. If fate paired me with an idorr, it couldn't be angry with me, at least.

Probably.

A bunch of their heads lifted as they looked at us, and Ravv put a hand to my lower back, making sure I didn't stop.

"How long does it take for your souls to catch?"

"It can be instant, or it can take time."

Veil, that was nerve-wracking.

His hand remained on my back as we walked slowly through the town. When some of the idorr murmured friendly greetings, we greeted them back. I didn't feel any tug on my soul, unfortunately, even when the adorable furball cubs ran over.

Ravv crouched down to greet them, his expression soft as he scratched them behind the ears.

My heart melted a little at the sight, though I had to keep that quiet. I kneeled beside him, petting the babies too. One of them snuggled right up against me, and I smiled at the soft brush of fur.

"So if I don't bond with any of them today, it doesn't mean it's hopeless?" I asked.

"Not at all."

I laughed as the cub I was petting started licking my arm, urging me to continue rubbing its fur.

"Aren't you sweet?" I teased the little guy.

A soft nose brushed my shoulder as a large female idorr approached me. *"He hasn't quite figured out how to communicate with the fae yet,"* she murmured.

Her voice was calm, her body relaxed.

Veil, I hoped she would bond with me. Or her soul would bond with mine, I supposed. I could use that level of quiet confidence in my life.

"Well, he's beautiful," I told her. Her eyes were soft as she sat down beside me and lowered her massive head to rest against my leg. I scratched her head with my free hand, and she closed her eyes as she relaxed.

After a few minutes, the cubs ran off to play together. A few more of the adults came over and plopped down beside us, so Ravv and I chatted with them. He told them about Jirev when they asked, and explained our bond, as well as the dragon over our heads. None of the idorr seemed very concerned about the Demon, but that didn't surprise me since I'd seen how laid-back Gleam was.

My soul didn't connect to any of the beasts', so eventually, we thanked them for their company and headed out to find Gora and Jern.

CHAPTER FIFTEEN
LAELI

"Veil, I'm tired of pretending not to like you," Ravv grumbled to me, as we walked with an appropriate amount of space between our bodies.

"I don't think you're selling it well, either," I agreed. "You're not growling at me nearly as much as you used to."

"I promised to be nicer. I'm not breaking the damn promise," he growled back.

My lips curved upward slightly at the irony of his words paired with his growl.

"Where are Gora and Jern living?" I asked him.

"Coarse put them in one of the homes furthest from the cult and the mated fae. It's on the east end of the city, overlooking the ocean. You'll be a few houses down from them after the eclipse."

My throat swelled slightly at his mention of my future without him.

I really needed to put more distance between us... I just didn't want to.

"Can you show me my house?" I asked.

He agreed and tucked his hands in the pockets of his shorts.

My eyes scanned row after row of homes and shops, everything mixed together as it lined the streets. The city seemed to go on forever, especially while we walked on foot. *"Are all of these homes full?"*

"No, only a fraction of them are occupied. The city was built to house growing families and a thriving society long before the cult came into play. It'll be centuries before we build it back to what it was, even if we manage to clear out the rest of the cult and get the mated fae living back on the surface."

I saw everything with new eyes, knowing all of that.

Suddenly, the massive city and rows of homes seemed more sad and eerie than hopeful.

There had to have been fae living there, once. The streets must've been full at some point.

The fae may have enjoyed the fighting, but the horrors of war were still horrors.

"Are there many fae where I'm going to live?" I asked him.

"Plenty. It's where the strongest of our kingdom's warriors live; the home was mine, before Ria tried to kill our parents and I took the throne."

My head jerked toward him, my eyebrows lifting in surprise. *"You're giving me your old home?"*

He lifted a shoulder. *"I don't need it. I haven't lived there in centuries."*

Right.

It wasn't really his home. He wouldn't have given it to me if it was. His feelings for me were only because of the bond, and they would end with the eclipse, too.

If only I could figure out a way to stop developing feelings for him...

We continued walking, both of us lost in our thoughts. I itched to take his hand, but it was still buried in his pocket, which was probably a good thing anyway.

My stomach rumbled as we neared the houses, and Ravv growled at me. *"You didn't have breakfast?"*

"Someone abandoned me in a room all night and insisted I stay put."

His anger vanished, though his jaw clenched. *"I'm sorry."*

"Stop apologizing to me. If you want to be better, be better."

He jerked his head in a nod.

I hesitated, and then added, *"Thanks for caring enough to apologize, though."*

He nodded again, the movement slower and softer.

"This is Jern and Gora's house," he told me as we stepped up to a thick, icy door.

I rapped my fists against it and winced at the hardness. It may as well have been stone.

I heard murmuring on the other side of the door, and then it opened just a crack.

Gora's suspicious eyes met mine—and then relaxed. She tugged the door open, and Jern yanked me in for a tight hug.

"Veil, we were worried about you!" he exclaimed, pulling away to look me up and down.

Physically, I knew I looked fine.

Emotionally, the last few weeks had been tremendous. And not in a good way, for the most part.

At least I was out of the cellar. I had to keep reminding myself of that.

"You look great!" he added, eyes bright and happy.

"So do you. Look, you've finally got some squish!" Both of them had filled out a bit, and it made me happy for them. They had on long sleeves and pants, much warmer clothes than me or any of the fae. Gora didn't match the typical fae women's style, but I imagined short dresses were far too cold for someone who wasn't bonded with a fae.

Jern grinned. "Finally!"

He dragged me in for another hug, and Gora squeezed us both.

It was strange to see them clean. To see them *happy*.

"Show me your house," I told them. "Tell me everything. Do you have jobs? What have you been doing?"

"I'll wait outside," Ravv said, staying on the doorstep when Jern shut the door. *"Ask them for food."*

"The journey here was long and painful," Gora admitted. "But the fae have been friendlier than we expected. They gave us this place to live, and the first week, they kept it stocked with food for us. They asked us to help out on their farm, and have been paying us plenty to do so."

"We eat like kings," Jern agreed, still grinning.

My stomach chose that moment to rumble.

"Speaking of *kings*..." Gora eyed me.

"We're just friends. *Barely* friends," I said quickly.

"I was going to ask if he's been feeding you."

Oh.

"He usually stuffs me so full of food that I'm sick. We just got back here, though, so he's still trying to figure out the dynamic."

"Then we get the pleasure of feeding you," Jern winked at me.

Ravv growled into my mind, and I fought a snort. "Tell me about your farming."

Jern started throwing some food together for me. I hadn't watched anyone cook since I was a child, so I found myself watching his movements. Something about the motion was familiar and peaceful, though it brought back memories.

So many memories.

I tried hard to focus on their stories, but my thoughts were going back to the damn past again.

I could nearly envision my mother in Jern's place, cooking as she told stories with a smile on her face.

My throat swelled with emotion, but I forced myself to act like nothing was wrong.

Jern and Gora didn't know my story. They didn't know what had happened to my family, or how I had ended up in the cellar. I'd heard them whisper about their own pasts together, but it wasn't something I'd ever discussed with either of them.

Still, I was fine.

Everything was fine.

Their food couldn't compare to what the chefs in Jirev made, but I appreciated it anyway. They had to buy their own ingredients and figure everything out themselves, and I respected that.

I'd need to learn how to cook, too.

And get a job.

Veil, what would the fae let me do? I didn't have any skills, and my magic was more of a liability than anything, especially around things like plants, which could burn. There was no reason ice fae would need a human with fire magic. I certainly wasn't a warrior, either.

My bittersweet memories pushed that worry away for another day while I continued chatting with the couple as if nothing was wrong.

Eventually, I reached out to Ravv, to make sure he was doing alright. *"Is your ass numb yet?"*

There was no response.

Fear clenched my stomach as I thanked the couple and slipped out of their house. That fear heightened when I found Ravv sitting a few feet from the entrance, with his back to the house and his head on his shoulder. I dropped to my knees beside him and put a hand on his throat, checking his pulse.

It beat rhythmically against my fingers, and I let out a relieved breath.

Sleeping.

He was just sleeping.

"Ravv." I brushed my hand against his face, but he didn't stir. *"Ravv,"* I said a bit louder, speaking into his mind again.

He finally lifted his head, cracking tired eyes at me and frowning. "What happened?"

"You fell asleep." I brushed a few of his messy curls off his forehead without thinking, and then withdrew my hand quickly.

My gaze darted around us, but I didn't see anyone else. That didn't necessarily mean they weren't there or watching.

"You can show me my house another day," I told him, pulling my hand back and standing up.

He looked exhausted, and proved that he was when he didn't argue with me.

We walked back to the castle quickly. I tried to memorize the route as we wove through streets until we finally reached the massive structure. Then, I tried to remember the path through the castle as we headed to Ravv's room.

I still wasn't tired when he locked the door behind us and climbed into bed, dragging me into his arms the moment he was settled. I was still feeling a bit dark after all those damn memories had filtered their way to the front of my mind.

"At least today's over," he said into my hair.

"It's the middle of the day."

"It's yesterday for me." His lips brushed my head once, and then again. "I'm glad you're here."

As insane as it probably made me, I was glad I was there too.

He fell asleep quickly, leaving me staring at the ceiling. More memories of my mother slowly filled my mind until tears leaked from my eyes. The salty water didn't wake Ravv up, thankfully, as I cried for the woman I'd loved so damn much.

Veil, life had been easier when I could pretend the past never happened.

I needed a way to separate myself from all of the memories that had started returning after we faced the Beast... but I was starting to think that was an impossibility. My memories demanded to be heard, and no one could listen but me.

Eventually, I managed to quiet my mind long enough for a nap, and sleep's embrace was exactly the blissful escape I needed.

"Move over," Gleam said into my mind, as she nudged me with her nose.

I lifted my head, meeting her gaze with bleary eyes.

She nudged me again, and I scooted back against Ravv.

His hand landed on my hip and squeezed roughly. I thought I heard him mumble something, but couldn't tell what he'd said as I pressed my backside to his erection and used it to guide him backward.

His hand on my hip tightened again, and he pulled me closer until his erection was nestled between my ass cheeks.

My body flushed with heat.

"Gleam is here," I said into his mind. *"Move over."*

He didn't budge.

"Move over, Ravv," I repeated, pushing against him.

He finally slid across the mattress, dragging me with him, then muttered something that sounded suspiciously like, *"reek,"* and promptly fell back asleep.

One furry body plopped down right up against me—and then another followed on the other side of it, shaking the bed.

I lifted my head and found myself eye-to-eye with Coarse.

He stared at me.

I stared back.

A few minutes passed before he closed his eyes. His head was resting on Gleam's back, and she was already snoring again.

No longer tired, I found myself staring up at the ceiling. My heart beat quickly, my mind returning to the past.

My mother's smile flashed through my thoughts.

My father's hug.

My sister's laugh.

Tears flooded my eyes, and I squeezed them shut.

Veil, I needed a distraction.

Sleeping more wasn't going to do me a damn bit of good.

My stomach rumbled, and I placed a hand on it, silently shushing it.

"I can take you to the dining hall," Coarse said, his voice low and rumbly in my mind.

My first instinct was to turn him down just because I remembered how angry he had been the first time I saw him. But, I wouldn't be able to find the food on my own, and it wasn't really safe for me to leave alone.

"Okay," I whispered back, wiping the tears quickly. *"Thank you."*

It took me a few minutes to wiggle my way out from between Ravv and Gleam, and Ravv made a few grumpy noises when I did, but I eventually broke free.

I wrapped my arms around my middle as I followed Coarse out of the room, both of us peeking both ways before we slipped into the hallway. The doors swung shut silently behind us, and my feet didn't make a sound on the hard, smooth ice beneath them.

"Thank you," I repeated to Coarse, as we walked.

He only grunted in response. It wasn't much different than what Ravv would've done, I knew.

"Stay close," he told me as we turned a corner. *"I don't know who will be in there. When we're inside, I'll let you know which fae to avoid."*

It felt too repetitive to thank him again, so when he glanced at me, I nodded.

He didn't seem angry at all anymore. Just a bit growly, and I could handle growly.

We stepped into a room fairly similar to the dining hall back in Jirev, and I looked around at all of the tables scattered through the room. Most of them were made of ice, like the castle itself, but all of the chairs looked much softer and cozier. There were a few rugs on the floor too, warming the space up. Though I questioned the wisdom of a rug in a dining room, it brought the space to life in a way I appreciated.

...and worried I might burn.

Veil, I needed to keep my magic under control.

There were only a dozen or so fae in the room with us, alongside their idorr companions, so at least it wasn't too loud.

Elwynne waved me over, and relief spread through me.

She would prevent it from getting too awkward.

There was an open seat at her table, and one of the fae sitting beside her shifted seats at her request, his bonded idorr moving too. The man on her other side got up and walked through a door nearby, but his idorr remained sitting, so I assumed he was coming back.

I took the chair that had been vacated first, and Coarse folded himself into the space beside it, lowering his head to his paws but keeping his eyes opened and narrow.

He hadn't been joking when he mentioned protecting me.

Elwynne introduced me to everyone around the table, and the man sitting beside her eventually came back with a plate of food. He was just as massive as Ravv, with dark brown skin, and deep crimson hair braided and tied up in a huge bun. He gave me a dramatic bow as he did, winking. "It's a pleasure to meet you, my queen."

I snorted.

As if I'd ever be anyone's queen. Even if Ravv decided to pursue that whole life-partners thing, I would never be a ruler.

Elwynne gave the man a good-natured smack on the shoulder, grabbing the plate from his hands and setting it in front of me. "Sit down, Orvay."

He grinned as he stepped back around her and took his seat again. "Can't say I ever expected Ravv to fall for a squishy little human with red hair."

My face warmed at the insults.

"Sometimes it looks orange," Elwynne tossed back, winking at me. "And she didn't used to be squishy. I think he takes pride in the way he's fed her enough to soften her up."

Damn, I hadn't realized the conversation could get worse.

"It's just because of the bond," I admitted, tugging my sleeve down to show them the glowing handprint. I noticed fascination in most of their eyes, more than anything else. Tugging my sleeve back up was a bit of a war, since I'd gained weight and all. "There are no real emotions."

Most of them looked unconvinced, but thankfully, none of them asked any more questions.

"You've bonded with Coarse too?" one of the women asked, her voice curious.

Coarse growled.

"No," I said quickly. "He's just here to make sure no one tries to kill me since I snuck away from Ravv while he was sleeping."

Elwynne grinned, shaking her head at me. "Bad call, Laeli."

"I couldn't stay trapped in that room any longer. It was starting to feel like another prison." I started on my food, hoping it would get the subject off of me.

No luck, though.

"What was it like to live in a cellar?" Orvay asked.

"About like you'd imagine. Dark. Humid. Uncomfortable. Lonely. Everything was made of stone, so I couldn't burn it."

Grimaces went around the table.

"One of the other human girls was trapped in a tower, though. I'd take a cellar over a tower." I tried to lighten the mood, but the words were at least partially lie.

I was afraid of heights, but Nissa had been allowed outside. She'd felt the sun on her face and seen other people, even if they were unpleasant people to see.

I'd only had Jern and Gora. And they were great... just not great enough that I wanted to spend all of my time with them, without any kind of reprieve.

"Damn. What about the third?"

"Oh, Kaelle was in a cave. She actually liked it, though." I changed the subject, before it turned to something in my past that I wasn't willing to discuss. I could barely think about those memories, so sharing them was out of the question. "Which of the events did Loire win? No one told me."

The question was like lighting a fire inside all the warriors. They launched into a debate over which events they'd won, versus which ones they would've won if they'd chosen the correct warrior to fight in it. According to them, they could've taken all of them.

The confidence didn't surprise me at all after my experiences with Ravv, though. And anyway, it wouldn't do them any good not to believe in themselves.

Eventually, the group of fae at the table disbanded. Some went to bed, others went to train, and the rest went to a tavern.

Elwynne and Orvay remained seated though, their gazes lingering on me.

"Stop staring at me," I grumbled at them, brushing hair out of my face.

"We're not staring at you," Orvay said with a grin. "We're trying to figure out how long you have until Ravv wakes up and realizes you're gone."

Elwynne rolled her eyes at him. "He's joking."

He mouthed, *"I'm not joking."*

"You're right; he'll be furious if he wakes up and I'm gone. I'd better get back." I flashed them both quick smiles.

"I'd recommend a shower, too. You smell like a man." Elwynne waved her hand in front of her nose.

I grimaced.

I'd hugged Jern, which I wouldn't apologize for, but she was probably right that Ravv would be annoyed by his scent on my skin and in our bed when he finally woke up.

And I didn't want to be alone in the silence with my thoughts, anyway. Showering would be a distraction, if just a short one.

"Thanks." I nodded at Elwynne before I slipped away.

Coarse walked with me silently, leading the way when he realized I was still clueless as to where we were in the castle.

We got back to the king's space without any problems, and I locked the door behind me again. It occurred to me that I shouldn't have left it unlocked in the first place, and I felt a bit guilty.

Coarse plopped back down in bed with Gleam, and I remained by the doorway as I stared at Ravv for a moment.

Veil, he was gorgeous.

Made entirely out of chiseled muscle and battle-honed strength. Confident, deadly, and sure.

What would I give to have even a fraction of those qualities?

More than I could even comprehend.

My eyes closed, and all I saw was fire.

I wasn't ready to sleep again.

Elwynne was right about me needing a shower, and showering definitely defeated climbing my *squishy human* self into bed with that gorgeous creature. So, I stripped and slipped beneath the water, embracing the warm, blissful peace of the shower.

CHAPTER SIXTEEN
LAELI

My mind wandered as I scrubbed my hair.

Ravv and I hadn't had a chance to reestablish what our relationship truly was since the Beast's attack. It could have been gone completely, or it could be what it had been before the attack... which had been a tentative friendship bordering on more.

Most-likely, it was somewhere between those two options. Ravv had mentioned being tired of acting like he didn't want me, so he wasn't completely impervious to whatever he'd felt for me.

Despite that, whatever we were would end with the eclipse.

I closed my eyes and forced myself to accept the truth.

Ravv and I had no future.

Even if we were attracted to each other, there would be no real commitment. He would never choose me as his queen, and I could never let myself rely on him.

I'd survive. I had to believe that.

My mind went back to the fire, though.

Back to the loss, and the trauma.

I shuddered, still needing a distraction. I'd trapped myself in Ravv's room again, and there was no way out.

Which meant nothing to distract me.

Except...

My mind went back to the way Ravv had touched me in that shelter.

Theoretically, I could distract myself just by slipping a hand between my thighs. It would be a bit weird to learn how to touch myself in Ravv's shower, but he was the one who told me not to leave the room.

Which meant... I was going to do it.

I slid a hand between my thighs, then breathed in sharply as I dragged my fingers over the sensitive bud there. No one had ever taught me the name for it, but I knew Ravv had paid a lot of attention to it.

Slowly, I circled it.

My body shuddered.

Veil, that felt good.

My breathing picked up as I continued touching myself, not entirely certain how to make myself climax. Ravv had just kept going until it happened, so I supposed that was the best method.

"What are you doing?" he asked, as tension swelled in my lower belly.

I didn't answer him.

He growled, *"I'm the only one who gets to make you shatter. Take your fingers off your clit."*

A moment later, the bathroom door rattled.

My gaze jerked toward it, and my fingers stilled.

"Unlock it." Ravv's voice was low and deadly... but I took great pleasure in pissing him off, so I ignored him again. *"I will break my own damn door down,"* he all but snarled at me.

But... I still wasn't going to give him what he wanted.

There was a loud noise, and the door broke inward.

I spun to face Ravv just in time to watch him step into the bathroom as the door crashed into the wall, his eyes somehow both hot and tired.

The man didn't say a word as he crossed the space between us in three steps, pulled my hand out from between my thighs, and replaced it with his own. I was pretty sure I had a rule about nothing sexual happening, but that rule was going in the garbage, because I wasn't about to stop him.

My fingers landed on his chest, and I took a staggered breath in as he stroked me lightly, walking me backward until my ass hit the wall.

Why did his touch feel so much better than mine?

"I'm the only one who brings you pleasure," he said roughly into my ear, as my body flushed and arched in response to his touch.

He caught my wrist with his free hand, lifting it to his mouth and wrapping his lips around my fingers. His gorgeous eyes were locked with mine as his chest rumbled at the taste of me.

The pleasure built rapidly, and I cried out as I shattered on his fingers. His chest rumbled again, and he held my eyes as he lowered to his knees.

My chest heaved as he waited for me to say no—and when I didn't, he parted my thighs.

I grabbed his hair for support as he opened me up for him, parting my folds so he could get a good look at me. *"Look at this pretty, wet core,"* he murmured into my mind, leaning in close and inhaling my scent.

My entire damn body flushed.

The flush grew when he flicked his tongue over my bud, rumbling, *"And somehow you taste even better than you look, Lae."*

The nickname snapped me back to the past.

Back to reality.

Back to the fire, and the terror, and the—

His tongue dragged over me again, and a cry escaped me.

My hips jerked.

My body trembled.

My mind was clear again, focused solely on the moment I was living.

Ravv lifted one of my legs over his shoulder, giving him better access to me. His finger teased my opening, and I cried out again as he slid it inside me, stretching me.

His tongue moved faster, the pressure growing more intense as he dragged me closer and closer to the edge again.

I had never felt so full... or so hot.

My body writhed and rocked in desperation.

I cracked my eyes open and stared down at Ravv. Seeing his face at the apex of my thighs, his hands gripping me, filling me...

It was too much.

I cried out as I lost control again, my body clenching around his fingers as the waves of pleasure rolled through me.

It was bliss.

Veil, it was bliss.

My head pressed harder to the wall as I struggled to catch my breath.

"You did so damn well, Lae."

The praise made me feel good.

Really, really good.

He stood up and released me long enough to grab the soap, dragging the thick bar to my hair. I didn't tell him I'd already washed it as he pulled me away from the wall, his body so tight against mine that I could feel him breathe. His erection pressed against my lower back while he massaged my scalp.

"Thanks," I whispered into his mind. *"I can wash myself."*

"No." He continued his massage. *"And thank me by telling me the next time you need a release."*

"That would feel like breaking some unspoken rule between us, and you're busy, anyway."

"Then we set new rules." His hands slid down my neck, and I groaned when he tilted my head forward to massage the muscles there.

The conversation was starting to feel like the end of one we'd had in the bathing pool in Jirev... and I didn't mind that.

Not at all.

But I still wasn't sure he really wanted to continue growing closer. *"You don't owe me anything. I forgave you for bringing me into your mess, remember? I can take care of myself in every way."*

And if I couldn't, which seemed fairly likely, I'd figure it out.

"I didn't ask whether you could, I told you that you're not going to," he growled back. *"You're mine, Lae. That means you're mine to take care of. I'm sorry I left you alone in here for so long, but it won't happen again. My new rule is that you tell me when you need to get off, and I touch you when I want to see you lose control. Make your own rule in retaliation, or don't."*

Veil, he was ridiculously good at getting what he wanted.

I supposed that made him a good king.

But I had to reestablish some semblance of control in our relationship. And while he was the king, all I really had control of was myself.

"My rule is that we don't have sex."

He jerked his head in a nod.

"That means no asking me. No suggesting it or mentioning it either," I added.

If we were together that way, it would change everything for me. He would be my first, and that would inevitably mean something to me.

"I'll always respect your 'no' when it comes to sex, Lae. That's a boundary I won't cross."

I had known he wouldn't argue about it, but his confirmation still made me feel better.

"Any other boundaries to add?" he asked, his hands sliding down my chest and lingering on my breasts. *"You get to make demands just as much as I do."*

I hesitated to voice my thoughts.

I really didn't want to admit what I was thinking.

"You're not with any other women, right?" I finally asked him. *"Romantically?"*

He scoffed into my ear. *"I told you I'm faithful, female."*

"I know. It's just..." I trailed off, biting my lip.

"Tell me what you're thinking, Lae. You know I'll be truthful with you, so give me the same courtesy."

I sighed. *"You know everyone, which makes me feel like I have no power in this situation. You're the king, and I'm nothing. There's no balance."*

He was silent for a long moment.

"And now I've offended you," I grumbled. *"I knew this was going to happen."*

"You haven't offended me. I'm thinking."

I waited.

He started massaging my breasts, and I closed my eyes, relaxing against his shoulder as he did.

"If we were still at war, your magic would make you a great asset," he finally said. *"Our enemies couldn't use their ice with you on the battlefield, which would be a massive advantage."*

"I'd burn them, too," I pointed out.

"Double advantage, then." He went quiet for another moment, still palming my breasts.

I enjoyed it too much to stop him.

"There are many places in my kingdom where we have to manually break ice," he finally said. *If you could control your fire a bit, you could replace numerous weapons and many, many hours of labor."*

I hadn't considered that. Living on a glacier *would* mean cutting through ice frequently.

"I can try. The other human women have no control over their magic, though, so it might be hopeless," I reminded him.

"Your magic is not the same as theirs. It's all life magic, but plants, wind, and flames are all vastly different. They'll have unique triggers, and different natural levels when it comes to energy and life."

I supposed that made sense. Nissa had told me that her magic burned through her energy quickly, while my power simply remained warm until I lost control of my emotions and caught fire.

"Do you think I could control it enough?"

"It's worth attempting." His lips brushed the side of my head. *"Things will feel more balanced as you get settled here. I'll ask a few of the idorr to stick with you for protection so you can move into your house now rather than waiting. I want you to feel comfortable and confident about your place here."*

"Thank you." Gratitude swelled in my chest.

"I told you to thank me by asking me to touch you."

I snorted. *"You should know me well enough to know I'm too prideful for that."*

He chuckled, low and rumbly. *"I would be too. Just kiss me, and I'll know what you want."*

There was some... uncertainty in his tone.

He knew my first time had been with that fae in the hallway, and had never tried to convince me to give him my second. I thought maybe he was just trying to give me the space I'd asked for. Or maybe he wanted me to ask him myself.

But there was always the chance he just wasn't interested.

"Do you even want to kiss me?" I asked him.

"I just kissed your core, Lae. Do you really need to ask?"

Right.

That was an emphatic yes.

"I don't know how to instigate those things," I admitted. *"And mentally, I really haven't been in the right place for it since the attack. I'm not sure I ever will be."*

"You will. When you want something, grab me and take it. I'm yours." Ravv's voice lowered. *"As far as me holding all the power in our relationship, you should know that's not true. All it would take for you to seal our bond is to repeat the vow I already made. If you decided to, you could claim me, and I'd be helpless to fight it. Our social positions may not be equal, but you possess the true power between us."*

He caught me by surprise with that.

I tried to recall the words, and they popped into my mind as if by some kind of magic.

"Sillah ovim rett warum."

The urge to speak them hit me, though it wasn't so strong I couldn't ignore it.

I pressed my lips together anyway, just to be safe.

He was right; I was in control of our relationship, not him. If I wanted to, I could make the rest of his life extremely difficult by sealing our bond.

I wasn't going to do that, of course, but knowing it was an option made me feel slightly better.

"I forgot about that," I admitted to him. *"What does the vow mean?"*

"The exact translation vanished when the gods were lost. The oldest of our fino believe it's something along the lines of, 'my heart and life are yours'."

That was much simpler than I would've expected.

His hands finally left my breasts, sliding down my hips and over my ass slowly. My eyes closed as he cleaned my core, his fingers torturously-slow on the sensitive, aching parts.

"You're so damn soft," Ravv murmured into my ear. The brush of his lips made my skin erupt in goosebumps as he continued cleaning me. "Tell me how Jern touched you in your prison."

Those words snapped me out of the bliss I'd been feeling. "What?"

"You said he was the first to touch you. Tell me how." He nipped at my ear.

"No."

"Yes."

"No, Ravv."

"Yes, Lae."

I huffed.

He nibbled on my earlobe, making me shudder. And the bastard was still stroking me, which felt incredible.

"He didn't touch me," I finally said. "That was a lie. We were nothing more than friends."

Ravv's fingers stilled on my core. "Did you touch yourself while they were in the room with you?"

I squeezed my eyes shut. "No."

"Then your climax in the forest was your first, ever?"

"If you hold it against me, I will *kill* you," I shot back.

"Answer the question." His teeth dragged over my earlobe again.

"Yes, it was my first."

"Veil, Lae."

My face flushed. "You are *not* allowed to mock me for it."

"I'm not mocking you." His words were low and almost reverent. "I'm grateful that you trusted me enough to ask me for that, and I regret once again making you wish you hadn't by withholding the truth from you."

Oh.

The heat in my cheeks faded. "Thank you."

Instead of telling me to withhold my thanks again, he simply leaned down and brushed his lips against my cheek.

My eyes closed at the soft, intimate touch. It couldn't have meant as much to him as it did to me, but I relished it anyway.

His fingers resumed their motion on my core, and my body tensed at the pleasure of it.

"I'm going to watch you climax again," he murmured into my ear, his free arm sliding up my waist until the weight of my breasts rested on it. "While knowing that no one else has ever seen you come undone."

The flush returned to my face. "That sounds possessive."

"Oh, it is." His lips caught my ear lobe and pulled lightly as he increased the pressure of his touch. The man had me crying out a few moments later, working my body as if it had been created just for him.

And considering the intensity of our connection, maybe it had.

CHAPTER SEVENTEEN
LAELI

By the time we made it out of the shower, I was absolutely boneless, and Ravv's cock was so hard it looked painful. I considered offering to touch him, but I wasn't sure I was ready for it, and it didn't seem like the right time.

He pulled on a pair of shorts while I put my undergarments back on—the fae called them scanties—and then we climbed back into bed together, wearing nothing else. There was no light streaming into the castle, so I knew it was the middle of the night, and Bright and Coarse had left at some point during our shower.

My face warmed with the realization of why they'd left.

I was noisy.

"Is Gleam upset that I scared them away?" I asked Ravv, as he dragged me to his chest.

"Of course not. She and Coarse have their own room, and she's constantly telling me I need to occupy myself with a woman to lighten up."

I snorted.

That did sound like Gleam.

"You used to *occupy yourself* plenty, didn't you?" I countered. He hadn't been with anyone in around a century, if he'd been honest about that, but he definitely didn't act inexperienced. "And why did you stop having sex, anyway?"

He made a noncommittal noise. "After the initial excitement of adulthood wore off, it felt hollow. Even before I stopped, I was only sharing someone's bed for an eclipse once every few years, when particularly drunk. Sex is very selfish for fae."

His hands began to move over my abdomen and hips slowly, and I frowned. "How is it selfish?"

"Both male and female are only there to take what they need from each other. The female fae makes commands, the male follows them until she's found her climax, and then he does what he wants to reach his own. There's no giving—only taking."

"So you never touched a female fae just to make her feel good?"

"Of course not. I never gave of myself physically unless it was to get something in return. I find myself intrigued by the idea, now."

I opened my mouth to say something, but Ravv yawned behind me, so I closed it.

He needed his rest.

But... I respected him, for what he'd told me.

I really, really did.

"Your skin is so damn soft, Lae," he murmured into my ear as his hands settled—one on one of my breasts and the other trapped between my thighs, gripping the thick muscle there. "Sleep now."

By the time I considered protesting, his chest was already rising and falling steadily against my back.

Images of Ravv touching me again filled my mind.

Him touching me in the shower.

Feasting on me in some sort of closet.

Tonguing me while I rode his face.

That last one lingered the longest, until the feel of thick, hot fingers on my core roused me from sleep.

I groaned as they slid over my bud—my clit—before dipping into my opening then sliding against me again. The slick heat felt blissful.

The fabric of my undergarment was tight on my hips, straining as it held his hand close to my core, until he tugged it down far enough that it didn't block his access to me.

The bed shifted, and then he was dragging me further up the mattress, backward, so I faced away from him. A cry escaped me when he sat me on his mouth, and then *devoured* me.

My hands landed on his bare abdomen as I caught myself, and my eyes were nearly level with his cock.

Ravv worked me so fast, all tongue and teeth and fingers. Cries escaped me as I lost control, pleasure rolling through me.

Veil, I wanted to touch him.

He kept licking me, tasting me, and touching me, even as the pleasure faded.

Ravv wasn't done with me, and maybe I wasn't done with him.

He snarled against my core as I gripped his erection over his shorts. The thick hardness of him surprised me, even though I had felt it against me so many times.

His teeth caught my clit, and I cried out loudly at the intensity of it.

His fingers joined his mouth and tongue, spreading and filling me. It dazed me for a moment—and then I focused on his cock again. He was throbbing in my grip, and it fascinated me.

I wanted more.

I pushed the stretchy shorts over him, freeing his erection. The sight of it had my lips parting as my hips rocked against Ravv's face.

He was so damn huge—and the head of him was already slick with the evidence of how much he enjoyed the way I tasted and reacted to him.

Ravv snarled again as I dragged a finger over his slickness. His erection bobbed for me, and I wrapped my fingers around the length of him again.

I didn't really know what I was doing, but he said he could use his hand to get himself off.

When I squeezed, he bit down harder on my clit, and I *screamed*.

The climax hit me, hard.

My body jerked as the pleasure cut through me, my eyes glued to Ravv's cock as he lost control in my grip, throbbing and releasing all over my hand.

I struggled to catch my breath as he kept feasting on me, his tongue moving slower to give my body time to recover.

"Show me how to touch you," I breathed, as I finally released his erection.

"No." He growled the word into my mind. *"Let me focus on you."*

"I want to focus on *you*," I shot back, shivering as one of his fingers slid to my asshole and dragged over the sensitive skin.

"Just enjoy what I'm doing to you."

"Give me what I want, and I will."

He snarled at me again—but finally peeled me off his face and flipped me to my back. I landed with a huff, and he tugged my undergarment the rest of the way down my legs before tossing it to the ground.

He left his shorts where they were, so I leaned over and pulled them down to his knees, revealing the rest of him to me.

Veil, he was gorgeous.

Massive, muscular, and still so damn turned on.

Ravv grabbed my hand as he kneeled beside me. He wrapped my slick palm around his erection, and slowly dragged it down the hard length of him.

All words died in my throat as I stroked him with his help—once, twice, and a third time.

He gritted his teeth and grabbed one of my thighs, pulling me closer before his fingers hooked inside me.

"How many times can you climax?" I asked him.

It felt like a stupid question, but I didn't think he'd find it stupid.

"I usually stop after one. Theoretically, there's no limit." The words were a growl through a clenched jaw, and heated me further.

His eyes closed as I peeled his hand off mine, so I was free to touch him how I wanted. Changing the motion, I rolled my hand just a little. His face twisted in a silent snarl, his hips jerking and his cock somehow growing even harder.

I continued working him until he erupted again, and satisfaction settled in my chest.

"Veil, Lae." The words were gritty and harsh, but not in anger, his chest rising and falling rapidly as he opened his eyes.

His fingers were still between my thighs, stroking my clit and buried inside me. I was breathing fast, my own hips moving with the need that had swelled inside me.

"You're the sexiest thing I've ever seen," he growled, pulling my hand off his cock. He lowered himself to the bed until his face found the center of my thighs, then grabbed my slick hand.

My mouth went dry as he lowered it to my core, then rubbed my fingers over my wetness, combining the evidence of his pleasure with mine.

He inhaled deeply, and his chest rumbled loudly.

An image flashed through my mind—one of his cock sliding into the slick heat of my core—and I wanted it.

Veil, I wanted it.

But—

I cried out as he slid three fingers inside me, stretching me while he ate my clit with renewed fire.

"You'd better soak this damn bed. I want you sweating, writhing, and desper-ate," Ravv said into my mind. He dragged his teeth over my clit again, and I cried out as another climax hit me.

I was a panting mess when I came down from the high, so he got exactly what he wanted.

Honestly though, I couldn't complain either.

My stomach was growling and the sun was shining brightly by the time we cleaned up and made it to the dining hall.

Ravv was keeping his distance from me again. Even though I knew it was only because his people wanted us dead, it still messed with my mind.

I wanted him to hold my hand.

To touch my arm.

To drag me close.

It was disorienting to go from touching so much to acting like we didn't want to be near each other at all.

We sat with a few of his warriors again, though Elwynne and Orvay were both noticeably absent. I knew two of them from dinner the night before, and they both said something about it. When I explained that Coarse had gone with me, Ravv thankfully didn't get mad.

He did tell me that I wasn't allowed to leave his side without letting him know where I was going again, though.

After our late breakfast, we headed out to the idorr portion of town. I played with the cubs while Ravv asked them for their help protecting me, and when a few of the unmated idorr agreed, we headed off so I could see my house.

Ravv and I left the distance between us as we walked with all three of the idorr who had become my temporary protectors. Two were male, and one was female. I couldn't remember their names, but I would memorize them when I wasn't so nervous about seeing the house Ravv had given me.

It seemed strange that he gave me his own home, even though he wasn't going to live there. It made me wonder what the rest of his people would think—and whether I'd eventually lose my house if he decided he wanted it back.

Though I didn't want to admit any of that aloud, I had to consider it.

What would I do if I never bonded with an idorr, and lost my house? I could move in with Jern and Gora. They would let me, but I really, really didn't want to do that, for all of our sakes.

I could go back to Jirev. None of the kings had been *nice*, but Kier's city and people had seemed welcoming enough. I could offer to do... well, honestly, I didn't know.

Maybe I needed to find a way to get in contact with the gargoyles. The gargoyle man who'd captured me in the Sands had mentioned me helping in their forges. If I could do that, I'd have some use. But I didn't know how gargoyles felt about humans, or whether I'd be safe in the Chasm with them. And it was the Chasm, so instinctually, I didn't want to live there.

Then again, Ravv had said they could use me to melt ice to make their lives easier. He could've been making it up in an attempt to help me feel better about my shitty magic, but there was a chance it was true.

He led me up to the door of the smallest house on the street. It was made of ice, like the others, but was a simple, no-nonsense building.

As I took in the shape of it, I decided that I liked it.

Maybe I even loved it. Only time would tell.

He opened it up without any resistance or keys. I knew the fae only locked their doors when they were inside, so that didn't surprise me.

I stepped inside behind him and one of the idorr, my gaze scanning the space. It was simple, with two bedrooms, a kitchen, and a living area with a comfortable-looking couch. Both bedrooms had beds in them, and there were rugs over most of the smooth ice floors, but none of it looked lived-in.

Yet it was mine, at least for the moment.

And that made me love it.

"Thank you," I whispered, as I dragged my fingers lightly over the soft fabric on the couch. I'd have to be careful not to burn it, but I would manage.

"Save your thanks."

When I glanced over my shoulder at him, I found his lips curved upward just the tiniest bit. He said into my mind, *"You'll still spend every night with me, either here or in my castle."*

"That doesn't exactly say we don't have feelings for each other."

"My people expect me to be protective and possessive while we're mates—and while you're keeping me hidden from the Demon. No mated male would sleep far from his female, regardless of his feelings for her."

"The Demon's still flying above us, so if I'm a protector, I'm a terrible one." I gestured upward.

"He doesn't know what I look like, and you've concealed my magic from him," Ravv countered. *"He would have to burn the whole city to find me, and even then, he wouldn't recognize me. His magic prevents him from purposefully killing anyone but his target, so you're doing as good a job as anyone could ask for."*

I didn't really believe him, though his words did relax me slightly. *"As long as you don't think it'll get us killed."*

"I can protect you."

"Not while you're sleeping."

His scoff told me we were never going to agree on that topic, so I changed it. *"Alright, we'll spend our nights together. I'm going to learn how to cook, too."*

Ravv's continued scowl told me he didn't love my subject change, or idea about cooking.

"It's going to be great," I told him, though I didn't really believe it myself. *"Now, can you show me where you think I could be useful? I can try to melt some ice."*

He grudgingly agreed, and we slipped onto the backs of the idorr who had agreed to stick with me.

It took nearly an hour on the beasts' backs. Finally, we reached the part of the city beyond the fae-made rivers and streams that fed their crops

Ravv remained on the idorr's back as he introduced me to Cree, who was apparently in charge of keeping the rivers flowing. He was one of the roughest-looking men I'd ever seen, with a thick, scraggly orange beard, and eyes that glowed black. His body was covered in scars, and he was built even thicker than Ravv.

"What do you want, Highness?" the man grumbled.

"Laeli has offered her magic up to help with the ice dams."

The man looked at me.

A long moment passed before he finally looked back at Ravv and shook his head. "No."

Ravv's eyes narrowed. "I wasn't asking. She can take care of the dams faster than any of the rest of you." He nodded to me, and I slipped off the back of the idorr I was seated on.

"Fine." The man strode away.

I looked at Ravv, and he waved me toward Cree.

I hurried after the guy, with two idorr following me. Ravv remained where he was, watching me intently.

"Tell me if anything goes wrong, Lae. I want to know everything," the king warned me.

I shooed him away mentally, the same way he'd shooed me with his hand, and he chuckled into my mind.

CHAPTER EIGHTEEN
LAELI

I followed Cree to the river, and immediately saw the problem. The water was actively freezing, with ice slowly spreading from a set of rocks that felt like they possessed magic of their own. As it spread, it slowed the river's flow and started freezing the water.

There were dozens of massive metal tools on racks near the ice, and one fae was positioned on each of the icy rocks, hacking at it.

"This is the dam?" I asked Cree. The handprint on my arm was already aching with the distance between Ravv and I, but I was trying to ignore the slight pain.

Cree gave me an affirmative grunt. "The ice swells and spreads every night, and we spend every day keeping the water flowing."

"What do the rocks have to do with it?" I asked him.

"They're enchanted, and part of the glacier's magic. This land was originally a prison, so there are enchantments everywhere to keep it frozen and prevent crops from growing. We fight through it." He looked out at the two other huge fae and their large weapons.

All three of them were men, but I assumed Ravv wasn't concerned about them. He was certainly possessive enough to attempt to keep me away from anything he thought was a threat to either of us.

I did have two idorr by my sides though, and I'd have three to help protect me when the one carrying Ravv returned.

"You break the ice over and over again, every day?" I asked him, surprise coloring my voice.

Cree grunted again. "Our other option is to starve."

I supposed I'd be willing to break ice every day if it was the only way to fill my belly. I certainly would've done it for food a thousand times over if given the opportunity when I was trapped in the cellar.

"Last I heard, you can't control your flames," the man said, his voice even.

Panic started to swell in my chest, and I ignored it fiercely as memories of the fire in my childhood home blossomed to life. "I'm learning."

"You're still young." The man studied the river for another moment before calling out, "Pirr, trade places with Laeli."

I blinked.

Already?

With no instructions?

I supposed he couldn't give me instructions to help control my own magic. I'd have to figure that out on my own, if it was even possible.

When one of the fae stepped off the rock, I strode toward it like I wasn't absolutely clueless.

I *was* absolutely clueless, though.

My heart beat erratically as I carefully placed one foot on the frozen rock. The pain in my handprint had vanished, at least. The surface was slick beneath the warmth of my bare foot.

I didn't dare put my second foot on it, and instead lowered to my knees on the stone. Even that felt a bit slick.

I could feel the icy magic pooled in the stone, thrumming with life. It was as if someone's life force had been embedded in the rock itself.

Where my magic touched it, the power seemed to recoil and shrink away.

I focused on my emotions—on my anger, frustration, and helplessness —and waited for my fire to ignite.

After a few moments, it burst to life beneath my palms, and the magic within the stone reacted immediately. The ice pulled back as my fire flooded the space, overwhelming the cold power.

I pushed harder, forcing the flames brighter and hotter until they met the icy magic and burned against the enchantment.

The ice fought back, hard and unyielding.

My fire burned on, and on, and on.

Some vague part of me sensed that the warring magic was draining my power, but I was too set on destroying the icy enchantment to pay any attention to the strain.

Finally, the ice started to melt.

I distantly felt a bead of sweat trickle down my forehead and face before sliding down the center of my chest.

There was a slight tremble to my hands.

I ignored that, too.

My stomach clenched as my determination wavered.

Veil, my energy was fading fast. Faster than the enchantment was melting.

That didn't bode well for me.

I tried to pull back, to conserve the tiny bit that remained, but failed.

Panic replaced focus as I fought the leash on my magic and tried to get my flames back under control. They flared brighter in response, burning against the power within the stone. Despite my pull, it continued draining me more and more.

I sucked in a panicked breath as my body began to sway.

The weakness in my limbs was thick and heavy.

The world started to spin around me.

Veil, I was burning myself out again.

This burnout felt bigger and fiercer, though.

My body trembled, and my knees did too.

The trembling was too much.

One of my knees slid off the edge of the stone. As my center of gravity shifted, the rest of me followed my knee, and I plunged downward.

The water engulfed me as I fell unconscious, and my last thought was of the comfort I'd felt when Ravv held me in his arms that morning.

CHAPTER NINETEEN
RAVV

"Cree can protect her," Gleam chastised me, as she and Coarse walked up to my side. *"The rest of the idorr can too."*

I remained where I was, leaning my back to the wall while I watched Laeli kneel on one of the enchanted stones that constantly froze the river. *"I have a bad feeling about this,"* I told her.

She plopped down beside me. *"Your feelings aren't always accurate."*

"Which is why I let her go," I grumbled.

Laeli wanted the chance to prove herself. Though she had nothing to prove, I would allow her that opportunity.

She needed to know that I would support her, if I was ever going to convince her to be my life partner. The woman still thought she was my lesser, for whatever damned reason.

"Something is off," Coarse said, standing on Gleam's other side and staring out at the glacier with narrowed eyes. All we could see was the ice, the river, and a strip of the ocean. If we squinted, we would see the tiniest bit of the Endless Wilds off in the distance.

"I agree. Have you seen anything to be suspicious about?" I asked him.

"No."

I hadn't either.

But there hadn't been any sign of the cult since we'd been back, which was a terrible omen. Ria's people always went silent in the days before one of their attacks.

She would be looking for us, and she'd see my bond with Laeli as a sign that I was fragile. On top of that, she'd expect it to mean my warriors and I were siding with the mated couples in the city below.

That alone would make us a target.

"They don't usually kill unmated fae, and you're technically not mated," Coarse said.

"This situation is not usual or technical. They will kill as many of us as they can. I—" The words died in my throat as I watched Laeli's magic burst to life.

Her fire blazed over the stone, and my eyes widened slightly as I watched it engulf the ancient magic none of my people could affect.

She blazed so brightly that I couldn't see her through the flames.

"There," Coarse growled, and my attention snapped to the side of the river.

I studied it for a moment before my eyes finally caught the movement.

Someone was running toward the river.

Not just toward the river—toward Laeli.

Toward my *mate.*

A second thought didn't cross my mind as I sprinted toward the coming storm.

"Watch my female," I growled at Gleam and Coarse, who snarled together in response.

Both of them wanted to fight, but there would be nothing left to fight for if they had time to hurt her.

Gleam stayed on my tail as I leapt over the river and launched at the fae sprinting toward my female. I threw my magic into my blood and skin, and my icy armor and claws swelled for battle.

The moment I saw the fae's face, I recognized him as one of Ria's closest friends.

We had been friends once too, before the two of them joined the cult.

Now, mine would be the last face he saw.

He rolled to the side fast enough to dodge most of my warriors—but I wasn't most of my warriors.

My claws sliced through his throat.

He ducked backward, his eyes full of surprise as he grabbed at his neck.

The damned cultists thought they were as strong as those of us who had gone to war for our kingdom for centuries, but they were wrong. They were just a hell of a lot better at hiding than we were.

"Where's Ria?" I growled at him, while his blood dripped off my claws.

His eyes stormed, but he didn't answer.

It was better to send them a message than to waste my time on torture, so I went at him again.

His next motion was clumsy. Too clumsy.

He swung at me, and I ignored the burn of his sword as it cut lightly through my ice and into my side.

My claws sliced through his chest—where I found his heart, and cut through the organ without hesitation.

The man fell to his knees, gasping for air as his body began to shut down.

I was already searching the horizon, looking for more cultists.

There.

I turned toward one—but through the corner of my eye, saw Laeli slip off the rock she'd been kneeling on.

The water engulfed her, and I started to move.

"I've got her. Focus on the attack," Coarse growled into my mind as he and two other idorr dove in behind her.

I hesitated for a heartbeat.

He could keep her safe.

I trusted that.

But the woman was *mine*.

Leaving her to her own devices... veil, it would kill me.

The fae woman I'd noticed dove into the water after Coarse, and a roar exploded through my chest.

I was engulfed a moment later, grabbing the woman. Her foot collided with my chest, but I ignored the painful impact as I threw her up onto the river's bank before hauling myself out too.

Cree's spear was already buried in her chest when I made it to my feet. The weapon pinned her to the ice while she took her last breaths. Though I knew she was a cultist, I didn't recognize her, so there was no satisfaction in the kill.

"Two more headed into the city. One male, one female. Her hair was the same shade as yours," Cree barked, the same way he would've if we were on the battlefield.

"Take the male," I growled back, already sprinting toward the city. He stuck close to my heels, and I finally caught a glimpse of Ria's hair as she and her ally parted ways.

He went around the city's walls, and she headed inside.

I pushed myself harder, tapping into my magic to make the ice work beneath me. The distance between us shrank with every step, but I found myself reaching out to Gleam.

"Coarse has her?"

"Yes, and the other idorr and I killed another two cultists. We don't see any other threats."

"Is she conscious?"

"No. But she's breathing, and Coarse doesn't see any blood."

At least she was alive.

"We'll take her back to the idorr portion of the city while you deal with the other threats. She'll be safe with us," Gleam said.

The words didn't bring me the relief they probably should have.

I was already having flashbacks to the moments she was with the raiders, when I knew her life was at risk and yet I couldn't reach her.

"Thank you." The words were hard to get out.

Ria wove behind a few buildings, and I cut down a street that would lead me to the same place her path would take her.

Toward the castle.

I threw every damn ounce of my energy into it as I ran, pushing myself harder and faster.

This wasn't just one battle—this was the war, and if I could kill her, I could end it.

Or at least buy us enough time to find the rest of the damn cult.

I turned a corner and plowed right into her.

Ria didn't scream—she threw a kick to my abdomen, and then tried to free herself from my arms the way she had a hundred times when we trained as children.

I turned her over as we slammed to the ground, so her front took the brunt of the impact.

With one sharp motion, she slammed a small, ice blade into the same place the other cultist had cut my side.

The pain surprised me enough for her to roll us both over, but I tightened my grip on her, grabbing her by the arms as my back hit the street.

"Learning new moves, Ri?" I drawled into her ear.

If I could piss her off, she would grow sloppier, and I needed her sloppier because I couldn't kill her from our current position.

She laughed, but the sound didn't ring with the joy of our childhood. It was bitter, and cruel.

As much as I didn't want it to, it made my abdomen clench. Her blade vanished from my side, and blood began to leak from the deep wound.

"Not as many new moves as you, Ravv. It doesn't get much newer than taking a *human mate*." Though her words were slow and sarcastic, she was still fighting my hold.

"I'm sure your eyes and ears in my kingdom have told you exactly why I did," I growled back.

"A bond for any reason is a death sentence, as you know well." She finally managed to land an elbow to my wound.

I grunted as she wrenched herself free of my grip, flying to her feet.

Her blades grew quickly in her hands as I stood and charged toward her.

She spun away, slashing at me, but I was already moving again.

The dance went on, the similarities in our fighting styles coming through while we moved the way we had as children, with me on offense and her on defense. Neither of us gained or lost the advantage, even though we both bled from a number of wounds.

My fae slowly lined the streets, watching the fight, but none of them intervened.

"*Laeli needs your blood,*" Gleam said, not distracting me enough to give Ria an opening. "*She's fading. Whatever she did to that stone took too much of her magic, and I don't think her body can replenish it on its own.*"

Veil.

I shouldn't have let her risk herself in an attempt to be useful.

I should've protected her, the way I was supposed to.

How many times would I fail this woman?

"I'll be there soon," I promised.

I snarled aloud, moving faster and hitting harder. When I finally saw an opening, my clawed and spiked fist slammed into her temple. She crumpled to the ground, but I wasted no time.

"Grab her," I ordered Orvay, meeting his gaze long enough to see him nod before I sprinted toward Laeli.

I reached her a few minutes later, finding her in the home Coarse and Gleam kept in their portion of the city. She was curled up on the edge of one of the massive round cushions the idorr preferred to use as beds, her hair still dripping water and her skin paler than I'd ever seen it.

"Veil." I dropped to my knees and pulled her into my arms, carefully easing her onto my lap. *"Give us a moment, please."* Though I didn't look at Gleam and Coarse, they knew I was speaking to them.

"Be careful with her," Coarse growled at me.

I narrowed my eyes at him. *"She's my mate. I'm always careful."*

He glowered at me. *"Our souls connected when I pulled her from the river. She's my companion; protect her better."*

The revelation caught me by surprise, but in the moment, there was nothing I could do but focus on saving Laeli's life.

So I finally jerked my head in a nod, lowering my gaze back to the fragile woman in my arms.

When I convinced her to solidify our bond, she would grow stronger. Our magic would knit together, and she would become just as immortal as I was. Her body would heal faster, and she would be able to move much more quickly.

But it was too late to seal anything now, and even if we did, there would be far too many consequences.

She'd need to drink from me if she was going to survive.

Though I was still bleeding from many wounds, I sliced through the skin at the base of my neck before hauling her higher and setting her mouth against me.

"Drink, Lae," I commanded her, tapping into her mind so the words echoed there, too.

She didn't respond.

I repeated the words, louder, and she finally moved.

Her teeth pressed lightly against my skin as she took my blood into her mouth. A moment later, they cut into me, flooding me with the same fierce pride that had hit me the last time I fed her.

Blood rushed to my cock as she started to rock a little, moaning and groaning softly against my skin. My hands stroked her lower back. She was much colder than usual—she typically radiated heat when her desire grew. Even at her coldest, her skin always felt warmer than my own.

My cock ached and throbbed as she drank, until my eyes closed and the world began to spin. "You'll have to stop, Lae."

She slowed.

"Ria wounded me too badly. I need some of my blood to heal myself."

She pulled away, gasping for breath. When I forced my eyes open, I found her dazed. Her eyes were dilated, and her face was red with the lust coursing through her veins. She probably hadn't heard everything I said. "What? You're hurt?"

I dipped my head a bit.

"Where?" She tried to slide away, but I held her too tightly.

"I'm fine. I'll heal."

"No. Show me." She pushed on my chest, but her touch was too light to move me. "Ravv," she growled.

"Lae," I growled back.

"You're an ass."

I made a noise of agreement, closing my eyes again to fight the spinning of the room.

"Are we—" She cut herself off. "I just heard Coarse's voice in my head. It felt different than usual."

"You're bonded." I was growing more tired by the minute.

Healing her had thoroughly drained my energy.

"Veil, really? He's grumpy, though."

"Only when Gleam pushes him, which she does often. He likes it more than he admits." I brushed my lips against her forehead.

"Show me where you're hurt."

"Later." I tugged her closer, and she pushed at me again.

"We need to wash up, at least. And I'm freezing cold."

"You burned yourself out," I grumbled at her.

"I almost killed the enchantment in that stone; I could feel it." Her voice grew more excited, though she was still leaning against me heavily. "If I'm more careful, I can get rid of it entirely next time without knocking myself unconscious."

"No."

"We'll agree to disagree." She patted me on the arm, as if comforting me.

"You're not doing it."

"We can talk about it later. Take me home."

I grumbled, but carried her out of the house. Everything was still spinning a bit, and moving felt much more difficult than usual, but I managed.

Laeli lowered her head to rest on my shoulder, her face tucked against my neck while her legs wrapped around my waist.

Gleam and Coarse fell into step with us as we walked.

"You need a few bandages," Gleam warned me.

"I'm fine."

"You're not. It'll scare Laeli if you pass out from blood loss."

"I'm not going to pass out from blood loss."

"You said that last time, too."

I grumbled again but couldn't disagree.

Gleam said, *"We'll find some bandages. Watch her carefully so Coarse doesn't get as grumpy as you."*

I scowled at her, and she winked at me before slipping away.

Coarse growled at her, then growled at me, before following her away.

"They're kind of adorable," Laeli whispered to me.

"Ridiculously so," I agreed.

She snorted, and I couldn't stop a ghost of a smile from curving my lips.

"Between Gleam, Coarse, Elwynne, and Orvay, you've been paired with couples for a long time," she said.

"Unfortunately."

She smiled against my neck. *"You like it."*

"I enjoy seeing them happy," I admitted.

"But…"

"It grows lonely from time to time. I think it would for anyone. I saw my parents together enough to believe that fae are meant to exist in pairs."

She grew quiet for a moment.

A long, long moment.

I wondered if she was also thinking that fate had paired us perfectly, but doubted it. She was far less certain that we suited each other than I was.

Because I knew Orvay would've taken Ria back to the castle, I didn't dare take Laeli there, and headed toward my old house instead. I tried to prepare myself for the emotional impact that would accompany seeing her sprawled across the bed that had been mine back when life was so much simpler.

CHAPTER TWENTY
LAELI

Ravv pulled my dress over my head as he stepped into the shower with me and turned the water on. My eyes shut as it started falling, raining over my head and rolling down my face.

"Veil, you're freezing," Ravv grumbled, setting me down on my feet. When I wobbled, he stepped up close, spreading one hand on my abdomen to hold me in place with my back against his front.

"You're the cold one," I shot back. "Geez, are you *made* of ice? You usually feel warm to me."

"Yes, I am made of ice. I have no idea why I would feel warm to you. You're my personal fire at this point." He dragged his hands up to my breasts and squeezed, making me want him. If I wasn't so damn exhausted, I would've considered asking him to touch me, but I didn't think I could stay on my feet that long.

"I see. You just like me for my warmth."

"Yes, that's the only attractive quality you possess," he drawled, squeezing my breasts again. "Heat. Just heat. I'm disgusted by your ass, breasts, and mouth."

I snorted. "Seems believable."

"Very." He lowered his lips to my throat and slowly kissed up the column of it until he reached my earlobe and sucked lightly. "I want to taste you again."

Despite his words, he looked absolutely exhausted, and a bit dizzy too.

My legs trembled. "I don't think I can stand that long."

He gave me an unhappy rumble. "In bed before you sleep, then."

"Deal."

He released my earlobe and reached for some soap, but found none. "Damn. I forgot to restock it."

My lips curved upward.

The fact that he'd forgotten something mundane made him seem more human to me, as silly as that was.

"I'll head out to grab supplies while you're asleep."

"I still need to check your wounds," I reminded him. "I might be in better health than you right now."

He made a noise of disagreement. "They're small wounds."

"I'm starting to think that means you're pretending not to be in pain." I leaned away from him, turning slightly. My eyes caught on a bright red wound on his side, and widened. "What is *that*? Veil, Ravv! Who did you fight?"

He released me reluctantly. "It's nothing to worry about. It'll heal fast."

I bent closer so I could see the wound. "It's still bleeding. If it wasn't something to worry about, it wouldn't still be bleeding." I poked at it, and he swore.

"Don't touch it."

"I thought it wasn't something to worry about," I shot back.

"It's not." He gritted his teeth. I was pretty sure it was out of pain, not anger, for once.

"Who were you fighting? What happened?" I repeated the questions he'd ignored.

"Ria finally came after me."

I blinked.

It took a minute for the admission to set in. "*Ria*, Ria? As in, your twin sister Ria?"

"Yes." He swore again as I pulled him further into the water—and again when I moved his arm so the shower would wash his wound.

"What happened?"

"She finally hunted me down herself. There must only be a few cultists left."

"So she's desperate," I said, leaning down again so I could see the wound better. My lips twisted in a grimace as I did. "The coloring on this is weird. Do you think she could've poisoned you? Can fae even be poisoned?"

"Yes, we can be poisoned." He was gritting his teeth. "But her blade was ice, and it's difficult to poison an ice blade. She would've had to dip it before she left, and carry it all the way here."

"That doesn't mean she didn't."

"It makes it unlikely."

"Okay, but I'm telling you, this doesn't look good. Go check the mirror."

He gave me an exasperated sigh, but left me and my shaky legs in the shower while he went to the mirror. When he reached it, he stared at himself for far too long before shuffling back.

"Well?" I asked.

"It's poisoned."

My eyebrows shot upward. "Is there an antidote, or are you dying? I feel like you should be more worried about this."

"There's an antidote. Gleam was almost back with the bandages, so she's heading out for it now. It's nothing to worry about."

I huffed at him. "You really need to stop saying that."

"You really need to start believing me."

We were never going to agree on that. "Did Ria beat you?'

He scowled at me. "I'm not dead, am I?"

"Well, you *are* poisoned." I gestured to his side.

"Only a coward who can't win with skill alone uses poison. I'm not surprised my sister is one of them. She was always a poor loser."

I rolled my eyes at him.

He shut off the water and pulled me close, lowering his nose to my hair and inhaling deeply. "Veil, you smell good."

"I smell like a river," I mumbled against his chest.

"You smell like my mate."

My chest burned with his words.

He wrapped me in a towel, and then did the same to himself but tied it at his waist. The way he moved was strange as he walked me back to the bed. I studied his tense shoulders and the tight way he was holding his abdomen. "You're in pain, aren't you?"

"I'm fine."

I didn't believe him. "Ravv."

"Lae," he growled back.

"Tell me the truth."

He growled again....

But said nothing.

"Veil, Ravv. Seriously, what is your problem?"

The man couldn't conceal his wince as he lifted a hand to rest on my hip.

I put both hands on his chest and steered him to the mattress. He reluctantly let me push him, taking one step back, then another, until he reached the mattress and sank onto his ass.

"Take your towel off," I said bluntly.

It was almost... an order.

He narrowed his eyes at me.

I narrowed mine back.

Finally, he undid the towel and it fell onto the bed.

Though my gaze caught on his erection, and I wanted to comment on it, my eyes moved quickly to a wound on his thigh. It was angry, red, and bleeding lightly.

I looked him up and down, then climbed onto the bed to see his back, taking stock of his injuries.

Damn, there were a lot of them.

"Your sister is good," I remarked, grimacing as I wiped a bit of blood from one of the smaller cuts. It was a miracle he was still awake, considering that he'd healed me and bled plenty from his own wounds.

He made a noncommittal noise. "It wasn't a typical fight. We grew up practicing together, so she knows how I move."

"And you know how she moves?"

He confirmed it.

"Would she have been the queen, if she hadn't joined the cult?"

"Yes. I never wanted the throne, and she did. I would've vastly preferred a life in this house, away from the drama."

"Really?" He had me curious. "What would you like about it?"

"There would be no important decisions to make. No one's life in my hands. I could spend my days breaking ice when we weren't fighting, and I could walk off the battlefield without the guilt of my people's blood on my shoulders."

"If you defeated the cult and your parents came back, would you give them the throne?"

He chuckled, his back still facing me. "In a heartbeat, if the people would follow them. When they ran away, they ensured that our warriors would never allow them to rule again."

My lips curved upward a bit sadly. I wished there was some way to make that happen for him.

His eyes were looking a bit unfocused, and worry curled in my stomach.

"I think you should rest. Climb under." I pulled the blankets back. Though I needed to cover his wounds, Gleam and Coarse hadn't returned with the bandages and antidote.

I still wasn't sure about the bond connecting me to Coarse, which made me hesitant to use it. But, I was worried about Ravv, so I finally reached out.

"Are you getting close? He's not doing good."

"We're almost there," the idorr said, his voice surprisingly un-grumpy.

I hadn't expected to end up bonded to Gleam's mate, but I couldn't say I hated the idea. He would protect me, as he'd proven when he pulled me out of the river. Our connection would make it harder when Ravv and I went our separate ways, but I would figure out a way to make it work.

"And you have the antidote?"

"We do."

The steadiness in his voice made me feel slightly better.

Having Coarse would help me avoid relying on Ravv, I realized... and that was a very good thing, because I was really starting to worry that I was becoming dependent on him.

"Thank you," I told Coarse.

"You owe me no thanks. I would help my mate save her king even without our connection."

Right.

I bit my lip, really uncertain about how the dynamic of our bond was going to work.

That was something to worry about later, because at the moment, I needed to focus on Ravv.

His eyes were closed and his breathing was even, but I put the back of my hand on his forehead to check his temperature.

Veil, he really was cold.

Then again, I was too.

The doors to the room swung open, and Gleam and Coarse slipped inside. She had a dark blue fabric bag hanging from her jaws, and set it next to me on the bed.

"The bandages will stick to wet skin, so you'll need water. Make sure your hands are dry when you put them on," she said. *"And he'll have to drink the antidote."*

"Thank you."

She climbed carefully onto the bed, leaving me to play healer.

Though I was flooded with uncertainty, I opened the bag and peeked inside. The bandages looked thick and tough, and felt the same when I brushed my fingers against them. They were a light color that would nearly match Ravv's skin, too.

The bandages would have to come after the antidote, though.

It was a small vial of liquid in a strange yellowish-green color. The shade of it didn't make me think it would cure anything, but I knew nothing about healing.

I uncorked the liquid and inhaled, nearly gagging at the scent of it. My eyes watered, and I pulled it away from my nose.

"The fae usually dump it down the person's throat and hold their jaw closed," Gleam explained.

I nodded, fighting a grimace as I parted his lips.

The man barely budged.

"I need you to drink this," I said into Ravv's mind, but he didn't stir.

His lack of reaction made me worry more, so I just muttered a curse under my breath, and tipped the vial back.

As soon as the liquid met his tongue, Ravv's body bucked. I held his jaw closed as tightly as I could while he fought me. The antidote finally went down, and I let out a long breath.

After smoothing his hair back, I slipped off the bed and headed back to the bathroom for another towel. I soaked it in the sink, and then went back to Ravv's side.

He was still pale and cold, but I had to hope the antidote would work.

"How sure are you that was the right cure?" I asked Gleam.

"Sure. There are only two poisons that can be made from the plants that grow on the glacier, and the other one causes vomiting. It's not deadly, so it's only used to be a nuisance."

That was better than completely uncertain, at least.

If he didn't start recovering... well, then we'd have to start trying to figure out what else it could be.

I nodded and focused on the wound on his side first. It was already a bloody mess again, and my jaw was set in a grimace as I cleaned it up, then pressed a bandage to the skin with a dry hand.

The edges stuck perfectly, and I smoothed them just to make sure they were on correctly.

Moving on to the next cut, I found a bandage in the right size, cleaned the blood off, and covered it.

The room was nearly silent as I continued with both idorr watching me work. My movements grew confident as I got used to the motions, and

Ravv's coloring started to improve a little too. That made me feel more certain we were doing the right thing in how we were taking care of him.

My body still felt cold and tired, so when I was finally confident that every inch of the king had been patched up, I let myself collapse on the bed and fall asleep.

I woke to the sound of soft swearing.

My eyes cracked open, and I looked around the room, a bit disoriented.

My gaze was drawn to the silhouette of a massive man in the bathroom, his bare body turned to the side.

It took me a moment to realize what he must've been doing.

"Don't mess with my bandages," I warned, stumbling out of bed.

Veil, I was more exhausted than I realized.

"Go back to sleep," Ravv growled back.

I ignored him, swatting his hands away as I stepped up to his side. My hip bumped the countertop a bit harder than I planned, and he growled at me again when I winced.

"Be careful with yourself, Lae."

"Says the man who's bleeding from a hundred different cuts," I mumbled back. He'd peeled the bandage about halfway off the wound on his side before I reached him, so I pulled on it a little as I leaned in to look closer.

The discoloration had mostly faded, but it still looked pretty damn grisly, and had bled through the bandage at some point.

"I think you need more of the antidote," I admitted.

"There are two more vials in the bag," Gleam said from the bedroom.

"You'll have to drink it after I replace this," I told him.

"I've got it." He tried to pull my hands off his abdomen, but I shooed him away.

"You healed me. Now I heal you."

"If you're offering your blood, you know I'll have to turn it down until you've recovered."

I hadn't been offering that... but it was a good idea. I should've considered it sooner.

"You'll drink from me," I decided.

"*No,*" Ravv, Coarse, and Gleam all growled together.

"I drank from you, so it's only fair," I pointed out.

"You're barely awake right now. When your magic returns, you can heal me if I still haven't recovered. Until then, my teeth don't go anywhere near your throat."

"I'm sure you could drink my blood from some other part of me, if you tried."

He narrowed his eyes at me. "Don't tempt me, Lae."

I narrowed mine back. "Don't resist me, Ravv."

With that, I ripped the bandage the rest of the way off his wound.

Colorful curses spewed from his lips as he bent over, trying hard to remain on his feet. I put a hand beneath the water, wet his skin with it, and then pressed the new bandage to his wound with the other hand.

He groaned. "You're vicious."

"My viciousness turns you on." I dragged a hand lightly over his bare erection, making his body tense.

"Veil." He dragged me closer and lowered his forehead to rest on the top of my head. "You're right."

"I know."

After he drank the second dose of the antidote, I slipped an arm around his waist and tugged him back toward the bed. Neither of us was in the right shape to act on his desire, so we just collapsed back in the bed together. When he'd pulled me to his chest, I whispered, "What happened to Ria after you beat her?"

"I left her to Elwynne and Orvay. They should've taken her to the castle and chained her."

My stomach twisted. "Do you have a prison?"

"Most kings have prisons, Lae," he murmured.

"But do *you*?"

"I do. It's usually empty, though." He brushed his lips to the back of my neck. "There's nothing you could do to land yourself there. You're safe here."

I hoped he was right.

And sitting in his arms, I was comfortable enough to let myself believe him.

CHAPTER TWENTY-ONE

LAELI

W e slept for the majority of the next two days, with Gleam and Coarse bringing us edible, if questionable, food sporadically.

Ravv only had two wounds left that weren't entirely healed by the time the third day came around. My body was growing warmer by then, but my magic was still so small and weak that I could barely touch it at all.

I'd never burned myself out so thoroughly before, so I was surprised that my power continued to be inaccessible.

Still playing along with the façade about us not liking each other, Ravv left distance between us as we walked down the ice street, toward the castle. Gleam walked at his side, and Coarse walked at hers.

I was still uncertain about my bond with him, but there was no way out of it, so I knew I needed to figure out a way to get over it.

I was glad to have bonded, because it would mean I had an idorr on my side and wouldn't have to be alone, but Coarse was typically grumpy or angry. His connection to Gleam and Ravv was an even bigger problem, too, or would be as soon as the eclipse passed.

My fingers slipped into the pockets of the worn dress I'd gotten in the Timeless Sands. That dress had been through the veil and back with me, so it had a special place in my heart.

I'd have to figure out what to do about Coarse later.

"We're still pretending not to like each other, right?" I asked him mentally, as we walked.

"Most people will know we've been together sexually at this point," he said. *"Someone in the castle will have heard us and spread the word."*

A flush stained my cheeks. *"We haven't had actual sex."*

"They'll assume we have. Neither of us has been a quiet lover."

"So?"

"So, we have to decide what story we want to tell them. I'd prefer the truth." His gaze met mine, steady and soft.

"What's the truth in this situation?"

"That we intended the mate bond to be temporary at the beginning, but now have feelings for each other. If the cult already wants us dead, I see no point in pretending otherwise."

Veil.

He was admitting he had feelings for me, but what did that mean for our future? And what did I want it to mean? That, I still didn't know for sure.

My cheeks warmed. *"I don't know what I want to tell them. I'd rather we decide what we're going to be on our own, and let everyone else know after."*

He nodded, and his eyes finally focused on the city around us. *"We'll keep up the façade until you're ready, then."*

I tried to ignore the way my heart sank just a little, even though I was still refusing to admit the truth about what I felt for him.

• • •

I remained silent as we slipped inside and headed down a few flights of stairs. Every fae we passed acknowledged Ravv, and most of them did the same for me. It was strange to be recognized that way, but not unpleasant.

We passed a few hallways before we reached the bottom of the stairs. I itched to take Ravv's hand for comfort, but forced myself not to.

Maybe I should've agreed to Ravv's idea about telling the truth.

The smell in the prison made me shudder, and he gave me a concerned glance.

It wasn't the scent of old blood, or death. The prison honestly didn't smell like it had been used any more frequently than he claimed. It was just the scent of being underground that triggered me.

I met his gaze, not letting him see the fear that made my hands tremble in my pockets.

I wasn't in prison.

Ravv wouldn't trap me.

No matter how many times I repeated it, I couldn't seem to convince myself though.

"It's alright if you need to wait outside," he said, his voice gentler than I expected.

"No." My voice was steely. Or at least, I hoped it came out that way.

I followed Ravv into the dark hallway. There were very few lights, which made me more nervous even though I could see just fine.

We found Elwynne and Orvay leaned up against a wall, their shoulders pressed together. They weren't speaking, but they grinned when they saw Ravv.

"Has she said anything useful?" he asked.

"No, she hasn't," a feminine voice called from inside the cell to the right of them. "You know, my people will be making plans as we speak. In the time it took you to recover, they could've already infiltrated your walls."

"She's been like this the whole time," Elwynne said.

Ravv nodded, and his eyes flicked to me. *"Wait here."*

I obeyed his command until he'd disappeared inside Ria's cell. When he had, and I was sure it was safe, I stepped up next to Elwynne so I could see inside the cell.

The chained woman's hair was the same color as Ravv's, but where he was built thick, she was all sharp angles and toned muscles.

"Careful." Elwynne's warning was barely more than a whisper.

I nodded, my gaze lingering on Ria as her lips curved up in a wicked smile. "Hello, Ravv."

"Tell me how many people you have left and where you've hidden them, and I'll do what I can to spare them," Ravv said calmly.

Her smile widened. "At least give me the respect of asking reasonable questions."

"If your war was reasonable, you wouldn't have killed a child in our parents' city. Your tirade became a joke the moment you ended an innocent life."

Ria's smile vanished. "That was an accident. A casualty of war."

"And yet my war, one that dragged on for centuries, didn't take the life of any children."

Her face twisted in a scowl. "So I'm a monster now?"

"You've been a monster since you tried to kill our parents in the middle of a damn eclipse," he growled at her. "Since you pulled others to your cause, corrupting more fae simply because you were *afraid*. All of us feel fear—and yet none of us turn to murdering our own damned families."

"Don't act as if you're better than me," she spat. "You walked in here with a plan to cut my heart out of my chest. You're just as much of a killer as me, *brother*."

Ravv didn't argue, or deny her accusation.

Instead he stepped forward. Though I closed my eyes, I heard a wet squelching noise that made my stomach turn.

Ravv's voice was low as he said, "May the souls you have wounded guide you to a better future, and may your next life be one of hope, understanding, and love."

Another squelch followed as he pulled his hand from Ria's body.

I stepped back without looking to see if he held her heart, my stomach still churning.

A few minutes passed before Ravv emerged from the cell, his hands in his pockets and a dark expression on his face. Gleam rubbed up against his side, and he slipped his fingers into her fur as he said quietly, "Now, we carry her body to the city below, so her people see that she's lost, and the mated can see that we want to establish peace."

Orvay dipped his head.

"Any warriors who side with them die too," Ravv said. "We're fighting with the mated, and anyone who objects can bring it up with me."

"We'll spread the word," Elwynne said simply. "Who will you take to the city with you?"

"Whichever warriors are most suspected to side with the cult."

"I'll have a group together by lunchtime," Orvay agreed.

"Thank you." Ravv slipped onto Gleam's back, and she headed up the stairs without pause.

The couple was surprised by his gratitude, exchanging looks I couldn't read before turning back to me. "What have you done to him?" Orvay asked, his voice a bit playful.

"Barely anything," I admitted. "He's the one doing things, and I'm just dragged along for the ride."

As if on cue, his voice touched my mind. *"I need you close for the next few days. It's not safe for you to be alone right now."*

Coarse nudged me with his nose, and I slipped onto his back. He carried me off toward Ravv and Gleam, and I buried my fingers into his fur.

It was a strange sensation, to ride on the back of the beast I was bonded to. There was a different level of trust and safety in it. I didn't feel at risk, or in danger, despite my lack of relationship with Coarse. I just felt... secure.

We followed Ravv and Gleam around the city for the next few hours. Ravv stopped or dismounted to speak with fae every couple of minutes, but I remained on Coarse's back for most of it. That feeling of security I'd felt riding with him only grew stronger, as more time passed.

Just before it was time to meet the warriors to take Ria's body, we stopped for lunch at a small shop in the middle of the city. When I told Ravv I wasn't that hungry, he asked for extra on my plate.

I rolled my eyes at him, but when the food was put in front of us, ate as quickly as I could so we weren't late.

Though I was contemplating his idea to stop hiding our relationship, I was still uncertain. I had enough to worry about on my own, and was still fighting off the feelings of being trapped that had returned when I stepped into the castle's prison. They warred with the memories that had started coming back during the Beast's attack, leaving my mind a mess.

Wanting a distraction, I glanced up at the sky. My gaze followed the gleaming red belly of the dragon soaring in slow, wide circles over the glacier.

I didn't know if he was trying to scare us, or if he could sense the elves' shield, or... if maybe he didn't want to attack us?

That seemed like a ridiculous idea, but I didn't understand why else he hadn't attacked yet, so my curiosity was growing.

At the castle, we met a group of fae waiting with a body covered in black cloth. A shudder rolled down my spine at the memory of Ravv stabbing her, and I tucked my face close to Coarse's fur. He hadn't spoken more than a few words to me while we ran around the city, and I hadn't spoken much to him either.

We were both still reluctant to discuss our connection, I thought.

I needed to fix that, though.

He rubbed up against Gleam's side after Ravv dismounted to speak with a few of the fae gathered.

"I'm sorry," I said quietly to Coarse.

"For what?" he sounded grumpy again, but I didn't mind.

"It doesn't seem like you wanted to be bonded to anyone, so I'm sorry for trapping you in this," I explained.

He was silent for a moment.

A long, long moment.

"I suppose it could seem that way," he finally said.

We started walking, staying at the back of the group with Ravv and Gleam at his command.

"There are many idorr who despair at their lack of a bond. I focused all of that energy on my mate instead, so I wasn't prepared when our souls connected. I'm uncertain how to care for and protect my female while also being your companion. I have lived a long time without needing to worry about that."

That made sense, and I didn't blame him for it.

"I'm sorry. It's weird for me, too. I hoped that bonding to an idorr could help give me some sense of stability when the eclipse separates me from Ravv, so I think maybe we both just need to adjust our expectations."

"I have made it clear to the king that our connection outranks his to you, and he will face my wrath if he hurts you," Coarse growled into my mind. *"A mate comes before a companion, but you are not his mate."*

The words stung, but I needed to hear them.

My eyes burned a bit, too.

"He's the first sliver of stability I've had since..." I trailed off, closing my eyes and taking a shaky breath in. *"Since my family died. There was a fire on my thirteenth birthday, when my magic came in. I woke up surrounded by flames. They died—they all died. The ones we didn't lose to the fire, we lost to the king's men's swords."*

"You were a child, Laeli. Children can never control their magic. Don't carry the guilt for something you never would've done on purpose. Blame the fates or the gods for giving you that magic, but never yourself."

I wasn't sure how to respond to that, but his certainty lightened the heaviness weighing on my chest. *"Thank you for saying that."*

"You need to believe it," he grumbled at me.

My lips curved upward in a small, sad smile. *"If only it were that easy. I don't know how to make myself believe it any more than I know how to make myself stop relying on Ravv."*

"The king is generally a safe male to rely on," the idorr admitted. *"I trust him with my female's life more than I trust her with it."*

I snorted. *"That's terrible."*

"Gleamingeyes knows how protective I am of her. My trust in the king has nothing to do with her, and everything to do with him. He is an honorable male."

"You're not making it any easier for me to come up with excuses to put distance between us," I said with a sigh. *"He might be honorable, but it seems like he has no desire to stay with me after the eclipse breaks our bond."*

"I doubt that's true. Have you asked him? I've never seen him care for a woman the way he cares for you. Your bond is not as meaningless to him as you think."

My throat swelled. *"Maybe I'll talk to him about it."* I changed the subject, before I got too emotional. *"Have you and Gleam had any cubs yet?"*

"No. We had no desire to become parents during a war. Perhaps in the future, we will decide to try."

I respected that, tremendously.

If I had kids, it wouldn't be for a long, long time. I'd need a fae lifespan to make it possible at all.

We continued speaking as we ran, covering ground on the glacier as we headed to the city of mated fae. I'd been nervous about talking to Coarse, but I was so damn glad that I'd pushed past it. We weren't so different after all.

I even learned why he'd been so grumpy when we first met—because Gleam hadn't told him when she slipped away with Ravv in the middle of the night as they headed out to find me. He was angry because he had been worried about her.

Though I laughed inwardly at the story, it occurred to me while he was talking just how similar I was to Ravv's bonded idorr... and just how similar he was to mine.

I wondered if that might mean something for all of a heartbeat before focusing back on Coarse's story.

CHAPTER TWENTY-TWO
LAELI

One of the suns had already set, and the other two were going down, when we finally reached the thick crevice that was the entrance to the other city.

"We sent word to warn my parents that I'm bringing fae who may want them dead," Ravv said into my mind, as the first of our group slid into the crack. *"They'll be waiting at the gates to fight. Stay at the back for your safety; I don't want you involved."*

I wasn't going to argue in favor of my fighting abilities, so I nodded.

The fae holding Ria's body slid down, and Ravv and Gleam followed them.

Though I would've hesitated, Coarse slid down behind them.

My stomach jumped into my throat as we launched toward the ground below. My terror was tangible, until we landed smoothly.

Even then, my heart still galloped as my chest rose and fell rapidly. I gripped Coarse's fur tight enough to be afraid I was hurting him.

"Close your eyes," Coarse growled into my mind.

I, of course, did the opposite.

My eyes flew open, my head lifting so I could see what was going on.

My heart about stopped altogether when I saw the battle that had broken out in front of the metal gates. A couple fought viciously at the head of the group, and I knew they had to be Ravv's parents.

Among our people, the fae and idorr seemed to have turned on each other, and I couldn't tell friend from foe. I caught a flash of Ravv's face as he launched into the fight, ice claws and sharp shards erupting over his skin. He tore through the warriors with ferocity, working with some of them to kill others. I had no idea how he could tell the good ones from the bad ones, though I assumed he'd been filled in on which were most suspected to be working with the cult.

"Let me get down, and you can fight too," I whispered to Coarse.

"No." His voice was calmer than expected. *"The king and my mate have it handled."*

The words stunned me, but we stayed where we were.

I watched the fighting fae fall one by one, until Ravv stood in a group of those he must've trusted, with his parents behind him. His chest rose and fell quickly as his gaze scanned the faces of those left alive.

Finally, his eyes landed on one last man.

The man took a step backward—and then took a final strangled breath before my king tore his throat out with his clawed hand.

The contents of my stomach nearly came back up.

I covered my mouth, refusing to acknowledge the nausea. It was hard for me to face violence, but I knew Ravv was keeping his people safe.

Keeping *me* safe.

Given the opportunity, that man he killed would've likely killed me too.

The gore was still difficult to see, though.

"Someone grab the body," Ravv commanded.

I itched to ask him what had happened and how the battle broke out, but I knew the time wasn't right.

We would talk later.

...probably.

I could hope, at least.

Coarse and I stayed at the back of the group as Ravv led the other fae up to the gates of the city, where his parents stood, wearing icy armor that was splattered with blood.

"We're here to negotiate for peace," Ravv said evenly.

"She's dead?" his mother asked. Her voice wasn't quiet, but her expression was grave.

He gestured toward one of his men, who carried the body up to them.

Ravv's father carefully pulled the fabric back, and he and his mate stared at their daughter's face for a long moment before he gently covered her again.

His mother wiped at her watering eyes with a shaky hand. "It's over."

"Nearly. In the coming weeks, I'll find the cult's hideout to make sure they've all been eliminated. My most trusted men and women are working through the ranks of my warriors right now, making sure we've identified any who fear mate bonds and may retaliate."

"We can come home, then," his father said.

"Yes."

There was a moment of silence.

It was... more tense than I expected.

"We'll prepare our people for the move. When you come to let us know you're ready, we'll head back up with you," his father added.

"Agreed." Ravv started to turn away.

"Can we keep her body?" his mother asked quietly. "I'd like to bury her myself, and leave her with wishes for a kinder future."

"Of course." He didn't bother turning around, giving the order to the man holding her body before climbing onto Gleam's back.

Ravv's eyes moved slowly over me, making sure I was alright as Gleam strode past the rest of the warriors and their bonded beasts. She began to run toward a path off to the left of the slanted wall we'd come down.

Coarse remained where he was, planning to stay at the tail-end of the group so we didn't have our backs to anyone.

My eyes caught on one of the women in Ravv's group.

While the others were funneling out, she and her companion lingered a bit too close to his parents, who were both wiping at watery eyes, too engaged in quiet conversation to notice her.

"Do you see her?" I asked Coarse.

"Yes. If she moves toward the king's parents, she dies."

When a small ice blade appeared in her hand and she took a step, he wasted no time.

Coarse crossed the distance in a heartbeat, catching her off guard and removing her head from her body with his claws.

The woman's bonded idorr roared her fury, lunging toward Coarse. Her claws caught me in the arm as he dodged her, and I bit my tongue to hold back a cry.

He snarled back, slamming into her with his shoulder. She cried out again as she skidded backward, and then as his claws tore into her side.

When she retaliated, he moved enough to protect me from her claws.

I made myself as small as I could on his back while they traded blows, her injuries far worse than his. Ravv wasn't snarling into my mind, so he must not have known what was happening.

Ravv's parents and their bonded beasts joined the fight a moment later, and then it ended quickly.

I squeezed my eyes shut to avoid looking at the female idorr's body while Coarse traded words with a few others who had come to our aid. Soon, we had started down the path that would lead us out of the city.

Ravv and Gleam were so far ahead of us that they didn't see or smell our blood.

"Should we tell them?" I whispered to Coarse.

He grunted. *"I'd rather she lick my wounds in private."*

My lips curved upward a bit.

But Ravv wouldn't lick my wounds—he would be furious that I'd been injured without him noticing.

It would be easier to deal with his fury when we weren't on an hours-long trek back to his city... but he would feel betrayed if I waited that long to tell him.

I couldn't stand the idea of him feeling like I'd betrayed him on the same day he'd had to kill his own damn sister, so I couldn't wait.

"I'm going to tell him," I whispered to Coarse.

He made a noise of agreement.

I reached out to Ravv. *"Hey."*

There was a pause. Though I could feel his attention on me, he remained silent. I couldn't imagine the toll that day must've taken on him, and wasn't hurt by his silence.

"I need to tell you something without you panicking or growling at me," I added.

Another moment of silence passed.

I figured that was as much of a confirmation as I was going to get. *"After you left, there was a female fae who lingered too long. She looked suspicious, so Coarse and I were watching her. When she pulled out a knife and moved toward your parents, Coarse killed her, and then fought her bonded idorr."*

I saw his head jerk back toward the group before his eyes caught on me.

Quickly, I added, *"I'm fine, of course, but the idorr's claws caught me on the arm. I'm only bleeding a little, but—"*

He and Gleam were already charging through the group. The other idorr and fae dodged him without hesitation, giving him room.

Ravv plucked me off Coarse's back as Gleam snarled at her mate, poking and prodding at him with her nose. We skidded to a stop, and Coarse remained still while Gleam checked and licked every one of his wounds, growling and snapping her teeth at him.

Ravv was doing the same to me as he ripped the torn sleeve off my dress and studied my wound closely, then wrapped it tightly with that fabric. Though there was no licking involved, he was growling at me too. I could see the wound on his side bleeding through his bandage again, but something told me it was a bad time to bring that up.

"I'm okay," I repeated to him.

He said nothing as he held me tightly to his chest, leaning lower on Gleam's back so we wouldn't fly off when she started to move.

Coarse let Ravv and Gleam have their way. He gave me a deadpanned look when Gleam took off at an angry run, and he said, *"Does that really seem like a male who plans to let you go when the eclipse breaks your bond?"*

I didn't answer him, because the truth was too hard to believe, especially in my state of mind at the moment.

It had been a long, rough day... but we were all alive.

And we would figure everything else out when we got back.

CHAPTER TWENTY-THREE
LAELI

It was dark and cold by the time we finally reached the castle. My body was exhausted and achy, and Ravv seemed insanely tense.

Gleam and Coarse slipped into their own room after leaving us at the door to Ravv's. Though I knew there was a good chance they'd come back in to snuggle up with us later, I figured they knew we needed a few minutes to talk.

Ravv scooped me up and carried me into the bathroom, turning on the shower before stripping the rest of my clothes off. His movements were harsh, and there was frustration evident in the way he'd set his jaw.

I put my hands on his face when he set me down on my feet. We weren't beneath the water yet, but it rained down off to the side of us. "Just breathe, Ravv."

"I'm breathing," he growled back at me.

I narrowed my eyes at him. "Talk, then. Tell me what's on your mind instead of ripping my clothes off. If you're angry with me, tell me why. We're awful at communicating, and we need to fix that if we're going to survive even just until the eclipse."

"I'm not angry with you. I'm just..." He let out a rough breath. "Veil, I don't even know. I'm not ready to talk."

"Then tell me what I can do to help you."

"Drink my blood." He didn't so much as hesitate, and his gaze went right to my wounds.

They weren't small, and there were four of them in a row, so I could understand his concern.

But given the massive cut that had started bleeding through the bandage on his side again, I couldn't do what he wanted.

"Are you going to drink from me first?" I countered.

He scowled at me.

"If you tell me your wound isn't a big deal one more time, I will castrate you," I warned.

"You might need my balls someday, mate," he countered.

"And you might get your ass kicked by my flaming feet if you imply that we're going to have kids before you even tell me whether or not you want to be with me after the eclipse."

His lips curved upward the tiniest bit—and then they were on mine, and veil, he *kissed* me.

My first kiss was nothing compared to the way Ravv's mouth met mine. He kissed me the way he touched me, like he needed me and would do whatever it took to have me.

My back hit the wall, and he tore my undergarments from my body as his mouth made love to mine. His hands were everywhere—hot, slick, and perfect.

Mine buried into his curls, pulling him closer and tighter as we devoured each other, desperation growing between us.

I wanted more—I wanted him.

All of him.

The thickness of his cock rocked against my clit, and I nearly demanded he strip his shorts off and fill me. Only his mouth on mine stopped me from making the command.

The intimacy of it was all-encompassing.

It was overwhelming, in the absolute best way.

And veil, I never wanted it to end.

When he dragged my mouth to his shoulder and growled at me to bite him, I couldn't resist the command. My teeth buried in his shoulder, and his cut into mine.

We gasped together at the bliss that filled us both.

Our bodies moved against each other as we drank, our souls seeming to intertwine.

But it wasn't enough.

I wanted more.

"I need you inside me," I breathed into his mind, not daring to pull my mouth from his skin. He felt and tasted too damn good.

"You're sure?" I could feel how much effort it took him to ask me, rather than taking what I'd offered.

"Now, Ravv."

"Veil, you're perfect." He freed his erection and lifted me higher in one smooth motion.

His cock slid inside me, slow at first. The way he filled me was overwhelming—my breath stalled for a moment, until he squeezed my ass and growled at me to breathe.

I sucked in air, and he slid further in.

And further.

And further.

I thought he hit the back of me when a burst of pain had my stomach tensing, but he eased against it, and the pain faded into an achy, brilliant bliss.

Moans and pants escaped me as I released his shoulder, too overwhelmed to focus on anything but the way he stretched me.

"Tell me how you feel," he commanded me, withdrawing his teeth from my shoulder and capturing my mouth again. I could taste my blood on his tongue, and it was so much more of a turn-on than I could've imagined.

"Full," I breathed. *"So full."*

"You fit me perfectly." He sucked lightly on my lip before releasing it. *"I'm going to move, now. It'll probably feel strange at first. Lose yourself in the sensations, and the pleasure will follow."*

He thrust his hips, and my lips parted in complete and utter silence.

The pleasure that rolled through me was so much bigger and fiercer than what I was expecting. My body trembled with the force of it, and a soft cry escaped me when he repeated the motion.

"Veil, you're tight." The way his chest rumbled against mine when he spoke aloud made me dizzy with need. I was so damn close to the edge, and he knew it. "I'm going to fill you with my pleasure, Lae. When you go off, I go with you."

He thrust again, and I screamed.

Wave after wave of bliss washed over me as I jerked and rocked and moved. He slammed into me, managing not to hurt me as he roared, flooding my channel with the thick heat of his release.

We came down from the high, sweating and panting. My arms were draped over his shoulders, and his face was buried in my hair. The shower was still on at our side, but neither of us even noticed the damn thing. Outside the sweat and pleasure, we were as dry as the Sands.

"Veil," I whispered.

"That had better be a good veil," he grumbled at me.

I laughed, still a bit breathless. "So good."

"Then beg me to eat you while you're full of my seed."

I laughed again—so hard I nearly snorted. "No. I told you, I'm never going to beg you. The power dynamic between us is already a mess."

He gave me a deadpanned stare. "Stubborn female."

"If I were any less stubborn, you'd clean your floors with me."

He chuckled. "I wouldn't."

"No, but you'd get tired of me. You need someone just as strong as you."

He made a noise of agreement. After a moment's pause, he added, "You said I've never told you whether I want you after the eclipse."

"You haven't." I fiddled with the curls at the back of his head.

"I told you in Jirev that even if we couldn't be mates, I wanted you as my life partner. We're fated, Lae. To me, that's forever. Even if we weren't, I've come to enjoy fighting with you too much to go back to sleeping alone. I thought you understood that, or I would've made it clear long ago. I've been giving you the space you demanded because you're not certain—not because *I* have any doubts."

My throat swelled, and my eyes stung.

"I think I knew that," I admitted softly, not meeting his gaze as I continued playing with his hair. "It was just easier to believe you were pushing me away than to accept that I might want more."

"I'm not trying to make your life harder." He adjusted our position, and his lips brushed my throat once, and then again.

"I know. I think maybe *I* am, unintentionally. I'm not sure how to live life anymore, now that I'm free. It was always just about survival before."

"Your strength got you here. Now, you have to learn how to trust yourself." His lips brushed my throat again. "And me."

"I already trust you. I'm the problem here." My lips curved in a sad smile.

"Stop fighting with yourself, then. If I ask you what you want, what's your gut reaction? Without thinking, doubting, or questioning?"

"You," I whispered.

His chest rumbled against mine. "Good answer."

I laughed softly, and he lifted his head from my hair, brushing a few strands off my face. His expression was soft, and achingly-sweet. "Can I stop giving you space?"

"Yes."

His lips captured mine, and he kissed me slowly. Intimately. His cock was still buried inside me, hard and thick and perfect, but the kiss wasn't about pleasure.

It was about *connection*. About hope, peace, and veil, maybe even a little bit of love. Not that I was anywhere near ready to pull out *that* word.

He released me after a moment, then rested his forehead against mine. His eyes closed, and mine did too.

I almost *felt* his mood change as his grip shifted, going from holding me securely against him to holding me like he was afraid I'd leave him.

A few moments passed before he spoke quietly. "I killed my sister today."

My smile faded, and I wrapped my arms around him tighter. "I know. I'm sorry. You didn't have another choice."

"Elwynne or Orvay would've done it for me. I just..." he let out a harsh breath. "She was my responsibility."

Ravv had said that his crown was heavy, and I knew that was the truth in many ways. More than he'd even shown me.

"Your people respect you fiercely because you do the hardest things yourself. *I* respect you fiercely for that. Most kings would hand out the worst tasks to the people they trust, but you don't ask anything of anyone that you wouldn't do yourself. You should be proud of that, even if it's shitty today, tomorrow, and next week. You might not want to be king, but that doesn't make you any less incredible at it."

He grimaced. "Don't lie to me. Tell me I'm a miserable asshole."

"You're an asshole, but a good one." I pulled him closer, and he didn't protest the motion.

"If you're trying to make me hard for you, it's already worked."

I laughed. "You're still inside me. I know you haven't gone soft." I brushed a kiss to his cheek. "Tell me about your parents."

"Tell me about yours," he countered.

My smile vanished, and I tried to slip out of his grasp. He helped me slide off his cock, but held me in his arms even more tightly afterward.

"If I was as good a man as you say, you would've already trusted me with their story, whatever it is. You think I haven't noticed you lost in your memories? I see flashes of your past through our bond, Lae. I keep waiting for you to trust me enough to tell me."

My throat swelled, and I tried to pull away.

He held me tighter, gripping me to his chest. "You know that Ria tried to kill my parents. It was in the middle of the night, following an eclipse. Everyone was exhausted. I went to her room to see if she wanted to go for another round of drinks, to buy a few more hours until the alcohol sickness set in, but she was gone. When I tracked her scent to my parents' bedroom, I found that she'd tied them to their head-board and was torturing them, slowly. Relishing their pain."

My eyes widened with horror.

"She was drunk, and raging out of her mind. I dragged her from the room and made her tell me what had happened. She had fallen in love with a mated man who claimed he would leave his female to run away with her."

He continued, "When she went looking for him as the lust set in, ready to run away, he admitted he would never be able to leave his mate and asked her to spend the eclipse in bed with both of them. She murdered both him and his mate that night, and it turned her against not just them, but mated couples as a whole. When we went back in to release our parents, they were already gone."

The revelation was so insane, I could barely breathe.

"She lost her damned mind when we found that room empty, and tried to kill me too, but was too drunk to manage it. I hauled her back to her room and spent the night getting her sober. When the morning came around, she acted sorry for what she'd done, to convince me it was alright to sleep. Then, as soon as I let myself rest, she slipped away. I hadn't seen her since, until today."

"I'm so sorry," I whispered.

He squeezed me tighter.

Closing my eyes, I let out a shaky breath.

I felt better after I told Coarse some of what had happened. And I trusted Ravv even more than I did my bonded companion, as insane as that may have been. So... I had to tell him.

"My magic came in on my thirteenth birthday, and I woke up engulfed in flames," I began.

Ravv held me while I told him everything. He wiped my tears when I cried, and when I apologized for the tears, he licked them off my face.

I could tell that was just to get a pathetic little laugh out of me, but I appreciated it anyway.

When I finally finished talking, he turned off the water we had never stepped beneath, then hauled me to the bed. We would shower in the morning.

Breathing felt easier without carrying the secrets of my past on my shoulders alone.

My mind felt clear, for the first time in far too long.

I curled up in Ravv's arms, my bare body resting against his as he held me securely, and for the second time since we'd met, I let myself imagine what it would be like if we were fully mated.

And veil, it was perfect.

CHAPTER TWENTY-FOUR
LAELI

Ravv woke me up early the next morning with his face between my thighs, and then made love to me until I was so damn exhausted I was ready to go back to bed.

Instead of sleeping more, we went to a shop nearby, grabbed an assload of the fertility suppressant herb, ate a quick breakfast, and then went out with Gleam and Coarse to search for the cult's hiding place.

Though Ravv didn't say it, I knew the chance of us actually finding the hiding place were incredibly slim. There were dozens of other pairs of warriors scouting the glacier too, but the ice could be dangerous, and that made the search even more difficult than it already was.

We were so exhausted when we got back that night that all four of us collapsed in bed together. Gleam's sweaty, furry back was nearly plastered to my face, but Ravv's body was pressed to mine, so I didn't care.

The next few weeks passed by in the blink of an eye.

The dragon flew massive loops around the glacier, as if he was studying all of the fae from above while we searched for the cult's hiding place.

We got back to the house halfway through the fifth week of searching, ready to collapse back in bed with the food we'd grabbed from a shop nearby, when someone knocked hard on our door.

"We found it!" Elwynne called from outside.

Ravv didn't waste a moment, throwing the door open and waving her, Orvay, and their bonded idorr inside.

Their eyes were bright, and there was dried blood on both of their hands and arms.

"How many?" Ravv demanded.

"Four." She rattled off their names, but I didn't recognize any of them.

"Did you lose any?"

"Nope. All dead." Orvay's grin was vicious.

Three others had attacked the city and been killed for it in the past weeks without any other casualties, too, while we were off searching.

"Veil, we might actually be done with this mess," Ravv ran a hand through his already-wild curls. "You'll have to lead me there."

I fought a grimace.

My entire body was sore from the constant riding, but I couldn't say that. Not when they'd finally caught the people who had been plaguing them for so long.

"Of course," Orvay agreed.

"How far?" Ravv checked, glancing at me with a bit of concern.

We couldn't be apart without pain, and it had been a long day already.

"I can handle it," I told him.

"It's about a four-hour ride," Elwynne said.

Veil. It would be morning by the time we got back.

Ravv shook his head. "We'll leave with the first sunrise."

I blinked.

Elwynne and Orvay blinked too.

Coarse let out an amused huff and plopped down on the ground beside me, his mind brushing against mine. *"And you thought this male would walk away from you after the eclipse."*

"You need to see it. I'll sleep in the morning." I closed the box of food I hadn't yet started.

"Lae," Ravv warned, his chest rumbling unhappily. He sat down beside me and reopened the box. "Your health matters more."

"More than the security of our city?" Elwynne checked.

He flashed her a glare. "The city isn't at risk. You took care of that already."

"A few more of them could've been out foraging," Orvay pointed out. "We cleaned up and buried the bodies just in case."

"We can't risk waiting." I started to close the box once again.

Ravv ripped it open yet another time, leveling me with that glare he'd turned on Elwynne. "If you want to convince me of that, you'll need to fill your stomach."

"I'm not starving anymore. Look at all of this." I gathered the squish on my belly in my hand, through my simple, soft black dress.

"I'm not watching all of *this* fade." He grabbed my belly the same way I had. Somehow, it was much sexier when he did it. "You eat, or we don't go."

I heaved a sigh, but knew that fighting with Ravv about food was pointless. We had stopped hiding that we had feelings for each other, but we'd been gone searching all day every day, so none of his people really knew what we were to each other.

Elwynne's eyebrow lift, and Orvay's snort, told me they had figured it out.

"We knew you were together romantically," Elwynne said, plopping down in a chair opposite of mine and grabbing Ravv's fork. Orvay sat next to her, and after she took a bite of Ravv's food, she gave Orvay one.

"We knew you were together romantically too," I pointed out, as Ravv took my fork long enough to load it and fill my mouth again.

"The difference is, we're not bonded." Elwynne gestured between herself and Orvay. "There's no magic pushing us to stay together."

Ravv countered, "You're also not being hunted by one of the elves' assassins."

"Still. I like the freedom of being together without anything forcing us," Elwynne said. "If one of us changes our mind, we can part ways without a problem."

If one of them changed their mind, they could part ways without a problem?

I fought not to wrinkle my nose at the idea.

Maybe I liked the idea of a mate bond more than I cared to admit. I supposed I had lived so long without stability that I wanted the guarantee of it.

If I was going to be with Ravv for an extended period of time, it wouldn't be with the knowledge that we could part at any time. I'd tie him to me in every way there was, so he knew I was his without question, and I knew he was mine with just as much certainty. And if we ever fell out of love, we would figure out what we had to do to fall back *in* love. Our bond would be a vow that we would do whatever it took to make things work for us, for the rest of our existences. It was a huge commitment, but there was a lot of security in it.

Then again, even a mate bond could be manipulated, abused, or ignored. Ria had seen clear proof of that.

I wasn't about to argue about mate bonds with ancient fae, though, so I kept my thoughts quiet.

We all ate quickly, then headed out once again.

The ride was long.

Really, really long.

And a bit cold, too. It was difficult for me to get a chill thanks to my bond with Ravv and my fire magic, but not impossible, and the glacier at night made me shiver a bit.

The Demon in the sky seemed to be sticking closer than usual to us too, which was nerve-wracking.

By the time we finally reached the hideout, with an entrance that was nothing more than a crack between two chunks of ice, I was struggling to keep my eyes open. My body was pressed to Coarse's back, and his movements were steady enough that I didn't need to hold on tightly.

"Stay out here," Ravv murmured into my mind. His hand brushed my back before he and Elwynne slipped inside, while Orvay stayed out with me.

I didn't want to think about what might be happening inside the hideout, so I focused on Orvay. I had never spent much time with him, and I found myself studying him a bit curiously.

He hadn't said anything during the conversation about mates a few hours earlier, and that made me wonder how he felt.

He noticed me eyeing him, and his lips curved upward in amusement. "You're stuck on the conversation earlier, aren't you? Humans believe in marriage more than fae believe in mating."

I sat up a bit. "I guess. Why wouldn't you be comfortable promising everything to each other when you've been together for so long?"

"I'd love to make Elwynne my mate," he said bluntly. "But she grew up in a family of nomads, so she feels safer knowing she has options."

"Aren't you afraid of losing her, then?"

His smile widened. "I won't lose her. If she tries to leave me, I'll follow her until I've annoyed her enough that she takes me back. Eventually, she'll realize she doesn't want to live without me in any life, and she'll become mine permanently. I'm a patient enough man to wait for that day."

As I opened my mouth to ask another question, Ravv and Elwynne came back out.

"It's still empty. If there are any more cultists alive, they're not here. My guess would be that the only ones left alive are those still hiding among our warriors, and there can't be more than one or two we haven't uncovered at this point," Ravv said, his eyes landing on me immediately. They moved over me slowly, as if he was making sure I was in the same shape he had left me.

It didn't exactly thrill me to find out that we'd gone all that way for nothing, but Ravv would be able to rest easier after seeing the hideout, so it was worth it.

"Ready to head back?" Elwynne asked, scratching her bonded idorr behind his ears.

Ravv started to say something, but a huge rush of wind cut him off.

My head jerked upward as a flash of gleaming red caught my eye, and panic flooded me.

"Get inside!" I yelled at Ravv.

He stepped in front of Coarse instead, protecting me with his own damn body.

The Demon landed in front of us a heartbeat later, shaking the glacier beneath our feet. I clutched Coarse's fur as he tensed for the fight.

Ravv's ice claws and shards coated his body, and Elwynne's and Orvay's swords appeared in their hands.

But the demon shifted into the form of a man—a gorgeous man, with light skin and thick, curly crimson hair. He was even bigger than Ravv and Orvay.

Rather than attacking, he lifted his hands up as if in surrender.

None of us moved.

"I'm not here to kill you," the Demon called. "My curse drives me to track my targets, but I won't be forced to act on the urge to take your life for a few more weeks."

"What do you want?" Elwynne demanded.

"To make a deal with you."

A moment of silence followed his response.

"We're listening," Ravv finally growled.

"I want you to kill me," the Demon said.

There was a long, long pause.

I studied the man. He didn't look like a monster. He looked... tired.

"Why?" Ravv asked, his fury shifting to angry confusion.

His voice was weary as he admitted, "My curse controls me entirely, and I'm tired of being its prisoner. Death would be my only escape."

His words struck me hard.

I knew what it was to be a prisoner. To wish for a way out—*any* way out.

"What about mating?" I asked him.

His attention jerked to me, and Ravv gave a low, threatening growl.

"Mate bonds change your magic. What if taking a mate could alter your curse?" I added.

"This may all be a game to him," Ravv warned me. *"Do not risk yourself in any way."*

I didn't think it was a game to him, though. I knew suffering well enough that I didn't think anyone would be able to lie to me about it with any amount of success.

The Demon studied me for a moment. "And what if I make the female like me?"

"Then you'll have to make sure she falls in love with you, or she'll hate you for it," I said bluntly.

He studied me for a long, long moment before he shook his head. "I have taken too many lives as it is." His attention moved back to the fae with me. "Find a way to kill me before the eclipse, or my curse will force me to take your life. Your elves' shields may stop my brothers, but they'll be useless against me."

With that, he shifted back into his dragon form and launched into the sky.

I let out a breath I hadn't realized I was holding as he disappeared above our heads.

"We move, *now*," Ravv said harshly.

Our bonded idorr ran like our lives depended on it the whole way back to Loire.

The second sun was rising when we reached the castle, and I expected Ravv to go back to his room with me so we could get some sleep. Instead, he left me with a searing kiss at the door, and a warning to get some rest, before striding away to begin developing a plan.

Being left behind didn't hurt anymore, because I knew he was just taking care of me the best way he knew how. I wasn't a warrior, and all of us knew it.

Gleam collapsed in bed with me while Coarse followed Ravv to the meeting he likely had Elwynne and Orvay putting together, and I fell asleep almost as soon as my head hit the pillow.

My growling stomach woke me a few hours later, and I looked around blearily before realizing I was all alone.

Ravv was...

Veil.

Still in a meeting?

My handprint was throbbing a bit, but it had started to do that even when there was only a small amount of distance between us.

LOLA GLASS

"Where are you guys?" I asked Coarse, not wanting to disturb Ravv if he was still having a conversation.

There was no response.

I tried again, and got nothing once again.

Gleam was still snoring, so I didn't dare wake her up. I'd been up all day and night, but she had been *running* the whole time.

On second thought, I hoped Coarse was asleep too.

Though I was reluctant to interrupt him, I knew Ravv would be furious if he found out I was hungry and hadn't told him, so I reached out. *"Are you still awake?"*

"Unfortunately. Still planning with my generals," he admitted. *"Are you hungry?"*

My lips curved upward at the way he had practically read my mind. *"Yep."*

"I'm in an office just down the hall. Turn left outside our room, and walk down to the third door on your right. You can sit on my lap and glare at my people while I convince them to settle on a damn plan."

My smile grew a bit at the idea of sitting on Ravv's lap while he growled at his generals.

I swapped my dirty dress for one of his shirts before slipping out. I really needed a shower—and to wash all of my clothes—but he did too, so I'd wait for him.

Halfway down the hall, the door I'd been heading to opened, and a man stepped out.

Ravv's voice met my ears for a moment before the door shut behind him.

The man stared at me as I neared him, and I opened my mouth to say hello in passing.

He moved so fast, I barely saw him swing his fist at my face.

The pain of the collision didn't register as my world spun for a heartbeat, and then went black.

When I came to, my head felt like someone had taken a hammer to it. My body felt like it was turning too, but I could feel a muscular form against my back, so I knew that wasn't real.

My mind moved sluggishly, and the sharp pain in the handprint on my arm was enough to make breathing a struggle.

Some part of me could hear Ravv and Coarse speaking into my mind, demanding to know where I was and what had happened, but I wasn't functioning well enough to connect with them. Their voices and the bonds were there, but I was too weak to get a hold on them.

I forced my eyes open just a crack, and inhaled sharply when I found myself looking down at the city below us. My abductor and I stood on the roof of the castle, with just a thin strip of ice in front of our toes to keep us from plummeting.

Wind blew lightly at me, and I could feel my flames trying to ignite but failing.

Heights—veil, I did *not* like heights.

It was a good thing my mind wasn't working correctly, or I would've been a shaking, sweating mess.

"You have hunted and slaughtered us, but we will not cross the veil in vain!" the man holding me shouted to the crowd that had gathered at the base of the castle. My body stilled as he lifted the sharp edge of an ice blade to my throat and pressed hard. It nicked my skin, and a drop of warm blood rolled slowly down my neck. "The king's mate dies with me, leaving you with nothing but a broken crown, while the Demon of the Weeping Skies burns you all to ash."

Ravv and Coarse roared into my mind, deafening me to the sounds of the man behind me and the fae below.

The last few times I had been captured, I froze.

I couldn't move, or think.

This time, I forced myself to fight those urges. I had to speak—if I didn't, I would die. "Our bond isn't sealed," I managed to say. "We're not mates."

"You have a bond, and that's dangerous enough," the man spat into my ear.

A soft cry escaped me as he dug his knife deeper into my skin. More blood rolled down my throat until it disappeared into the dark fabric of the large, soft shirt I had taken from Ravv.

Ravv's voice boomed into my mind, growing clear for just a moment. *"I'm almost there, Lae."*

He needed me to delay the cultist.

It was my only chance at survival, so I forced my blurred mind to focus just a little longer.

"I didn't ask to be mated," I whispered. "I didn't know what he was doing when he said the vow. We don't—"

"Shut up," the man snarled at me. "You lost the right to live the moment that handprint appeared on your arm. You are a threat to Evare, and—" His words halted, and his hand dropped away from my throat. The knife was still too close for comfort, so I didn't dare move.

After a moment's pause, he stumbled.

A scream pierced the air as we plummeted off the ledge—*my* scream.

I fell for a moment—the longest moment of my life—until a strong hand caught me by the ankle. The yank of the grip was painful enough to make me scream again, until my body slammed against the icy wall of the castle, and the shock of it silenced me.

The fae who had cut me continued to fall. I heard yells and cries erupt below me, but none of them processed.

Everything spun faster as more pain flooded my senses.

Ravv spoke into my mind, his words sure and calming, but I barely heard them.

The grip on my ankle began to pull me back up onto the roof.

The crowd and world hung below me, and the terror held me captive.

I finally cleared the ledge, and a pair of warm arms wrapped around me. I inhaled Ravv's scent deeply as his chest rose and fell, and I could nearly feel his fury spiraling out of control.

The smell of him calmed me, though the world was still spinning. I wasn't sure what that fae had done to me, but it wasn't right—I wasn't right.

My stomach churned, then, and I moaned.

Ravv parted my lips, leaning in and sniffing my breath. Curses burst from him as he hauled me up off the roof and back into the castle. He snarled commands at someone—I couldn't focus well enough to know who—as he stormed back through the hallways.

My knees met the cool ice floor of our bathroom just in time for me to lean over the toilet and vomit the contents of my stomach.

The sickness was more violent than anything I'd ever experienced before. It hit me again, and again, and again. Ravv's hands were on my arms, in my hair, on my shoulders. At some point, he had a cold, damp cloth on my forehead that felt so good I could've cried.

When my body was empty and my mind delirious, he carried me to the bed. His voice was soft and kind, his grip gentle but firm, and I managed to doze for a few minutes before the vomiting started again.

At least I wasn't on the roof anymore, I thought briefly, before losing consciousness to the sickness.

CHAPTER TWENTY-FIVE
RAVV

I tied the end of Laeli's long, thick braid before brushing a kiss to her forehead and slipping out of bed.

The fury coursing through me was thicker and fiercer than anything I'd ever experienced before.

The bastard had cut her throat.

He had poisoned her.

He had nearly *killed* her.

After I had been sitting in a damn meeting with him through the entire night.

I had trusted him... and it nearly cost me everything.

My gaze lingered on her small, fragile form. She was strong of will, but soft of mind and body. My female would never be a warrior, and I would never ask her to become one.

But veil, I needed her safe.

I needed her healthy and fiery, challenging me at every turn and grinning as she did.

She deserved a male who could protect her better than I had in the time since I'd found her, but there was no one better suited for it.

And the veil knew I couldn't let her go.

She was mine.

I began to pace the room as I thought over the possible ways to keep her safe. Staying with her at all times was the best idea, if not an entirely reasonable one. She was independent enough to need her space, and would never agree to a constant guard, especially if I was that guard.

Of all the possibilities, one lingered at the front of my thoughts.

Sealing our bond.

If we sealed it, I would have more complete access to her mind. She would be able to use my magic as her own if she needed to, which could help protect her as well.

Most importantly, she would heal like a fae. She would have our senses and speed, rather than the ones of a human, which would enable her to watch her own back more closely.

And perhaps at the very pinnacle of the reasoning, she would have our immortality.

My immortality.

My magic would make her mine, for as many years as we could manage to stay in Evare. It would bind her to me and me to her in a connection that would stretch far beyond the bounds of a lifetime.

She would be mine to love, protect, and care for through our *eternities* together.

I wanted that with her.

I didn't just want her to be mine, I wanted her to be my mine *permanently*.

Laeli cried out in her sleep, pulling me from my thoughts as I crossed the room to her. A moment later, I was holding her upright as she emptied her stomach into the toilet. Nothing came up except bile, but I had been drugged with the same herb on two different occasions, so I knew the pain and misery of the illness.

"I'm here," I murmured into her ear, as I lowered her back to the bed. Gleam cuddled up beside her immediately, nuzzling her cheek to comfort her. I'd need to get water into her system within an hour or two, assuming she worked the same as a fae. It would all come back up, but the alternative was dehydration.

Then again, humans were weaker than fae. What if she could get dehydrated more easily?

I couldn't risk that, so I filled a glass of water in the sink and brought it back to Laeli.

I brushed a hand lightly over her forehead as I sat down beside her. She was clammy, but not cold. "Lae, I need you to take a small drink."

She groaned softly in response.

I put the glass to her mouth, and she opened it just a little.

A small stream of water trickled between her lips, and her face twisted in a grimace as she swallowed it.

I set the glass down when she pulled me closer, laying beside her as she pressed herself against me. I let myself close my eyes for a few minutes, knowing we'd be back in the bathroom soon enough.

Orvay and Elwynne were dealing with the backlash of what had happened on the roof, so I didn't have to worry about that. At my insistence, they had gone to bed for a few hours after the plans had been drafted, leaving me to work on convincing the generals.

If I hadn't been awake when the bastard took her...

Veil, I couldn't allow myself to think about it, or sleep would become an impossibility.

"Wake me if I don't notice when she starts feeling sick again?" I asked Coarse. Though Gleam was asleep, Coarse was watching my female with tired eyes from where he guarded the door. He had been sleeping

in the meeting room when Laeli was grabbed, and I knew he felt guilty about it.

He nodded, and I let myself drift off.

Fifteen minutes later, we were in the bathroom again.

The cycle continued, with the pauses between visits growing longer over the next twenty-four hours. I made sure Laeli had enough to drink, even though it killed me to see her so sick. I made her take a little of my blood a few times to keep her strength up, but it barely helped.

In the four days that followed, her stomach slowly normalized, and she was able to start eating small amounts.

It was another two days after that before she recovered enough to ask to leave our bedroom. Gleam and Coarse were off in their own space, catching up on sleep without our interruptions now that they knew Laeli was fine.

"Ravv," she grumbled, releasing her grip on me and rolling to her back. All she had on was one of my shirts again, as she preferred them to sleeping in her scanties. "I need to go for a walk, and I'm sure you have things to do too. I'll lose my mind if we stay in here. You won't even tell me about your plan to take down the Demon."

"Because you're not going to be involved in that plan." I brushed a few strands of hair off her face. She still looked paler than she should've, and I'd need to feed her more than usual when she was recovered enough for it.

"That doesn't mean you can't tell me about it."

I scowled. "I don't want you in any more danger than you already are."

"Knowing what's going to happen won't put me at risk, Ravv. And I deserve to know the plan." Her eyes were narrowed at me. "If you're going to start keeping things from me again, your bed will suddenly get very cold, and very empty."

"You would miss me too much." I slid a hand beneath her shirt, slowly dragging it up one of her thighs. My palm brushed her abdomen, and I teased the dip of her belly button with a finger. The scent of her desire slowly tainted the air, making my cock harder than it already was at the sight of her.

"You'd show up and grovel," she said, her lips curving just slightly.

"I would." I slid my hand back between her thighs and dragged a finger between her folds, fighting a growl when I found her even more slick than I expected.

Her gaze suddenly grew soft, and she threw her arms around my neck, pulling me in for a hug and squeezing me tightly. "Thank you for taking care of me. I already said it, but thank you. I know I'm a frustrating patient to deal with, and you've been amazing."

I left my hand between her thighs, pulling her closer with the other arm.

The best *thanks* would be to let me touch her, but I'd take a hug too.

"You're supposed to say, 'you're welcome'," she mumbled against my neck.

I blinked. "You're welcome."

Her lips curved into a smile against my shoulder. "Does no one ever thank you?"

I considered it. "I suppose not."

"Veil. I'll work on saying it more." She pressed her lips to my shoulder. "You're going to tell me about your plan when you're more relaxed about everything that happened."

"...okay."

Laeli's hand slipped into my shorts, and my cock throbbed as she gripped it.

She pushed my back to the bed, then slipped one of her legs over my abdomen, turning around so her ass was to me. I swore as her lips wrapped around my cock—and swore *viciously* when she lifted her ass off my abdomen, showing me every slick fold she had. She wore nothing under my shirt, and I'd never been so grateful for that.

"No touching," she warned me, gripping the hilt of my cock as she wrapped her lips around me again.

I growled back at her, grabbing her thighs and opening her wider.

She released my erection, shooting me a warning look over her shoulder. "No touching, Ravv. You took care of me—now I get to take care of you."

"You can take care of me by letting me make you scream."

Her eyes gleamed wickedly. "Oh, I will." My cock throbbed, and she turned back to it. "Let go, now. You can touch me again when I'm swallowing your pleasure."

Her lips engulfed me again, and I forced myself to release her. I gripped the blanket as she bobbed her head over my length, taking me deep into her throat.

She was so damn perfect, her ass and core bare for me while my shirt hung off her slight frame, revealing the underside of those heavy breasts.

Veil, I wanted them in my hands. On my chest. In my mouth.

Her core was visibly slick with her desire, her hips and ass rocking and swaying as she worked my length, dragging me to my climax too damn quickly.

My hips jerked as I lost control, snarling and flooding her throat with my release. My face was buried between her thighs before my pleasure ended—and she was crying out with her own climax moments later, commanding me to fill her.

I, of course, obliged.

Enthusiastically.

Until she was sweaty and panting, wrapped in my arms and letting me press my lips to those perfect breasts as many times as I wanted.

And when she asked about the plan again, I told her everything.

She didn't like the idea of us killing the Demon, even though she understood him wanting to be free from his curse. I knew she saw herself in him, despite the difference in years and magic between them.

And though I would never admit it to her, in that moment, I started working on another plan.

One that would satisfy my female while still giving the demon the freedom he wanted.

CHAPTER TWENTY-SIX
LAELI

When I finally managed to convince Ravv to let me out of our room, the first place we went was the dining hall. Elwynne dropped into the chair next to me as we finished eating, and she wrapped her arms around me for a quick hug.

"I'm glad you're still alive," she said, flashing me a grin.

"Me too."

"I'm not going to let her die," Ravv growled at both of us, taking our empty plates and striding toward the kitchen.

"I wish I could do something to help while you guys take the dragon down," I admitted to her, my eyes following Ravv across the room.

Veil, the man was gorgeous.

And the fact that he'd taken care of me through my sickness... well, it made him even more attractive to me.

"I can't imagine waiting inside, absolutely helpless," Elwynne agreed.

"Oh, I can't stay in the castle. Ravv won't be able to focus if he's in that much pain from being away from me. Me and Coarse are going to stay close, but out of the fight. We'll stick to the shadows."

She frowned. "Ravv will be distracted if you're close."

"After what happened the last time we were separated, he'll be more distracted if we're apart." I lifted a shoulder, trying not to let my mind wander back to the roof.

It wandered anyway, and a shudder rolled through me.

She looked a bit concerned. "Are you okay?"

I forced a smile. "I'm fine. When do we attack?"

"We're waiting for the king to give us a day and time." She glanced at Ravv as he sat down beside us again.

He studied me for a long moment before looking back to her and saying, "Tomorrow morning, at dawn."

"I'll spread the word." She gave me another quick hug before leaving.

There were others in the dining room, but none of them were staring at us. Or at least, I hoped they weren't.

"You look upset," Ravv said, his forehead creased.

"It's nothing." I brushed hair out of my eyes, and he narrowed his at me. "My mind just went back to the roof." My fingers brushed my neck, where the wound no longer existed. His blood had healed it while I was suffering the poison's effects, but I was starting to think I'd be able to feel it for the rest of my life anyway.

His gaze darkened. "You're not scared someone else will hurt you?"

"No. I think you're having everyone checked and rechecked for cult involvement." I squeezed his hand, and he calmed slightly. "I just need a distraction, I guess."

My mind went back to our bedroom, and my cheeks flushed at the idea of spending a few more hours that way.

I certainly wouldn't complain.

We had been so focused on looking for the hidden cultists that we hadn't had much time to get to know each other's bodies. There had to be some things we hadn't tried...

"If you want to go back to the river and attempt to break the magic on the rocks, the answer is no," Ravv said.

"I do want to try that, but not today." I leaned closer to him, and he tilted his head so I could whisper into his ear. "I was thinking maybe you can teach me something new?" I flashed him a mental image of me with my mouth on his cock earlier.

His eyes flashed. "How new?"

"Surprise me."

His lips curved upward wickedly, and he stood, pulling me to my feet with him.

Ravv slipped his fingers between mine and towed me down the hallway.

"Where are we going?"

"You'll see."

I wanted to insist on an answer... but I was too excited to risk spoiling it, so I stayed quiet.

Our shoulders brushed as we walked side by side, alone in the hallway as we went deeper into the castle.

We turned a corner, and the smooth, even walls of the hall slowly began to grow rougher and change shape.

"I'm going to need an explanation before I start to feel like you're about to murder me," I murmured to Ravv.

He barked out a laugh, and my lips curved upward a bit. *"There are caverns beneath the castle—magical ice caves that run hundreds of miles below the surface. They stretch beneath the Glittering Sea and continue below the mountain range of the Weeping Skies. A few branches even continue below the Endless Wilds and can take you all the way to the Aching Chasm, if you know how to navigate them."*

My eyes widened. *"How do you navigate them?"*

"Ice magic." He lifted my hand to his lips and pressed a kiss to the back of it. *"We're not going exploring. The caves closest to the castle are well-mapped and extremely safe, unlike some of the lower ones. The caves have magic of their own, and some are interesting. You'll see."*

I tensed a bit with his explanation—not because of the magic, but because we were heading underground.

"Does it smell like your prison?" I asked him.

"No. It smells like the sea down here, so you shouldn't be affected. Give it a minute and you'll start to smell the salt."

Relief rolled through me, and sure enough, the smell of salt slowly filled the air.

The walls began morphing further as we walked hand-in-hand. The ice became more crystalline, glittering in bright blues and soft purples. It grew jagged in some places, jutting out in wickedly-sharp icicles, and smoother in others, forming waves and swirls. All of it looked like art to me, and veil, I had never been exposed to art like that before.

It took my breath away.

"Legends say that centuries ago, these tunnels were full of pixies," Ravv murmured.

"Pixies?"

"The tiny version of fae, with crystalline wings." He held two fingers apart to show me how small they would've been. *"No one knows why they vanished, or if they really did exist. Some of the most ancient fae will tell stories about them, but fae that old begin to lose their minds, so they're unreliable."*

My eyebrows shot upward. *"Are you going to lose your mind too? How close are you to being too ancient?"*

He laughed. *"We call it immis when they lose their minds, and all immortal beings can get it. None of our fae have been lost to it for a long time, because we've had our war to focus on. Immis comes on with boredom or loneliness. Before the cult, fae used to take mates as soon as they felt it begin to set in.*

There were many couples mated as friends just to keep the madness away. Some still live now, in my parents' city."

"Mated couples don't get immis?"

"No. They live for each other, and that gives them purpose." He lifted my hand to his lips again and brushed another kiss to the back of it.

"Maybe the pixies were all lost to immis, then. Or to the cult."

"Or perhaps there is more in these caves than we realize."

I didn't like the sound of that.

He must've felt me shiver, because he tucked me beneath his arm and pulled me closer. *"We're almost there. Fae frequent these caves, and no one has ever been harmed here. You'll see why we like them, soon."*

I nodded, though I was still uncertain.

Clearly, I didn't have the best relationship with anything underground.

We came upon an opening to a smaller cave, and I peered inside. There were glittering, glowing crystals dotting the walls, sending bits of light everywhere and reflecting off everything.

"Veil," I murmured, staring into them.

"Couples come here to make love beneath the lights, or dance below them. Sometimes both at once, or to do so while others do the same," Ravv said, his breath brushing my ear and making goosebumps erupt on my skin.

Worry curled in my stomach. *"Have you brought a woman here before? I'm like the fifth girl, aren't I? Or the hundredth?"*

He laughed—loud and booming. *"No, Lae. The caves are far too intimate for casual sex. Fae come here with their life partners, not for drunken pleasure."*

Though I still didn't love the *life partner* label, it was a lot better than a potential future without him. I wouldn't necessarily mind being alone, but veil, I'd miss Ravv if we parted. He had become more than just my lover; he was the best friend I'd ever had. He was stubborn, but so was I, and I'd started to enjoy making him growl at me.

I wanted to ask him if he'd ever consider sealing the mate bond with me, but I didn't want to ruin the moment. I'd never been somewhere as beautiful or as magical as the caves, and I wasn't ready to let them go yet.

We resumed walking, passing the large opening to another cave. Steam flooded the space, and yellow and orange ice shone softly behind it.

"There are hot springs in there. Some fae enjoy heat play in their love-making. The water would feel nice to humans, but it's a bit painful for us."

"A pleasure and pain thing, then," I said.

"Mmhmm." He nipped at my ear as his hand slid under the large shirt I was still wearing, and stroked my thigh lightly.

My body warmed at his touch, and he pulled me closer with his free arm, so his erection pressed against my ass.

"And multiple couples use these caves at the same time?" I whispered.

"Sometimes. It depends on the couple, and the cave. Some fae are too possessive."

"How would you know if anyone else was already in there?"

"With your ears, Lae." Ravv nipped at my earlobe.

Right.

He added, "If they want to be alone, they'll throw a small ice barrier over the opening, like this." A short, thin sheet of ice appeared over the cave's entrance, blocking it completely. "If they want it soundproof, they just thicken the ice."

In the blink of an eye, the ice disappeared again.

His tongue trailed down my throat, making me flush hotter, and his fingers brushed my core.

"Can anyone remove the ice just like that, though?"

I didn't have anything against people who were interested in orgies, but I personally didn't find the idea appealing. After living with Jern and Gora, I'd heard enough of other people having sex for my whole life.

"No, it's much harder to alter ice that isn't your own. If I build a barrier, there are only a few fae in the city strong enough to take it down—and taking a barrier down here without permission would get a fae murdered in a heartbeat. We are warriors, after all." He resumed walking, and since I was pressed against him, I did too. "Most of the male fae who make love in the caves with others around ask their females to leave their clothing on. We aren't particular about nudity, but it's one thing to see a fae's body and a completely different thing to watch their lover enter it."

My eyebrows shot upward again. "You've been down here to watch before?"

"When I was young and inexperienced."

I supposed that wasn't surprising.

We passed the entrance to another cave of hot springs, and another cave full of ice sculptures. All of the sculptures were of men with massive ice erections jutting upward.

I didn't ask for a description of how that one was used, or allow my mind to consider the possibilities.

Ravv's breath brushed my ear again in front of that cave as he murmured, "If you ever want to ride an ice statue, it will be a statue of *me*."

I snorted—and then my humor died with a thought. "Tell me there's not a statue of you in there."

He chuckled. "There's not."

He went still for a moment though, and when I looked back at him, I got the feeling he was using his magic to check each of the statues.

A relieved breath escaped him after another minute, though, and he repeated, "There's not."

We passed a few more caves with interesting lights and crystals before we came to the final one at the end of the tunnel. It was smaller than the others we'd passed, and the ceiling was covered with even more of the crystals from the first cave. I let out a relieved breath when I didn't see any statues or ropes or anything.

"You scared me," I grumbled at him.

He flashed me a grin. "You scare me all the time, Lae."

That was fair.

And veil, his grin was heart-stopping.

A barrier closed over the entrance, making it entirely private.

"So which kind of possessive are you?" I asked him, as he turned me in his arms so our eyes met. I was pretty sure I already knew his answer, but I had to ask anyway. "The kind that puts up barriers, makes his female wear clothes, or is all about nudity?"

He didn't even pause to think about it as he lifted me off the ground. "The barrier kind. The very, very thick barrier kind."

My thighs wrapped around his hips, and he gripped my ass as he adjusted my position. I inhaled sharply when the length of his erection pressed against my core, hitting my clit just right.

"Now, if we were in a crowded room, and no one knew what we were doing..." he rocked his hips just slightly, and a soft cry escaped me. The lights dancing off our skin only made the moment more intimate. His voice was gravelly as he said, "I've always had a fantasy about making love on my throne, during a party."

A groan escaped me as he started walking, rocking his cock against me with every step. "A party?"

"Mmhm. It makes me hard to think about whether we could get off without letting anyone realize what we were doing."

My shoulder blades hit the wall, and his fingers lightly traced my back entrance.

"Who is this we?" I managed to ask.

"You and me. On my throne, during the eclipse. I throw a party in the castle every time it comes around. I have since I became king."

Since his sister had hurt his parents.

It was a distraction, an—

"Ohhh," I groaned as his finger dipped into my channel before sliding down to my back entrance again. He'd played with it a little, but had never gone any further than teasing it a bit.

"We need to talk about you not wearing scanties when you're in public, Lae."

"What about it?"

"I'm going to start seeing it as permission to spread these thighs whenever I want, and wherever I want," he rumbled. "In my office. On my desk. In my library. In my hallway."

"Veil," I groaned, as the tip of his finger slid inside my back entrance. "What are you doing to me?"

"You wanted a lesson." He lowered his head to my breast and caught my nipple through his shirt that I'd stolen. I sucked in a breath, rocking against his erection where it rested on my core. "You're going to learn about ice."

"Ice?" I echoed, already breathing a bit raggedly from the way he had his finger in my ass.

"Ice," he agreed. "I need you good and wet before we start. Are you wet for me, Lae?"

"Yes," I breathed.

"I'll decide that." He eased his erection away from me, making me groan again, but in frustration. At least, until he lifted me away from the wall and set me on the ground...

And then settled his face between my thighs, releasing my ass in favor of opening me up wider for him.

Ravv lowered his nose to my core and inhaled deeply, his eyes burning their gorgeous purple color. The glow reflected off the crystals on the ceiling, mixing with my red-orange and sending lights of both colors all over the cave. "Not ready yet," he growled, and then dragged his tongue over my clit.

A cry escaped me as he licked me slowly.

"Show me your breasts," he commanded, his eyes hot as he tasted me.

I tugged my shirt upward, pulling it up to expose them to him.

His chest rumbled in satisfaction, and my hips jerked at the vibration while his tongue worked slowly down the center of me.

Veil, he was going to lick *every* inch of me.

If he wasn't looking at me like I was the sexiest woman he'd ever seen, I would've been petrified.

"Shirt off completely," he said.

I peeled it over my head, and he rumbled for me again. His finger found my back entrance once more, using the slickness to begin working into me.

"Play with your breasts for me."

I stared at him, waiting for some kind of clarification. He had made it clear that he was *not* okay with me bringing myself pleasure on multiple occasions.

"Now, Lae." His teeth scraped my clit in punishment, and I swore, jerking my hips to chase the pleasure that followed it.

"That's not my job," I shot back.

His eyes gleamed wickedly. *"Good. Hands above your head."*

My eyes were narrowed at him, but I lifted them.

His ice restraints grew over them, pinning them in place.

I took in an unsteady breath... and then let it out too.

I was fine.

Ravv hadn't trapped me.

I could free myself with my magic if I needed to, but I wouldn't need to. He would never do that to me.

"You're safe with me, Lae. Always. You tell me to stop, and I stop at any time," he said, his voice steely. His mouth was still on my core, his tongue against my clit, but it wasn't moving.

I met his gaze and nodded.

"Ready?" he asked.

I jerked my head.

He scraped his teeth over my clit again, making me buck before he pulled his face away. His fingers ran over the bud, but they felt different. Smoother, and harder.

Ice.

He'd covered them with ice.

He dragged them around my clit slowly as he worked his finger inside my back entrance. My body rocked and jerked desperately, and I neared my climax. He increased the pressure on my clit until just before I lost control, and then halted.

My chest heaved, and my body throbbed.

So close—I was so damn close.

"Ravv," I hissed at him.

His eyes were still wicked. "The lesson's just starting. You don't get to climax until it's through."

I groaned at him.

"You know I won't let you out of here until you can barely walk straight, Lae." He dragged his ice against my clit again, and my whole body shuddered. "You'll get what you need, and more."

I trusted him, even though I hated being patient.

I opened my mouth to say as much—but then a thick, smooth column of ice slid inside my channel, and all thoughts died in my throat.

It was...

I...

Veil.

His fingers dragged over my clit again, and I shuddered hard, so close to the edge.

"You look so damn good with my ice in your core, Lae. These pretty lips part perfectly for me." He dragged a bare finger slowly around the ice that filled me, pausing to tease my clit a few times. "You're going to take more."

I couldn't breathe well enough to ask him how he thought that was even possible. I was so deliriously close to the edge, I could hardly function at all.

Ice engulfed his finger, buried inside my back entrance—and then slowly, so slowly, expanded.

My breaths grew even shallower.

I swear, I almost saw the veil.

"When you climax for me, I want to hear you scream," Ravv said, dragging his tongue over my clit.

My hips jerked.

I rarely screamed—only when we'd gone so many rounds that I couldn't remember my own name until he said it in my ear.

"I'm not leaving this cave until you've screamed for me three times, so go ahead and stay quiet. I could do this all night."

He was going to kill me.

The bastard was really going to kill me.

I—

He sucked my clit as he slid the ice in my core out, and then back in, and it was over.

I screamed, and screamed, and screamed as I climaxed, and climaxed, and climaxed.

I'd never felt so much pleasure, and the smirk on Ravv's face when I came down from the high told me he knew it, too.

"I'll count that as three," he told me, as the ice that filled me slowly disappeared.

I let out a relieved breath when it was gone, my heart still pounding fiercely.

"That was the hottest thing I've ever seen, Lae. I'm so damn proud of you. Next time, you'll take my ice and my cock together."

Veil, I couldn't even imagine.

We would definitely save that for another day.

"How do you want me?" I gestured to my drenched core.

"Just like this."

He lowered his tongue to my clit, working me until I was ready for more —and then he made love to me beneath the glittering lights until I could've sworn I was sparkling too.

By the time he carried me back to his room, the words of our bond repeated through my mind as if trying to force their way through my lips.

"Sillah ovim rett warum."

"Sillah ovim rett warum."

"Sillah ovim rett warum."

I wouldn't speak them, of course... but I had to wonder what it would feel like if I did.

CHAPTER TWENTY-SEVEN
LAELI

The next morning came too soon.

I put an actual dress on for the first time in too long, and undergarments, too.

Ravv caught my face between his hands before we slipped out to meet Gleam and Coarse in the hallway. He tilted my head back, and I looked into those gorgeous eyes of his. "I need you to be careful today. I'm worried about you, Lae. I need you to come out of this whole, healthy, and safe."

"I'll be careful." My lips curved up in a sad smile. "But only if you will too. The Demon doesn't feel a drive to kill anyone except you. That makes this riskier for you than everyone else."

"I'm not worried about me." He pressed his lips to mine.

It was a soft, gentle kiss that had nothing to do with pleasure or desire —another kind I was coming to adore. I could get used to kisses about nothing but intimacy and comfort.

His forehead pressed against mine.

"Promise me, Ravv. Swear you'll look out for yourself first."

"I can't make that promise. I'm the king; it's my responsibility to put my people first."

"Before your mate?"

"No. My people come before me, but not you. Never you." He brushed his lips against mine again.

"It would kill me to lose you," I said quietly. "I've survived a lot, but I don't think I could survive that. I need you to stay alive."

He closed his eyes and let out a long breath. "I'll protect myself with the same ferocity that I protect my people," he finally said. "I don't want to leave you any more than you want me to leave, Lae. Especially not while this is silver, instead of gold." His fingers brushed the handprint on my arm, and I shivered.

"If you die now, I'll be forced to take someone else as my mate in revenge," I whispered.

His eyes gleamed, and he growled. "Veil, you're perfect."

With that, he pinned me to the wall and kissed me.

By the time Gleam and Coarse joined us and my king released me, my lips were swollen, and I was nearly dizzy with happiness.

We met a massive number of fae out in front of the castle. The Demon was still flying slow circles overhead, the way he always was, and I let myself wonder if he was really just going to let us kill him.

All terror aside, he was an incredible creature. I'd never seen a dragon before, but he was majestic. His scales glittered like gemstones in the sky, and I had to wonder why anyone thought of dragons as demons. Sure, they could breathe fire, and were known for being vicious, and...

Well, maybe I didn't have to wonder.

But still, he was beautiful.

Wasn't there any way around killing him?

"*What would happen if we left him alive?*" I asked Coarse, as he stayed in the shadows of the large ice buildings we ran beside. Ravv was close enough that my handprint was throbbing, but I wasn't in actual pain.

"*He would eventually be driven to kill Ravv. Letting him go isn't an option.*"

"*What if we trapped him somehow? Or made a deal with him?*"

"*Making a deal with an assassin is never wise, Laeli. His magic will drive him to uphold the agreement he already made. He will have to throw everything he has at killing Ravv.*"

I knew that.

I did; I knew it.

But I didn't want it to be the only option.

He had seemed so tired, and so sad. Was he really a monster if he was suffering so much that he'd request to be killed?

"*What if someone formed a mate bond with him?*" I asked. "*Do you think it would change his magic? Or stop his drive to kill Ravv?*"

"*Your magic only hides the king's because it's his opposite.*"

"*Or because we're fated mates.*"

"*But how would we find the Demon's fated mate?*" Coarse countered.

He was still right, and I was still wasting my time trying to think of an alternative.

"*If he's truly the man he claimed to be when we met him, he doesn't deserve to die,*" I finally said. "*He deserves a chance to be free.*"

"*It may not be possible at all.*"

"*But it might be, and isn't the possibility worth something? What if we could save him?*"

"*Some people don't want to be saved, Laeli, and there is nothing we can do to change their minds.*"

My gaze landed on the dragon above us.

Coarse was right, but I wished he wasn't.

The Demon landed as we reached the outer edge of the city.

The fae yelled battle cries as they sprinted across the ice with their bonded idorr, but the Demon didn't blow fire.

He didn't roar or swing his spiky tail.

He simply bowed his head and prepared to die.

The fae with the scale-breaking weapons were at the front of the group. Those with the brutal strength were behind them. Ravv led everyone. Most of his generals had wanted a grander, more elegant plan full of moving parts, but Ravv had refused. There was no need for elegance in slaughter.

I watched all of them go, my eyes stinging as they lingered on the Demon.

The fae neared his massive form without a moment of hesitation.

My eyes slipped down to Ravv and Gleam at the front of the army, and I noticed them slow, as he shouted a command I couldn't hear.

The warriors around and behind him slowed too, until everyone on the battlefield stopped entirely.

I silently reach out to Ravv's mind, to see if I could pick up any of his thoughts, and heard him yell, "This is not a fight, it's an execution."

The Demon growled something back.

Ravv shouted back, "I won't kill you for being tired of living, Demon. Do you think you're the only one who grows weary of this world or the mantle you carry?"

There was a long pause, and the Demon asked what the alternative was.

Ravv called, "There are caves beneath my city. Even when your magic is at its strongest, you won't be able to escape the depths of them to find any target or agree to any more kills. If you try to shift and fly free, the ice will end you. Its magic prevents it from melting or being broken, just like my city's. If you truly wish to die, die with honor, traversing caverns of ancient magic even more powerful than you."

The Demon roared, and Ravv roared back.

After a moment's hesitation, the rest of the fae army roared with both of them.

The assassin shifted to his man form, and Ravv offered him a hand.

Coarse snarled into my mind and Gleam's about his mate carrying the Demon—and she must've snarled something back to him, because he cut himself off quickly.

I could've sworn the Demon's eyes locked with mine for a moment as Gleam cut through the middle of the army, carrying the assassin back toward the castle, and to the caves.

Though I hadn't asked Ravv to spare him, I couldn't help but wonder if he had heard something I said to Coarse... and if somehow, I had changed his mind.

Ravv apologized for the pain I would feel as he led the Demon into the caves with a dozen of his fiercest warriors. He wasn't willing to leave them alone with the assassin, so I spent the day hunched over in bed, trying to breathe through the agony.

All of the men were between my king and the Demon constantly, at my insistence. I would've rather gone with them, but Ravv had snarled at me when I even suggested that.

It was a battle I knew I wouldn't win with him, so I didn't bother fighting about it.

We spoke through our bond nearly constantly, my second requirement to Ravv going underground. Though I didn't want the assassin to die, I was still worried he would attack my king. Thankfully, he didn't.

Outside of me and my pain, the rest of the kingdom had erupted in a roar of dancing and drinking in celebration. They considered the battle won, simply because no one had died. Their music shook the castle's walls with its volume, and their drunken songs floated through the hallways at all hours.

Elwynne and Orvay stopped by to bring me food a few times throughout the day, seeming a little more drunk each time, but they were happy drunks. They apologized for my pain and asked me to join their revelry, but I refused every time.

When the suns went down, my pain still hadn't eased, but Ravv was finally on his way back out of the caves. He growled at me to accept Elwynne and Orvay's invitation for the sake of distraction. So, the next time they showed up, I let them drag me into the party.

Between the pain and the music, I couldn't hear myself think at all. It was actually rather glorious. I accepted the first drink they gave me— and when it dulled my pain, I accepted a second, third, and fourth. I danced, sung, and celebrated, losing myself in the party.

Eventually, I collapsed on a couch, snuggled up with Elwynne while Orvay cuddled her from behind, and fell asleep.

I woke up to a familiar growl. "Who touched her?"

Veil, my head throbbed.

My stomach, too.

I looked down at myself to see if I looked as if I'd been touched.

Normal black dress.

Normal red-orange hair.

Normal breasts, no nipples hanging out.

"I dunno. We all danced with everyone. It didn't turn into an orgy or I would've gotten both of them out," Orvay mumbled back, his voice insanely slurred.

He had been drinking longer than me, but I couldn't imagine it was possible to feel any more terrible than I already did.

The pounding in my skull was getting even more painful.

I almost preferred the poison to the alcohol sickness.

I felt the bed shift beneath me—err, the couch?

Elwynne groaned and clutched me tighter. "No, Orr."

"I'm behind you, Wynnie." He patted her on the head.

She released me, rolling slowly and clumsily to face her lover.

"You reek, Lae," Ravv said into my hair after he hauled me into his arms. My legs wrapped around his waist as he walked, and he held me close.

"My mom used to call me that," I whispered.

"I know. Does it bother you when I use it?"

"No, I like it. It brings happy memories, not just sad ones."

He squeezed me tightly. "I think we've had this conversation before. You're still drunk, aren't you?"

"Not sure." I pressed my forehead to his neck. "I like you."

"I like you too." His lips brushed my arm. "I'll find you something to eat, then we'll get you showered and back to bed."

I nodded. "Thanks for saving the Demon for me."

There was a moment of silence as he opened the door. "I couldn't very well kill him after you saw how sad and lonely he was," Ravv finally said, setting me on my feet in the shower. "Stay here. I'll find food and water."

I nodded, leaning against the shower wall and closing my eyes. The water rained down on me, and it felt nice. It felt *cleansing*.

Ravv came back soon with food, and we both showered and ate, then collapsed in bed together.

A few hours later, we headed out to the city below the surface. Our group was bigger than it had been the last time we went there, and

Coarse told me that was to help bring more people and their things. We had a group of unbonded idorr with us too, to carry some of the younger fae who had never had a chance to bond with a beast.

My head and stomach ached from all the alcohol the night before, but Ravv rode on Coarse's back with me to make up for the time apart. The warm comfort of his presence eased the hurt, and his stories made me smile.

The gates opened as soon as we reached the bottom of the crevasse, with Ravv's parents waiting just inside them.

We were at the back of the group, so we watched our fae and idorr spread into the city in assigned pairs, keeping an eye on each other just to make sure there weren't any cultists left hidden among us.

When we finally reached the gates, Ravv lifted me off Coarse's back and slid his fingers between mine as we approached his parents. There was pride in his voice as he said, "Mother, Father, this is my female. Laeli, these are my parents."

"It's nice to meet you." I nodded at them, hoping I didn't come off as awkward as I felt. I knew there was still strangeness between Ravv and his parents because of the way they'd abandoned him, but we seemed to be ignoring that for the moment.

"Hello." His mother smiled, her expression kind and genuine. "My, you are beautiful."

My face warmed. "Thank you."

She stepped forward and put her arms around both of us for a tentative hug. "It's good to see you happy, Ravvi."

I bit back a snort.

Ravvi?

I loved it.

He looked a bit uncomfortable with the hug, so I leaned into him a bit when his mother finally released us and stepped back. His fingers dug into my hip, and I had the feeling it was for comfort when he pulled me closer.

"Your magic feels unusual," Ravv's dad said, his eyes a bit narrowed. "It's warm."

I was kind of flattered that was the identifier he used. It would've been rude to point out the weight in my breasts and ass, or my weak muscles.

"Laeli is human. Her power is the opposite of ours; heat and fire. Life, to our death." Ravv said bluntly, his eyes narrowing right back at his father.

"If you seal the bond you've begun, our people will follow you," his mother said, almost eagerly.

At least she didn't care about my humanity.

His father's expression softened a bit, too.

"If we seal the bond, it will be because we wish to be together for the rest of this life and every other that follows. I don't care whether your people follow me; we are at peace now, so there are no battles to drag them into. If they don't approve of their king, they can leave. Now, we have people to help." Ravv led me away from his parents, and I squeezed his hand for reassurance.

"That could've been worse," I whispered.

"It certainly could've. Thank you for staying at my side."

"Of course." I brushed my lips to his cheek, and noticed a fae child watching us curiously as Ravv pulled me closer.

We spent hours helping others pack their things and load their bags onto the backs of the idorr who would carry them, and then spent a few more running back to the city. By the time we ate a massive meal that the castle's cooks had prepared for everyone, and started helping with the unpacking, the suns had already set.

We worked until I could barely keep my eyes open, and then Ravv hauled me back onto Coarse's back, and held me to his chest as the idorr carried us back to the castle.

CHAPTER TWENTY-EIGHT

LAELI

The days began to fly by after that. Ravv and I hadn't discussed what would happen after the eclipse, but I didn't really think we needed to. As much as I would've loved to seal our mate bond, I wasn't letting myself obsess over it. We knew we would stay together, and that was what mattered.

I started working in the castle's kitchens to help feed the returning fae while they got settled, and Ravv left me with the chefs while he helped people move in. Our handprints ached more than usual with the distance, so he tried to stay as close as possible, and that made it manageable.

It didn't take long to learn how to cook, and I found myself looking forward to it every morning. I enjoyed the simple chatter with the other fae men and women who cooked professionally, and the bustle of it all.

A shipment of ridiculously large and delicious produce came in from Jirev one day, with a note from Nissa that made me grin.

Laeli,

I hope you're doing well! Kierden finally seduced me into his bed, and I think we might stick together for good. Only time will tell. I have to have a mate bond with someone to keep my magic in check, and I think he's too possessive to let me bond with anyone else, so we'll see what happens.

In other news, I've become a farmer! As ridiculous as it sounds, I think it's my life's passion.

How are you? Is Ravv still possessive? Have you guys gotten together, or are you going to part after the eclipse?

Come visit soon!

Nissa

P.S. if you need a place to live, I can always use another set of hands on my farm! I have so many extra plants, it'd probably be a relief if you burned some of them.

I paused what I was doing long enough to scribble out a reply so the fae from Jirev could take it back with them.

Nissa,

I knew you'd end up with Kier when you checked him out in that cage the first night we met. You would've let him ravage you there and then!

Ravv and I are still together! I don't think we're going to seal the mate bond, but he's dropped the whole "life partner" thing the fae here seem to do, and neither of us plans to walk away. His possessiveness only seems to have grown, so I'll be interested to see how different he is when the bond is gone.

I don't really have a passion in life. Guess I'm still figuring that out! I've been having fun in the kitchen these last few days, so maybe I'll spend my life cooking. At least my heat is useful here!

Have you heard from Kaelle? I hope she's not still afraid of Vayme. We might need to rescue her after the eclipse if she is.

Come visit me too!

Miss you!

Laeli

The warriors who'd brought the letter were happy to take it back. They didn't seem bothered about the journey they'd taken, and it made me think about what Ravv had said about *immis*. They needed a purpose to keep their sanity, and maybe some people would enjoy running back and forth between cities.

I supposed it was better than sitting on your ass day in and day out.

The night before the eclipse, I started cleaning up for the day, assuming we'd be going back to our homes just like always.

"No, no, no." One of the other cooks plucked a sponge out of my hand. "Tonight, we cook, so tomorrow, we can revel."

I lifted my eyebrows. "All night?"

She grinned. "All night."

My lips curved upward. "Alright, then. Let's do it."

Ravv came looking for me shortly after that, stopping at the entrance and frowning when he saw me working on some pastries I was still trying to master baking. Gleam wasn't with him; Coarse had spent his days helping the fae moving in, and he'd let me know a few minutes earlier that he and Gleam were heading in for the night.

"You're not cleaning up?" Ravv asked me.

"Sorry, Highness, she's cooking most of the night!" one of the other ladies called out, winking in my direction before she looked back at him. "We're keeping your woman."

His lips curved upward.

My stomach clenched as I realized it was our last night with the bond. Our last night being able to communicate mentally.

"I can't leave them to cook alone. I'm becoming part of the team," I admitted to Ravv.

"Then I'm staying too," he said simply.

I stopped and blinked.

So did everyone else in the kitchen.

"Do you even know how to cook?" I asked Ravv.

"No." He grabbed an apron off the hook he'd seen me hang mine on every night. "You can teach me."

"I barely know how to cook," I protested.

"We trained you well. You can do it." One of the other women elbowed me, in the side this time.

"I'm not spending the night before the eclipse away from my female, Lae," Ravv said.

"Alright, alright, come on." I waved him over.

He washed his hands and then stepped up beside me. I taught him how to measure out the ingredients, which was overwhelmingly simple, and we were both quiet as we worked.

"This is surprisingly easy," he remarked to me after a while.

"I know! It's relaxing too."

He made a noise of agreement. *"The company doesn't hurt, either."*

I flashed him a playful smile. *"Are you thinking about propositioning one of my co-chefs, Ravvi?"*

He chuckled, and I felt multiple sets of eyes on our backs as we continued working. Neither of us turned around to check. *"I'm far too busy thinking about how many ways I'm going to take you tomorrow to consider anyone else."*

My face warmed, but I couldn't stop my smile from growing.

A few of the other chefs' life partners joined us, and one of them seemed to be among Ravv's closest warriors. Though the warrior started a conversation with him, Ravv ended it quickly. He didn't seem grumpy or irritated... just calm and contemplative.

The mood was comfortable and upbeat while we cooked, and Ravv's body brushed mine every chance he got. If he wasn't using his hands for cooking, they would've probably been on my figure too.

.   .   .

It was late by the time we finished everything and headed home. Ravv took my hand and slipped his fingers between mine, still quiet. My shoulder brushed his as we walked.

We walked to our room in the castle in silence. I wasn't sure what he was thinking—and in a few hours, I'd have no way to ask him other than out loud.

I wanted to collapse in bed when we got back, but I smelled like the food we'd cooked for dinner, so I headed for the shower, and Ravv followed me.

"We've made a lot of memories in here," I remarked, as I stripped and then slid beneath the falling water. My eyes closed as it washed over me, and I sighed at the feel of it.

Ravv's gaze lingered on my form as I cleaned myself, and for once, he didn't join me. I was still curious about what he was thinking, because he didn't look upset or angry. Just calm, and quiet.

He had a towel ready for me when I was clean. I stepped out, and he wrapped it around me, brushing his lips against my cheek and squeezing my breasts lightly through the fabric. "You're the most beautiful woman I've ever seen. Thank the veil for these perfect, human curves."

I laughed, and kissed him. "You're weird tonight."

"I've just been thinking a lot." His expression grew rueful.

"About what?" I dried my hair as much as I could with the towel, then padded out of the bathroom.

"About life."

"You're going to have to be more specific." I stepped into the closet, pulling one of his shirts out and slipping it over my head as he leaned against the doorway. "Life without me? If that's what you're thinking about, I'll have to fight you. And I know I'll win, because you won't hurt me, even if you've decided to cut me loose."

"Not life without you. Veil, I hope I never have to think about *that* again." He studied me. "Life without the bond."

Oh.

There was a small lump in my throat, and I couldn't stop my gaze from moving to the soft silver glow on his palm. I'd miss that when our bond was gone.

I'd miss a lot of things about it, honestly.

The mental connection, most of all.

"I've been thinking about that too," I admitted.

"What have you been thinking about it?"

"No, I'm *not* the one spilling my thoughts on that first. I already know that humans have different ideas about bonds, and marriages, and mating, than the fae, so I'm almost confident we don't agree." I tried to step past him, but he caught my hips and dragged me close.

When I squeezed my eyes shut, he tilted my head back, and waited.

Finally, I opened them.

Those gorgeous purple eyes of his were staring down at me like they were searching my soul.

"I love you, Lae," Ravv said.

The words were soft, but certain.

My throat swelled. "You what?"

"I love you. You make my life better, so damn much better. I love talking with you, fighting with you, laughing with you. I love the way you think, and the way you feel so damn intensely. I love you." His calm confidence wasn't overwhelming, or overpowering.

It was just... perfect.

My eyes burned as my emotions swelled. He brushed his mouth against mine, but I pulled away before the kiss could turn into anything else.

"I love you too," I admitted. "I've known for a while, but I thought I'd scare you away if I said it. You make me happy, Ravv. Happier than I ever knew I could be. And even more than that, you make me feel safe, in every way."

His lips curved upward, his eyes glittering with emotion, and then he kissed me again.

I could nearly *feel* his emotions bleeding into mine through the bond.

His fierce love.

His overwhelming gratitude.

His flooding peace.

When he pulled away, his hands gripped my face. My lips were swollen, and we were both breathing fast as our foreheads pressed against each other.

Ravv spoke again, his voice lower and rougher. "I'm not ready to let the bond go, Lae. I'll never be ready to let it go. Seal it with me. Be mine in this life, in the next life—in *every* life."

Tears swelled in my eyes. "Are you sure?"

"I've never been more certain of anything." His words rang with honesty. "If it's not what you want right now, I can wait, but—"

"I want it," I whispered.

"You do?" His eyes widened, just slightly.

He was *actually* surprised that I wanted to be his mate.

"Of course I do." I buried my fingers in his curls. They were longer than they'd been when we met, and I hoped he'd leave them like that. Veil, if I was his mate, I could *ask* him to leave them like that. "I always wanted the bond, but I thought you were just going to ask me to be your life partner forever."

He chuckled. "I'd have to be a far less possessive male to accept that fate."

"True. I should've realized."

"You should've."

His lips brushed mine again.

My throat swelled as the words of the bond rang in my mind.

Finally, I could say them.

"*Sillah ovim rett warum*, Ravv," I whispered. "My heart and life are yours."

The magic of our bond swelled and thickened in my chest.

Ravv's eyes glimmered slightly, and he repeated the vow he hadn't meant when he said it in my prison all that time ago. "*Sillah ovim rett warum*, Lae. My heart and life are yours."

The bond grew within both of us as he leaned in and kissed me, and kissed me, and kissed me.

And even though the eclipse was coming soon, even though we'd spend the next twenty-four hours dragging out every ounce of pleasure we could from each other, we made love more slowly and more sweetly than we ever had before.

CHAPTER TWENTY-NINE
LAELI

I woke up an hour or two after we went to sleep. The filthiest dream I'd ever had was still running through my thoughts, and I was soaked between my thighs.

My mind was on Ravv and his damn fantasy—him sitting on his icy throne with me dressed in a fancy, glittering gown, perched on his lap. A party raged around us, but we were both blind to it, all of our efforts focused on hiding what we were doing—and bringing each other pleasure, as he touched me and entered me below the billowing skirts of my dress.

A glance at his raging erection, and a flicker of an image coming from his side of the bond, made me wonder if they had been my dreams at all.

His hand brushed my thigh, and the sight of the bright golden glow coming from his palm made pride swell in my chest.

My lips stretched in a smile when I saw the golden handprint wrapped around my bicep, too.

I could hear music playing somewhere in the castle, telling me the party had already started. The windows didn't let in much light, so I knew it had to be early still.

His hand moved over my thigh again, slower.

"Your fantasy is going to kill me," I told him, brushing hair off my damp forehead.

"The smell of your desire is going to kill me first." He slid his hand between my thighs.

My body clenched as he dragged his fingers over my clit roughly.

"The first time I take you today will be on my throne, Lae." His teeth caught the sensitive skin on my neck, dragging lightly.

"You're really serious about that?"

Ravv made a noise of agreement. "We have to do it now, before the party becomes an orgy." He nipped at my throat again, then released me and slipped out of bed, taking a long moment to look at me. His hand slowly stroked the length of his cock as he stared down at my bare body. "Veil, you're stunning."

I was too busy staring at his mismatched eyes to process what he'd said. One of them was his own gorgeous dark purple—but the other had changed with our bond, and now glowed the reddish-orange of my own.

"You're starting the eclipse by refusing me sex?" I asked, sitting up slowly as I tried to ignore the need burning in my veins.

I had never felt such fierce desire on an eclipse as a human—and it was still so early.

Ravv released his cock and stepped into the closet for a moment, then emerged with a thick, billowing dress. The same one from my dreams.

Err, his dreams.

Maybe with the connection between our minds strengthened, more of our thoughts would mix like that. I was honestly a bit excited to find out.

Ravv caught my hand and tugged me out of bed, then pulled the dress over my head. He eased my arms beneath the delicate straps, and arranged my breasts so they weren't bursting from the bodice.

When he finished settling the fabric, he pulled on a pair of shorts, then his hands slid into my dress from behind.

A slit.

There was a slit at the back of it.

That damn fae king.

His hand slowly dragged over my thigh, and I moaned aloud. "I'm terrible at being quiet, Ravv."

"You'll do fine." He dragged his teeth over my shoulder as his hand found my bare clit again, and slowly teased the oversensitive bud. "Do this for me, and you can punish me in any way you like. If you want to make me spend the rest of the eclipse with my face between your thighs and my cock weeping without your touch, I will."

I groaned at the mental image, and he continued working my clit until I cried out with my release, my body tensing with pleasure as it warred painfully with need. "I just want you inside me."

"You'll have me, Lae." He continued working my clit. "I'll be yours to command."

"Fine. Let's go," I whispered.

His hand left my center, and I fought a whimper as he swept me up off the ground and hauled me down the hallway.

The music grew louder as we approached the celebration. We passed people already dancing and reveling in the hallways, none of them naked or doing anything sexual, which confused my need-addled mind.

"It hits harder for those with a partner," Ravv murmured into my ear, before nipping at it. "It's worse this time because we're bonded. Everyone else has a few hours before they feel it this strongly."

We reached the throne room, and veil, the need was only growing fiercer.

I wanted Ravv.

I *needed* him.

I was going to lose my mind if I didn't have him.

He walked me to the throne, barely sparing a growled greeting for the people who said hello or exclaimed about our sealed bond. The music was loud enough to hide his growls, and I vaguely noticed that most of the female fae in the throne room wore dresses similar to mine.

It must've been a tradition or something—and he'd gotten me a dress to make sure I fit in.

My legs shook with the weight of my desire for him.

He finally sat down on the throne and pulled me onto his lap. His erection was against my ass, his hands on my waist.

Everyone was looking at us for a greeting, so he bellowed something about a successful and enjoyable eclipse. The crowd roared their approval, and the music grew even louder.

The groups of fae danced together, their bodies moving nearly as one, and soon enough, there wasn't an eye on us in the room.

My abdomen ached with need.

My body quaked and quivered.

Ravv fluffed my dress, slyly opening it at the slit so the skirts billowed around both of our legs. One of his hands remained on my waist, and the other slipped beneath my skirt.

He slowly pulled one of my legs up until my knee was against the throne, and then did the same with the other. The movement lifted me to meet his cock—and my skirts kept our movements hidden entirely.

"You're doing so damn well, Lae," Ravv murmured into my mind, as my body trembled with need. *"I'm going to make you feel incredible."*

He freed his erection, and his hand was hot on my skin as he found my slit through my slickness.

"Close that pretty mouth, mate," he said. *"The sounds of your pleasure are for my ears alone."*

I clamped my jaw shut as he eased me downward until finally, the head of his cock met my opening.

I bit down harder to stop myself from crying out—and even harder when he pulled me down further. His erection was thick and hard as he filled me, and my pleasure hit as I sank down onto him.

Ravv's fingers worked my clit lightly, and the climax hit hard. He held me in place as the pleasure rocked me, hiding what we were doing from the fae in the room.

"That was perfect," he growled. *"And you're going to do it again for me."*

Veil, I was going to do it as many times as he let me.

The need was still so damn fierce.

He pulled me down again, until my ass met the tops of his thighs. The warm bareness of his skin there made me shiver.

He swore softly, his hips jerking slightly as his cock swelled inside me. My breathing grew staggered as he thickened—and then lost control.

Ravv held me still as I went over the ledge with him, my jaw still clenched and my body finally relaxing slightly with the relief of the quick releases.

"Look at the crowd," he said into my ear, after his pleasure had faded. One of his hands stroked my thigh lightly beneath my dress, and the other was still on my hip. "They know you belong to me—but they have no idea how completely I have you right now."

The world spun with his words, and the way his hand was moving closer to the apex of my thighs.

"Tell me you're mine, Lae."

"I'm yours, Ravv," I breathed. *"You said I'm yours. Prove it."*

He snarled softly against my ear, and finally touched me.

The pleasure hit me hard.

I had to clench my jaw so tightly it was painful to stop from crying out, but I did it.

And the pleasure went on.

And on.

And on.

We were on that throne for at least an hour—maybe two—before Ravv finally decided our appearance had been enough and hauled me away.

When we reached our room, we didn't make it to the bed.

He had me pinned to the wall and was slamming into me from behind before the door shut behind us.

And veil, it was perfect.

The rest of the day—and night—passed in what felt like a dream.

A very, very sexy dream.

We made love in the bed.

Against the wall.

On the floor.

In the shower.

In our clothes.

In our *ripped* clothes.

Veil, we even did it upside down.

I had never imagined an eclipse could actually be enjoyable, but damn, I'd hold on to the memories of our time together until the day I died.

CHAPTER THIRTY
LAELI

I woke with a smile on my face, curled up in Ravv's arms and blissfully relaxed. He kissed me slowly, and then murmured, "I have a surprise for you."

My eyebrows lifted. "More than just the dress yesterday."

His lips curved upward. "Yes."

We slipped out of bed, and took a long, slow shower to clean off all the evidence of the *fun* we'd had on the eclipse.

After we were dressed in clean clothes, Ravv took my hand and led me down the hall, to the left. My gaze flicked to the door his meeting had been in, and I expected to feel fear with the memory.

Instead, I felt nothing.

The castle wasn't responsible for what had happened, and I'd seen my captor die.

We stepped past that door, and a few others, before we reached the end of the hall.

"What are we doing?" I asked, curiously.

He didn't answer as he twisted the doorknob and stepped inside the room, leading me in after him.

My eyebrows raised when I took in the space.

It was three times as big as Ravv's bedroom, with a huge bathing pool, a larger bathroom, and a massive closet. There was even a small kitchen in one corner.

Ravv set me down on the edge of the massive bed, and then sat beside me. There was a fancy box with a large bow beside him, but he didn't pick it up.

I stared at him, waiting for an explanation.

"You told me once that the power dynamics in our relationship were distorted. I came up with a way to fix that but couldn't make it happen until now." He pulled the lid off the box, and my eyes went wide.

Inside, there was a thin, silver band studded with jewels.

He lifted it from the box, and then set it on my head. "The announcement is spreading through the city right now. Loire finally has a queen again."

Tears stung my eyes. "I can't be the queen. What would I even do with my time?"

"Whatever you want. If the king fights on a battlefield, I think the queen can cook as many pastries as she likes." He gestured to the room. "We needed a bigger living space, of course. One that's not just mine, but ours. We can still stay in the house when you prefer it, but—"

I flung my arms around his neck and kissed him, hard.

He grabbed me, kissing me back without hesitation.

"This is perfect," I said against his lips. "You're perfect."

He chuckled. "I'm certain you won't feel that way next week."

"I will. I might want to smack you, but I'll still feel it."

He laughed, his expression relaxed. "The closet is full of dresses, too. I measured you while you were sleeping a few weeks back. You haven't been gaining weight for a while."

My eyebrows shot upward. "Are you serious?"

"Yes. You needed new dresses that were actually made to fit this gorgeous human body, Lae." He squeezed my thigh.

"Not so human anymore." I gestured to the glowing handprint on my arm. It glowed bright and clear, declaring to us and the rest of the world that our souls had become one, permanently.

"Human in the ways that count." He tucked my hair behind my ear, and then traced its curve with his fingertip. "And here. I love these little ears."

I couldn't fight my smile.

"We need to stop by the kitchen for breakfast, and then there's something else I want to show you," he told me, standing smoothly. "And you're wearing one of your new dresses out. One without sleeves."

"So you can show off my handprint?" I teased.

"So I can look at it anytime I want and remember that you'll never be free of me again."

I laughed, and he flashed me another grin before he disappeared into the closet.

We strolled out of the castle together, hand-in-hand, shortly afterward. Our bellies were full with food we'd found left over from the party, and we kept looking at each other and grinning.

At his insistence, I wore the delicate crown Ravv had made for me, and though I was self-conscious about it, I was also proud that he considered me worthy.

And glad that we'd figured out the weird power dynamic.

It would take time to really establish how things would work between us in the kingdom, but we would figure it out. I had no desire to start making any leadership decisions or to take any type of a queenly role, so it wasn't as if I'd step on Ravv's toes.

Unless he asked me to stop cooking.

I'd started enjoying it far too much.

We walked through the streets of our city, and the sounds of children laughing and playing floated through the air. They would spend all day outside after being locked in their rooms with books and snacks throughout the eclipse, Ravv told me. Like humans, the eclipse didn't affect fae until they reached maturity.

It took a long time to reach the outer edge of the city, but I was so content that I didn't mind. Ravv and I shared stories of our childhoods, laughing about how we had both come to understand what actually went on during an eclipse, and holding on to each other tightly. Coarse and Gleam would be resting and enjoying each other's company, so we didn't try to interrupt them.

When we finally slipped out of the city, we followed the river to the place where I'd burned myself out a few weeks earlier.

"This is what you wanted to show me?" I asked him curiously, as we approached the icy stones.

"Just wait. You'll see." He squeezed my hand lightly.

When we were close enough to see the rocks, surprise lifted my eyebrows. I had expected to find the river frozen over, since no one was there to break the ice.

Instead, I watched the water run smoothly, without taking pause.

The stone I hadn't touched was still covered in an obscene amount of ice that stretched over halfway into the river, but the one I'd focused my magic on only had a thin layer.

I had almost done it.

I had almost erased the magic completely.

And it was more than enough; the water was flowing just fine.

Satisfaction flooded me. "I did it. I burned away most of the enchantment."

"And that saved multiple fae an endless number of hours, day after day," Ravv rumbled. "You should be proud of yourself. You're stronger than you know."

I *was* stronger than I knew.

And veil, I *was* proud of myself.

I wasn't the same woman I had been in the cellar. I wasn't scared, lonely, or desperate. My luck wasn't bad, at all.

Not anymore, at least.

I had been rescued by a gorgeous fae king, who became my mate.

I had been brought to a magical city where my power was useful, not dangerous.

And I had fallen in love with a man who had become my closest friend.

It seemed safe to say that somehow, I had become the luckiest woman in the world.

BONUS SCENE
LAELI—A FEW MONTHS AFTER THE ECLIPSE

"*Damn, this is hot,*" I hissed at Ravv.

I was typically a fan of that particular aspect of my newfound faeness; the way the temperature changes affected me. The lukewarm water in our shower felt blissfully warm thanks to the change.

But the hot springs in the caves beneath the city? Them, I didn't like so much.

Ravv pulled me closer, murmuring into my ear, "You'll adjust."

"Unlikely," I managed to say.

He chuckled against my back, his arms around my bare middle. There was a thick ice wall up over the entrance to the small cave, giving us a bit of privacy.

His lips trailed slowly down my neck and over my shoulder as I tried to relax in the heat of the water, but really, I felt like I might melt or just be cooked through at any moment.

I could hear the humor in his voice when he asked, "Are you turned on yet?"

I swatted a hand at his face, but he caught it and dragged it to his lips for a kiss.

Visiting the hot springs *had* been my idea...

A poor one, apparently.

"Don't pretend you're hard. I feel you against my ass, and you're not any more into this than I am," I grumbled at him.

"You keep me too well-pleasured to feel desire in this infernal heat." His lips brushed my shoulder again. "Though I'm sure you could convince me with enough effort."

I had no more desire to put forth that effort, though.

I'd give it a few more minutes to see if I could adjust, but if not, we'd enjoy each other's bodies some other way. It wasn't as if we lacked ideas.

Fanning my face, I said, "Veil, how does anyone live in Jirev? It must feel like a boiler if hot water feels like this."

"It's miserable," Ravv agreed. "The Endless Wilds possess their own beauty, but it's the kind I'd rather experience in passing."

"Same." I closed my eyes and swallowed thickly. "I don't know how much more of this I can take."

"I'm ready whenever you are." His hand brushed my hip.

Nope, my body didn't react.

It was too busy trying to sustain itself in the hellish water.

"You're still going to make love to me, right?" I asked.

Ravv scoffed. "You should know me well enough not to have to ask, Lae."

"It's the heat. It's boiling my brain," I mumbled. "Alright, I can't take any more."

Ravv lifted me out of the water.

I groaned when my ass met the cool stone beside it. "Never again."

"I'm sure you'll forget how this went and decide you want to try again." He plopped down beside me and slicked his curls off his sweaty forehead. My gaze followed the gorgeous golden glow on his palm, reminding me that he was mine, permanently. "And I'll agree, because I'm hopeless when it comes to denying you."

"You argue with me all the time," I protested. My feet were still dangling in the water, and I didn't mind it as much as I expected.

"About how much you eat and how much you work, because I want you healthy and by my side constantly."

"About what I wear."

"When I want to see you take it off, yes." His eyes gleamed as he opened my thighs, pulling one of my feet from the water to spread me wider as he lowered his face to my core.

I couldn't help my sharp inhale at the first stroke of his tongue against my clit. "Ravv."

"Lae." He rumbled against me. "You wanted to find pleasure in the springs. Technically, you're still in them."

My gaze flicked to my leg, dangling over the edge so my foot was submerged in the hot water. I moaned as he licked me again, my hips bucking for him.

His tongue dragged over me again, and I gasped, hooking a thigh around his head.

He gripped my thigh with one hand as he opened me with the other, giving him better access to my body.

"Sounds fair," I managed to say.

"Very." He sucked lightly.

My hips jerked against him, and he released my thigh to pin my hips down where he wanted me. My foot started to rise from the hot spring, but he pinned it in place too.

"Your foot stays in the water."

I groaned, and he nipped at my clit.

I gasped, and he filled me with ice.

When I unraveled, he growled that I was perfect—and then replaced the ice with his cock.

My foot stayed in the water as he filled me, cries escaping me as my ecstasy swelled.

"Tell me again that you don't like the hot springs," he growled into my mind, tilting my hips as he thrust in again, dragging us both to new heights of pleasure.

"I don't—" I cut myself off with a moan. *"I—"*

The words failed me.

All words failed me.

We found our climax together, and my cries melded with his roar as he lost himself inside me.

"Damn," I breathed, pulling my foot from the scalding water and resting it on Ravv's ass. "You're a professional."

"So you tell me." He eased himself to a seated position, dragging me up with him so he remained buried inside me. My hot foot rested against his back, but he didn't mind. "Next time, your head hangs over the ledge while your hands are in the water."

"Veil."

He gave me a gravelly chuckle. "You wanted the experience, Lae. You're getting the experience."

"Or you could stand in the water, and I could lay on the stone," I suggested.

"No." he kissed my shoulder.

"Ravv," I protested.

He lifted me a bit, and I swore as he sat me back down on his cock, even deeper. "You're mine."

"Fine," I heaved a sigh, though my body was still throbbing with need. "Do your worst."

His chest rumbled. "You get my best, Lae. Always." He lifted me again, turning me around—and then he slid into the water to his thighs, standing on the seat while he hissed his pain. My legs wrapped around his backside, my hips hovering over the water, but his grip was firm enough that I knew he wouldn't dunk me.

His hand smacked my ass lightly, and I bit my lip to stop myself from grinning. "Your ass will take the pain you wanted," he gritted out, still buried inside me, and still insanely hard.

Slowly, he pulled out, and then plunged inside me again.

My cries echoed through the cave, growing louder and louder until I was sure the entire castle above us could hear them.

And when I shattered, I took Ravv with me.

The pleasure was so damn intense, I almost could've been convinced I crossed the veil with my climax.

I was so damn glad that I'd let him make me his queen, because veil, he'd certainly learned how to treat me like one.

EPILOGUE
RAVV—MANY YEARS LATER

"Are you sure this is safe?" I eyed my very pregnant mate, gripping her hand tightly as I walked beside her. We'd taken one last trip to the icy shore of one of our beaches, so we could watch the waves in peace once more before our baby joined us.

"It's a chunk of ice, Ravv. I think I can walk on a chunk of ice without managing to off myself," she drawled back.

"Ice becomes very dangerous when you're pregnant, Laeli," Elwynne called from where she sat on the beach, cradling her newborn. The golden handprint on her shoulder glowed brightly beneath our suns, and Orvay leaned over to press a kiss to it.

Elwynne and Laeli had managed to get pregnant at nearly the same time without discussing it, even though a handful of decades earlier, they had both proclaimed that they would never be mothers.

Change was a natural part of life, though. When my teary-eyed mate told me she had decided she was ready to be a mother, I simply took her into my arms and told her how wonderful she would be at it, then offered my baby-making services.

She had smacked me for that last bit—but I clearly knew what I was doing.

"Who knew?" Laeli tossed back.

"Every male fae with any good sense," I grumbled. "Especially the ones with mates who run hot."

"You're all a bunch of overprotective bastards," Laeli agreed, though her words were full of fondness. She had grown used to my protectiveness long ago, and though she would never admit it, she loved it.

"What are we going to name him?" she asked me. "I think he needs a strong fae name."

"I think *she* needs a dainty human name," I countered.

We had been making bets on the baby's gender since nearly the moment we found out she was expecting.

The bets only grew grander as her abdomen swelled. Currently, the winner was set to earn six months free of any type of labor, including cooking, cleaning, and anything else they could come up with.

My female would need the time off after growing my massive baby, after all—in her words, not mine.

Laeli didn't know I'd asked Alida, one of the elven leaders, what gender the baby was when she'd visited last.

Or that our little boy would have her hair, and my eyes. I would've told her, if I hadn't known she would be furious with me for spoiling the surprise.

Pride swelled in my chest at the thought of him.

Life with Laeli had been a great adventure already, and it would only get livelier when another little soul joined us.

Coarse growled as one of his and Gleam's cubs came running over to us, bumping his little head into Laeli's leg a little harder than he probably realized.

"Careful," I growled at her, as she stumbled.

I couldn't growl at the cub, after all. And Lae was used to my grumbling.

"I'm fine," she insisted, though she gripped my hand just the tiniest bit tighter.

"You're always fine." I eased a little closer, so I'd be ready when she lost her balance, whether it was the fault of an idorr or her straining ankles.

"I'll take that as a compliment," she tossed back with a grin.

I couldn't fight the grin that slowly spread on my own face in response to her expression. "You should."

"Oh, I know." She winked at me—and then lost her balance with a shriek.

I caught her easily, and she huffed out a laugh as she stared into my eyes. Those gorgeous firey orbs glittered with humor, and her hands weren't even steaming.

She trusted me to catch her when she fell, and that made me a proud mate.

"Thanks, Ravvi."

"Any time, Lae." I brushed my lips to hers before setting her on her feet, back on the damn ice. "Be more careful next time."

She grinned at me again. "What would be the fun in that?"

I chuckled, recapturing her hand.

A century earlier, I would've roared with laughter if someone told me I'd fall for a small, flaming human woman. Now, my eyes brightened every time someone said her name.

Truly, she had become my everything.

And I had never felt more fulfilled in my life.

THE END
(Keep reading for a peek at Kaelle's & Nissa's stories!)

DARK & DEADLY PREDATORS

PREDATORS

KAELLE & VAYME'S STORY

To all the fairytales that preach love at first sight

CHAPTER ONE

VAYME

Wind tugged my hair as my gaze swept the rocky mountainside.

It had only taken a moment to realize the town at the base of the mountain didn't hold the female the elves had sent me to find, but she had to be somewhere nearby.

I scratched my bonded xuno, Strong, behind the ears as I continued scanning the mountainside, until...

There.

A flash of blue caught my eye.

A tiny, fragile-looking woman stepped out of a hidden cave and looked down at the town below. Her skin was pale and her dress was both dirty and oversized, but her lips were curved in a soft smile, and her cobalt hair blew around her lightly in the wind.

There was an itch beneath my skin, a tingle of magic in my spine telling me there was something important about her.

Her gaze snapped to me, and her happiness vanished as her eyes seemed to stare into my damn soul. I should've been too far for her human gaze to see me through the trees, but there was nothing else around that she could've been looking at.

She vanished back into the cave as quickly as she had appeared, seemingly just as excited to become my mate as I was to make her mine.

Veil, this was going to be a nightmare.

CHAPTER TWO
KAELLE

I stepped back into the cave, lifting my hand to my heart as it hammered in my chest.

Someone—or some*thing*—was out there. Its aura was like nothing I'd ever seen before. Darker, deadlier, and so much stronger.

Some part of me was drawn to the danger of it, but I knew I couldn't risk myself that way.

My cave was where I belonged.

It was safe for me, and for everyone else.

Though it wouldn't be of much use against a deadly force radiating as much power as the *thing* outside, I shut the thick stone door my family had built into the cave for me and locked it, too.

My chest rose and fell rapidly, and my fear grew thicker, which meant my wind would be picking up.

I had to calm myself before I created a storm.

Before I destroyed what little my family still had.

Before I—

There was a loud knock on the stone door.

My body went still.

My wind blew harder, whipping my hair and dress around.

I would've seen my family on the path leading up the mountain if it was them or anyone else in the town.

And that meant that *thing* I'd seen out there was knocking.

It knocked again, louder.

My heart beat faster.

"Don't make me break down the door," a masculine voice growled.

Veil.

It was a man.

A man with a dark, deadly aura.

Our veil separated our world from the next, and we cursed by it frequently for a reason unknown to me, but this man was certainly and solidly on my side of the veil.

My head jerked toward the back of my cave, looking for a hiding place, but there was nothing.

My cave *was* my hiding place.

It was safest—safest for me, and for everyone else, and—

Ice slowly grew over the door, and my panic grew fiercer.

The only magical beings in Evare with ice magic were fae.

And fae were warriors. Dangerous, vicious warriors, who killed without thought and rode on the backs of magical animals just as deadly as their riders. And—

The door shattered like glass.

The cave started to spin a bit as my fear grew more intense.

I was safe in my cave.

I needed to stay in my cave.

The man stepped inside.

The first look at him made the spinning stop completely.

He was *massive*. At least a head taller than the tallest man I'd ever seen, maybe two heads taller. And he was built like an ox, with wide shoulders and insanely thick muscles.

His hair was brown, falling wildly to his shoulders, and his beard was trimmed close to his chin. His skin was tan, his eyes glowed a bright shade of silver, and his ears were long and pointed. All he wore was a pair of black pants and some dark fabric wrapped around one of his hands, too.

But his aura... it was thick, powerful, and dark. It felt like *death*.

I tried to open my mouth to ask him not to kill me, but the words didn't come out.

He crossed the entire cave in three steps before he stopped in front of me, studying me silently.

I tried again to ask him not to hurt me, but failed.

The man let out a long, frustrated sigh, and then said the words, *"Sillah ovim rett warum."*

I didn't know what they meant, but I felt the tingle of magic in my veins as something within me responded to them. I inhaled sharply as I watched the man's aura swell—and then *change*.

The edges of his darkness began to glow the soft, barely-there blue of my own aura.

My gaze dipped to my hands, and I saw the edges of my faint blue begin to blacken.

"What did you do to me?" My panicked whisper escaped before I could consider the words, and my gaze jerked up to the man's.

He didn't answer me; instead, he grabbed my waist.

A shriek escaped me as his grip *burned* me, and he tossed me over his shoulder before striding out of the cave without a backward glance.

My magic swelled in my chest, and the wind whipped harder and faster, increasing its constant drain on my energy. The growing intensity of it didn't seem to bother the man, but it scared me badly.

I plead with my magic,

"Don't storm, don't storm, don't storm."

But the wind only continued to pick up.

"Don't speak into my mind," the man growled back, his voice just as clear as my own thoughts. *"Our bond will expire with the eclipse."*

But the eclipse, the day all three of our suns were aligned and caused extreme sexual desire in anyone mature, was still nearly three *months* away...

And what kind of bond was he talking about?

"My magic," I managed to say. "It's getting out of control. If I can't calm down, it'll turn into a storm. A massive wind storm. The last one destroyed a dozen towns and a whole kingdom."

"They should've been built stronger, then." The man stepped out of the cave, and I bit back a scream when I saw the monstrous gray wolf waiting outside.

I tried to shrink away, panicked enough to beg, "Leave me here. Please, leave me here. I don't have whatever you want."

He set me on the wolf's back. "All I need is your magic."

"You don't want that," I whispered. "My magic kills people."

"Then you'll fit in with my fae." He climbed onto the back of the wolf with me, and his body pressed mine against the wolf's fur.

"I won't hurt you," a masculine voice I assumed was the wolf's murmured into my mind.

When the beast started to move, I buried my fingers in his silky fur, my body weak and unused to the movement. His aura was just as wide as the man's, but it was a strange gossamer silver that made it far less intimidating.

More wind whipped at me—natural wind, as the wolf ran.

For some reason, the natural wind calmed me enough that my magic's tug on my energy slowed slightly.

I squeezed my eyes shut against the fear that was still swollen in my chest.

"I'm called Strongpaws," the wolf said to me, as he ran. *"To the fae, Strong. Tell me your name, human."*

"Kaelle," I whispered back, though the wind whisked the word away as it left my lips. I reached out to the beast's mind and repeated, *"Kaelle."*

"It's a pleasure to meet you, Kaelle. Your magic is very powerful."

"It will drain my energy soon enough, even if I don't create a storm," I admitted.

"It's draining my bonded companion's power as well," the wolf agreed. *"Can you stop it?"*

"I can't. It's not controllable. It has a mind of its own, and responds to my emotions when I get really scared." Which rarely happened in my cave... but I wasn't in my cave anymore.

"We will have to outrun it, then." The wolf was much more upbeat about the idea than I expected. *"Do not fear the speed. Vayme won't allow you to fall."*

"That's the fae's name?" I asked softly. He pronounced it almost like a more elegant version of the word "name", with a "v" in place of the "n".

"Yes. Vayme Vuuth, one of the three fae kings."

My eyes widened. *"He's a king? Why did he come after me?"*

"Unfortunately, that is his story to tell, not mine. Hold on, Tempest."

Tempest.

Veil, what a terrible nickname.

I had spent eight years trying to control my wind, only to be called a wind-storm by my captors.

The fae at my back pressed me tighter to Strong as he picked up speed, and despite the war in my heart and mind, the storm that had been brewing within me eased to a violent, whipping wind.

Neither Vayme nor Strong chastised me or urged me to calm it. But that didn't ease my fear... because I had just been stolen from my home by a vicious magical warrior, and his bonded beast.

With my wind draining my energy, it wasn't long before dizziness overwhelmed me.

I whispered to Vayme and Strong that I needed to stop and eat something, but they didn't hear me, and I slipped into unconsciousness soon after.

When I opened my eyes, I found a furious fae warrior leaning over me, glaring heatedly.

Fear had me shrinking away, and my wind picked up rapidly.

"What is wrong with you?" Vayme growled.

I tried to tell him it was nothing. That there was just never enough food to keep me going with my magic constantly consuming my energy, but the words didn't come out.

He was absolutely terrifying, and clearly despised me.

Strong's furry head eased Vayme away from me, and my breathing grew slightly easier.

Only slightly.

I noticed the trees above me, and the relatively even dirt beneath me.

"What ails you, Tempest?" Strong asked me. His voice was measured, and calm.

"My family brought food when they visited from town, but there was never enough, or any money for more," I whispered. It was easier to speak mentally than out loud.

"You need sustenance," Strong said.

Vayme vanished from my line of sight, and I closed my eyes as I let out a shaky breath.

The wolf's voice was contemplative when he asked, *"What do you fear? The king will not hurt you."*

"He stole me from my home. You both did. Why would I believe you have no intentions of hurting me?"

The wolf blinked. *"You lived alone. In a cave, far from others of your kind. It rather seemed like we were rescuing you."*

"My cave was the safest place for me and everyone else. I put people in danger just by being near them," I whispered. *"And whatever Vayme did to me, it certainly wasn't for my own sake."*

My aura was still blackened along the outside, as if it had been burned by the king's.

Strong blinked again. After a long moment's pause, he finally lowered his head toward me, almost like he was bowing.

Vayme returned, and I felt a surprisingly gentle hand on my wrist before a familiar soft fruit met my palm.

"Eat," he commanded me.

I lifted it to my lips and took a small bite, careful to keep my gaze fixed on the branches and sky above my head so I wouldn't have to make eye contact with the king.

"Why are you hungry?" he asked me. Though his tone wasn't kind, it also wasn't cruel.

I took another small bite of my fruit, not wanting to explain myself to him.

Considering the size of him and his muscles, he likely had no idea the extent some of us suffered for food. My town had been thriving, before my first storm. So had all of the others around us.

And then I'd woken up surrounded by gusts of wind at thirteen-years-old... and I had panicked.

When I panicked, the winds picked up.

And picked up.

And picked up.

Until my tornado was ravaging our land, violently destroying without purpose or restraint.

Even eight years later, we still hadn't recovered. Everyone was hungry —and it was my fault.

"Her family brings her food. There hasn't been enough for anyone," Strong explained.

My face warmed at the king's frown. "The town looked fine. There were far more fruits and vegetables than they would need to keep themselves alive, even without the grain they were also growing."

My defenses rose.

What was he trying to say?

That my family had starved me on purpose?

I refused to believe that, even as my mind returned to the soft curves of my mother's figure, or the strength in my father's build.

They wouldn't have done that... would they?

"You were mistaken," Strong said calmly to Vayme, broadcasting his thoughts so we could both hear them.

I was no longer certain what to believe.

We remained where we were as I ate the entirety of the fruit. By the time I was done, my belly ached with fullness.

My town had large fields, but there were so many mouths to feed, and they had to sell some of those crops to the kingdom nearby to fund the other necessities they couldn't grow themselves.

They wouldn't leave me hungry. I couldn't believe that, for the sake of my own sanity.

Vayme tried to give me some type of crackers after I'd set the fruit's pit on the dirt, but I shook my head.

I was too full to eat anything else without making myself ill.

Though his expression was stony, he put the crackers away and lifted me onto Strong's back. My fingers buried in the soft fur, and Vayme's body pressed against mine once more as the beast began to run.

The motion and wind kept my thoughts blissfully silent as Strong ran. We stopped for an evening meal as the first of the suns began to set, and I managed a few of the hard, tough crackers, before we started again.

Darkness set in around us as the last of Evare's three suns went down, and I found myself peering at the forest around us. I could see in the dark without any problem, for some reason. I had to assume it was because of whatever Vayme had done to me to give me his magic and change our auras.

It was the middle of the night before we finally stopped beside a river. My body was so tight and achy that Vayme had to lift me off Strong's back, because I could barely move myself.

Vayme was silent as he pulled food from the large bag he wore on his back, handing me more of the crackers he'd given me for dinner. I'd only managed four of them, but the stack he gave me held six.

My gaze flicked from the crackers to the man, and I found him watching me.

I wanted to tell him I couldn't eat them—that my body would feel sick, and he could keep the food—but still felt uncomfortable around him. It was harder to speak when I felt uncomfortable, especially when factoring my soreness and exhaustion into that discomfort.

"You need to eat more than you are. You'll never make it back to the fae lands on a few crackers and one piece of fruit. We'll slowly increase your diet until you're taking in enough food to provide the energy you need."

My face flushed as anger swelled in my chest, but I stayed silent.

He had not only stolen me from my home, but was also trying to control me with food.

And yes, eating was a necessity, but I had been surviving just fine. I didn't have a lot of energy, but I hadn't needed it. And the less I ate, the faster I would go unconscious when my magic raged out of control, which was...

It was a way my family could've been controlling me, too.

I still couldn't consider that, though. They weren't controlling me; they loved me.

Bitterness flooded me, and I took a bite of a cracker, trying to hide my emotions.

Vayme wasn't my friend.

He wasn't my ally.

I felt his eyes on me while I ate, but I didn't look at him.

CHAPTER THREE
KAELLE

My belly was swollen by the time I swallowed the last of the cracker.

"We'll bathe before we sleep," Vayme said.

My body went rigid.

Veil.

What if he touched me?

What if he—

"Alone," he said quickly. "You bathe alone. I also bathe alone."

I didn't relax much, though his words calmed the majority of my fears.

"I'll wait here. Strong will accompany you," he added.

I considered my options. Arguing might be best—though my chances of winning were slim. The massive fae king could always throw me in the river if I put up too much of a fight.

And truthfully, I was filthy, and had been for far too long. There was a tiny trickle of fresh water that spilled out of the stone on one of the walls of my cave, but that was the only water source on the mountain.

Or at least, on the part of the mountain I had the energy to explore. I walked around a little most days to keep myself from going mad, so I'd seen as much of it as I could before my body grew too exhausted to continue.

Anyway, that trickle of water was for both drinking and bathing. I had two buckets—one for each purpose. It took about a day to fill one to the brim, so most of the water was to drink. The remainder, I used with a wet cloth to try to keep myself clean.

It was more difficult than it should've been, given that my magic tended to hit me with all sorts of dust and dirt.

A bath sounded... well, blissful.

I hadn't been truly clean in longer than I cared to consider.

When I looked at Strong, he stood and padded toward the river.

I eased myself to my feet, wincing at the pain in my legs and chafe inside my thighs from gripping Strong's fur between them.

Though I still felt Vayme's eyes on me, I continued ignoring his gaze as I slowly made my way to the river.

When I reached the water, I glanced over my shoulder to make sure I couldn't see Vayme. The side of his muscular shoulder and arm protruded from behind the tree he sat up against, but he was facing away from me, and far enough that I didn't think he would try to look at me.

It wasn't as if the man seemed attracted to me, anyway.

Hopefully, he wasn't waiting for me to drop my guard so he could attack. I didn't have much of a guard, so if he was, he was waiting for something he likely wouldn't even notice.

"My companion is a male of honor. He won't take liberties with you," Strong said, noticing my nerves. *"You have nothing to fear from us, though I understand it may be hard to believe that."*

I dipped my head, not feeling the need to say anything else.

Gingerly, I eased my dress off. A glance down at my bare thighs made me grimace and look away. The skin on the inside of my legs was patchy and red, and while most of it wasn't broken, I had multiple popped blisters where my undergarments met my thighs.

"You're hurt?" Strong's voice sounded in my mind.

"Where?" Vayme's low, growly voice echoed through the forest, making me shiver. When I looked over my shoulder to make sure he hadn't turned around, I found him in the same position as before, though much more tense.

Strong stared at me, waiting for me to answer his question.

I said nothing, just stepping down toward the water, dressed only in my undergarments. They had started off in one piece that covered my breasts, torso, and lady bits, the same way most human undergarments did, but my parents hadn't had the money to bring me any new clothing since that first storm I created.

I hadn't grown around my middle or chest since I was thirteen—really, I may have shrunk—but I did get a bit taller. So, I cut the undergarment in the middle with the one small knife I had, turning the garment into two pieces. It had been uncomfortable after that, so I'd cut it down a few more times until I could live with it.

After I cut them, the lower hem of the top piece fell to the middle of my ribcage, and the top hem of the bottom piece rested at my belly button.

The fabric was worn and scratchy, but I was still grateful I had it.

After the destruction I'd caused, I didn't really deserve even that.

"Tempest?" Vayme growled, the second demand more threatening than the first.

I ignored the lump in my throat and said quietly, "A captor shouldn't be concerned with his captive's health."

Silence followed.

A long, tense silence.

When I glanced at Strong again, his expression was distant, and I got the feeling he was conversing with Vayme privately.

I waded deeper into the water, and my eyes fluttered shut as I suppressed a groan.

Veil, it felt incredible. I wished the water was colder to ease my muscles, but the lukewarm was so pleasant, I wouldn't complain.

I stripped my undergarments off and tossed them to the dirt beside the river, then scrubbed myself with sand from the bottom. It felt like I was peeling away a whole layer of old, dirt-crusted skin.

"My king apologizes for not thinking to bring soap," Strong murmured into my mind.

I rolled my eyes, facing away from the wolf.

His apology was so unlikely, the remark was ridiculous.

Light wind blew the water around me as I scrubbed at my scalp with my fingers, and then braided my hair behind my head. Since I had nothing to tie it back with, I just left it hanging. It had been a long time since I last cut the blue waves, so they fell below my ass. If I had any amount of freedom in the fae lands, I'd ask someone to cut the strands.

Though I assumed we were headed to the Endless Wilds, a fierce jungle the fae were known to live deep within, Vayme and Strong hadn't mentioned them specifically.

I wrapped an arm around my breasts as I slowly waded back to the edge of the river, marveling at the pale shade of my skin. It had been so long since I'd seen myself free of dirt that I didn't even recognize the color.

A gleam of silver caught my gaze as I reached for my undergarments, and I froze when my eyes landed on my hip.

There was...

A massive handprint.

A massive, *silver* handprint.

It glowed softly, clearly brought on by magic.

My mind went back to the moment when Vayme had grabbed me in the cave.

I had felt burning, but I hadn't paid attention to where it was, specifically.

It seemed safe to assume the burning had been right where his hand-print was.

I quickly examined the rest of myself to make sure he hadn't branded me anywhere else, and relief made my shoulders sag when I found nothing but bare skin.

And the damn handprint.

I forced myself to remain calm as I grabbed my undergarments and scrubbed them with a stone beneath the water. Though it was nowhere near as effective as soap would've been, it was far better than nothing.

My mind rolled through everything I knew about Vayme and his magic as I cleaned the fabric.

He was a fae, which meant he had ice magic, but I didn't know if he had any other power on top of that.

He could move extremely fast, and was stronger than any human.

He was immortal.

He was connected to Strong.

His magic had settled in my veins beside my own, and in doing so changed both of our auras, which were physical manifestations of our souls. That meant he had changed my soul.

We could also talk mentally, though he'd commanded me not to.

Vayme had also said he needed my magic for something, and seemed uninterested in my body. My magic seemed wicked, and fae were said to be wicked beings.

I wasn't sure how the handprint fit into his plan to use my magic, but I assumed it was a representation of the connection he had created between us when he said those foreign words.

As I remembered that moment, a shiver rolled down my spine and the words echoed in my mind.

"Sillah ovim rett warum."

What did they mean?

My lips formed the shape of them.

"Sillah ovim rett warum."

"You must not speak the vow," Strong said, his words sharper than I'd ever heard them.

My head snapped to the side as I looked at him.

"If you speak the vow, you'll seal the bond."

"What is the bond?" I asked.

He said nothing.

Frustration swelled in my chest, but I hid it.

If I angered the fae king, he could hurt me.

I needed to stay calm, despite the wind that had begun whipping through the trees and snapping against my exposed skin.

Control.

I had to stay in control.

I bit my tongue to stop myself from saying the words that were itching to escape.

Veil, I was frustrated with the situation. Really, really frustrated.

I needed a way to voice that emotion without it coming off that way, so the king didn't have an excuse to attack me.

I developed a plan as I continued scrubbing my undergarments, and then enacted it, musing, "If you don't tell me what the bond is, I have no real reason not to seal it. It connected the king's magic to mine—perhaps if I repeat his words, it will further connect us, and I'll be able to share his immortality."

Strong stared me down, as if daring me to try.

I tilted my head back. "What were the words again? *Sill* something..."

Strong's chest rumbled with a warning growl.

Satisfaction curled in my abdomen.

This conversation would tell me exactly where I stood with the king and his bonded beast. They could lie as much as they wanted with nothing on the line, but if I had a bit of control, they would either react violently, or they would tell me the truth.

"No, I think it was *Sillah*," I said. "*Sillah ovim...*"

"Cover yourself, Tempest," the king commanded from within the forest, and then I heard his heavy footsteps on the dirt. I lowered myself deeper into the water, so I was covered below my shoulders.

Did he really think my name was Tempest?

He hadn't bothered to ask me for it, and he must've heard Strong call me that before, so maybe he assumed that really was my name.

His angry, silver eyes collided with mine, his chest rising and falling quickly. "The bond between us is a mate bond."

His words stunned me into silence.

I didn't know much about magical beings, but I had heard the stories mention their mates. A mate was like a husband or wife—but magical, and permanent.

"You do not need to know why I established the bond between us, but you should know that it will disappear when the next eclipse arrives, unless you speak the words to seal it. If you do that, the connection will be permanent. A mate bond doesn't vanish when one crosses the veil; it carries through every world that follows after death. Our souls would be bound together for the rest of our eternal existences."

I said nothing, too stunned by the admission to speak.

"Strong tells me your undergarments have injured you, so you will wear the spare clothing I brought for the remainder of our journey. Should you cooperate peacefully, I will return you to your town after the eclipse has passed. Should you seal our bond, I will lock you in another cave myself."

He set a bundle of fabric on the ground, then strode back to his tree and sat down.

My heart beat quickly in my chest, fear clouding my mind. The wind had picked up even more, as well.

When I looked at Strong, I found him looking away from me.

That shouldn't have stung, but it did.

I was still alone. I couldn't let myself believe otherwise. All I had and could trust was my family, and that would always remain true.

I abandoned my old undergarments by the river and stepped out as carefully as I could, trying to keep my feet in the grass and weeds so I wouldn't coat them in dirt. My wind blew me dry quickly as I picked up the shirt and pants Vayme had left.

They were fae-king-sized, but the fabric was softer than anything I'd ever felt. I would have to tie knots in them to hold them up, but I could manage that.

I slipped the shirt over my head and looked down at myself. The long sleeves fell past my fingertips, and the bottom hem nearly hit my knees.

It took a few tries to roll the sleeves up to my wrists, especially with the wind blowing around me, but it slowed a bit as I stepped into the pants and began feeling more secure than I had a few minutes earlier.

The thought of a mate bond was a bit terrifying, but it was no longer a mystery to me. I understood the connection between myself and Vayme as much as I could without a better, calmer explanation, and that put me at ease. Whether he liked it or not, I had a small amount of control over our situation.

He had stolen me from my home, but I could trap him in our bond as retribution if he didn't agree to return me to my cave. And by sealing our bond, I could ruin his life if he did anything to harm me. Sure, it would ruin my life in the process as well, but what more did I have to lose? I had already been abducted and dragged away from the only home I had ever known, and I would never be able to locate it again or make it back on my own.

My lips curved upward just the tiniest bit.

I wasn't as powerless as I had thought.

CHAPTER FOUR
KAELLE

Vayme created a tiny, rectangular shelter of ice before he left so he could bathe. He told me in no uncertain terms that we would have to share it for safety, too.

I wasn't looking forward to sleeping beside him, but didn't bother arguing. It seemed safe to assume that our mate bond would make us both uncomfortable in some ways, and that there was no way around it.

I also wasn't under the impression that he *wanted* to sleep beside me, so that made it less nerve-wracking. Neither of us would try to snuggle.

Though I had read plenty of books with sex in them and knew how it worked, being hidden in a cave hadn't led me to experience anything related to intimacy. I had been curious before, but I certainly didn't want to learn anything about that from Vayme.

I stepped into the shelter and tried to get comfortable on the thick bed of ice. I didn't have a mattress in my cave, but I had a bundle of straw and blankets that were far preferable to solid ice.

Though I was exhausted, I found myself tossing and turning, trying to get comfortable.

Vayme eventually joined me, and I rolled onto my side, facing away from him. He was so big that my body pressed against the ice while he got situated.

My arm started to go numb, and I itched to move again, but bit my cheek and forced myself to remain still.

Vayme fidgeted a bit, and I inhaled sharply as his thick arm brushed my ass. He grunted an apology, and my cheeks burned.

Veil, it couldn't get less comfortable.

"You don't have a blanket in your bag?" I finally whispered, moving a bit so feeling would return to my arm and hip.

"No."

I closed my eyes and forced myself to stay still.

Maybe if I could ignore the numbness and discomfort long enough, I could sleep.

"Your magic's pull is getting worse," he growled a few minutes later.

My frustration swelled thicker. "I'm just going to sleep outside." I tried to get up, but smacked my head on the roof of the shelter and crashed back down to the ice.

Vayme muttered something under his breath, then rolled onto his side and lifted my head up, setting it on his thick bicep to rest.

I sucked in a breath when my face met the muscle, but my wind died down noticeably as I managed to find a slightly more comfortable position. Though my back brushed his chest the tiniest bit, and my cheek was pressed to his arm, I found myself starting to relax just a little.

There was a smell on his skin—something light, that reminded me of the scent of fresh rain in the wind.

It calmed me, and soon enough, lulled me to sleep.

• • •

Vayme made me eat crackers and fruit before we headed out with the first sunrise. We'd only slept a few hours, so I was too disoriented to protest.

My stomach heaved and rolled for a bit when Strong started to run, but it adjusted soon enough, and we continued on.

Three days later, we reached what Strong told me was near the outer edge of the Aching Chasm. The dirt was a deep crimson red color that made me nervous, but we didn't go anywhere near the deadly drop-off that housed an unknown number of gargoyles and who knew what other magical beings. Strong told me that the edge of the Chasm was safer than the Timeless Sands, and there was no way around traveling through one or the other.

I believed him.

Vayme and I only exchanged a few words each day. He fed me, and I ate whatever he gave me, even though the amount kept increasing. We shared the shelter in silence every night, and I always used his arm as a pillow. The only time we spoke was when I told him I needed to stop to heed nature's call, or he told me we needed to pause so I could eat.

The days were endlessly long.

I had too much time to think.

Far too much time to think.

And the more I thought about the cave and my family, the more I remembered the way my parents' bodies had grown thicker in the years since the storm, while mine remained painfully frail.

The more I thought about that, the more Vayme's words seemed to repeat in my mind.

"The town looked fine. There were far more fruits and vegetables than they would need to keep themselves alive, even without the grain they were also growing."

I didn't want to believe him, but he'd had no reason to lie.

And the more I considered it, the more I wondered if it was true.

My magic was dangerous. *I* was dangerous. Neither myself nor my family had ever argued against that. It was a frequent topic, in fact.

"It's too dangerous for you to leave the cave, Kaelle," they'd say.

"Your magic is deadly," they'd add.

"We're all still starving from the last time you lost control," they'd remind me.

The first two, I knew were true.

I *was* dangerous.

I *was* deadly.

But what if they weren't still starving?

What if they had starved *me* because they were afraid of me? What if they had only visited me to keep track of my magic?

I couldn't let myself think about that too much, because every time I did, it made my eyes sting.

If they were really afraid of me, I had to believe they would've killed me.

But at the same time... what was the point of destroying a weapon you could use in your favor?

The town had struggled against the reign of a cruel king in a nearby kingdom when I was a child. I could remember my parents talking about the taxes no one could afford, and the terrible soldiers who would come to enforce them.

They hadn't mentioned the taxes since my storm had destroyed all those towns and that kingdom. I was sure they had rebuilt, but they hadn't been mentioned to me.

What if there was a reason for that?

What if they were lying to me, or using me, while starving me?

I didn't want it to be true, but some part of me knew it was a possibility. Maybe that same part of me had always known but was too afraid of myself to consider the truth.

Though I tried to push all of those thoughts and possibilities away, there was so much free time passing that they lingered.

And lingered.

And lingered.

Another day went by before we reached the Endless Wilds. When we entered the jungle, I found myself looking around in both terror and intrigue. The trees around us were so monstrous that the smallest one I saw was even thicker around than my cave was wide.

The trunks and branches were decorated with leaves bigger than me, and wrapped in huge, vibrant green vines. I couldn't see any of our suns through the branches far above our heads, and found myself counting the numerous rivers and streams we passed.

The Wilds were full of life in a way the Human Lands and the outer edge of the Aching Chasm simply were not.

Auras flew past us constantly, and it scared me a little. I wasn't used to being surrounded by so many creatures, and it worried me to know they were there without being able to see what, exactly, they were.

The constant change in colors and life around us drained me even faster than usual. My stomach growled, and I struggled to keep my eyes open while night approached.

Vayme looked a bit suspicious when we stopped for dinner, but he didn't ask how I was doing. He and I didn't talk enough for that.

We bathed in a river again that night, staying close but keeping our backs to each other for both privacy and safety. When we reached the shelter, I fell asleep even before he tucked his arm beneath my head.

I still woke up lying on it, though.

. . .

Three more long days passed as Strong ran. I had started to understand why it was called the *Endless* Wilds. Even at the wolf's incredible speed, it was still taking what felt like a lifetime to get through it.

It was long past the middle of the night when we finally reached the outer edge of a fae city called Jirev.

"Be careful here, Tempest. This is not Vayme's city, and he has little control," Strong murmured to me.

The words didn't make me feel any better.

Earlier that day, I'd tried to ask Vayme what to expect from the city, as well as a few other things about fae. He had told me I didn't need to worry about it.

That answer was frustrating, but I had been too exhausted to push him further.

My eyes scanned the city as Strong ran. The homes and shops had been carved into the massive trees all around us. They were connected by bridges of wood, branches, and ice, though the latter seemed to be melting in most places.

There were a ton of fae around us, and all of them had huge, vibrant auras like Vayme's. It was overwhelming, and I started developing a headache soon after we entered the city.

As we reached the more populated portion, the ache in my head grew to a sharp pounding that made my stomach churn.

I was in so much pain that I barely participated when Vayme stopped at a clothing shop. Since I could do nothing but stand there with my arms around my middle, he held a few dresses up to my figure before buying them. I was still wearing his clothes, and I supposed he would want them back.

Afterward, Strong carried us to a shop that sold food. Vayme sat us down in the far corner, and waved a male server down without saying a word.

Maybe I wasn't the only person he didn't like to talk to.

The man brought us food soon after, and I slowly worked on the soup and bread. The flavors were incredible, and I found myself wishing I didn't feel so awful, if just so I could enjoy the food more.

A different man with a terrible, shadowy aura came up and exchanged a few heated words with the king as I finished up my meal. While Vayme remained calm, I could see his energy begin to vibrate with whatever he was feeling.

When the man finally stepped away, Vayme's emotions were strong enough that I was nearly choking on the damn things.

I was dizzy when he hauled me onto Strong's back again, and my stomach churned when Strong started moving through the city, quickly.

We entered some sort of stadium, with a large metal cage in the middle of the room and rows of benches lining the outside. Vayme seated me just outside the edge of the cage, and the crowd roared around us.

Everything around me blurred as I tried to look at the fae, but I saw nothing except auras.

So many auras.

So many colorful, massive, *violent* auras.

Vayme's wasn't even an outlier. I'd thought he was some kind of a monster when we met, but looking around, I was forced to accept that it wasn't just him—it was all of the fae. Either all of them were monsters, or they were just powerful, ancient beings with magic stronger than I had even realized was possible.

My own aura was nearly as large as theirs, but it didn't affect me because I was used to it. It was soft, calm, and *mine*.

I noticed that Vayme's aura had left mine and Strong's, and my lips curved down in a frown.

That didn't make me feel safe.

Especially considering I couldn't tell what was going on.

Vayme and I were nowhere near friends or allies, but we were bonded, and that meant he would protect me.

Or I was *pretty sure* it meant that. It at least meant he wouldn't hurt me, if our time traveling was an accurate representation of who he was.

My head ached so intensely that I began to sway slightly. When I closed my eyes, I could still hear the fae cheering and roaring around me. Their auras were so intense, the colors leaked through my eyelids.

The more time went on, the more I started to wonder what shape I'd be in when it was finally time to leave the stadium.

CHAPTER FIVE
VAYME

It took every fiber of effort I possessed not to look back over my shoulder at the fragile human on the bench as I walked away from her.

Soon enough, I met Kier outside the large metal cage built for the violent fighting events our people put on. My fists were clenched as I fought my own mind and the damn newfound possessiveness.

Kaelle was safe.

Strong would ensure that.

My rage was too fierce to allow myself to stay by her side. I could hurt her.

Kier had been in the cage, bleeding, wrestling, and grinning, when I entered the stadium. He still wore a feral grin when he stepped outside the metal bars. "You're alive, then."

There was no love between us. His people, mine, and Ravv's had warred for centuries. We'd established peace for all our sakes, but that didn't erase the impact of so damn many years of fighting.

I had lost friends to his warriors, as he had lost friends to mine. And yet, we had been forced to put that behind us and focus on the future.

A future that wouldn't exist, if half my people had any say in it.

"For now," I growled. It nearly killed me to ask for help, but I forced myself to add, "I'm struggling to stay in control, and my human is fragile. I need a fight to release the tension before I harm her."

Kier jerked his head in a nod. The bastard had never turned down a fight in his life.

"With weapons. To first blood," I added.

Kier's grin returned, still wicked as he strode back into the cage with his arms opened wide. I followed him inside, and he announced the match.

I waited until he'd turned to face me before tapping into my ice to create the greatsword I preferred to fight with.

Our people roared around us as our weapons appeared. Their bloodthirsty voices were vicious, but that was to be expected.

"Ready?" Kier's ice swords were just as sharp as my own, but we wouldn't attempt to kill each other. We'd spent far too much time and effort building peace to tear it down with one foolish act.

I jerked my head in a nod, and we began.

He slashed toward me, and I blocked in defense. My movements were stronger and harsher than they should've been, but that wasn't surprising considering I'd spent more than two weeks traveling.

I slashed at him, and he dodged the motion easily.

Our speeds picked up as we settled into the fight, focused entirely.

Time passed, movements grew instinctual, and my mind slipped back to the conversation with Cev in the food shop.

My rage swelled, and I swung too hard, slowing myself by a fraction of a second. Kier took the opening. His sword caught my shoulder, and pain sliced through my fury. The cut wasn't deadly, but it wasn't shallow, either.

The crowd cheered as Kier stepped back, wearing that damn grin again. "Your human is distracting you."

Of course she was.

She was my damn *mate*.

The woman's smell alone made it difficult to keep my hands off her skin. The scent of her fear set me on edge—and veil, she was constantly afraid of me.

And Cev's threats...

My gaze flicked back to her just long enough to assure me she was okay before I focused on Kier. There was blood rolling down my arm, but that was hardly a first.

"Again?" he asked.

I jerked my head in a nod.

We settled into position, then began.

Though my motions were smoother and less rage-filled, eventually, control of my mind slipped away from me again, and the distraction cost me.

Kier won three more rounds before I was bleeding enough to take my mind off Cev, my brother, and Tempest.

The pain finally cleared my mind enough during the fifth match, and after a long fight, I defeated Kier.

He challenged me again, and I couldn't say no.

Partway through the sixth fight, Strong said quietly into my mind, *"Kaelle doesn't seem well."*

My gaze jerked in her direction without pause, and one of Kier's swords cut into the outside of my thigh.

I swore, looking back at the king and finding him a bit apologetic. His sword vanished from my leg, and I focused on the human for a moment.

My human.

She shouldn't have been mine, but veil, she was.

She looked fine from where I was, so I jerked my attention back to Kier when he asked, "Again?"

I couldn't refuse the fight, so I nodded, and we began once more.

Worry for my human pooled in my abdomen, but I didn't allow my mind or gaze to linger. I focused on what I was doing, until my sword finally carved into his back, ending the match.

"Come, now," Strong growled into my mind.

When my gaze flicked over there, I saw him holding up my female.

My *unconscious* female.

Kier's eyes followed my gaze. "Veil."

"Thank you." I lowered my chin toward him slightly. Though it was difficult, I ignored the fierce pounding in my chest and forced myself to make my way out of the cage at a normal pace.

"What happened?" I demanded as I went.

"I don't know. She was swaying a bit, but I thought she was just tired."

What if something was wrong with her?

The worry I felt with the thought was ridiculous. She was terrified of me, and even if she wasn't, I had vowed to take her back home after the eclipse.

Any feelings I developed for her would have to be inconsequential, despite her soft humanness and the look in her eyes that spoke to my damn soul.

To care for her would be to put us both at risk, and I couldn't allow that.

"We'll take her back to our room and find a healer if we can't figure out what's wrong," I said.

Strong agreed, and I adjusted her position before climbing on his back behind her. My body held hers securely against him, and I tried to keep my position stiff so the people who saw us wouldn't think anything of it.

I checked her pulse with my fingers to make sure she was alright. Thankfully, her heartbeat was normal, and she was still breathing steadily.

Strong got us back to Kier's castle quickly, entering the monstrous tree that housed it. The castle itself was larger than Tempest's town, but that reminded me of the way her people had starved her.

And that made me angry again.

I set her on the bed and checked both her breathing and pulse again. She was still functioning properly... so why had she passed out?

"Perhaps she loses consciousness at the sight of blood," Strong suggested.

"I was bleeding for a while before she passed out."

He considered it.

I did too.

Neither of us came up with a reasonable answer.

I started pacing the room to distract myself from my worry, and Strong rested his head on her abdomen so he could feel her breathing. She was still wearing my clothes—I hadn't asked her to change into her dress. She had seemed overwhelmed by the fabric in the shop, so I assumed she needed time to adjust.

What if it had been something more?

What if she was ill?

I continued to pace as my thoughts wandered, worry morphing into agitation and frustration at my helplessness. I didn't trust the other kings' healers. My brother was a healer, but he was back in my city, Vuuth. And as far as the Jirevs and Loires knew, he was dead.

Though there were many of my people that I trusted, Matían was the only one I trusted with my life, and now Tempest's. I couldn't trust any of them with the knowledge of my mating, and I certainly couldn't ask them for help.

My people were the reason I'd had to take the woman from her prison at all.

I continued pacing for another twenty minutes, until Kaelle's eyes fluttered a little.

In a heartbeat, I was seated on the edge of the bed, once again checking the temperature of her forehead and pulse at her throat.

Finally, her eyes opened. The wariness in the blue orbs made my chest constrict.

"What happened?" I managed.

It came out angrier than I wanted.

Her eyes closed again.

My jaw clenched as a moment passed, and another.

Finally, she whispered, "Fae auras are really bright."

I blinked, caught entirely off guard by her words.

Fae auras?

I'd heard of some demons seeing auras, but not a human.

"Since when can you see auras?" I growled at her.

Veil, I needed to stop sounding so angry with her.

Sure enough, Kaelle shrank away from me. "Since my magic came in."

I shoved a hand through my hair.

Her gaze caught on the cut on my shoulder, and her face turned a soft shade of green that contrasted far too prettily with the blue of her hair and eyes. "You're bleeding."

"I'm aware."

Her eyes shuttered.

Veil, I had no idea how to talk to her.

Every damn thing I did scared the woman.

"Is there a bath in here?" she asked me quietly, clearly intending to get away from me.

I didn't blame her.

If I was a small, terrified human female, I'd probably want to get away from me too.

"The bathing pool is there." I gestured to the corner of the room. I thought she'd choose the shower if I told her where it was, but didn't really want her out of my sight. Despite my own desires, I couldn't bring myself to lie to her, even by omission. "There's a shower in the bathroom. Water falls from the ceiling to clean you, if you'd rather."

Her eyes widened.

Everything scared her.

It should've made me want to push her away, but it made me want to wrap a damn arm around her and show her I could protect her. The desire was ridiculous, so I did my best to ignore it.

"No need to be afraid. Vayme will show you how it works," Strong said, stepping up to us and nuzzling her hand with the side of his face.

"That's okay, you don't have to," Kaelle said quickly.

"No, you shouldn't be afraid of our room." I paused, and then changed the wording. "*Your* room."

Strong shot me a look.

"*Our* room," I admitted, taking it back. "I can't sleep outside, or anywhere else. It's not safe for you."

She gave me the tiniest nod, and carefully eased her legs off the edge of the bed.

I should've tucked them beneath the blanket when she was unwell.

I should've... veil, I hadn't done a damn thing right with her.

I had no idea what to do with a woman.

She winced when she stood, and I grabbed her by the waist when she teetered. Though she sucked in a breath at my touch, she still looked dizzy enough that I worried she would collapse.

"I'll find someone to bring you food, Tempest," Strong said, as I held her upright and waited for her dizziness to subside.

She whispered her thanks.

Even after he was gone, she still didn't seem steady.

I tucked an arm around her waist and stepped a bit closer to her so I could hold more of her weight, and then started walking. She reluctantly moved with me, and her chest was rising and falling quickly by the time we reached the bathroom.

"What's wrong?" The damn words came out as a growl again.

"You're bleeding on me," she nearly whimpered.

She really *was* afraid of blood.

I withdrew quickly, and her knees knocked as she wobbled. When I caught her with a hand on her hip again, she stumbled toward me.

"I've never really been around blood," she said, her eyes squeezed shut. "I'm sorry."

"Don't apologize."

Her silence told me those words came out wrong, too.

I forced myself not to grit my teeth as I said slowly, "I am not angry with you. Situations where I have no control are... difficult for me."

"Imagine being in my shoes, then."

I blinked.

She had been stolen from the prison she considered home, by a deadly fae warrior who she was supposedly mated to, without any information as to why...

Veil.

That *would* be difficult.

I supposed I needed to tell her some things, but that would have to wait until she was clean and steadier on her feet.

"This is the shower." I showed her how to turn it on, and watched rapture fill her eyes as the water began to fall.

Her hand stretched out, and her rapture turned to wonder. "It's like rain."

I made a noise of agreement. "Can you stand on your own?"

Her lips turned downward, her wonder fading away. "I don't know. My head still feels like someone took a rock to it."

I grimaced. "Because of the auras?"

"Yes."

"You can bathe tonight, then."

"Is it even night still?" she murmured.

"It is."

Probably.

I shut the water off, and helped her over to the bathing pool. She eyed it, and then eyed me.

"I'll need to stay nearby, in case you lose consciousness again," I said bluntly.

I wasn't about to let the woman drown.

Her face reddened.

I needed to give her an alternative before she worried, yet again, that I was trying to steal her virtue. "I'll leave my back to you if you speak the whole time I'm looking away. That will be my guarantee you're not drowning."

The blush on her cheeks didn't fade, but it stopped growing redder. "I'll hum."

I waited until she finally started humming, and then turned my back to her.

Her hum was soft, but smooth. While the song she'd chosen wasn't one I recognized, it was calm and quiet. I found my eyes closing and heartbeat slowing as I listened.

There was soap sitting on a small shelf inside the bath, and its scent filled the air as she began to scrub herself clean. Tempest would feel much better after using it; there was still dirt in her hair that had probably been there for years.

I didn't allow myself to consider that. If I thought too much about it, I'd have the urge to go back to her parents' town and slaughter everyone who'd dared mistreat the small human.

Her hum continued as she washed. I retrieved a towel for her when she was finishing up, and handed it to her without looking back when she stepped out. Even without seeing the woman bare, my cock was thick and hard, which I didn't acknowledge.

Kaelle was still drying off when Strong reentered the room with a female fae I trusted, Kee. Kee gave my human a curious look, then shot me a lingering one after she set two plates down on a small table beside the bed.

Though she was one of the fae I trusted most, I had never been interested in her romantically the way she was interested in me. To take a partner, I would have to enjoy their presence and body in a way I hadn't ever enjoyed anyone's, so I didn't see a future in which I was paired off with someone in any way.

It had been centuries since I'd cared enough to spend an eclipse with anyone at all. The idea had grown unappealing after a few decades of finding satisfaction in every way possible.

And yet my body had responded to Kaelle every time I was near her. Despite her fear, despite her dislike for me, despite everything, I wanted the human in a way I hadn't realized I was still capable of.

Of course, I couldn't admit that to her.

She was still terrified of me, and her terror certainly didn't make me hard. It was her body and scent that did, particularly at night.

Strong started guiding Kee out, but she stepped away from him so she could walk over to me. I fought the urge to groan.

"Vayme," she said. Her voice was soft, as if we were lovers.

I fought the urge to look at my human, to make sure she wasn't getting the wrong idea, and growled, "*King* Vayme."

She nodded but didn't correct herself. "Some of our fae were worried when you disappeared. Giving a reason for your absence would help negate the effect of those who work against you. I can spread the word, if you want."

"Fine." The word came out an irritated grumble. "Tell them the other kings and I decided to make the events more memorable by stealing magical humans to fight in a battle. We went to the elves, to ask them where to find the humans, and then retrieved them. Now, we're back."

She put a hand on my chest.

I pushed it off with another growl. "I did not give you permission to touch me, female. Spread the news, and get out of my room."

Strong nudged her hip with his nose a bit harder than necessary, and she finally let him lead her out.

I turned to look at Tempest when the woman was gone, and found her strangely... red. Her cheeks were flushed, her eyes looked angry, and her fists were clenched.

Veil, fury was a good look on her.

I waited for her to say something, but she didn't.

Instead, she let out a few long breaths, turned her back to me, and put on the fae-style undergarments and black dress. Then she stiffly walked back to the bed, where she sat down and started on the food Strong had brought her.

The dress hung off her shoulders and showed a strip of her abdomen, before falling to the tops of her thighs. It highlighted the starvation she had been put through and made it difficult for me to fight my rage toward her family again.

I assumed her anger was about Kee touching me, but it could've been about the human fight I had mentioned.

On second thought, the fight was certainly the source of her anger.

I crossed the room and sat down beside her. "The human fight is merely an excuse the other kings and I came up with so we had something to tell our people, rather than admitting our mating. You'll have to fight, but you won't be at risk in any way."

She focused on her food, but her jaw was set in anger.

I... well, I had no idea what to say to her.

Clearly, my answer hadn't cheered her up.

So I remained silent while she ate, and then added some of my own food to her empty plate before starting on my own meal. She stopped glaring at me when I fed her, at least.

We ate quietly, until Tempest curled up on the bed. Without an excuse to share it with her, I stopped in the bathroom to patch my wounds. When they were covered, I headed over to the doors and tried to make myself comfortable on the floor while Strong snuggled up with my human.

It took some time, but eventually, I fell asleep.

CHAPTER SIX
KAELLE

I tossed and turned until Vayme started snoring, and then continued tossing and turning. My wind was irritating me, but there was still nothing I could do to stop it.

A few hours must've passed when I finally lifted my exhausted, frustrated gaze to Strong's.

He was already staring at me.

"You're worried about Kee," he said.

I closed my eyes again and ignored him.

If he knew her name, there was obviously something between her and Vayme.

"The bond will lead you to be possessive, Tempest. It's natural. If another male were to touch your body intimately, Vayme would remove his head."

"He would not."

"He would." Strong's words left no room for questioning, even though I still didn't think that was true.

"It doesn't matter. He didn't tell her we're mated, so obviously he doesn't feel any loyalty toward me. The bond will only last until the eclipse, anyway." I

threw an arm over my eyes to keep myself from opening them again. I needed to sleep, not obsess over a man I didn't even want.

My wind was still blowing through the room in agitation, draining my energy and making everything worse.

If Strong was right, the obsessing was just because of the bond, but it was still frustrating.

"He can't tell her or anyone else about the bond. Couples who seal their mate bond are often murdered in the fae kingdoms. There was a cult that killed mated couples many years ago, and enough of its members slipped through the cracks that the murders still occur."

Shock flooded me, and I sat up quickly. *"What? Why wouldn't Vayme tell me that?"*

"You're already scared of most things. If he told you someone might kill you for your bond, it would be one more thing to fear."

I was stunned speechless for a moment. Finally, I said, *"What if I'd told someone because he didn't inform me?"*

"Vayme would've killed them before they could spread the news."

"If he was really that concerned about my life, he wouldn't have started the bond between us and then signed me up for a fight."

"I can agree the fight was a bad idea," Strong said. *"But the bond was the only choice."*

Letting out a long huff, I dropped to my back again. *"Yet neither of you will tell me why it was the only choice."*

"You are easily scared," Strong reminded me.

My wind whipped around us lightly, but unfortunately, it didn't throw anything at the giant wolf.

I wasn't getting anywhere, so I changed the subject.

"Why are some of the fae bonded to giant bears and tree cats instead of wolves?"

"The bears are called idorr, and the tree cats are called esu." He pronounced the words eye-door and ee-sue. *"Different types of beasts call each of the kingdoms home. The esu are best suited for the forest, so they live in Jirev. The idorr are best fit for the glacier, so they stay in Loire. Not all beasts are willing or able to speak mind-to-mind with a fae they aren't bonded to, so don't take offense if you meet some who are not. The esu are known to be quite particular about it."*

That was interesting.

I eyed him, expecting him to offer the name of whatever he was called. He knew I had no idea about the proper name for... whatever he was.

He remained silent.

Strong was going to make me ask.

I waited another moment before finally giving in. *"What are the wolves called?"*

"We are xuno." He pronounced the word zoo-no. *"We enjoy the caves of Vuuth, so we remain there."*

"Caves?" My mind returned to the comfortable cave I had called home for so long.

"Yes. Our cave system is vast, and packed full of both magic and ice. It's much different than the small one you lived in."

"I loved my cave," I said a bit defensively.

"Then you will adore Vuuth."

I shook my head at him, and my stomach rumbled.

Though there was still anger in my veins, Vayme had trained me into having an obnoxiously large appetite that only seemed to be growing.

"Let's find you more food so we can both sleep," Strong said. *"I'll take you to the castle's dining hall."*

I reluctantly agreed, and we both slipped out of the room as silently as possible. The tiny fae dress I had on made me self-conscious about the thinness of my legs, and the way my ribs showed, but it seemed better to fit in than to draw attention to my humanness.

My worry that Vayme would wake up and yell at me for leaving the room faded as I put more distance between myself and the king. Strong walked at my side, and I slipped my fingers into his fur so I would feel a little safer. My wind was still blowing more obnoxiously than I liked, but I hoped it would slow as I ate.

We reached a large room full of tables of different shapes and sizes, and Strong led me to one at the far end. He murmured for me to sit down, and then slipped through a door nearby for a moment.

My eyes slowly scanned the room, and I found two dozen fae looking at me curiously. Their auras were still massive and intense, but since there were less of them, they only caused a slight strain on my mind.

My face still warmed, though, and my wind picked up a bit.

Maybe my humanness was still obvious.

Strong returned a moment later and swept the room with a warning glare. Most of the eyes left me, and he sat down on the floor at my feet.

My fingers buried in his fur again for security, and I remained silent as I waited.

A few minutes later, a fae woman I didn't recognize brought me three large plates of food. When I thanked her, she smiled and bowed her head toward me.

My face warmed, but I nodded back, then started on the food.

As I worked on my meal, a small, pale woman with red-orange hair stepped into the dining room and looked around.

Her gaze landed on me, and lingered.

Her aura was more toned-down than most of the fae's, its size and color along the same lines as mine. And she didn't have a bonded beast at her side, which made me wonder who she was.

She stepped through the same door Strong had used, and then came and sat down across from me and smiled. "Hey. You're human, right?"

I nodded.

If I was supposed to fight other humans, it made sense that I'd see them in the castle.

I should've put the facts together and realized what she was, but between my exhaustion and the overwhelm of my magic, I wasn't thinking properly.

"I am too. I'm Laeli," she said.

"I'm Kaelle." I paused for a moment, trying to think of something worth saying despite my tendency to grow silent when faced with new situations. Finally, I settled on, "At least I'm not the only one."

"There's another one of us too—her name's Nissa. She has plant magic, and she's mated to Kier."

Kier was the king Vayme had fought in the cages, when the magic overwhelmed me. His aura was just as intense and deadly as Vayme's. "He's terrifying."

"Is your king not?"

My mind went back to the way he'd growled at me, towering over me with that awful glare in his eyes, and I shuddered a little. "Vayme is worse."

Laeli leaned toward me slightly. I wondered if she'd realized she was doing it at all. "Did he abduct you too? Ravv likes to tell me he rescued me, which is technically true, but I'm pretty sure he would've stolen me away even if I'd been happy in my old life."

"Yeah. My village kept me protected in a cave outside town so I wouldn't kill their crops with my wind. There was never enough food to go around, even before my magic came in," I admitted.

She caught my hand and squeezed lightly. "I'm sorry. The king of my city kept me locked in a cellar beneath their prison, so I can imagine the misery of that."

Horror swelled in my chest, but I tried not to show it. "Veil."

"Yeah. At least we're free now."

I nodded.

Despite the difficulties of her past, the woman looked confident. Maybe even calm.

I hesitated, but finally voiced the question lingering in my mind. "How are you not scared senseless? You don't even look nervous about being here, and I feel like I can barely breathe through the terror."

Laeli smiled a bit and leaned toward me more. "The best way to stop being afraid is to act like you're not. The more confidently you carry yourself, the more people will believe you're confident, even if you're terrified on the inside."

I sighed.

I had really hoped there would be a simple answer, like some kind of magic.

"That sounds... difficult," I said.

"But worth it."

I nodded reluctantly.

Someone brought her a plate of food too, and we both grew quiet as we ate. She was clearly just as hungry as I was, if not hungrier.

Hearing that she had been held prisoner made me feel slightly better about my own situation. Technically, I had never been imprisoned. I had stayed in my cave by my own choice, because my magic was terrifyingly strong. Even if my family had been starving me to keep me weak, I could have left. I could've walked away at any moment, but I chose to stay, because I loved my cave.

Because I loved my family, too.

And that made me feel slightly more at peace with the horrible possibilities.

As I continued to eat, the exhaustion of the day—or days, as I wasn't sure what time it was—finally caught up to me.

I found myself sagging as I struggled to continue lifting my fork to my mouth.

Laeli studied me for a moment before asking, "Are you okay?"

"Yeah. I think I just need to go to bed," I whispered. "It's been a long week."

Or a long week and a half, I supposed.

"Get out of here, then." She waved me toward the door, and I nodded.

Strong stood with me, telling me to leave my plate where it was and lean against him as we made our way out. Even with him holding me up, the walk felt very, very long.

When we made it back, I collapsed in bed and slept.

And slept.

And slept.

Vayme eventually woke me with a touch to my shoulder. The touch was surprisingly gentle, and I wrestled my heavy eyelids up. My sleepy eyes collided with his intense silvers, and I tried not to suck in a breath.

Veil, the man was still terrifying.

Massive, and deadly in every way.

"You need to eat," he told me.

I nodded and slowly slid out of bed.

My feet hit the ground, and he caught my elbow to help me as I stood.

Now that I was awake, I could feel the yawning pit in my stomach painfully demanding I fill it.

I was still wearing the fae-style dress from earlier, but saw my old human dress hanging over the bathroom door, clean. Nostalgia hit me, and Vayme released my arm when I took it into the bathroom to change into it.

As soon as it was on my skin, I regretted the decision. The fabric was stiff and scratchy, and the fit was truly terrible.

I didn't want to admit as much to Vayme, so I tied my hair up in a bun and said nothing as we slipped out of the room.

We walked down the hallway, and when I looked at him, I saw what almost resembled hesitation in his often-stony expression. I wasn't going to push him to tell me what he was thinking, so I didn't remark on it.

Finally, as we reached the dining hall, his mind touched mine. The brush of it shocked me, considering he had told me harshly that I was never supposed to speak into his mind.

"You deserve to know more than I've told you," he said.

I did... but I couldn't say that.

It might encourage him to stay silent again.

When he glanced at me, I gave a small nod to show I'd heard him.

"The fae kingdoms have only just recently established peace," he said. *"I was the one to initiate the peace discussions, and some of my people despise me for it. Some of them prefer to fight, as they know nothing else. It has been centuries since couples have mated or brought children into our world, so our numbers are dwindling."*

We reached the dining hall, and I still remained silent. It was mostly empty, which made me wonder what time it was, but I didn't ask.

Vayme gestured toward a table, and I sat down while he went to the door to request food from what I suspected was the kitchen. When he joined me at the table, he put a fair amount of distance between us and resumed speaking.

"A decade ago, my brother disappeared during a battle. He was killed—or at least, we assumed so—but no one recovered his body. I mourned him severely. He was the person I trusted most, as well as my people's only healer. Rather than throwing myself into battle, I was determined to honor his memory by ending the war the way he had been trying to convince me to do for most of my time on the throne."

Vayme's words stunned me.

I supposed after all his anger and silence, I hadn't considered the king to be a *person*. Certainly not one with family or emotions. I hadn't really considered him to be anything except my captor, the stoic king.

He added, *"Only a few of my people were vocal about their desire to continue the war. They understood that I was mourning, and most looked forward to a future where we weren't in a constant state of losing our loved ones. Until two months ago, when my brother returned."*

I blinked.

"Matían swept into the city on the back of his bonded beast in the middle of the night, with a child in his arms. A young girl who looked like him, and carried a deadly magic in her veins. He told a story of getting severely injured in battle just outside Jirev, and being carried by his companion to the Timeless Sands while struggling to survive. Both of them had long been tired of the fighting, and decided not to return. They made it to an inn run by humans, and the woman who owned it offered housing if they would protect her inn from the nearby raiders for a few months in return," Vayme continued, pronouncing his brother's name *mah-tee-on*.

Our food arrived, and Vayme went on as we started to eat. *"He enjoyed the work, and the company of the humans. When the eclipse came, he spent it with the woman who owned the inn, and they agreed to continue sharing a bed afterward. Years passed, and one cycle, she found herself pregnant. They weren't in love, but Matían was thrilled to become a father. His daughter Pavia was born soon enough, without a lick of the magic that coursed through his veins, and both parents were relieved."* He pronounced his niece's name *paw-vee-ah*.

Though we kept eating, my attention remained fixed on Vayme's story. *"Halfway through her sixth year, she hugged their chef soon after waking. At her touch, the life leeched away from him, and the man collapsed on the floor, dead. She had already hugged Matían and ridden on his companion's back that morning, so he knew he and the xuno were immune to her magic. Her power was neither human nor fae, but a mixture of both."*

Vayme continued, *"Matían kept his lover from touching their daughter, but news of her deadly magic spread. Soon enough, they had the entire city hunting the little girl. He kept them at bay for a few weeks, but they finally got past his defenses and killed his lover. He swept his daughter away, buried his female, and then his bonded beast carried them both back to Vuuth. He begged me for protection, and I couldn't deny him. Not while my niece stared at me with sad eyes, the first fae child I had seen in centuries."*

Veil.

"With the power of death in her veins, Pavia was immediately loved by all in our kingdom, and many of my people wanted to go to war with the city in the Sands to take revenge against those who killed her mother. A rebellion grew among them when I refused—our people are bloodthirsty, and they yearned for the thrill of battle. Matían tried to convince them otherwise, but the rebellion only grew. They have declared me weak for refusing another war, and have made it their mission to end me so they can take that revenge," he said.

"They don't care that Matían and Pavia don't want war?"

"No. They want battle, at any cost. Should the news of our mating spread, others will take their side as well, and you and I will be hunted. Already, the faction that seeks war with the Sands has paid in blood and power for the Monster of the Aching Chasm to kill me."

My eyes widened with horror. *"One of the elves' assassins?"*

Everyone had grown up hearing the stories. The elves had twisted the magic of a few different magical beings, turning them into mindless killers who hunted those they were paid to kill. They were ruthless, deadly, and unmatched in power. Some even said they were vampires, too, awful beings that required the blood of others to survive.

"Yes. Myself and both other kings have been marked by the assassins, which is why I went looking for you. One of the elven leaders told us of human females with life magic that were hidden away in your lands, and gave us your location. Because our magic is death and yours originates from life, yours hides ours, so the assassins cannot hunt us through our power."

"So you're using us as shields?" I asked.

"We are."

Veil.

I was definitely right about him being selfish—and there was a decent chance I'd end up dead at the hands of the Monster because of that selfishness.

CHAPTER SEVEN
KAELLE

O ur conversation was interrupted by another couple who entered the dining hall. My gaze lifted to them, and I blinked when I saw Kier's aura melding with a vibrantly-colored human one. Kier was tall, with tan skin and wavy black hair that curled around his ears. One of his arms was wrapped in a tattoo that seemed to be in a language I didn't recognize, but otherwise, he didn't look angry or cruel.

The human with him had dark green hair that fell to her waist in waves, skin a shade lighter than Kier's, and wore a brightly-colored fae-style dress. Her eyes glowed green, and she didn't look standoffish, but she didn't look friendly, either.

They approached the table, and her gaze met mine as she gave a quick greeting. "Hi."

Kier stepped closer to her, his stance protective and eyes narrowed at us.

Vayme barely acknowledged them before focusing on his food again.

"Hello," I said quietly to the human, whose name I knew was Nissa. "I'm Kaelle. I think Laeli told me about you. You have plant magic, right?"

"Yep." She smiled, and I tried to smile back, but my mind was still racing through everything Vayme had told me.

Mainly, the bit where one of the elves' assassins was hunting him.

"He hasn't hurt you, right?" Nissa sat down next to me and gestured to Vayme.

My king lifted his eyes from his food to glare at her, and her king's body tensed again.

Despite... well, *everything* that had happened with Vayme, he definitely hadn't hurt me, and I couldn't leave her with that idea.

"No, he's fine. Thanks for asking, though." I took her hand and squeezed it to assure her. She looked surprised by the breeze she could undoubtedly feel blowing off my skin, but didn't ask me about it.

The fae woman who had brought me and Vayme our food reemerged with plates for Kier and Nissa, and the mood calmed as he sat beside her. I released her hand, and we were all quiet as we ate.

Despite the nerves that had me wanting to stay silent, I remembered my conversation with Laeli. She had told me that the best way to feel confident was to act confident, and... well, I wanted to try it.

So, I forced myself to speak up.

"Were you glad to leave your city?" I asked Nissa, as I finished eating.

"I was," she said, and didn't add to it. If her situation was anything like Laeli's, I didn't blame her for not wanting to share the details.

My gaze flicked between her and Kier, and my empathy grew.

I could certainly understand not wanting to share details with the king who had stolen her away, in particular.

Her question from earlier came to mind, and though it made me a bit terrified to do so, I asked softly, "Has he hurt you?"

Kier growled at my question, but she put a hand on his chest before he could attack me. "No. He hasn't."

I was fiercely grateful for her quick response, even though I had felt Vayme tense beside me, as if ready to protect me.

I nodded, and found my eyes wandering to the food that remained on Vayme's plate. Though my belly was deliriously full, I was still hungry somehow.

He silently placed some of it on my plate, and more gratitude swelled in my chest.

Nissa resumed eating as she asked me, "Do *you* miss your city?"

"Oh, I'm from a teeny, tiny town." I bit my lip, deciding it was better not to tell her that I had missed the town since I'd been moved into a cave for everyone else's safety. "Laeli was from a big city though, so I assumed you were too."

"My town was small, too. They would kill anyone who got close enough to try to take me."

My eyes widened.

My town had feared me...

But hers defended her?

"So they protected you?"

"In a way, yes."

I forced myself not to admit aloud that my mind had started going back to my own experiences.

If someone had tried to take me from them, would my parents have fought for me? Would they defend me, or kill anyone who tried to abduct me?

I had a sinking feeling that they wouldn't.

Nodding, I resumed eating while everyone grew quiet again.

"Have you seen any sign of the Monster?" Kier asked Vayme, as I scraped the last bite from my plate.

"Not yet. The ache in the rune has gotten worse, though."

The rune?

I looked over at Vayme curiously.

"I'll show you later," he said into my mind, once again surprising me by speaking to me that way.

"Mine as well," Kier agreed. "I assume they'll search the human lands after losing the trail of our magic there, and then return here."

Vayme nodded, and his expression, though still stony, seemed a bit thoughtful. "Should you need a place to hide, my castle is open to you and the female. They won't expect us to rely on each other."

"Thank you."

"The Monster is hunting you?" Nissa asked Vayme.

"She likely knows that the Beast of the Endless Wilds hunts Kier," Vayme told me, scowling as he said aloud, "Yes."

"Does he really drink *blood*?" I wondered, unable to suppress a small shiver.

Vayme's voice lowered. "I don't know. Pray we don't find out."

We only spoke for another minute before Nissa and Kier left to attend the violent events that were supposed to help the kings keep the peace. When they were gone, Vayme and I headed back to our room.

After the door was shut securely behind us, he unwrapped his palm. My gaze caught on its silver glow, and my eyes widened.

He showed me the back of his hand, pointing out a brand that glowed a crimson color. I noticed his aura moving around it, as if hurting or unhappy because of the marking.

"Veil," I whispered.

"I won't let the Monster kill you," Vayme said, as he rewrapped it. "I'm sure you're worried about it, and for good reason. I took you so your magic could protect me, but I won't let him hurt you if he does catch me."

"Thank you," I said quietly, though I doubted he could actually do anything if the Monster came for me. He was a warrior, and a king... but the assassins were monsters of legend.

Vayme slipped out soon after that to supervise the events and deal with his people. Strong led me to the castle's library at my request, and I spent the day and night with my nose buried in a book as I tried not to panic about the assassin hunting us.

The handprint on my hip ached a bit when he got too far from me, but he spoke into my mind to let me know that he'd stay close enough to prevent the ache from becoming true pain, so I survived.

The next day, Vayme dragged me out of the library. He'd decided I was going to train with the other two humans, so I'd be prepared for the ridiculous fight all of us would participate in.

Despite my reluctance, I tried to learn how to swing their stupidly heavy swords and move my body properly.

Two weeks passed quickly as we trained. My progress never quite satisfied the kings, and my body was never quite satisfied with the amount of food I ate. Though I gained weight quickly, I was still constantly hungry.

And I was still trying to come to terms with the fact that my family may have starved me on purpose.

When the day of the fight finally arrived, I was ready to get it over with so we could move on from Jirev. After the events were over, we would be going to Vuuth, which was made of caves.

Since caves made me feel much safer, I was looking forward to that security.

Laeli and Nissa made me dress in a ridiculous metal outfit that barely covered my assets for the fight. Nissa was attempting to get some sort of revenge on Kier, and Laeli was thrilled about it, but I was dreading the disgust Vayme would probably have on his face when he saw me nearly naked.

Though I wore fae-style dresses all of the time, and finally got a few inches of my hair cut so it didn't look scraggly, he had never seemed attracted to me in the slightest, so I had no hope that he liked the way I looked.

We still hadn't discussed the female fae who had touched him in our room that day, either. I assumed he was at the very least interested in her, if not actively *with* her.

Though we spent plenty of time together, he always slept on the floor in front of the door, and there was nothing romantic between us. We were becoming reluctant friends, I supposed, but I wasn't under the impression that our mate bond meant anything to him.

I was his shield, and nothing more.

Anyway, the fight had arrived, so all three of us humans headed into the cage with the man who was announcing the battle. The auras of all the fae in the stands had started overwhelming me and giving me a headache as soon as we entered the stadium, and it only grew worse as we moved further inside.

The deafening cheers melded with the raging rainbows of auras around me, and I fought to keep myself from lifting my hands to cover my eyes or ears.

The auras were insanely intense.

My gaze caught on one in the stands...

One that burned bigger and brighter than any of the others. Rather than shadowy or dark like Vayme's, it blazed like a fire.

It was so much larger than any of the fae's.

It had to be something important.

Or some*one* important.

Like... an assassin.

My gaze was still fixed on the massive aura, my head pounding and stomach rolling as Laeli called out to me, "Are you alright?"

My wind was blowing in agitation as I fought to keep myself rooted in place, my gaze following the aura as it began to move.

"I don't know," I said. "Something's wrong."

"What's happening?" Vayme's words were somewhere between worried and irritated.

"I don't know," I repeated. *"Maybe nothing."*

"You're staring at something," he growled back.

"An aura," I said. *"It's larger than anyone else's. I don't know why."*

Vayme said something else, but I didn't hear it properly. There was too much going on around me, and I was too overwhelmed.

Could the aura have belonged to one of the assassins?

I didn't know.

I would've expected their souls to be dark and deadly, not bright and fiery.

The announcer dragged us into place until the three of us faced each other, and then he shouted something. The crowd was too loud for me to make out the words, but I assumed it was the start of the fight.

He shut the door of the cage behind us, and the bright aura surged closer. The heady power of it made the pain in my head worse, and I pressed a hand to my temple as I fought the wave of dizziness that accompanied it. My other hand was on my sword, holding me up as I leaned against it, my face twisting in pain.

Slowly, the crowd's roaring quieted.

The fae in the stands had to be getting suspicious, but the noise and colors of the auras were so bright that I couldn't do anything but stand there helplessly. My wind was whipping my hair around, draining my energy, as well.

The aura neared the edge of the cage, and my heart sank.

An aura that bright and strong, coming straight toward humans who were mated to the kings...

There was no other option.

It had to be one of the assassins.

I whispered to the other women, "He's here."

The crowd had grown silent around us, but the colors of their auras were so, so loud.

"Who?" one of the other women asked me. I was too dizzy to tell which one.

"One of the assassins. I can feel him," I said.

The other woman asked, "How can you feel him? How do you know?"

"I see and feel auras. My wind comes from them. And his aura is *terrible*."

I knew the words made little sense, and his aura wasn't wicked or anything, but its fierce strength was so damn overwhelming. When paired with all the others around me, I couldn't even think straight.

"What are you waiting for?" one of the kings shouted from the stands. Not Vayme—he wasn't one for yelling.

My wind was so loud that the men couldn't have heard us. They didn't know that an assassin was there, or that he was at the entrance of our cage.

"What do we do?" one of the women demanded.

"I don't know." My gaze was fixed on the aura as it moved faster than should've been possible, right into the cage.

"We need to get everyone out," one of the other women finally said.

"Oh, it's far too late for that," a smooth male voice said. The aura appeared next to me, and I was so blinded by its intensity that I couldn't see, let alone breathe. "Which one of you is connected to Kier Jirev?"

He was looking for Kier, which made him—

"The Beast of the Endless Wilds," one of the other women breathed.

"Hello, sweetheart. Is Kier using your magic to hide his?" the Beast purred.

The commotion in the stands further blinded and deafened me to Nissa and Laeli's responses, if they responded at all. The auras were all moving, the fae were yelling, and my body started swaying a little. My wind was growing into a storm, and I was helpless to stop it as its drain on my energy picked up.

I was going to lose control and lose consciousness again, which could be a death sentence with the Beast nearby.

And if I was going to die anyway, I might as well take the fall for being Kier's mate, so Laeli and Nissa stood a chance at escaping.

The cage door started rattling as someone tried to break through. The Beast must've locked us in.

I started to say that I was Kier's mate, but just as I did, another woman blurted, "I'm mated to Kier. It's me."

"See how easy that was?" he asked.

Fire erupted alongside my wind, melding with the Beast's aura and making it impossible to see what was going on around us. From what little I could see, it looked like...

Like he was drinking Nissa's blood.

Vayme was speaking into my mind, but I was too out of it to hear the words clearly. My wind was blowing too hard, my panic was swelling too intensely, and my world was still too blurry with auras.

The Beast shouted, "Surely a fae king of any worth would at least attempt to defend the female he's claimed as his. Come out and fight, Kier."

My storm swelled.

"Tempest," Vayme's commanding voice finally grew loud enough to cut into my mind.

For once, I didn't hate the nickname, because it meant I wasn't alone.

The auras of the fae in the stands were fading, but fire and wind still filled my vision, making me stumble around the room as I tried not to get burned.

"Tempest, I need you to find the door and let us in. We're powerless out here," Vayme's calm, steady voice ordered me.

It shouldn't have grounded me, but it did.

"Look for my aura. Get the door open," he repeated.

"Use your magic so I can find you," I managed to whisper back.

His aura flared, just bright enough for me to make it out through the flames. For the first time since I'd met him, I looked at his aura and felt not afraid or uncertain, but... safe.

I ran through the fire, toward the pooling darkness of his soul. My wind blew hard enough to keep me from getting more than a little burned, until a large hand collided with my torso through the bars of the cage. My forehead nearly smacked the hot metal, but a pair of intense silver eyes met mine as his other hand caught my head, stopping and steadying me again.

"Get it open," he said.

My shaky hands found the lock and got it undone quickly. Vayme helped me throw the door open, then yanked me into his arms, hugging me fiercely to his chest.

There wasn't time for comfort, though.

I jerked my gaze to Kier's, and words tumbled from my lips nonsensically. My head still pounded so hard I could barely think, and my whole body hurt with the effort to stay conscious. "Nissa told him she was bonded to you, and he bit her. He's drinking her blood. We didn't know he was a vampire. I didn't know. I should've warned everyone."

My storm was still brewing, the winds rattling the cage as the magic grew more out of control.

"Laeli's on fire," I added. "She can't stop it. I—"

Kier interrupted me, his gaze moving to Vayme, who still held me firmly. "Get her out of here. Go to the elves. Tell them if their assassins kill any of our people, *including* our mates, we will consider it an act of war and will come for them as one."

Vayme dipped his head in a nod, then threw me onto Strong's back.

"We can't leave," I said into his mind, my panic still swelling as Strong took off. *"I have to make sure the other women are okay. They—"*

"Your magic will be the death of all of us if we don't leave, Tempest. A storm will give the Beast the advantage he needs." Vayme's voice was still calm, but his words struck me silent.

I was dangerous.

Veil, I was deadly.

Of course, they needed to get me out of there.

My eyes stung.

I didn't fight anymore, letting the tears fall down my cheeks as Strong ran through the trees.

CHAPTER EIGHT
KAELLE

The fierce drain of my magic knocked me unconscious after a few hours, and I was lost to the blissful burnout. It wasn't the worst I'd ever had, but certainly could've been better.

By the time I woke up, it was the middle of the night, and Vayme was pacing in front of me. I seemed to have been set on my ass, with my back propped up against a snoring Strong's side.

We were still in the Endless Wilds, because the elves lived in a different part of them than the fae did.

A dozen esu, the jungle cats that often bonded with fae in Jirev, had caught up to us on the way out of the city. They stuck with us, intending to transport the elves back. I didn't see them, but assumed they were sleeping in the trees around us. None had tried to speak to me, and Strong said that wasn't unusual.

I didn't particularly feel like speaking to them or anyone else, anyway.

My metal lingerie was digging into my skin hard enough that I was bleeding in a few places. The edges of the metal weren't sharp, but they weren't made for riding on a xuno's back for hours.

Hopefully the metal hadn't cut Strong, too.

I sat up slowly, wincing at the pain of the movement. My headache was gone, at least.

"You're bleeding," Vayme growled, covering the distance between us before kneeling in front of me. His fists were clenched, and his jaw was, too.

"Just a little." I tried to bend the metal away from my skin, but only succeeded in making the cut deeper. "It's fine. I deserve it for losing control and putting my friends in danger."

"The other kings and I are the reason your lives are at risk; not you. It isn't your fault that you were given magic too wild to be controlled."

His words made my chest swell with gratitude and my guilt subside drastically. "Thank you."

"Don't thank me. I don't have any spare clothes for you, and I'm not wearing a shirt. You've been bleeding, and there's nothing I can do about it," he said through gritted teeth.

"If my magic's not my fault, my lack of clothing certainly isn't yours." I brushed hair out of my eyes, and he growled at me again. My wind wasn't tugging at the strands, at least. Burnout did have that advantage.

"Stay still. The more you move, the more you bleed."

"You're really concerned about this." I dropped my hand back to my thigh.

"Of course I'm concerned about this. You're *bleeding*, Tempest."

"Not concerned enough to use my real name," I countered, finding myself too at ease with Vayme to bother biting my tongue.

His eyes narrowed. "Tempest suits you better."

I scowled at him. "Maybe I should start calling you *Ice*, then."

"Names are beside the point, *Kaelle*." He emphasized my real name. "You're bleeding, and it's driving me mad. We need a way to stop it."

At least he *knew* my real name.

I hadn't been certain that he did up until that moment.

"I'm not going to ride with you in the nude, if that's what you're suggesting." My voice grew hotter, anger building in my chest. "I'm not any more attracted to you than you are to me."

It was a lie.

I was extremely attracted to him, physically, at least.

But he didn't need to know that.

"*Not any more attracted to me than I am to you?* What does that mean?" His eyes were still narrowed.

My face flushed.

He was really going to make me say it. "You have made it clear that you're not attracted to me. I'm saying that I'm not attracted to you either."

His expression grew a bit incredulous. "What could possibly have made you feel that way?"

"Everything?" I gestured to him, as a whole.

My face was still red, and I was starting to feel... untamed? I usually let my fear get to me, but new emotions had taken over. Emotions like embarrassment, frustration, and maybe even a little stubbornness.

"I have been attracted to you since the first day we met. I'm sure you've noticed my body's reaction." He gestured to himself.

To his... lower half.

My cheeks burned hotter. "I can assure you, I have *not*."

"Veil, Tempest. Give me your hand."

I didn't give him my hand.

His narrowed eyes morphed into a glare.

I glared back, though my face felt as if it were nearly on fire.

"I've smelled your arousal in the air after I shower. Give me your damn hand so I can prove you're not the only one who feels it," he commanded.

That revelation caught me off guard.

He had smelled how attracted I was to him?

I didn't know what to think about that.

I liked it—I definitely liked it.

But anything other than *like*, I wasn't sure.

I didn't want to let him win, but if I didn't let him prove it, I would always be wondering.

So... I finally gave him my hand.

"You know how the male body works?" he asked, as he pulled my palm toward his body.

Veil, my blush would never go away. "I've read about it."

"You've read about sex?"

"Yes."

The answer seemed to satisfy him enough.

My hand finally reached his body, and he slowly dragged the backs of my knuckles over his erection.

I sucked in a breath, taken aback by the hardness of him.

He was attracted to me.

He was definitely attracted to me.

I itched to ask him if I could see his erection, but assumed he'd find the question inappropriate, so I stayed silent.

Vayme released my hand, but I didn't move it away from him.

My gaze flicked to his face, and I saw his eyes fixed firmly on my hand, only a breath away from his... well, his cock.

He didn't look bothered, angry, or stony, for once. If I had to guess, I'd say he looked like he wanted me to touch him again.

Biting my lip, I lifted my fingers back to his erection, and slowly dragged them over the length of him.

Veil, he was huge.

The characters in the books had mentioned the size of males, but I had never been able to picture it, because I'd never seen a naked man before.

"You're attracted to me," I said quietly, reluctantly pulling my fingers away from him.

"More than I should be."

My stomach curled at the words, though not unpleasantly. My toes curled a little, too.

"I still can't ride on Strong's back in the nude. I'd feel uncomfortable."

"Not as uncomfortable as you would with the metal cutting into your skin." His voice had a growly edge.

"Do you have shorts on beneath your pants?" I asked him.

He blinked, surprised by the question. I'd seen the shorts he wore as an undergarment, though, so I knew he did. "Yes."

"Can I wear them? If I'm at least partially covered, I'll feel more at ease."

Understanding flooded his eyes. "You can take my pants, so we're both partially undressed."

I nodded and he stood, his hands going to the waistband of his pants.

Nerves hit me when I realized he was about to strip, and I said quickly, "I can wait until we're leaving. It's no problem to deal with the metal while we eat and sleep."

"No. The sight of you bleeding is driving me mad. After we get it off you, your body can start healing itself. The wounds aren't bad enough for you to need to drink my blood."

He stripped his pants off, and my mouth went dry as I watched. The powerful motion of his biceps, the way his body bent and moved...

The shorts he wore beneath them were tight. His erection strained against the fabric, and my throat closed as my eyes followed the length of it.

Veil.

The urge to ask him if I could see it—just once—hit me again, but I bit my tongue to keep my mouth shut.

I was being ridiculous, and I knew it.

He tossed the pants over a bush nearby, then stepped closer.

I tried not to stare at his erection, I really did, but I definitely failed.

He grabbed me by my waist and picked me up as if I didn't weigh a thing, then set me on my feet. "I'll break the metal with my ice to get it off you."

I grimaced. "Will it hurt?"

He scoffed. "Of course not. You know I won't hurt you." There was a pause. "Right?"

"Right," I agreed, my voice soft but honest.

He let out a relieved puff of air, and his fingers landed on the metal strips around my back.

"Can you try not to look at me?" I asked him, my cheeks reddening again.

"I can." His voice was reluctant.

"I guess it's okay if you look, as long as you don't judge my body," I said quietly, my face still hot.

He growled at me again, and pulled the metal away from my skin. I heard a quiet snapping sound, and the tension on my breasts grew significantly lighter.

There were a few more snapping noises before he eased the metal down my arms, freeing my breasts entirely.

My face burned as I felt his gaze on me, and I wrapped an arm around my chest. The cuts on the sides of my breasts and ribs hurt, and I could feel a few of them bleeding, but I ignored them in favor of covering myself.

Vayme bent closer to work on the metal wrapped around my lower bits, and his lips brushed my ear as I heard another snap of metal. "Your breasts are stunning, Tempest."

Suddenly, I didn't hate the nickname.

Not even a little.

Maybe it wasn't an insult at all. The fae respected power, so maybe calling me a storm was a sign of respect.

"The next time I imagine my mouth on them, I'll have an image of the real thing in my mind," Vayme added, his lips brushing my ear again.

Veil.

He had imagined his mouth on my breasts?

What else had he imagined?

I bit my lip hard to stop myself from asking.

There were a few more snaps of the metal before he slid it down my thighs, then helped me step out of it. He grabbed his pants, and I remained where I was as he eased my feet into the legs one by one. Though I itched to take control, I stayed still while he pulled them up and tied a knot in the waistband, so it rested on my hip.

He stepped behind me again, brushing his erection against my backside as he did. "If you knew how difficult it's been for me to keep my hands and mouth off you, you wouldn't worry about me *judging your body*." His hands landed on my hips and squeezed roughly.

I bit back a squeak at the pressure of his touch, and would've stumbled if he hadn't been holding me so securely.

Finally, after one last squeeze, he released me and strode into the forest. I turned to watch him go, and my eyes lingered on the bubble of his ass, so much harder to ignore without his thick pants covering it.

"Where are you going?" I asked him, a few moments too late to ask aloud.

"Foraging. I saw a berry bush back this way. Sit down by Strong and let your wounds heal."

I rolled my eyes at his instruction to *let my wounds heal*, but sat back down and peered at one of the cuts on the side of my ribcage.

My lips curved downward in a grimace at the sight of it, and my mind went back to what he'd said.

"Aren't bad enough for you to need to drink my blood."

What did he mean by that?

I hadn't heard of blood drinking for anyone but vampires... and fae didn't have vampiristic tendencies, did they? Vampires could only come from humans who became cursed by using some type of twisted, dark magic. I didn't even know where a person would find the kind of magic necessary to change themselves like that.

A day earlier, I would've sat and wondered in silence. But a day earlier, Vayme hadn't grabbed my hand to show me his erection, rescued me when the Beast showed up, calmed my guilt, or told me my breasts were stunning.

My perspective had changed when it came to him, I supposed.

I cautiously spoke into his mind again. *"You said something about drinking blood?"*

"Yes. Mates can drink each other's blood to heal," Vayme said, almost absent-mindedly. He seemed focused on whatever he was doing. Picking berries, I supposed. *"As far as I know, it works better after the bond is sealed, or if the pair is fated."*

"Fated?"

"Some couples' souls bond before they reach our world. A handprint will appear for them the first time they touch without a spoken vow between them."

My eyes widened. *"So we're not fated?"*

He didn't answer immediately, but finally said, *"I suppose there's no way to know, because I spoke the vow before I touched you. It's quite unlikely, though. Fated pairs are rare even among magical beings, and you're human."*

I was surprised he remembered the day we met so clearly, given how unhappy he'd seemed to be there and stealing me away.

"It doesn't particularly matter, though," he added.

"Because we're not going to stay together after the eclipse," I said quietly.

"Exactly."

There was a moment of silence.

Some part of me almost felt... sad.

Not at the thought of being separated from Vayme, of course. We weren't even friends.

But at the thought of going back to the silence and loneliness of my cave. Even if I had enough food, it would still seem far emptier after my time spent mated to the king.

"You're still going to take me back home, right?" I asked him.

"I promised I would, and I'm a man of my word," Vayme said.

Good.

That was good.

"But I'm not going to leave you there unless I know it's safe for you. We'll figure out what's going on with your family and your town, and ensure that you'll be safe and well fed, before I consider leaving you in that tiny cave. If a cave is all you want, I can provide you with as many as you'd like, even after the bond is broken."

"We'll see. I still love my family," I said, but the words sounded hollow.

If they had really starved me to keep me weak, I wasn't certain they deserved my love.

And I definitely couldn't risk my life by staying there, if they were willing to deprive me for their safety.

I was dangerous... but I still deserved to eat and have my freedom. I supposed Vayme had helped me realize that, as ridiculous as it seemed that he would help me with anything.

"Of course." His words were gentler than they had been. *"I'm heading back. Prepare to feast."*

My lips curved upward. *"What a feast it will be. Berries, berries, and more berries."*

He chuckled. *"A meal fit for a queen."*

I bit my lip to stop my smile from growing, but it was still lingering when he got back and sat down beside me. One of my arms was still wrapped around my breasts, but he sat without a shred of self-consciousness as he spread his muscular legs out in front of him.

Truly, the man was a masterpiece. It was hard to imagine anyone with muscles more sculpted or a body more perfect.

And he had brought me a huge basket of berries, each of which was only a little smaller than my fist. The basket was made of ice, and the food inside it only made him more gorgeous.

He handed me one, and we both started eating. Though we were quiet, it was different than our usual uncomfortable silence. It was calmer, and more peaceful.

Strong was still snoring, so we left a large bowl of berries for him without waking him up. He needed to rest.

When our bellies were full, Vayme built an ice shelter and slipped inside. Though it was exactly the same as the ones he'd made on our way to Jirev, it seemed different.

Or *I* seemed different, I supposed.

I tightened the knot on my pants before stepping into the shelter myself. My arm was still around my chest, but realistically, I knew that wasn't going to last all night.

Vayme had already seen my breasts, but he hadn't touched them.

I wasn't sure whether I wanted him to.

On one hand, it would probably feel good.

Really good.

On the other, it would definitely affect how I felt about him, and I wasn't sure I was ready for that.

Despite my uncertainty, I sat down beside Vayme the same way I always had when we were traveling together. When I lowered my head to the ice, he lifted it onto his arm like he always did.

And then, after a moment of hesitation, he placed his hand on my hip. The fabric of the pants I had on separated us, but my face still warmed at the gentle intimacy of the contact.

I scooted just the tiniest bit, so the back of my body brushed his a little.

His chest rumbled softly, and my throat swelled as he slid closer, so his entire front pressed to my back. His erection was against my ass, and his chest met the bare skin on my back, making me warmer. Though his grip tightened on my hip, it didn't move any closer to my breasts.

His voice was low and soft as he said into my ear, "Sleep well, Kaelle."

My throat swelled. "You can call me Tempest, if you want."

"Don't hate it so much anymore?"

"I mostly hated it because I thought you didn't know my name," I whispered.

He chuckled. "You've given your name to at least a dozen people since I've known you. I'd have to be purposefully obtuse not to."

"Maybe I thought you were purposefully obtuse."

"I am many things, but usually, not that." He squeezed my hip again. "Good night."

I mirrored his words as I closed my eyes, and by some miracle, managed to fall asleep.

CHAPTER NINE
KAELLE

We were moving again just a few hours later, after another breakfast of berries.

Though I was self-conscious at first, I quickly adjusted to traveling with my breasts bare. It felt natural, and forced me to grow more confident in my nudity.

Strangely enough, it even made me feel more comfortable with Vayme. He never tried to grab me or push himself on me, consistently remaining respectful.

We reached the elves late that night.

The Wilds didn't look any different when Strong and the esu stopped. When Vayme pointed out the shimmering, lace-like curve of a shield that kept everything except the elves out, I understood that they simply hid the entirety of their kingdom.

"What do we do?" I asked him, my voice heavy with exhaustion. I wasn't the one running, so I shouldn't have been so worn out, but I was.

"We wait. They'll send someone out to see us. If they're wise, it'll be one of their leaders."

I nodded, and Vayme pulled me against his back.

Since I wasn't sure whether the shield was transparent for the elves, or whether they could see through it, I kept an arm wrapped around my chest as I relaxed against him. He was strong and warm, despite the ice of his magic, and my breeze was a barely-there whisper. It still hadn't built back up to its full strength, and likely wouldn't for a few more days.

"Are you going to threaten them?" I asked Vayme silently, my eyelids lowering a bit.

"If I have to. I know their leaders well enough that I hope it's unnecessary, but I will if I must."

I nodded.

As we sat there, his arm slid around my middle, beneath mine. *"You can rest. I've heard that their city is vast, and it often takes time for them to come to us."*

"Thank you." My eyes drifted shut, and I relaxed against him further. My arm around my chest started to sag, and he simply lifted his own to hold mine comfortably in place.

I only dozed for a few minutes before the shield rippled, and Vayme woke me with a gentle squeeze to my hip.

Two women stepped out. Both had luscious curves, and wore flowy, elegant dresses. One had long black hair, big hazel eyes, and light brown skin. The other had dark skin, light red hair, and big lavender eyes. I had expected them to look more magical than they actually did, to be honest, because they looked much like the fae but with far less muscle.

The dark-haired one's lips curved wickedly as she purred, "Well, isn't that a pretty mate bond."

"Hello, Alida," Vayme said.

"Hello." Her eyes landed on me, and lingered. "Your magic is a breath of fresh air, you know. A cool breeze on a humid day."

"Every day is a humid day in the Wilds," Vayme's arm tightened around me. "And Kaelle is not looking to join the elves."

My head jerked a bit, surprised by the comment.

I hadn't known that was an option.

If it was...

Veil, maybe I'd consider it.

Then again, I didn't know anything about the elves except that they were mystical, and apparently appreciated wind magic.

I'd also finally started feeling more comfortable with Vayme, so it would probably be better just to stay with him.

"Why have you brought your human mate here, then?" the redheaded elf woman asked.

"The Beast of the Endless Wilds attacked Jirev and drank from Kier's human. He and Ravv sent me here to threaten you with the greatest war the Wilds would ever see," Vayme said.

Both women's faces grew grave, but Alida recovered the fastest, pasting on a nonchalant expression. "What do you want, then?"

"Your shields to protect us."

"Veil." Alida closed her eyes and let out a long breath.

"And the only other option is war?" the redheaded woman asked.

"Yes. Most of our fae are gathered in Jirev right now. We can remain there if that will make it easier, or Ravv and I can return to our own cities with our people."

"We could never defend against all three assassins at once. Protecting against even one is a stretch." Alida ran a hand through her hair, pushing the long, thick strands out of her face. "You're asking for too much."

"We are no happier about this situation than the rest of you. Far less, I'd say, considering our lives are on the line." Vayme's voice was neutral, but there was enough danger in its undertones to make me suppress a shiver.

"You don't understand how much the assassins despise us." Alida gestured to the shield behind her. "We turned our city into a fortress so we don't have to deal with them."

"You still don't have to deal with them," Vayme said calmly. "But if you don't, you *will* have to deal with us."

"Obviously we cannot take on three armies worth of fae warriors any more than we can handle the assassins. At least if we go with you, we can use your damn warriors as protection too if the assassins manage to break through," Alida said.

Vayme dipped his head. "You have a far greater chance of survival if you come with us. There is still a chance we could kill the assassins; we simply don't wish to find out."

The elves looked at each other for a few moments before turning back to us.

The redheaded woman warned, "We'll need a few hours to gather enough willing elves. You'll have to take whoever we can convince."

"As long as they can shield us, we don't care who they are."

Alida's eyes scanned the esu gathered with us, and then she nodded. Both women slipped back behind their shield, and my gaze tracked the ripple in fascination.

"That went well, didn't it?" I asked Vayme silently, still not entirely certain what to think about the elven women.

"As well as it could've," he agreed. *"That was Alida and Virre, two of the elven leaders. They won't have nearly as difficult a time gathering elves."*

"Are they queens?"

"No. The elves haven't had queens since they created the assassins. I imagine you'll meet the three ex-queens when Alida and Virre return."

"Why would the ex-queens help us?"

His fingers stroked the side of my ribcage lightly, and I shivered a little. *"They are the ones who created the assassins. They shaped the spell that made them what they are. All of the elves helped, but the queens were ultimately the powerhouse behind it."*

"I thought it was a curse."

"Perhaps it ended up that way, but it was unintentional. The males chosen were the weakest of their kind. They volunteered to receive the elves' changes and become their weapons, but no one realized what would come of the spell or the way those changes would affect them."

"Veil," I whispered.

"From what I know, the ex-queens have tried to alter the assassins' magic many times, and they carry immense guilt for what they did to the men. I suspect their guilt will drive them to join our protective party."

"That's good, I suppose. They must be strong if they were queens, and made the assassins what they are."

"Their magic is strong, but their minds may not be. Their guilt pairs with the natural insanity of an immortal life, which we call immis. We can only hope they remain sane."

"What is the natural insanity?" I asked.

"All immortal beings begin to unravel without a purpose. War gave my people purpose and prevented immis, but some other types of magical beings haven't been as lucky. We can only hope the queens are still steady-minded."

I nodded. *"According to the legends I always heard, there are no male elves. Is that true?"*

"It is. There are no female gargoyles either, so long ago, their groups used to form bonds. Now, both are alone." Vayme's fingers brushed my side again. *"I need to feed you. You'll have to come with me; I'm not comfortable leaving you alone this close to the elves' city."*

"Alright."

Strong lowered to his belly on the ground and dropped his head onto his paws. He would need to rest after running so much.

Vayme's hand slipped into mine, and he towed me through the jungle until we found a bush loaded with fruit I didn't recognize. He taught me about it while we picked it, and then while we sat down and ate. Surprisingly enough, I found myself enjoying his company.

We went back to the edge of the elves' shield after we finished eating, and sat down with our backs to a tree while we waited for them. Vayme offered to let me sit on his lap with my chest to his so I could stay modest while I rested, but I turned him down with flushed cheeks.

I fell asleep with my shoulder pressed to Vayme's side, his arm around my waist to hold me upright, and mine still wrapped around my chest.

Eventually, he woke me again.

I opened my eyes in time to see more than a dozen elves step out from behind their shield. Most of them were curvy, and all of them wore elegant, delicate-looking dresses. Their hair and skin were in a variety of shades and colors, and all of them were unique in their own way.

I noticed that three of them on the far side of the group had shimmering, curling golden tattoos on various parts of their body. One of them looked a lot like Alida, strangely, while another was tan with light pink hair, and the third was pale with golden hair. The pink-haired one had a firm grip on the other two's arms, but neither of them looked like they were considering making a run for it.

"Are those the queens, with the golden tattoos?" I asked Vayme, my gaze lingering on their markings as he stood and lifted me with him.

"Yes."

"I brought your defenders," Alida announced, gesturing to the group of women around her. Virre wasn't with her anymore, so I assumed she hadn't been one of the elves willing to come and protect the fae cities. "If the Beast was in Jirev yesterday, we need to leave now and move quickly."

"On that, we agree." Vayme stood. "The esu have offered to carry you. We will stop twice for food, but otherwise, we will run through the night."

A few of the women grimaced, but they all agreed.

"Here." Alida tossed Vayme a bundle of fabric, and he caught it easily. "So Kaelle doesn't have to hold her arm around her breasts for the next two days." She winked at me. "I'm sure there's a story there, but we don't have time to hear it."

My face warmed a bit. "Thank you."

"She speaks!" Alida exclaimed.

My face warmed further.

"Do not mock my female," Vayme growled. "We may need your protection, but I will not accept cruelty toward her."

Alida's lips curved wickedly. "Your female?"

"Until the eclipse, yes." The king's voice slipped back into its typical stony neutral.

I ducked behind a tree to slip the dress over my head, and when I smoothed it out, found that it fit better than I expected. My own curves were thickening as my body grew healthier, making me closer to the shape of the elves than the fae.

It was made of a soft, filmy fabric with a higher neckline than I usually wore around the fae, and didn't have sleeves. Though I liked the gray-ish-blue color of it, I found that I missed the soft fluttering of the fae-style sleeves around my arms.

I did like that the undergarments were built into it, though. That certainly made things a bit simpler.

The elves were climbing onto the backs of the esu as I stepped out from behind the tree. Two of the elf women shifted into wolf forms, which surprised me, but Vayme murmured to me that Alida and one of the ex-queens were sisters, and both were half shifter.

My king hauled me onto Strong's back after a long, lingering look at my figure, and my cheeks heated again when I felt his hardness against my ass.

Strong slipped into the forest, and picked up speed as the esu caught him.

We ran, and ran, and ran.

Despite my prior dislike for travel, I found myself not minding the endless journey when it meant Vayme held me so close.

A day and a half later, we reached Jirev again.

Exhaustion flooded every line of my body, but I was still upright, so I counted it as a victory.

The smallest hints of my magic had started to return too, which was a good sign.

Vayme, the elves, and I met the other kings at the center of Jirev. The jungle had filled with fae as we wove through the city, and the mood was far more solemn than it had been before we left. Nissa and Laeli weren't with the other men, which worried me.

While the elves divided themselves into three groups, Kier and Ravv filled Vayme in on what had happened while we were gone.

Kier had apparently admitted the truth about the kings' mate bonds, and the assassins hunting them. I could tell that worried Vayme by the stiffness in his shoulders, though he didn't voice it.

When I asked him mentally to find out what happened to Nissa and Laeli, he didn't hesitate to ask how the other humans were. Both other kings glanced at me as they told him the women were fine, and I relaxed a bit knowing all three of us had made it out alright.

"Do we have time to stop and see my friends?" I asked Vayme, as he slipped onto Strong's back again.

"Unfortunately, no. I won't know the threat my people pose to either of us until I've had time to speak with a few fae I trust. We need to get out of Jirev

quickly to make sure my enemies can't attack here. An attack now could break the tentative peace, and we cannot risk that."

I nodded.

"We'll visit again as soon as we can." He paused, and reluctantly said, *"Or I suppose we can stop in on the way back to the Human Lands."*

My stomach tightened at the thought of returning to my cave alone.

Of starving, and being confined to my tiny home.

Of stepping away from the freedom I'd gained.

I said nothing, because I wasn't sure how to respond aloud. Or how to process my emotions about it.

Luckily, Vayme was too concerned with the possibility of an incoming attack to notice my silence.

After a quick stop in the castle to grab our things and change our clothes, we headed out so he could gather his people.

CHAPTER TEN

KAELLE

I remained quiet on Strong's back while Vayme spoke with a group of his fae. My fingers tightened in the xuno's fur when he had a conversation with Kee, the woman who had made her desire for him clear in our room a few weeks earlier, but I didn't say anything.

Vayme and I still weren't really mates, even if we felt desire for each other.

Within a few hours, we were on our way to Vuuth, traveling through the Endless Wilds once again. The wind on my skin as Strong ran calmed me, and my own breeze's drain on my power was really slight.

Traveling with a large group of fae was surprisingly simple, since they were all bonded to xuno. We moved almost as quickly as we had while traveling alone, though my eyes continuously trailed over the fae and xuno in front of us. We were at the back of the group for our own safety, Vayme had said.

The elves remained near the back with us, and I found my gaze tracing over the three ex-queens who had stuck with us, including the one in wolf form. She looked much like a xuno, though she was a little sleeker, and her fur was the same shade of black as her hair. Even her glittering golden markings remained while she was in her wolf form.

By the time we stopped for the night, I could barely keep my eyes open. I leaned up against a tree with Strong curled in front of me, protecting me as he slept, while Vayme spoke with some of his fae.

The elves with us plopped down near me, looking just as exhausted as I felt.

The one with the pink hair rubbed some dirt off her cheek and murmured, "Can you turn up that wind, Kaelle?"

My lips curved upward a bit. "I can try."

I focused on my emotions—namely, the fear that I might die in the Endless Wilds—and the breeze picked up a little. Its response wasn't quite what I hoped it would be, but I was still recovering from that burnout. A little sleep would get me back to normal, I thought.

The pink-haired elf groaned in bliss, and I heard a few other fae echo the sound among Vayme's group.

"Are you alright?" he asked me, his voice alert.

"I'm fine. The elves just wanted to cool off a little."

"Good."

His mind slipped away from mine as he focused on what he was doing.

"Thank you." The pink-haired elf flashed me a small, tired smile. "I'm Ismaray. This is Orah and Meeri." She gestured first to the dark-haired elf, and then the golden-haired one.

"It's nice to meet you," I said, the words honest.

"Likewise." She brushed a little more dirt off her face. "Any idea how long this trip is going to be?"

"Let me ask Vayme." I repeated the question into his mind.

"We have two and a half days left. We'll reach the Weeping Skies tomorrow night, then we have a half-day trek through the Skies, and a whole day of travel through the caves before we reach Vuuth."

I repeated his answer, and the golden-haired elf, Meeri, grimaced.

Orah, the dark-haired one, leaned back against a tree and closed her eyes, resting. She'd spent both journeys in her wolf form, so she had to be even more exhausted than I was.

Ismaray pulled some crackers and dried fruit out of her bag, and made the other two women take some before passing them to me too. I thanked her and nibbled on the food, eating slowly to ease my stomach back into it after so much traveling.

Vayme returned while we ate, and he made me take more crackers and fruit from him. The elves' tasted different, so I didn't mind the variety.

When we were done eating, Vayme and I climbed into a shelter together.

"Are you sure we can sleep next to each other without making your people suspicious that there's more to our bond than survival?" I asked him.

"My people are already suspicious of that. I don't trust them any more than they trust me right now, so I won't let you sleep out of my sight."

I supposed there was no way to argue against that. Not if I wanted to survive the night, which I most certainly did.

So, I stayed quiet as I settled down against Vayme. His hand rested on my hip again while my head rested on his shoulder, and the quiet intimacy made my chest burn, though I didn't voice that.

"What if your people try to kill me?" I asked him quietly.

"Even those who hate me the most know that would risk their lives right now," he murmured back. *"The news spread widely that you're hiding me from the Monster. If you were to die, your magic would stop protecting mine, and the Monster would follow us to Vuuth. Their plan with the assassins hinged on me dying in Jirev."*

I nodded lightly.

That was good, I supposed.

"If that doesn't stop them and they still hunt you, I will relish the chance to send them through the veil. You are safe with me," he added.

I drifted off to sleep soon after, and despite everything, I did feel safe.

. . .

The rest of the journey unfolded exactly the way Vayme had said it would.

We spent the next day in the Wilds. The day after that, we were in the mountains of the Weeping Skies until lunch. After a quick meal of strange fruit that grew despite the ice and snow in the Skies, we slipped into a well-hidden entrance to the icy caves that stretched below the mountains.

My curious gaze followed the shapes and lines of the caves. They were far more beautiful than the one I'd lived in, a mixture of stone and ice that looked more like art than structure. Some of the caves had glittering walls and ceilings that made me stare in wonder as we passed them, and I noticed a few bubbling pools within them.

Though the caves smelled more of salt than my previous home, there was still a warm comfort to being underground that seemed to calm my soul. My fear eased as we continued, and my awe grew as I saw more of the beauty beneath the land's surface.

Why would anyone have chosen to live in the sweaty, hot Wilds when there were gorgeous caves beneath the Weeping Skies they could claim?

I definitely understood Vayme's preference for being underground.

We spent that night in the caves, and then the entire next day, too.

I felt more comfortable the further we were from the surface. I knew there was still danger in Vuuth, but I would always feel more secure hidden away from the world above.

When we finally reached Vuuth, I was so exhausted that it took me a minute to process what I was seeing.

The tunnel leading into the city was wide enough for three xuno and their riders to fit side-by-side. It opened up into a monstrous space that stretched as far as I could see. Veil, no, it stretched *farther* than I could see.

The city was shaped like an upside-down dome, growing lower in the center and higher on the outside edges. I could see stairs everywhere—grand staircases, and simple ones, too. Some of them were made of ice, but most were crafted from various shades and types of stone.

Down at the center of the city, deep in the lowest part, I could see a large formation protruding from the ground. It looked like a sculpture of some kind, but I couldn't make out what it was from where I stood.

My gaze followed the sculpture up, and up, until my eyes landed on the glowing stones above our heads that stretched above the city. They radiated light like the stars would've if they were on the surface.

"You like it?" Vayme asked me, his grip light on my hips.

"Veil, yes," I breathed, still stunned by everything I was seeing.

"This is only the top portion. The city stretches much further beneath the surface."

My eyes widened further.

Strong picked up the pace again, heading down one of the grander staircases as if he'd done it thousands of times.

He probably had.

It took some time for him to make it down to the statue that marked the castle's location, but when he neared it, my gaze scanned the shapes and curves of the large ice sculpture. It was...

"A sword?" I asked Vayme. *"Why?"*

"We are warriors, and we always will be," he said simply. *"And while it takes strength to wield a sword, it also takes wisdom to know when to put it down. The sword in the sculpture faces downward, to remind us that sometimes, it's better not to raise our weapons."*

I liked that, honestly.

The castle was built beneath the statue, and was far larger than I'd realized from above.

Strong made his way down a few more massive staircases. A handful of fae that Vayme told me lived in the castle led the elves to their rooms and headed to their own, branching off when they reached the right level.

All of them were gone when we reached a smaller, more private set of stairs. We spiraled downward until I couldn't see another staircase— and hoped I never would.

I looked around as we passed small, branched-off rooms connected to the large foyer area we were in. I couldn't see inside them at our speed, but I hoped I'd be able to look around later. Usually, I wasn't an incredibly curious person, but I supposed a lot about me was changing as I adjusted to being around the fae.

"This is my wing of the castle. It holds the king and queen's room, library, baths, kitchen, and armory. There are extra rooms for their children or trusted allies to occupy, as well. A few unmated and unbonded xuno guard the space, so you will always be safe here. The only other fae allowed in are Matían and Pavia, and they have their own rooms here right now," Vayme explained as Strong ran.

That made me feel more curious, too. I was looking forward to meeting the brother and niece that had apparently turned much of Vayme's kingdom against him.

Strong plopped down on his belly in a large bedroom that held a massive bed, along with a shower that had no walls to hide its occupant. There was a closet and a bathroom, as well, but otherwise, it was empty.

A few of the crystals I'd seen above the city littered the ceiling, glowing just enough to make me feel like I was looking up at the stars rather than a sheet of rock.

The walls and floor were gray stone, and the blankets on the bed were black, thick, and soft-looking. I itched to feel them on my legs, but assumed I'd get my own room. The masculine feel of the one we were in made me think it was definitely Vayme's.

The king helped me off Strong's back, and the xuno wasted no time before climbing onto Vayme's bed and promptly falling asleep.

My lips curved upward as the sound of him snoring slowly filled the air.

"I'll show you to your room," Vayme said into my mind, his voice a bit quieter than I expected. When I glanced at him, I found him already striding away from me, and I had to hurry to catch up.

Those legs of his were too damn long.

He still had his bag on his back, and led me across the large, open area that I'd assumed was a foyer of some kind. Upon closer inspection, it seemed to be some sort of a huge, rectangular sitting space.

We passed a handful of couches and large cushions. I noticed a xuno passed out on one of them, and when my gaze skimmed the room, I found another beast on a different cushion, watching the area directly in front of the staircase.

I hadn't noticed the xuno guarding the stairs, so that scared me a little. Its glowing eyes met mine from across the room, and the barely-blue of them reminded me of my own aura. Something about the energy felt feminine, and sent a slight tingle up my spine.

I looked away from her as we slipped into a bedroom half the size of Vayme's. It was otherwise identical to his, with the same exposed shower, bathroom, and closet, though the blankets on the bed were a crisp white color.

"Why are there so many rooms if this is your space?" I asked Vayme, wrapping my arms around my abdomen to steady myself in my uncertainty.

It felt strange to have him place me in my own room, entirely alone again. I enjoyed my own company, but... I didn't think I wanted to be alone anymore. I'd had enough of that in my cave.

"One of the earliest ruling couples had many children." He slipped into my closet and hung the dresses he'd gotten for me in Jirev, before dipping his head toward me slightly. *"Sleep well, Tempest."*

Receiving nothing but a nod made me feel even more uncertain.

But I nodded back, not wanting him to realize what I was feeling.

He closed the door as he left, giving me a quiet mental command to lock it, and I reluctantly did so.

With the bond between us silenced, and my room empty other than me, I let my gaze scan the space again. It lingered on the bed, but I suddenly found myself feeling a bit restless.

And a lot uncertain, honestly.

I'd started to think Vayme and I had something of a connection, and more than just because of our mate bond. He was attracted to me, and I was attracted to him.

But that didn't mean anything to him, so I supposed it shouldn't mean anything to me either. Our bond would still break with the eclipse, and we were safe in the king's wing of the castle, so there was nothing to worry about.

Or at least, I *hoped* there was nothing to worry about.

Other than the Monster of the Aching Chasm.

And the fact that his people wanted us dead.

Nope; nothing to worry about at all.

I huffed out a nearly-silent laugh and slipped out of my dirty dress, striding over to the shower. If I was too lost in my emotions to sleep, I may as well get myself clean before I climbed into bed.

Though the water felt only lukewarm, it was nice to scrub the dirt off my skin. There was no soap in the bathroom, but I'd survive without soap.

That was another thing I was uncertain about returning to in my cave, though; the filth. Being on constant alert about the amount of water in my buckets, and having only a few splashes of it to clean myself with every day was worrisome. I had never enjoyed that part of cave-living, but I wasn't sure I could manage it after being so clean for so long.

I pushed that thought away and scrubbed my hair before turning the water off. After drying myself with a soft, white towel I found hanging nearby, I slipped out of the shower.

Since there was no one around, I didn't bother putting any clothing on. There was no comb for my hair in the bathroom, so I left it in its awkward tangles as I tucked myself into the bed. My wind still danced over my skin, but it was light and gentle in a familiar way that relaxed me.

It felt strange to go to sleep without Vayme in the room, but I still found my lips curving upward as I stared at the ceiling of the cave. Despite everything, I felt safe again.

Safe, and comfortable too.

I fell asleep with a smile on my face, cuddling up with a squishy pillow that was a poor replacement for a muscular fae king, but good enough that it didn't keep me awake.

CHAPTER ELEVEN
KAELLE

I woke with an ache in the handprint on my hip that let me know Vayme had left me. I wasn't sure how large the king's portion of the castle was, but it couldn't have been large enough for the distance to cause me that much pain.

Slipping out of bed, I stopped in the bathroom to use the facilities, and found myself staring at my reflection in the mirror.

I had avoided looking closely in Jirev, and it had been a week since I'd really had the chance, on top of that.

But veil, I was different.

When I first got to Jirev, I had been gaunt and breakable. Now, I looked... healthy. Strong. My curves had filled in, and my face had too.

My hair, of course, was a wreck of blue tangles since I hadn't been able to comb it after washing it, but I even seemed to have grown into the color.

I stepped back a bit so I could see more of myself, and looked at the curve of my ass, the fullness of my breasts, and the softness of my belly.

Veil.

I was... beautiful.

Soft, curvy, and beautiful.

Not because of my family, or because of my cave.

Because of Vayme.

Vayme, who wasn't even interested in staying mated to me.

If his attention could lead me to grow so much stronger, what would a male who really wanted to be with me do?

Or what could I do, if I was in a position to take care of myself?

I stood up a bit straighter and headed to the closet, deciding I was going to learn how to do just that.

I was dangerous, but that didn't mean I couldn't live successfully. If anything, my power made me more capable, not less.

After a stop in the closet to slip my clothes on, I headed out of the room.

It was time to find a comb.

I managed one step outside the door before I halted.

There was a little girl with light skin and bright white hair laying on the floor right outside my door. Her chin was propped on her hands as she stared up at me with soulful, glowing, ice-blue eyes.

I stared back at her.

Her magic was death, wasn't it?

Her aura was as white as her hair, but teeming with life, strangely enough.

I fought the urge to take a step back, not wanting her to think I was afraid of her. Because I wasn't... I just didn't want to die.

"Pavia?" I asked, forcing my voice to remain calm.

She bobbed her head. "Who are you?"

Vayme hadn't said anything about me?

Great.

It wasn't as if I could tell a little girl I was her uncle's temporary mate, or that he and I were attracted to each other, but were absolutely nothing else to one another. She was young, and she had grown up human, so I wasn't even sure she knew what a mate was.

"Vayme's friend," I said. "Do you know where he went?"

She shrugged, remaining where she was on the floor.

"Is Strong still here?" I asked, trying again.

She shook her head *no*.

"Pavia?" A low, masculine voice that reminded me of Vayme's called from another room.

I froze.

That had to be his brother, didn't it? If Vayme was close enough to call for his niece, there wouldn't have been pain in my hip.

"In here," she called back.

I tried to step into my room again, but a large, masculine figure entered the sitting area before I could make my escape.

Unlike his brother's, his aura was a peaceful gray color.

My eyes widened as I took him in. The man looked so similar to Vayme —insanely similar. Their noses and eyebrows were shaped slightly different, but otherwise, they may as well have been identical.

He blinked at me.

I blinked back.

"Who are you?" Vayme's brother finally asked.

I didn't know how to answer him any more than I had his daughter. "Kaelle." There was a pause before I asked, "Where's Vayme?"

"I don't know. He didn't wake me when he left." The man eyed me. "Or arrived."

"You missed a lot, then." I let out an unsteady breath and brushed hair from my eyes. My tangled hair was the one thing I could tackle, and I needed to, since I was getting hit in the face by my own tangles. "Do you know if he has a comb?"

I knew the question was stupid as soon as it escaped me.

"A comb?" the man repeated.

"Yes, a comb. It's fine; I don't need it. I'll be fine." I tried to step back into my room.

"I have a comb!" Pavia stood suddenly. "I like your blue hair. You can borrow it!"

With that, she disappeared, moving faster than any human I'd ever seen.

Maybe she was only half-fae, but that half was definitely a boost above us humans.

"What are you to my brother?" Matían asked, still looking slightly suspicious.

"It's a long story." I sagged against the doorway, still fighting the urge to disappear back into my room. So much for the confidence I'd gathered. "I'm sure he'll tell you when he gets back from... wherever he is."

Part of me itched to reach out to Vayme, to find out where he was, but I didn't want to bother him. If he'd really wanted me to know where he was going, he would've said something.

"You could tell me," Matían said.

I supposed the basics of our situation were common knowledge. And if I wanted to be independent, it would be good for me to practice sharing what I knew with someone I didn't know. It was technically my information to share, anyway.

I lowered my voice. "Vayme is being hunted by the Monster of the Aching Chasm. Alida, one of the elven leaders, sent him to find me because my magic is life-based. I was human—I *am* human," I said quickly. "We're mated, just until the eclipse, so my magic will keep hiding his from the Monster's. There are elves with us now too, to protect the city in case he comes after Vayme."

Matían blinked.

"I've got the comb!" Pavia skidded to a stop in front of me, her eyes bright and happy. "Here." She shoved it at me, and I took it.

"Thank you. My hair is so tangled after traveling, I hope I don't lose this comb in it," I said softly, flashing her a quick smile.

She giggled. "I can find it for you if you lose it. Or my dad can; he's really good at combing." Her gaze jerked to him, and I saw the mischief in it. "Maybe he can comb it for you."

"Pavia," Matían warned.

"She's nice!" Pavia protested.

He groaned and shook his head.

Something told me he was fighting the urge to tell her that I belonged to his brother—if just temporarily.

"That's okay, I'm quite adept at combing myself." I winked at her and started on the tangles to prove my point.

Her smile returned. "Will you go see the xuno with me? I'm looking for a companion. My dad says it takes time to find the right one."

I glanced at her dad, and he answered for me. "Kaelle would have to ask Uncle Vayme if it's safe first. He might want to go with her."

She shot him a curious look. "Why?"

"Because she's his friend." He brushed the back of her hair lightly, far more gently than I would've expected from such a large man.

Vayme had proven himself gentler than I expected on a few occasions, too.

"His other friends don't ask him to go places," she pointed out.

Matían nodded slowly. "You're right."

She frowned. "Then why does Kaelle have to ask?"

When he didn't answer, she looked at me.

"It's a long story," I told her honestly. "Too long, if you want to make it to the xuno."

I didn't know how long it would take to get to the xuno, but I knew I could drag the story out for a good long while if I needed to.

She heaved a sigh. "Alright. You'll tell me later though?" Her gaze was expectant.

Veil, it was no wonder she had the city wrapped around her finger. She was damned adorable, and persistent too.

"I think that's probably up to your uncle and your dad. If they say so, yes."

She huffed. "They're too careful."

My lips curved upward. "On that, we agree."

She started to throw her arms around me for a hug, but froze before she reached me. I tried really, really hard not to shrink away from her, but veil, I was terrified she might kill me. She looked at her dad. "Is it safe? Will I hurt her?"

His gaze was uncertain as he looked at me. "How human are you?"

"Entirely. But Vayme's magic is in my veins."

He grew reluctant. "Better not, Pav. Just to be safe."

She sighed and peered up at me. "Sorry. I'm dangerous."

The simplicity of the apology and the lack of guilt in her voice struck me. I crouched down in front of her and said quietly, "I'm dangerous too."

She frowned. "But you said you're human."

"Some of us have magic."

Her frown deepened. "What's your power?"

"Look at my hair." I pointed toward the detangled strands, moving lightly in my breeze.

She studied them for a moment before her eyes widened. "You're blowing."

I had to bite back a smile at her description. "My power is wind magic. When I get scared or angry, I sometimes make storms."

"You *are* dangerous," she agreed. But she didn't say it like it was bad—she said it like it was amazing. "We're friends, even if I can't touch you," she declared. "The xuno miss me though, so we have to go. Bye!" With that, she ran out of the room.

Matían's gaze scanned the open space for a moment before he said to me, "You'll be safe down here. And you can reach out to Vayme if you need him, right?"

"Right," I confirmed.

"We'll try not to be gone too long. There's food in the kitchen, and there are books in the library if you're bored."

"Thank you."

He dipped his head in a nod, then left the same way Pavia had.

Alone again, I tried to remember what I had been about to figure out before I ran into them...

Independence.

Yay.

I looked to my left and right, trying to determine where I should go. While I was definitely hungry, I could also use a shower with some soap.

Deciding I'd stop in the kitchen to find food first, I headed out.

It took a few minutes, and a lot of peeking into doorways, but I found it without too much hassle. The kitchen was much larger than the one in my parents' house growing up, and it had a large icebox, which I knew was to keep food from spoiling so quickly. We'd had one about the size of my head when I was a kid, but the one in Vayme's kitchen was at least as big as two of me. Maybe even three of me.

The dining room seemed to be connected to said kitchen, with a few tables set up in the room. That also reminded me of my childhood home, which put me at ease.

I found some fruit in the icebox, and while I itched to eat some of the larger, more involved meals in there, I didn't want to anger anyone.

So, I took the fruit and sat down.

Everything was so quiet while I ate, it was almost a bit bizarre. I'd grown used to the noise of Jirev, and the constant wind of traveling, so the silence was strange.

Strange, but not unpleasantly so.

A few xuno walked past the open doorway while I ate, and while most gave me curious looks, none of them said anything. As she passed, my gaze lingered on the female xuno with the blue eyes who I'd seen the night before.

Something about her and her aura felt... important. I didn't know why, but it did.

I finished my fruit, then headed out to look for soap.

As I explored, I only found a few rooms on the whole floor with closed doors. Three, to be precise. It seemed safe to assume the two that didn't belong to Vayme belonged to Matían and Pavia.

I closed the door to my own room again as I passed it, just because the other three had.

The only soap I found in any of the rooms with open doors was in the bathing chamber, so I made my way back there when my exploration was done. There was no lock, so I simply left it closed.

No one else was around, anyway.

I stripped my clothes off as I looked at everything a bit more closely.

The bathing room had multiple pools in it, all of them much larger than the one in our room in Jirev. The ceiling was encrusted with some sort of glowing jewels that bathed everything in gorgeous color and moody light. They were a bit different than the ones I'd seen in the bedrooms, and above Vuuth, but equally beautiful.

I noticed steam coming off two pools at the far end of the room, and stopped to dip my toe in each of them to test the temperatures.

The baths grew hotter as I went further, and I found myself grinning at the blissful heat of the hottest one. It had been so long since I'd felt warm water that I likely could've spent all day in it.

Slowly, I sank into the heat, groaning again as it engulfed me. There was a small shelf near each bath with its own bar of soap on it, so after a few moments of soaking and relaxing, I grabbed the soap and started to scrub the dirt from my skin.

As I finished washing my hair and simply sat back to enjoy the beauty and peace of the room, I finally admitted a small, quiet truth to myself:

I would likely never want to leave Vuuth.

Not if the alternative was going back to my cave and spending the rest of my days starving, filthy, and alone.

Maybe I should have taken Pavia up on her offer to let Matían comb my hair after all; truly mating with a fae for love would be the best way to guarantee that I wouldn't get kicked out of Vuuth.

And I knew Vayme well enough to be sure his brother was a decent man, at the very least.

Then again, mating could get me murdered. And considering the king's possessiveness, flirting with his brother while I was mated to him would likely cause drama.

So... I wasn't sure how I was going to earn myself a place to stay.

I rinsed the bubbles from my hair and then gathered all of it into a bundle on the top of my head, closing my eyes and relaxing against the back of the pool.

Veil, maybe I would simply refuse to leave Vayme's bathing pool, and see what came of it.

CHAPTER TWELVE
VAYME

I slid off Strong's back, slipping my pack off my shoulders and striding to Kaelle's door.

There had been no choice but to leave long enough to announce my temporary mate bond to the fae who had remained in Vuuth. I also had to fight a few fae who challenged me for the throne in response, so I'd picked up a few things for my female as an apology for the pain in her handprint.

Grabbing a shirt had seemed like a necessity, so I could hide the bruises and cuts on my torso, as well.

I knocked on her door, then waited for an answer.

Silence was all that greeted me.

She couldn't still be sleeping, could she?

With a frown, I pushed lightly against the door, to make sure it was still locked.

It swung open without pause.

I stepped inside and looked around the space.

My female was gone.

My body tensed, and my gaze jerked back to the sitting area.

"She's in the baths," one of the xuno told me, apparently seeing my panic.

"Thank you." I walked to the bathing area and reached for the door, then paused.

Where were Matían and Pavia?

An image flashed in my mind—an image of my brother's body pressed to my female's.

Rage boiled inside me, and I saw red as I shoved into the room.

Kaelle's surprised gaze jerked to me from where she sat in the hottest of the pools. Her hair was piled on her head, sweat rolling down her neck and over the swell of her breasts.

My cock hardened at the sight.

She didn't try to cover herself in my presence, which only made me harder.

"What's wrong?" she asked me.

I blinked, my rage vanishing upon finding her both safe and alone. "Nothing's wrong."

She lifted an eyebrow. "You *stormed* into the room."

My jaw clenched at the reminder of the damn thoughts in my head. "Where's Matían?"

"Pavia wanted to go see the xuno, so they're wherever they would go for that." Her face was red due to the heat, but her expression was serene, and so damn beautiful my body ached.

I bit my cheek, hard, to stop myself from asking whether he had flirted with her.

She eyed me. "I told him about our mate bond. Hopefully that's okay."

Relief relaxed my shoulders.

My brother was an ass at times, but he would know better than to show interest in the woman I was mated to, even temporarily.

"Of course. The whole kingdom knows."

She nodded. "I wasn't sure how to explain it to Pavia, so she just thinks you and I are friends."

"Friends is fine." I slid my bag off my shoulder. "I know I'm late, but I brought you breakfast."

Her eyes lit up. "Really? Thank you."

She started to stand, but if her bare, wet body was exposed to me, I wasn't sure I'd be able to stop myself from touching her. "You can eat there," I said quickly, the words coming out gruffer than I intended. "I'll bring it to you."

The peaks of her nipples were barely above the water before she sank back in.

Veil, the urge to take them in my mouth was nearly overwhelming.

"Perfect." She flashed me a smile, and I walked to her side, sitting down next to the pool to pull food from my bag. "You could join me in here, if you want?"

Veil.

"The steaming pools aren't usually used for bathing," I said, focusing on the food as I opened the thick paper box of food I'd brought back for her.

"Why not? What are they used for?"

I tried not to let my thoughts wander to the nights I'd retreated to the pool in an effort to get my mind off whatever misery I'd dealt with during the day.

My voice was strained as I said, "Some fae find that the pain of the heat enhances their pleasure."

She blinked.

If her face hadn't already been red, something told me she would be blushing fiercely.

"I imagine it feels hotter for us than it does you, as my magic is only partly tangled in yours," I added.

"Oh," she finally said.

I wasn't even sure if she knew how to bring herself to climax, let alone had ever imagined the extent of the intense sex lives many of the fae pursued.

Silently, I cut her a piece of the massive pastry I had brought her. I hadn't stopped to eat, but I would wait until she was full to fill my own belly.

She took the utensil from me and wrapped her lips around it. Her eyes fluttered as she groaned at the taste, and I fought a smirk of victory.

I'd known she would like it.

"That is incredible," she said, after swallowing the food and handing the utensil back.

I reloaded it and handed it back to her, relieved we were past the previous discussion.

Silence lingered in the air as I continued to feed her, itching to be the one to put the food in her mouth myself. Instead, I let her do it, knowing she wouldn't take kindly to more help.

"Are you one of them?" she finally asked me.

"One of what?"

"The fae who find that hot water enhances their pleasure."

I stilled.

My cock strained against the seam of my pants.

"If you expect me to give you answers like that, you'll have to give me some of your own," I finally said, handing her another bite.

"Alright. Ask me something."

Veil.

She was going to be the death of me.

The curiosity in her eyes wasn't just curiosity—it was a sign she was growing more comfortable with me. It certainly hadn't happened overnight, and I wouldn't allow myself to do anything to make her self-conscious again.

"Have you brought yourself to climax before?" I asked.

"Yes." She took the bite and handed it back. "Your turn."

My eyes narrowed at her, and she bit her lip to stop herself from smiling.

"Tempest," I warned.

"You said we'd trade answers. It's not my fault you asked such a simple question." A strand of her hair slipped free of the rest, and she tucked it back up in the wet, twisted bun. "Does hot water enhance your pleasure?"

"At times," I said, a bit reluctantly.

Her eyes gleamed. "How often?" They widened, and the gleam faded. "And how many women have you brought here?" Suddenly, she was looking around the pool with an expression of illness.

It was my turn to ask her a question, but I couldn't leave her with whatever thoughts raced through her mind. "I've never brought a woman here, and I only use the pools for that purpose once every few months."

She let out a long, relieved breath.

"How do you bring yourself to climax?" I asked her, choosing my words more carefully. "And how frequently?"

Her eyes narrowed at me. "I didn't ask *you* for details."

"It's not my fault you asked such a simple question," I said, mimicking her reply.

She huffed at me, though it looked like she was trying to hide a smile again. "I was bored in the cave. I did it... probably once a day. Except during the eclipses, of course. I'm sure you can imagine how frequently I did it then." Her response was reluctant, and her eyes lowered to the pool as she considered her answer to the second question.

I handed her the utensil again, and she took another bite before finally speaking.

Her voice was soft, when she did. "I would usually lie on my back, on my bed. Now, I realize how uncomfortable it was, but it was the most comfortable part of my cave. I would slip my hand between my thighs and work myself until I climaxed, letting my mind wander to the things I'd read."

My cock throbbed at the mental image she painted for me, of her on her back in that cave, sweating and crying out in pleasure.

Otherwise, I forced myself not to react.

"Have you touched yourself since we met?" I asked her.

She met my gaze and wordlessly shook her head. "Have you?"

"Once. In the shower, while you slept." I'd wanted to many, many more times, but we were rarely apart. And when we were, I was always doing something with my damned fae.

"What did you picture?"

I was still worried about scaring her away, but lying to her would only hurt her. "You," I finally said.

Her eyes narrowed at me. "I'll need more details than that."

The mental images flooded me at her reminder, and I pushed them toward our bond. Her eyes flew open as the image of her with her thighs open, my face buried between them as she cried out in bliss, filled her mind too.

"Veil," she breathed, her chest rising and falling rapidly, dragging my attention back to the swell of her breasts. "How many women have you been with?"

My gaze snapped to hers, my forehead furrowed. "Why would that matter?"

Her eyes were a bit dazed, and hooded, too. "It doesn't. I just want to know. Have you had sex with anyone since our bond started?"

"Of course not," I growled. "To ask that is to question my honor, Tempest. Only the worst of males would consider sharing his bed with another female while mated, even temporarily."

"I'm sorry. I didn't know." She reached up and retwisted her hair, as it had started falling. "I—" she hesitated, and stopped herself.

I hadn't meant to scare her into self-consciousness again. I appreciated her comfort far too much for that.

"I'm not sure how many women I've been with," I admitted, reloading my utensil with another bite and handing it to her. She slowly took it. "It's been a few hundred years since I've shared a bed with someone, and it's rare for me to think back to those times in the past."

Her eyes went wide. "A few hundred years? Why?"

"I spent a few decades taking my pleasure any way I wanted it—so long as the other person consented, of course. It grew dull and unappealing, so I stopped. If I need a release, I can get myself there easily enough. Sex is selfish for fae, and for me, there was little satisfaction in sharing someone's bed simply to take my own pleasure."

Her expression grew understanding. "Before my magic came in, my mother spoke to me about sex a few times. It embarrassed me, but she wanted me to know what to expect so I could protect myself in case anyone in town tried anything. She told me that the greatest joy in sex was to see the pleasure of the one you love."

The idea was fascinating, truthfully.

Fae women gave the commands for the most part, when it came to sex. A male followed a female's commands until she reached her climax, and then did what he wanted until he took his. Neither worried about each other, or particularly cared how the other felt.

To be in a relationship where your own pleasure wasn't what mattered most would be something entirely different.

"You're looking at me strangely," Kaelle said, leaning over to steal another bite of the massive pastry I'd brought her.

"I'm thinking."

"Okay." She continued eating while my gaze lingered on her, my thoughts moving slowly but comfortably.

What if I had a life-partner or mate who would allow me to bring her pleasure the way I wanted to, as frequently as I wanted to? What if I had a female who would touch me or taste me, simply because she wanted to see my reaction?

Veil, it would be a different life.

A different *world*.

A world where I dragged my female into closets to ravage her with my mouth between the endless meetings I was forced to attend.

A world where I could sit her on my lap and touch her beneath my table during those endless meetings.

A world where I could come home to a woman who meant everything to me. One where she would see the exhaustion in my shoulders and take it upon herself to talk to me, to taste me, to sit on my cock simply because she wanted to make my day better and trusted me to bring her pleasure.

To share my life with someone in that way would be... glorious.

"Did you already eat?" Kaelle asked me a few minutes later, pulling me from my thoughts.

"What?"

She repeated the question, and I shook my head. "I planned to eat after I knew you were full."

She shot me a curious look. "Why? We could eat together."

The words struck me.

I didn't *have* to be alone.

Perhaps I had already found the woman who would be my perfect life-partner. Kaelle was softening to me, and besides that, she was gentle and kind. She had suffered more than most of us could imagine, despite the short number of years she had lived, yet it hadn't made her cruel or harsh.

And she wanted the same kind of relationship I had just realized I wanted.

"By my count, you owe me three answers," I finally said to her.

"Alright." She took another bite. "I'll only answer them if you're going to eat too, though."

I reached back into my bag and pulled out my box of food. When I opened it, her mouth nearly watered at the sight of the savory, fragrant food she had never eaten before.

Setting it down between us, I pulled out my own utensil and filled it, taking an emphatic bite.

Her lips curved upward, and she took one of her own.

I was still worried about scaring her, but I didn't think we would progress if I didn't push her a little. "If I were to ask to slide into the water with you and bring you to climax with my fingers, what would your response be? Theoretically, of course."

Her eyes went wide. "Theoretically, I would say yes."

My cock throbbed. "And if I were to ask you to slide out of the water and spread your thighs for me so I could taste you?"

"Still theoretically?" she whispered.

"Of course." I took another bite, though food was the furthest thing from my mind.

"Theoretically, I would slide out of the water and spread my thighs for you." Her voice was soft, and a bit wobbly.

My cock throbbed again, harder.

"And if I were to tell you to show me how you bring yourself pleasure?" I asked.

"I would tell you to show me how you climax first."

I was going to lose control in my damn pants if she talked to me like that.

Forcing myself not to react visibly, I filled my mouth to stop myself from growling an order for her to get out and prove it.

Kaelle opened her mouth to say something, but before she could, the door to the bathing rooms burst open and my niece came barreling in, hollering, "Uncle Vayme! I missed you so much!"

She crashed into me, and I caught her with a grunt, hiding my damn erection with an arm. My brother stepped into the room behind her, and I fought the possessive tension swelling within me. "I missed you too, Pav."

She heaved a sigh. "I still didn't convince one of the xuno to bond with me."

"It'll happen when the time is right." I gave her a quick squeeze, and my gaze lifted to Matían.

When I found his eyes trained on the ceiling, mine jerked back to Kaelle, who had sunk lower in the water so just the tops of her shoulders were showing.

I fought a snarl at the thought that my brother might have seen more of my female. Fae were comfortable with nudity, but I couldn't stand the idea of him seeing my mate bare.

"Give me a moment with my friend, and we'll meet you outside," I told Pavia, squeezing her lightly before releasing her.

"Alright. Hi, Kaelle!" She waved at my *friend* before running out of the baths, and Matían wisely left with her.

"I'll install a lock on the door," I told her, taking another bite of my food before closing the lid on both boxes and stacking them.

"Probably a good idea." She eased herself to a standing position, and my gaze lingered on her figure before she turned and slipped out of the water.

Her bare ass was nearly as nice to look at as her breasts, but my gaze lingered on the handprint on her hip. Something about seeing the mark of my palm on her skin was intensely satisfying.

As she dried off, her back still facing me, Kaelle said quietly, "You should probably know, Pavia suggested Matían comb my hair for me earlier. She told him I could make him happy. She obviously doesn't know about our connection, so it was nothing against you—but she might suggest something like that again, and I don't think you want to be surprised by it."

My anger surged.

Not at my niece, but at my damn brother. I knew it was ridiculous to feel that way, but veil, I couldn't help it. "Thank you for letting me know."

She nodded.

My gaze slid from my handprint to her ass again as she pulled on her undergarments and then tugged her dress over her head.

I needed to get her something... smaller.

No, not smaller.

Something with a cut out over her hip, so I could see my handprint any time I wanted.

My mind was made up as I grabbed our boxes of food and stood. "We can pick our earlier conversation up later."

She flashed me a curious look. "Can we?"

My gaze swept over the curves of her form, barely hidden by the black dress she wore. "We *will*."

Kaelle's lips curved upward, and she followed me to the door. Her breath brushed my back as she whispered, "I look forward to it."

CHAPTER THIRTEEN
KAELLE

Vayme was good with Pavia.

Very, very good with Pavia.

Though his energy level wasn't at the same fierce speed of hers, he spoke to her easily and she replied with the excitement I was coming to realize was natural for her.

I ate far too much food while she filled him in on everything that had happened while he was away. There was tension in my lower belly from the desire that had gone unsatisfied after our little interruption, but I ignored it.

Eventually, Pavia got bored of talking to Vayme and made her way over to one of the xuno. From what the little girl had said about the beast, I assumed she was Matían's companion, Wicked. Despite her name, she seemed sweet.

"What do you intend to do to keep your human alive?" Matían asked Vayme, his voice low as he gestured toward me.

"She's going to charm my people," Vayme said bluntly.

I blinked.

I *what?*

Matían gave me a skeptical look before shooting it back at Vayme. "She's not exactly... charming."

Asshole.

I hated that he was right.

"Of course she is," Vayme growled back.

I blinked again.

He was either insane or just delusional if he actually believed that.

"She has been through more than most of our people can comprehend. They might be asses, but they love Pav because of her story, and they'll love Tempest for the same reason."

"I thought her name was Kaelle." Matían shot me another skeptical look.

"It is," I said. "And where's Strong, anyway?" Maybe a subject change would fix things.

"He's been chasing a female for the past few years, and has begun trying to convince her to mate with him again," Vayme said, his gaze still on me. "Think about it. Pav lost her mother—you lost yours too."

"Because you abducted me," I tossed back.

But we both knew that wasn't really true.

He had abducted me... but I had lost my mother long before he showed up in front of that cave. I had lost her the day I created that storm, or perhaps the day she tucked me away in that cave.

Or veil, maybe I'd lost her the first time she lied about everyone not having enough food—the first time she'd starved me.

I wanted to argue that it wasn't true, that my family had taken care of me as well as they could. But I could no longer deny the healthy weight of their bodies or the way they had never even bothered to bring me water to clean my skin with.

They had lied to me over, and over, and over.

Vayme didn't disagree with me, but he didn't look away, either.

"How am I supposed to use that to charm them?" I finally asked him. "I can't just walk around telling strangers that I spent the last eight years of my life on death's doorstep in a tiny cave."

"Why can't you?"

I scowled at him.

"Think about it—didn't Laeli do exactly that? She would randomly mention her years of starvation in her cellar, and it made people feel for her."

"I'm not Laeli," I protested.

"Thankfully," Vayme agreed. "But if you happen to meet my people, and mention your past while you do, word will spread. They will look at you differently. And while it may not save my life, it could protect yours."

I heaved a sigh.

"You were starving for *eight years*?" Matían asked me, his expression entirely different.

"Yes," I admitted.

"Veil." He looked at Vayme. "You're right. It's a shitty plan, but there's a chance it might work."

"Isn't it kind of manipulative?" I asked them both.

"It is," Vayme agreed. "But my people won't be concerned with morals when they try to slaughter you, so you can't be concerned with them while you try to save your life."

I supposed if that wasn't a good enough excuse, nothing would be.

"Did you try the same thing with Pavia to stop the people who want war?" I checked.

Matían looked at Vayme. "No. Maybe we should, though."

"It couldn't hurt. I'm just not sure how we would achieve it," Vayme said. "We can't ask Pav to try to convince adult fae not to go to war."

"No." Matían drummed his fingers on the table, thinking.

"What if she took some fae with her to visit her old home?" I asked.

"No," Vayme growled, at the same time Matían said, "Out of the question. They could hurt her."

Right.

Bad idea.

"What if you sent a group of the most bloodthirsty fae to pick up some of her mother's old things? If you told them they can't start a war, but they can kill everyone who attacks them first, it would change their opinions, right?" I checked. "If fae warriors are as strong as you said, a group of them could handle a city in the Sands, I think. Why would it have to turn into another war?"

"We don't know how the rogues would respond if we took down one of their cities," Matían explained. "They could see our attack as a sign that we want war, even if we don't hurt anyone else."

"It's a long journey from the Sands to Vuuth, or even to Jirev. Without your bonded beasts, it would be even longer. The chance of anyone having the desire or the strength to pass through the Wilds to get all the way here, and *then* start a war, seems really slim," I countered. "Especially if they're mostly human. Do you really think a bunch of humans are going to attack the fae if they know they have an alternative? I can tell you, they won't. They were afraid of me, and I'm one of them."

Both men studied me.

It was a bit unnerving, and I felt warmth spread over my face. "If you're really worried they'll see it as an act of war, you could send messages to the towns and cities nearby to let them know that it's *not* an act of war, but one of revenge. I don't think anyone would be surprised by fae taking revenge; you're known as brutal, icy warriors."

My cheeks continued warming, and words continued spilling from my lips. "You say your people want war because they love Pavia. If those fae manage to take the throne, they could do a lot more damage than just killing a handful of humans stupid enough to challenge them. They could ravage more of the Sands, including innocent children or men and women who have no desire to fight. I—"

Vayme put his hand on mine.

The gesture was simple, but sudden enough and intimate enough that I cut myself off.

"You're right," he said.

The words surprised me so much, they stunned me to silence for a moment.

"I am?"

His lips curved upward slightly. "Yes, Tempest. You're right. Giving the bloodthirsty what they want, with guidelines, could potentially solve the problem. It won't satisfy those who despise me enough to send the Monster after me, but it could make enough of a difference to tip the scales back in our favor." He glanced at Matían, who gave a grudging nod.

Vayme's brother was looking at me differently again, and I didn't know what to think about it. "It's a good idea," he finally said.

"It is," Vayme agreed.

Pavia chose that moment to run back over, her cheeks pink and her expression happy as she grabbed Vayme's hand. "We need you to play too."

"I thought of something even more fun," Vayme said, leaning closer. "Do you want to go to the shops with Kaelle? She needs some new dresses."

"Yes! And she needs a comb," Pavia said eagerly.

"Then we'll get her a comb. Perhaps we can find a blue one, to match her hair." He winked at Pavia.

She burst out laughing before grabbing my hand. "Let's go!"

Vayme, Matían, and I all froze.

There was supposed to be a chance her touch could kill me.

One by one, we let out long breaths when we realized I was fine.

Vayme's magic must've been strong enough to protect me from Pavia's.

I let her tug me to my feet, and followed her toward the xuno I knew her dad was bonded to.

"I'll protect them," Matían told his brother, striding toward us.

I saw the sudden storm in Vayme's eyes.

He wouldn't want me alone with Matían and Pavia. Though he trusted his brother, I knew the bond would make it difficult to watch me leave with another man.

"Come with us," I called to Vayme, and then added mentally, *"I'm tired of the ache in my handprint."*

"My people will be less accepting of you if I'm at your side," he said.

"Then I'll have to be extra charming, I suppose." I added, *"And it'll be easier to be charming if I'm not in pain."*

His lips curved upward the tiniest bit, though the expression was a bit grudging. "Fine."

"I'm going to ride with Vayme," I told Pavia, giving her a quick smile.

"Okay! Be nice to her, Uncle Vayme," Pavia called out.

"I'm always nice," he called back.

She snorted. "If you were always nice, you would have more friends in the empty rooms."

I bit back a laugh at her sass, and the sight of Vayme's rueful grin.

"Can't argue with that, brother," Matían tossed back, looking highly amused.

Vayme shook his head, capturing my hand and striding toward the female xuno I had noticed on two different occasions, the one with the light blue eyes. "Would you be willing to carry us to the shops, Soft?" he asked aloud.

"Will you buy me a treat?" she countered, speaking into both of our minds.

He chuckled. "Of course."

"Then I'd be happy to." She stood and stretched a bit before dipping her head toward us.

Vayme lifted me onto her back—though he had to know damn well at that point I could get on myself—and slipped on behind me.

"Is your name Kaelle, or Tempest?" she asked me, as she headed up the stairs behind Matían's companion. Speaking mind-to-mind with me was all the permission I needed to do the same with her.

"It's Kaelle. Strong started calling me Tempest, so Vayme did too. I've tried to talk them out of it, but I think it's a lost cause at this point."

She chuckled into my mind. *"Surely they could have come up with a better nickname."*

"You would think," I agreed.

"Perhaps I'll have to call you by your given name to balance out their unfortunate one."

My lips curved upward. *"I certainly wouldn't complain."*

"Kaelle it is, then."

She continued running, and my curiosity got the best of me. *"What do you know of Vayme and Strong? I've been around them so consistently that I've never heard an outside opinion, other than from my human friends."*

"Hmm." She considered it. *"I have known both for too long to give a truly unbiased answer, but I'll do my best. Both are males of honor, but not without flaws. Strong grows smitten with a new female he knows will never truly consider a mate every few decades. He currently pursues Vibrant, who will certainly never mate with the king's companion."*

"Interesting."

"Mmhm. The king himself is a more peculiar creature. Though confident and the strongest fae in our city, both physically and magically, he keeps to himself. He rarely pays attention to the females interested in him, and politely declines any offers he receives. The man prefers books and weapons over all else, and has few fae he truly trusts."

"Why?" I wondered.

"I don't know. I suspect some fae would blossom with the stability of a mate bond, but because of their ridiculous stance against mating, they deprive themselves of that which they need. Unconditional love can lead to a truly beautiful amount of security."

I thought about Vayme and his quietness. He'd even seemed a tiny bit awkward with me, a few times.

And I wondered if she was right. Was Vayme someone who yearned for the stability of love, perhaps without realizing it?

I certainly believed what Soft said. Finding out that my family had likely been my jailers and that I was alone in the world, made me feel far more uncertain about myself than I had ever felt before. I had nothing to fall back on, if I failed.

Did Vayme feel that way too?

Being able to trust him to protect me had been just about life-changing for me. I knew he wouldn't abandon me, because he needed me to stay hidden from the Monster. And I knew he wouldn't hurt me, because he was a kind man despite the roughness of his personality.

All of those things had made it easier for me to open up to him. I was getting more comfortable speaking my mind with him, because I'd grown more certain that doing so wouldn't change anything about the way Vayme treated me.

"Thank you for sharing your thoughts," I said to Soft. *"I appreciate your honesty. It gives me much to think about."*

"Of course. Thank you for trusting me enough to ask."

Her words surprised me, but in a good way.

CHAPTER FOURTEEN
KAELLE

We reached the shops shortly after my conversation with Soft ended, and Pavia was immediately at my side, dragging me toward the stone buildings. The crystals above Vuuth glowed much more brightly than they had the first time I'd seen them, creating similar light as our suns, but more glittery and spread out.

Vayme and Matían wore similar neutral expressions as they followed me and Pavia. Though there were a lot of auras around, they weren't anywhere near as concentrated as they had been in Jirev, so I was alright.

Pavia towed me into the first shop, and proudly declared to the woman running it that she needed a comb for her uncle's friend.

The woman smiled and looked at me. "The king's *friend?*"

I blushed a bit. "Yep."

She laughed. "I think we can manage to find a comb. This way."

Pavia maintained her hold on my hand as we followed the woman deeper into the shop, where we found a row of toiletries. My eyes widened at the sight of all the different soaps, lotions, and perfumes. At the end of the row, I saw a basket of combs in varying sizes and shapes. I was at a loss for words, having never seen so many options in one place before.

Pavia released my hand and ran over to the combs, then started going through all of them in a painstakingly slow attempt to find the best one.

"There's a better selection at Pera's shop across town," the woman said, noticing my surprise. "I try to keep some of everything to save people a bit of time, but the best choices will be there."

"Oh, no, this is perfect," I admitted. "I grew up in a tiny town." I bit my lip, knowing I was supposed to throw in more about my past than I necessarily wanted to share. "And then I lived in a small cave for eight years, so I've just never seen so many products like this before. It's a bit magical."

Sympathy flooded the woman's eyes. "Oh, dear."

"Yeah. I suppose they have shops like this in Jirev, but Vayme was so busy that the only one I saw had clothing in it." I flashed her a small smile, and her eyes softened even more as they flicked to our male company, waiting near the door to give us space.

"He's a good king. I'm sure he'll treat you well even after your bond fades."

"He will," I agreed.

She grabbed a basket off a pile I hadn't noticed and handed it to me. "While little Pavia finds you the perfect comb, why don't you look through everything else to find the scents you like most?"

"That would be great. Thank you."

She flashed me another smile before handing me the basket and slipping away.

I started sniffing the soap bars, and glanced over at Pavia. When I saw Vayme beside her, holding up a few different options, my lips curved upward, and I went back to sniffing.

There were so many choices, I had no idea which to pick. All the different smells were a marvel. I liked the majority of them, but was uncertain which one I would truly want to smell like. It was a silly thing to wonder, but I wondered anyway.

There was a soft brush of skin against my arm, and I jerked my head to the side. My eyes met Vayme's, and I relaxed again.

"Difficult decision?" he asked, his voice quiet and unassuming.

"Unfortunately. I don't particularly know how I want to smell."

"Your scent doesn't need soap's enhancement. You smell plenty delicious without it."

My cheeks warmed, and I wasn't sure whether to thank him or try to come up with some sort of clever retort.

He noticed my uncertainty and added, "Point out your favorites, and I'll tell you which will pair the best with your natural scent."

Gratitude swelled in my chest, and I pointed out the five I liked the most.

Vayme sniffed all of them briefly, and put three in my basket without an explanation or question.

"Oh, I don't need three soaps," I told him quickly. "Just tell me which one will smell the best, and I'll pick that one."

"All three of them will smell nice. A queen would have a whole shelf of soaps to choose from, and are you not my queen, if only temporarily?" His eyes were piercing, and I felt as if they cut into my soul.

"I don't really think that's how it works," I finally said.

"I get to decide how it works." He grabbed another two bars of soap, a few jars of lotion, and a handful of glass bottles holding some other kind of soap I didn't know the use of.

My body burned with something between desire for him and embarrassment for myself, but I tried to ignore it. "What are those?" I gestured toward the strange soaps.

"Conditioner. It will make your hair easier to comb through."

Veil, it sounded like a gift from the lost gods themselves. I spent far too much time detangling my hair. "Thank you."

"A female doesn't thank her mate for providing for her."

"The proper response is *you're welcome*," I said, brushing up against his side.

He stiffened at the contact—the way one would when they were in pain.

I jerked away quickly, assuming he had hated the touch... but then I noticed the darker patch of fabric on his black shirt.

He rarely wore shirts.

Was he injured?

"What happened?" Without thinking, I grabbed the bottom hem of the fabric and lifted it up so I could see his abdomen. My jaw dropped when I saw a thick cut, not bandaged or covered at all. "Vayme!"

"I'm fine. A few of my fae challenged me after I explained about the Monster hunting me and about our connection. I won."

"What if you hadn't won?" I demanded.

"I would be dead," he said calmly.

My heart dropped into my stomach, and I let go of his shirt.

If he didn't care whether he lived or died, how could I ever let myself rely on him the way I'd started to?

"I've got them!" Pavia exclaimed, running up to us with a stack of combs.

"Nice work. Let's see what you found."

She beamed, and held up not just one or two combs, but six.

Six combs.

"Six?" I flashed Vayme a dark look.

"You need a big one for getting out the big tangles, and a small one for smoothing the rest of them," Pavia explained quickly, taking my attention back. "Vayme said you get a lot of tangles 'cause of your magic. And combs are *really* easy to lose."

"That's true," I managed to say. "And you must've picked out the best ones, because these are really pretty."

She beamed again. "I did."

I wasn't sure whether to laugh or to rip said tangled hair out. Both options seemed equally reasonable.

Vayme picked out a few other toiletries for me—all in multiples, of course—and then paid for everything. He helped the woman running the shop put it in one of the fabric bags all of the fae seemed to like, and followed me and Pavia out.

The king mentioned a clothing shop, and I shot him an exasperated look as Pavia dragged me toward one. She wore the same black dresses most of the fae seemed to prefer, though hers were shaped a little different to cover more of her. I had to assume that was her father's doing, because the fae women didn't seem to care about showing their bodies off.

I felt similarly after the weeks I'd spent among them. And my current dresses were a bit too tight, but I didn't really mind. The fabric was smooth and soft, so it wasn't as if I was in pain.

Though Pavia immediately started loading my arms with black fabric, my gaze kept wandering to the colorful dresses tucked at the back of the shop. Nissa had always worn colorful dresses when we were in Jirev, and something about them just seemed... happy.

And strong, and confident.

I wanted to feel those things, too, but I didn't want to disappoint Pavia, so I stayed quiet.

Vayme prowled over to me with a blue dress dangling from his fingers. It was a light, faded blue, more like the color of my aura than my hair. "Tempest is going to try this on, Pav," he told her.

"It's blue!" she exclaimed.

"I know. It'll look pretty on her, don't you think?"

"SO pretty! Can I have a blue dress too?" She looked around for her dad, but he wasn't in the shop.

"He went to get Soft and Wicked," Vayme told her. "I'll ask them to make you a dress to match Kaelle's."

"I don't even know if I'll like it," I protested, as Vayme led me toward the curtained area for trying clothing on. His hand was on the small of my back, and it felt nicer than it should've.

Particularly considering he didn't care whether he lived or died.

I needed to distance myself from him, so that when he left me, it didn't break me. A fae warrior should be a safe person to care about, shouldn't they?

My frustration swelled as I tried the dress on, and grew more intense as I looked at myself in the mirror.

Vayme was right. I looked stunning in the damn thing. And the missing fabric on the sides—which seemed to be fashionable among the fae— showed the print of the bastard's massive hand on my hip perfectly.

I let out a soft huff before pulling the curtain open and gesturing to myself. "Well?"

"Veil, you're gorgeous," Vayme murmured, his gaze moving over me slowly.

My face warmed

"SO gorgeous!" Pavia exclaimed. "Why do we even wear black?"

"That's a good question," her uncle replied, his gaze lingering on my midsection, and probably the handprint easily visible there.

"What's that?" she pointed to the handprint on my hip.

"A magical tattoo. You can ask your dad about it." Vayme ruffled her hair, and she squealed, pushing his hand away.

The seamstress who ran the shop came in and exclaimed over how good it looked, and how she could make it fit perfectly. She took my measurements and quickly altered the blue dress while I told her a little about my past.

Vayme decided I needed a few *more* dresses, so they both had me choose my favorite colors. All the shades I picked were blues, pinks, and purples, and Pavia requested matching dresses to all of mine.

After making a few more stops, we met up with Matían and the xuno and headed back to the castle. As much as I didn't want to admit it, my gaze kept sliding down to the light blue fabric fluttering in my breeze, and it made me happy. I knew it was silly for a piece of clothing to have that power, but it did.

Pavia was a ball of even more energy than she had been when we arrived. She told her dad and the rest of us all about the colorful dresses we were going to wear, how delicious the treats he'd bought her were, and how much she loved Vuuth.

I supposed it was important to remember that she had spent most of her life running an inn with her mother, before losing her, and was then brought to a new city. I'd started to feel like she was a bit spoiled, but a little girl who'd so recently lost everything she knew deserved to be spoiled, to ensure she knew how safe and loved she was.

As I watched her, I couldn't help but wonder how differently my life would've turned out, if someone had been beside me after the storm, telling me I wasn't a monster for what I had done. Those had been long, lonely, difficult years, made harder by my parents repeating how dangerous I was every time I saw them.

The more I thought about it, the more I remembered my father starting the conversations—changing the subject away from the books I'd been reading and back to how important it was for me to stay in the cave, to protect everyone from myself.

Still tired from the traveling, and a bit subdued with the weight of my thoughts and memories, I murmured a *thank you* to Soft and scratched her behind the ears before heading back to my room. Vayme had the bags of things he'd bought me, but I didn't need any of them at that exact moment.

Except maybe the combs, because veil, my hair was a tangled mess.

I closed the door and locked it, then leaned against it, resting my back and head against the thick stone.

My eyes shut, and I let out a long breath.

Everything was so... new.

I wasn't sure what to do about any of it, honestly. Or how to feel.

On one hand, I did feel better than I had in my cave. So much better, in so many ways.

But my emotions were insanely conflicted, and my thoughts were the same.

Mainly, I was struggling with knowing that everything was going to change again after the eclipse, so I couldn't let myself get too comfortable.

And it didn't help to know that Vayme didn't care whether he lived or died, which meant I couldn't allow myself to rely on him or trust him the way I'd begun to.

I wasn't tired enough to sleep, but I didn't want to go back out and face Vayme after what I'd learned. My room was basically empty, though, so there was nothing to do in there except shower.

And if I showered, I would inevitably remember my bath... and my conversation with Vayme.

My cheeks warmed.

I could always bring myself pleasure, but something told me I would have a hard time keeping my mind separate from the king's if I did that. And if he knew I was doing it, I was fairly sure he would find a way to involve himself, either by sending me more mental images of his fantasies or asking to join me.

Maybe I would've been interested in that earlier, but knowing what I did about his fights, I wasn't willing to let myself grow even closer to the man. He had likely been bleeding during our conversation about sex, of all things, yet he hadn't even bothered to tell me.

I walked over to the bed and collapsed on it with a huff.

The whole situation was a mess.

The intensity of a mate bond, without the feelings that should naturally precede it.

The intimacy of a relationship without the promise or expectation of anything past the eclipse.

Veil, I wasn't sure how to deal with any of it, or how to stop myself from growing more attached.

There was some chatter and commotion outside my room for a few minutes, and then silence that told me Pavia had probably left again.

A minute after that, there was a knock on my door.

I squeezed my eyes shut, not sure who I hoped it was. At least with Pavia, I didn't have to make conversation or have difficult discussions. Even with the difficulties, I'd probably prefer talking to Vayme than Matían, so that was something.

"Tempest?" Vayme called out.

I debated whether or not to feign sleep.

"Can we talk?" he added.

I really didn't want to talk, but couldn't see a refusal actually working in my favor, so I reluctantly slipped out of bed. It took a minute to unlock the door, but when I got it open, I found myself face-to-face with a massive, gorgeous king. He was leaning against the doorway in a way that somehow made him even more attractive.

Though I tried to hide the way I sucked in a breath at the sheer presence of him, I probably failed.

"Hi," Vayme said quietly.

"Hi." I slipped my hands into the pockets of my dress, trying to come off more aloof than I really was.

"Are you okay?" he asked me.

"Yes."

"You seem upset. Did I do something?"

I blinked.

He wasn't going to let me get away with my aloofness, apparently.

His gaze lingered on me, waiting for an answer.

Though I wanted to lie, close the door, and disappear back inside the room, he was giving me a chance to tell him exactly what was wrong. It would've been ridiculous for me to stay quiet, given the situation.

"You don't care whether you live or die," I said.

It was his turn to blink.

I gestured to his side, where I knew his open cut was. "You were in multiple fights that could've led to your death today, and you didn't tell me about them, or even take care of your wounds afterward. I can't rely on someone who can't be trusted to take care of himself, so I need to step out of this... whatever we are." I took a physical step back, to prove my point.

His forehead creased.

"I'm not upset with you; I'm upset with me. I should've realized where we stood sooner. So yes, I'm okay, and no, you didn't do anything wrong. I'm just... I need more distance." I started to close the door, but he caught it with a thick hand.

"We're mates, Kaelle." His gaze wasn't hard, or angry, but it was... intense. "*Whatever we are*, is mates."

"Temporarily," I countered. "As soon as the eclipse comes, we're nothing. So *whatever we are* is a reasonable statement. You know my history; you should understand why I can't just embrace being mates until the eclipse and walk away without looking backward. I need stability."

I tried to close the door again, but he was too damn strong. It didn't budge.

"I never said I wanted you to walk away without looking backward." Vayme's voice was steady.

"No, but you *vowed* to take me home."

"Did I say I was going to leave you there?"

My eyes narrowed. "You're a king. You're not planning on living in that tiny cave with me. There wouldn't be enough water—and you'd die of starvation much faster than me."

"I'm not letting either of us starve," he growled at me. "I'm going to take you back so you can confront your family to get the full story, and then I'm going to drag your ass back to Vuuth, where I know you'll be safe and healthy."

"And alone. Away from you."

"I never said that either."

"It was implied!" I exclaimed, tossing a hand out toward him. "Our bond is going to break, and fae don't take permanent mates anymore."

"We do take life partners." He captured my hand and lifted it to his lips. My heart hammered in my chest as he slowly brushed a kiss to my fingertips, and then to my knuckles, where he lingered.

"What are you saying?" I was growing flustered, and I didn't like it.

"Our bond will end with the eclipse, but that doesn't mean *we* have to end."

CHAPTER FIFTEEN
KAELLE

My eyes widened at the suggestion that he didn't want our bond to be temporary. Or at least, didn't want some aspects of it to be temporary. "We've only known each other a month, Vayme."

"A month during which we've spent almost every moment together. I'm not suggesting we make vows; I'm saying the decision is ours to make, regardless of the bond breaking. We can stay together when we're no longer mates, if we wish to."

"Why would you want that?" I asked, my voice growing softer. "I'm human, remember? As soon as the bond is gone, my magic's effect on me will grow stronger again. The more emotions I feel, the faster it drains my energy. I was only conscious for a few hours a time in that cave."

"You were starving."

"And your magic wasn't there to ease mine. Everything will be different without the bond."

"Everything became different when the bond was created. We can handle another change," he said, his gaze steady.

"And what if we can't?"

"We deal with that when it happens. *If* it happens."

"That's easy for you to say, Vayme. You're a king. You're a warrior. If things end between us, you still have *everything*." I gestured to the rooms behind him, the castle above us. "I have nothing."

"I'll provide you a home and fill it with supplies. I'll help you find something to occupy your time, too."

I huffed. "I didn't ask for that. I—"

"I know you didn't. I would do all of it out of selfishness, on my own behalf."

I scowled. "How could that possibly be out of selfishness?"

He dragged my hand away from his lips and set it on his chest, over his heart. I could feel the steady, constant beat of it, and it warmed me.

"My body hasn't responded to the presence of a woman in centuries, Tempest, yet I find pleasure simply watching you breathe. You're clever, you're kind, and yes, you're delicate—but beyond your delicacy is a fierce strength of both mind and will. Your body is attractive, but your soul? It captivates me. And yes, it's incredibly selfish, but I'm not willing to let you walk away from me."

My own heartbeat was faster than his, my breaths shorter, too. "I don't know if I would be willing to agree to be life partners, after the eclipse. Even if things were perfect, I would age like a human, and you'd remain immortal. We could never be equals without the bond connecting our magic. And Vayme, I believe in marriage. I believe in making vows and keeping them. I believe in choosing someone every single day, even when it's hard. I believe in devotion, and love."

"I didn't consider your lifespan," he admitted.

"You don't want a mate bond." I brushed a few strands of hair out of my eyes. My wind had blown them there, and the veil knew I couldn't control that. "It wouldn't make sense to consider starting any kind of a relationship when we don't want the same thing."

"I've lived long enough to know that the best things in life often don't make sense." He tilted my chin back, so our eyes collided. "And I have nothing against mate bonds. We'll have to kill any cultists hidden among my people who come after us if we seal ours, but luckily for you, I excel at killing."

I scoffed. "Even if all of that is true, it doesn't negate the fact that you could've died multiple times today, and you didn't bother to tell me! You could've been bleeding out while we were talking about sex, and I still would've been oblivious because you decided not to tell me. I woke up with pain in the handprint—for all I know, tomorrow, I could wake up *without* it."

"I won't let that happen."

"Why should I believe you? You don't care whether you live or die, Vayme. How can I let myself develop feelings for someone like that?"

He stepped closer and caught my face between his hands, leaning his head closer to mine. "I want to live, Tempest. My life wasn't at risk in any of those challenges."

"You already said it was!"

"No. I said that if they won, I would be dead."

"Which is exactly the same as saying your life was at risk," I shot back.

"I've fought in hundreds of challenges in the past few centuries. If any of my fae could beat me, they would've done so by now." His voice was ridiculously calm.

"That is one of the stupidest beliefs I have *ever* heard."

"I am very good, Tempest. I don't say that with pride, or overconfidence. I say it as a fact. I am very, very good. I have never been close to dying in a challenge, and I never will be."

I pushed his hands off my face and stepped back, shaking my head. "Maybe that's good enough for you, but it's not good enough for me. You lost when you fought Kier. I—"

My head jerked to the side as I heard Pavia's voice in the spiral stairwell leading down to the king's space. When I looked at Vayme, I found him still staring at me, waiting.

"Just go," I finally whispered, gesturing him out of the room.

He stepped inside instead—then locked the door behind him and leaned up against it.

I huffed. "Vayme!" My voice was soft enough that Pavia hopefully wouldn't hear through the door.

"This conversation isn't over." His voice was even quieter than mine, though it still held his complete certainty.

"Of course it is. I'm never going to see it the way you do. I will *never* be comfortable with being close to someone whose life is at risk so frequently."

"Give me a solution, then. You're my temporary queen—come up with a better alternative. If I step down in the next challenge, the fae who takes over will be worse. They will create more wars. They will kill more humans. They will attack the kingdoms we just made our allies."

My throat went dry. "What?"

"Give me an alternative, and I will take it," he said, his gaze steady.

"I..." I began, and trailed off. He had a point, as much as I didn't want to admit it, and wasn't comfortable with the cost of it. "Do you kill them after you beat them?"

"I don't. I wouldn't have any people left by now if I did."

"So what's the consequence if they lose?"

"Shame. We are warriors; there are few things worse than losing a fight."

I ran a hand through my hair—or started to, extracting it when it got caught in the tangles.

Then, I started to pace just a little bit. My wind tugged at my skin and hair, but it actually felt fairly nice.

"I don't want you to fight," I told him.

"I know." He watched me pace. Though his expression was still neutral, there was something in his eyes that almost seemed *happy*.

"If there's no way around it, there would have to be a limit. One challenge a day—actually, a week would be much better, or even a month. And there would need to be a real consequence for them when they lose. Shame isn't achieving anything; if it did, no one would be challenging you right now. Give them a terrible job for the week until the next challenge, or something. A blow like that to their pride would probably be more effective."

His gaze grew thoughtful. "That may be doable."

"And *if* I were to consider any kind of a relationship, I would want to be there when you fight. I wouldn't be able to sit at home, knowing your life was at risk. I would need to see the healer tend to you afterward, or bandage your wounds myself or something."

"You don't like blood."

"I would get used to it, if I loved someone who was constantly bleeding," I shot back.

"Okay," Vayme said.

I stared at him for a moment. "Okay?"

"Yes, okay." He stepped toward me and caught my hands, stopping me in my tracks. "I can respect that the challenges affect you differently than they affect me, and I will change how they're done."

"Well, that was easier than I expected."

He chuckled softly. "It—"

A small fist banged on the door.

"Kaelle?" Pavia hollered. "I have treats!"

My stomach still ached a bit from our last treats.

When I opened my mouth to say so, Vayme put a finger to my lips to quiet me, stepping up even closer.

I eyed him curiously.

His mind touched mine for what felt like the first time in ages. *"If she thinks she'll succeed at getting us out of our rooms by pounding and yelling, we'll never have a moment of peace. Matían will talk to her. Give him a minute."*

I sucked in a breath as he slowly dragged his finger over my bottom lip, and remained silent as he continued to do so while we waited in silence.

"Pav," Matían called out, his voice faint thanks to the door and walls separating us from them. He said something else, but his words were muffled enough that I couldn't make them out individually.

She groaned, but didn't yell again.

My eyes were still locked with Vayme's as the silence slowly returned.

"I'm going to kiss you," my king murmured into my mind. *"If you have any objections, now is the time to voice them."*

I didn't have any objections.

His lips met mine. It was sweet, but nothing like the fiery passion I'd expected.

I started to pull away, but before I could, he tilted my chin further. His tongue parted the seam of my lips, and I stumbled backward at the sudden intensity of his taste in my mouth. His tongue stroked mine, and one of his hands landed on my hip. He stepped closer, pressing against me as he kissed me, going slow enough to give me time to figure out how to kiss him too.

My fingers lifted to his shirt and dug into the fabric as he started walking me backward without pulling away.

My ass met the wall, and the rest of my back followed until I was pressed against both it and Vayme.

Every inch of me was hot, despite the wind blowing through the room.

My heart pumped hard in my chest, my hands sliding further up his neck as I hung onto him, pulling him closer.

One of my legs hooked around his waist, and he lifted me higher. I groaned into his mouth when his erection met my core, hitting me perfectly.

"Veil, you taste incredible," Vayme growled into my mind, releasing my mouth long enough to drag his lips and tongue down the sensitive column of my throat.

I struggled for breath, clinging to him as he made me feel things I'd only ever dreamed of before.

"I don't taste that good. You're just out of practice," I whispered into his mind.

Vayme's rumbly chuckle made my lips stretch in a smile as the back of my head hit the wall. He sucked lightly on the skin above the curve of my breast, making me desperate for more.

"Let's fix that, shall we?" He moved to the side just a little, and his hand found the apex of my thighs.

I gasped at the contact, and he captured my lips again to keep me quiet as he slowly stroked my clit. His fingers were big, and his touch was rougher than my own, but veil, he was so damn perfect at it.

My hips rocked and swiveled desperately as he worked me slowly through my undergarment, dragging me closer and closer to the edge. His mouth was hot on mine, swallowing every sound I made. My fingers buried in his hair, gripping the strands to anchor myself as he brought me closer to my climax.

Finally, it all became too much.

I shattered.

The pleasure hit harder than I'd ever experienced—and lasted longer too.

His mouth stayed on mine as his fingers dragged it out for me, his touch soft but confident.

"Veil, you are good at that," I sighed. *"I don't even want to know how good you are when it hasn't been a few centuries."*

He chuckled. *"You're going to find out, Tempest."*

The words made my toes curl, and heat swell in my abdomen. I couldn't even imagine how good his touch would feel without my undergarments separating us.

"Are you still bleeding?" I whispered against his mouth.

"It doesn't matter." He recaptured my lips, but I eased them away from him.

"It does to me."

He gave me a long look, then eased away from me. I remained where I was, one of my hands settling over my heart and the other resting on my abdomen. Vayme slowly peeled his shirt over his head, exposing his chest to me.

I'd seen him half-naked every day we'd known each other... but one of my hands flew to my mouth as I stared at him.

He looked *terrible*.

Cuts were scattered over his torso, most small and healing, but two were still wet and leaking. Nausea turned my stomach, but I forced myself to ignore it.

If I wanted to prove I could be there for his fights, I couldn't be squirmy around blood.

"Veil, Vayme."

"You've seen me bleeding before." He stepped closer.

"It's worse now that I care about you."

His lips curved upward. "I can accept that."

"And you're not going to have a healer look at them?"

"I've survived hundreds of cuts like these, if not thousands," he said. "I don't need a healer. They'll be gone in a few days."

I hoped that wasn't an underestimate, because I hated that he was wounded at all. "Do you have bandages?"

"In my room."

I nodded, letting out a shaky breath. "Alright. We'll go to your room, and I'll patch you up. Hopefully without passing out."

"I'm not going to let you pass out again," he said, his voice low. "I've made every possible effort to keep you from getting overwhelmed by the auras; if my wounds are going to knock you out, you won't take care of them."

"It was a joke, Vayme. I'll be fine." I patted him lightly on the arm.

He didn't look convinced, but I grabbed his shirt off the floor and handed it back to him. "You can strip again for me in your room. We don't want Pavia to see you bleeding."

He jerked his head in a nod, and tugged the shirt back over his head. When he caught my hand, I let him lead me out of the room.

As we reached the door, he halted and said into my mind, *"You'll have to change so my brother can't smell your pleasure."*

I blinked.

His eyes narrowed. *"Has he smelled your pleasure before?"*

"Um... I don't think so. I was in the pool when we were talking earlier, so it's unlikely."

The response satisfied him. *"We'll have to be careful about keeping the doors closed so I don't have to fight the urge to remove Matían's head from his body."*

"Maybe we should just not do anything in my room? It'll be easier to keep Pavia out that way. She's already used to not going into your room, and seems to have an affinity for mine."

My suggestion satisfied him further. *"My scent will be more completely entangled with yours that way, too."*

"Are you going to be this possessive around everyone?" I asked him.

He considered it as I changed into one of my tight, black dresses, giving the soft blue one a lingering look as it joined the other dirty clothes.

Vayme's gaze tracked my every move, his eyes hot as they devoured my figure. *"Not quite. We're sharing a living space, so he's much closer than anyone else would be, and we're brothers, so there's a different dynamic. I had him and Pavia living here to ensure their safety after they first arrived, but it would be more than safe for them to find a home of their own now. Everyone adores Pavia."*

"Oh, I don't want you to kick them out because of me," I said quickly, straightening my dress and tugging to make sure it was in place.

"I would never. I'll simply ask Matían if he would feel comfortable moving out. If he wouldn't, I'll deal with the discomfort."

"He'll hate me," I protested.

"He was living with his lover in another land, allowing me to believe he was dead, for nearly a decade. If he despises you because I want privacy with the first female I've taken to in multiple centuries, he possesses far less intelligence than he's led me to believe. The bastard's lucky I didn't kill him for letting me believe him dead for so long."

I guess it didn't sound as bad when he put it that way.

We stepped out of the room hand-in-hand, but halted when we found Pavia laying on her belly in front of our door again.

Her head was in her hands, and her eyebrows were furrowed as she stared up at us. "What were you doing in there?"

Veil.

My face heated.

"Talking," Vayme said calmly.

"About what?" Pavia asked.

"Kaelle's feelings. She's tired of combing her hair," the king said.

He was a far better liar than I was—though I *was* tired of always combing my hair.

"Me too," Pavia said, looking at me.

"Perhaps we should both cut it short," I suggested.

Her face fell. "My mommy loved my hair. I can't cut it."

My throat swelled. "Then we'll have to practice our braids, won't we?"

She gave me a small smile, and nodded.

"We're going to keep talking in my room, Pav. Have fun out here." Vayme rustled her hair, and her smile grew a little bit as she nodded again.

"You can't kick them out," I said quietly to him, holding his hand a bit tighter as we crossed the large space. I nodded at Soft as we passed her, and she dipped her head in return.

"I won't," he reassured me. *"But I doubt Matían will want his daughter consistently at risk of being exposed to just how thoroughly I enjoy bringing you pleasure."*

My face heated.

"There are no other children in the city, but it may be good for her to make friends with some of the fae outside the castle. He's mentioned before that she would benefit from time spent growing herbs and plants, and with the seamsters and seamstresses. She was used to staying busy at the inn, so she's having a hard time adjusting to the quiet of life in my rooms. He's been hoping she'll bond with a xuno to give her that extra protection, so he doesn't have to worry as much," Vayme added.

I couldn't blame him for that. Or for wanting to keep her busy—she certainly had the energy for it.

"I'll speak with him tomorrow," Vayme said. *"Tonight, I'm yours."*

My face flushed as he opened the door to his room and gestured for me to walk inside, but I didn't protest.

Only a fool would've turned down an invitation into a fae king's bedroom, after all.

CHAPTER SIXTEEN
KAELLE

Vayme stripped his shirt off again while I locked the door behind us, and despite his wounds, I found myself studying his body with thinly-veiled desire.

The man was a masterpiece.

He strode into the bathroom for a moment, and returned with a bundle of bandages, a pair of scissors for cutting them to size, a towel, and a cup of water. I wasn't sure what the water was for.

"Where should we do it?" I checked.

"The bed would be easiest." He gestured toward it, and I headed that way.

Vayme surprised me by sitting his massive self on the floor, his back to me as I sat on the mattress behind him.

He explained quickly how the bandages worked—you just had to wet the wound and skin around it, then apply them with a dry hand—and I nodded my understanding.

Though it made me nauseous at first, my illness eased as I slowly cleaned him and patched him up, eventually moving from my seat on the bed to the floor so I could better get the wound on his side.

Things had changed between us, and it seemed like we were both still trying to figure out the new dynamic.

"Were you ever in a relationship, before?" I asked Vayme, as I finished up with the final wound on his chest.

"No. I suppose I don't really even know what it requires," he admitted. "My parents have never mated, so their connection has taught me nothing about the bond, either. You were never in a relationship, were you?"

"Oh, no. I was only thirteen when I went to the cave, so that would be... weird, to put it in the politest way."

He chuckled. "Did anyone other than your family ever visit you? I imagine you were close with the others, since your town was small."

"We were all close before the storm, but they hated me after it. My parents said that much, at least. I really only saw them a few times a month, and they never stayed long. My brother only visited once a year or so. I should've been more suspicious of them."

"You were young, and they convinced you that your magic made you unworthy of anything more than they gave you. Leaving there as strong as you did is a testament to the strength of your mind and soul, Tempest." His words were quiet, but firm.

My eyes stung a little. "Thank you."

He brushed a few tangled strands behind my ear, though we both knew my wind would sweep them away again soon enough. "This will be a first for both of us. You'll have to tell me when I do something wrong, so I can learn."

"And you'll have to do the same," I whispered.

His lips curved upward. "I can't see you doing anything wrong."

A quiet laugh escaped me. "Prepare yourself for it, because—"

His mouth captured mine before I could finish what I was saying. I parted my lips for him without waiting for a nudge, and his tongue stroked mine.

All thoughts disappeared from my mind as he kissed me slowly and intimately, as if there was nothing else in the world he would've rather been doing. I migrated onto his lap as the kiss went on, and his hands moved over my thighs and ass, slowly touching and exploring me.

Though he was hard against me, he made no effort to push me for more.

My breathing picked up, and my hips started to move as I rocked against his erection. It hit me perfectly, dragging me closer to the edge and making him growl. His grip on my body grew rougher, his hands on my ass as he helped me move.

His mouth was still on mine, swallowing my cries again as I lost control once more. I came down from the high panting, and he released my lips to let me catch my breath.

His lips brushed my ear. "You're so damn gorgeous."

I was too dazed by the double hit of pleasure to respond. My lips felt as if they'd be swollen for hours, if not days, after all the kissing, yet I was already wondering how Vayme would respond if I kissed him again. My body was blissfully warm, and veil, I wanted more.

"You're really good at that too," I whispered to him, earning a chuckle.

"I can do far better."

"I'm sure you can."

His lips landed on mine again—the kiss still slow and intimate. My fingers slid into his hair, tangling in the thick, soft strands.

A soft squeal escaped me as he lifted me off the floor and set me on my back on his bed. He didn't break the kiss, but his body stretched over mine, strong and warm.

"I would never hurt you," he said quietly into my mind, as he continued kissing me.

"I know." I did. I knew he wouldn't hurt me, and I trusted him. He had proven that he respected me, despite the insane number of differences between us.

"We'll have to stay quiet." He pulled away from me and settled on his knees between my thighs, opening my legs to him. I was still fully clothed, but the way he stroked my legs told me he didn't care.

"Okay. Just cover my face with a pillow or something if I get loud." I wasn't positive where the night was headed but was absolutely on board no matter where it went.

After so many years in that cave, I was finally free, and I was going to live my life however I wanted. And while there was a gorgeous fae king interested in my body, I was certainly going to take advantage of the situation.

Vayme's hands slid back up to my ass, where he squeezed lightly before hooking a finger in the bottom of my undergarments. His eyes met mine. *"May I?"*

"Please."

I watched him slowly peel the fabric down my thighs, taking the opportunity to touch as much of my skin as possible in the process. The undergarment hit the floor, and he opened my legs wider.

His gaze was hot as he took in every inch of me. Any fear I would've had about him seeing me bare was gone thanks to those moments in the Wilds, when he'd stripped me naked and told me how gorgeous I was.

"You're absolutely drenched for me. Veil, I can't wait to have my tongue on you. Sit up."

My abdomen was tight with desire, so I sat up without a question.

He was sliding my dress over my head a heartbeat later, stripping me further. My face warmed as his chest rumbled at the sight of me, his hands sliding over my exposed abdomen and covered breasts. *"You have no idea how badly I wanted to touch you when we were traveling toward the elves."*

"I do, actually. Your constant erection made it pretty clear." I brushed my foot over his hardness, making his gaze grow hotter.

"Finding your fire, Tempest?" He undid the clasp of my remaining undergarment and slid the fabric from my chest, revealing my breasts to him.

His hands slid over them, making me fight to keep my hips from jerking.

"Or my inner storm." I brushed my foot against his cock again. *"I want to touch you."*

"You can, after I've tasted your climax on my tongue and watched you bring yourself pleasure as well."

I flushed hotter.

"I believe you told me you would show me how you bring yourself release if I showed you my own first." He lowered himself to his belly, relaxing between my thighs. My entire body clenched in response to the sight of his face above my core. His eyes were locked with mine still, and I realized he was waiting for me to respond.

"I did."

"And?"

My throat swelled as he lowered his nose to my core and inhaled deeply, taking my scent into his lungs. Veil, taking my scent into his very *being*. His hands were still on my breasts, gripping them firmly.

I managed, *"And I certainly haven't changed my mind."*

His chest rumbled with satisfaction. *"Good. Now, I want your hands in my hair when I lick you. Show me how you feel about the way I touch you, since we're staying quiet."* He waited and watched while I slid my fingers into his hair, tangling them in the strands. *"Just like that. Ready?"*

I jerked my head in a nod, my eyes glued to the gorgeous, massive man.

He lowered his lips to my core and lightly dragged the tip of his tongue over my clit.

I barely managed to slam my jaw shut in time to stop myself from crying out at the intensity of the sensation.

He slowly continued working me, in no hurry to pick up the pace.

My hips started to buck and my grip on his hair grew tighter. It took every ounce of effort I had to stay quiet as he made love to me with his

DARK & DEADLY PREDATORS

mouth, dragging me back to the edge of my pleasure with far too much ease.

His hands landed on my hips and held me in place when my motions grew too desperate, and the heat of his grip was too much.

I shattered, biting my cheek so hard it bled as the pleasure cut through me so damn fiercely. He didn't pull away from my core or even slow down, the strokes of his tongue still steady on my clit.

I tugged his hair until he lifted his gaze to me. Though my throat was dry at the sight of him pleasuring me, I said into his mind, *"Give me a moment."*

His eyes narrowed.

"I bit my cheek," I added, fairly certain the unimportant wound would distract him long enough to recover.

He released my clit with a suck that made my hips jerk roughly against his hold, and slid up my body enough to look into my mouth. "Open," he said.

I opened my mouth, showing him the bleeding wound in my cheek. His forehead knitted in concern as he pulled my lips open wider so he could see it better.

"It's alright," I said around his fingers.

"It's not." He pressed lightly against the outside of my cheek, and I winced at the pressure on the back side of my wound. "I don't want you bleeding without reason, Tempest."

"It's hardly any blood."

"Blood is blood." He nearly growled the words at me.

Maybe I shouldn't have made him take a break.

Deciding I needed to distract him, I slipped my fingers into the waist-band of his pants and tugged lightly, murmuring, "You said you were going to touch yourself for me."

His eyes dilated slightly at the reminder, but he scowled at me anyway. "You're bleeding."

"I want to watch you climax."

His eyes dilated further, and he undid the fasteners on his pants in two sharp motions. "This conversation isn't over."

"Agreed," I lied.

The conversation wasn't over... but I'd effectively ended it.

He pushed his pants down his thighs, and when his erection sprang free, I went still.

Utterly still.

His cock was absolutely huge.

How would it fit inside me?

Maybe fae women had larger vaginas—or stronger ones?

"It'll fit," Vayme said, his eyes gleaming with both desire and something that resembled humor.

My thoughts must've been strong enough to bleed into his mind.

"You won't take me until I've stretched you thoroughly with my fingers, and we both decide you're ready for me," he added into my mind. *"Do you fear me?"*

"I don't," I said honestly. I wasn't sure we would fit together... but I certainly didn't fear him.

He spread my thighs with his knees and let his gaze slowly trail down my figure. My eyes were glued to him as he dragged a hand down the thick length of his erection.

Veil, that was the hottest thing I'd ever seen.

He lifted my hand to rest between my thighs and said in a low voice, "Show me."

I touched myself lightly, barely paying any attention at all as I watched him stroke his cock again.

And again.

And again.

His fingers felt far better on my skin than my own did, but watching him... it made me hot, everywhere.

My hips jerked in response to my touch as his breathing picked up, the head of his cock dripping a bead of pleasure onto my abdomen.

My eyes followed the drip, and lingered.

"You're going to wear my pleasure on your body tonight, Tempest. Where do you want it?"

Where did I...

Veil.

My breathing hitched as his mental images flashed through my mind.

His pleasure on my breasts, as he massaged them.

His pleasure on my abdomen, as he cleaned me with a towel.

His pleasure coating my core, his fingers slick as he touched me with it.

"That one," I said, without a heartbeat to consider it.

"Then show me how you make yourself climax."

My hips jerked, my fingers moving quickly while my eyes stuck to Vayme, watching his body respond to every stroke he gave himself.

I was close—so damn close.

But not close enough. It hadn't been long enough since my last release. I was on the edge, and couldn't push myself over it. Not while clenching my jaw so soon after so much pleasure.

My eyes burned with frustration, and I groaned softly, *"Veil."*

"Arch your back for me."

I didn't hesitate to do so—or to freeze, when Vayme's thick thumb trailed over my entrance, and dipped inside me.

Though I'd tried that once or twice, it had never been very pleasurable for me. One touch from the king told me it was different when he was the one doing the touching.

"Do you trust me?" His eyes lifted to mine as he continued to tease my entrance.

I jerked my head in a nod so quickly it was nearly painful.

With one hand wrapped around my thigh, he tugged me closer, and pressed the head of his cock to my slit.

My breathing stalled.

Was he—

Were we—

Did I—

Veil, he was huge.

He dragged his cock up my center and back to my slit before stopping it there and pressing against me lightly. It wasn't enough to stretch me, just enough to make me insane.

And veil, to make me want him so much it made my head spin.

He lifted my hand to his cock. *"Use me, Tempest. Unravel yourself for me."*

It was so much more intense than anything I'd ever done before.

It was absolutely *insane.*

And yet I found myself slowly dragging the head of his cock over my clit, dipping him against my slit before dragging him back up.

He was smooth, hard, and foreign—and it was so insanely hot, I couldn't take it.

His hand covered my mouth as I cried out with my release, my body tightening with waves of pleasure even though there was nothing to tighten around. The thought of his thick cock inside me as I lost control only made the pleasure fiercer.

He snarled softly as he tugged my fingers from his erection and jerked a hand down his length once, and then again, before releasing all over my core. The warm heat of it was so foreign—and so, so good.

"Veil, you look incredible covered in my pleasure," he swore into my mind. His hand still muffled my cries as he dragged his fingers through the slickness of his release, and over my clit again.

I was so damn sensitive, my hips jerked, and my mind spun.

"Roll over."

I didn't even consider ignoring the command, rolling to my belly and propping my arms on the bed.

"Hands and knees," he said.

It was an order, but it was so simple and direct, without any disrespect in it. He knew how he wanted me, and that was the easiest way to get me there.

His hands were on my hips, lifting my ass as I raised myself to the position I'd been instructed to.

"I'm not going to take you from behind yet, Tempest. Tell me if I do anything you don't like."

"Okay. I—" I cut myself off as his fingers dragged over my clit, and a moan escaped me.

His hand smacked my ass lightly, not hard enough to sting, but hard enough to make my body clench and wonder if more was coming.

I wasn't sure why, but veil, I wanted more.

The thought made me so damn wet between my thighs, I felt my pleasure and his roll down my legs.

"Pillow in your mouth," he said.

I bit down on the pillow.

"You're going to feel my fingers, now. There may be a small amount of pain, since it's your first time. I won't know if it's too much unless you tell me, understand?"

"Yes," I whispered.

Veil, the way he had taken over was so damn hot.

More pleasure rolled down the insides of my thighs as he toyed with my clit a little more—and then slid a finger inside my channel.

My words died.

My thoughts died.

My sounds died.

The feeling—veil, it was so much.

So, so much.

"You're so damn tight. I can't wait to feel you around my cock."

I let out a strangled breath as he added a second finger and slid them in until he hit something near the back of my channel.

"Relax, Tempest," he murmured into my mind, slowly pressing against whatever he'd hit.

My face twisted at the slight pain until he broke through, and it ended as suddenly as it had begun. He growled into my mind as his fingers slid in deeper. *"Veil, you feel good."*

The words didn't even process in my mind.

The intensity of what he was saying, the insanity of what he was doing... with my ass in the air and my tits on his bed and his fingers buried inside me... everything was so unreal.

He pulled out long enough to slide another finger in, then his spare hand found my clit, and it was over so fast.

I cried into his pillow as my hips rocked desperately, the climax hitting me so damn hard there were no words to describe it. It was so vastly different than any pleasure I'd felt before—so much deeper, and wilder, and more *free*.

I came down from the high faster than I wanted, my mind still blank of anything except shock at how good I felt.

"That was perfect, Tempest." He stroked my clit lightly. The slickness of his release was still on my core, and still dripping down my thighs. *"Veil, I can't wait to watch your body swallow my cock."*

The words made me want him—fiercely.

Insanely.

Desperately.

I opened my mouth to say that, but a loud knock on the door silenced me.

"What?" Vayme growled.

"The Monster has been spotted outside the city. The elves' shields are holding, but your council wants to develop a plan in case he breaks through."

My heart nearly stopped.

Vayme let out a rough breath before replying. "Give me a minute, and I'll meet with them."

"Alright. Kee is on the stairs along with a few others, so be quick," he said.

My throat swelled at the mention of the woman who had touched his chest in his room that day. Kee. He seemed to trust her—and she certainly seemed to be interested in him, because I'd never seen anyone else touch a fae they weren't in a relationship with like that.

She hadn't known we were mated, though. Maybe that would change things?

And his hand was still buried inside me; that would definitely change things.

Or at least, it would definitely change things for me.

I suddenly felt very, very self-conscious on the bed like that, exposed so completely to him.

Just as I started to move, he slid his fingers free of my body, and then his tongue dragged slowly up the inside of my thighs. His chest rumbled at the taste of our mingling pleasure, and he said nothing of the meeting. I sat up with my legs dangling off the edge of the bed, much more uncertain than I wanted to admit or accept.

"Shower with me," he said into my mind, rising to his feet and offering me a hand. I took it, though I knew the fae well enough to know he wanted to wash the scent of what we'd just done off his skin.

"So we're keeping what just happened a secret?" I asked him, more uncertainty swelling in me as he grabbed his bar of soap and scrubbed himself quickly.

"Not really." He took his soap to my skin, the motions much gentler than when he'd washed his own. I itched to use my new soap, but I was fairly certain he'd dropped the bag in my room before he had kissed me. *"I'd rather my people not know the specifics of how I make you climax, but it doesn't need to be a secret that I do. Our plan hinges on the bond breaking, but that doesn't mean we can't share a bed."*

That... didn't relax me.

Maybe it should've, but it didn't.

I wasn't sure what to do about it, or how to feel.

So, I changed the subject. *"How long is your meeting going to be?"*

"Long, probably. You should sleep in here while I'm gone."

I cringed inwardly, and debated how to turn him down before finally saying, *"I think I'd rather stay in my own room. It'll be nice to have my own space again."*

He nodded silently. *"Let me know when you're going to sleep."*

"Okay. I can finish up, if you want to get going. I know they're waiting on you."

He grimaced but agreed.

My gaze lingered on him as he finished drying off, pulled on a pair of pants, and then strode out of the room.

"I'll stay close enough that the handprint will barely ache. Please be safe." He paused in the doorway, hesitating, and then shook his head and slipped out of the room with one last, *"Lock the door behind me."*

I only waited until he was gone before padding to the door. Water dripped off my skin, but I wanted to lock it... and maybe see if there was anything to hear as Vayme left with his friends.

I opened the door just a breath and put my ear to it, listening closely.

"How long has he been outside the city?" I heard Vayme ask.

"Not long. He just arrived," a female voice explained.

Though my throat constricted, I knew they were only talking business. And if Vayme hadn't been with any women in that many years, it was really, really unlikely that he would find himself suddenly attracted to her. It seemed safe to assume he had known her for a long time, since there were no new fae being born and whatnot.

The problem wasn't that I didn't trust him... it was that I didn't understand their relationship, or friendship, or whatever it was, and she had certainly seemed interested in him the last time I saw her.

Their voices faded, and I carefully closed the door.

Rather than locking it, I dried myself off as quickly as possible, slipped back into my dress and undergarments, and then stepped out of the room.

Staying in there without Vayme seemed wrong since he'd left to deal with whatever was going on with the Monster. Whatever we were wasn't solid or certain, so I needed to make sure I had enough space to protect myself.

Thankfully, Pavia wasn't playing out in the foyer area when I stepped out. Matían eyed me with something near curiosity, but I just gave him a quick nod before disappearing into my room and locking the door behind me.

A long breath escaped me when I collapsed against the stone, and I closed my eyes.

There was so much uncertainty... and it was going to drive me mad.

At least there was nice-smelling soap to wash myself with. Maybe it would help me forget my worries.

CHAPTER SEVENTEEN
KAELLE

Unfortunately, the soap didn't wash away my problems.

It did smell nice, though.

And the soap to make my hair softer was even more of a miracle than I'd hoped for. My comb glided through the strands easily after using it.

I let Vayme know when I was going to bed, and received a quick good-night that only made me more uncertain.

He hadn't asked me to let him know when I woke up, so when morning came around, I didn't reach out to him.

Matían and Pavia—well, mostly Pavia—invited me to go see the xuno with them, and since I had nothing else to do, I agreed.

I wasn't about to snuggle up on a xuno with Vayme's brother, so I asked Soft to carry me. She agreed readily, without asking for anything in return.

The handprint didn't occur to me until we were on our way out, and Vayme was growling into my mind, *"Where are you going? Are you safe?"*

"I'm fine. I'm going to see the unbonded xuno with Pavia and Matían. Soft is carrying me."

He seemed to relax slightly. *"Stay clear of the city's edge. The Beast could have told the Monster what you look like, so he may be watching for you."*

"Are they friends?"

"I don't know. It seems likely."

"Well, I don't plan on going far. Besides, the handprint would probably hurt too much if I did."

"That's true." Vayme's response was still gruff. *"You didn't let me know you'd awoken."*

"I didn't know you wanted me to."

"Tempest, I worry when I don't hear from you. Next time, let me know."

I sighed aloud so he didn't hear, my uncertainty swelling, but agreed. *"Alright."*

"I've got to get back to the meeting. I have word spreading that the challenges will be based on a list now, and will only occur once a week. Some of my people are gathering volunteers to retrieve some of Pavia's mother's things, as well."

It was nice to be filled in on that, since he had taken my advice. I would've preferred to be involved in the conversations about it too, but I did understand that Vayme was likely the only person who saw me as a temporary queen. To everyone else, I was just a human shield to protect him from the Monster.

"Okay. Thanks for letting me know."

I felt his hesitation through the bond, but he finally said, *"You're welcome,"* and left it at that.

"Is everything okay?" Soft asked me, her mind touching mine.

"I'm not sure. It's hard to say," I admitted. *"Something's wrong, I think. I'm just not sure how to put it into words."*

She chuffed—the closest thing she had to a chuckle. *"That's difficult."*

"I know. I think I'm just bothered that I still don't really have a place with Vayme. I think technically we're... dating? But we have this mental bond that

makes things intense, and I'm not even sure what it means to be dating from a fae's perspective. He said to tell him if he did something wrong, but I'm also not sure what's really considered wrong." I huffed out a laugh. *"It's pathetic."*

"It's not pathetic. I think most beings—xuno included—struggle with the beginning of a relationship. Everyone has their own definitions and ideas of things, and it's hard to make them align. I imagine it's harder when one of you is a human and the other is fae."

"That's a good point."

"If you're confused, the king likely is too. He's old and stuck in his ways. I don't think he was joking when he told you to let him know if he did something wrong; something wrong probably meant something that bothered you or frustrated you."

A laugh escaped me. *"Something tells me he wouldn't appreciate being called old and stuck in his ways."*

"It's true though, isn't it? And direct communication makes life much easier for everyone." She winked at me over her shoulder as she slowed to a stop.

"You're right. I think I'll just have to talk to him about it whenever he gets back from this meeting he's at." I slipped off her back, and scratched her behind her ears after I landed beside her. *"We should be friends. You know how to deal with this place a lot better than me, and you see things more simply than I do."* After a pause, I quickly added, *"And I mean that as a compliment."*

She chuffed again. *"Then we will be friends. As a friend, I should warn you, it's likely that Vayme will send Strongpaws to stick with you through the entirety of his meetings. He will worry about you."*

"See, this is why I need you." I flashed her a smile, and she gave me a wolfish grin.

Pavia ran over and grabbed my hand. "Come on, Kaelle! We need to find you a xuno to bond with too!"

Soft's grin widened as she followed while Pavia dragged me into a portion of the city that looked packed full of xuno.

For the next few hours, we met, talked to, and scratched every beast we could manage, trying to establish bonds. Soft told me facts about each of them, and I had to stifle laughs a few times.

When Strong showed up to keep an eye on me, I laughed aloud, and Soft and I exchanged grins again.

Eventually, we made it back to the king's rooms, and I found my mind wandering while I watched Pavia play a game with Matían's companion.

Of course, my thoughts kept returning to Vayme and his meetings. Something about the way he had left, and how we had communicated in the moment, rubbed me wrong. I was trying to figure out what it was.

After a while, Pavia called out, "Kaelle, come play with us!"

My attention jerked to her, and I found her waving me toward her.

"No one likes to be commanded, Pav. Ask politely," Matían warned.

She sighed dramatically, but asked politely, so I agreed.

When I'd played long enough that I could sit back down on the cushion —with Soft on one side of me and Strong on the other—my mind went back to my interactions with Vayme, but I still couldn't figure out what the issue was.

Both Soft and Strong snuggled up with me in my bed that night. Strong stared at her like he expected her to leave, and she stared back at him with narrowed eyes.

I found myself looking between them, wondering what was going on, but didn't ask. They would tell me if they wanted to.

Neither of them said a word to me as their stare-off ended and they got comfortable. I wasn't sure what to think about that.

"How is it going with the female you're pursuing?" I asked Strong, after we had all settled. I hadn't seen Vayme all day, and had barely heard from him, which added to the uncertainty I was feeling.

"Not well," he grumbled.

I scratched him lightly behind the ears, and he closed his eyes as he relaxed. *"How does one pursue a female xuno, anyway?"*

"Compliments. Gifts. Snuggling. Spending time together. The same way one pursues a human female, I imagine."

I nodded. *"Why isn't she interested?"*

"She wishes to remain unmated until her companion selects a mate."

"And you don't?"

"Vayme is mated, remember?" He nudged the handprint on my hip with his paw.

"Only temporarily."

He made a noncommittal noise, but said nothing.

"What does that mean?" I eyed him suspiciously.

He studied the ceiling intently.

"Strong," I warned.

"Tempest," he countered.

I huffed in frustration.

"He is truly an irritating male," Soft agreed, broadcasting her thoughts so both of us could hear.

My lips curved upward, and I set a hand in her fur so I could scratch her too.

"Don't try to turn my companion's female against me," Strong growled at her.

"Your companion's female is my friend, Strongpaws."

He glared at her, and I couldn't suppress my curiosity any longer. *"What's going on between you?"*

"Nothing," they said at the same time.

I looked between them, not believing them in the slightest.

"Strongpaws and I were friends when we were pups," Soft finally said, her eyes focused on mine as she ignored the xuno on my other side. *"Our friendship grew into romance, and we decided we would create a mate bond. The day we were going to seal it, he bonded with Vayme, and then introduced me to his companion as his friend."*

Strong was staring at Soft, his eyes still narrowed. *"Many beasts choose not to take a mate until their companion does."*

"And many take mates whenever they find the male or female they wish to bond with," she countered.

He scoffed. *"I went to find you that night, and you were already gone."*

"I'm not daft. I know when I'm not wanted, Strong." Her use of the short-ened version of his name sounded like an insult, and while I liked Strong, I silently cheered for her for it.

"You were always wanted. My circumstances changed, but my emotions did not."

The flatness in her gaze told me she didn't believe him.

Not even a little.

She closed her eyes, effectively ending the conversation. Though Strong growled again, he didn't press for more.

"I love the way you stood up for yourself," I admitted just to Soft.

"Powerful males are impressive, but they will take anything you allow them," she murmured back. *"With a powerful male, a female must determine what she's comfortable with, set her own limits, and respect herself enough to enforce them."*

I studied the smooth stone ceiling, considering her words. *"You're right. I think maybe that's my problem with Vayme. I'm not very good at standing up for myself, or setting limits."*

I supposed that was what I had done when we discussed mate bonds, though.

He had been plenty receptive when I told him I wasn't willing to consider a relationship without the potential for it to end in a mate bond. When I said that, he had adapted his thoughts and expectations to suit me. That seemed... significant.

He likely hadn't realized it would make me feel uncertain when he left with Kee to attend his meetings. Or that he had never explained the full extent of their relationship, friendship, or whatever it was. He heard the Monster was outside the city, he showered, and then he left. There had been plenty of time for me to speak up, but I had stayed quiet.

Vayme was a good man, but he was also a fae warrior, and a king on top of that. He was direct and clear in his communication, so it might not occur to him that I could be hesitant about communicating the same way.

The fae were certainly confrontational, after all.

"You can learn," Soft said simply.

"Thank you." I scratched hers and Strong's fur lightly. As I did, I decided that when Vayme got back, I was going to ask him plainly about his friendship with Kee to hopefully settle my mind on the subject. Until then, I needed to figure out exactly what I was comfortable with, so I could set those boundaries.

I was still thinking when the xuno fell asleep, and the quiet sound of their snores made my lips curve upward slightly.

"Tempest?" Vayme's voice was grumpy in my mind.

"Don't sound so excited to talk to me," I murmured.

My sarcasm earned the tiniest chuckle from him.

"Have you gone to sleep yet?" I asked.

"Unfortunately, no. I don't recommend getting into politics. It takes far too long to make any decisions. Every warrior thinks himself a strategist, and veil, the discussions are endless." He sounded far wearier than I expected.

"Are you almost done?"

"I doubt it." He heaved a sigh. *"Tell me about your day. We're having a second dinner break right now, and I want to strangle everyone else in the damn room."*

Though I'd been hesitant and a bit uncertain when he first reached out, speaking with him calmed me. I told him about everything I'd done with Pavia, but left out the conversation between Soft and Strong, since I wasn't sure what he knew about it.

We chatted about the xuno I'd met that day for a bit, and then he sighed again. *"Someone just came to drag me back in. I've got to go. You're tucked into bed?"*

"Yes." I focused hard on the sight of my body curled beneath the blankets, tucked in with Soft and Strong, and felt the tiniest whisper of his satisfaction.

"Sleep well."

"Try to get out of there soon so you can rest," I murmured back.

He made a noise of agreement, but I knew him well enough to doubt he would really try to end the meeting. He didn't want to disrespect anyone he liked, and he was the kind of man who would surround himself with people he liked at the head of his kingdom.

My eyes lingered on the ceiling as I got back to considering what kind of relationship I wanted. Eventually, I drifted off the same way.

CHAPTER EIGHTEEN
VAYME

The next few days passed far too slowly, full of meetings and empty of sleep. I only managed an hour or so each day, and never caught Kaelle while she was home. Pavia kept her busy, which I supposed I should've been grateful for, though I was itching to have her at my side in the damn meetings.

I finally made it down to my wing of the castle five mornings later, and found Kaelle curled up on a cushion with a book, scratching Soft's fur absentmindedly as she read. Strong was snoring quietly on her other side, and her book was resting on his head. She wore a light purple dress that made her look calmer, and my handprint showed clearly through the cutout over her side.

I stopped at the bottom of the staircase to simply look at her for a moment.

Veil, she was the most beautiful woman I had ever seen.

Her hair blew lightly in the soft breeze emanating from her skin, and her expression was set in a calm, relaxed position as her eyes scanned the pages of her book.

She was stunning.

And I had missed her more than I realized. There was something comforting about her. Something peaceful and happy, unless I'd scared her or made her angry, of course, though I tried not to do that.

Kaelle's eyes lifted from the book's pages after a moment, and her eyebrows lifted in surprise when she saw me.

I crossed the room to greet her, and she said, "I was starting to wonder if you'd ever come back." Her voice was quiet, and despite the bit of playfulness in it, I didn't think it was a joke.

Had I done something wrong?

I had itched to ask her to join the meetings, if only to sit on my lap and let me stroke her legs while my fae debated.

Veil, I'd been starting to wonder if I'd ever come back too.

The only reason I hadn't asked her or invited her was because I knew she would enjoy herself more with Pavia, and it seemed selfish to ask her to suffer through it with me.

"As was I," I admitted, offering her a hand.

She eyed it but didn't take it.

Worry curled in my abdomen.

I had certainly done something wrong, but was too exhausted to try to figure out what.

"The challenge is tonight. I assumed it would worry you less if I showered and rested beforehand," I told her, my hand still outstretched. "I would like you to join me."

She eyed my hand again, but then lifted her gaze to mine. "That *would* worry me less. But I'm not feeling particularly comfortable with where our relationship stands right now, so I don't think joining you is a good idea."

I blinked at her.

That was fair, but... surprising.

And I wasn't sure why she was uncertain, truthfully.

"What worries you?"

Both of us turned our gazes to Pavia's bedroom as she bounded out. Her face lit up when she saw us.

She sprinted across the room in a light purple dress nearly identical to Kaelle's. Her hair was braided away from her face, and she shrieked, "Uncle Vayme!"

I caught her as she launched toward me, and lifted her for a hug. "Good morning, Pav."

"You were gone sooo long!" she exclaimed. "I worried about you!"

My gaze flicked to Kaelle.

If Pavia had worried about me, how had my female felt? She didn't know anyone in my city except my brother and his daughter.

Perhaps that was why she had refused my hand.

"I'm sorry. Hopefully I can get everything taken care of soon, so we have more time to spend together," I told my niece, setting her back down on her feet.

"You look worried," she remarked, staring up at me for a moment. "Kaelle is worried too."

My gaze and Pavia's both jerked to Kaelle, who gave Pavia a small smile. "I'm okay, Pav."

"Pavia?" Matían called, as he strode out of the room. He looked surprised to see me, and when he asked what all had been decided, I gave him a quick summary. He nodded as I finished up, and said, "We're going to visit the xuno again, Pav."

She groaned. "I want to stay with Uncle Vayme."

"Uncle Vayme needs to catch up on sleep."

"Fine." She stepped over to Kaelle and grabbed her hand. "Let's go."

Matían looked at me, the humor in his eyes telling me I was going to have to deal with *that* part myself.

"Unfortunately, I have to stay and talk to Vayme this time." Kaelle covered for me, tugging lightly on the end of Pavia's braid. "You'll have to keep an eye out for potential companions for me."

Pav groaned. "I have to go alone?"

"I'm right here," Matían drawled.

She sighed. "I'm always with you."

"Because you're lucky." He leaned over and plopped a kiss on her forehead. "Let's go."

She shot Kaelle a desperate look, and Kaelle mouthed, "I'm sorry."

I caught my female's hand as they slipped away, not giving her the chance to turn me down that time as I led her to my room.

Veil, I was exhausted.

After I made things right with my female, I would sleep.

"I believe I've upset you somehow," I said to her, studying her from the side as we walked.

She nodded, but said nothing.

Though I itched to ask for more—or demand answers—I held my tongue. She needed to decide on her own to tell me what the problem was.

"You were gone for a long time," she finally said. "I know what you were doing was important, and we spoke mentally, but it's not the same as seeing you. It was hard not to think the worst."

She needed reassurance.

I should have invited her to the damn meetings.

Changing directions, I led her to the baths instead of my room. She gave me an inquisitive look as we slipped inside, and I closed the door behind us—locking it too.

Kaelle eyed the lock with surprise. "You had it put in?"

"I did. No one can attend my damn meetings for me, but many fae can install a lock." I released her as I stripped my clothing and then slipped into the nearest pool.

She sat on the ledge and let her toes dangle into the water. I grabbed the soap and started to scrub my skin. Though I would rather have pulled her in with me, I understood the importance of our conversation coming first.

I admitted, "I wanted to ask you to come to the meetings with me, but I didn't want you to feel obligated. In most situations we would have disbanded every evening, but with the Monster outside the city, it seemed unwise to dismiss everyone. We had fae creating distractions, tests, and diversions to see how hard he would try to break through the elves' shields to get in, and whether the elves could feel the impact on their magic. Walking away would have been difficult, and could have led to my death."

She nodded. "I don't blame you for staying; I understand why you did. It's just hard for me to feel sure, considering everything."

I needed to make her understand the way I had ached for her, and thought of her day in and day out. Veil, the Monster could hunt me down and end my life, and I'd pass into the next life with her name on my lips and her smile in my mind.

But there was no way to force anything with her. And even if there was, it wasn't what I wanted. I wanted her to think of me the same way I thought of her.

Constantly.

Obsessively.

With far more emotion than I wanted to admit.

I couldn't convince her of any of those things in the moment though, so there was only one thing to do.

I took her hand in mine and met her gaze with my own. "I'm sorry, Tempest."

She blinked, seeming surprised by my apology, and said nothing.

I lifted her hand to my lips and pressed a kiss to the back of it, giving her a chance to gather her thoughts.

"I think I would feel more comfortable if I could be sure of a few things," she finally said. "If I know I'll see you every day, it won't feel as if you've abandoned me. If you tell me about Kee and let me see you interact with her, I won't feel as if you're spending your time away from me in her bed. And I know those things aren't logical, but they're what I feel, so they're important to me."

My jaw clenched.

I had forgotten that she saw Kee touch my chest in Jirev. I should've remembered that and realized Kaelle would be uncomfortable with it even though nothing had ever or would ever happen between us.

I forced myself to regain control of my breath and mind before I said, "Those are reasonable requests."

She nodded, but looked a bit uncertain. "Then why are you angry?"

"I should have predicted your discomfort sooner and done something about it."

She bit her lip. "We can communicate mentally, but you can't read my mind. I should've spoken up sooner."

"Tempest, if a man had put his hands on you in front of me, I would be fighting a very powerful urge not to kill him... or he would already be dead."

Her face flushed a bit. "I don't think that's a compliment."

"It's a promise." I brushed my lips to the back of her hand again. "Next time, I will drag you into my meetings and sit you on my lap, so you're certain my people know who I belong to."

She sighed and ran a hand through her hair, pulling it away from her eyes and tucking it behind her ear. Her wind wouldn't leave it there for long, but she knew that. "This whole thing is overwhelming. I couldn't stop thinking about you, or missing you, even when I was angry or frustrated. I think it might be easiest if we end whatever we have, or just leave it at sex so neither of us gets our heart broken. Our lives don't exactly seem compatible, and—"

I put my hands on her thighs, rising to my knees on the stone seat inside the bathing pool. Her eyes collided with mine, and I held her gaze steadily. "It would have been easier for you if I left you in your cave, wouldn't it?"

She grimaced, but nodded.

"It would've been easier if I had let the war continue, or if I let the Monster end my life. Easy is not *better*. I'm sorry that I hurt you, and I will do everything in my power to prevent it from happening again, but ending our relationship isn't the answer. And it *is* a relationship. If another female attempts to seduce me or touch me in a way that dishonors you, I will promptly end her life. Even Kee knows that, and has kept her distance."

"You're really stubborn," she said.

"I am a king, Tempest." I squeezed her thighs lightly, where I still gripped them. "It's part of the job."

"I think you're more stubborn than the average king," she countered.

My lips curved upward. "You must not have had a conversation with Kier or Ravv, then."

"I guess not." Her smile was small and reluctant, but genuine. "Alright. We can continue our... *relationship*. But if I don't see you every day from now on, I'm going to have to be done."

"I understand." I dipped my head. "It won't happen again."

She didn't look quite convinced, but didn't protest.

"I have a request," I said, squeezing her thighs again lightly. "I would like us to share a room and a bed. I have had a difficult time sleeping alone since we've been back from Jirev."

Her face reddened slightly. "You've hardly slept at all, because of your meetings."

"And that sleep has been restless," I agreed. "I worry for you, and I itch to have you in my arms when you're not with me. If you're not comfortable sharing, I understand, but I would vastly prefer it."

She bit her lip, considering it, and I gave her time to think it through. "Alright," she finally agreed. "But you can't kick Soft out. She's been cuddling with me, and she's started to become my closest friend."

"Soft?" My eyebrows lifted in surprise. "And Strong hasn't said anything?"

"They fight sometimes and exchange glares, but otherwise no. I know they have a history together, but they don't bring it up very often."

"Well, I have nothing against sharing with her."

I would ask my companion how he felt about it, but I wouldn't sleep apart from my mate if he hadn't spoken out against it. Even if he had, we would discuss it until we reached a reasonable understanding and agreement.

"Okay. I'll move my stuff after you leave," she said.

I shook my head. "We'll move it together, after we're done bathing. I'm not leaving you again. The challenge is tonight, and you're coming with me."

She grimaced, but nodded. "Are you worried about it?"

"No. I've fought Ivel many times, and usually walk away with no more than a scratch or two."

She only looked slightly comforted by that.

One of her hands lifted lightly to my hair, catching a strand and sliding softly down the length of it. I fought the urge to close my eyes and lean into her touch, or lay my damn head on her leg.

The days had been very, very long.

"I missed you," she said quietly. "I didn't realize how much I would."

Though the words were a bit sad, pride swelled in my chest upon hearing them. "I missed you too, Tempest."

I wrapped a hand around the back of her neck and leaned in, brushing my lips to hers. She sighed softly at the contact. Her toes dragged against my erection before she hooked her leg around my ass and used it to pull me closer. My cock met the fabric over her core, and she groaned lightly into my mouth.

I released her long enough to tug her dress over her head, exposing her undergarment-clad body to me.

"Veil, you are stunning." I took her breasts in my palms and worked them lightly. "I'm going to taste your pleasure on my tongue when you're wet enough for me."

She moaned at my words, and watched with hooded eyes as I slowly removed her undergarments, baring her to me.

I certainly didn't deserve to see her like that, but damn, I was grateful she let me.

One of my hands coaxed her legs open for me while I lowered my lips to her breast and took her nipple in my mouth. I fought the urge to bring my ice into play. She wasn't ready for it—I knew she wasn't ready for it —but veil, I wanted to watch her react to my magic.

She moaned and moved against me, opening her legs further. The scent of her desire was so thick, it surrounded me like a second skin.

"Are you wet enough?" I murmured into her mind.

"Yes."

I released her nipple and kissed my way down her abdomen, lifting her hands to my hair before I dragged my tongue over her clit.

The taste of her exploded on my tongue, so damn erotic I nearly found my release then and there.

She cried out, her fingers tangling in and tugging on my hair as she rocked against my mouth. I worked her clit, and slowly slid a finger inside her channel.

Veil, she was so damn tight and hot.

My cock swelled, and I nearly lost control yet again.

Her hips jerked, and I worked her until she reached her climax, her voice loud, frantic, and desperate in a way I had only imagined.

A snarl escaped me, and I stroked my cock roughly as I found my pleasure, releasing into the water.

"Ohhh," Kaelle moaned, dropping to her forearms on the smooth stone of the floor. "That was amazing. We should never try to be quiet again."

I chucked, flicking her clit with my tongue again and making her hips rock a little in the process. "I'll talk to Matían today."

"You're sleeping today, and fighting," she reminded me.

"I can do all of it." I dragged my teeth over her clit, and she sucked in a breath.

"Veil, you're making it really difficult to stay away from you."

I chuckled. "Good."

CHAPTER NINETEEN
KAELLE

"Bathe with me," Vayme said. When he looked up at me with his face between my thighs, he was too damn gorgeous for me to say no.

"Alright." I wasn't sure how far I should let us go. He had very nearly entered me the last time we were together. I had been moments away from asking him to do so.

But after so many days apart, I was less certain.

I did expect that his idea of time passing was different than mine. It likely hadn't even occurred to him that I would be upset. And even though I was still cautious, I did believe him when he said it wouldn't happen again. Vayme had never lied to me.

He dragged his tongue over my clit one more time before pulling me into the water and sitting me on his lap. When we were settled, the length of his erection rested against my core in a way that made me ache for him.

Part of me wanted to just get it over with. If we had sex, the act would likely stop feeling so big and important, which would be nice. But at the same time, I doubted he would agree to sex just for the sake of *getting it over with.*

Maybe if I didn't phrase it that way...

His lips brushed my neck once, and then again, before he leaned back. The movement slid his cock against my core, and I fought to keep my thighs from clenching in desire.

"Veil, you feel too good," he growled against my throat.

"I want to get it over with," I whispered.

He went still.

Dammit, I knew I should've phrased it differently.

"Sex," I added quickly. "I want to get sex over with. I know we got kind of close, and—why are you growling?"

His fingers dug into my thighs. "Sex will not be something you and I *get over with*, Tempest. I had far too many years alone with my hand to ever allow that. When I enter you, it will be because I've made you so damn desperate, you won't settle for anything except my cock. Understand?"

"Not really. I—"

"I will not budge on this."

"Stop interrupting me." I hit him on the arm, the smack soft enough that I could barely hear it, despite my wet hand.

His eyes gleamed wickedly, and he remained quiet.

"I was trying to say that I'm nervous, okay? It makes me nervous. I'd feel better if we got it over with, because it wouldn't be looming over me anymore. I understand wanting to wait—and I can wait. But there's some part of me that feels it looming. I think your reasoning is just as legitimate as my own, but that doesn't mean I agree with you."

His wicked gaze softened. "I suppose I didn't consider that. We will meet in the middle, then. When you decide you want me, you climb on me, and take me. It's your first time, not mine. The choice should be yours."

His words warmed me and calmed me at the same time, but I wasn't entirely sure I liked having all of the responsibility and pressure on my shoulders. "Thanks, I think."

"You think?"

"What if you don't want me when I want you? What if you're not ready, and I—"

"I'm ready for you this second," he said.

I didn't mind the interruption so much, that time.

"I was ready for you in those damn meetings. I kept imagining you climbing on my lap without anything beneath your dress, and taking my cock without letting anyone in the room know. You could take me any damn time or day, and I'd want you. No questions asked, no hesitation given. My pause is for your sake, not mine."

Heat curled in my belly.

He had fantasized about that?

I stored the fact away for later, in case I might be able to use it.

"Okay." I nodded. "When I want you, I'll take initiative."

"Good." He lowered his lips back to my throat and sucked lightly on the sensitive skin there. "Now, you're going to ride my fingers while I wash you. I need to make sure you're ready to take me, whenever you decide to do it."

"Well, I won't say no to that."

Vayme turned me around on his lap so my back was to his chest, then grabbed his bar of soap. He dragged it slowly up my arm and then to my breasts, where he slowly circled my nipples with it, one at a time. The combination of grit and slickness was enough to make me flush with need, especially as his fingers slowly stroked my clit.

"Did you touch yourself while we were apart?" he asked me, his voice low in my ear. Goosebumps emerged on my skin, and my hips jerked against his hand.

"Did you?" I asked him, not wanting to be the first to admit it.

"I didn't. If I'd had time enough for that, I would've sought you out so I could bring you pleasure first, and coat you in my release. Seeing my pleasure on your skin brought out something deeply wild within me, and I'm curious as to how I'll feel if it happens again."

A snort escaped me. "What a compliment."

"It is. I can't say I'm ever wild." His teeth dragged against my throat, making me shiver as he worked my nipples with the soap and my clit with his fingers. "Did you?"

I bit my lip, and he slowly slid the soap between my breasts, moving it in a lazy trail downward. My body ached and throbbed, but his fingers stopped moving.

"Answer my question, or I'll give you a reason to, Tempest."

"What does that m—ohhh." I cried out at the coarse pressure of the soap dragging over my clit.

It was slick, gritty, and rough...

And it nearly shattered me just like that.

Maybe I liked my pleasure the same way Vayme did.

He held the soap against my clit, but trapped me in place with his free hand so I couldn't move against it. "Tell me, or you'll leave this pool aching for my cock."

Though it was a threat, I recognized the arousal in his voice, and the throb of his erection against my backside. The threat wasn't a warning or a challenge—it was a game.

"Make me," I whispered.

His teeth dragged over my throat, and he grinded the soap against me just for a moment. Just enough to make me reach for his hair and take hold of the strands, gripping them tightly.

He worked me again, and halted again before I reached my climax.

"Give me my pleasure, and I'll tell you," I breathed.

He chuckled. "That's not how this works, Tempest."

But I needed boundaries. He needed to see us as equals. He could order me around, and I could have a bit of fun following those orders, so long as he knew how to follow my orders too.

I sucked in a breath as he worked me with the soap again, taking me even closer to the edge before stopping.

"Get me off so I can stroke your cock and watch you cover my core with your release," I said.

His body went rigid.

My lips curved upward just a little, even as I panted for breath.

I had more control in our relationship than I had realized.

As I thought that, the words to seal our bond drifted through my mind.

"Sillah ovim rett warum."

I forced them away.

Obviously, it was the wrong time. There probably wouldn't ever be a right time.

"You don't want to pleasure me," he finally said, his voice straining.

"Of course I do. I've been itching to touch you since the forest, Vayme." I took a page from his book and sent him a mental image of me stroking his cock.

He gritted out a curse, and dragged the soap over my clit again, making me rock against his grip. "You'll answer my question after you've climaxed?"

"Yes."

He bit down lightly on my ear, grabbed my breast in his free hand, and started moving the soap harder, and faster.

My breath hitched and my body rocked violently, responding with thrill to that tiny bit of pain mixed with pleasure. It wasn't long before I was crying out, my voice flooding the bathing chambers again as pleasure rolled through me from head to toe.

Veil, it was so much better when I didn't have to be *quiet*.

I pushed his soap away from my sensitive skin and slipped out of his arms, then out of the bathing pool.

He had loved it when I worked my clit with his cock, so I'd give him that —and more—for letting me have my way.

"Get up here," I told him, taking charge again.

His eyes burned with heat, and he rose to his feet as I spread my legs wide for him.

"Lean closer and put your hands on my thighs. Hold on to me, but don't touch me otherwise. This is about you," I said.

The man's eyes could've burst into flames.

I sat up enough to take his cock in my fingers, and he swore as I gripped the massive length of him. Though I didn't know exactly what I was doing, I had seen him bring himself pleasure, so I had a pretty damn good idea.

"Do you like when I take control?" I asked him, my eyes on his as I held him securely.

"More than I ever would've expected," he gritted out. "I couldn't stand it when other females did—but I find myself so damn eager to please you, all it does is make me want you more."

"Good answer," I whispered, and stroked him once.

His hips jerked as he thrust into my hand, and I let go of him, making him snarl at me.

"I'm in charge, Vayme. If you want me to change the way I'm touching you, you tell me," I warned.

He swore again, but didn't fight me as I took his cock in my hand and guided him back to my core. His hands gripped my thighs in a way that turned me on more than it probably should've.

His breathing picked up as I worked my clit with his cock, stroking his length every moment or two. The way his body trembled told me he was desperate to take charge himself—but he didn't ask me to do anything differently, so he must've been enjoying what I was doing.

"Stop," he gritted out, as his cock grew even harder in my fist. His fingers dug into my thighs so hard, they had to have been leaving bruises. Bruises I'd wear with a thick, heady pride. "Stop, or it's over."

I interpreted his words to mean he was about to climax, and wasn't ready for it yet, so I stopped and waited. He throbbed in my fist, and though we both panted for breath, neither of us did a thing except stare at each other.

"I won't last much longer," he finally said, when the throbbing had slowed. "Have the last of your fun. When I've finished, it's my turn to have my way with you."

Thrill coursed through my veins at his words.

I dipped my head in a nod and started slowly moving him over my clit again. "You like how I look with your release on my core. How would you like to see it inside me?"

His eyes flared with heat, and his fingers dug deeper into my thighs. "Don't taunt me, Tempest."

In response, I dragged his cock down to my slit and moved my hips a little.

Curses spewed from his lips as the thick head of him pushed against me just the tiniest bit. I pulled away long enough to stroke the length of him, and then repeated the motion, taking just the very tip of his cock. He wasn't even stretching me—I was in complete control, and he wouldn't thrust inside me, no matter how badly he wanted to.

I lifted my hips, my gaze fixed on my core as I met his cock, and the tip of him stretched my entrance just a tiny bit.

Vayme's nails cut into my thighs as his body trembled, and his snarls and curses filled the air as he found his climax.

His pleasure drenched my ass and slit as he released. His chest heaved as he came down from the high, and he pulled his cock away as his hands left my thighs. My body arched as his hands dragged over my ass, collecting his release and lifting it to my core.

I watched in dry-mouthed shock as he pushed his pleasure inside me again and again, filling my body further with the warm thickness of his release.

Then, he dragged his fingers over my slick core—and leaned over me, lifting them to my lips.

His eyes were hot, his chest still rising and falling rapidly as he gave me a single order. "Taste us."

I was going to argue, but his fingers pressed against my mouth, and the desire to fight didn't even cross my mind.

My lips parted, and his fingers slid over my tongue. The delicious heat of his pleasure and the saltiness of my own assaulted me, and I couldn't help but moan.

"Swallow," he said.

I swallowed.

His fingers stroked my tongue and the inside of my mouth slowly, before he finally withdrew them. Then his lips caught mine, the kiss slow and salty and so damn intimate it made my world spin.

He withdrew after a moment, leaving his forehead against mine as we both breathed hard. "The next time you want to torture me, Tempest," he said in a low voice. "Use your mouth."

Veil.

With that, Vayme removed my hands from his hair and set them on the ground on either side of my ass.

As I opened my mouth to ask him why he had, thick cuffs of ice grew over my thighs and wrists, holding me where I was.

My thoughts stumbled, and then froze for a moment. What he'd said came to my mind... something about it being his turn.

I supposed that was fair. And there could hardly be a way to take more control than to literally restrain me where I was, spread open and completely bare.

He slowly kissed each of the bruises and tiny cuts his fingers had left in my thighs, and then sank into the water, his predatory gaze moving over me. "You're even more stunning with my release dripping out of your body like that. Perhaps this will have to become our tradition after I take you—watching my pleasure drip out of you, drenching that pretty little asshole."

My face flushed. "Vayme."

"I let you take control the way you wanted it. It's my turn, now." His eyes lingered on me as he retrieved the bar of soap and slowly washed his hair. Mine lingered on him too, watching the flex of those massive muscles and the way his hands moved over his body.

By the time he finally made it back to me and slowly licked every damn inch of me, stretching my channel with his fingers as I climaxed, I was so damn ready to have his cock inside me, it was ridiculous.

Vayme dried me off before drying himself. His lips moved over my shoulder and neck as he held me in his arms, and then his forehead rested against my head too. "I'm so damn glad to hold you again," he murmured into my ear. The man sounded absolutely exhausted, and I felt bad for keeping him up.

"Let's get you to bed," I said.

"After we move your things." He brushed another kiss to my throat. "I'm not letting you get away from me that easily, Tempest."

I tried to frown, but my lips curved upward of their own accord. "I'm not trying to get away from you."

"Not anymore. I'll keep you satisfied enough that you never have a reason to," he agreed.

His hands moved with the towel as he dried me off, and it was strangely intimate. I wouldn't have expected that intimacy, but I found myself enjoying it.

It was probably a bad idea, but veil, I could get used to having a massive fae king's arms around me like that more often.

We moved my things to his room—our room—and then collapsed in bed together. I had my book, and neither of us wore anything but our undergarments.

The intimacy of that was even more intense than him drying me off, but I didn't let my mind linger on it. We still hadn't promised each other anything, after all.

Even if the words of our bond had started ringing through my mind again, with more insistence.

"Sillah ovim rett warum."

"Sillah ovim rett warum."

"Sillah ovim rett warum."

I couldn't say them; I knew I couldn't.

And yet they kept repeating anyway, as if taunting me with a life I could have, if I decided to take it for myself.

Of course, I was smart enough to know those urges were a lie. If I sealed my bond with Vayme without him being certain he wanted to stay with me, we wouldn't work anything out. We would be tied to each other forever, both physically and mentally, and he would despise me for it. It would be a nightmare.

So, my mouth stayed shut, even if my mind didn't.

"Sillah ovim rett warum."

The guarantee of stability that I wanted, but could never take.

CHAPTER TWENTY
KAELLE

Vayme slept with his face buried in my hair and his body plastered to mine. Holding my book was a challenge, but I enjoyed the physical contact too much to move away.

A few hours passed before the door swung open and Strong came strolling in.

"We'll need to leave for the challenge soon," he said to both of us, eyeing our positions with interest.

Vayme stirred, taking a deep inhale of my hair and letting out a soft groan that made me warm.

"I'll give you a few moments," Strong said, padding out of the room.

Vayme's lips found my neck, and sucked on it lightly as his hands slipped between my thighs.

A quiet gasp escaped me as his fingers brushed my core.

"Vayme," I whispered in protest. Though I wanted him to touch me, Strong had said we needed to leave. I had heard Pavia talking faintly when the door opened, so I knew she was back.

Which meant we had to be quiet.

"I need to watch you unravel before I carry you out before my people as if on a platter," he said into my mind, sucking my neck a bit harder. *"And I can smell your desire, Tempest. You're reading a steamy book, aren't you?"*

My face flushed.

It was becoming something of an obsession—both the king, his body, and what he could do to me.

"That answers that question." He worked my clit through my undergarment, and I gripped his arm to anchor myself. *"But you owe me another answer. Did you touch yourself while we were apart?"*

My face burned, but pleasure still curled in my abdomen. *"I did."*

"How many times? Where? Alone?" His growled demands made my toes curl, though his fingers had stopped moving on my core.

"Of course I was alone. In my shower, so your brother wouldn't smell anything. I knew you were concerned about the smell. And... well... every day. Sometimes twice." My cheeks may as well have been on fire. *"I kept thinking of the way you had kissed me and touched me. The way I used your cock, and the way you had me on my hands and knees, too. I couldn't help it. I feel like you started a fire in me, and I don't know how to put it out."*

"I don't want that fire to go out." He dragged his fingers over my clit. *"I'm sorry I wasn't there. I'll make up for the lost time, starting now."*

He made love to me with his fingers and mouth before he coated my breasts in his pleasure, and then we reluctantly washed the scent off before we finally slipped out of the room.

Strong didn't look surprised by the extra time it had taken, and Soft looked a bit amused.

My face heated, but Vayme reassured me that the xuno weren't bothered by sex the way humans were. It was natural to them.

He left me with Soft and Strong while he slipped away to talk to Matían, and I scratched Strong for a moment before going back to Soft.

"So you stood your ground?" she asked me.

"I did. It was easier than I expected."

DARK & DEADLY PREDATORS

"And it will only get easier." She stood and stretched. *"We're going to the challenge?"*

"Unfortunately, yes."

Her face formed a vicious grin. *"Good. It's been far too long since I watched someone bleed."*

A laugh escaped me, and Strong padded over, looking a bit suspicious.

Soft flicked her tail. *"We're talking about the challenge, not about you."*

He didn't reply, though his gaze grew a bit less narrow.

Vayme came striding back out then, and leaned in to brush a kiss to my head before he lifted me onto Soft's back. *"You'll keep an eye on her?"* he asked the xuno.

"Of course. Kaelle and I are friends, Vayme."

The way she addressed him like he was her equal rather than her king made me fight a grin.

"Thank you." He scratched her behind the ears, then stepped back to Strong's side and slipped onto his companion's back.

The xuno took off without waiting for instructions, and I leaned down further, gripping Soft's fur lightly as she ran.

We made it up the staircase and out of the castle soon enough, and then we were moving fast.

"Where is the challenge going to happen?" I asked Vayme, as we went.

"We have our own version of the stadium in Jirev," Vayme explained. *"Without a cage, of course."*

I nodded, though that last bit didn't seem as obvious to me as it apparently was to him.

"If you grow dizzy from all the auras, ask Soft to get you out long before you go unconscious," Vayme warned me.

I agreed, though I probably wouldn't do as he asked.

I could survive a little dizziness.

. . .

The crystal lights above Vuuth were fading as if the suns were going down as we traveled through the city. It wasn't far, so we reached the stadium soon enough.

I found myself peering down at the large stone cavity in the ground. Shaped much like the city itself, it was rounded, with seating that rose in layers around a pit in the middle. The benches were already full of fae, who were a mesh of loud energy and laughter.

I was more used to the insane number of auras than I had been when we first reached Jirev, so I could still function properly, and hoped I could do so through the entirety of the fight.

When I brushed my mind against Vayme's again, I did so as gently as possible. *"Will anyone try to kill you while you fight, now that word is out about us being mated?"*

"It's possible, but not likely. To attack me in public would be a death sentence, even for my enemies. The majority of my people still want me as their king, even if they don't want to admit it. Our kingdom is stronger with me on the throne."

Soft and Strong made their way through the fae and xuno on our journey down to the very bottom of the pit. There were no empty benches, though I spotted a few small gaps and wondered where Vayme would want me to sit.

He led me to a bench full of fae I recognized from Jirev, and they made a little more space for me to sit between them. I noticed Kee right behind me, and my face warmed as my discomfort grew.

"You are the queen, even if it's temporary," Soft murmured into my mind. *"Act like it."*

She was right.

I turned around and gave Kee a small smile. "Hi, I'm Kaelle. I think we sort of met before."

She mirrored my expression. "We did. It's nice to officially meet you, as the king's mate."

My smile grew a bit brittle.

Kee studied me for a moment before she added, "I'm sorry if I made things less comfortable for you in Jirev; I wasn't aware of your bond. I would never knowingly touch a mated male in any romantic manner. King Vayme seems happy with you, so I'm glad you're here."

My discomfort lessened slightly.

Only slightly.

"Thank you."

She nodded, and I turned back toward Vayme.

His gaze moved over the people around me without lingering on anyone in particular before it landed back on me, and he nodded. *"This is going to work."*

"It sounds like you're trying to convince yourself."

His lips curved upward, but rather than responding, he bent down and captured my mouth in his. My hands slid into his hair as he kissed me passionately, staking his claim on me for everyone around us. The overwhelm of their auras slipped from my mind, and my body relaxed at the intimate contact.

I was safe.

Vayme would protect me.

Nothing bad was going to happen.

Some of the fae in the stands cheered, while others fell silent.

When he pulled away, the king murmured into my mind, *"Trust me."*

I did, so I nodded.

It was the rest of his people I didn't trust.

My eyes lingered on his backside as he strode down into the fighting portion of the arena while the crowd roared around him. All he had on were his usual pants, but after hearing about the fae who fought naked in Jirev, I was grateful for the pants.

When Vayme reached the center of the circular space, he slowly turned, holding his hands out at his sides and calling, "Where is the challenger?"

The auras swelled through the crowd as their energy level rose. A massive man and xuno with average auras swaggered down through the stands, and I remembered Vayme telling me that the man's name was Ivel.

Unlike Vayme, Ivel *was* naked.

And apparently turned on by the challenge he was about to fight, or the crowd's reaction to it.

I flicked my gaze back to Vayme quickly, and found his eyes on me again. Something told me he was making sure I wasn't checking out his competitor too closely.

When I flashed him a small smile, I felt his mind brush against mine as if to let me know he'd noticed the gesture.

The men met in the center of the arena and shook hands. Neither of their positions were stiff, but neither man looked entirely relaxed, either.

Vayme needed to win to hold his throne... and Ivel needed to win if he wanted to become king. And now, there was likely some other consequence hanging over Ivel if he lost. Vayme and I had discussed that, but he hadn't told me what they settled on as punishments when he was in those meetings.

Obviously, it wasn't the right time to ask.

I didn't have to though, because the crowd finally quieted, and Vayme's voice boomed through the arena. "As you all know by now, the consequences have changed for challenges. Death is no longer the goal or punishment. The loser faces the harsh reality of a year working in the deepest farm, without reprieve during an eclipse."

A hushed, unhappy murmur rolled through the crowd.

They were used to frequent battles for the throne, without any real consequence for the challenger. Though I didn't know what their deepest farm was, it didn't sound very pleasant, and the crowd's reaction solidified my suspicion of that.

"Every challenge loss that follows the first will increase the time spent at the farm," Vayme added. "The second will be five years. The third will be ten. The fourth will be fifteen, and so on."

The crowd went silent at that.

Fifteen was so damn many. I could understand that fae saw the passing of time differently than humans, but they still lived each of those days, and I couldn't imagine anyone really wanted to live them in a truly unpleasant situation.

"Do you understand the terms?" Vayme called out, his gaze lowering to Ivel.

"I do." Ivel didn't look uncertain, but he didn't look entirely comfortable, either.

That meant he was taking the challenge seriously. I hoped Vayme would do the same.

Both men nodded at each other. Ice weapons appeared in their hands, and the fight began.

They were so fast, my eyes could barely follow them around the space.

Their bodies spun and swung, moving through the battle as if it were a dance. They moved too quickly for me to have any idea what was really happening or who was winning, unfortunately.

But their auras and those all around me continued to grow stronger as the fight went on.

My head began to throb, and dizziness slowly but steadily set in. I tried not to react to it, but keeping my eyes open grew more difficult as the strain began to work against me. My wind picked up its pace, but no storm built.

Soft pressed against my legs, reminding me that she was there and that I was alright. Though we didn't speak to each other, her presence let me know I wasn't alone.

By the time the fight came to an end, I couldn't see people anymore; just auras. The crowd was cheering again, but they had barely stopped, and I was pretty sure they would continue to cheer regardless of who won.

I forced myself to focus, until I saw Vayme's aura standing tall and strong while Ivel's was on the ground. That had to mean my king won, right?

Thank the veil.

No one had touched me during the fight or tried to attack me, as far as I knew, so that was good too.

Vayme called out to the quieting crowd for a few moments, and then I watched his aura move in my direction. He lifted me off the bench without a moment's hesitation, then slipped onto Soft's back with me. The warmth of his body and familiarity of his aura were calming as he pressed me against her soft fur, and she moved.

No one tried to kill us, thankfully.

Maybe his kingdom was more at peace than he suspected.

Or... maybe his people were waiting to see how his new challenges went before attacking us at one of them.

I supposed there would be no way to know which one was accurate until more time had passed.

"How hurt are you?" I asked him quietly.

"Barely. Only a few cuts. There's a deep one on my abdomen, but the others are only scratches."

I supposed if he was bleeding, that would explain some of his warmth against my back.

"I'll patch them as soon as I can see normally again," I said.

"Don't worry about me, Tempest."

I was fairly sure that our bond meant I would *always* worry about him until it was broken, but I didn't say that aloud.

Closing my eyes, I squeezed them against the onslaught of dizziness that accompanied Soft's motion. She wasn't unsteady, but veil, she moved fast. And speed did not work with my overwhelm. Not at all.

My stomach rolled, but I clamped my jaw shut.

I was *not* going to vomit.

My willpower was swaying too when we finally reached Vayme's wing of the castle.

He thanked Soft, who said something in response that I couldn't make out perfectly, and added something else to Strong. Pavia's voice sounded in my ears too before he began carrying me away.

I assumed we were headed to his bedroom until he murmured to me that we were going to the bathing pools to help calm me. The pools sounded like something that might actually help, so I whispered an agreement as he continued onward.

CHAPTER TWENTY-ONE
KAELLE

Blissfully warm water engulfed me as Vayme slipped into the same pool he'd found me in on the first day. I let out a soft groan at the feel of it, leaving my eyes closed in hopes that it would help me regain control of the dizziness that was overwhelming me.

He slowly and carefully peeled my dress over my head, tossing it to the side and leaving me in my undergarments. His arms wrapped securely around my middle, holding my back to his chest as I relaxed.

"I can—" I started to tell him that I was ready to patch his wounds, but he shushed me. His voice was calm and level, so that made me feel better.

I let out a soft sigh, but remained quiet as I waited for the dizziness and nausea to fade.

Vayme's hand moved lightly over my hip, relaxing me further as his erection rested against my ass.

Eventually, the overwhelm began to lighten up.

I opened my eyes after it did, looking around the room slowly to make sure I could see normally again. Everything looked okay, so I glanced over my shoulder at Vayme, and found those gorgeous silver eyes of his staring at me.

"Feeling better?" His voice was low and gravelly, and it gave me goosebumps.

"Mostly."

"Good." He leaned in and brushed a kiss to my forehead before he dragged me back against him and pressed another kiss to my temple. "You scared me."

"You knew there was a good chance that would happen, though."

"That doesn't make it any less worrisome, Tempest. I don't like seeing you hurting, particularly when there's nothing I can do about it."

I supposed I couldn't blame him for that. And veil, I was grateful he felt it, too.

I changed the subject, though. "Did you have any problem beating him? I couldn't really see much even before the dizziness got too strong."

"No. I know how Ivel moves, much to his frustration. He left bleeding far more than I did."

The answer satisfied me. "I'm glad."

"As am I." He brushed his lips to my temple again, and we relaxed against each other as the pounding in my head continued to fade.

"You probably need to rest," I said quietly, after a few more minutes had passed. "And I need to bandage your wounds."

He made a noncommittal noise.

"Vayme."

He leaned in and brushed his lips against mine lightly, calming and quieting me before he said simply, "You can patch me if you'd like, but I can sit here as long as you're enjoying it. It was only one fight; I'm fine."

I sighed, but relaxed against him again. "Alright. We can wait a few more minutes."

It was already the evening, and while I'd gotten plenty of sleep, the combination of my wind's drain on my energy and the overwhelm of my magic had exhausted me completely.

The peaceful heat of the pool slowly relaxed me more and more, until I slipped into the soft embrace of sleep.

Some part of me felt Vayme lift me out of the water and dry me slowly before setting me in bed, where I fell back asleep the moment my head hit the pillow.

When I woke up, I felt more than a little disoriented looking around the darkness of Vayme's room.

"Easy." His soft, thick murmur near my ear relaxed me, and I found his body pressed against mine.

"I'm supposed to bandage you," I mumbled, tripping over the words with the weight of sleep still hanging onto me and trying to drag me back in.

"I took care of it. Go back to sleep, Tempest."

Nodding lightly, I closed my eyes and lowered back onto the pillow before I fell asleep.

When I woke up for real, the castle felt quiet.

Very, very quiet.

Pavia must not have been there, because it was never so perfectly quiet when she was. As much as I liked her and her noise, the peace was nice too.

"You smell so damn good." Vayme's voice was gravelly in a way that made me shiver. His chest was pressed against my back, and one of his arms was wrapped around my abdomen, while the other was tucked beneath his pillow. His body was so tight against mine, I could feel every line of his erection between my thighs.

"So do you."

His arm released my waist so his hand could find my hip, and he slowly dragged his palm up the curve of my body. I still had my undergarments on, and part of me was grateful to him for not taking the liberty of undressing me while I slept.

The other part of me wished he had taken the liberty, so he could ravage me with a little less effort.

His hand skimmed my side again. "Do you feel better about the challenges now?"

"Mostly. I still need to see your wound," I whispered.

He abandoned my hip long enough to catch my hand and drag it to his abdomen, where he ran my fingers over the soft roughness of his bandage.

That shouldn't have satisfied me, but it did.

"You were more affected than I was. I wasn't going to let you patch me up when you couldn't see straight, Tempest." Vayme's lips brushed my shoulder, and he set my arm back down where he found it. Then, he resumed moving his hand over my hip. "I have to admit, I slipped away for a few minutes while you slept."

My stomach tensed. "You did?"

"I did. Pavia called out to me that she was leaving, and I had to say goodbye."

Oh.

My body relaxed.

"Where did she go? Back to the xuno?" I asked.

"I'm sure they'll be there later. Matían packed their things and headed to my parents' house. He's decided to stay with them until he determines which part of the city he wants to live in. I offered him the floor above this one, and most of my xuno as guards, but he doesn't think he and Pavia are in danger. I don't think they are either."

"Was she crying?" My stomach tensed again, this time with guilt.

"No. She's excited to stay with her grandparents, she was just worried she would never see us. I assured her that we would visit, and she perked up. She's excited to be on the city's surface, where she can see the lights change and try more new things."

His response eased my guilt. "I'm glad."

"As am I." He brushed his lips over my shoulder again, continuing to run his hand up and down my hip. "And think about it—we have all this space to ourselves."

My stomach curled for an entirely different reason. "That sounds nice."

"Mmhm." He pressed a kiss to my throat, and lingered there. "Did you know that mates can heal each other by exchanging blood?"

My throat swelled. "I think you mentioned that before."

"Good. Remember that for the future. And fae heal much faster than humans—so if something ever happens, and you're badly wounded without a way to get back to me, you'll need to seal our bond to ensure your survival."

The remark surprised me thoroughly.

I blinked, then blinked again.

And again.

And again.

Finally, I said, "You *want* me to seal the bond? What happened to not being convinced, and deciding what to do when we either fell in love or didn't?"

"I would not want to continue living in a world where you don't exist."

Veil.

That was... intense.

"Well, I'll try not to get wounded," I finally said, not willing to agree to what he'd suggested.

"That is a given, Tempest." His hand continued stroking the curve of my hip.

I changed the conversation topic before we went any deeper on the topic of mating. "Are you close with your parents? You've hardly mentioned them before."

He didn't answer immediately, and I wasn't sure if he just didn't want to talk about it, or if he was trying to decide what to say.

Finally, he said, "I'm not close with them. My parents are... unique. When I was conceived, they were simply friends who were bored with life and edging on immis—immortality's insanity, if you recall. Neither of them was willing to consider mating to prevent it, so they decided to have a child to give them purpose. It worked, so they had another as soon as possible afterward. They had planned to each take one of us and raise us separately, but before Matían was born, they fell in love."

I blinked.

He was right; that was unique.

Vayme continued, "They were still against mating, and didn't particularly want me after they found purpose in loving one another. When Matían was born, they saw him as evidence of their love, while I was simply a defense against immis that they no longer needed. It resulted in clear favoritism, and I was constantly being told to be more like Matían."

My heart ached for him.

"It didn't matter that I'd never lost a fight, or could best men forty times my age in games of strategy. Their dislike showed regardless of how hard I tried in every aspect of my life, how many things I mastered, or how quickly I learned. I wasn't Matían, and I never would be. The previous king took me under his wing, so I moved to the castle as soon as I reached adulthood. The war began, and I became his closest advisor. He wasn't a good man, but he was an intelligent one, and he saw my value," Vayme said.

He went on, "When he died in battle, he gave me the throne, believing that I'd have the best chance at keeping our people alive as long as possible in a war we had all started to realize would never end. Matían eventually joined the ranks of my most trusted fae, despite our childhood, and became the only one I did really trust. When we thought he died, my parents blamed me for his death, and started the uprising against me. They quieted when he returned, but the damage was done."

My throat swelled with emotion for his sake. His family had tried to have him killed for something entirely out of his control—or had at least turned his people against him for it. "Veil."

"You are not the only one whose family treats them improperly." His lips brushed my shoulder again. "We cannot control how anyone treats us, but we can control our responses to them."

"I'm surprised you didn't kill them," I whispered.

He chuckled softly, rumbling against my back and warming me as he did. "Killing is often the answer, but not always, and I have always tried to be fair. Despite their treatment of me, they're not necessarily bad people. Their disapproval during my childhood made me work harder. Because of it, I became someone I'm proud of. I suppose the pain of it will never be gone completely, but it has faded drastically in the years that have passed, and became nothing more than an occasional sting. When I stopped expecting them to treat me the way I used to hope they would, it took away their power to hurt me."

"Veil, Vayme," I repeated. "I'm sorry."

He chuckled again, his hand still moving slowly over the curve of my side. "You don't need to apologize, Tempest. Nothing that happened was your fault. You being beside me will simply give my parents another reason to compare me to Matían, but the handprint on your hip will force them to keep their mouths shut. Even they know better than to insult the king's mate, however human she is."

My face warmed. "You wouldn't hurt them, would you?"

He didn't hesitate. "I would. I would take no pleasure in it, but they would force my hand. Not retaliating against an insult to my mate would be a crime against you, and would put you at great risk. My people must know that I will protect my female at all costs. I would never let you become a target because of my refusal to act on an insult."

My body warmed. "I don't think that should make me feel good, but it does."

He brushed his lips to my shoulder again. "I'm glad." My stomach rumbled, and he heaved a sigh. "I've been neglecting my duty to you."

"I'm perfectly capable of feeding myself. There's always food in the icebox, and Pavia got mad at me when I didn't help myself to it, so I've been careful to always eat what I want."

"At least *someone* made sure you were fed," he grumbled, clearly annoyed at himself.

"Look at these curves. They would start to disappear if I was starving again, Vayme. I'm doing just fine, so don't be angry with yourself." I squeezed a hip, followed by one of my breasts.

His hands did the same, and a satisfied rumble escaped him.

I added, "You're trying, and the next time you have meetings, we're going to make sure we still spend the nights and mornings together, so it's alright."

"The next time I have meetings, I'm going to drag you there with me."

I laughed.

He hauled me out of the bed, padding out of the room without bothering to grab me a dress. I didn't mind being in just my undergarments, since our wing of the castle was empty except for the xuno.

We would definitely be making our way back to the bed...

Or perhaps we wouldn't bother with the bed at all.

My lips curved upward at the thought, and Vayme kissed the smile off of them before he set me on the table—literally, on top of it—and strode to the fridge.

All he had on was the tight shorts he wore as undergarments, and veil, I wanted him to take them off.

CHAPTER TWENTY-TWO
KAELLE

I remained sprawled across the table while he put two bowls of food in the device that warmed them, and waited for it to work its strange magic. It had come from the human lands, according to Pavia, but no one in my town had owned one.

Vayme leaned up against the wall nearest to it, and his eyes slowly skimmed my figure as he folded his arms over his chest.

My body warmed, and I tried not to let myself get too flushed at the sight of him.

But veil, the man was gorgeous.

"Open your legs for me," he said into my mind.

I looked over my shoulder to make sure there were no xuno near enough to see into the room, and found the space clear.

Slowly, I parted my legs. There was fabric covering my core, but it was slim, so it wouldn't conceal much.

His chest rumbled in satisfaction, and I slowly dragged my fingers lightly over the top of the fabric that covered my clit. His rumble grew louder.

"Free your cock for me," I said into his mind, echoing his order.

He didn't hesitate to step out of his shorts, or wrap his hand around the thickness of his erection.

Damn, he was gorgeous.

"Take them off," he commanded me.

I didn't have to ask what he was referring to.

Knowing it would drive him mad, I slowly undid the fastener on the undergarment around my breasts, and then stripped the fabric off even more slowly.

His chest was rumbling, the man nearly growling, as it hit the floor.

He grew louder as I slid my remaining undergarment down my legs. I got an actual growl when the fabric landed on top of the other piece.

"I don't know why you ever wear clothing," he said into my mind, making me warmer as he dragged his hand slowly down his cock again.

"Something tells me you would have a problem with me walking around your city naked." I opened my legs again for him, then dragged a finger over my clit, making him snarl.

"You don't wear clothes in our home anymore. Now, they're reserved for the eyes of everyone but me."

"Then the same rule applies to you."

"Agreed." He strode across the room and captured my hand, lifting it to his mouth and wrapping his lips around my fingers. *"I want your ass in the air while I eat you on this table, Tempest. Now. I intend to stretch you with my ice, so you're ready when you want my cock."*

I flushed with his words, but veil, I wanted all of that.

...I just didn't want to let him have his way. He needed to be absolutely certain that we were equals, and that I could give orders just as well as he could.

So I countered, *"Why don't you sit down while I eat you first?"*

He laughed—the sound was rich, and so damn joyful it made me hotter. "With pleasure."

His ass met the edge of the table, and wetness pooled between my legs as I slid down to the seat in front of him. His erection was so damn huge, and I honestly wasn't positive what to do, but I would figure it out.

Leaning in, I gripped the base of his cock and then wrapped my lips around the head of him.

Vayme snarled, and his hands buried in my hair. His grip wasn't tight enough to cause me pain, but we had established that neither of us was against mixing pain and pleasure a little.

He dragged me further down his cock, showing me what he liked, and I groaned as I bobbed over him.

Veil, the taste of him would drive me mad. It made me feel powerful, strong, and sexy.

I had control of the king's pleasure.

I could pull away at any moment, leaving him wanting more, or I could give him the release he needed.

My body sang with pride at those thoughts, and I met his eyes as I told him with my lips still wrapped around him, *"Don't take over, Vayme. It's my turn."*

He jerked his head in a nod. Though his grip on my hair didn't loosen, he didn't try to pull me back down.

My motions grew more confident as I sucked and bobbed, taking him deeper as I became comfortable with it.

His growls and snarls told me how much he was enjoying it—and the tight grip of his hands in my hair only intensified the sensation for me.

I slipped a hand between my thighs, and he snarled into my mind, *"If you touch yourself, you give the control back to me. I won't allow you to take your own climax while you taste me. That pleasure is mine alone."*

Veil.

I left my aching core alone, bringing my hand back to his thigh as I changed the angle of my mouth.

Curses spewed from his lips as I worked him, and finally, he roared. Tremors rolled through his body, and he forced himself to stay still while I swallowed his release.

His chest rose and fell rapidly, his gaze intense as I met it from below him. His hands loosened in my hair, just enough that the grip was no longer painful. *"I have never allowed a female so much control over my pleasure before, Tempest, or even considered it. You must tell me if I push you too far or hurt you too much in my effort to stop myself from taking what I want."*

I nodded, releasing his cock from between my swollen lips. A bit of his pleasure slid over the bottom one as I let go of him. When he noticed, he snarled again, dragging me into his arms and kissing me.

The brutality of his mouth on mine made my head and body spin.

Veil, he was too good at that. Too damn good at that. Something about the raw, rough strength of the way he did everything made him irresistible to me.

He ended the kiss and turned me around, lowering my forearms to the table as he set me up on my knees and lifted my backside. A squeak escaped me when he dragged my ass over the ledge of the table, sitting me on his face while the back of his head rested against the stone.

"Always so damn drenched for me," he growled into my mind.

His tongue found my clit before I had the chance to respond, and a cry escaped me as my body jerked desperately in response.

I wanted him.

Veil, I wanted him.

All of him.

I opened my mouth to tell him as much—but then he bit down on my clit, and tilted my hips to change the angle of my core. The tip of something hard pressed against my entrance, rendering me silent.

Ice.

He had mentioned his ice.

And stretching me, so I was ready for him.

His tongue stroked my clit lightly, as if soothing the pain he'd caused.

But I didn't want it soothed—I wanted more.

"This ice isn't as thick as my cock, Tempest. You can take it." He slowly slid the tip inside my entrance, stretching me open.

All words died as he slid it deeper.

And deeper.

And deeper.

It was nothing like his fingers. It was so much bigger, and harder, and—

I cried out as he bit my clit again, the ice still slowly filling me and stretching me. When it finally hit the back of me, I felt so damn full, I didn't even know what to say or how to think.

"That's right, Tempest. It's new, but so damn good. Move for me. Get used to the sensation, and use it the way you want to." He sucked my clit lightly, and my hips jerked as another cry escaped me. The motion changed the stretch of the ice, and was so foreign, I couldn't help but repeat it.

Soon enough, my hips were jerking desperately as I rode Vayme's face, my cries growing louder and longer as I neared the edge.

But I didn't want to climax with his ice inside me—I wanted *him*.

"Stop," I whispered.

He didn't hear me—and didn't stop.

"Stop, Vayme," I commanded.

He halted where he was, his teeth on my clit and my body aching, so damn close to the edge.

"Take the ice out," I said.

He snarled at me from below, and didn't do as I'd said right away.

"Take the ice out," I repeated.

He slowly withdrew it, though I knew he could've made it vanish altogether if he wanted to.

My hips jerked and my body trembled.

"Sit down on the bench," I managed.

Some measure of fury and concern warred in his eyes, but he slowly sat down.

When I eased over the ledge and sank onto his lap, his fury and concern vanished—replaced by overwhelming fire.

He lined his erection up with my slit when I met him, keeping his hands off my thighs. He had promised that I could take his cock whenever I wanted him—and he'd realized I wanted him right that moment.

Slowly, I let gravity pull me down over him.

And down.

And down.

We both panted for air.

My fingers dug into his hair and gripped so tightly it had to have hurt. His landed on my hips and squeezed me, kneading me, urging me to continue without pulling me down himself.

The stretch of him was blissful. He felt so damn much better than his ice—and I wanted more.

I was gasping for air when my clit finally met his skin as he bottomed out inside me. He was breathing almost as rapidly as I was.

"You'll never be free of me now, Tempest," he said into my mind, the words hot and gravelly. *"Every part of this body is mine."* He squeezed my hips, my ass, my waist, my breasts. *"No one else has ever touched you—or ever will."*

"A few minutes ago, you were still against mate bonds," I panted out, speaking aloud.

"A few minutes ago, I was a fool." He bit down on my throat. "This body is mine. This blood is mine. This *cunt* is mine." The filthy curse made me throb all over, and I wasn't even moving against him. "I'll kill anyone else who thinks about touching you, bond or no bond. If you ever consider taking another male's cock, you'll spend weeks chained to my bed while I torture you with climax, after climax, after climax, until you forget your own name or why you would ever think about walking away from me."

The world spun around me as I started moving my hips, just lightly. "That sounds intense, Vayme."

"It's everything, Tempest. Everything. *We* are everything." He thrust deeper inside me, and I gasped for air. "I will never be done with you. Not in this life, and not in the next. You take care of me too perfectly—and fit me too well." He thrust again, and I cried out louder as my pleasure swelled.

What was he doing to me?

What was he—

He thrust again, and it was over.

I screamed as the climax hit me like a damn boulder. It was so much more intense than I'd ever expected, and so much *better*.

My pleasure went on for what felt like forever as Vayme roared and filled me with his release, marking me in a way no one else ever had.

We both panted as we came down from the high, our bodies pressed together tightly and intimately. I started to climb off him, but he held me securely where I was, narrowing his eyes at me. "You're going to hold me inside you until I hear you say that you belong to me completely."

A breathless laugh escaped me. "Vayme."

"I'm not joking."

I laughed again, harder. "It's always a battle for control with you."

"Just the way you like it." He captured my mouth in his, and kissed me until I had to pull away to suck in more air.

"I belong to you, just as completely as you belong to me," I finally breathed.

"That's right, Tempest." He kissed me again, just a soft brush of his mouth on mine. "Now, I need to feed you." He stood smoothly, and I gasped when he held me in place, leaving his cock buried inside me.

By the time he'd retrieved our food, it was cold again. My face was even more flushed, and I was nearly dripping with the effort to stop myself from rocking violently against him to take what I wanted.

How did I still want more?

What had the man done to me?

He must've plucked that thought from my head, because he murmured,

"I started a fire in you, remember?" He nipped at my throat as he sat back down, and I moaned uncontrollably.

Vayme lifted me from him long enough to turn me around, and then sank me back down over his cock a heartbeat later, with my back to his chest.

Soft, desperate sounds escaped as I fought the urge to rock against him.

"You fit me so damn perfectly, Tempest. Feel how tight that is?" He thrust in just a little.

I definitely felt it.

"Veil, you can't help but tighten around me, can you?"

"No," I breathed.

He released his grip on my thigh and grabbed his utensil, filling it with food and bringing it to my mouth.

"Not hungry," I managed.

"Eat, or this ends." He thrust inside me again, just as lightly as before.

I moaned, and forced myself to take the bite.

"Just like that." He sucked on my throat a bit, holding me in place while I chewed. When I'd swallowed, he rewarded me with another thrust of his hips—and a drag of his fingers over my clit that sent me over the edge.

I screamed again, rocking and jerking as he snarled about how perfect I was, and lost himself inside me again too. I didn't even bother trying to get off him after that one—the man wasn't done with me. That much had become clear.

He fed me a few more bites of the food, giving me time to breathe as he held me.

He said into my ear, "Feel where we connect, and how drenched we both are."

I was no longer trying to take control. Vayme could have it; when I wanted it, I'd take it back, and he'd let me.

For the moment, I was happy to be at his mercy.

I lowered my hand to my core, and slowly ran it over the place my body stretched to take his. I trembled as I felt myself there—as I felt *us*.

He was right; his release and my pleasure were all over both of us.

"Touch yourself, Tempest."

I moaned, but followed the order... and soon enough, I was losing control again, adding to the wetness we'd already created.

CHAPTER TWENTY-THREE
KAELLE

Eventually, we made it back to the bed. I was still struggling to understand how fae were so damn good at sex.

It wasn't like that for humans.

Or at least if it was, no one had written a book about it. And I was pretty sure they would've written about it if they'd realized it was possible.

So... fae had to just be really good at sex.

I certainly wouldn't complain.

After we napped and then took a long shower together, we headed out to the shops to pick up some of the herb that suppressed fertility. It had been a long time since Vayme had any reason to take it, so he didn't have any, and I obviously didn't either. It could be taken a few days after having sex and still prevent pregnancy, so neither of us was concerned about it, but we did want to make sure we took it as soon as possible.

Vayme held me close to his side as Soft and Strong walked behind us. They were just as far apart as they always were, and when Vayme noticed me eyeing them, he asked why.

"I don't know. Wishful thinking, I guess," I murmured into his mind.

His forehead wrinkled.

"Soft told me about how they used to be together," I explained.

The wrinkles smoothed. *"What did she say?"*

"They were both with me, actually. Soft said they were about to seal a mate bond when he bonded with you and introduced her to you as a friend. He'd changed his mind because his companion was unmated. He said he went to find her that night, but she had already left with her things because she knew when she wasn't wanted. When he said she was always wanted, she didn't believe him, and the conversation ended."

Vayme nodded. *"Strong speaks of her rarely, but when he does, he does so with reverence. I've long believed him to still be in love with her."*

My eyes widened. *"Really? She said he never chases any females who could actually end up mating with him, so clearly she keeps track of him. Maybe she has feelings for him too."*

"She's right. Perhaps we need to figure out a way to nudge them to have an honest conversation. They were best friends, once." He eyed them too. *"I'm not sure how we'd achieve that."*

"Neither am I," I admitted.

"Hmm. We'll continue to consider it."

I agreed, and we continued walking. The light pink fabric of my dress rustled in my wind, reminding me...

"I need to find some shorts to wear under my dresses, kind of like your undergarments," I told him.

He frowned, so I gestured down to the light hem, rustling in the breeze. *"I don't want to know how many fae have already seen my ass."*

Vayme's eyes narrowed. *"We'll find someone who can make them today."*

A few hours later, we stopped at Vayme's parents house, with a large quantity of fertility suppressant in his pocket, and a pair of tight shorts around my ass. I wasn't looking forward to meeting them, but we knew we needed to stop in and see Pavia so she didn't worry that we'd abandoned her.

His arm wrapped around my waist when we knocked on the door, and he held me close to his side as we waited for someone to answer.

A tall, muscular fae woman pulled the door open. Her face wasn't as severe as I expected based on what I knew of her, but I didn't let that sway my opinions.

"Hello, mother," Vayme said simply.

She studied us for a long moment, her gaze critical.

Vayme's fingers didn't tighten on my hip, and he didn't pull me closer. Despite what he'd told me, his position was full of confidence.

I supposed he'd had a long, long time to wrap his mind around the dynamics in his family.

"We're here to see Pavia," he added.

"You're not going to introduce your temporary mate?" his mother finally asked, her gaze lowering to me. It was far less critical than I expected, though a long way from friendly.

"I'm Kaelle." I didn't offer her a hand, though I did give her a small smile.

"Are you going back to the human lands after the eclipse?" she asked me.

"No." I didn't bother hesitating. "We'll visit, but I belong with the fae."

The woman didn't look convinced. I found it ironic that she expected me to be introduced but hadn't introduced herself, so I was also unconvinced. I supposed we had that in common.

"Uncle Vayme!" Pavia's excited shriek cut through the air, and a moment later, she was surging past her grandmother. She threw herself at Vayme, and he caught her easily in the arm that wasn't wrapped around me. His chuckle made my lips curve in another smile—a genuine one, that time. "I missed you so much!" she exclaimed.

"I missed you too." He squeezed her lightly.

She released him suddenly, turning her gaze to me, and her face lit up when she saw me. "Kaelle!"

I was the next to catch her, though I did so with a soft "oof," and probably a bruise or two.

She dragged us inside, and proudly showed us both her room and every xuno in the house. Vayme's parents both had companions who were mated to other xuno, and both pairs had pups running around the house. They were so damn adorable, it made my heart swell.

We spent an hour there before Vayme excused us, and then we headed back to his rooms—our rooms.

We spent the rest of the evening putting the fertility-suppressing herbs to the test, while trading stories of our lives between rounds.

We fell into a rhythm, after that, and the weeks passed by quickly. Vayme dragged me to meetings, and I listened in rapture, offering my opinion when asked.

And he asked frequently.

He explained his history with Kee to me, too. She and Matían had been together romantically for a decade when they were all young, and the two parted as friends. She didn't understand why that meant Vayme wouldn't consider anything with her, but I did, and it erased my questions.

I spoke with her many times, and she was always kind and respectful to me. We even traded jokes on a few occasions, so I had no choice but to let go of my grudge against her.

Vayme and I spent an obscene amount of time making love, and I kept waiting to grow tired of it, but it didn't happen. When we weren't naked together—and even sometimes when we were—we talked.

And talked.

And talked.

He told me stories of his life, and I told him of the books I'd read.

Sometimes, we wondered about the veil together, and what truly happened before and after our current lives. Those discussions made us hold each other a bit tighter. The idea of spending not just one lifetime together, but all of them, grew more appealing by the day.

The Monster was still waiting just outside the city, moving through the tunnels and checking the strength of the elves' shield. It had held against him without fail, even when he attacked it, which relieved all of us. Sometimes he disappeared for a few days, but he always returned, which worried us tremendously.

Vayme had offered to take me down to the deepest farm to calm my curiosity when I admitted I wanted to see the place. Apparently, it was very deep and exceptionally dark, with a strange smell and without crystals to light it. There, they grew multiple types of necessary food that couldn't grow beneath the lights in Vuuth.

Being down there was difficult on the minds of those who went, so there were only two fae who remained permanently. Those fae didn't mind the depth or darkness like the others did. Everyone else was a part of a rotation to spend a week down there every few years. I was intrigued, but not intrigued enough to be interested in that long of a trip quite yet.

The group of fae who had gone to the Sands returned with stories of razing the militia that had killed Pavia's mother, and the number of challengers on Vayme's list dropped dramatically. There were still enough challengers for one fight a week, but many, if not all of them, believed in the cause of the cult that had massacred mated couples long ago.

He didn't end their lives, but he and the fae he trusted kept track of their names and began an investigation into each of them. If any of them were found to be connected to the cult, they were thrown in prison instead of taken to the deepest farm, just until our bond was broken.

Vayme would kill them if they truly ended up posing a risk to us, though.

We had yet to be attacked by any of the possible cultists, but Vayme assumed the ones he hadn't thrown in jail were holding out hope that the Monster would do that job for them.

The challenges were still difficult on me, mostly because of the auras, and I suspected they always would be. I'd started to recover faster after they were over, at least.

As we neared the eclipse, Vayme grew more tense, waiting for the Monster to attack. He seemed certain that the assassin would do something.

I grew quieter as it came closer, having a hard time imagining how things would change when the bond was broken. I couldn't help but wonder whether Vayme would no longer want to be with me when the magic holding us together was gone.

The words to seal our bond had begun to echo through my mind in a maddeningly-rhythmic fashion, as if pushing me to speak them.

"Sillah ovim rett warum."

"Sillah ovim rett warum."

"Sillah ovim rett warum."

I still wanted that security, but I also still knew I could never take it.

So, I ignored the constant strain on my mind, forcing myself to say nothing at all when the need grew too strong.

"Sillah ovim rett warum."

I respected Vayme far too much to seal a bond I knew he may not truly want, even if it was driving me mad.

A few days before the eclipse, Vayme, Strong, Soft, and I walked into one last challenge before our bond would break. Soft and Strong were reluctantly becoming friends again, and I'd noticed them staring at each other when the other wasn't looking.

Vayme suspected that the eclipse would push them to admit their feelings for each other, and we both looked forward to seeing the outcome.

Soft set me down on my usual bench in the arena, and I forced my breathing to remain calm and steady in an effort to stop the auras from overwhelming me.

Veil, there were so many of them.

My wind rustled my hair and dress, but I paid it no mind, focused on retaining control.

The fight began, and I followed it as well as I could despite the ache blooming in my head. Though my eyes still couldn't keep up with the fae movements, I'd learned how to tell who was in the lead by a few physical clues, and the motion of the auras.

Vayme was clearly winning, so I let my focus fade from him as the fight went on.

Closing my eyes, I let out a long breath to fight a wave of dizziness.

Veil, I was getting really tired of how easily I grew overwhelmed. It was ridiculous. I—

Ice flooded my mouth, and my eyes shot open.

I was no beginner when it came to ice. Vayme and I had used it in just about every way possible, I thought, so the ice didn't terrify me.

Or it wouldn't have terrified me, if it didn't taste so *wrong*.

I knew the taste of Vayme's ice, and that wasn't his.

Soft's head jerked in my direction, and her eyes widened as they collided with something behind me.

I didn't turn around to look.

I couldn't, because there wasn't time.

A thick hand encircled my throat, and a masculine arm went around my middle.

Soft lunged toward me, but the man holding me ripped me off the bench too quickly.

The ice kept me silent as he tossed me over his shoulder, then *ran*.

Soft's voice cut through my thoughts as she cried my name, sprinting after me. I sucked in a sharp breath through my nose when I felt the connection in our minds hit harder—and then *change*.

It swelled into something thick and permanent, altering the interior edges of my aura and *veil*, changing my soul.

Companions.

We were companions.

It felt so damn right, it nearly brought tears to my eyes.

The man holding me landed on the back of a xuno, and pinned me against its neck as the beast sprinted away.

"I'm not far behind you. Try to hit them with your wind—try to slow him," Soft urged.

Though slowing my captor would slow Soft too, I focused on my fear like she had asked.

My wind began to whip around us faster and wilder, cutting through the city as the man holding me sprinted. The xuno's fur blew into my face and mouth. I tried to wrestle myself away from the beast and his companion, but even with my storm brewing, the fae's grip was too tight.

The wind built, and built, but he kept running.

When I managed to turn my head, I saw Soft. She was close behind, but not close enough to take him down.

"I won't be able to stop the wind if it gets much bigger," I called out to her, my fear beginning to swell out of control with the wind. My last storm had destroyed the town I loved—what if this one could do the same to Vuuth?

What if my captors hurt me?

What if they *killed* me?

I knew starvation better than I knew myself, but I had never truly considered my death before, and it was terrifying. I wasn't ready to pass through the veil—I wasn't ready to move on from Evare.

"Don't stop it. Show the city the wrath of their queen," Soft snarled back. *"If they're going to allow someone to take you or hurt you, they deserve to pay. These warriors can fight; show them that you can too, Kaelle."*

I jerked my head in a nod before the fae man shoved my head back against his bonded xuno's neck. It was hard to breathe through the creature's fur, and I let that struggle fuel me.

Me, my fear, and in response, my magic.

The wind whipped around us, growing as the xuno continued to run. Its drain on my energy had become so intense, I knew it was already nearing the largest storm I'd ever created—if it hadn't gone over yet.

Strong and Vayme's nickname for me would be proven by the end of the hour.

"Where are you?" Vayme snarled into my mind. *"What happened?"*

I couldn't answer him; I had to focus on my storm.

On my life.

I had to stay alive, no matter the cost.

He continued speaking to me, but I tuned him out. I had to.

"Give it more, Kaelle. Give it everything," Soft commanded me. *"We're near the edge of the city. If they get you through the elves' shield, the Monster will find you, and he will use you to get to Vayme."*

Veil.

I pushed every ounce of my energy at the storm, urging the wind to take all of it. To *use* all of it.

My mind began to spin, and life began to fade from me rapidly. I wasn't dying—not yet—but the burnout would hit, and it would hit hard.

"If the Monster takes me, do whatever you have to do to keep Vayme away from me," I whispered to Soft. *"I don't care what the Monster does to me—just don't let him hurt Vayme."*

"The Monster will do whatever he can to get the king out," she warned. *"Do your best to look weak and pathetic. Do whatever you have to, to make him think you're not a threat."*

Before I could respond, the xuno beneath me skidded to a stop, and the fae launched smoothly off his back, sprinting.

My head bounced against his shoulder as I wrestled against the complete exhaustion of my burnout. My wind was no longer coming from my skin. I had left it all behind me, in the city. Though my storm would rage, it would do so without my guidance.

More terror struck me when I saw the aura of the man—the assassin—in front of me. It was like the Beast's, thicker than any of the fae's and even more vibrant. It was alive with colors, brighter than Nissa's flowers or the Endless Wilds or anything else I'd ever seen.

The colors swirled, shifted, and combined as the man they belonged to sprinted toward me faster than even the fae could move. I was in his arms a heartbeat later—and my gaze met Soft's on the edge of the city before she and everyone else were so far behind me that I could no longer see them.

Stabbing pain blossomed in my handprint, reminding me that I was supposed to be at Vayme's side.

Gray stone stretched above my head for a breath, before the thick overwhelm of my burnout dragged me into the dark bliss of unconsciousness.

CHAPTER TWENTY-FOUR
VAYME

Kaelle's funnel clouds tore through my city, sending ancient fae warriors running for their lives as Strong sprinted through the streets. My female's scent had been wiped away by her winds, and there was no sign of her anywhere.

Blood dripped down my leg as I leaned tighter against my companion. I didn't urge him onward; he didn't need my encouragement.

Not when the female he loved was beside my mate.

Someone had grabbed my Tempest, and Soft had followed her—that was all I had been told. Now that her magic was sending my people running for their lives, they would surely regret not standing up to help their queen.

If her power damaged my city, it would be pure revenge.

"They were moving toward the edge of the city!" a man on the back of his bonded xuno yelled as we passed him, pointing me toward the largest entrance before hauling away from an incoming funnel.

Fear for my mate pounded in my chest, and Strong ran harder, veering in that direction.

"Seal the bond," I ordered Kaelle, my voice growing more desperate by the moment. I couldn't feel her mind against mine—she was either trying not to hear me, or unable to listen. *"Seal the bond, so you can heal like a fae."*

The pain in my palm was ferocious, and my desperation swelled as we reached the edge of the city. There, we found Soft in a vicious battle with a male xuno whose fae companion was already dead at his side.

They circled each other, both already bleeding and snarling.

I didn't loosen my grip on my companion, lowering my head as he launched into the fight with a roar. Despite his issues with Soft, the two of them worked together to down the other xuno quickly.

They stepped away from his body, chests heaving.

"That was my kill to take," Soft snarled at him, ramming his side with her shoulder.

He let her throw him a few steps backward, snarling, *"What in the veil were you thinking?"*

"He's a traitor," she spat. *"He helped his companion steal mine, and they gave her to the Monster."*

Her companion?

Had she bonded with...

No.

"The Monster has Kaelle?" I roared.

"Yes. And someone must've gone to the elves about her storm, because their damn shield is no longer just keeping him out; it's keeping us in."

I was off Strong's back and running toward the entrance again, my head tucked and my shoulder forward. My body slammed into the shield like it was made of stone, and I roared again as I staggered backward.

Soft stepped between me and the shield before I could ram it again. *"This is not going to help anything. She made me vow to keep you away from the Monster, anyway."*

I glowered at her, daring her to repeat the words as I said aloud, "Nothing will keep me from my mate. We'll go to the elves and force them to take down the shield."

I looked out at the city below us, and the storm ravaging it.

There would be some damage, but Vuuth was certainly built strong enough to survive any amount of wind. There was no way to know how long it would last, though. She'd said her last storm had destroyed many towns and a kingdom, but hadn't told me how long it went on.

"She will never forgive you if you let her magic kill your people," Strong said, quietly. My gaze jerked to him, and he added just to me, *"I know the price of a female's refusal to forgive, brother. And it is not a price you want to pay."*

"I'd take her hatred over her death, every moment of every day," I growled back.

"She burned herself out more thoroughly than she ever has before. It will be at least a day before she's recovered, probably more like two or three." Soft said, her gaze tracking the funnel clouds as well. *"That's enough time to get your people into the castle for their safety, and talk to the elves to come up with a way to get her free, or at least to protect her until the eclipse comes. If she's unconscious for three days, the Monster may miss his chance to kill you entirely."*

"And he may kill her in revenge," I argued.

"There's no way to know without talking to the elves. The queens are here; they know the assassins better than anyone else."

Though I wanted to snarl at her, to throw myself against the damn barrier again, and again, I knew the xuno was right.

The Monster had taken my female as bait, so he wouldn't hurt her.

Or at least, I could pray to the lost gods that he wouldn't.

I found the ex-queens tucked in a room together. Orah, the half-shifter, was curled up on her bed in her wolf form. Meeri, the blonde, was painting in the corner of the room, her arms and dress nearly as covered in paint as her canvas. Ismaray, the pink-haired one, was pacing the room, her dress swaying around her as she walked.

"Tell me you know where to find my mate," I growled at Ismaray.

"I heard the Monster took her," she said, her face tense with worry.

I fought a snarl and jerked my head in a nod.

"He won't kill her. The monster—he's not cruel," Ismaray said quickly. "None of them are. Not really. We twisted them with our spell, but they were good men before we did. The Beast is the most bitter. He might hurt her, if he had her, but the Monster won't. The worst he'll do is drink her blood to stay alive."

Another roar nearly burst through my lips at the thought of the Monster's mouth on my female's soft, delicate skin.

"No, it's a good thing," Ismaray said, brushing hair from her eyes in agitation. "He's not going to kill her. The curse will push him to kill you, but if you stay in the city until the eclipse, he won't be able to get to you. He'll bring her back then, or at least walk away from her."

"She is in pain because of our separation. I am not leaving her in his grasp," I spat. Even if I wasn't a man of honor, to leave my female with a creature that could hurt her with a blink of his eye would be insanity.

"If he kills you, he takes your magic," Ismaray shot back. "The last thing he needs is more magic. Those men are going to destroy Evare if we let them—and this is your chance to help stop him. A little pain is a small sacrifice."

"I will not allow the Monster or anyone else the opportunity to hurt my mate," I said, my voice growing lower and more feral. "You will remove the barrier around my city, or I will consider it an act of war against my queen."

Her eyes flared with anger, her shoulders straightening and her chin lifting as the royalty in her past surged to the surface. "We were brought here to keep you and your mate *alive*, Vuuth. If either of you die, my people will be at war with *three* fae kingdoms. I don't care whether you like it or not—this is the best chance of survival for both of you. The shield stays up, you stay in, and the Monster stays out. Kaelle will be fine."

I snarled and surged toward her, my sword materializing in my hand with a tug of my magic. I slammed into another shield, and met Ismaray's glower with my own.

Both of our chests rose and fell quickly.

"I will have enough warriors outside this room to end all three of you the moment your magic runs out, if so much as a hair on her head is wounded," I gritted out. "I created our peace, and you can be damn sure I'll create war if anything at all happens to my mate, whether I'm in here or out there."

Ismaray's fists clenched. "She has a far better chance of being killed by accident in one of your battles than by the Monster. I will not lower the shields. Leave us."

With that, her wall forced me and the xuno from the room, then slammed the door behind her.

I swore and began pacing the hallway, reaching out to Kaelle again, and finding only silence.

I shoved my non-aching hand through my hair. "I'll go mad waiting to hear from her. Veil, I need a way through that shield."

"We have no way to break an elf's magic. Focus on your people," Soft said, brushing her side against mine. *"Ismaray knows the Monster, and we do not. If she says Kaelle is safe with him, I trust her."*

"We'll see if there's anything we can do to help the wounded, and then find out who was friends with the fae and xuno we killed," Strong said, nudging my other side. *"Worrying about Tempest won't help her. She'll want your people taken care of—and her enemies slain. We will cleanse the city of cultists while we wait for her to wake."*

As much as I despised the idea, and the awful pain in my palm, it seemed like the only real solution. Throwing myself into finding and killing the traitors in my city would distract me long enough for my female to wake up, at least.

And if I found out the Monster had hurt her when she regained consciousness... well, then I'd find a way through the damn elves' shields, even if it killed me.

CHAPTER TWENTY-FIVE
KAELLE

My mouth was dry and my stomach hollow when I finally woke. The pain in the handprint on my hip was worse than it had ever been before, and my entire body was trembling.

Then again, that dizziness could've been coming from the fact that I'd burned myself out thoroughly, and had no idea how long I'd been asleep. It could've been *days* since I passed out.

My stomach tensed painfully as I remembered everything that had happened just before I burned out.

I'd been captured by a fae and xuno.

I'd bonded with Soft.

I'd created a bigger storm than I'd ever realized I could.

And I'd been given to the Monster, to use as bait to lure Vayme in.

Fear suddenly cut through me, and I reached out to my mate. *"Vayme?"*

"Tempest." There was thick, fierce emotion in his voice. *"Are you okay? Has the bastard touched you?"*

"I don't know. I think I'm alright. The handprint hurts so bad that if he did anything to me, I don't think I'd even know," I whispered back.

He snarled into my mind. *"The damn elves have me trapped in my city, with a barrier between us. Seal the bond so I know you'll be okay if he hurts you—so I have enough time to break through the elves' magic."*

My body stilled even as the words to seal it rolled through my mind.

"Sillah ovim rett warum."

"I'm not sealing our bond just because we're afraid. That's a terrible reason to seal a bond," I said, as the words repeated again.

"Sillah ovim rett warum."

Veil, I couldn't seal it. Not when we hadn't even agreed that we wanted to be together permanently. Vayme's fear for my safety would fade eventually, and I couldn't bear it if it morphed into regret.

He had mentioned wanting me to seal it before, but only when overtaken by pleasure or lust—not in a moment of rational thinking. We certainly hadn't proclaimed love to each other either, though I knew without doubt that I was in love with him.

"It could be the worst reason in the world, and I'd still encourage it," Vayme growled back.

"Just let me see what the Monster's doing. I'm in so much pain, I don't know if I could even say the words of the bond aloud right now anyway. How are you functioning at all?"

"I'm fueled by fury," he gritted out.

If I wasn't hurting so bad, my lips would've curved upward at that answer. It didn't surprise me in the slightest. *"Give me a few minutes."*

He didn't like that idea, and told me as much, but I tuned his voice out anyway as I slowly wrestled my eyes open just a crack.

The space around me was eerily still, without the tiniest sign of my wind. I'd well and truly burned myself out, and the violent way I was trembling made me wonder if I was going to recover at all.

If illness struck... well, then Vayme may have been right about me needing to seal the bond.

Its words repeated in my mind at the thought of it.

"Sillah ovim rett warum."

"Sillah ovim rett warum."

I was struggling to focus on what was physically around me, but forced myself to do so anyway.

I was on my back, and seemed to be tucked away in a small pocket within a slightly larger cave. A pair of large bare feet were pacing off to my side. The aura around them was definitely the same one I'd seen when I was given to the Monster.

If I scooted forward, I would've been able to tilt my head to look up at his whole figure. But, when I tried to scoot, all I managed to do was cause myself enough pain that I had to bite my lip to prevent myself from crying out.

The pacing in front of me stopped for a moment—and then a large knee hit the floor, and a pair of piercing red eyes met mine.

I sucked in a sharp breath at the sight of his face.

Veil, he was *beautiful*.

With pale skin, facial features sharp enough they could have been chiseled from stone, and wavy silver hair tied up in a bun, he certainly didn't *look* like a monster.

Then again, looks could be deceiving. After all, I looked like a small, weak human, and my storms could have still been raging through Vuuth.

"Your king hasn't come for you," the Monster growled, his voice somewhere between angry and annoyed. I wasn't sure whether his anger or annoyance had a better chance of keeping me alive, honestly.

I opened my mouth to try to tell him that the elves were holding Vayme hostage, but the words wouldn't come out. I was shaking too much, and all I managed to stutter out was, "Elves."

He snarled and stood again, resuming his pacing.

"Tempest?" Vayme demanded.

"I'm alright. He realized I'm awake and asked about you. All I could get out was, 'elves,' and it made him mad, but he didn't react violently. He has me tucked in a small space within a cave. I don't feel like I'm in danger."

"Show me."

I sent him a mental image of the cave around me, and his next growl wasn't nearly as angry as the last one. *"Ismaray told me the Monster wouldn't hurt you. She's one of the queens."*

I remembered Ismaray from our journey to Vuuth. She had shared food with me. *"Something tells me you didn't believe her."*

"Of course I didn't believe her," he grumbled at me. *"I threatened her with war, multiple times. She wouldn't relent. If not for the fierce strength of her shields, I would've gotten through them by now to kill her."*

My lips would've curved upward if I'd been anywhere other than where I was.

Something about knowing that the fae weren't all-powerful made them feel more... real, I supposed.

"How long until the eclipse?" I asked Vayme.

"Only a few hours, now. It will begin at the first touch of morning, and both my connection to the Monster and our bond will fade as it sets in."

Good.

That was good.

Well, not the bond fading. That was terrible. But we needed to be free of his connection to the Monster, so *that* was good.

"Can you bring food when you come for me? And water?"

"Of course," he growled.

My chest warmed at the thought that I could trust him to rescue me. *"How much damage did my storm do?"*

"More than I expected, but less than my people deserved." His words calmed some terrified part of me I hadn't known how to vocalize. If my magic had cost me Vayme, the same way it cost me my family, I wasn't sure how I'd react or what I would do. *"The last of the winds are slowing as we speak. It won't take more than a month or two to repair the damage, and now, people will respect you much more as my queen. You know how weakness is seen in my city."*

I certainly wouldn't mind his people respecting me more, though I hadn't necessarily been mistreated. I supposed they would think before deciding to try and abduct me again, at the very least.

"I spent my time cleansing my kingdom of that damned cult while you were unconscious," Vayme added. *"It will be safe for you when you come back—even after we seal the bond."*

"I don't think we ever agreed to do that."

"We didn't. I've decided I'm going to convince you."

I would've laughed if I didn't ache so badly. *"How do you plan to do that?"*

"In whatever way works, Tempest. Any advice?"

"No. I think you'll have to figure that one out yourself."

"I intend to."

Vayme began packing things, and our conversation grew quieter and slower as he focused his effort on what he was doing. I wasn't sure how he was moving so damn well, but I supposed he'd gotten much more used to pain in his long life than I had in my years in my cave.

"You're alright?" Soft said quietly into my mind. *"The king seems to have calmed some."*

"I'm okay," I reassured her.

We chatted for a while, and she told me everything Vayme had left out, including the gory details. I hadn't wanted to know all of them, but I did appreciate being treated as an equal, and that Soft would leave no secrets between us.

The Monster continued to pace as the hours went by—until eventually, he vanished.

"He's gone," I whispered to Vayme, worry curling in my abdomen, alongside the cramps.

My pain and dizziness were getting so bad, I was starting to worry I'd pass out again.

The Monster's roar rolled through the caves, and I heard a loud thumping sound.

Vayme sent me a mental image of the Monster slamming his fists against the elves' barrier. My king seemed to be standing just inside of it—just out of the assassin's reach.

And the Monster looked possessed. He'd shifted to his stone form, being a gargoyle, but his face and eyes were twisted with something I didn't recognize at all.

The curse on him must've been truly awful, because when I saw him earlier, he had looked *normal* for the most part.

He roared and attacked the elves' shield for what felt like a few more hours... until his noise finally faded.

Soon after, the pain from my handprint started to fade as well.

"The brand is nearly gone," Vayme said into my mind. His voice was distant, and though my throat swelled with worry, I knew it was normal. *"The bond will be too, soon. Strong waits with the elves, to tell them when the Monster has gone, and Soft will bring me to you to ensure we can stay in contact."*

"Okay," I whispered back. *"Thank you."*

"I'm the one who dragged you into this mess. Don't thank me for that."

Vayme sent me a mental image of the Monster's insanity fading from his eyes—and then of the Monster dipping his head toward him as if in respect, before the assassin turned and walked away.

"I'm coming for you, Tempest. Never doubt that," Vayme said into my mind.

I cried out softly as the last of the pain in my handprint vanished. A new feeling cut through my chest as the ice in my veins melted away. The darkness on the edges of my aura faded out until there was nothing left but my own pale blue, and the inner ring that represented Soft.

"The elves will take the barrier down as soon as they're certain the Monster is truly gone," she said into my mind. *"They're being stubborn, but Vayme recognized the cave you showed him, so we'll get to you soon enough. It won't be long."*

"Thank you." I closed my eyes and let out a long, slow breath.

Despite the chill in the air without Vayme's magic to keep me warm, my body was beginning to heat already, responding to the start of the eclipse far sooner than it ever had before. I supposed it made sense that my time bonded to Vayme had changed me more than it seemed, even without his magic lingering in my veins.

The eclipse's heat would be torture, especially while I was so exhausted from the burnout and my lack of food.

At least the painful handprint was gone. Something told me I'd miss it the moment I looked down at my hip and found it bare, but I couldn't let myself consider that. Not while I was alone in a dark cave, with my vision growing worse by the moment, and my body still trembling slightly.

The moments passed by painfully slow. Soft checked in every few minutes while I waited, and I had a feeling Vayme was growling at her to do so, making sure she was keeping me sane.

Wetness blossomed between my thighs, and I found myself shifting positions every moment or two, as the need grew thicker and more overwhelming.

After so many weeks full of so much sex, my body seemed clueless as to how to ignore that desire, but I wasn't about to touch myself while tucked away inside a tiny cave, waiting for Vayme and Soft.

I was sweating, panting, and soaked *everywhere* when she finally let me know they were on their way. I rolled out from beneath the small stone lip slowly, lifting myself on shaky arms just to prove I could. I tucked my knees below me, holding them together firmly as I sat up and waited.

And waited.

And waited.

I'd just started to worry I might collapse in a pile of drenched, awful need when Vayme and Soft finally reached me.

He launched off her back and was pulling me into his arms so damn quickly, I hadn't even seen him move.

Tears stung my eyes as he gripped me tightly to his chest.

Neither of us said a word as he lifted me up onto Soft's back, keeping my body securely against his. His erection was pinned between us, but I knew that was the eclipse's fault and not mine.

"I'm glad you're safe," Soft said to me, her voice straining in my mind.

All of us were struggling with the damn eclipse's effects, including her.

"Me too. We'll talk more tomorrow."

I felt more than heard her agreement.

Vayme's jaw was clenched ferociously tight as she carried us, and I bit my cheek so hard I could taste blood as I fought my body as well. When she finally reached Vayme's chambers and found Strong waiting, he brushed up against her side possessively, giving me a small lick on my arm to tell me he was glad to see me.

I couldn't hear their conversation as Vayme hauled me off her back and toward our room—his room—but the way Soft's side brushed Strong's too made me hopeful.

And then the door shut behind us, and my hope was forgotten.

Vayme set me down on the edge of the bed, peeled a bag I hadn't noticed off his back, and ripped the top of it open. He pulled out a massive box of fruit, bread, and cheese, handing me a chunk of bread without a word.

I accepted it, but narrowed my exhausted eyes at him.

There was only one thing I wanted, and it wasn't food.

CHAPTER TWENTY-SIX
KAELLE

He handed me a glass of water off the table beside the bed, too, rather than giving me what we both knew I wanted.

"Vayme," I said.

"Tempest." He managed to keep his voice steadier than mine. "Eat, so I can ravage you without fear that you'll pass out again."

"You say that like it's happened before." I lifted the glass to my lips and took a slow, reluctant sip.

I wanted his face between my thighs or his cock driving into me, not *water*.

But he did have a point.

And I was already light-headed.

He narrowed his eyes back at me. "I'd be scarred for the rest of our lives if you passed out while I was inside you. Eat the damn food."

"Touch yourself while I do, then."

He blinked.

"The eclipse affects you even more than it affects me, right? Because you're fae? I don't want you hurting. Bring yourself pleasure, and I'll eat."

His eyes blazed, and he unfastened his pants.

I took a bite of the bread in response.

His gaze burned into me as he peeled the fabric down his thighs before stepping out of it entirely.

My body somehow flushed even hotter at the sight of him, bare, hard, and straining. Though his desire was because of the eclipse, I let myself believe he was straining for me.

He stroked his cock once, and shuddered violently.

My toes curled.

"Your clothes reek of the Monster," he said, voice low and gravelly. "Take them off."

I set my bread and water down long enough to take my dress off with shaking hands.

He stroked his erection again, gritting out a curse.

I warned, "Don't hold back. You know I won't judge you for losing control quickly, Vayme. Especially during an eclipse."

He gritted out another curse as he stroked himself again—and snarled as he found his pleasure, releasing on the pants he'd stepped out of.

"Veil, you are so damn hot," I whispered, my body nearly tingling with need.

"The bread, Tempest. Eat it *now*."

I picked it up and started on it again.

"I want you bare." His voice strained again as he covered the distance between us. His fingers traced slowly over the edges of my undergarments, making me tremble again, for an entirely different reason. "Tell me you're mine for the eclipse, Kaelle."

"I'm yours for the eclipse. I've been yours for a while."

"And you will be mine *forever*." His fingers brushed my nipples, and my back arched a bit. "Take a bite, now."

I took a bite.

He slowly traced the lines of the fabric over my breasts, his cock throbbing and jerking in response to the feel of me. My toes were curled, and I was struggling to keep eating, but forced myself anyway.

Vayme finally peeled it off me, exposing my breasts. A low growl escaped him, and he stroked them as if they were something sacred, something he wanted to *worship*. Staying where he'd put me was a struggle I was starting to lose, but the bread was only half-gone. I knew I still hadn't eaten enough.

"I want your release on my skin," I nearly whimpered to him.

"Work on your food, and you'll get it." He pinched my nipples between his thumbs, and I cried out, so damn close to the edge of my climax. I was going to lose my mind if he didn't give it to me, if he didn't—

His fingers brushed the fabric covering my clit, and I cried out, grabbing his arm and gripping it tightly. My body jerked as the climax cut through me, the pleasure hitting hard and fast.

It wasn't enough.

It wasn't anywhere near enough.

But it calmed me just slightly, anyway.

"You're so damn gorgeous, Tempest." His voice was low and strained again. "Eat, so you can take my cock."

I moaned at his words, taking another bite of the bread when he snagged it from me and lifted it back to my mouth.

His free hand stroked his cock for me, and I watched, flushed and needy.

"Your breasts will wear my release as soon as your bread is gone, Kaelle." He held his erection, waiting for me.

I groaned, but took another bite.

He stroked himself again, and I quivered.

The pattern continued until the bread was gone—and Vayme had snarled again, coating my chest in his pleasure.

He made me drink water after that, and then made me eat the fruit and cheese.

The last thing I wanted in the moment was cheese, but he was worried about me, and I was too needy to refuse.

He peeled the undergarment away from my core and down my thighs as I ate, and then slowly teased my core with his tongue until I was done and crying out again.

Our movements grew jerkier, our thoughts beginning to fade as the eclipse started to take over completely.

As soon as I'd eaten the last of the food, Vayme rolled me to my hands and knees, lifting my ass and tilting my hips. Finally, he parted my thighs and slammed into me. I cried out as he slid home, giving me what I needed and craved. His fingers teased my clit as he dragged climax after climax out of me, losing himself inside my body over and over again until I was trembling again.

Despite the eclipse's haze over our minds, he noticed the trembling and carried me into the kitchen, still impaled on his cock. My world spun as he forced me to eat bite after bite, his erection throbbing inside me.

When he was finally satisfied with how much I'd consumed, he pinned me to the icebox and made me climax there a few times—before carrying me to the bathing pools.

We spent the rest of the eclipse there, until our energy was finally spent.

As the eclipse's remaining intensity faded away, Vayme left me on the seat of the hottest pool, hauling himself out of the water that must've been burning him while his chest heaved. "Veil, Kaelle."

"Veil," I mumbled in agreement.

My body ached madly, though it was an extremely satisfied sort of ache. I hoped I wasn't bleeding.

I leaned the back of my head against the edge of the pool, waiting for my racing heart to calm.

I usually despised the eclipse, but I certainly hadn't hated anything we'd done. Now that it was over, I didn't think I'd ever felt so relaxed in my life.

As I rested, though, my mind ran over the spot Vayme's consciousness used to occupy.

It felt... empty.

Maybe *I* felt empty.

It was probably a side effect of the missing bond, as well as the sudden loss of his cock in my channel. I would survive it.

Though perhaps it might make me feel a bit lonelier.

I sighed softly and squeezed my eyes shut.

"That didn't sound like satisfaction," my king rumbled unhappily.

"Oh, I'm satisfied," I mumbled. My mouth didn't seem to be working quite properly; I needed more food and water.

He growled at me, then stood and strode out of the room. I knew he'd be back, so I waited where I was.

Sure enough, he returned with enough food to feed my entire town, and had multiple glasses of water tucked beneath his arm.

I eased myself out of the water as he set the food down beside the pool. He reached out to help me, but I waved his hand away. I couldn't help but notice his bare palm, free of our silvery marking, as he did. "Just worry about the food, Vayme."

He gave me an unhappy look, but pulled his hand back without touching me.

I finished off an entire glass of water before starting on the food, and silence set in between us as we ate. It was peaceful, though my satisfied bliss was fading into a calm sort of sadness.

I missed having his mind bound to mine.

I kept sneaking looks at my hip, too, bare of the handprint all my dresses had put on display. I hoped it wouldn't make me sad when I put one on and had nothing to show but the soft flesh of my hip.

"My mind feels far too quiet," Vayme finally said, slicking a few strands of wet hair away from his face. "I don't like it."

"I don't like it either," I admitted. "But it's probably for the better, isn't it? Your people still don't take mates."

He scowled at me. "I'm their king. I don't follow their traditions; I make my own."

"That's another terrible reason to form a mating bond, Vayme."

"What would be a good one, then?" He studied me, his gaze intense.

"I don't know... love? Attachment? The realization that one's life would be poor without the object of their affection as a part of it forever? Mating is permanent; it should come with a certainty that the person taking a mate will never change their mind, even when both mates inevitably grow and change. Shouldn't it?"

"Of course it should." He leaned toward me, placing both of those massive hands on the stone between us as he did. "Tell me, Tempest, do you love me?"

My face flushed, and I threw the question back at him. "Do *you* love *me*?"

"I thought I made it obvious that I did."

My eyebrows shot upward. "*Obvious*? How?"

"I asked you to seal our bond. I protected you, and provided for you. I—"

"Those actions could just as easily be driven by guilt, or responsibility. You only asked me to seal it because you didn't want me to die, remember?"

"What man wants the woman he loves to *die*?"

I lifted a finger to stop him, my hand trembling a bit yet again. "You *never* said you loved me."

"Well, I certainly thought it. I love you, Tempest. I love the way your smile lights up a room, and the way you challenge me. I love your quiet strength, and having you in my arms. I love you. I want you to be my mate permanently—not just to keep you alive, but to make you *mine*. So I get to keep you through this life, and every one that follows. So I get to feel your pretty little mind entwined with my own. Is that clear?"

"Very," I whispered, stunned by his words.

He loved me.

He really did want to mate with me.

He *loved* me.

Vayme popped another berry into my mouth, clearly not waiting for me to proclaim my love in return. Maybe fae didn't expect that—maybe they didn't worry as much as humans.

Or maybe he just didn't want to pressure me into speaking about feelings he didn't think I had.

Or... maybe I'd spoken too soon.

Because he leaned back, his body position casual but his gaze lingering on my face. "You didn't answer my question."

"I suppose I didn't." I brushed hair away from my eyes with a shaky hand. My wind still hadn't returned, but I was sure it would after I rested.

He waited.

I fought the urge to bite my lip and go silent, admitting, "I've loved you for a while. I'm not sure when it happened, exactly, but I do. I love you.

You make me feel safe and happy, and that's so much more than I ever expected for myself."

The intensity in his gaze shifted to a warm simmer. "Veil, I'm glad. I think I'd have to lock you in my room until I convinced you otherwise if you said no."

I laughed. "You wouldn't."

The challenge in his eyes told me he would most certainly consider it, at the very least.

His foot brushed the side of my thigh slowly, but the physical contact shocked me. A slice of pain erupted in my hip, and I yelped as I jumped a bit.

My gaze jerked to my side, and my lips parted as I watched his handprint reappear on my skin. "How..." I trailed off, not sure how to finish the question as I looked up at him.

His expression was just as shocked as my own. "We're fated."

I stared at him in silence, eyes rounded.

"Our souls bonded before we reached this world, Tempest. They're making that known to us now." The pride in his eyes swelled. "I suppose now I understand why the other females were so damn unappealing."

"I can't feel you in my mind, though."

"It's not a full bond—just a handprint, to let us know that our souls are connected. A bond from the world before doesn't have to be recreated in this one."

My chest warmed. "So we made an agreement to be together before this life."

"We did."

"Maybe I really do belong with the fae." I reached for his hand, and he slid closer to give it to me. Emotion burned in my throat as I studied the soft, glowing silver on his palm.

The first time we started a bond, he had been frustrated. It wasn't a good start—not in the slightest.

Now, we could change that.

I lifted my gaze to Vayme's. "I love you. *Sillah ovim rett warum.*"

Joy swelled in his face as our souls and magic began to knit together again, and a feeling of rightness washed over me. *"Sillah ovim rett warum, Tempest. I love you more than life itself."*

Tears stung my eyes as a fierce tingle rolled through me. Our auras began to change again, but unlike that first day in my cave, I didn't sit there and watch.

Instead, I surged toward my king—my *mate*.

He hauled me onto his lap, capturing my mouth and kissing me deeply as our souls and bodies changed, sealing the connection we both wanted so desperately.

There was no brutality, and no roughness, but... maybe a little pain.

He wrenched away from me a moment later, his nostrils flaring. "I smell your *blood*, Tempest."

"I don't think my human body was made to survive an entire eclipse with a fae king," I admitted sheepishly.

The anger I'd expected flooded his gaze—but there was much more of it than I had expected. "I hurt you?"

"It didn't hurt in the moment."

He growled at me, set me on my ass, and parted my legs. My gaze was nearly glued to the marking on his palm—now glowing bright gold, rather than soft silver. There was no way a little fabric could hide that glow, which thrilled me.

"Vayme," I protested, as he inspected me slowly, and thoroughly.

"It's not as bad as I thought," he said after a few minutes, dragging his tongue lightly over my clit as if in apology for getting angry.

My body shouldn't have reacted.

It really shouldn't have, after everything we'd done.

But something about hearing Vayme proclaim his love for me made me want him, just one more time. Just to solidify... *everything*.

"You can make it better," I suggested.

He flashed me a narrow-eyed look. "Absolutely not."

I heaved a sigh, staring up at the ceiling. "We're mates now. For real, this time. I think that should earn me the right to whatever I want, for the night at least."

"Technically, it's already tomorrow."

The bastard stroked my thighs and abdomen lightly, as if that would make me want him less.

But a wicked idea came to me—one he wouldn't be able to turn down.

The more I thought about it, the more certain I was.

"You could let me drink your blood."

His hands went still.

"That would heal me, wouldn't it?" I asked.

His fingertips dug into my skin, and he finally answered. "It would. And you should know you are entitled to my blood any time you want it, Tempest."

I eased myself up to my forearms. "Would you like it if I did, though?"

"Of course. It's supposed to be one of the most intimate things a couple can do."

"Then it's only fair we try it." I started to sit up the rest of the way, but Vayme caught my waist and lifted me carefully onto his lap. The length of his cock pressed against my core—hard again, despite the eclipse we'd just gotten through.

"No sex," Vayme warned me, as I studied his neck in an attempt to figure out how I was supposed to drink from him. My teeth weren't very sharp, after all.

"I would never," I lied, leaning toward his throat. His expression told me he didn't believe me any more than I believed myself.

I felt some strange kind of magic swirl in my lower belly, and a few of my teeth lengthened and sharpened.

His fingers dug into my ass as I slowly pressed my teeth to his throat. A soft gasp escaped me when the flavor of him flooded my mouth, and it quickly rolled into a groan when the shock morphed into a fierce, hot desire. It wasn't completely unlike the effects of the eclipse—just sharper, and focused entirely on what I wanted from Vayme instead of on my body alone.

I moaned, rocking my hips against his erection. It would take far more than that to bring either of us to climax after the eclipse, but veil, it still felt incredible. His nails dug deeper into my ass, and I rocked harder, encouraging him to lose control. I'd never minded the tiny cuts he left me—and now, he could heal them nearly as fast as he left them.

"*Bite me too,*" I said into his mind.

"*I don't need your blood.*" His voice was strained, and his nails dug in deeper.

"*I wasn't asking, Vayme. Bite me, now.*"

He growled at me—but listened.

We groaned together as the pleasure heightened, and his hips jerked desperately.

"*I need you inside me,*" I breathed into his mind, the flavor of his blood still in my mouth and through my damned veins.

"*Tempest,*" he warned.

"*You can give me your blood again tomorrow in apology.*"

He grunted. "*I'm hopeless at refusing you.*"

"You want me too much."

"Undoubtedly." His hands glided over my ass, lifting me enough to line us up. *"Take what you need, mate."*

I sank down on him, and rode him until I screamed.

Somehow, it felt even better knowing that he was mine.

And not just mine—my *mate.*

CHAPTER TWENTY-SEVEN
KAELLE

Vayme made me stay in bed for *days* after the eclipse. And not the fun kind of *staying in bed*—the kind of *staying in bed* where your mate feeds you more food than you can safely eat, and assigns two massive xuno to make sure you can't get out.

Then again, he also stayed with me through most of those days. He did attend a few meetings, but they were about fixing the mess my storms had made, so I forced him to leave me long enough to go to those ones.

Soft and Strong had spent the eclipse together, and seemed to be moving on from their past. They were all over each other, and it was adorable.

When Vayme finally accepted that I was fine, we emerged from the castle and made our rounds, letting the people closest to him know about our bond. Word had already gotten out because he had attended meetings, and the glow on his palm was impossible to hide, but telling them in person seemed important.

We stopped at his parents' house to tell his family that evening—well, to tell Matían and Pavia. His parents were there too, but we didn't particularly care about them.

Matían opened the door with a grin, having already heard the news, and congratulated his brother with a massive hug. I made sure my congratulatory hug was a quick half-hug, because I knew better than to do anything that might make Vayme think I cared about his brother with more than a familial fondness.

Some scars ran too deep, after all.

His parents gave us both stiff embraces, which we returned just as stiffly.

Not all relationships could be mended, or needed to be.

If Vayme wanted to be close with his parents, I would support him, but until then, I'd survive awkward hugs and conversations. And if he never wanted to, I'd support that too.

Pavia waited patiently for her turn at the very end of the line, standing behind everyone else with a grin of her own... and a tiny xuno at her side.

"You found your companion?" I exclaimed to her, as I bent down so she could throw herself at me the way she always did.

"I found my companion!" she shrieked, hugging me fiercely. "And you're my uncle Vayme's mate!"

I laughed. "I'm happy for you! And yes, I'm his mate."

"Yay!" She pulled away, still grinning. "What's a mate?"

My gaze flicked to Vayme, and he shrugged.

I supposed if she'd grown up around humans, she probably didn't know.

"It's like a husband or wife, but with magic. Me and Vayme are going to be together forever, even when we cross the veil. Look." I pointed to the glowing handprint on my hip, revealed in almost its entirety by the cutout on my dress.

Her eyebrows raised and her lips parted. "Your magical tattoo changed. It's pretty!" She flashed her dad a quick look, and then leaned in close, cupping my ear with her hands and whispering, "We need to find my dad a mate. I think it would make him happier."

I bit back a laugh, pulling away and nodding with a solemn expression. "Let's do it."

Her lips stretched in a wide grin. "Yay!" She hugged me again, then finally gave Vayme his hug.

"I'm second now, huh?" he teased her, tickling her side. She giggled, wriggling in his arms.

When she leaned in and whispered to him, she told him the same thing, her whisper loud enough that all of us could hear. His face grew just as serious as mine had, and he agreed, "It will be our next mission."

Matían looked amused more than anything, and dragged her into his arms as Vayme and I greeted her new companion with scratches behind the ears.

It wasn't perfect... but veil, I loved it anyway.

It took a few more weeks to make sure everything was settled in our kingdom, but when it was, we headed out with Strong and Soft, as well as three bags of supplies.

Thanks to the shiny new mate bond Strong and Soft had, they ran with their sides brushing each other every now and then. Strong and Vayme had both tried to persuade me to ride on his back, but Soft and I had exchanged grins and refused.

Powerful males were impressive, after all, but we had to put our feet down sometimes.

My mate was keeping good on his promise to return me to my cave, though the way he was keeping it was vastly different than either of us had intended when he made the promise.

We traveled much slower, since there was no rush. Vayme gave me a list of beautiful sights we could see on the way, and didn't complain once when I made him go to every single one of them, even though a few were just outside of Jirev, and one was all the way over by Loire.

When we stopped to visit Laeli and Ravv, we found them mated, much to my shock. I spent a good portion of a day cooking in their castle's kitchen with Laeli, laughing up a storm as we traded stories. We spent the evening at one of their city's apparently famous parties, drinking and dancing until Vayme and I slipped away to spend the night alone together.

They had so many mated couples and fae children in Loire, it made my mind spin—and made me hopeful for a future where Vayme and I weren't the only ones in Vuuth with a bond.

When we made it to Jirev, we spent a day there too. Nissa had written me a letter, apparently, but whoever agreed to give it to me had never bothered to do so. My king growled a promise to find it, and make sure that never happened again.

He wanted me to be able to connect with my friends, even if just through letters.

I spent a day there in the fields with Nissa, though we mostly just walked around, chatting about everything under the sky. We told each other our stories, and talked about how long we wanted to wait to have kids—a *long* time—and said all the things we'd felt like we couldn't, back when we first met.

It made me feel like I'd found closure for all the time we spent there, and that calmed me.

After one last night in Kier's castle, we finally headed back toward the human lands, and toward the family I didn't want to claim as my own.

We spent every night in an ice shelter, with my head on his arm and his body pressed tightly to mine as he murmured to me about how damn much he loved me.

I still thought I would always feel safer surrounded by stone, but with my king by my side, I wasn't afraid anymore. And to me, that was what mattered above all.

CHAPTER TWENTY-EIGHT
VAYME

Kaelle was quiet as we traveled the last few hours to her parents' town. I didn't push her for her thoughts, knowing she would share them when she was ready.

"Let's stop at my old cave first," she murmured to me and the xuno, as we approached.

Strong turned, heading in that direction, and Soft followed.

When the xuno stopped, we dismounted. I took Kaelle's hand when she slowed near me, and she shot me a small, grateful smile.

I knew she hadn't really worked through everything she learned about her parents. Not entirely, at least. Scars like that took far more than a few months to heal, but I would make sure she was never healing alone or questioning her worth while she did.

She gripped my hand tightly as she led me inside her old cave, taking a moment to study the door. I remained far enough behind her that I could support her without being overbearing as she did.

We didn't speak a word as we walked around it. It had been overrun with water while we were gone, the bucket beneath the trickle missing completely. Whatever she had used as a bed was gone too, along with her books, and everything else that had once made it feel like a safe, warm space to her.

"They took my things," she said quietly into my mind. *"I wonder if they mourned me, or if they were just glad to have the items back."*

Anger swelled within me for her sake, but I didn't voice it.

I stopped her there and pulled her into my arms, hugging her fiercely. *"You know I love you, Tempest. We don't have to do this."*

She swallowed hard enough for me to hear it. *"I know, but I do have to do it. I have to find out, or I'll always wonder."*

Though I understood, I hated that it would likely cause her pain.

"Alright. As long as tonight, you're going to curl up in my arms and tell me everything you felt here."

"I will. I'll probably explode if I don't," she admitted.

I couldn't chuckle at her soft joke. Not when I knew she was struggling, and there was nothing I could do to help.

"You're helping me just by being here, Vayme."

I squeezed her tighter. *"Say the word, and I'll get you out of there in a heartbeat."*

"I know. Thank you." She tilted her head back and brushed a kiss to my lips. *"I love you too."* With that, she stepped away and pulled me behind her. *"We're walking there. I know riding the xuno would look fiercer, but I want them to see how strong we are. There's always a chance they might try to attack us, though I don't think they have any weapons. I think I was their weapon."*

"Then they will be doubly afraid when you walk in beside a fae male, wind blowing through your hair."

She laughed softly. *"I suppose. I'm not sure I should want to make them afraid, but I'm also not entirely against it."*

"If they fear your strength, they aren't worthy of it."

Kaelle squeezed my hand in response.

We made our way down the mountain, with Soft and Strong remaining close at our sides.

The town's members began to gather soon after we started our walk. I imagined the gossip flying through town—their human prisoner had returned with a man holding her hand. Was she there to kill them, or had she truly believed herself to be loved?

There were enough people gathered when we reached the bottom of the mountain that I had to assume the entire town was there.

A soft-looking, middle-aged, human woman with tanned skin and blue hair stood at the front of the group. A man around the same age was beside her, with pale skin and dark hair. They had to be her parents.

Another man around Kaelle's age was with them, though he looked very, very uncertain. His hair was nearly the same shade as my mate's, giving away their relationship as siblings.

"Kaelle!" her mother cried, running toward us and throwing her arms around her daughter. My mate held my hand in a death grip, but hugged her mother lightly with her free arm.

Her mother added, "We were so worried about you! Where have you been?"

Kaelle released her, and her mother's gaze flicked to me. She looked back immediately, as if noticing my height for the first time. Kaelle had asked me to tie my hair up, so everyone could see the points of my ears and realize what I was, and I hadn't protested in the slightest.

"I was rescued by King Vayme of the fae," Kaelle said, her voice steady. I was damn proud of her for that steadiness.

Her mother's expression of worry cracked slightly. "Rescued? What do you mean?"

"Do you think I was blind to your treatment?" she asked, her voice quiet but strong. "To the softness of your body and the frailness of my own? You starved me, mother." My mate's eyes lifted to everyone in the town, many of whom seemed to be taking steps back, either to get away from me or Kaelle. "You all starved me."

"Your magic was dangerous," her mom countered, her voice losing all kindness as quickly as it must've gained it. "You destroyed so many towns, Kaelle. Your magic made you a monster."

"It's Queen Kaelle, to you. Unlike you, the fae respect strength, and I am now mated to King Vayme." After a moment to let the shock of her statement set in, she added, "I was a *child* when I lost control of the magic I didn't know existed. You starved your own daughter; if one of us is a monster, it certainly isn't me."

"That is *enough*," her father said, stepping up beside his wife with a red face. His fists were clenched, and the bastard actually looked as if he might swing at my female. "You will not disrespect your mother."

I didn't care what his relation was to her—if he swung at my mate, he would die.

"If you try to attack me or my king, he will end your life faster than you can blink," Kaelle warned her father. "You have no power over me anymore. None of you do."

She looked out at the town, and let the breeze blow through her hair for a moment as her father's face reddened more.

Wisely, he didn't make a move against either of us.

She mused, "My king offered to bring a battalion of fae warriors with us. It would only take a few to raze this whole damn town to the ground, wouldn't you say?"

My gaze scanned the space quickly. "I could manage it myself, given ten minutes or so. No battalion needed, Tempest."

A few of the people slipped back into their homes, hoping they could hide from the storm that may or may not be coming.

It wasn't coming, but they didn't know that.

Her lips curved upward softly, and she nodded as she looked back at the town. "Anyway, I thought about it, but decided it would be far better revenge to leave you here, suffering in the fields for every coin you need. While you suffer, I feast on fae delicacies and enjoy every moment of my immortal life with the fae king I adore—who worships me just as much as I worship him. If you had loved me, perhaps I would take you with me, and offer you the same happiness. Instead, I leave you with the tiniest sample of the joy that could have been yours."

I unclipped one of our large supply bags from Strong's back, tugged the strings to open it, and tossed it toward them. The top layer of candies and other desserts we'd brought for that purpose spilled out onto the dirt, all of it wrapped pristinely in a plastic that would dissolve slowly, over time.

"You will never see me again, but in some part of my heart, I still wish you the best." With that, Kaelle dipped her head toward her family, slipped a leg over the back of her companion, and took off.

I lingered, stepping up to her father with my sword in my hand. The ice was so damn familiar it may as well have been a body part.

I let the edge of the blade kiss his throat, and said in a low voice, "As her father, you were meant to protect my female. I will return after your death and curse your grave, to ensure you are incapable of hurting another child the same way in the next life."

The redness vanished from his face as he paled.

Humans knew little of fae magic; he likely had no idea that I was incapable of cursing anyone. Even if he doubted it, the threat alone would haunt him.

After a long enough pause to scare him nearly to death, I finally released him and tossed a leg over Strong's back.

He howled viciously into the sky, and Soft echoed his howl in the distance. Then, he snapped his teeth at the town members, and took off after his mate.

We caught Soft and Kaelle quickly, and my female threw herself into my arms, taking in deep breaths of air as tears leaked down her face.

I held her tightly, letting her cry as long as she needed to. She was mine, I was hers, and she knew I would never leave her.

· · ·

Her sadness followed her for a few days, but by the time we stopped at one of our last destinations, it had faded into a steady resolve.

"Thank you for saving me," she murmured, as we stared out over the edge of the Aching Chasm. My arm was wrapped around her, and she was tucked against my side. None of the beings and creatures that lived within it had any reason to venture to the surface, so we were in no danger. Even the Monster within would remain down below until he had another contract—and then, he would hunt his unfortunate target.

"Thank *you* for saving me," I countered, brushing a kiss to her cheek.

Her lips curved upward. "I suppose I did."

A chuckle escaped me. "You most certainly did, Tempest."

Her smile grew wistful. "Laeli and Nissa seemed so happy working in the kitchens and fields. Do you think I should find something like that? A passion?"

"You seem happy attending meetings," I pointed out. "The other humans don't want to act as queens, but that doesn't mean you can't."

She admitted, "I really do enjoy the meetings. Especially when you use my ideas." She flashed me a grin, and I laughed. My voice carried over the chasm, and her body relaxed against mine.

"I appreciate your thoughts tremendously, as I always have." I squeezed her tightly. "Eternity will be blissful with you, Tempest."

"Or at least a whole heap of fun," she murmured, still wearing a smile of her own.

"Of that, I am certain." I brushed another kiss to her cheek, and she turned in my arms, taking my lips in hers.

I couldn't care less what the future held, so long as I got to hold the woman I loved through it all.

CHAPTER TWENTY-NINE
BONUS SCENE
KAELLE—A FEW MONTHS LATER

Vayme had taken to letting me sleep in while he attended the most boring of our meetings in the morning. Though I knew he was trying to be sweet, I had told him to wake me up.

He had just decided not to.

Luckily, I had come up with the perfect way to make sure he started listening to me.

I slipped my shorts off, put on one of my longest dresses (it still only fell to the middle of my thighs), and padded up the stairs.

Was I being sneaky and underhanded?

Slightly.

Did my mate deserve it?

He most definitely did.

I felt his irritation with whoever was talking as his mind brushed up against mine, and was careful to keep my thoughts and emotions neutral so he wouldn't realize I was up to anything.

I must've done it well, because when I stepped into the meeting, he looked surprised to see me.

"What are you doing out of bed?"

"Just needed to stretch my legs."

"Queen Kaelle," a few of the people in the meeting murmured, bowing their heads respectfully in my direction.

"Hello." I flashed everyone a quick, soft smile, crossing the room and taking a seat on Vayme's lap.

His hands reached up to adjust my position, and stilled on my ass and side when he found them bare.

A warning rumble rolled through his mind and into mine.

"This is your fantasy, right?" I asked him.

"You're going to be my death, female."

"I'll take that as a yes."

"If anyone in this room realizes I'm bringing you pleasure, they die," he warned me, dragging a finger over my clit.

My wind blew hard enough to keep my scent from growing detectable, I hoped.

"Understood." I bit my tongue to keep myself quiet. I'd had a lot more experience since the last time we tried to stay silent, so I was pretty sure I could manage it.

Everyone was used to my presence, so the meeting resumed easily, and the conversation began again.

I forced my breathing to remain even as Vayme slowly lifted me off his lap just enough to free his cock, and then worked my slickness over the head of his erection before easing me down on him.

My throat swelled as he filled me for the first time in... two days? Veil, it had felt like a lifetime.

Both of us remained silent, though I could feel the power in the tension in his muscles.

"There's no way to do this without giving it away," his voice strained in my mind.

"Then we'll sit here until the meeting ends, and find our pleasure after it's over," I murmured back.

It would be a bit torturous... but we could survive the torture.

"You're insane, Tempest."

"And you love me for it."

His lips brushed my shoulder. *"That I do."*

It was the longest meeting of our lives—but when it finally ended, Vayme filled me in on something that had been decided before I got there as an excuse as to why we weren't leaving with everyone else. They all made their way out, and then finally, we were alone.

He iced over the door, then finally threw me onto the table, leaving my ass hanging off the ledge. "You're perfect," he snarled, as he drove into me.

A breathless laugh escaped me at his words—but it turned into a frantic cry as he dragged me to the edge, and then over it.

Veil, it was good to be mated.

EPILOGUE
KAELLE—MANY YEARS LATER

"*Veil, they are adorable together.*" I wiped tears from my eyes as Pavia kissed her new mate beneath a trellis of flowers that had been brought all the way from the deepest farm just for their celebration. Pavia had wanted a human-like wedding, so she'd gotten it.

"*You think everything is adorable right now,*" Vayme murmured back, his hand slowly stroking my bare, swollen abdomen through the cutout on the side of my dress.

"*It's the pregnancy hormones. They're going to kill me,*" I said with a sigh.

"*You know I won't allow that.*" He brushed a kiss to my forehead. "*And this time, you're right. They're adorable.*" His gaze flicked to the xuno pups wrestling off to our side. "*Though perhaps not quite as adorable as that.*"

Soft was growling at the clumsy little pups, trying to get them to behave, but they rarely listened. And Strong took so much amusement in their hard-headedness that I wasn't sure they ever would.

A soft laugh slipped from my lips. "*You're right. It would be hard for anyone or anything to be more adorable than that.*"

His lips curved upward, and he brushed another kiss to my forehead, still stroking my abdomen lightly. *"Our baby will manage it."*

I choked back a laugh. *"Veil, I hope so."*

He chuckled softly, and we all stood as Pavia and her mate moved through the crowd, eyes bright and fingers intertwined. We were at the front, seated across from Matían and his mate, so we exchanged grins with them both before Pav stopped to hug them, and then us after.

More tears stung my eyes as she whispered to Vayme, "Thank you for always loving me."

I started full-on crying when I heard my mate murmur back, "It was a privilege, Pav."

Veil, I was so glad Vayme had dragged me out of that little cave and forced me into such a beautiful life—and so damn proud of myself for learning how to become strong enough to survive it.

AFTERTHOUGHTS

I had written a few cheerful paragraphs to close out this series, but I can't lie at the end of a book.

I just can't.

So here's the truth.

Shortly before I started this series, I had a miscarriage in a country I don't live in, while I was there for a book signing. I got home and finished what I had been working on, and then had to start a new series.

My emotions were shot, my anxiety was through the roof, and I was writing cheerful, hopeful books at a time when I was struggling to feel very cheerful or hopeful.

I buried myself in my then-current idea of a perfect book by toning down the humor and sarcasm and adding more plot. I planned fancy paperbacks and hardcovers, and I made it happen.

These books were a distraction from my grief.

They were something to get me through while I came to terms with what had happened as much as you can in a situation like that.

I still loved writing them... but I didn't feel them in my soul, the way I have with other books in the past. I don't know if I could've felt any stories in my soul at that point, honestly, and that's okay. It was nice to have a challenge and a goal while I struggled with my emotions and mental health.

But now that this series is finished, I find myself realizing I don't want that idea of perfection anymore.

I want the humor and the sarcasm back. The cheer and the hope, too.

I want *me* back.

So, I do still plan on writing more in Evare, but I'm going to be shaking things up again. My next series will be called Claimed by the Wolf, and will take place in the Broken Woods with the mysterious shifters lovingly called "assholes" by Ravv.

As always, thank you so much for reading!
All the love,
Lola Glass <3

PS one last thank you to the ladies in my Facebook group who won the giveaway to help me create a few characters for the series! Kiah, I hope you love how Matían and Pavia turned out!

STAY IN TOUCH

If you want to receive Lola's newsletter for new releases (no spam!) use
this link:
LINK

Or find her on:
FACEBOOK
TIKTOK
INSTAGRAM
PINTEREST
GOODREADS

ALL SERIES BY LOLA GLASS

Standalones:

Wildwood

Deceit & Devotion

Claimed by the Wolf

Forbidden Mates

Wild Hunt

Kings of Disaster

Night's Curse

Outcast Pack

Feral Pack

Mate Hunt

Series:

Burning Kingdom

Sacrificed to the Fae King

Shifter Queen

Wolfsbane

Shifter City

Supernatural Underworld

Moon of the Monsters

Rejected Mate Refuge

ABOUT THE AUTHOR

Lola is a book-lover with a *slight* romance obsession and a passion for love—real love. Not the flowers-and-chocolates kind of love, but the kind where two people build a relationship strong enough to last. That's the kind of relationship she loves to read about, and the kind she tries to portray in her books.

Even though they're fun stories about sassy women and huge, growly magical men ;)

Milton Keynes UK
Ingram Content Group UK Ltd.
UKHW041304150524
442626UK00011B/26

9 798869 167262